An Army of Angels

A Novel of Joan of Arc

An Army of Angels

Pamela Marcantel

St. Martin's Press ✖ New York

Design by Nancy Resnick

Map by Claudia Carlson

Library of Congress Cataloging-in-Publication Data

Marcantel, Pamela.
    An army of angels : a novel of Joan of Arc / by Pamela Marcantel
        p. cm.
    ISBN 0-312-15030-X
    1. Joan, of Arc, Saint, 1412-1431—Fiction.   2. Christian women saints—France—Fiction.   I. Title.
    PS3563.A6324A89   1997
    813'.54—dc20   96-31791
                                                                    CIP

First Edition: March 1997

10 9 8 7 6 5 4 3 2 1

For my mother,
for my cousin Paul Marcantel, who loved La Belle France,
and for all upon the earth who suffer for their truths

Contents

Acknowledgments

Though almost every book begins with only one person, it usually passes through many hands before finally making its way into print, its character influenced meanwhile by everyone with whom the author interacts. It is therefore fitting that I take the time to thank those individuals whose input, assistance, and encouragement were invaluable in my writing this book and seeing it published.

A hearty *Merci beaucoup!* to my friends in France, who generously opened their homes to me while I conducted my on-the-spot research: Brigitte and Boubker Intissar, and Monique and François Widemann. My heartfelt appreciation also to Monsieur Robert Joseph of Patay, whose knowledge of the battle fought there between the English and the French in 1429 was most impressive and helpful. And thanks as well to Frances Hébert, my cheerful interpreter, who let me drag her all over France without once complaining.

Special thanks to Judith Marymor, who read the draft as it took shape, assured me that it was good, and offered suggestions for improvement when the need arose; to George Garrett, who graciously gave of his time and encouragement; to C. Brian Kelly for sharing his extensive knowledge of Jehanne's military career; to Elizabeth Outka, whose humor and optimism cheered me on, and whose efforts led to my acquiring representation for the manuscript; to Leslie Breed, not only a superb literary agent but a warm and caring friend; and to Hope Dellon, editor extraordinaire, whose professionalism and sensitivity improved the novel in ways I had not foreseen.

And lest they feel left out, I would also like to thank my family, friends, and co-workers, those loving individuals who, if they thought I was crazy to take on such a huge project, never mentioned it.

N

English Channel

Die[

Rou[

Seine River

Northern
France

Loire River

St.-Florent

Tours

Chinon   Loch[

Ste.-Cathérin[
de-Fierbois

Poitiers

Vienne River

Orléans
1428-29

B. de St.-Pouair (Paris)

B. du Pressoir Ars (Rouen)

B. des Douze Pierres (London)

B. de la Croix Boissé

Porte
Bannier

Porte de
Paris

Road to Chécy

B. de St.-Loup

B. de St.-Laurent

Porte
Regnard

Porte de
Bourgogne

Ile St.-Antoine
Tourelles

Ile Devant
St.-Aignan

Grande Ile-aux-Boeufs

Ile Charlemagne

River Loire

B. du Champ
de St.-Privé

B. des
Augustins

B. de St.-Jehan-le-Blanc

0   1/4   1/2   3/4   1 Mile

Portereau St.-Marceau

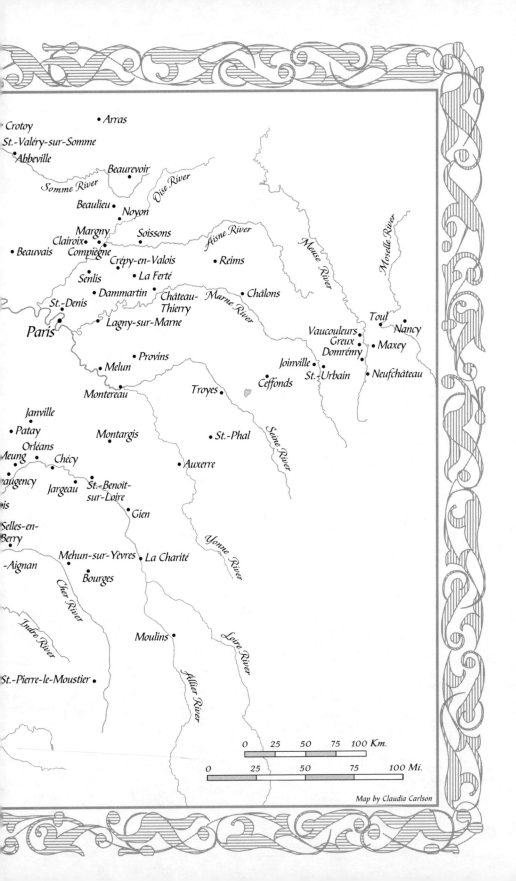

Crotoy

St.-Valéry-sur-Somme

Abbeville

Arras

Beaurevoir

Somme River

Oise River

Beaulieu

Noyon

Margny

Soissons

Aisne River

Clairoix

Compiègne

Crépy-en-Valois

Reims

Beauvais

Senlis

La Ferté

Dammartin

Château-Thierry

Marne River

Châlons

St.-Denis

Lagny-sur-Marne

Meuse River

Moselle River

Paris

Toul

Vaucouleurs

Nancy

Greux

Domrémy

Maxey

Provins

Joinville

Melun

St.-Urbain

Neufchâteau

Ceffonds

Montereau

Troyes

Janville

Patay

Montargis

St.-Phal

Seine River

Orléans

Meung

Chécy

Auxerre

Beaugency

Jargeau

St.-Benoît-sur-Loire

is

Gien

Selles-en-Berry

Yonne River

-Aignan

Mehun-sur-Yèvres

La Charité

Bourges

Cher River

Indre River

Moulins

Loire River

St.-Pierre-le-Moustier

Allier River

0   25   50   75   100 Km.

0   25   50   75   100 Mi.

Map by Claudia Carlson

Rouen Castle

February 20, 1431

The long table was crowded end to end with the most inviting food she had ever seen. A dazzling melange of meats and vegetables, soups and desserts, stretched the entire length of the room, tempting her to draw closer, to sample the array of smells and tastes. Breads, dark and light, were piled next to succulent cheeses of every variety, and the board groaned with meatpies and mouth-watering cakes so cleverly fashioned in the shapes of flowers and animals that they took her breath away. The assault to her nostrils made her shrunken stomach rumble with pain. She was so hungry, was always so hungry, she knew that if she began eating she would never stop. She reached for a fat capon, and—

"Wake up, you bitch!" A violent boot kicked her shackled feet.

She jerked, still curled up on her side, her mind springing to groggy wakefulness.

John Grey, captain of the guard, hulked over her with his hands on his hips, a threatening grin spread toothlessly across that familiar beard. His large body emitted the nauseating odors of urine that had dried to a dark patch across his codpiece and the crusted perspiration of many seasons. Between green stumps that were once teeth a morsel of heavy sausage clung, mocking her empty belly, and even at this distance she could smell the foulness in his breath. Hatred gleamed in soul-dead blue eyes embittered by longtime service in his king's wars, years which had given him and his comrades a crude fluency in the French language.

He grabbed her tunic with both hands and pulled her to a standing position. The long, greasy blond hair hanging to his shoulders brushed against her cheek as she inhaled his stench.

The shackles around her wrists clinked a little as she pulled herself free of his grasp. "What is it this time?" she asked testily, her words escaping into the freezing air in small puffs. Although she swayed a little from exhaustion and lack of nourishment, she was full awake now, and vigilant.

"New orders," he barked. "We're to smear you with sulfur and burn you this very night."

She reeled with confusion. Not long ago the guards had told her that she had been ransomed and would be freed within the hour. At that time, her hopes had risen in a prayer of thanksgiving. The King had delivered her! How they had laughed when the time came for them to inform her that there would be no release and she realized that they had been playing with her.

Now they were telling her the opposite. Was this another cruel hoax, or the truth? Catherine had promised that she would not be executed. Yet in Grey's humorless eyes there was no reprieve, no hint of mercy. It had really come this time; his menacing triumph meant that this was no jest.

She sank to her knees and made the Sign of the Cross. Oh, God, she prayed, give me the courage to bear Your will!

A burst of raucous laughter came from the three English soldiers. She raised her head and saw that the other two were still sitting on their stools next to the door, with tears streaming down their cheeks as they cackled at their joke. Grey's savage grin ridiculed her, and he waved a dismissive hand.

Turning his back to her, he sauntered across the straw-heaped floor to join his friends. He sat down on the third stool and reached for a mug of the potent English ale that waited on the narrow table where he and his comrades took their meals. After taking a long pull, he wiped his mouth with the back of his hand.

"Had you going there, didn't I?" he rasped in his thickly accented French. A conspiratorial glance set the others into another gale of oafish laughter. She could hear even John Barrow—on guard outside the cell—chortling at the jest.

She eased herself onto the block to which she was chained, and hugged the warmth of her body against the bitter wind. Her first night here, they had stolen the warm cloak given her by the lady from Abbeville.

"It is a sin to mistreat me so." She frowned, relief slowing her heartbeat and emboldening her speech. "You should all beg God's forgiveness."

"Oh, should we, you French slut?" asked William Talbot, youngest of the three, whom the others called Billy. "Who the bloody hell do you think you are to lecture us about sin and God, when it's you who's the bleeding witch?"

"I am not a witch." Her face burned with indignation. "I am a prisoner of your little king. I have been unjustly accused, but God has told me that I shall be delivered from all this."

"Oh, yes?" Grey queried sarcastically. "And when will that be, I wonder?"

"In God's time. Within three months."

"Rubbish," countered Julian Floquet, whose ample girth reminded her of Tré-moïlle, the King's chancellor. "The only release you'll have is when the Church condemns you and we get the chance to send you to Hell where you belong."

"I'm already in Hell," she retorted, "and you are all demons sent to torment me. But I shall escape. God has given me His word that I shall be released through a great victory, and there is nothing any of you *goddons* can do to prevent it!"

2

Billy hawked up a mouthful and spat at her. The spittle fell short and slapped into a foaming puddle onto the stone floor.

She had been in this place since shortly before Christmas. The benign summer in captivity at Beaurevoir had melted into autumn, and autumn had eventually frozen into bleakest winter. Upon reaching Rouen, the English had brought her to the castle and dragged her up the eight steps that ended in this hexagonal, darkened room, six feet across, whose only daylight came through a small slit of a window, and was further illuminated at all hours by a single torch in a wall sconce near the door. Her captors had flung her across the room to the darkness of the opposite wall. They clapped irons around her ankles, then chained them to a long wooden block, an arrangement that she would later find enabled her to take only small, restricted steps. Then they locked an iron band around her waist and slid another, heavier chain through the rings attached to it. Lastly, they fastened that shackle to a large ring in the stone wall directly beneath the arrow slit, making it impossible for her to avoid the blasts of cold wind that whistled into the cell from the north. They wound a longer chain about her body at night.

These five jailers, John Grey and his comrades—two of whom stood guard outside the cell at all times—were soldiers in the English army attached to Richard Beauchamp, earl of Warwick and loyal lieutenant to the duke of Bedford. With his superior gone to take the field against the loyalist French, Warwick was guardian to the royal ward Henry. He was said to be fiercely dedicated to his king and his overlord and would unhesitatingly carry out any orders they commanded. The woman could well believe him capable of anything. She had discovered that the moment she reached Rouen, when he rushed to view the witch for himself.

He had stood over her, tall and well built, with a handsome nose and close-set gray eyes, holding a torch while they shackled her to the far wall, his steady gaze as cold as the December wind and empty of pity for his prized captive. He said nothing, just peered at her for a moment before he left. But it was enough. She had seen the leader; it was foregone that his men would be the same, or worse. Her dismaying intuition proved correct, for though she had found the English in general to be as hardened to charity as he, these in her cell were the lowest of them all.

No matter how fiercely she tried to forgive them as she knew a Christian should, she could not stop herself from hating these vile men. It was not so much because all three of her guards were filthy, clad as they were in breeches worn every day for the years since they were last acquainted with soap and water. She was not clean either. The rancid odors of long-unwashed bodies crowded the cell, and now it was only when one of them moved, fouling the already fetid air, that she even noticed their filth any longer. Sharing their condition, she did not fault them for it. She detested these men because their minds were as loathsome as their persons.

Sleep, chief among the things for which she yearned, was her enemy, for it was while she dozed that she was most vulnerable to their predatory mischief. The original denizens of her cell had attempted outright rape shortly after she arrived, and it was only through God's grace that the earl of Warwick had heard her screams and run to save her. After rebuking the men in their harsh native language, which she did not understand, he replaced her captors with these, who while not making a clear-cut move to violate her body, nevertheless harried her ceaselessly. Even so, she needed to maintain watchfulness, for this was the deepest *donjon* of the enemy's rotting Hell. She kept the hose laced so tightly about her waist that the strings cut into her flesh.

They did not leave her in peace but always woke her through trickery, and it seemed that the Devil never tired of inspiring them to novel and disgusting acts against her. Sometimes they only brought unidentified men, English lords and a multitude of hard-faced churchmen, to gloat over and insult her. Worse, on other occasions the *goddon* soldiers disturbed her rest simply for the pleasure that tormenting her appeared to give them. She would fall into a doze only to awaken to a sword prodding her buttocks or tracing a line down her backbone. Or they would wait until she slept, then suddenly start banging their pewter cups on the door or the wall, frightening her back into consciousness. She often awoke to find one of them standing over her and an English paw stroking her thighs or her breasts. Once, she had wakened to the smell of excrement, and when she opened her eyes found a large human turd steaming on her chest just a few inches from her face. That had given them a new source of merriment, to see the abhorrence with which she hurriedly sat up and flung the thing from her tunic.

The reasons for their doing all this hardly mattered. She knew only that she was weary beyond her capacity to endure it. Imprisonment was bad enough, without the physical exhaustion that blurred her vision and left her lightheaded and confounded. She promised herself that when she got out of here, she would sleep for a week. And she would have that feast she had dreamed about.

The very worst of their outrages, passing even the sleeplessness they forced upon her, was the food they kept from her. She was given only what they did not want, remnants of poorly cooked meat clinging to capon skeletons and legs of lamb, every now and then a hunk of hard bread. In the beginning she had disdained their leavings, too proud to let them know how hungry she was. But now she prayed that when they tossed the bones to her, something edible would remain for her to gnaw upon. Memories of even the simplest meals long past haunted her daily life, and she would have wept for what she could no longer have if she had not promised herself that she would never give her enemies the satisfaction of seeing her occasional despair. Tears could never move to pity those so far from God's love. When hatred began to stir within her, Marguerite returned to counsel charity, reminding her that these were lost souls who despised themselves for their very lack of compassion.

Although she had difficulty hearing Them through the constant disturbances and her mind-numbing terror, she was certain that her Counsel were always with her. They were her courage and her shield, pristine moonbeams from God gleaming through the swamp that had become her life, and without Their steady love and sustenance, she knew that she would readily tumble into a raving, black madness. Even as she sat upon the block that held her shackled feet, warily eyeing the despicable creatures who guarded her, she inwardly chanted her connection to God, and to Them.

Lord Jhesus is my strength, I will fear no evil, Lord Jhesus is my strength . . .

Beautiful child of God, you are His own precious one, His soldier and His jewel.

Deliver me from this evil, I beg you! I don't know how long I can endure it.

As we have promised, in God's time a great victory shall liberate you. Bear your martyrdom with faith, and He will help you to come into the Kingdom of Heaven.

What can I do to help myself?

"We're going to burn you, witch," hissed a voice beneath the flickering torch. Billy's malicious giggle chattered at her from across the room.

She made herself ignore them. She strained to hear further.

Your accusers will bring you before them to confront their lies, and when they do, you must answer them boldly. Remember that they do not have the power to harm your soul.

When does it begin?

Their agents approach you even now.

Footsteps sounded upon the flagstone steps leading to the cell, and a man said to the guards outside the room, "Open up, in the name of Bishop Cauchon."

She could see torchlight and a flash of unfamiliar faces through the barred window near the top of the door. A key rattled in the lock and the guard swung it open. Three of them, monks this time. Two wore the dark-hooded white robes of the Dominican Order, while the third was clad in a simple black tunic. A round cap hugged his head, and there was a silver cross swinging from his neck.

They passed the jailers and walked toward her. At one time she would have stood in the presence of priests, but she had become so accustomed to their comings and goings that they no longer awed her, and these men of the Church were no doubt her adversaries. Besides, she was weaker than she wanted to admit, so feeble that when she stood up at all her knees buckled. So she remained sitting.

"Jehanne, I am Brother Martin Ladvenu," said the shorter Dominican. His smile was kind, almost tender, in a thin face whose dominant feature was pensive brown eyes. "This is Brother Isambard de la Pierre," he introduced the other white-robed monk, heartier in build than Ladvenu.

"And I am Brother Jehan Massieu," said the man in black. An aspect of sad humility rounded his shoulders.

"We have come to summon you officially to appear tomorrow morning at eight o'clock before the ecclesiastical court," Ladvenu said. "Do you understand?"

"Yes," she answered. "I am to be put on trial. Are you my judges?"

"No," said Isambard, taking in her worn appearance. "Brother Martin and I are assessors who will counsel the court in matters of canon law, and Brother Massieu will be your usher, your escort to and from the proceedings."

A corner of her mouth went up. "Who have you assigned to counsel me?"

Ladvenu shifted his feet and crossed his arms. An uncomfortable look darted from Massieu to the Dominicans. "I am sure that the court will appoint someone of your choosing," Isambard replied.

She sighed. "It is not necessary. I have my own Counsel."

"As you wish."

She could feel something, elusive, tantalizing, that made them different from the gloating churchmen who had been to see her earlier. Ladvenu and Massieu looked almost as though they did not want to be here. Isambard, the tallest and somehow more like the others than his companions, stared at her with cool, gray eyes. "Do you accept the summons?" he asked.

She nodded, aware that she had no other choice.

"Is there anything you need?" Ladvenu tossed a glance at the indifferent guards. "Can we bring you anything?"

"I would like very much to hear Mass, Brother, and to take Holy Communion. It has been a long time since I was allowed that. Even at Christmas, the English did not let me."

The monks exchanged a swift look among themselves. Isambard could not meet her pleading expression and cast his eyes at the irons around her wrists.

"We shall tell the bishop that you asked for the Holy Sacrament," responded Ladvenu in a low voice. "Meanwhile, bless you, child." He made a Sign of the Cross over her, a small one so the guards would not notice. And then the men of the Church turned away quickly and departed from her.

Oh, please, dear God, make them allow me to receive Your Son. Give me that at least.

"We're going to burn you, witch." Floquet moved one cheek on his stool and farted loudly. His comrades laughed.

She eased herself off the block without taking her eyes from the soldiers, and moved into a seat against the wall with her knees drawn up to her chin. She knew instinctively that they had had their fun and, for a while at least, would not disturb her further. It would be all right for her to nap a little before they locked her in chains for the night.

BOOK ONE

Preparation

Bless the Lord, O my soul! . . . You are clothed with majesty and glory, robed in light as with a cloak. . . . You make the winds your messengers, and flaming fire your ministers.

PSALMS 104:1–4

CHAPTER ONE

Domrémy

1425–28

When Jhanette was a child it was said that fairies dwelt within the overhanging branches of the Ladies' Tree, guardian of the village fountain. The old people claimed to have seen them sometimes, when they went to drink the waters as their ancestors had done for centuries. They explained to the young that a healing spring deep beneath the earth gushed forth from the ancient Mother's breasts, and that the fairies were the stewards of this gift to her children. The elders swore that when summer was high, you could see flickering lifeforms from the hidden world dancing in the shadows under the magical tree. One of Jhanette's own godmothers and her namesake, Tante Jehanne Aubry, vowed by the Holy Virgin that she had actually seen the fairies with her own eyes.

From the time she could think for herself, Jhanette did not believe that. Her mother had taught her that shadows were shadows only, and that all water was given by God, Lord of the entire earth. Fairies and unicorns and such existed only in old legends and had nothing to do with anything real in the world. Jhanette was not alone in her skepticism. None of the children of Domrémy really believed in the stories, since none had actually seen the fairies. At least, they all claimed they did not believe.

But in summertime, when the days were long and the countryside alive with the scent of secret possibilities, it became easier to put aside doubt and to lose oneself in the early morning mists shrouding the fields all the way down to the river bottom. In those moments, when nature hummed her alluring tune and beckoned the mind to explore her undisclosed places, the supernatural seemed possible, even certain.

Sometimes, during festivals or other reprieves from the demands of daily life, the village youth hung flowery garlands on the magnificent, ancient branches of the Ladies' Tree, offerings to the invisible fairies who perhaps existed after all. It was a custom that went back to the time when Domrémy still had a lord who lived in the castle, the Château-de-l'Ile, in the middle of the Meuse. In the old days, the Bourlémonts often brought their picnics to eat under the shade of the tree's meandering greenery, and long after the family had died out and the castle fallen to ruin, the villagers continued to go there for the same purpose. In good weather the Ladies' Tree was the central public meeting place where farmers could swap communal planting strategies while their children danced, pretending that they played under a grand, sheltering canopy.

Jhanette and her friends Hauviette and Mengette, on their way to pasture with Domrémy's collective herd of cattle that very morning, had stopped briefly to leave flowered necklaces on the beech. Then, forgetting about the mythical sprites, they began to splash water on one another from the not-quite-sacred fountain, giggling and squealing.

"Jhanette!" Hauviette shrieked. "See what you've done? Now I'm all wet!" Her dimples crinkled deeply, belying the seriousness of her speech. Although only eleven years old, she was a pretty child with wavy light brown hair and eyes the color of twilight. The women of Domrémy predicted that she would marry well when she came of age in a few years.

Jhanette often felt envious of the village beauty, then said a hasty prayer to the Holy Virgin to forgive her sin. She knew that no one could say that Jhanette was comely, nor did they. She had been unusually sober, even austere, from the time she was small; her mother sometimes joked that Jhanette had been "born old." Everyone said that she resembled her father, whose black brows were a band across his forehead, giving the impression of a constantly impending frown in a square face accented by a mustache, full lips, and a strong, stubborn chin. Although she loved her father deeply, she sometimes wished she could have possessed more delicate features, then felt guilty for the wish. God in His wisdom had not made her attractive, certainly not as good a prospect for a gainful marriage as Hauviette.

But then, what did it matter anyway? she asked herself, remembering that vanity was as much a sin as envy. Someone would take her to wife, and that someone would perhaps be moved by God to treasure her in spite of her looks.

At thirteen, she was sturdy, with strong, knotlike muscles, and a shapeless dress the color of dried blood hanging on her stocky frame. It tied at the waist and dropped to the tops of the mud brown shoes her father had bought last year from old Anatole the cobbler. Like her older brothers, she would have been swarthy anyway, but her skin was further tanned from a lifetime spent outdoors, and at this time of year especially she was a deep bronze. The sun had turned a patch of skin pink at the end of her wide-based, practical nose. Thick black hair as straight as a horse's mane was always coming loose from its braid and falling into her face above dark, widely spaced eyes. They were liquid with dreamtime but could become enflamed when she lost her temper, which was often enough. When she walked she moved with the competent, no-nonsense stride of her earthbound class.

A sudden handful of cold water made her gasp. The other girls were laughing at her stupefied expression.

"I'm going to get you, Hauviette." Jhanette grinned.

She began to chase her friends around the fountain, the three of them squealing and splashing each other until the fronts of their dresses were soaked. The cattle in their charge started to dance restlessly at the disturbance, a few trotting with tentative steps down the dusty street.

"Hey, you girls!" yelled a booming masculine voice. Gaston the blacksmith, hands on rotund hips, stood in the doorway of his forge glaring at them, his forearms gleaming muscles of smoke-darkened sweat. "What are you doing there? Aren't you supposed to be taking those damned cows to pasture? Look, they're already starting to run away!" He gestured broadly at the lowing truants.

The girls immediately quit their game, mumbling apologies with an abashed curtsey. Jhanette picked up her stick from the wet ground next to the fountain and began to urge the laggard members of the herd toward the pasture, while Mengette ran toward the bemused animals, waving her own stick above her dark head.

"Stop!" she called ludicrously, as though the cattle knew what she was saying. Jhanette and Hauviette snickered, but carefully, since Gaston was still watching them. He was certain to tell their parents that they had misbehaved on their way to pasture. All seriousness now, they hurried the herd along with their sticks commanding the strays, hoping that their present diligence would blunt his memory by day's end. And yet, so careless had they been that it was several minutes before the girls had rounded up all of the animals and were ready to make their way to their grassy, flower-patched destination.

A low bottomland, the pasture bordering the Meuse east of the village was large enough to feed Domrémy's herds of cattle and sheep. Just north of it the men cultivated the fields some years, always leaving one parcel of land fallow that it might be used the following season. Last summer when they brought the livestock here, the girls could see the distant figures of their fathers and brothers sweating under the summer sky as they cut the season's first wheat. On this July morning, however, last year's field was unused. The farmers of Domrémy were in the field, past the stand of trees to the north, and did not notice that the herd arrived at pasture after it should have.

That was earlier, when the sun was just coming over the thatched roofs of the village. For much of the morning the girls played at identifying shapes in the fluffy clouds above the river. Now it would soon be midday, and having finished their meal of cheese and bread, they lay on their shawls under the shade of an oak less distinguished than the Ladies' Tree, bored and dozing in the summer heat.

Jhanette secretly detested having to take her turn herding Domrémy's animals to the fields. She hated the monotony of minding them all day and bringing them in when the sun went down. There was never anything to occupy her when she was here. All the village children had to obey their parents and perform this important duty when the lot fell to them. She knew that. She was aware that it was a sin to play truant, but boredom aside, she abhorred it most of all because it prevented her from being where she wanted to be.

On those occasions when she was lucky enough to be shepherding alone, she sometimes stole away from the grazing animals and ran across the fields to the

Bermont Forest, to the chapel of Our Lady of Bermont. It was a secluded sanctuary where she felt most at peace, and she thought it the holiest spot on earth. Usually, lest her absence be discovered, she took only a few moments to kneel before the crude wooden statue of the Holy Virgin and say a quick prayer before starting back again. But sometimes, it was easy for her to elude the world's boundaries and, in no time at all, plunge into a profound serenity where reality had a center and that center was nowhere that could be touched. Lost in the stillness of that sacred place, she found herself in a deep, tranquil garden of the soul. Beyond thought, beyond emotion, she hovered in eternity while the rustic walls hummed around her and time lost all definition.

When she returned with an inevitable jolt, the changing shadows cried out that indeed a great deal of time had sped past her. Alarmed, she always shot to her feet. But no matter how late she was, she remembered to end her time there by asking forgiveness for her miserable sins—for teasing her little brother, Pierre, for disobeying the rules to be there at all. Invariably, she felt cleansed when she reluctantly rose to return to the fields.

Today, however, she did not have the luxury of visiting Our Lady, not with Hauviette and Mengette as chaperones. Although they had been her two best friends since they were all infants, Jhanette would never have shared her secret journeys to Bermont with them. Even if they did not resent her leaving a responsibility which they all must share, their raucous company would have marred the tranquility of that mystical spot, as sometimes happened when they went there in the open with their parents' consent. To them it was just a lark, a diversion, and they could not understand why Jhanette was so *serious* about it.

Jhanette knew that her friends loved her, but could not understand her devotion to something outside of their everyday concerns. They mocked her relentlessly whenever the bells from St.-Rémy rang and, crossing herself, she knelt to pray.

"Jhanette is always on her knees," Hauviette would laugh, unmindful of the bite her words carried and the loneliness Jhanette felt as a result.

How could Jhanette explain that she heard God's voice in the bells, pealing past comprehension of all else and settling into the foundation of her soul like a quiet friend? She had tried once, when the three of them were smaller, but the depths of her admission had eluded them and their mockery only sharpened. So by now she had learned to ignore their jokes, and kept her thoughts—and the sting inflicted by her friends' barbs—to herself.

Anyway, even if they had understood, Mengette would never have been able to keep Jhanette's absences from the flocks secret. Mengette was small-boned and swarthy, with close-set, quickly darting eyes that took in everything above a long, too-pointed nose. She talked constantly, saying very little but chattering on gaily nonetheless. "Mengette the Songbird," Jhanette's mother called her. Even now she was babbling disjointedly about the new baby her mother was carrying, and didn't they think Richard Aubry, the mayor's son, was good-looking, and she was making a new dress for herself that she hoped to have finished within the week, and on and on.

Jhanette, wishing only to feel the warm wind on her face and to hear the leaves stirring overhead, felt herself tempted to tell Mengette to be quiet. Instead, she sat up.

Less than half a league to the east, the land rose to great sloping hills that looked purple against the grassy valley. This side of the river, the herd was grazing with placid unconcern across the emerald field. Every now and then a cow flicked winged insects from her body with an irritated swish of her tail. At the edge of the herd a calf was nursing at its mother's teat, pulling on the pink udder while the cow nonchalantly ground grass protruding from the sides of her mouth between her great teeth. Where the sloping pasture met the riverbank, cattle refreshed themselves in the shallows before ambling back to feed on the sweet grass. The air steamed with droning flies and the odors of summer grass and cattle.

"Let's do something," Jhanette said.

"What?" asked Hauviette drowsily, not bothering to open her eyes. She was lying prone on the shawl she had spread over the thin grass.

"I don't know." Jhanette shrugged. "Let's have a race or something."

"Oh, Jhanette, I don't feel like racing you." Hauviette pouted. "You always win. Besides, I'm comfortable here."

"I'll race you, Jhanette," Mengette volunteered. She leaped to her feet. "What'll we race for?"

Jhanette picked up the bunch of garlands they had made earlier, after exhausting the cloud game, and carelessly cast aside when the novelty of weaving them had worn off. "These?"

"Agreed." Mengette nodded emphatically. She was standing above them with her hands on her thin hips. Her body, swaying with restlessness, seemed already in motion.

"Hauviette, you'll have to watch us to judge who wins." Jhanette looked down at her sleepy friend.

"I don't wish to," the girl groaned petulantly.

Jhanette got to her feet, chuckling. "Come on." She took Hauviette's hands and pulled her to a standing position.

"We'll race from that tree over there"—she pointed to a tall beech on their right—"to that little one over there"—her arm swept leftward—"and then back again. Come on."

They walked into the hot, brash sunlight, with Hauviette dawdling a little. Dodging soft platters of manure, Jhanette and Mengette trotted to the starter tree, scattering cows as they ran. Jhanette fixed her concentration on the halfway point, which was not very far away. She knew that she would easily win. The two of them hitched their skirts up to their knees and belted them at the waist with their aprons. Jhanette could see Mengette tensing for Hauviette's signal out of the corner of her eye.

"Go!"

Jhanette darted forward, at once leaving Mengette behind her. She heard Hauviette shout, laughing, "Oh, Jhanette, I can see you flying above the ground!"

Jhanette was running so fast that she certainly felt that she was soaring. The grass whipped against her bare calves in little prickles and she seemed as weightless as air. She made an easy leap over a steaming cowpile and ran on effortlessly, well ahead of her slower friend. When she got within striking distance of the small beech she tapped it, then sped back toward their starting point, passing Mengette as she turned. Mengette could never hope to keep up with Jhanette even when Jhanette held back a little as she had just now.

Hauviette jumped up and down, applauding. Flushed with merriment, she bolted toward them, flowers in hand. She put the wreaths around Jhanette's neck and kissed her cheek.

"You're the fastest and the best," she proclaimed, her blue eyes alert now and dancing with affection. Then she added sweetly to a sullen Mengette, "And of course, Mengette, you're the second fastest in the village after Jhanette, everyone knows that. Do you want to pick some more flowers?" she asked the victor.

Jhanette shook her head, too winded to speak right away and feeling a little dizzy from the heat. "No," she gasped, taking in great gulps of air. "I think I'll go back to the shade to catch my breath."

"Come, Mengette, let's pick some of these little yellow ones," Hauviette offered. "If we weave them with the pinks, they'll make a beautiful garland."

Jhanette waved them on, still breathing deeply. She started back toward the shawls lying in the large oak's shade. As she approached the tree, she was surprised to see a boy standing in the darkness beneath its branches. From her position she could not see him clearly enough to establish his identity. With the sun-bleached cottages of Domrémy at his back, he was only a dark shape. She thought from his bearing that he might be Gérard, a local farmer's son.

Before she could draw near enough to be certain, he called out, "Jhanette, go home, your mother needs you."

She stopped. "All right." She turned toward her two friends, who were still picking flowers, tittering and goading one another playfully. Jhanette cupped her hands around her mouth. "I must go home," she called to them, "my mother wants me."

They waved to her distractedly, and with a great sigh she removed the flowered necklaces and dropped them onto the grass. When she looked toward the tree again, the boy had vanished.

Thinking little of it, she took off toward home, across the pasture and down the narrow winding lane into the village. This deep-rutted path, worn down by scores of trampling feet and pungent with animal droppings, brought her to the main street. If one followed it to the north from the direction Jhanette had just come, it eventually took the traveler to Vaucouleurs, the nearest royal town of substantial size. In the opposite direction it made its way to the walled market town of Neufchâteau. Down this road in spring and summer came mendicant monks and minstrels and soldiers of the king, bringing stories and news of what was happening with the war. But they never lingered, for Domrémy was just a stop on the road to more important destinations.

Jhanette turned south. Her father's cottage was on the far southwestern side of Domrémy, and to reach it she would have to run through the streets. She passed Gaston's smithy again but this time did not see him, only the smoke that slithered like a dark serpent from the bedraggled roof of the forge. The sound of his hammer clanging against metal told her that he was inside, hard at work and probably mending a plow or making a horseshoe. It was just as well; she was in no mood to offer explanations after this morning's chastisement.

She ran on, past the wood and plaster houses lining the main road. Steep, rolling hills loomed at the western edge of the village, giving it a wall-like sense of protection. From every direction came the smell of baking bread and roasting meats. In a few hours it would be suppertime. Tante Beatrice saw her from her kitchen window, and called out, "Jhanette, where are you going in such a hurry?"

"Home!" She waved. "Maman sent for me!" She did not slow down.

Agnès Barrey looked up from her hoeing when Jhanette sprinted past her garden, but she did not have a chance to fling the question that sprang to her lips, for Jhanette was already gone. She rounded a corner between the mayor's bungalow and the communal bakehouse and disappeared.

She could see the spire of the church by now, pointing toward Heaven between the thatched roofs. Although built of mud and timber like most of the other structures in Domrémy, the church had a proper tiled roof and squatted comfortably next to the cemetery, assured of its place in the life of the village. Jhanette's dead brother and sister, both born before her and taken to Heaven when they were a few hours old, lay buried among the slate headstones dotting the graveyard.

Jhanette slowed her pace a little and wiped the sweat from her face and neck with the end of her skirt. Her cottage was just ahead, at the bottom of the hulking knoll that flanked the village on the south. A curl of smoke from the familiar, sloping roof hinted of baking bread.

The small house was one of only three in Domrémy constructed from stone. At least part of it, the residence itself, was stone. Its dark tiles and worn, sun-polished coat of whitewash gleamed in the relentless sunlight. On either side of the front door two small windows opened to the street. The largest gave illumination to the main room where Jhanette's parents slept and the family gathered for meals. The other lit the bakehouse, which doubled as Jhanette's bedroom. Above it another window opened to her brothers' loft, hung with onions and cured hams.

The barn was a ramshackle wooden affair that clung like a beggared kinsman to the proud domicile of Jacques Darc and his family. There were great gaps between the boards holding up the thatched roof, and through them Jhanette could see chickens flapping in their cages. A manure heap almost as tall as a man sat at the point where the barn connected to the house. Out of sight behind the barn were Papa's vegetable garden and the privy.

Jhanette wiped her wet face again. Letting her breath out, she trotted toward the cottage's open door.

The whole house was stifling with the sweet odor of baking bread. Isabelle Romée was sitting on a bench at the rugged wooden table, repairing a tear in her husband's shirt. Her hands, gnarled and weathered by labor, took tiny, neat stitches in the dull fabric. She was very old, Jhanette thought, forty-six or so, with grandchildren from her oldest son Jacquemin. Light from the window fell across her braided hair, once brown but now streaked with silver and held in place by a blue kerchief. The gray eyes above her plump cheeks shone in fervent testimony to an earthy but loving character. Maman was heavy-boned and stout, and the ample breasts that had nursed so many babies drooped almost to her waist. It was from Isabelle that Jhanette had inherited her faith and her single-mindedness, for once Maman got something into her head she invariably got her way, no matter how loudly her husband protested. She liked to travel far on pilgrimages to well-known shrines, where she could pray that a miracle would come to save the kingdom and grant perpetual safety in their lives.

Isabelle looked up from her sewing.

"Here I am," Jhanette announced, red-faced and a little winded. "What do you need of me?"

With vision still accustomed to the heady sunlight, she could just distinguish the puzzled expression on her mother's round face. "What are you talking about, Jhanette? I have no need of you now. You're supposed to be at pasture."

"Didn't you send for me, Maman?" Her eyes swept the darkened room as she tried to focus better.

"I did not." Isabelle, clad in the frayed woolen dress that she wore in summer, held her interrupted work with an expectant frown. A skein of heavy thread lay on the table within easy reach, next to the iron scissors.

Jhanette felt a pang of dismay at the vexation in Maman's voice. She loved her mother so much that it sometimes tore at her heart, and she experienced guilt on those rare occasions when she was naughty. She felt such now, even though she had done nothing wrong.

"But a boy told me you sent for me," she said defensively.

"What boy?" Isabelle's tone was more curious than angry.

"I thought it was Gérard Thévenin. It looked a little like him."

Her mother gave an impatient sigh. "Well, he was just having a jest at your expense." She rubbed the end of her nose with a fleshy hand and picked up her sewing. "Now, go back to where you *are* needed."

Jhanette felt her face flush with humiliation. "Yes, Maman," she mumbled.

Head down, she left through the door that opened onto the garden. It would be quicker if she took the back way to the pasture, and besides, she was so embarrassed that she had no desire to encounter any more adults. She would cross the side road and make her way behind the houses, out of sight.

Still smarting, Jhanette sauntered through the cabbages toward the street. As she walked by one of the rows, she happened to look down and saw that a few adjoining leafy heads bore chewed holes and the imprints of small teeth. "Rabbits," she muttered. She stooped and pulled the spoiled vegetables from the soil and tossed them away, then tamped down the vacant crevasses with her hands.

Rising, she saw that there was a swarm of bees buzzing in her path, flying around her father's flowers, which faced the general direction of the church. She stopped to wait for them to get out of her way.

But they did not. They would not let her pass. When she moved to the right, they followed her, and to the left as well. She obeyed them and stood still.

As though of one well-coordinated mind, they began to dart back and forth in front of her face. They swooped and dove at her in what she could swear was a predetermined pattern, diving now across her vision, then buzzing into her ear.

Fascinated, she examined the rapidly beating wings, too quick for the human eye to discern clearly, suspending the small furry bodies in midair. She felt the hive defy her to keep pace with them, ask her to go with them. *Bzzzz, bzzzz,* their voices gradually increased in volume until they drowned out any other sound, *Bzzz, bzzz, bzzzzz.*

She felt a lightheaded sensation flying in and out between her ears. The bees seemed to have the power to take her with their graceful maneuvers, across and back, around and across, in the high summer heat. The sun's blazing radiance shifted, softened, somehow became muted and stimulating in a single instant. It was a thing more real than the time and place around her, now beginning to recede into a shimmering, swirling light. Her surroundings slowly melted away except for that steady drone of the bees, humming through her ears and all the way down to her feet. The heightened sound increased in volume, coalescing into a roaring wind that entered her tailbone and shot a bolt of energy up toward her head. There it burst between her eyes and became an explosive radiance.

She no longer apprehended the bees, for the light was in her, through her, all around her, making her body tingle vibrantly until there was no body, only ex-pectant mind and that rushing wind. From the heart of the sunburst there emerged a panoply of faces, overlapping, each gently replaced by a successor in delicate waves of ever-shifting features. Jhanette saw the beautiful presence of a small, genderless child whose innocence began to alter and refine, maturing in the blink of an eye into the aspect of an ancient brown-skinned male. He had no beard and his head was completely hairless, and from his serene essence there emitted wisdom and compassion as bright as a hundred torches.

There were so many, dissolving and transposing into one another, now here, now gone! The pace was overwhelming, suffocating, almost too much to stand, but the curious countenances flashing past her sight had magic shining about them. Intrigued, she found herself unable to turn away from their faces. Old and young, male and female, they flashed before her. She saw a young blond woman with a burning-ice gaze metamorphose into an olive-complexioned boy with cu-riously slanted dark eyes. The youth aged quickly and became a mature woman covered in long, iridescent feathers. This wondrous creature looked gracefully to the side and raised a winged arm. Then she stretched, reaching out to the light with yearning and sorrow and regret. She opened her shimmering wings and raised them slowly over her head, and when they were at their highest, a flame erupted from her feet, transforming her into a living conflagration. With a triumphant flap of her great, flashing wings, she flew into the center of the magnificent, windswept Light.

A Presence began to throb at its source, as powerful as a heartbeat, and from it there emerged the glowing essence of a man from Eternity. Jhanette could not see his face, which evaporated whenever she tried to look at him, as though his power were gently insistent upon shifting her attention to his eyes.

His eyes.

They were a clear, wondrous blue and in their depths she saw mirrored an emanation of the most profound Love conceivable: all-encompassing, nurturing, awesome in its constancy, beyond words, beyond anything in her experience or in her imagination. She was enfolded in it, her existence confirmed by it, and she knew that here was all safety and meaning. He smiled at her with a tenderness that pulsed in her heart and took away her shallow breath. Enraptured, she saw only him. When he spoke, a lyrical sweetness, seductive in its commanding humility, tingled within her spirit.

Beloved Jehanne, dear Daughter of God, the King of Heaven has heard your prayers, and gives His pledge that He will be with you forever as He has always been. You are His special one, the one who was born for glory on earth and in Heaven.

Wh-What must I do?

God has accepted your love. Continue to pray, keep your faith, Child of God, and honor your family. We shall speak to you again.

Dumbfounded, paralyzed, she asked, though her lips did not move: Who are you?

It is too soon. You must be patient.

The musical whisper was without rebuke.

The wind picked up, taking his voice away, and he started to fade into a gray mist swimming with minute particles of colored light. The gale that replaced him raged in Jhanette's ears, sweeping to a roar that became a terrible cyclone of light and color. She swayed dizzily toward unconsciousness; overcome, she sank to her knees and closed her eyes. She was spinning in space at a terrifying speed, around and around. She wrapped her arms about her head to slow her fall. She scarcely breathed.

The wind gradually slowed; its potency weakened, then stopped altogether. As the Presence receded into the humming of the bees, the exhilaration sizzling through Jhanette's body diminished and collected within her galloping heart, and she returned in time to her father's garden, on her knees in the moist earth.

Traces of the apparition's love hung like a charged mist in the hot air. Suddenly chilled despite the sun, Jhanette's body quaked with a vehement, involuntary shudder. Her heart sprinted in her ears; her numbed mind raced with terror and she could not move, afraid that the uninvited visitation would come upon her again. But when after a few moments it did not reappear, she opened her eyes and cautiously looked about her.

This was just her father's garden, same as always, and she was still on her knees in the cabbages. High above in a normal sky, the sun illuminated her surroundings as a few diaphanous clouds floated overhead like lazy boats. The thatched roofs of nearby houses glinted just as they always did in summer when the sun was high. Up on the ridge to the south, the Bois Chenu, said to be haunted and seldom approached, still waited darkly for autumn nut gathering. The bees had dispersed and become only insects again. The episode, whatever it had been, was ended.

Jhanette got to her feet unsteadily. Like a sleepwalker she shuffled toward the street, feeling no sensation in her legs. She could still see it all, yet not really *see* it, for she had not seen it at all, at least not with her physical eyes but with some part of herself that she could not name.

Daughter of God, he had called her.

Of course, we are all children of God, aren't we? she reasoned, dazed. Why would he address me so? And who was he, what did he want with me? His words echoed in her head: *Born for glory on earth and in Heaven.* What glory? She was just an ordinary child, living in an ordinary village.

It was the race, she thought, desperately trudging along the riverbank behind the houses nearest the pasture. I was tired and then I ran home and I was too long in the sun, and that's all it was. She wiped the sweat from eyes that did not register the island in the river and its ruined castle. Yes, that's all it was, it won't happen again. Yet even though that's all it was, she could not tell anyone about it. They would think her mad or possessed, and perhaps she was.

The sudden bong of the noon bell startled her so that she jerked in alarm. Her teeth clamped down hard on her tongue and she tasted blood.

She knelt hastily in the grassy dust and, crossing herself, implored the Holy Virgin not to let it happen again. Then, to be especially sure that it would not, she asked for protection from St.-Michel, the warrior angel entrusted by God to fight the Evil One and to weigh the souls of His people at the moment of their deaths.

The family had fish for their evening meal. Jehan, the oldest son still living at home, had caught them, two beautiful big trout. When Jhanette returned to her cottage after Vespers, their mother had already gutted and cleaned them, and they were simmering in the iron pot that dangled from a hook within the soot-blackened fireplace. Ordinarily, Jhanette would have welcomed the odor of *court-bouillon,* but tonight her anxious stomach rebelled and she tasted a salty nausea swelling at the back of her tongue.

She had been most apprehensive about going home. She was afraid that her face would betray the shock she still felt, as it had when she returned to Hauviette and Mengette.

"Jhanette, are you all right?" Hauviette inquired with concern. "Is your mother ill? You look so pale."

"I'm well, and so is Maman," Jhanette replied, shaping her face into a neutral expression. "She didn't want me after all. I guess Gérard was just playing a trick on me."

Her friends exchanged a doubtful look.

"I didn't see Gérard, Jhanette." Hauviette frowned.

"Neither did I," Mengette agreed. She put a hand on Jhanette's arm in an uncharacteristic attempt to be comforting.

"He was standing right here, under this very tree!" Desperation gnawed at her mind. If the boy was not Gérard Thévenin, as she had supposed, who was he? And why had her friends not seen him? The other two girls made no reply but continued to look anxious.

"I know what it was!" Jhanette exclaimed, hopeful common sense rising to replace dismay. "You were too far out in the field to see him, but I was coming toward this tree to rest, and I was close enough to see him standing in the shade. Yes, that must be the reason!"

Hauviette's expression changed to relief. "Of course, you are right," she soothed, "that makes perfect sense."

Mengette mumbled assent, but in the glance that she and Jhanette shared, there was a tacit acknowledgment that something odd had happened that morning. And they all knew that none of them would mention the incident ever again, neither among themselves nor to anyone else, least of all to Gérard Thévenin.

Much later, Jhanette was still thinking about the mysterious boy. When the setting sun told them that it was time to return home, the girls drove the herd down the cowpath toward the village with their animated conversation, forced and uneasy as it had been throughout the afternoon, pealing across the cooling fields. An unuttered sense of mystery and its attendant denial snapped at their heels and followed them all the way. By the time she reached her cottage, Jhanette had disciplined her thoughts and marshaled her face into her normal demeanor. Nevertheless, her palms were sweaty and nausea fluttered through her midsection. She could still see the unbidden countenance of the noontime specter.

"Oh, there you are, Jhanette," Jehan exclaimed. "See the fish I caught today!" He beamed, gesturing toward the fire where the headless trout bubbled.

Her seventeen-year-old brother was as muscular as his father but much handsomer, his dark visage less fierce and not yet as weathered. Like his younger sister, his eyes were widely set on either side of a strong nose, but his features were more regular and refined than hers. His ebony hair, cut short for summer, hugged the back of his neck. He had already removed the reeking shirt and washed his perspiration-caked torso clean of chaff and mud. With a casual hand on his hip he grinned at Jhanette, glowing with pride. His two hunting dogs were jumping at his feet in a bid for his attention. The female yipped and tried to nip his hand.

Jehan did not intend to be merely a farmer as his father was. He hoped someday to become mayor of Domrémy, an open secret that everyone acknowledged and approved, for he was endowed with natural leadership and confidence and could speak well. The villagers liked him, and he knew how to make certain that they continued to like him. He had a resplendent smile.

Jacques upheld his son's ambition even though he himself had not yet been able to attain that high office but had to content himself with being sergeant, the third most important man in the village. Still, he had worked hard to attain that station, and had become one of the representatives to the local château owned by the Bourlémont heiress. For a man originally from Ceffonds in Champagne, who had started out with few resources, it was no mean accomplishment.

Jhanette tried to smile at her brother, but the most she could manage was a feeble upward turn of her mouth. "Smells good."

Actually, the cottage was suffocatingly close, what with the cooking fire and the sweaty, unwashed bodies, but by now the fish stew was a little more inviting than it had been when Jhanette first walked in the door. Maman's bread smell mingled in comfortable familiarity with the simmering kettle's contents. A stack of earthenware bowls waited on the planked table next to a pile of spoons and a sharp knife. Maman had already filled everyone's cup with wine and put it before his or her place at table. Jhanette could hear her in the little side room, taking another loaf from the mouth of the clay oven.

Trying not to be noticed, twelve-year-old Pierre slunk to the table with his head lowered and grabbed a spoon. He was trying to hide something, Jhanette could tell by the way he sat on the bench, shielding half of his face with his hand.

Inattentive to his youngest son, Papa did not see Pierre's attempt to hide, at least not yet. He took off his shirt and flapped it against his furry chest to cool himself, then stooped over the bucket near the door and splashed water onto his face, rubbing his neck with vigorous swipes. Isabelle returned with the towel-covered bread clutched in both hands and put it on the table.

In the everyday interior of the cottage, Jhanette's awe-inspiring vision seemed ridiculous. She seized the thought with relief: This is home and everything is normal.

"I helped catch them," piped up Pierre, forgetting to hide his face. "Jehan lured them, but I helped pull them out of the river."

"Yes, yes, we know your contribution, Pierrolot," his brother said with a sarcastic laugh.

Pierre responded by sticking out his tongue. There was an ongoing rivalry between the two brothers. Pierre adored Jehan and wanted to be like him, so Pierre strove to do everything his brother did, which annoyed Jehan no end. He regarded the little tagalong as a pest whose only purposes in life were to intrude into his achievements and disturb his privacy. When Pierre fell flat on his face in an attempt to outdo Jehan, the young man did not let him forget it.

He saw something now that made him grin. "Where'd you get that black eye, Pierrolot, eh?"

The treacherous hand flew to his cheek. "Shut up," the boy muttered with an anxious glance at his father.

Jehan went to Pierre and, putting his head next to his brother's, draped an arm around his shoulder. "What's the matter, little pea, you been picking on the big boys?"

Outraged, Pierre took a swipe at Jehan, who instinctively held up his arm to ward off the blow. At the same time he clapped his younger brother on the ear.

"That's enough!" their father roared. He pointed to the long, sturdy table that he had made long ago when he was first married. "Sit down," he ordered. "I don't want any of that in this house. Save your fighting for your trips to Maxey."

"What trips, Papa?" Pierre asked with feigned innocence. He was fairer than his brother and sister, more like the blonds in his mother's family. Like Isabelle, he had gray eyes. They peered at the world from behind a shock of mousy brown hair, cut as short in back as Jehan's. But he was not as handsome; his face was short and his jaw too wide, and when he grinned, he appeared to be all teeth. He always insisted on knowing everything that was happening, even when it was none of his business. Pierre was the family opportunist, with a reputation for being sneaky and self-serving. But he was only rarely that way with Jhanette. Most of the time he felt too guilty to take advantage of her, and he loved her even when they squabbled.

"What trips?" Jacques Darc loomed over them both threateningly, his large, workworn fists planted firmly on his hips. "You know very well what trips I mean, the ones you take to fight with the boys from Maxey." He lifted a callused hand in a command for silence from his son, who ventured a protest while self-consciously covering the offending bruises.

"I suppose you got that black eye from falling over a log or something, eh?" Jacques' mustache harrumphed. "Yes, yes, I know all about how you really got it. I don't want to hear any more about it."

Jhanette listened to this exchange in knowing silence as she washed her sweat-smeared face and grimy hands in the bucket of water near the door. Because she was the last in the family to use it, she had first to scoop grass from the water's surface, thankful at least that any dirt was by now at the bottom of the bucket. She was looking forward to the bath she could have on Sunday, when Isabelle would fill a tub for her in her bakehouse bedroom.

She knew very well that her brothers sometimes went on nighttime excursions to the nearby village of Maxey, bent on violence; almost all the local youth did. Maxey was loyal to the duc de Bourgogne and his swinish allies the English, whose false king of France, Henry VI, was a mere infant. It was natural that the boys from Domrémy would express their opposition to the invader and their loyalty to the Dauphin Charles. On a long-ago night, Jhanette's older brothers, Jehan and Jacquemin, had secretly taken their nine-year-old sister with them, but she had been afraid to go back any more. She feared the ferocity of those en-counters and—most of all—that her parents would find out.

"Jhanette, bring the fish to the table," her mother said, taking her place on the bench next to Jehan. The dogs trotted to their master and made themselves comfortable at his feet, slurping and begging with their eyes. Jacques had by now sat on his wooden stool at the head of the table. His authority held back further bickering between his sons.

"Yes, Maman." She carefully wrapped a dingy rag around the handle of the iron pot and lifted it from the hook where it hung suspended above the still glowing fireplace. She hoisted the cauldron with ease, then brought it to the table and placed it before her father. He raised the cover and leaned over the ensuing cloud of mouth-watering steam with an appreciative sniff.

Jhanette sat down on the bench beside Pierre, opposite her mother and older brother. Jacques made the Sign of the Cross, and the family followed his lead. They folded their hands and bowed their heads. "Bless us, oh Lord, and these the gifts of Thy bounty which we are about to receive," Papa recited.

There was a chorus of "amens." They crossed themselves, then began sending the bread around the table. Jacques divided the tender fish with a spoon and passed each member a heaping bowl. They ate in ravenous silence for a few moments. Jhanette negotiated the fish scrupulously, picking apart the delicate meat in a cautious search for hidden bones. Once, when she was five, she had swallowed a fishbone and her father had to pick her up by her feet and clap her smartly between her shoulder blades until the bone popped out of her throat. The panic she had felt at not being able to breathe remained a vivid recollection, so she had been careful with fish ever since.

"Zabillet," her father said suddenly, chewing a portion of moist fish. His lips were greasy and a morsel hung from one end of his mustache. "I had it from the damoiseau of Commercy today that skinners in the employ of the *goddons* have been seen near Joinville during the last two weeks."

"Oh, Jacques, no!" Isabelle's normally unruffled face blanched.

"Skinners, Papa!" exclaimed Pierre, his light eyes wide with fear. "Do you think they'll come this way?"

Jacques shook his head, still chewing. "I don't know, but we all need to be a little more careful." He swallowed, then tore a hunk of bread with his large teeth. "We have decided to bring our herds onto the Bourlémont property for the time being. I don't think the skinners would dare to attack the walls of the Château-de-l'Ile, but I'm going to recommend to the mayor that we send one or two men out with the children when they go to pasture, just until we know it's safe." Turning to Jhanette, he asked, "Did you see anything unusual today when you were out with the cattle?"

The bread she was eating stuck to the roof of her mouth and she grew pale. She shook her head and whispered, "No, Papa."

Jacques' thick brows knitted into what she knew from experience was not really an expression of anger. She felt fearful nonetheless. His eyes narrowed, but he said nothing more and she experienced a jolt of relief.

"I'll go with them tomorrow, Papa," volunteered Jehan, his jaw set grimly.

Jacques smiled at the boy. He felt an enormous pride in all his children, but Jehan was his most esteemed son, though he conscientiously tried not to show it, especially not before Jhanette, the child he loved best. A strong bond linked him to her, a tie that he had felt since he first held the squalling infant in his arms. It was why he knew beyond all doubt that tonight she was holding back something. At the same time he also knew that she was a good girl, pious to an unusual degree and obedient in all things. He was curious, but decided not to press her.

Instead, he nodded to Jehan. "Very well, you may go with them tomorrow."

"May I go with them, too, Papa?" Pierre requested. "I'm strong enough to fight any skinner who might show his ugly face."

"No," Jacques answered with particular emphasis. "I need you to help me to plow the winter field. Besides," he added sarcastically, "you have not yet learned to hold your own even against the boys from Maxey. Jehan will go with the herds tomorrow, and that's final. Be sure to bring a stout stick with you," he told Jehan, "and take the horn as well, so you can signal the rest of us if you need help."

"I will, Papa," swore Jehan, his face serious. A somber mood sat with the family like an uninvited guest for the remainder of the meal.

Skinners! And in the employ of the hated *goddons*, the English, so called because of their rumored habit of blasphemously swearing "Goddamn." Jhanette shuddered at the thought of them. It must be true; they must be near if the damoiseau de Commercy had heard of the raid. After all, he was the overlord of Domrémy and had access to important news.

Skinners were the most feared marauders roaming the countryside, renegade knights and mercenary adventurers paid for by whoever could assemble the most silver. *Goddons* or Burgundians, or even the Dauphin, it did not matter who paid them. They were truly loyal to no one and nothing except money and courage in war, and for these things they pillaged the unarmed countryside when their regular employment expired. They were notorious for their ruthlessness and lack of mercy.

Domrémy, situated out of the way of the main routes and protected by its poverty and the grace of God, was fortunate to have been safe so long from these human wolfpacks. Even so, no one knew when or if the village would suffer the fate of many of the surrounding towns and hamlets, which had had their crops burned, their livestock stolen or killed, their houses looted and destroyed. And the skinners notwithstanding, even though official Burgundian sovereignty in this part of the world offered some protection, there was no way to ensure that the skinners' equally Satanic allies, the *goddons*, would leave the people in peace.

Jhanette's stomach knotted when she thought of the English and the Burgundian traitors. Sited along the Meuse River, in the duchy of Bar and part of the greater province of Lorraine, half of Domrémy was technically under Burgundian control, but almost everyone Jhanette knew was loyal to the Dauphin and to his partisans, the Armagnacs. It was unwise to make one's politics publicly known, so most people went about their business and kept their mouths shut. For longer than anyone could remember it had been this way, and everyone had grown resigned to it. Yet in their hearts they longed for peace, and in the quiet of their souls they prayed for deliverance from the English-inspired scourge.

The family finished their meal in uncharacteristic silence. Jehan spooned the leftover *courtbouillon* into his bowl and took it to the door. He picked through it carefully with his fingers and threw the bones out onto the grass, then put the bowl on the earthen floor. The dogs attacked it and began lapping the last of the stew, trying to nudge one another out of the way. Jhanette helped her mother to clear the table and wash the dishes in the large wooden tub that Isabelle had earlier left standing. Then they all knelt for their evening prayers, Jacques leading the way.

Jhanette felt most secure at this time of day in the circle of her family when they gave themselves over to God's guidance and strength. She had experienced this feeling of safety ever since her mother had patiently instructed her babyish speech to form the holy Latin words. It was a communion that was so total, so connected, that nothing else mattered in the face of that loving enclosure, not the English, not the Burgundians, not even the Dauphin.

Prayers concluded, they all made the Sign of the Cross. The two boys scrambled to their feet and up the ladder to the loft where they slept. Jacques and Isabelle would not be leaving the main room, for their bed was in the corner, behind a wooden partition that Jacques had built. Jhanette turned toward the bakeroom where she slept alone.

"Jhanette?" Her mother's voice stopped her in mid-stride.

She turned, forcing her expression into a semblance of guilelessness. "Yes, Maman?"

Isabelle put a cool hand to her daughter's forehead. "Are you all right, my darling? You've been pale all evening and you're much quieter tonight than usual." Her brow wrinkled in loving concern, and the frownlines at the corner of her mouth turned downward.

Jhanette longed to put her head on Isabelle's pillowlike breasts and tell her about the strange things that had happened to her that day. Instead, she smiled wanly. "I'm just tired, Maman. The sun was very hot today, and I suppose I ran about too much." It ripped at her heart to tell such a lie to her mother, but what else could she do? Even she had no inkling what had occurred, and she did not want to trouble her parents with the idea that their daughter might be mad.

"I'm all right, really." Smiling, she kissed Isabelle's rounded cheek. "Good night, Maman." Isabelle returned the kiss and laid a hand to Jhanette's cheek, a hand that Jhanette squeezed affectionately. "Good night, Papa," she said, pressing her lips to Jacques' stubbled face.

He made no reply but did remember to return her kiss. She turned away from her parents and did not notice the disconcerted look they exchanged behind her back.

Jhanette's room was small and dark, with one tiny window. A band of moon-light fell across the dirt floor and halved Jhanette's cot. She quickly slipped out of her homespun dress and hung it on a peg next to the bread oven. Then she knelt beside the straw-stuffed bed. She folded her hands and whispered a prayer to the Holy Mother and to all the saints that they would keep her and her family from harm and that, most of all, they would not allow a return of the *Thing* that had spoken to her so mysteriously that day. She crossed herself and got into bed, then pulled the blanket over her naked chest. Feeling that her pleas had been heard, she fell asleep.

She had the Dream that night. She was seven years old when she first experienced it, and over the years it had recurred once in a while. She was yet again the dark-skinned man in the familiar long white robe belted with gold, and on her feet she wore strange shoes that were only straps of gilded leather. Her head was shaved so that it gleamed, and she somehow knew that that was a badge of office, as was the jeweled ring in the shape of a green beetle on the forefinger of her left hand. In the Dream she felt at home in the majestic stone edifice whose immense columns supported a ceiling inscribed with strange symbols. She could read them when she saw them, but lost their meaning when awake.

She was once more in the circle formed by others dressed like her, and the energy they generated together as they held forth their hands was vigorous and masterful. It was always like this, and it had no end. The Dream faded into a mist, and before she knew it, the mist had become unconsciousness.

In retrospect—and only much later—it would occur to her that the girl who returned to the fields that day from her father's garden had somehow split in two. There was Jhanette, who went about her everyday life in a fog, performing her chores and speaking to her friends and family as though nothing extraordinary had happened to her, while only marginally aware of the world about her.

And then there was Jehanne. Some deep part of herself had emerged as though having waked from a deep slumber, while in truth the other half had died on her knees in the cabbages that midsummer day. She knew with a profound mourning that she would never be the same again. She withdrew into an immeasurable, private part of herself, never to return as Jhanette and feeling at first unbearably alone.

She did not expect that it would happen again, in the one place where she thought she would be most safe.

Bermont Forest was at its most quietly beautiful on that peaceful late August Sunday. It had not rained for two weeks, but the weather was unusually cool for summer, the sky a brilliant, cloudless blue. The menace of a skinner raid had temporarily passed, and since Sunday was the day of rest, with Mass finished, Jehanne's mother gave her permission to go alone to Our Lady of Bermont. Ecstatic at her unexpected independence, Jehanne reveled in the long walk from her cottage, across the fields and into the woods, through the reed-choked lowland.

Leaving behind the clamor of the village, she surrendered to the lure of the surrounding wilderness and felt as alert as a forest creature. Her senses were attuned to the chirping sounds about her. A crow cried raucously overhead and, smiling, she watched it glide smoothly to a nearby oak. Somewhere very near a tiny thing scampered through the underbrush, too small to be a rabbit or even a squirrel, probably just a field mouse. The sun cut through the dense trees here and there in dusty shafts of airy illumination and fell in patches on the forest floor. Through the beeches a young deer was feeding on sweet grass. He was not even a year old to judge by his nascent antlers, and the sleek brown neck rippled gracefully as he bent to rip the grass from the earth. Suddenly, he raised his head and looked at her.

Their eyes met across the distance, and for several moments they stared at one another, neither moving. In that silent interaction there was no fear, no difference between them, simply a benign curiosity. The fawn turned in profile for only a moment, then like a dignified paladin moved out of sight. Jehanne smiled and raised her hand in a silent farewell.

There was a spring on the other side of the valley, and she stopped briefly to take a cool sip from the babbling, clear water. She loved this forest, so different from the forbidding, boar-infested Bois Chenu. It was as grand as any cathedral could possibly be. Its ancient familiarity seemed to evoke some forgotten, mystic memory, and it was because of this place that she had learned to experience—to *feel*—the presence of God. He was in the wind that made the high trees move majestically; in the sunshine, and in the stone gray clouds that sometimes obscured the sun before the sky shed her nourishment upon the earth; in the living things, both large and unobtrusive, that made their homes here. His butterflies and His birds were as holy as the angels. Jehanne felt His love in each moss-covered stone. The death and resurrection of His Son was reflected in every tumbled, snow-broken branch and in the new leaves that replaced them in spring. At times the beauty of the world so overwhelmed her that she had to behold it for a few moments through tears. She wiped her eyes on her dress sleeve, then, stepping over a fallen, rotting log, scrambled up the hill.

There it was, in the center of the little glen encircled by trees, her haven, the old intimate who knew her every secret and never judged her. Hardly anybody ever came here but her. Squirrels and rabbits ran in and out of the place, blithely unaware of its sacredness, and their droppings spotted the groaning floors. Jehanne smiled at the rickety walls that creaked when the wind blew from the west. She did not care that it was little more than a shack. Better to be closer to God and the land, she thought. She skipped across the clearing to the chapel which sat waiting patiently, inviting her to enter.

Breathing deeply of the musty air, she took in the odors of old leaves and weatherbeaten wood. Whenever she came to this place, she always felt with a mild and sudden shock the power pulsing within its walls like a knowing heart. She approached the altar reverently and knelt before the stark crucifix. She reached into her skirt pocket and took out stone and flint, and the remnant of a candle. When the candle burned, she put it into a tiny pot at the Blessed Mother's feet. Above her head and a little to the left, the Virgin's carved smile blessed Jehanne in the silence, and the Holy Child, chubby-faced and holding a dove in His over-large hands, beamed in comfortable familiarity. Jehanne made the Sign of the Cross and said a heartfelt *Ave Maria.*

She shifted her gaze to the symbol of her crucified Lord Whose effigy was carved in wood upon the cross. The craftsman had not been a master woodcarver but a local farmer who enjoyed the use of his knife, and Lord Jhesus' body, like those of the Virgin and Child, was unnaturally rigid and clumsily executed. But in the face, that open-mouthed, suffering face, the artist had managed to capture an aura of implacable self-sacrifice in sublime balance with a fully resigned heart.

What would it be to die like that? Jehanne wondered. What must it feel like to have nails hammered into one's hands and through one's feet, and then to hang from those same bleeding, agonizing wounds until death? She could imagine it all, could suffer just as *He* had suffered, for her and her sinful origin. Jehanne's hands stiffened and she felt the life streaming from her body. She swooned into a drifting place.

Slowly, imperceptibly, she merged into stillness, the great Mystery permeating her soul deeper than ever before. She floated gently into a bottomless well, focused only on the cross, falling down, down, into the light at her soul's inception. As a warm blanket of repose wrapped itself around her, the fire within began to move upward toward the top of her head, where it burst into hundreds of stars.

He emerged from the great ocean of souls and universes, his eyes just as she remembered them, supremely exquisite in their power and inexpressible love. After all that worry, she was calm and astonishingly unafraid of him now. She felt rather than saw his smile.

Dear child of God, you are His beautiful one, His most beloved.

Who are you? As before, her lips did not move, yet she heard her words.

A messenger from the Lord of Heaven. I have come to tell you of the condition of your home and of the destiny for which you were born.

His face evaporated into a softly muted, humming light, and she saw a vast battlefield on which two mighty armies were engaged. Arrows whistled into the bodies of screaming men, many falling impaled in their tracks amid flashing swords. The kings leading them were pitted against one another in a desperate, bloody struggle to the death.

The weaker one staggered to his knees, and it seemed his death was imminent. Just as his life force ebbed near extinction, an angel from God, winged and delicate, lighted upon his shoulder and whispered in his ear. The king revived, and brandishing a sword of pure flame high above his head, cried, *I am the rightful Lord of this land, and my people shall not be slaves!* With a vigorous stroke of his weapon, he sent his enemy, howling in anguish, running toward the sea.

The scene changed and Jehanne saw a spacious city rising to meet her. The inhabitants were strangely dressed and rode in bizarre carriages that moved without being pulled by horses. A tremendous statue of a knight on horseback stood in the center of the city's square, and when she asked who he was, she heard,

That is no man; that is Jehanne the Maid, who saved France from the English.

A sudden swirling cloud of light enveloped her, blotting out the city, and she saw the Messenger once more. What does this mean? she asked, instantly fearful.

Do not be afraid, for this is your destiny, to rally the Dauphin and help him to attain his proper place as King, that he may expel the invader from his bleeding and exhausted realm and hold it in trust for God.

But I am only a poor girl, she protested, I know nothing about fighting and warfare.

You will know what to do when the time comes, because God will be your General and we will be your Counsel. It is what you were born for.

Who are you? she asked again.

I am Michel.

St.-Michel!

There was a glimmer of a smile.

As you wish. There are two others who will soon speak to you, and they are Marguerite and Catherine. Mark them well, they are your helpers in your Great Work.

What must I do?

You will be told when the time is right. Meanwhile, continue to pray, revere God, and be mindful of the love of your family.

The image began to fade and she felt his presence recede. The light surrounding her moved into the vibration of the world, and she found herself again looking at the wooden crucifix above the altar. Rapt tears cascaded down her sunburned cheeks. He was not gone, not yet, for she could still feel him shimmering against her skin.

"Take me with you," she whispered.

It is not yet time.

The words were faint, a distant echo inside her head. When after several moments it became clear that there would be no further communication, she crossed herself with a trembling hand, rose, and started the long walk home.

The harvest season soon came to occupy Jehanne's days, and there would be no more walks, surreptitious or otherwise, to Bermont for a time. Whereas during high summer she had for the most part only household work to perform with Isabelle, now her father needed every available hand in the fields, and enlisted her strength as well as her brothers'. Even the eldest son, Jacquemin, came from his home in Vouthon to help. Jacques also hired the blacksmith and his three sons as reapers. They would be paid with grain and a few *écus*. As the hot days shortened into autumn, they brought in the wheat and barley.

It was dusty, thirst-summoning work, swinging the long-handled scythe through dry shafts of golden grain from the rising of the sun until it set. The men, naked to the waist, their shoulders gleaming redly beneath a fine layer of chaff, worked ahead of Jehanne. Her braid was tied up beneath one of Maman's kerchiefs, and she could feel the sun burning her bare neck as she collected the fallen wheat and bound it into bundles, afterward stacking the cereal behind the mowers in the already denuded portion of the field. She had helped in the fields like this since she was eight and was accustomed to it. This work was her duty.

Sometimes while they worked they sang old regional tunes going back no one knew how far, Jacques' warbly, off-key baritone soaring above the voices of the others. It was something he had done since his children were very young to keep them from becoming bored and to flag their exhausted spirits. There was usually very little conversation among them, for this was serious business and their survival depended on it. Once all the grain was mowed and loaded onto the wagons bound for the mill a little west of Greux, the jests and laughter could begin.

On market days all the farmers from nearby villages sold their surplus yields in the nearby town of Neufchâteau. The bounty of God had been most generous that year, and Jehanne and her family made the two-league journey with their neighbors. There were also hogs to be slaughtered and salted for the long winter that lay ahead. Jehanne and Pierre picked vegetables from the garden, which they kept carefully weeded. During those weeks, Jehanne was always engaged with others and at night was so exhausted that after a hastily devoured evening meal and prayers, she fell thankfully into bed and numbed slumber.

There were no further waking messages from St.-Michel during this time. Constantly occupied and never alone, Jehanne had little chance to give his absence much thought. Even so, there were moments when she was able to muse over the strange apparitions.

At first, after she returned from Bermont, she had felt that she was walking three feet above the ground and found it easy to believe that she had truly seen St.-Michel. But as the necessity of total involvement in her outer world increased, the memory of Bermont started to erode around the edges, and by the time the harvest was in, she was arguing with herself about whether it had any merit, or indeed if it had even happened.

Why, a part of her asked, would God want a country girl with no training as a warrior even to think about saving France when there were fine generals and knights to do it for Him? Besides, the Dauphin would never listen to her, no one would; she was too poor and insignificant.

Oh Jehanne, Jehanne, the other half chided, don't you know that God can do anything?

Yes, she countered, but you cannot, and anyway, Papa would not allow you to go. It had only been a dream, a waking dream but a dream nonetheless. No, not exactly a dream perhaps but definitely a fantasy, a daydream of glory, and that was a sin. This was her place, here in Domrémy with her family and their small life. To contrive otherwise was wrong.

Still, something was happening to her inside, something unnameable, teasing, just out of reach. The world had lost its innocence for her, and she would no longer see the river as only the river, or the trees and cottages as ordinary. Everything was tied together; it all made perfect sense. Yet she could not reach out and touch it because every time she tried, it shifted, its song forever alluring but beyond her grasp.

By the time the September moon rose to light the cooling nights with its amber face, she decided that the vision had really transpired, but who was that being of light who claimed to be St.-Michel? Since he had tempted her with the sin of vanity, he might actually be a demon, perhaps even the King of Hell himself. She must be vigilant and not listen to him if he came to her again. As she worked, she prayed to the Blessed Virgin to protect her, virtually chanting "deliver me from evil" in a hopeful, whispered litany.

But as Jhanette labored in the fields and pulled vegetables from the garden with her little brother; as Jhanette helped her mother stack baskets of produce in the crowded market at Neufchâteau, trying not to gawk like a bumpkin at all the people; as Jhanette forced herself not to vomit when Jacques removed the hog's entrails from its soulless carcass, Jehanne slept. And as she slept, she dreamed.

When the slumbering girl could not protest, Michel took her traveling through a shadowland which in daylight she never remembered. He revealed a dreadful, tarlike wasteland that felt like Death, crawling with beastlike creatures who moaned their despair in the darkness and begged for deliverance. Lost and forsaken, they fell upon one another ferociously, clubbing, raping, killing little by little, using all manner of horrific means and writhing in the death throes of their spirits. A loathsome creature, dark, hairy, just barely recognizable as human, lunged at another and drove a knife into him. Jehanne recoiled in dismay, for she saw that in the blink of an eye she had become one of those shadowy brutes, hulking in the deep and reeking mud. And just as certainly, she knew that a poisonous kernel of hatred, growing deep within her, had banished her to this place.

The sun seemed to appear suddenly above the desolate horizon, but it was not the sun after all; it was the Christe, brighter than a thousand suns, too bright to look at all at once. He spread His glowing arms and fire shot out of His fingertips, and where the flames fell, Light rained on the desolate, blackened earth and on the wretched beastlike creatures. The earth grew green beneath the shower of fire, the beings assumed the shapes of men and women, and everything gleamed with a dazzling, preternatural light. The people dropped to their knees and praised God.

Jehanne heard a magnificent voice say, *All honor to the Divine Sovereign and to the children of the earth who have healed themselves of the ancient curse of ignorance, for you who were dead to Love are alive again.*

It was a great truth that united the whole of existence, and the dreaming Jehanne, awed by its elegant, powerful beauty, recognized the implications with a flash of insight. She was aware with a simple knowing that she had seen far into the past and future and into the mirror of Eternity all at once.

The radiant, familiar face of Michel appeared, and he smiled at her.

Do not fear me, dearest one, and do not fear yourself most of all. For I have spoken to you truly and have made this agreement with your Soul, to guide you through the wilderness you have chosen to traverse. The journey will test you sorely and will break your heart, but it is the road to your Resurrection. God has sent us, and we will never leave you.

Jehanne's consciousness rose toward the surface of deep water, and she was staring at a duplicate of herself dressed astoundingly in burnished armor overlaid by a cloth of fine ivory linen. In her right hand she carried a standard, a glorious white banner on which was painted the world safeguarded by two angels, and above it all Christe and the words *Jhesus-Maria*. She could not read when awake, but she knew their meaning now.

As she moved into the shallows, random images began to flash in and out of her vision, bits and pieces of half-remembered conversations with her mother and father, with her brothers and the villagers she encountered every day. Her mother was telling her that it was time for the dream to be over now because it was dawn, but she didn't want it to stop, it had all been so beautiful and so disturbing at the same time. She didn't want to wake up, not yet.

Isabelle was standing over her bed, shaking her shoulder and telling her that it was time to get up. Jehanne sat up in the semi-darkness and rubbed her eyes as her mother left her to dress. She had dreamed something: she could feel it yet not remember it. She knew that it was important, very important, but it was gone.

It was soon forgotten altogether as she busied herself with helping Isabelle prepare the morning meal. But the feelings and thoughts of the dream swirled and eddied and created tidepools of realizations deep beneath the surface, lingering throughout the day and beyond.

On the Feast of All Saints, Jacques gave his wife a measure of beautiful linen he had secretly purchased at market, paid for by money from his surplus crops. He gave Jehanne a simple, modestly gilded ring. Its flat face was square and the left edge had "IHS" scratched upon it, the right "MAR." A tiny "M" adorned the raised shoulder next to "MAR," while the opposite was engraved with a cross. Jacques had bought it from a wandering merchant who read the words to him at Jacques' insistence before he exchanged it for money. He did not intend to give his daughter a blasphemous token, even if it did bear a cross within the indecipherable letters. The man swore on his soul that the ring said, "Jhesus-Maria." Satisfied, Jacques exchanged it for three *écus*.

Jehanne gaped at it open-mouthed, then flung her arms around her father's neck. When she slipped it onto the third finger of her left hand, she found to her delight that it fit perfectly.

"Jhesus-Maria," she whispered, admiring the ring's rude simplicity. She knew those words from somewhere, had heard them recently, not connected to her religion as such, but from someplace else hanging in the back of her mind. It meant something very precious, more valuable than all the gold in the world.

She vowed to wear it always, through the long years she envisioned stretching to her death in a far distant future.

The messages came to her with increasing frequency during the fall of that year as the leaves fell from the trees and the nights turned chilly. Sometimes while she sewed with Isabelle before the fireplace, she could feel a Presence, unmistakably feminine, vibrating near her. She began to know things without being aware of how she knew them. She sensed before it happened that the calf born in mid-November would have only three legs and would die within the week. In her imagination she saw Jehan Lingué's hayrick catch fire and spread across a third of his stubbled field before it could be extinguished, and so it happened. It was as though someone were whispering these things to her, instantaneously and without words, and she slowly started to accept the premonitions as a part of her daily life. But still St.-Michel did not return.

By the first Sunday of Advent she was no longer afraid of her inner adventures. She could feel herself changed and changing, within and without. She had grown a little taller by the time her birthday came around on Twelfth Night, and having reached a height of five feet and two inches, there she stopped. She no longer found pleasure in the frivolous company of her friends, and shrank from the wintertime celebrations she had once anticipated with joy. People started noticing that a calm intensity had come upon Jhanette and that at times she seemed far away. She was still Jhanette, of course, yet the puppyish animation that had sparked her childhood had vanished, replaced by a germinating quiet maturity. Her dark eyes, always dreamy, now glowed with an occasionally ardent fire unconnected to any displays of her well-known temper. When Isabelle expressed her apprehension about Jhanette to the other matrons, they laughingly assured her that Jhanette was just becoming a young woman and was no longer a child. What could be the harm in that? In a few years she would be married, and a mother herself in a few more, so there was no reason for Isabelle to worry.

Her mother would have been even more disconcerted had she known that Jehanne had no intention of marrying anyone, ever. As a child she had seen herself, as everyone else in Domrémy did, in a world that altered little from generation to generation, where one grew up, married someone—probably from the village or one nearby—and had a family. But the humble village life, the day-to-day sameness that she saw reflected around her, was starting to become swallowed up by her ongoing visions of a very different future.

In late February she acquired a confirmation from Ste.-Catherine that her will and God's were perfectly aligned: Marriage was not to be a feature of her life. The vision of herself as a soldier was a true one sent by God, and she had been born for no other purpose. The revelation left her much relieved. In St.-Michel's shining aspect, she had beheld all the love of Heaven, and when compared to his supremely devastating sweetness, what passed for human esteem withered into bestial insignificance. Every day, she saw all around her that even the most loving people held others accountable for their own miseries. They did not express their inner selves to one another and so never understood others. Thus, they quarreled and sulked and refused to accept love's gift.

God did none of those things. His great Heart was a perpetual hearth to warm the human spirit, an overflowing Bowl of understanding; He alone was the mighty Slayer of loneliness Who merited Jehanne's unqualified devotion. She also knew perfectly well that only the purest in heart and body could see God, could hear His messengers. If she allowed human love to claim her, perhaps she would never know Them again. She took a holy oath that she was willing to remain virginal as long as it should please Heaven.

As the angel had foretold, other beings of Light began to enter Jehanne's awareness, one at a time. Ste.-Catherine came to her first, soon after the dreams given Jehanne by St.-Michel. She manifested initially in foggy slumber, afterward becoming an enveloping, softly humming energy. Catherine literally introduced herself when Jehanne lay dreaming. She was darkly exotic and very beautiful. There was a youthfulness about her, a teasing, challenging quality, yet rooted in practicality and given over with such love that Jehanne could not resent the hard questions Ste.-Catherine had for her.

You are being asked to assume a great burden, you know. Are you aware of the sacrifices you will be expected to make?

Yes, I think so. Well, maybe I—

You do not know. It is permissible not to know, Jehanne. Only the unwise assume that they always know.

Help me to know, she begged, help me to be wise.

Very well. You may begin to learn wisdom by answering another question: Are you willing to follow our instructions and our guidance?

Oh, yes!

And why is that?

Because it is the will of God. Because it must be done and St.-Michel has shown me that I must do it for the glory of God.

For the glory of God, and not the glory of Jehanne? Come now, is there not a yearning for glory in Jehanne, for an escape from her village, a thirst for greatness?

Jehanne squirmed uncomfortably. Is greatness wrong? Is glory?

Glory is not wrong in the right measure. Glory is not wrong in the right way. And the person who knows that is truly great.

I do not understand what you mean.

Just as armor protects the physical body in battle, so too an armored spirit is one who accepts glory as the world defines it as though it were the most dangerous arrow, and therefore does not allow it to wound the balance within. A soul that is without armor will be vulnerable to adoration, to an imbalance in its identification, and will forget that a glorified soul is one who has found its way back to its Source. It is for the glory of your soul that you asked to be born.

I see now. I will not forget, I promise.

Catherine laughed merrily, but with a benevolence that made Jehanne's spirit warm.

You will forget many times, but we will be there to remind you.

The conversation nested in a subterranean cave during her waking hours, and when it had been there for several weeks, Jehanne came to feel Ste.-Catherine ever by her side, murmuring insights and revealing future events even when no words were audible. Sometimes an idea would pop into Jehanne's head and she would know that They had given it to her. Jehanne could always feel Ste.-Catherine but never actually see her when awake as she had seen St.-Michel. Though, to be honest, she had never actually seen him either, except with that part of herself for which she had no word. Nor would she ever behold Ste.-Marguerite with the eyes of her body.

The winter snows had already begun to melt before Jehanne felt Ste.-Marguerite. She would come and then depart, a less constant whisper than Ste.-Catherine. Her mood was different from Ste.-Catherine's, subtler and very ancient, like that of an omniscient, all-forgiving mother. Her urgings were oriented toward Jehanne's finer instincts, toward generosity of spirit and gentleness of demeanor, even when Jehanne felt impatient with Pierre and his childish whinings. The female Guides at times conferred with St.-Michel, and although both sometimes appeared in dreams, their power was distinct from Michel's, more like conversations with loving but uncompromising Teachers than the visionary whirlwind that was the Archangel.

Spring came and with it torrential rains that swelled the Meuse River and threatened the Château-de-l'Ile. Jacques and his sons—along with the other men in the village—ransomed the island from the river by diverting its flood into smaller, man-made streams. When the rain stopped and the water receded, already blooming trees and grass burst forth into April, and the planting season. As six months earlier Jehanne had helped bring in the fruits of the previous year, now she lent her muscles for the next crop.

Through it all she heard her Counsel. She grew accustomed to Their hushed voices, and even when They said nothing to her at all she knew They were there. They were there through the summer and into the days of long shadows. They taught her, chided her, challenged her, dreamed with her. It was They, Ste.-Catherine told her, who had sent the mysterious Dream to her from childhood. When she asked why, Jehanne was given that the purpose had been to awaken her. When she asked what it meant, she heard: IT IS YOUR HERITAGE.

She pressed for further information, and felt Ste.-Catherine withdraw.

As the months passed, she felt herself becoming better at functioning in two worlds. The imbalance created by Their first appearances shifted back toward the center, making her more fully present with her family and friends again rather than only half aware of what they were saying to her. At the same time, she was growing more comfortable with her Voices. The split had begun to heal, and with it came a new sense of power that filled her with potent light and increasing conviction. The seasons made their round once more, and the seed They had planted grew into a healthy sapling.

Jacques was in a foul mood during breakfast. Last night he had had that same dream again, and it had left him even more shaken than the first time, over a year earlier. In it he had seen Jhanette riding away forever on a horse accompanied by armed men wearing heavy armor. She had looked through him blankly from her horse, then rode on as though she had no care for him and for her weeping mother. The experience was bad enough the first time, but to have seen it all once more was almost more than he could bear, and his heart seethed with anger and fear.

Although an unworldly provincial, he was a man. He knew what the lives of soldiers were like; he had heard their tales of conquest in the taverns he occasionally visited on market days. He had no doubt what soldiers would do to his Jhanette if she were to follow after them, and rather than see her disgraced he would drown her in the river. He must see her safely married before she lost her heart to some passing warrior. After all, she was sixteen now and of the age for matrimony.

Jacques sat at his place at the head of the table without saying anything, glowering at the bread and cheese set before him. An aura of pent-up wrath hung over him and his unexpressed fears crackled in the scowl that infected the room.

No one dared say a word. Pierre nudged Jehan under the table with his foot. When he had his brother's attention, he wrinkled his brow quizzically. In response, Jehan put a light finger to his lips with a subtle shake of his head. Isabelle placed a tankard of milk before her husband, and when he merely grunted she bit her lip and shot an anxious glance at Jehanne. Then she took her place at the table next to her older son.

Jehanne divined, without understanding the reason, that her father's anger had something to do with her. She could feel his fury crossing the table directly to her, like a dark river of trepidation enveloping her and settling with a tightness in her chest. She had the premonition of an impending storm and was determined not to provoke its onslaught.

"Papa, do you want us to plant the north field today after we finish the wheat?" Jehan asked casually, trying to break the dreadful silence. He had an idea what was going on.

A few months before, his father had confided to him in a shaken tone that he had dreamed that Jhanette would run away with a soldier, and that if Jacques caught her at that, he would drown her in the Meuse. If Jacques were unable to bring himself to do it, Jehan must, he ordered. Jehan humored his father yet secretly dismissed the dream as just a dream. Jhanette had plenty of good common sense, and besides, she was not the sort to run off with some martial lover. But she was old enough to marry, his father was right about that.

Jacques slammed a draught of milk down his throat, then wiped his mouth with the back of his hand before taking another bite of bread. He nodded but still did not look at anyone. "If you have time to get started," he answered.

There were other matters on his mind besides that disturbing dream. He had an audience with the damoiseau de Commercy today. It was early March now, and one of Jacques' duties as sergeant of the village was to turn in to his liege lord the taxes collected from Domrémy, along with an annual report. Although he could not read, he knew some ciphering and was able to keep track of accounts. But he dreaded this meeting today. The year had only been a moderately good one as far as the village yields were concerned. The quality of the grain and vegetables had been poor, and there was very little surplus from the harvest. Money was scarce and now the people were grumbling loudly about the tax. So, as their official representative, Jacques was obliged to tell the squire that his vassals were unhappy. His lord was not by nature a generous and compassionate man, and these were difficult times for the realm. Jacques understood only too well that the damoiseau needed enough money from the village to bribe starving mercenaries to leave Domrémy in peace. Caught between his friends and neighbors, and his lord, he had been irritable after last night's town meeting and went to sleep feeling trapped in his potentially volatile position.

A man accustomed to confronting a problem and taking direct action to solve it, he resented the helplessness that now faced him. Domrémy's relations with its lord had been historically cordial. The village was blessed in its safety from outside hostile forces, unlike some areas of the country where the *goddons* and the skinners roamed at will either in alliance with the local lord, or because he looked the other way. Jacques loved his family with a fierce protectiveness, and the thought of their suffering the fate of other peasants in other places often infuriated him and threw him into a black, helpless despair.

Then there was groundbreaking for the spring planting to be started. The earth was still as hard as granite, making plowing difficult and laborious. Thank God his horse was strong and still young enough to do the heavy work. There were some unfortunate farmers nearby who had no horse and either had to rely on their own strength to plow, or borrow a horse from a neighbor. Nevertheless, he did not like to leave matters in his sons' hands. They were strong enough, no question about it. Jehan was twenty and more like an equal, a friend in fact, than a son. Pierre was technically a man at fourteen, but his scheming, quietly rebellious nature was not always amenable to accepting Jehan's authority. Jhanette had not worked regularly in the fields for two harvests, except when the load was especially heavy, but spent her days helping her mother around the house. She was no longer a child; she was a young woman now, and it was fitting that she should contribute to the family by using the skills meant for women. Still, Jacques often wished he had her additional strength to help in the fields, that she were not growing up.

Jacques was not by nature an inwardly turned man. Now he felt an unfamiliar sense of guilt for his suspicions about Jhanette, raging against the power of his dream. He knew his daughter was not brazen and seductive like some he could name, nor was she frivolous. She could be outspoken when provoked but for the most part kept a quiet part of herself in reserve.

Of course, that was in her favor. She possessed the peasant-stock common sense Jacques expected in a daughter of his and would not be led astray by anyone. And, truth be told, his love for her was not so blind as to make him think her pretty enough to tempt some passing suitor.

Yet his nocturnal experience had been so *real*. He had clearly seen her riding away with soldiers, perhaps—God be merciful—mercenaries or even the dung-eating *goddons*. His heart writhed when he thought of it. He could not bear to sit there any longer with his misgivings, her mystified glances rebuking him for disloyalty. He swallowed the last of his milk with a great gulp and slammed the mug upon the table.

He stood up. "It's time to get to work," he muttered brusquely.

His sons knew it was a command. They stumbled to their feet quickly, Jehan knocking the table with his knees so hard that it clattered and almost overturned. Pierre stuffed the last of his bread into a mouth already crammed full of cheese. Jacques was out the door before his offspring were into their cloaks.

Jehanne stood up and took the pitcher containing the last of the milk to the door, then emptied its remaining drops into the grass beside the cottage wall. She helped her mother put away the last of the bread and ate a small hunk of leftover cheese. When they had removed all traces of breakfast, the two of them sat before the fire and sewed patches on the clothes that required mending. Soon April would come, and they would be able to use the new wool from the sheep to spin yarn for clothes to replace the ones that were threadbare and beyond salvation.

Jehanne had seen, in her mother's glances during breakfast, that Isabelle knew the reason for Jacques' peculiar temper. Plagued by curiosity, she nonetheless dreaded the answer. "Maman," she asked, curiosity winning out, "why was Papa so gruff this morning?"

Isabelle sewed doggedly for a time, her eyes lowered to her work on Pierre's trousers. She appeared to be struggling with herself, and Jehanne thought at first that she would not reply. Finally, Isabelle stopped sewing and looked at Jehanne, her face conflicted with love and worry. "He has had a dream, Jhanette," she said tersely.

Jehanne waited. She knew there would be more.

"He dreamed last night that you—that you ran away with an army."

Isabelle's daughter gasped and her face drained of color. Isabelle did not notice Jehanne's consternation because she had again put her eyes to sewing. Jehanne was thankful that she had a chance to recover from her shock before she was forced to reply.

"He had that same dream many months ago," Isabelle continued. "The first time, he thought it was just a silly dream, but Jhanette"—she paused, suddenly eager for reassurance, and put a hand on Jehanne's knee—"he is really frightened now, and so am I. Promise you won't run away from home with soldiers, it would break our hearts." Her reserve had crumbled and her stout face pleaded with her daughter.

Jehanne's eyes filled. She put down her sewing and embraced Isabelle. "Don't worry, Maman, please," she whispered in Isabelle's ear. The older woman squeezed her tightly as though, still unassured, she was afraid that her child would be torn from her arms any minute.

Jehanne disengaged herself from Isabelle's embrace and looked deeply into her mother's eyes. "I promise you, Maman, I shall never do anything to disgrace our family, you must believe that. I love you all very much, and I wouldn't ever want to cause you sorrow." She really meant it. Her heart was waging war with her head even more intensely than it had been before this morning.

Almost three years had passed since They first came to her. It had taken nearly a year for her to fully trust Them and to begin to trust herself. The latter had been the hardest to accomplish. Until They came she thought of herself as ordinary, but They had shown her that she was not. She had great strength and courage and willpower, and furthermore she had support from Heaven. With the passing months, They had taught her many things, chief among them that this was her time of preparation for her Great Work. She accepted without question that They were from God, and while at first reluctant, she knew now with an ardent faith that she was His agent.

As Michel had promised, They spoke to her about the condition of the kingdom. Jehanne had grown up knowing that the English had taken vast French lands through countless political marriages between the extended families of Anglo-Norman and French kings. It was a tradition that went all the way back to duc Guillaume de Normandie, conqueror of the English. She had always known, as did even the lowest beggar, that the late King Charles VI—God rest his poor soul!—had been mad. While the English and their ally, the traitorous duc de Bourgogne, schemed to divide the fractured realm further, the Dauphin Charles lived in exile from Paris, rejected by his mother and deprived of his place as rightful ruler of his kingdom. In a pact with the *goddon* devils, the Queen Mother had declared her son a bastard and enticed the witless King to leave his throne to Henry V of England. But God took Henry to Him before the king could receive his ill-gotten inheritance. Now England had only his very young son to contest against the Dauphin for the kingdom of France.

Jehanne had long since heard all of this. She had listened to stories of the royal family ever since she could remember, sitting upon her father's lap while Jacques discussed politics with his friends. But her Counsel told her even more about the destiny of France than she already knew. They told her that the Dauphin was under the special protection of Heaven, hence no harm could come to him. It was the task of his soul to learn how to carry the burden of responsibility, with the companion lesson that it is sometimes necessary to fight for what one knows is one's due. The Dauphin, as God's chosen shepherd of the land, was to be given the task of expelling the English from France, and through him the French people would begin to heal their battered faith. The time would come, St.-Michel assured Jehanne, when France would be a mighty, unified kingdom and a power in the world.

But before that could happen she, Jehanne, would have to convince the Dauphin to take the first steps toward coming into his destiny. That would be difficult, but there was no doubt that Jehanne would triumph. The Dauphin was like a closed flower, in need of encouragement to bloom. Long denied authority by his mother's dark control, and tormented by the suspicion that he might be a bastard, Charles knew nothing of the powerful warlord asleep within his soul. It was the will of God that he should awaken it, for his own sake and that of his kingdom.

Within the last year Jehanne's Counsel had told her that the time was drawing near for her to begin her journey to the Dauphin at his court-in-exile in Chinon. Rumors of an impending attack from the English to conquer France once and for all were rife in the countryside, and the Counsel affirmed that it was so. Recently, They had given her instructions to start her journey in May, just two months away. Although They did not actually speak to her in words, the idea did occur to her that she should approach Robert de Baudricourt as a first step in the direction of Charles' castle.

Vaucouleurs was the nearest garrisoned town to Domrémy loyal to the Dauphin, an Armagnac island in an otherwise Burgundian sea, and Robert de Baudricourt was its commander. A man of noble birth, he was military governor, putting him in a position to provide Jehanne with both an introduction to the Dauphin and an armed escort to Chinon. The biggest obstacle would be in convincing him to listen to her. Ste.-Catherine told her that he would turn her away at first, but then would accept her once he realized that she really was sent by the King of Heaven to rally the Dauphin. Comforted and encouraged, Jehanne had been making plans for several months.

But now to have her father see her secret design in a dream! She had long since been lulled into believing that her inner life was unbreachable. Her father's revelation made her feel vulnerable and exposed. His awareness, even if he did not understand what he had seen, would almost certainly compel him to watch her very carefully from now on. She chafed at the difficulty she foresaw in getting away to Vaucouleurs at all. A few months earlier, Jacques had spoken to a young man from Toul about the possibility of the man marrying her, and that had thrown her into a panic until Ste.-Catherine assured her that God would see to it that she never married. Nevertheless, Jehanne feared that something could go wrong unless she planned her escape carefully.

Swept along in an undercurrent of unease, another part of Jehanne wrestled with burdens of conscience that her Counsel had been unable to soothe completely. Until They came, her disobedience and dishonesty to her parents had consisted of her clandestine sojourns to Bermont Forest and that one-time-only expedition to Maxey with her two older brothers when she was little. But this was very different from small sins because Jacques and Isabelle would never be able to understand what she was now getting ready to do. She ached for them and the future when they would realize that she had gone away.

Your parents know in their souls what you were born to do, Ste.-Marguerite assured her, and they accept it in their souls. Your father's dream shows that he is aware of your destiny, but his mind cannot yet accept it.

He is in pain; they both are. How can I leave them if it will hurt them even more?

IF THEY ARE IN PAIN, IT IS ONLY BECAUSE THEY ARE UNWILLING TO OPEN THEMSELVES TO THE VOICE OF SPIRIT WHICH WOULD SOOTHE THEIR AGONY. IT IS A CHOICE THEY MAKE, JEHANNE, WHICH DOES NOT ULTIMATELY CONCERN YOU, FOR YOU HAVE CHOICES OF YOUR OWN THAT LIKEWISE HAVE NOTHING TO DO WITH YOUR PARENTS. AS LONG AS YOUR INTENTION IS NOT DELIBERATELY TO HURT THEM, YOU HAVE NOT SINNED.

Even though I know in advance that it will hurt them?

Even then. Give your family the freedom to decide how they will feel when you have gone. In so doing, you will perform a true act of love. Do not be afraid to go out into the world, the time has come when Domrémy can no longer hold you.

I am afraid, she admitted.

YOU WILL NOT BE ALONE.

Thus armed, she waited restlessly for May when she would begin her journey.

CHAPTER TWO

Venture Outward

May–December 1428

hen he finished breakfast, Robert de Baudricourt found that a line of
petitioners had formed in the courtyard outside the run-down hilltop
castle that served as his headquarters. He groaned aloud at the sight
of them. There would be squabbles between townsfolk and soldiers to be settled,
among denizens of small villages in his district, matters both civil and criminal
upon which he must rule. It was not so bad during the cold months, when people
remained for the most part indoors and therefore did not have much opportunity
to cause trouble among themselves. But he especially detested the warmer seasons
and the quarrels they encouraged, and now, with spring full upon them, his docket
was crammed with citizens and their piddling complaints. It promised to be an
exhausting day. By nine o'clock, Robert Liebaut, sieur de Baudricourt, was already
a busy man.

He hated the provincial post to which he had been assigned as governor. Stuck
in this miserable pesthole with nothing official expected of him but to judge petty
lawsuits and punish his own rowdy soldiers from time to time, he silently cursed
the Dauphin for not ordering him into the field. In his late thirties, he was a
strapping, bandy-legged fighting man bred from minor nobility, and such inac-
tivity rankled his pride. He wanted to do something *useful* for a change instead
of staying holed up like an old man, or a coward. Indeed, there were times when
he wondered why he did not just throw in his lot with the Burgundians and be
done with it. At least they were willing to fight. But he hated the English passionately, more than he hated this dull life, and if the Dauphin was a fool, he
was nevertheless the soul of France. Baudricourt vowed that he would rather die
than live under a rule meted out by the usurpers. So he chafed within and carried
out his duties with bitter resignation.

"Who's next?" he yawned, addressing Bertrand de Poulengy, who stood beside
and slightly behind him, leaning casually on Baudricourt's chair.

Poulengy was his captain and trusted friend, thirty-six years old, and like Baudricourt, the son of a minor noble. But where sieur Robert had to break backs every now and then to get anything out of the garrison, Poulengy was easygoing and popular with the men under his command. He was taller and wirier than his stocky, darkly bearded superior, and in the gray eyes that peered at the world with sober good humor his rough warriors found a steady, dependable advocate. He was often present during Baudricourt's sessions with the people, quietly observant, saying little except when the governor asked for his advice. He was here now in that capacity.

"A girl from Domrémy, daughter of Jacques Darc," he gave in languid reply. "You remember him, he was one of the representatives in the villagers' dispute with the damoiseau of Commercy over the tax they owed him."

"Big man? Large black mustache?"

"The very same."

"You know him, don't you?" Baudricourt lifted a thick eyebrow.

Poulengy nodded. "Yes, I've known him a long time. Good sort, him and his wife. Good family."

"And the girl?"

He shrugged. "Just a girl, quiet type, doesn't say much. I don't know her very well."

"Well, what does she want?"

"I don't know, she wouldn't tell me. She said she had a message that she could deliver only to you." He smiled mischievously at Baudricourt's exasperated look. "She's accompanied by her uncle."

"All right." The governor sighed. "Let's see what she wants." With a flip of his hairy hand, he signaled the man-at-arms standing guard at the door to let them in.

A small, gaunt man entered the chamber hesitantly, both hands clutching his hat before him. He appeared nervous and an apologetic expression flickered across his face. Dressed in a homespun shirt and thick woolen hose that crinkled at his knees, he looked to be about forty-five. There was nothing noteworthy about him, just another peasant, going bald. He bobbed his head in apprehension.

Baudricourt had become a discerning reader of men, and he could see by the way the man shifted his feet and fumbled with that crumpled hat that he was here reluctantly. "Yes?" the governor growled.

"Good morning, sir, my name is Durand Lassois, and this"—he quickly gestured behind him—"is my niece, Jhanette. It is she who wishes to speak to you." The stooped man stepped aside, his gaze lowered to the floor.

The girl came forward. She smiled at Poulengy, whom she recognized. At first glance she seemed typical of her class. She was not tall, but of the sturdy peasant type, obviously strong and accustomed to hard labor, judging by her muscled arms and sun-darkened complexion. She wore a wine red, coarsely spun wool dress, and on her feet were handmade leather shoes. Her hair was as black as night and fell in a disorderly braid across her left shoulder, lying finally upon her breast. In contrast to Lassois, she did not comport herself as a timorous peasant but looked boldly at Baudricourt with heavy-lidded brown eyes that were simultaneously otherworldly and impassioned.

"Well?" Baudricourt asked, vexed at the lack of awe for his station that she silently communicated. "What do you want?"

She smiled slightly and inclined her head forward, her eyes never leaving his. "I have come, sir, with a message from my Master for you to deliver to the Dauphin." The rural accent was pure Lorraine, but her voice had a low, striking timbre, as confident and steady as her gaze. There continued to be no trace of deference in her stance but rather an unexpected composure, as though she were speaking to an equal.

Baudricourt was further annoyed. "A message?" He frowned. "What kind of message?"

Her slippers clapped softly upon the brick floor as she took a couple of steps toward him. "My Master says that the Dauphin should be careful with the army and not engage in battle until mid-Lent, when my Master will give him the help he needs."

The governor, taken aback by her impertinence, shot a glance at Poulengy. "Isn't it for the Dauphin to decide what he should do within his own kingdom?" he asked sarcastically.

"The kingdom is no concern of the Dauphin, but of my Master," the girl retorted, her eyes never leaving Baudricourt. "Nevertheless, it is the wish of my Master that the Dauphin shall be the crowned and anointed King of France, and shall hold the kingdom in trust for my Master. I am further instructed to lead the Dauphin to his coronation."

A pained expression formed on Baudricourt's shaggy face, and he glanced up at Poulengy as though to ask, Is this a joke?

The captain's eyebrows arched in an amused reply.

"And who, I might ask, is your 'Master'?" Baudricourt had had enough of this impudent nonsense.

"The King of Heaven," she said evenly.

Poulengy gasped in astonishment. Baudricourt felt the air leave his lungs as though he had been punched in the stomach. He inhaled sharply and exploded into howling laughter. Relief echoed through the stone-walled chamber in great *ho, ho, ho's.*

It was a joke after all; that or the girl was simply addled. So an otherwise dull morning had been sparked by a little unforeseen entertainment, but a jest in bad taste all the same. Still laughing, he wiped away the tears, then waved his hand toward the sheepish Lassois.

"Take her back to her father, and tell him to box her ears." Very slowly, his eyes raked her up and down. A lascivious grin sneaked across his beard-encircled mouth and he said to the dignified, still-intent girl, "Or maybe, if she likes to play with soldiers, she can stay in Vaucouleurs a little longer. My men would enjoy having some new meat fresh from the country."

Lassois took Jehanne by the arm and tried to steer her in the direction of the door. "Come, Jhanette," he murmured.

She allowed herself to be pulled but continued to stare dauntlessly at Baudricourt. Her face was blank, unreadable, and the soldier felt unaccountably discomfited, as though somehow overpowered by her. He wanted her out of here, now.

"Go!" he barked.

The vassal Lassois asserted himself and pushed her outside, all the while bowing and apologizing for his niece.

When they were gone Baudricourt laughed again, a little too heartily to be entirely convincing to either himself or his friend. Truth was, that girl had disturbed him.

When she first began speaking about her "Master," his spirit had lifted with hope, for Baudricourt had long wished that the Dauphin might somehow acquire an ally powerful enough to help him to expel the English. True, there were the fierce Scots, with their frightful, wailing pipes and savage integrity, but they were few in number. Baudricourt had not known how open to an elusive hope, however flimsy, he still could be, even to the point of listening to some farmer's balmy daughter. He was as irritated at his own lurking capacity for naïveté as he was at that irksome girl.

But he had to admit there was something about her that was compelling in a way he could not define. She had conveyed her "message" matter-of-factly, and her words notwithstanding, she did not appear to be mad. She was as common as the earth from which she had sprung, and when she spoke, her country accent disavowed guile or conceit. At the same time a cloak of authority lay upon her, and however outlandish, the well-spoken declarations seemed to originate far above her station, suggesting a nobility alive in some fundamental part of her. That was the most disturbing thing about her: a natural, salt-of-the-earth appearance at odds with an uncommon composure. Had it not been for the insanity of her words, Baudricourt could have been moved by her.

Of course, it was all a load of horseshit. If God spoke to anyone at all—and he very much doubted even that—He would probably communicate with highly placed churchmen conversant in matters such as God, and Heaven, and so forth, not with some peasant's daughter from the frontier. And why God would want to help the Dauphin was beyond comprehension. Charles might or might not be the legitimate heir to the throne, but he was also a frivolous dolt who often compromised his own tenuous position and the welfare of his people in exchange for money from any and all, even—so rumor had it—from Chancellor de la Trémoïlle, the Dauphin's prime minister and likely tool of the Burgundians.

In any event, Baudricourt found it impossible to believe that God would have a hand in politics in the first place. The war had been going on for a long time without any apparent Divine intervention. No, the girl was simply not in her right mind, despite her demeanor.

Baudricourt turned his attention to the other cases awaiting his decisions. He ordered a man-at-arms flogged for murdering a comrade with whom he had quarreled over a gambling debt. Later, he settled a dispute between two antagonistic landlords. By afternoon Jehanne had become an amusing anecdote he had half forgotten.

Jehanne was not discouraged by her audience with Baudricourt; on the contrary, she felt jubilant. She did not even mind the soldiers' sniggering catcalls that followed her and Durand across the courtyard and down the steep hill to the street. She had introduced herself into the governor's awareness and taken the first step toward breaking through his resistance. Her Counsel had told her that he could be convinced, though not easily, because he was disheartened and bitter.

You will find it necessary to give him patience before he will hear you, Ste.-Marguerite told her as she rode home to Burey-le-Petit with Durand. When he sees that you are sincere and determined, he will send you to Chinon.

When will that be?

When it is time. You will know. Meanwhile, in order to succeed you must become fortitude itself and endure in God.

Jehanne knew that patience was not her strongest point. Still, she was getting better at it all the time. After she made up her mind that she was going, she had waited a whole long week to ask her parents for permission to visit her mother's cousin, also called Jehanne, and her husband, Durand Lassois. The Lassoises lived only a league from Vaucouleurs in the village of Burey-le-Petit. It seemed to her that if she was to find her way to Robert de Baudricourt, she would need to put herself as near him as possible. She was not acquainted with anyone living in Vaucouleurs itself, so she would have to take a risk and rely on Durand, whom she called "Uncle" out of deference to his advanced age of forty.

Obtaining her parents' permission to visit her cousins had been easier than she had hoped. What with Papa's moods, Isabelle agreed, it would do Jehanne good to spend a week away. Jacques objected, but Maman was persistent and prevailed in the end.

Once she was under the Lassois roof, Jehanne bided her time for another five days. She helped her namesake around the house and spent quiet evenings with Jehanne and Durand. Because she was fond of them and felt marginally guilty for using them to gain her objective, she decided to tell them as much as they could understand without revealing things she should not. As opportunities presented themselves, she dropped hints here and there that she had experienced something over the last few years that had greatly changed her. Finally, two nights before her last full day in Burey-le-Petit, she confided in the couple.

She made her bid that evening while the three of them sat before the fireplace after supper. Durand was whittling a little wooden horse, a skill he had learned as a boy. As he cut, his sharp knife flicked tiny wings of birch into a growing pile on the floor. His wife spun strands of wool through her long fingers, humming a little tune in cadence with the spinning wheel. Jehanne sat on a low stool near the fire. First one side was cold, then the other. Every now and then, when the heat started to really burn her face and arms and it seemed her dress would ignite, she had to move her seat to a new spot.

They had spent the evening meal talking about family matters, which issued into an uncomfortable discussion for Jehanne about her possible future with the young man from Toul. When Jehanne Lassois asked her if it was true that her father had recently betrothed her, Jehanne evaded the question by stating that she had not met any young man, and her father had not told her of any plans he had made for her. She was grateful when they did not inquire further.

At last, a break in the conversation gave her the opening she was waiting for.

The words came haltingly at first, then a little faster. She did not reveal the particulars of her encounters with her Teachers, to whom she referred collectively as "God." Still, she told them in shortened form about her first visitation and how frightened she had been. She spoke about the way she had felt during the vision in Bermont, her account impaired by the inadequate words. She revealed how subsequently she was given foreknowledge of things that soon thereafter came to pass. God was always comforting and wise, she said, and He had taught her to be patient and to have pity on the suffering kingdom. But she warily avoided any mention of her mission. She would have to choose the right moment for that.

Durand had stopped whittling his horse early on, and as Jehanne finished speaking, his face was focused intently on her, eyes narrowed in dubious concentration. Jehanne Lassois was so engaged with what her young cousin was saying that her spinning wheel had stopped with the wool half-spun in her hands.

"I know in my heart the messages are from God, because He has never lied to me that I can tell and He's always told me to pray and honor my family. And the marvels I've seen! I can't begin to describe them."

"What sort of marvels, Jhanette?" Durand asked. He was not sure of her, she could tell by the way his eyes probed her earnestness.

She looked at his homely features, measuring how much she should say all at once. Durand was one of the kindest men she knew, but she could not be sure how he would respond to what she was now going to propose.

"God told me to give a message to Robert de Baudricourt," she said, sidestepping the question for which there was no coherent answer.

Husband and wife exchanged a surprised look. "What message?" asked Jehanne Lassois. There was clearly concern in the woman's normally jovial face.

"I cannot tell you that, I'm sorry. The time will come when you will know everything, but right now I can't tell you; I don't have God's permission. But Uncle Durand"—Jehanne pleaded with his quietly resistant eyes—"I need your help to meet with sieur Robert."

Durand wagged his head, trying to chuckle but unable to muster genuine humor. "I don't know, Jhanette, sieur Robert's a busy, important man, I don't see how I could. . . ."

Like a great serpent nesting at the base of Jehanne's spine, something within her awoke. Almost casually, it seemed, it stretched, sending its vigor all the way up to her head, and she was instantly flooded by a Power blazing from her spirit, charging her body. The ends of her hair appeared to crackle with it and her hands buzzed so that she thought they were glowing. She felt her essence swell, then take up the entire room with the vast resources of her will. She was unconquerable and irresistible.

She sat forward on the stool, her posture stressing her passionate conviction as the Power raced through her blood. "Uncle Durand, I promise you that I have truly been commanded by God to speak to sieur Robert. This is not a trivial thing but is very, very important. You must help me, please. What I do is the will of God."

Durand faltered as the Power struck him. He shook his head like a dog just emerged from a bath. Resisting her, he looked back down at the block of wood. "Do your parents know about this?" he muttered.

He had stumbled but not fallen, and Jehanne knew she had yet another obstacle to sidestep. She decided to chance rejection. "No. And I need for both of you to promise you will not tell them. Not just yet."

Jehanne Lassois' eyes glimmered with the trace of a conspiratorial smile, and she said to her husband, "Come, Durand, take Jhanette to see sieur Robert."

He shook his head doubtfully, lowering his eyes to the aimless slices his knife made into the hard wood. "I need to think about it."

"But, Uncle Durand," Jehanne said with urgent exasperation, "tomorrow's my last day here; I go back home the day after. If you are to take me to Vaucouleurs, it must be tomorrow!"

His wife began to importune him with her own pleas. Aware that the battle was almost won, Jehanne exulted in her ally. But Durand was uncharacteristically stubborn, and it had taken the two Jehannes the rest of the evening to convince him to yield to his cousin's request.

Riding beside him now in his farm wagon, she felt a twinge of guilt follow her initial elation. He had said nothing of consequence to her since leaving Baudricourt's headquarters. He drove the wagon in a slow silence, and Jehanne could feel his humiliation as though he had voiced it.

"I'm sorry, Uncle Durand, I didn't mean to embarrass you." She bit her lip uneasily. She felt very sorry for this kind man whose life had been one of sadness and toil. His parents had died in a skinner raid when he was ten, his brother in a minor skirmish fighting for the Dauphin. Yet he somehow did not appear overburdened by his misfortunes. His earth-darkened hands gently held the reins which he now flicked, clicking his tongue in a command that his horse understood.

"Sieur Robert is an important man," he mumbled, "and I don't think you accomplished anything by speaking to him that way, Jhanette."

"I had to speak to him that way, Uncle," she protested. "Everything I told you and Jehanne last night, everything I told sieur Robert, it was God's truth. He *has* bidden me to give this message to the Dauphin, because God wills that the Dauphin shall be King and drive the *goddons* from France!"

For what seemed to Jehanne a long time, Durand drove without responding. Finally, when they reached the road that turned to Burey-le-Petit, he reined in the horse and looked at her.

"Let us not speak any more about today, Jhanette. I know you believe in what you have seen, and perhaps you are right. I am only a farmer and I don't know about these things. But sieur Robert did not believe you, and you must let the matter drop." His practicality and limited imagination pleaded for her understanding.

She nodded. "Promise you won't tell Papa. He would never let me out of the house again." Her eyes filled, and Durand smiled, creasing his face into even deeper valleys.

"I promise."

He was true to his word. When Jacques came to fetch her home next day, the Lassoises expressed their joy at having hosted Jehanne and relayed their greetings to the rest of the family. Neither cousin mentioned anything about the journey to Vaucouleurs. Jehanne hugged and kissed them both in a grateful farewell. She assured them that she would see them again soon.

That summer of 1428, refugees from farms and villages to the west funneled through Domrémy bound for what they hoped would be safety in Vaucouleurs and in the duc's capital at Nancy. They traveled singly and in family groups, on foot and driving wagons laden with their few worldly goods. Jacques and Isabelle, together with their neighbors, gave them food and shelter, and Jehanne sacrificed her bed to two small children. Frightened by the ordeal of sudden flight, the uprooted babbled that the Burgundians had massed a great free company which had already put to the torch much of southern Champagne. Together with the English, they had begun a series of raids throughout the countryside, fiercer than any in the last few years, burning and looting as the helpless population fled before them. There were hundreds of them, the refugees said, and they were as ravenous as locusts. It seemed that this time the *goddons* and the Burgundians were making a united effort to remove all signs of human life from the kingdom's rural areas.

Worst of all, they were headed toward the east, and Lorraine.

While his wife and daughter fed the half-starved, unexpected visitors, Jacques listened grimly to their tales, his mind whirring with possibilities. That very night he called together the mayor and the village council. In anticipation of impending flight, he offered to make a special trip to Neufchâteau next day on behalf of Domrémy to arrange for sanctuary within its walls. He was gone for three days. While there, he made plans for his family to stay at the inn of a woman well known to them from their journeys to Neufchâteau on market days. Her real name was Renée Waldaires, but she was called La Rousse in honor of her russet hair. A stoutly built widow whose three grown children lived in the town with their families, she had ruddy cheeks and a loud, gregarious nature. Her late husband, Louis, had known Jacques since they were boys together at Ceffonds.

July came, and skinners commanded by the Burgundian governor of Champagne, Antoine de Vergy, were rumored to be on the rampage just a few leagues from Domrémy.

In an atmosphere of near panic the residents of Domrémy and neighboring Greux threw together what they could carry and loaded their wagons. Everyone stayed awake that first night, ready to leave at the sound of the churchbell or the horn. After hours of tense uncertainty, dawn found many exhausted and unfit for work or flight.

For a few days nothing happened. When no menacing shapes appeared on the ridge ready to swoop down upon them, day-to-day village life resumed and continued much the same as always. Just when they were beginning to feel that the threat would pass them by, the sentry they had posted a couple of leagues west of town came riding back, shouting the alarm. A great cloud of dust from many horses was headed their way.

While the churchbell pealed its urgent signal, the farmers ran home from their fields and collected their families. They departed hurriedly, driving their animals through the waning light of day. The total populations of Domrémy and Greux, some two hundred and thirty people, left the villages deserted as they walked and drove in anxious silence. The last to leave set their own fields ablaze to deny forage to the skinners.

Maman's chickens, caged and covered with burlap, chattered noisily in the back of the wagon next to the spinning wheel, propped up by sacks of grain. Jacques' children prodded the livestock along under the moonless sky. The jingles and creaks of horse harnesses were interspersed with terse commands from the mayor for them to hurry along. At the edge of the flock a lamb, bewildered by the activity, bleated loudly for its mother. The blacksmith's youngest son ran to it, flapping his arms, and shooed it back to the herd. Riding in the back of her son's wagon with her feet dangling toward the ground, old Tante Jehanne Aubry clutched her rosary and whispered a prayer for their safety.

They had not gone far when Jehan Morel, Jehanne's godfather, shouted an alert to the rest of the caravan. An unnatural glow in the sky behind them had affixed itself to the one they had created, and with sinking hearts they realized that their homes were being sacked and burned in their absence. A few of the women began to weep, and seeing their mothers distraught the young children also cried. They were as homeless now as those unfortunates they had sheltered just a few weeks earlier. But at least they were safely away, Jehanne thought; they were all together and unharmed, by the grace of God.

By the time the villagers staggered through the gate past the walls of Neuf-château on that sticky summer evening, the market town was already swollen with the throng of other rural refugees. Domrémy's neighboring farmers from elsewhere in Lorraine, having seized the opportunity to sell their harvests to the hungry, were loudly hawking vegetables and fruit, chickens and grain, from carts they had hastily positioned end to end in the congested streets. Soldiers summoned to support the garrison at Vaucouleurs threatened their way through the sea of unwashed bodies. Everywhere was noise and confusion, stirred about in the dusty torchlight beneath hundreds of shuffling feet. Unsure of where to go, those who had arrived penniless huddled together at the wall nearest the market. The odors of animal manure, cooking food, and smoke blended into one great stench.

Jacques and his sons muscled their horse's way through the crowded market-place and down a side street no less packed than the square. The inn where they would stay was at the end of the alley, just past the butcher's shop on the corner. After he drew rein, Papa ordered the boys to wait outside with the wagon while he took Maman and Jhanette into the inn.

From across the noisy tavern, La Rousse saw them and began to shove her way through the monks, soldiers, merchants, and refugees. She welcomed Jacques' exhausted, trembling family with hugs and a friendly smile. She had saved two rooms for the family, she said, one for Jacques and his sons, the other for Isabelle and Jehanne. She offered the women food and wine, and after they had the chance to fill their stomachs they were able to take their ease somewhat and to put aside for a little while thoughts of the home they had abandoned. Still fright-

48

ened and worried for their future, Jehanne got a little tipsy from the wine. She was much relieved when the time came to go to bed. She slept huddled next to Maman, and relived the flight in her dreams.

That night the men of Domrémy formed their loaded wagons into a circular enclosure behind the inn. They posted rotating sentinels from their ranks to guard their livestock and their goods from thievery. After sunrise the children were given the task of feeding the animals with the kitchen slops La Rousse and other innkeepers allowed them to take away.

Jehanne's family stayed in Neufchâteau for two weeks. With nothing else to occupy their time and to show their gratitude to La Rousse, Jehanne and her mother helped in the kitchen and served the other guests who filled the hostel to overflowing. It was not labor that they minded; they considered themselves fortunate to have a room to themselves. Many who had fled the skinners found it necessary to sleep on the floor of the downstairs tavern, next to the very tables where they took their meals.

Despite God's mercy to them, and the adventure of being in Neufchâteau, Jehanne longed to return to Domrémy, if indeed the village still stood. Apprehension about their home ate at all her family. It was something they dared not utter out of fear that God would condemn their ingratitude and visit upon them a worse fate. So each of the Darcs bore his or her unease in impassive silence.

Jehanne's sleep continued to yield disturbing, vaguely remembered dreams. She begged St.-Michel for news of home, yet on the subject he and her other Guides were mute. Jehanne was so intent on her fears of destruction that she was unprepared for trouble from another quarter, and when it came she was taken unawares.

His name was Paul LeMaire and although Jehanne had certainly heard of him, she had never met him until that day when he sought her out at La Rousse's inn. He was twenty-two years old, a farmer from Toul and distant cousin to her sister-in-law. It was he to whom Jacques Darc had spoken about marriage to Jehanne.

That afternoon she was in the pension's stifling, busy kitchen, chopping onions for the lamb stew that would be served for supper. Her stinging eyes were watering heavily when one of the serving girls announced that she had a visitor. Jehanne's first reaction was relief at the interruption, coupled with a mild curiosity.

Then, suddenly excited, she thought, Perhaps it is a message from sieur Robert, perhaps he has reconsidered and is ready to send me to Chinon!

She wiped her eyes and beaded forehead on her wet apron, then hurriedly plunged her hands into a bucket of water to rid them of the onion odor. She was still drying them on a rag when she left the kitchen and entered the tavern.

The tall young man with brown hair and blue eyes was sitting at a table near the kitchen door. He was neither handsome nor ugly, merely average-looking. His farmer's clothes, while not grand, were clean. When he saw her he stood and, smiling, greeted her by name and introduced himself.

Jehanne blanched and drew her dark brows together above her nose. She grunted in acknowledgment of his existence.

He invited her to sit with him at the table. Wearing a frown, she slid onto the bench opposite him.

"Your father has given me permission to ask for your hand," he said with a confident smile, "and so I'm here to do just that." He was very sure of himself, and Jehanne could feel that he considered this meeting just a formality.

"My father has misinformed you. He has not asked how I feel about this." Her stomach knotted and something like a cornered animal started racing through her head. But she willed her face into a neutral mask.

LeMaire's jaw dropped. "What do you mean?" he said with a disbelieving attempt at a laugh. "It's all arranged that we'll be married sometime next year."

"It's not arranged with me. I'm not going to marry you or anyone else, not next year or any time." Her actively hostile voice spat at his presumptuousness. She was angry at Jacques, too, for trying to sell her off as though she were a sheep or a cow. She wondered what dowry her father had offered this muscular young man.

He recoiled from the antagonism in her downturned mouth and flaring nostrils. "I don't believe this," he said, simultaneously shaking his head and smiling in amazement. "Are you telling me that you're going to disobey your father?"

"I was born to obey a higher Authority than my father, and I will not marry you."

It was his turn to be angry. All traces of his former friendliness evaporated as his face reddened. He stood up abruptly, and glared at her.

"We'll see about this. I'm going to have you before the diocesan court in Toul, and I promise you, you will marry me with your consent or without it!" Flecks of saliva sprayed from the side of his mouth as he spoke.

Equally resolute, Jehanne stared him down. He turned on his heel and strode heavily from the inn, more daunted by her than he would ever have admitted.

Only when he was gone did she allow her fear to surface and she trembled, sweating profusely, her mouth as dry as linen.

YOU HAVE NOTHING TO FEAR, JEHANNE, Ste.-Catherine whispered without words. NO ONE WILL FORCE YOU TO MARRY THIS MAN. YOU ARE DESTINED FOR OTHER THINGS, AND THE TIME IS NEAR FOR YOU TO EMBARK UPON A VERY DIFFERENT PATH.

Jehanne hoped that Paul LeMaire would simply forget about her. But when she had been in Vaucouleurs for eight days, he did have her called before the church court in Toul to answer a charge of breach of promise. Jehanne pleaded with her enraged father to revoke his offer to LeMaire, or at least to allow Jacquemin or Jehan to accompany her to Toul. Every bit as obstinate as his daughter, Jacques insisted that if she went against his wishes for her welfare, she would have to go alone and thereafter bear the consequences. Isabelle supported Jehanne, but this time was not able to prevail against her husband. So while her family remained in Neufchâteau, Jehanne went to Toul alone.

The long, exhausting walk and the resulting legal procedure would thankfully blur in her memory and become just an unpleasant matter that was soon finished. Fatigued by the journey that had taken her the better part of the day to make, she stood before the bishop and two of his clerical advisers and answered their questions forthrightly, as her Guides had instructed. She felt Them near, filling her with courage and the Power.

No, she did not know Paul LeMaire, she responded, she had only met him that one time. She had not been aware of her father's plans for her and had never made any promise to Paul LeMaire or to anyone else. She pointed out that in view of her distaste for LeMaire and her utmost reluctance to marry him, it would be better if he chose another woman rather than live in miserable wedlock with someone as resentful as she. The authorities agreed and released her from the charge.

When news reached Neufchâteau that the skinners had moved on to the northwest, the men of Domrémy gathered together their families and loaded their wagons with the meager household goods they had so carefully guarded from theft. They drove a reduced number of cattle and pigs anyway, for a few had been stolen despite their best efforts. An equal number, freely given, had become meals in the homes of their hosts. After all, they were honest and proud of the fact that, while temporarily displaced, they were freemen, not beggars. So, although they left Neufchâteau with less than they had brought, they went knowing that they owed no debts there, pride girding them for the journey home.

But when the protective city walls were well behind them, confidence vanished and foreboding began to mount as the caravan entered the forsaken chaos left by the skinners.

For as far as they could see, the land was as black as the bowels of Hell. Normally a billowing green, the soft hills rose and fell bereft of any life at all. Even the insects were gone. Gnarled and charred by flames that had spread from a nearby wheatfield, a small stand of trees bent toward earth gouged with the hoofprints of many horses. A solitary house that had adjoined the plot of land no longer existed; only the pitiful remnants of supporting beams remained, lifted like arms in supplication to Heaven. The battered reflection of a large brass bowl peeked from the ground where it had been trampled by a warhorse, and near it an iron pot's dark mouth gaped at the travelers. Beside that, there was no indication that anyone had ever lived here.

Most unsettling was the absence of sound. A sinister quiet surrounded the occasional victorious trumpeting of the crows circling the sky in lazy loops. The only other animal sounds came from their own dogs and snorting horses. There were no twittering songbirds or singing crickets, just that black, deathlike silence hanging over the sunlit destruction. The crows followed them for half a league or so, then winged away toward the south.

The train lapsed into a dazed, morose silence as they made their way north through the ravaged landscape. No one dared utter the unthinkable, which soon became manifest nonetheless.

Domrémy had been burned in great part and thoroughly ransacked. Only three houses, those constructed of stone, stood unburnt. The former wood-and-mud dwellings were charred, skeletal hulls. Stunned families began to pick through the rubble that had once been their homes. Gaston the blacksmith stopped in front of the pile of ashes where his forge had stood, and after a moment his oxlike shoulders began to shake in great sobs. A woman's teeth-rattling wail rent the quiet town, provoking muffled tears from others. Though overjoyed to see her own family's cottage much as they had left it—with only the garden looted and the fence trampled—Jehanne was flooded with dismay to find that the nearby church had been destroyed.

The ruined steeple slouched at an odd angle atop the gray, ash-covered mound. Its scorched cross was as lopsided as the world around it. Once the building's proudest feature, the tiles lay scattered and broken among the wreckage. The stone baptismal font where Jehanne and everyone she knew had been christened was caked with thick soot, its holy water gone. The altar was just a large, smoke-blackened block. The skinners, agents of Death though they were, had not bothered to touch the cemetery.

What manner of men would burn a church? Jehanne raged. One might as well burn Christe Himself! Her heart tore with hatred and furious tears coursed down her face. She craved revenge upon the turncoat Frenchmen who had done this dastardly thing.

Suddenly, unbidden, Ste.-Marguerite's compassion blew through her.

Do not hate, Jehanne, she heard as she stared miserably at the ruined church in the eerie twilight. Hatred only fuels the darker aspects of one's own nature and gives power to that which is not of God.

But they have burned this House of God! They have blasphemed the King of Heaven!

The King of Heaven is everywhere; have you not felt Him in the fields and forests? Nothing that man does can ever harm God, only in his ignorance, himself. The men who did this are fearful and lost to God's love for them, though God does not love them the less for it. Do not allow this to trouble you further. If you would support the will of God, forgive your enemies, and when you do, you will know that you have no enemies.

Jehanne wiped away the tears with the back of her hands and looked about her. Her family and neighbors—those few lucky enough to still have homes—were shuffling to their houses like tired, dazed ghosts. The mayor and his family were not among the fortunate, and Jacques was urging them into his own house. They would all have to make sacrifices and double up this night. Jehanne knew she would sleep on the floor while one or perhaps two of the guests took her bed. These were her friends, people with whom she had shared joy and fear and everything else in between. It was her duty, the way to show her gratitude to God for having blessed her family and spared them the ordeal of pain and personal loss.

Lights began to gleam dimly from the few intact cottages as their fireplaces came to life. Up and down the moonlit street Jehanne could hear keening women and crying children who would not be comforted. Papa must have made a fire inside, for a soft glow danced behind the larger of the two downstairs windows. Jehan's dogs were slobbering around his feet, getting in his way and hindering his efforts to help Pierre unload the heavily piled wagon. Jehanne knew she should help them.

A new resoluteness rose within her and her face hardened. Is it time for me to go back to Vaucouleurs? she asked the coming night.

NOT YET, Catherine replied. YOU NEED TO BE LESS ANGRY FIRST. THE VOICE OF SPIRIT WOULD NOT FLOW THROUGH YOUR WORDS NOW.

Jehanne flushed to the roots of her hair. Half-comprehending chastisement, together with an unfamiliar, rebellious impatience, tried to overtake her. She was seized by a helpless desire to do something *now*, anything to stop this madness that men called war.

She took a couple of deep breaths and allowed calmness to rise to the surface of her mind. They are right, she told herself, I cannot let myself hate. I must not forget that the Burgundians, even the English, are also Christian children of God and redeemable in His sight. Oh, God, help me to kill my hatred!

A sudden breeze caressed her face and quietly moved her hair. How long will it be? she wondered.

GOD HAS PROMISED THE DAUPHIN HIS HELP BY MID-LENT, WHEN HE WILL SEND A MIGHTY WARRIOR AND A HEAVENLY ARMY TO CHINON.

She trembled a little as the wind came up again. The night was growing cool, and she smelled distant rain, charging the air through the coming dusk. She began to walk toward the old wagon whose cargo her brothers were still unloading.

Is Baudricourt the warrior? she asked, knowing the answer the instant she formed the thought.

THE WARRIOR IS ALSO THE SERVANT, ONE MOST BELOVED BY GOD.

The wind whipped up, stronger now, the rain inched nearer, and lightning could be seen on the horizon like razors cutting through the iron gray clouds. She heard the word as a whisper that seemed to waft through the quietening, saddened village and across the ridge into the Bois Chenu.

YOU.

The residents of Greux found that any crops which had not been hastily and prematurely harvested were gone. Since the villagers themselves had burned the fields, that was hardly a surprise. What did amaze them was that although a few houses had been torched, miraculously, most of the village still stood. A great cry of relief went up from the villagers at the sight of the home that God had spared for them. This was not so bad, really. And because Heaven had been merciful to them, they gave thanks by putting their energies at the service of their less fortunate neighbors. So the next day, when the residents of Domrémy plunged into rebuilding their village, they found their friends from Greux ready to assist them. By week's end they had restored to livable condition almost half of the cottages and barns that had been lost to Antoine de Vergy's unholy horde. They planted gardens they could harvest during the winter to stave off starvation, but their crops had been lost, and with them prosperity for the coming year withered before it had a chance to bear fruit. They lived frugally and prayed for help from God. With the church burned, Jehanne found it necessary to walk to Greux to hear Mass. Through the summer and into autumn, life gradually regained a semblance of normalcy; but beneath the surface all Domrémy remained shaken, the villagers' security no longer as certain as it had once been, no longer something to be taken for granted.

On October 12, 1428, the siege of Orléans began when English forces under Lord Salisbury defeated and then garrisoned the city outposts and formed a ring of intermittent earthworks around the city, north, west, and south.

News of the catastrophe reached Domrémy the first week of November by way of a small group of mendicant friars. Things looked very bad for the city, said the monks. They had not been there personally, but rumor was that the garrison was undermanned and Orléans would not be able to hold out for very long. Jacques and Isabelle listened to the tale with pitying hearts, but Orléans was far away. Bad as these tidings were for the kingdom, the people of Domrémy had their own miseries.

The last few months had been hard for the village. Food was available but not plentiful; there was no harvest except the winter crops needed for survival. Money was either wanting or carefully cached, buried in gardens. The villagers continued to live in terror that the Burgundian skinners would return, descending upon them like birds of prey, and it was forbidden for anyone to venture any considerable distance from home.

Jehanne's parents, particularly her father, watched her carefully. Jacques had not forgotten his disturbing dreams of her leaving with soldiers, nor had he forgiven her refusal to marry the man he had chosen for her. Hard as he tried, he could not hide his resentment and distress. He spoke to her only when necessary, and then his words were gruff and wounding. Thinking that she simply did not like Paul LeMaire, Jacques began a worried search for another matrimonial prospect for his daughter.

She could barely tolerate living under her parents' roof any longer. For several months she had known that Jehanne Lassois was pregnant and would give birth by mid-January. She prayed that she would be able to convince Jacques and Isabelle to allow her return to Burey-le-Petit to assist in her cousin's delivery. Meanwhile, she fretted like a leashed dog. Her Guides counseled patience, assuring her that her parents would be moved by God to allow the journey.

Christmas came, bringing December snows that deeply covered the land. On that holy night, Jehanne lay restlessly in her bed, listening to the howling blizzard outside her window. She felt Them hovering in the darkness, and knew by the familiar tingling in her hands that Ste.-Catherine was with her.

YOUR MOMENT HAS COME. YOU WILL HAVE MUCH TO DO IN A VERY SHORT TIME.

How short?

A YEAR AND A LITTLE MORE FROM THE TIME YOUR KING RECEIVES YOU.

And then?

The question resounded in her head but she received no answer. There was no sound except the raging storm.

A thousand plans whirled through her mind like hawks on a summer's day. There is so much to do, she thought drowsily. God now commanded that she relieve Orléans before seeing the Dauphin crowned King. In the future the English would go back from whence they had come so long ago, and the brave duc d'Orléans would return from the London prison he had inhabited since the humiliation at Agincourt, thirteen years past. Her Counsel had predicted that all of these things would happen. While They did not specifically direct her toward the latter two tasks, she knew that with God's help she would be able to accomplish them. Catherine's silence just meant that she would be free to do as she wished once her mission was complete.

Jehanne turned over onto her side and pulled the stiff woolen blanket up to her ears. Her consciousness melted into sleep and she plunged into the Dream again.

CHAPTER THREE

Messenger of God

January 12–March 5, 1429

There were two downstairs entrances to the house. On one side an iron-oaked door wide enough to permit a wagon's passage swung open to the street, and it was here that Monsieur le Royer worked with his apprentices, making and repairing wheels. The other, smaller door permitted admission into the residence.

This room, a parlor where the couple ate their meals, boasted a large fireplace to the right of the door. A simple wooden crucifix hung over the mantel, just above Madame le Royer's spinning wheel. The family cat was curled up into a ball at her feet, sleeping. A little farther from the fire, the planked table had been cleared of the evening meal by servants an hour ago. The Royers were not rich, but they could afford a cook and cook's helper. Jehanne could hear them chattering in the kitchen behind the parlor.

On the opposite wall firelight glimmered against the room's two windows, long and latched in the middle. With the sun having set, they were shuttered to the early evening. In daylight, when it was not too cold out, their panels of real glass opened to the busy passage of soldiers and sweetmeat sellers and messengers from the German Empire to the east.

The cozy fire's illumination was more than sufficient for Jehanne to see her work. She sat on a bench across from her hostess while the two of them spun wool on the large wheel. Or rather, Madame Catherine was spinning. It was Jehanne's task to wind the strands around her hands as the thread left the instrument. She hummed along happily with the little tune her hostess was singing. Jehanne loved this room; its warm atmosphere communicated propriety and hospitality.

With a smile for Jehanne, Madame Catherine began another song. She was tall and slender, neatly dressed in a gown of dark blue wool. Although her face was smooth and youthful, the white wimple that covered her shoulders hid hair brushed with strands of silver. Her demeanor was decorous, almost prim, Jehanne thought. She knew that if her parents could see her now, they would not mind her being here. Jehanne was sure that they would like Madame Catherine and Monsieur Henri.

Tonight, with supper over it was just the two women in the house, not counting the servants. Monsieur le Royer was out with his apprentices, enjoying a few draughts of wine at a tavern. It was a place he patronized regularly, and not just for drink. He made important business connections there, Madame said, and often picked up news of doings in the kingdom brought by thirsty travelers.

Jehanne liked the couple very much and felt comfortable under their roof. She knew that the Royers returned her esteem and, more importantly, believed in her and her mission. She had returned to Vaucouleurs knowing that it would be necessary for her to gain local support in order to persuade Baudricourt. After all, she reasoned, if many of the townsfolk could be convinced, the governor, know-ing that the entire population could not possibly be mad, would escort or send her to the Dauphin. To that end, she announced her intentions to Catherine le Royer upon her arrival.

"Haven't you heard the old prophecy," she asked her astonished hostess, "from St.-Bede and Merlin of ancient times, that a maid would come from the forests of Lorraine to save France after it had been ruined by a woman?"

Jehanne had half-listened to the tale in childhood, at the time thinking it just another legend told by the old folks. She had forgotten all about it until Jehanne Lassois reminded her of the well-worn fable. At the recall something clicked in her mind, making her shudder in abrupt comprehension. The destructive woman could only be Isabelle de Bavière, mother of the Dauphin, who had deceived the King, then sold her own son's patrimony to the English after declaring him a bastard.

And the maid? That was as plain as sunshine now.

Madame le Royer was indeed familiar with the prophecy, and having already heard about Jehanne's mission from Jehanne Lassois, was instantly satisfied that she was speaking with the very Maid foretold by the august sages. So she made Jehanne most welcome, and proudly accompanied her young guest to daily Mass. Jehanne had been here for a little over a week, after first staying with her cousins for fifteen days. Occasionally, between assaults on Baudricourt's stubbornness, she returned to Burey-le-Petit to help Jehanne with the new baby.

She had finally won over Durand. Shortly before the baby came into the world, she predicted that it would be a boy and that he would have a full head of black hair. When an amazed Durand saw his son for the first time and found that her prophecy had been correct, he asked her how she had known. She replied that God had given her the information. The thunderstruck man dropped to his knees before her, making her feel ill at ease and a little flattered all at once.

But what he was doing was wrong. She immediately told him to rise, adding that she was only a servant of God, not an angel to be worshipped. From that time on, he had believed and done all he could to help her. It was Durand who arranged that she stay with his old friends the Royers in Vaucouleurs. They were good Christian folk who helped to influence others in the town to support Jehanne.

By now all Vaucouleurs was abuzz about her. She often chatted with the soldiers who hung about the governor's palace. At first scornful and disbelieving, they had come around when they realized that she could not be frightened away by their obscenities and their lewd proposals. They were only men, after all. They knew common sense when they heard it, and hear it they did in her questions about the siege of Orléans: How many *goddons* were there, and how were their forts arranged? What weapons did they have? Jehanne saw respect creep into the soldiers' faces as she listened to their serious answers, given almost apologetically, for Orléans was some distance away and information was wanting. Finally, their gruff manners notwithstanding, they truly believed in God; Jehanne had gotten them to admit that. It had not taken long for them to surrender to her newfound Power.

Baudricourt was another story. She went to the governor every day and always he turned her away, saying that he was too busy to see her. She knew that this was not true because Ste.-Catherine said so. The Guide also told Jehanne that Baudricourt was worried that his friend René d'Anjou, duc de Bar, would give his fealty to the English as his father-in-law, the duc de Lorraine, had been pestering him to do, and that the *goddons* would overrun Lorraine, thus endangering Baudricourt's own life. With so much on his mind, Jehanne's mission was of little importance to him. Stung by his refusal to listen to her and fretting peevishly for the day when he would send her on her way to Chinon, Jehanne was only somewhat appeased by her Guides' continued admonitions of forebearance.

She had departed Domrémy shortly after her seventeenth birthday. She dared not tell her parents farewell for fear that they would stop her. Nonetheless, she felt a tug at her heart as she kissed them good-bye, since for all she knew she might not ever see them again. But she did say farewell to Mengette as she rode through the village in Durand's wagon, and she bade *adieu* to others she chanced upon. She did not have the courage to seek out Hauviette, and since God did not put her friend in her path, Jehanne left Domrémy without seeing her. Guilt and soreness of heart left her with a feeling of empty betrayal, for Hauviette had been her best friend of all. Now it was done and there was nothing she could do about it. She wondered if Hauviette still loved her when she discovered that Jehanne had gone.

There was a sudden sound of heavy footsteps outside the Royer door, and Jehanne jerked at the insistent, masculine knock. The cat at Madame Catherine's feet pricked up his ears and darted into the darkened corner between the fireplace and the kitchen. Slightly alarmed, Madame stopped spinning and passed the pile of wool in her lap to Jehanne. She stood up and went to the door.

When she opened it, a man rushed past her as though she did not even exist.

"Where is she?" he asked. Then seeing Jehanne still sitting before the fire, he smiled.

He was not very tall for a man. A heavy fleece-lined winter cloak covered his clothes and brushed against the tops of his boots. Right away, Jehanne noticed the sheathed dagger in his belt. When he removed his cap, she saw that his light brown hair was long, almost to his shoulders. Brown eyes danced like an elf's above a long, straight nose. It was a remarkable face, square and clean-shaven, verging on handsome, and vibrant with an adverturesome character. Jehanne guessed he was in his late twenties. Under his arm he carried a bundle wrapped in gray wool. He approached her and she stood up.

"Sweetheart," he said with a teasing grin, "what are you still doing here? Does the king have to be driven from his kingdom and all of us become English?"

"Who are you?" Jehanne wondered, a little offended by his familiarity. She had seen him before in the company of Bertrand de Poulengy, but did not know his name.

The man bowed to her. "I am Jehan de Nouillompont, at your service. But most call me Jehan de Metz. You may, too. So?" He spread his hands, still baiting her with his winning smile. "Why are you hanging about this miserable place?"

A little wary, she decided to ignore his jocular tone for the moment. "I've come here because it's a royal town," she responded, drawing herself up with dignity. "I need to ask sieur Robert de Baudricourt either to lead or to send me under escort to the Dauphin." Frowning, she gave way to the petulance stored within her heart. "But he takes no notice of me or what I have to say. Never-theless, before mid-Lent I've got to be on my way to the Dauphin, even if I have to walk my legs to the knees!"

"My, my, you're determined, aren't you?" He shook his head in a lampoon of serious wonder. "Why don't you send someone else instead? Me, for instance?" Metz's eyes twinkled and he gave her another grin.

She flushed and took a deep breath, one reflecting her rising anger. "Now, what good would that do? There's no one else in the world, not a king, nor duc, nor even the betrothed daughter of the Scottish king, who can regain the Dau-phin's kingdom." She looked away from him into the fire, and said so quietly that she almost whispered, "There's no one who can really help France but me."

Metz looked her up and down. "Think a lot of yourself, eh? Don't you know that's why God made soldiers, to save kingdoms and so forth? Why, you're just a little girl!"

Her eyes shot to him and she felt the familiar Power surge through her. "I promise you," she answered testily, nostrils flaring, "I would rather be home spin-ning beside my mother, because I know these things don't belong to my station. Yet God wishes that I go and I'm going to do what He wills!"

"Easy, easy." He came to her and gently placed a slender hand in hers. "I just wanted to see if what I've heard about you is true." His countenance softened, and she knew that he was finally serious. "I believe you," he said with sincere conviction, "and I swear by my faith that, with God's help, I will lead you to the Dauphin. When do you want to start?"

She burst into a grin, joyful relief flooding her spirit. "Better now than tomor-row, and better tomorrow than the day after!"

He laughed heartily and she joined in. They had both forgotten Catherine le Royer, who was watching the scene with a vaguely puzzled expression.

"Do you want to journey in your own clothes," Metz asked, taking in her long, brownish dress, "or would you rather go disguised as a boy?"

Jehanne heard Catherine gasp as she gave him an enthusiastic, "By all means, let me wear men's clothing! It would be more comfortable for the journey and probably safer." A sudden shyness burned her face.

"I thought you might say that," he chuckled, "so I brought you these." He produced the bundle from under his arm and handed it to her.

When she unrolled it, she saw that it was a cloak. Folded within were a shirt and a black doublet, leggings, a cap, and stout boots.

"I'm sorry they're not grander," Metz apologized. "They belong to one of my servants who's about your size. If you wish, I'll have others made for you."

"This is fine," she answered, sweeping her eyes across the simple clothing. "Thank you."

He rubbed his chin thoughtfully, studying the braid that fell across her breast. "That'll have to come off, otherwise the disguise won't be very convincing." He turned to Madame le Royer. "Do you have any scissors?"

She nodded mutely, aghast at the turn the conversation had taken.

"Well then, come, woman, fetch them," Metz ordered somewhat irritably.

Against her better judgment, Madame Catherine did as she was told and hurried upstairs.

Metz gestured toward the bench. "Come, Jehanne, sit down. I'll cut your hair for you. Oh, don't worry," he smiled at her mistrust, "I always cut my men's hair. And"—he added with a twinkle in his eye—"I've never beheaded anyone yet."

She laughed a little uneasily and put the pile of clothes on the table. Then she returned to where she had been sitting when Metz arrived.

All of this was so unexpected! As in a dream, she loosed her braid and ran her fingers through the long hair. She flung it over her shoulder so that it hung down her back.

Madame Catherine reappeared with the scissors and handed them to Metz. His mouth turned up at her in a contrite smile. Taking a small handful of Jehanne's hair, he began to cut.

"You know," he remarked casually, "you've caused quite a stir since you came here. Everyone's talking about you and your desire to go to the Dauphin."

"What do they say?" She knew that he was making conversation to put her at ease while he chopped away at her hair, and she felt a grateful affection for this man whom God had sent to her.

"They believe in you. Well," he amended, "many of them do."

"And the others?" She was aware that he could not see the amused look on her face.

"They think you're an enchantress. Are you, little saint?"

Jehanne grimaced as though struck. "I'm neither," she snapped. He was making fun of her again. She was more irritated by the mocking nickname than by what people thought of her.

"I'm sorry," he responded quickly, "I did not mean to offend you. I was only jesting."

She looked up at him and saw embarrassment and genuine regret in his eyes. Her face relaxed. "Your apology is accepted."

Metz placed his free hand atop her head and turned it away from him. "Careful,

I don't want to cut you." He snipped away in silence for a few more minutes. The cold scissors nibbled against her neck and up toward her ears. Then without warning, he announced, "Finished." He brushed the stray hair from her neck with his hand.

Jehanne put a hesitant hand to the haircut. The back of her head was cropped all the way up to the base of her skull. She could feel her exposed ears and naked temples. How short it was! She stood up and looked at the floor. It was covered with fallen black hair, long and abandoned.

Jehanne stooped to pick it up. Her hair. All gone, cut off. What would her father say if he could see her now? She sought Metz's eyes and saw by his smile that he was not displeased with his work.

Madame le Royer, on the other hand, looked at her in shocked astonishment. The older woman came forward and took the discarded hair from Jehanne, her wide eyes never leaving Jehanne's denuded head.

"Now," Metz said authoritatively, "let's see what you look like in my servant's clothes."

Jehanne went to the table and picked up the bundle. Her shoes clattered up the stairs to the bedroom where she slept. All the way, her heart thumped in anticipation.

She closed the door behind her and removed her dress, which she tossed on the bed. Her hands shook with excitement at the feel of the unaccustomed masculine garments. The shirt was a gray linen that scratched loosely against her nipples. She put her feet into the tightly woven leggings and pulled the garment up over her hips.

So this was what it was like to have one's legs encased in cloth! She had never imagined what a liberating feeling it could be. No wonder men felt so vigorous and masterful, wearing such wonderfully freeing things! True, the shirtsleeves were too long and the leggings bunched up around her ankles, but the boots were a near fit. The warmest garment was the winter doublet, heavy and quilted with fleece.

A mood of exhilaration swept through her, and feeling a little giddy, she snickered. She contemplated the door, all at once afraid that they would laugh at her.

But they did not. Metz whistled softly and scratched his head. Madame Catherine gaped at her, open-mouthed.

"You make a handsome boy, Jehanne," Metz joked.

She answered with a nervous laugh. "More than a pretty girl, eh?"

"Turn around," Metz instructed with a circular motion of his finger. It did not escape Jehanne's notice that he had sidestepped her question.

As she obeyed, she could feel the heat of their appraisal. She wiped her sweating palms on the tunic. When she again faced them, she saw that Metz had his hands on his hips.

"Not bad," he said humorously, with exaggerated but genuine approval. "I think that'll do quite well."

Madame Catherine's disagreement was evident in her stunned silence, but Jehanne was unconcerned. Her hostess would recover from her shock and come around when she understood that it was necessary. Everyone would, once they realized that Jehanne had the support of Heaven to do what she deemed fitting to obey God's commands.

Jehan de Metz did not immediately take her to Chinon after all. He explained that before he could escort her anywhere he would have to gain permission from his superior, Baudricourt. Disappointed to find the same obstacle remained, Jehanne flew into a fit of outrage and lectured him soundly on honesty and promises unkept. He calmed her down with an explanation that his offer still stood, but that she would need to be patient while he worked on Baudricourt's resistance. She was tired of being told to be patient; her nerves were beginning to fray, and she determined to go alone if necessary.

Instead, she enlisted the escort of the pliable Durand and his friend Jacques Alain. They had gone only a short distance from Vaucouleurs, as far as the shrine of St.-Nicolas-de-Septfonds, when she had a premonition that they should turn back. These men were only farmers, not warriors, and would offer little protection against dangers lurking in the countryside. So, reluctantly, she obeyed her intuition and returned to the exasperating safety of Vaucouleurs.

She resumed her occupations of badgering Baudricourt for an audience and attending Mass whenever she could. After she put on men's clothing, people in the town at first scarcely recognized her as the farmer's daughter from Domrémy. Even if Metz had not told her, she would have known by the awed and sometimes dubious looks they gave her when she was about that they were discussing her strange new look and her avowed mission. Her name was on everyone's lips. In the streets she heard, "The Maid," in whispers as she passed. She had come to know the soldiers of the garrison quite well, knew their names and those of their wives and children.

And yet, as wonderful as all of this was, it was not what she wanted. She felt like a horse yearning to run but held back by a short tether. The more desperately she tried to hurry events, the more frustrated she became. There were moments when she thought she would explode. She had to get to Chinon! Madame Catherine said that Jehanne reminded her of a very pregnant woman who wants more than anything for the child to be born at last.

Finally, after four weeks of turning her away, Baudricourt came unannounced to see her at the home of Henri and Catherine le Royer. He arrived in the late afternoon, bringing with him the curé of Vaucouleurs, Jehan Fournier. Jehanne knew the priest well from her attendance at daily Mass and confession. She smiled at him in greeting, noting with a vague curiosity that he was wearing a stole over his black habit as though he were going to perform a ritual.

Baudricourt rudely ordered Catherine le Royer from the room. When she was gone, Fournier raised his hand in a formal manner and said to Jehanne, "In the name of Jhesus Christe, our most Sovereign Lord, I adjure you to stand apart from us if you are of the Fiend; but if an agent of God, approach us now."

Jehanne dropped to her knees without hesitation and crept toward the priest. She embraced his lower legs, then looked up at him. "Shame on you, Father," she said in a low rebuke. "You have heard my confession almost every day. You know I am from God."

The curé blushed all the way to the roots of the gray tufts that protruded from beneath his cap. He was about sixty years old, not a bad man, and she regretted having to remind him of his duty. But the moment she touched him, she divined that he had never had a mystical experience in his life and thus failed to recognize her as one of God's own.

She rose to her feet and looked Robert de Baudricourt squarely in the eye. "I have been told by God that today the Dauphin has suffered a great loss near Orléans."

"What kind of loss?" His eyes narrowed into distrustful slits, and she felt his continuing absence of faith despite the ritual he had observed.

"I do not know," she replied, her voice calm and sure, "I only know that it is true."

He made no answer but turned on his heel and left the house. Père Fournier flung an uncertain glance at her, then followed the governor into the street.

Well, that was worth nothing, she observed with an unhappy sigh. Is that to be all?

No, she told herself, it is just another step. Her Counsel would not have brought her all this way for nothing. She reminded herself of the visions They had given her of the future, and she took heart from the memory of what she had experienced in the Bermont chapel on that momentous summer day. She could not give up hope, no matter Baudricourt's stubbornness.

"My lord will see you now," the little page announced importantly.

Jehanne had been sitting with Durand in the antechamber of the duc's bedroom for over two hours, a delay that annoyed her profoundly. She had been summoned here by the lord of Lorraine and therefore should have been admitted into his presence right away. Hiding her displeasure as best she could, she stood and went with the page. Durand remained on the bench in the old castle's antechamber.

Charles II, duc de Lorraine, lay in his enormous bed propped up against two plump pillows, holding a bandage to his arm. The doctor had just bled him and was silently packing away his healing instruments. A bare-headed steward stood near the duc's bed in anticipation of his needs. The only light came from a small window, and at first Jehanne could barely see the old nobleman in the dimness. His hair, streaked with washes of gray, was long and matted, and Jehanne was repulsed by the deathly pale, wrinkled face. His small eyes, rimmed by circles of crimson, gave her a curious, searching look.

"Approach me," he ordered in a voice as coarse as sand, waving a feeble hand in Jehanne's general direction.

She took a few cautious steps toward him.

"Closer," the duc whispered. He was very tired, and grimaced as though uttering the word had worn him further.

Jehanne came forward until she was near enough to touch him. She could see now the effects of ill health in the old man's pallid face, in those sunken, yellowed eyes and cracked lips. She was wrung with pity in spite of what she knew about him, for he smelled ancient, musty. Like Death.

Not only was he a Burgundian ally of the despised English, but it was well known throughout the land that he had put away his lawful wife to take as mistress a vegetable seller's daughter, mother of his five children. Jehanne was dismayed when a messenger from the duc had come to her in Vaucouleurs to fetch her to his lord, whom she did not trust. Yet she had had no choice but to answer his call. The duc de Lorraine was her regional overlord, and it was her duty to obey him. But her overriding obligation was to the Dauphin, and she determined to deal prudently with the duc.

"So you are the maid who has the district's tongues wagging?" he rasped distractedly, almost as though he were just thinking aloud. His eyes squinted at her in the inadequate light.

Before him stood a young person of nearly unknown gender but for her breasts, dressed in too-large men's clothing, her short black hair giving her the look of a youth of fifteen or sixteen. His spies had recently informed him of this young vassal with prophetic powers and devout nature who claimed to be touched by God. For some time now, the duc had suspected that he was dying. When he heard of this girl, he hoped that his own prayers had finally been answered; perhaps she would be able to keep death from him. He had tried everything else and was desperately fearful of the Judgment his life's end would bring him.

"I am Jehanne the Maid from Domrémy," she answered.

Struck by the confidence in her voice, he croaked, "I am very ill, probably dying. What cures should I take?"

"I have no cures for you, my lord, because I am not versed in those things. I want only to go into France."

"How might I regain my health?" the duc pleaded, giving no indication that he had heard.

"I do not know," she repeated, relieved that his purpose did not directly concern her mission. "However, I will pray to the Holy Mother for your health if you give me your son-in-law and a few men as escorts to go into France."

It had occurred to Jehanne during her journey to the duc's capital at Nancy that it might be possible to turn this commanded audience to her advantage. She remembered what Catherine had said regarding Baudricourt's worries about duc Charles' son-in-law, René d'Anjou. Very recently Jehanne had heard that now that he had reached the age of majority, he would soon forswear the Anglo-Burgundian alliance that his wife's father had forced upon him during his regency. René d'Anjou, high-spirited and popular with his subjects, was a skilled soldier, nevertheless sensitive enough to write poetry. It would do Jehanne much credit if she could enlist the young duc to take sides openly with the Armagnacs, and that might persuade other lords likewise to change their allegiances.

Suddenly alert, duc Charles asked with a suspicious growl, "What do you want with my son-in-law? And why do you wish to go into France?"

"Duc René is a strong young warrior," answered Jehanne placidly, "and would be a safe escort to the Dauphin. I have news of prophecy for his kingdom."

So the stories were true, she was indeed endowed with miraculous powers! The old man tried to sit up. She could probably help him after all.

"I cannot send my son," he said. "Just tell me, what must I do to be cured?"

Jehanne's spirits sank with the realization that this old man was haunted by his wasting body, and would be of no use to her.

Her face became cold. "Renounce your mistress and return to your legal wife. Only then will God hear your prayers."

The duc's mouth dropped open, and he looked so comical that Jehanne was tempted to smile.

There was a time when he would have had her punished for her impertinence, but now the prospect of death wiped out every other consideration. Clinging to hope that she somehow possessed the secret to life, he begged, "Is there no charm you can give me? No herbs or spells that could restore my body to health?"

"I shall pray for you, my lord," Jehanne said gently, moved to compassion for this once-powerful and now obviously very frightened man.

"Thank you." He sighed with a humility that surprised her. He sank back into his pillows. "I am tired now." The wrinkled eyelids closed in pain, and he licked his lips. Turning his head to his steward, he said, "Give her some money and a horse."

In the lengthening shadows, the duc struggled to see Jehanne. "Safe journey," he whispered.

She was dismissed. The steward waved her toward the door. Bowing to the duc unnoticed, she turned and left him to die, if God willed it.

Bertrand de Poulengy and Jehan de Metz were waiting for her in the le Royers' parlor when she returned to her lodgings in Vaucouleurs. Madame Catherine was with them, sewing. The men vaulted to their feet as Jehanne entered the house.

"Here she is!" Metz cried with a delighted smile, his whole face aglow.

"And we have some news for her that will make her most happy!" Poulengy, normally composed and even a bit sardonic, matched his friend's elation with a grin that widened his long, narrow face.

"What news?" She frowned at her new friends, in no mood for the jests she assumed lay in wait for her. The duc de Lorraine's refusal still weighed upon her like remembrance of his unhealthy pallor and approaching death.

Beaming, Metz put his hands on her shoulders. "The day you left, we received word that there was indeed a great battle near Orléans. You were right, the Dauphin suffered heavy losses from the *goddon* forces of their lord Fastolphe, and now sieur Robert believes you."

"He's going to do it, Jehanne," Poulengy exulted. In the playful light he looked little older than a boy. He draped one arm over Metz's shoulder and the other over hers. "He's sending you to the Dauphin."

"What?" She could scarcely believe it. "Is this a joke?"

"Not at all—"

"No joke," assured Metz, "and best of all, we're going to escort you!"

"Really?" Her face lit up as excitement rushed to replace the fatigue and disappointment she had felt on the return trip from Nancy. "We're actually going? When?"

"We leave at dawn tomorrow," Poulengy answered.

Metz picked up a bundle from the table. "And the people want to you have this."

She opened it. Fresh-washed clothes, men's garments on the order of what she was currently wearing but cleaner and more her size. She stared at the hooded brown tunic in amazement, her mouth open. The two men glowed, as pleased as children.

"You shouldn't go to the king dressed in a servant's clothes," Metz volunteered with a hint of his old playful manner.

"There's this as well," said Poulengy. He picked up a sheathed sword from the table. She had failed to notice it until this moment. "We mustn't forget this."

Her arms were too full for her to take the sword, so Poulengy held it out for her to examine. It was a simple, roughly crafted weapon with a hemp-wrapped handle and a recently polished blade, a sword that had apparently seen much use. Jehanne longed to feel its weight.

"We're really going," she repeated, as though entranced. Now that the moment was actually here, it had an aura of unreality about it.

The two men nodded, still grinning broadly. Poulengy said, "A week ago or more, sieur Robert sent a letter to the Dauphin by his swiftest messenger, telling him to expect you. You've won, Jehanne; you've finally worn him down."

"Of course, we helped," Metz said with mock importance, "my friend here and I with our eloquent powers of persuasion."

Jehanne guffawed through her nose. No longer fatigued at all, her entire being hummed with victory.

"What really convinced him was your conduct before the curé," admitted Poulengy. "He was much impressed that you didn't fall to the floor and foam at the mouth as a witch should."

"That's because I'm not a witch," she said with a laugh.

"We know that, don't we, friend?" Metz remarked confidentially to Poulengy, pretending that Jehanne was not present.

"We know that," the tall man assented in a comical deadpan.

"To the tavern!" Metz suddenly cried, raising his arm dramatically.

"Oh, no, I can't—" she protested.

"Yes, you can," they insisted. "We need to celebrate your victory."

Jehanne looked across the room at her hostess, forgotten in all the excitement. Madame Catherine's needlepoint dangled limply in her hands and her mouth hung open. But not for long. "Lucien!" the woman shouted toward the kitchen. "Lucien!"

The cook's husband, drying his hands on the bloodstained apron tied around his waist, came from the kitchen. "Yes, Madame?" He looked around the room at the others.

"Lucien, Jehanne wishes to accompany these gentlemen to the tavern." Madame Catherine's nose wrinkled in involuntary distaste. "You will please go with them."

Jehanne smiled. Old Lucien was a farmer recently arrived in Vaucouleurs—a refugee from the skinners—who had taken an oath never to return to his home.

Unaccustomed to fighting, he would be useless as protection in the event something threatened Jehanne. He was virtuous and respectable, though, and she knew that that was why Madame Catherine had chosen him as a chaperon. It was a gracious gesture.

"Thank you, Madame," Jehanne said.

Madame Catherine nodded, smiling in spite of herself at the joy in Jehanne's eyes.

Reassured, Jehanne allowed the soldiers to drag her out the door and to the tavern. These were her companions now, her God-sent escorts to Chinon, and for a couple of hours on that winter afternoon, her comrades in wine.

It stormed very noisily all night, and through the morning water bombarded roofs and gushed down streets, turning them into small rivers. The party of travelers agreed not to set off until late afternoon, when the downpour moderated into mere rain.

Jehanne's escort of six met her at the Royer home. Poulengy gave her a stout leather satchel, which she packed with her old red dress, and on top of that, the clothes from Metz's servant. She was wearing the traveling attire the people had provided, a fine pair of black leggings and a short tunic covered by a leather hood that extended across her shoulders. She pulled it over her head as she made ready to step out into the rain.

The servant attached to Poulengy—Julien, he was called—took the bag and Jehanne's sword and strapped them to her saddle. The horse snorted, sending a little cloud of steam into the cold air.

Madame Catherine was weeping. She dabbed her eye with the hem of her apron and kissed Jehanne's cheek. "God go with you, my dear," she whispered.

Jehanne returned the kiss, then in a thrill of elation hugged a flustered Henri le Royer. She felt an overflowing gratitude and affection for these good people who had so believed in her that they had even helped to finance her journey.

Metz's rain-soaked servant stood holding her horse, and she mounted the animal and took the reins from him. She waved to the Royers with a buoyant smile.

From the shelter of their doorway, they waved back. Madame Catherine wiped her nose and called out, "Safe journey!"

Metz gently spurred his horse and the group started down the deeply muddied street.

Vaucouleurs teemed with hope and goodwill on this February day. Jehanne was amazed to see that people all through the town had turned out to bid them Godspeed. They shouted it from doorways and waved down to the riders from houses and shopfronts. Every few feet soldiers had hung the royal banner, a splendid blue field emblazoned with golden fleurs-de-lys, from a window. The more intrepid citizens stood in the rain, in mud above their ankles, invoking God to give Jehanne a successful journey. A group of mud-splattered children, mostly boys, chased after the trotting horses. As the group rode past the church, Père Fournier sprinkled a blessing of holy water and Jehanne's comrades crossed themselves without stopping.

Her eyes filled with tears and the frigid rain, which she was almost too excited to feel. She had to bite her lip to keep from crying out loud. They were finally leaving, she was going to the Dauphin, and—God be praised!—France would soon be free. For all these good people she had come to know during the past six weeks and for many like them throughout the kingdom who had suffered so terribly, the war would soon be over. The long-elusive peace for which they had prayed would be theirs at last. Jehanne's heart soared as she acknowledged the shouts of blessing with a triumphant wave of her hand.

But before they could really be on their way, there was one more stop to make.

Near the northernmost edge of the wall, they coaxed their horses up the mucked street to the old château that commanded the town. If Jehanne looked back over her shoulder, past Poulengy's hooded, dripping form, she could see the red-tiled buildings below partially hidden by a veil of dense, gray rain. The party reined in their horses at the door to Baudricourt's headquarters, long the site of Jehanne's obstinate attacks, and as though having expected them, he came out to greet them clutching his cloak tightly around his shoulders, his hairy features turned up to her in a wet, squinting grimace.

"Thanks for the sword, sieur Robert." She was genuinely grateful. Poulengy had told her that the sword he gave her last night was actually from Baudricourt. She was touched that one who had so resisted her would have made such a heartening gesture.

"You're welcome," he muttered, feeling a little embarrassed.

He still thought this was a crazy idea, but oh well, he was tired of fighting not only her but his own soldiers, not to mention the townspeople. And the girl had been right about the French losses before Orléans; that was uncanny and made his flesh crawl.

He had gotten the Dauphin's response to his letter early last evening via the royal courier, Colet de Vienne. Surprised the hell out of Baudricourt, too, that the Dauphin was willing to have her approach Chinon. So now the decision had been made by Charles and the matter was out of the governor's hands. Who knew? The girl might even be able to accomplish something with her outlandish schemes. Perhaps she was from God as she claimed. At any rate, if she failed it would not be on his head.

Colet was among the riders. His duty done, he had to return to Chinon anyway, and would be one of Jehanne's escorts.

Baudricourt raised his right hand and addressed the mounted men. "Swear by Our Lord and all the saints to protect this girl and bring her unharmed to the Dauphin."

They lifted their own hands and took the oath. Then Baudricourt said to Jehanne with a resigned sigh, "Go, and come what may."

The group turned their horses down the street running the length of the city's wall. Then they passed through the gate called the Porte de France, to the top of the ridge and out of Vaucouleurs.

Besides Metz, Poulengy, and the royal messenger, there were three others with her, two of them servants. Julien de Honnecourt and his twin brother Jehan, sixteen years old, were pages to Poulengy and Metz, respectively. The last, a quiet older man attached to Colet, was called Richard the Archer. He was said to be deadly with the crossbow that hung within easy reach on his saddle. That weapon had been Colet's protection on the journey to Vaucouleurs, and it would be handy for the return trip in case they needed it. Richard was a hired soldier, actually a Scotsman in the service of the Dauphin. He neither knew nor cared about Jehanne. For him, this was just another assignment.

The twins, on the other hand, were as boisterous as puppies. Poulengy had to give them a good tongue-lashing and strict orders to behave themselves after he caught them pelting one another with bits of cheese when the group rested under a sheltering tree. Thereafter, they settled down, much to Jehanne's relief. These boys were almost as bad as Jehan and Pierre when they tussled.

There was a long ride ahead of them before they could get to their first lodging place. As the day passed into late afternoon, the party increased their pace across the undulating landscape. They slowed only to ford the swollen streams that soaked their boots and left Jehanne's feet so numb that after a while she could no longer feel them. Her hands were ice blue lumps, and she gripped the reins and the front of her saddle in desperation, praying that she would not fall off her horse and be swept away in the swirling brown water. Seeing that even these smaller streams had been transformed into courses of racing water, all of them knew how perilous travel would be after nightfall.

Suddenly, the skies opened further and the chilling rain became a torrent again, accompanied by great streaks of lightning and cracks of thunder which frightened the steeds and made them difficult to manage. Even before the light faded visibility was practically gone, and Jehanne wondered how her companions knew where they were going in this curtain of rain. She could hardly even see *them*. To her the men were dark, cloaked shadows perched upon their mounts in sheets of flashing water.

They rode on doggedly through the roaring wind and the downpour and the night. Jehanne could not remember having ever been so tired. In a way, she was grateful for the bad weather; it meant that she could not fall asleep in the saddle. The punishing storm, combined with her fear of being unhorsed and a back-of-the-mind impatience to get to Chinon, prevented dozing. She promised herself that if she could hang on while her horse struggled up this slippery hill and across one more stream, her persistence would be rewarded with a warm fire and dry clothing. She breathed through gritted teeth as her horse raced after Metz into a branch-slapping forest.

A little after dawn they reached the monastery of St.-Urbain on the Marne near Joinville, some eight leagues from Vaucouleurs. It was truly Providential, Jehanne thought, what with the ferocity of the storm, that sieur Robert had made prior arrangements for them to stay at the monastery after their first night on the road.

Poulengy told Jehanne that when Baudricourt knew for certain that the Dauphin would see Jehanne, he had sent a courier to the monks of St.-Urbain informing them that they should expect a party of seven within the next two days. Traveling in the group was the girl who claimed to be sent by God to the Dauphin. While officially neutral in its politics, the abbey secretly supported the

Dauphin Charles. Its abbé, Arnould d'Aulnoy, was, conveniently, Baudricourt's kinsman. But in any circumstance it was the Christian duty of monks throughout the kingdom to give shelter to travelers, and St.-Urbain had a singular reputation as a sanctuary going back almost three hundred years.

Abbé d'Aulnoy himself greeted them at the gate and ushered them into the refectory, where the monks had laid out a supper of bread, cheese, roast fowl, and wine. While her companions eagerly arranged themselves around the table, Jehanne asked for, and was given, permission to go to the chapel before she dined. With an inclination of his head, a silent monk led the way through a door at the darkened end of the room.

They moved down a long corridor lit every few paces by fetid torches hissing in wall sconces. The skirt of the monk's habit swished rhythmically as he walked ahead of her, and she could hear the *click, click,* of the rosary about his waist. A muted blast of thunder suddenly rumbled, sounding like someone dropping his boots upon a floor above their heads.

The prayers of the chanting community became louder as they approached the heavy, arched door at the end of the hallway. The monk pushed it open without saying a word to Jehanne. When she nodded her thanks, he did not appear to notice. He went ahead of her as silently as a shadow, and took his place with his brothers.

The chapel was lined with thirty or more monks standing in ornate, carved stalls of dark wood. Their cowls were pulled down over their faces so that it would have been impossible to establish their identities even had Jehanne known them. Not wishing to disturb them and interrupt the beautiful music that issued from their throats, she tiptoed quietly to the back of the room. Dropping to her knees onto the cold stone floor, she made the Sign of the Cross.

She looked up at the distant altar and the crucifix hanging above it. A statue of St.-Benoît stood in a nook to the right of the altar. On either side of the sacrificial table, tall candles burned and rows of votive lights flickered opposite the saint's effigy. Jehanne closed her eyes and said a *Pater Noster* and an *Ave Maria*. The music pulsed all around her in a steady, unmetered heartbeat so that the very walls seemed alive with the voices of angels. The hair on her arm raised in prickles of quickening light. A cool fire flooded her neck and shot to the top of her head, and she was overtaken by love, familiar and nurturing.

Oh, thank you, my dear Counsel, for allowing us to find this blessed place safely!

No harm can come to you, Child of God, you are under the protection of Heaven. You have nothing to fear on your journey to your king.

Will he truly accept me?

He shall; that is God's promise to you. And to give him confidence in your mission, there is something you must tell him.

She listened intently as St.-Michel imparted to her the sign by which the Dauphin would know her. It was something very sacred, known only to Charles and to God, and Jehanne realized without having to be told that it would be forbidden for her ever to reveal it to anyone but the Dauphin. She let the

Archangel's words penetrate her heart. In the chanting candlelight, she locked them into a safe place deep within her.

As was proper for a female visitor, Jehanne spent the night in the abbey's guest-house. Tired though she was, she tossed and turned and slept very little. Through much of the next day while her friends slept in the stark cells of the monastery proper, she prayed in the chapel. Upon rising, the men were confessed and before dusk the company heard Mass with the monks of St.-Urbain, Jehanne for the second time that day. After a supper of cold mutton, bread, cheese, and wine, abbé d'Aulnoy gave them enough provisions to last for several days. Then he blessed them, and they mounted up and rode off into the darkness and the fog.

The rain had stopped and a low mist blew from the mouths of the horses, clinging stickily to their harnesses and saddles. A sliver of moon strained to show itself through the smoky pall floating across it. Jehanne hugged the damp cloak about her shoulders.

When they reached the Marne, they found that it had overflowed its banks. They had to ride a league downstream before they could establish a safe passage across the river. At its shallowest point they swam their horses to the other side. The current was strong nevertheless, and Jehanne gasped sharply as the freezing water came up to her chest, enveloping her in sudden dismay. But in the next moment, she recalled the promises made by St.-Michel and fear flew away from her, into the night.

The travelers made good time through the countryside by avoiding the deep-mucked main roads. Citing his experience in war, Metz had insisted that they take shelter during the daytime in abandoned buildings—barns and farmhouses—and move only under a shield of darkness. He thought it prudent to bypass even the smallest towns while they were still in Burgundian-held territory. In these matters Jehanne deferred to his leadership and that of Poulengy, who sometimes offered advice and ideas to his friend.

Beyond St.-Urbain, they began to encounter the occasional deserted village, two of them that night. Eerie shells silent under the indifferent sky, they were surrounded by desolate fields that while still recognizable as having once been cultivated, were now overgrown and full of briars. Untamed flora, winter-brown and withered, invaded deserted cottages and crawled through once-busy streets and over toppled fences. Nature was encroaching in a gradual effort to reclaim everything, as though to trumpet its dominion over a fragile, vanished humanity.

Jehanne and her comrades rode through them silently, almost reverently. She was haunted by the probable fates of the former inhabitants. Perhaps these hamlets of five or six families had been abandoned because of skinners' raids or the plague, that other recurring scourge from God. The reasons hardly mattered, really. What was certain was that where there had once been the hum of busy lives, only a vine-covered extinction remained. But these places were nothing compared to what waited ahead of them.

On the second night from St.-Urbain the group had not been on the road for more than an hour, and it was just starting to turn dark. In their path a swathe of bright rose poured across Heaven, up and up from the horizon, until it bled into purple clouds ringed in gold. It was as though God had spilled two paintpots whose contents then mingled to form another color.

Jehanne was admiring God's handiwork when Metz said that he smelled smoke. The others did not catch it at first, for it seemed to come and go like an easily dismissed illusion. But the closer they rode toward the source, the more insistent it became. The odor of burned wood was eventually joined by another, stronger, and retchingly nauseating. Jehanne thought she recognized the stench of a slaughtered hog.

They reached the top of a low ridge and looked down. Discernible in the twilight, embers lit some time earlier were still pulsing in the corpses of fifteen or so cottages. The earth where they had stood was flattened into spots of smoking desolation so that it was impossible to guess what the buildings had looked like. Even from this high place, they were able to see further wreckage of war.

And the bodies. A few seemed to be moving.

Without speaking, the riders nudged their horses forward and they trotted down the ridge. Jehanne felt that she would choke on the fetor that was now overwhelming. She covered her nose and mouth with her hand, gaping in horror at what lay before her. She could not look at it, yet could not *not* look at it either.

They were all dead, perhaps forty of them. A farmer lay face down, his severed arm clutching the broken pitchfork he must have wielded in defense of his family. He had been decapitated and his head looked grotesquely toward his trunk. A few paces from him a young woman was on her back with her skirt pulled up above naked hips. Blood from her cut throat covered most of a face whose eyes looked in astonishment at the sunset. The front of her dress was ripped open and drenched in gore. She looked pathetic, indecent. An infant, soaked in blood from the swordcut in its back, lay across the woman's arm. A little further away, a very fat woman had been pushed onto her back. Her great breasts protruded from the torn dress, and like the younger woman, her privates were exposed.

Almost all the dead women had been violated, even a few children. Boys no older than eight had died trying to save their mothers and sisters. Older men, also. There was no life anywhere. The skinners had even killed the dogs. They must have taken the livestock for food, for there were no pigs or chickens among the slaughtered. A dead horse with an arrow in its neck rode the empty air in a rigid gait, probably killed by accident.

Jehanne felt herself reeling in the saddle. She grasped it as tightly as she could, trying to resist what was before her. Using her free hand to muffle the smell, she lowered her head until the dizziness passed a little.

Something moved. Over there, to the left. Jehanne got just an inkling of it out of the corner of her eye. When it moved again, there was a flapping sound like a man swirling his cloak around his shoulders. But it was not human. Another one moved and looked with remorseless arrogance at the riders.

Metz and Richard nudged their horses and took off toward the vultures, both men yelling with all their might. At the sounds of screams and pounding hooves, the filthy creatures squawked and flew away, complaining as they went like imps from Hell.

Jehanne could not bear it any longer. The smell of putrefaction, the horrific sights, were too much for her. She leaped down from her horse and threw up. She was shaking all over, her mind numb and helpless to form anything but a primal revulsion.

Her action prompted a general dismount. The twins hurled themselves to the ground and released their own abhorrence. They retched loudly, contributing another stench to the already unbreathable evening air. Unable to maintain his composure, the elegant Colet forgot his dignity and splashed his well-made cloak with vomit.

Richard and Metz rode back to them in time to hear Poulengy ask, "Jehanne, are you all right?" His voice sounded so normal, a token of sanity and stability. His horse's legs danced in front of her.

Jehanne spat onto the ground to rid her mouth of the evil taste. She nodded, wiping her mouth with the back of her tunic sleeve. Faintness had passed, and she really did feel better physically.

"Then we'd better be off," Richard said matter-of-factly in his thick Scottish burr. With his powerful beak, he looked like an alert eagle as he turned his head in all directions. "There's nothing we can do here, and besides, the men who did this are probably still somewhere around here."

Jehanne gawked at him, unable to believe his lack of humanity. "But we can't just leave them! We must give them a Christian burial and pray over them."

"We don't have the tools for that, Jehanne," Poulengy answered with genuine regret. "It would take us all night to dig deeply enough to bury all these people." In the near darkness, she could see that his eyes were sad for her.

"Yes, Jehanne, remember your mission," Metz reminded her. "We can't afford to tarry here, or in any one place for that matter."

She looked toward the murdered village. It seemed to whisper, *Pass on.*

Her friends were right, and she knew it. There was nothing they could do to help these people. What help the dead would get was from God. He would send an all-powerful army to avenge them and to drive the enemy back to his own land. Jehanne would pray for them. Next chance she got, she would go to Mass and dedicate it to these helpless souls who had died unshriven and in such terror.

The riders moved on. Behind them, Jehanne saw the birds of prey return to feast unhindered.

The company continued at a rapid gait through the darkened countryside, grateful that at this pace they did not have to speak. It was crucial that they remain set on their assignment, so they put aside shock and anger and crossed yet another river, then another. The thumbnail moon rose and slowly scratched its way across the sky. They might have covered two or more leagues before the night began to lift.

Soon the edge of the sun peered reassuringly over the top of the eastern hills. It seemed as if the horrors of the night had not been real at all. The massacre had indeed been a nightmare, the worst Jehanne had ever visited. But dawn was coming back, and with it everything that could be good in the world.

Just when the men were starting to worry that they would not find shelter for their day's rest, they came upon someone's abandoned home. The family who had lived here must have heard about the skinners before they descended upon their neighbors and fled to safety. The cottage was completely empty and unburned. It had an unhealthy, dank smell. These people had taken everything they owned with them except a bag of seed grain. Its contents were spilled across the earthen floor, and at the approach of human intruders, a pack of rats scattered from it like spies caught in a conspiracy.

The group made do without a fire lest the smoke attract unwanted attention. There could no longer be any doubt that the land was crawling with evil. Metz and Poulengy put the fear of the Devil into Jehanne by telling her that her name and the nature of her mission had spread so far that the Burgundians and the *goddons* would love to stop her from reaching Chinon. At first she assumed that they were joking again, but Richard vouched for their story and she believed him. The archer was so humorless that he must be telling the truth.

And then, there was the slaughtered village. Jehanne could see and smell it in her mind's eye, no matter how hard she tried not to.

She would not think about it. The men were correct to remind her to maintain constancy with what God had chosen her to do. Today she would rest and save herself for her journey. Chinon, she chanted internally, Chinon.

The men took turns at sentry duty. Wrapped in her cloak, Jehanne slept on the hard dirt floor between Metz and Poulengy. She was lucky to be traveling with these good soldiers, for they were also virtuous men, sincere Christians with whom she was completely safe. They were as warm as her brother Jehan's dogs. She slumbered dreamlessly while they snored beside her.

Most often over the next few days they rode at a brisk trot, sometimes slowing to spare the horses. Several times as they moved at a more leisurely pace Poulengy asked Jehanne if she would actually accomplish what she intended.

"In God's name, Bertrand," she replied with assurance, "don't be afraid. I have orders to do what I'm doing from my—my Brothers in Paradise. It is They who've told me that I must go into battle with the enemies of France and restore the Dauphin to his kingdom. So, you see, all of us are under God's protection."

She was aware that she was speaking to herself as well as to him. Ever since the burned village, she had sometimes nearly been afraid. But she felt Ste.-Catherine rustle through her heart, and remembered that the enemies of God would not harm them even though they had the power to destroy others.

She never discussed her Counsel with any of them. It was not that the Guides had forbidden her to do so; it was a subject They never spoke of. But her communications with Them were special to her, and she was reluctant to offer them for scrutiny—and perhaps argument—to anyone else. Besides, she was unable to put into words experiences for which there were no adequate words. She did not literally *see* her Counsel except in vaguely remembered dreams. She did not really hear Their Voices with her ears, though she certainly did hear Them. There was no language for the light and the silence through which she heard Them.

In any case, these men would not have understood. Although their faith was strong, they were firmly rooted in the world. Perhaps she would be able to share her visions with the Dauphin. Michel had revealed to her that the crown prince was devout in his fashion and often prayed for guidance and he was, after all, God's own chosen King. Surely knowledge of his role gave him the capacity to understand his destiny in all its splendid implications.

For this part, Poulengy was only somewhat heartened by Jehanne's confidence. While he felt a genuine affection for this girl with the one-pointed mind, he was not as devoted to religion as his friend Jehan de Metz, and did entertain doubts about Jehanne's chances of succeeding. It was, of course, possible that God had sent her to France in the kingdom's time of darkness. Yet when she spoke like this he felt a bit uncomfortable and suspected that she was not quite right in the head.

And then she would turn around and suggest something quite sound and sensible, and Poulengy was reminded that he had known her since she was a child, knew her salt-of-the-earth family. She was not mad, not at all. His faith in her always returned, only to flounder again when he asked himself what they were doing out here in this forsaken land.

He found himself tempted on occasion to make advances toward her. Though not pretty—her face had a coarse, country look—neither was she ugly, and she did have a beautiful little body. Freed now from the shapeless red dress and clad as a boy, she was strangely appealing. He wondered why he had never noticed her before when he visited Domrémy.

On the heels of such thoughts would come a deep shame. This was no barracks whore to be diddled, then tossed aside. Even if she did not scream and slap his face, he was reluctant to risk losing the singular camaraderie that he sensed growing between them. She was someone very special, that was certain. Her uniqueness glowed within those guileless eyes and in the inexhaustible faith that allowed her to endure the cold and discomfort of the saddle without flinching.

In his own way, Metz was as bedeviled by Jehanne as Poulengy. There was no doubt within his mind that she was the Divine messenger she claimed to be. Deep down he shared with Jehanne a profound love of God, though he characteristically played the jesting rake. It was not entirely an act, for he was a man who loved women. Quite often he had to admonish himself that Jehanne was a virgin and should remain so if she wished. That was not always easy to remember when she lay next to him at night, and it was sometimes with difficulty that he forced himself not to caress her as she slept.

Happily unaware of her comrades' turmoil, Jehanne rode with them feeling secure in their company. Sometimes they teased her, telling her that they were actually spies for the English, and she would laugh at their feeble attempts to frighten her. On other occasions, worn out by her piety, they pleaded with her to give God a rest for a moment and simply to enjoy the ride. She had never ridden anything but her father's old farmhorse, and found to her delight that horsemanship came naturally to her. Even when they had to ford rivers or climb steep hills, she was able to manage her animal with a skill that quickly came to match the others'.

She thought often of her family, especially her parents. What must they have felt when Durand told them that she was off to Chinon, as certainly he had done by now? She remembered her father's dream that she would leave in the company of armed men, and here she was.

But it's not like you dreamed, Papa, she thought; all will be well, you'll see. She prayed that God would comfort him and let him know that she was unharmed and not disgraced as he had feared. She gazed thoughtfully at the ring he had given her.

"Jhesus-Maria," she whispered, touching the tiny cross.

"What?" Richard the Archer scowled.

Jehanne tossed a glance at the mysterious man riding beside her. What an unpleasant-looking fellow he was, with that hard, craglike face and those cold eyes. She knew by the contemptuous way he treated her that he considered her just a silly woman on a fool's mission. He rarely spoke to her except to give some order.

She ignored his question and looked straight ahead at the back of Colet's horse. The animal was walking with a casualness that made the Dauphin's messenger appear to strut as he swayed with the horse's rhythm. Even dressed as he was now, in the plain clothes of a townsman, he could not hide his cultivated breeding. Colet's very being gave off a quality of refined scholarship. He had been educated at court, he told Jehanne during one of their stops, and could read Latin and Greek as well as French. When they began this journey, he had spoken to Jehanne with the hauteur his class reserved for hers, but just lately, he had started to become more amiable and she sensed that she had somehow earned a measure of his respect.

She turned halfway in the saddle to look at Metz. His hood was pulled down over his face, obscuring his eyes. In the moonlight she could not read his mood.

"When can we hear Mass?" she ventured. Hard as she tried, she could not rid her mind of the images of death. She needed to get herself to church, to pray for strength and understanding and for the souls of those she had not been able to save. Although she could feel Them with her every step of the way, she needed to speak to her Teachers in a place where God dwelled.

"Huh?" Her question jostled Metz to consciousness. He had been half-dozing in the saddle.

She repeated the request.

"Forget about that, Jehanne," he responded a bit testily. She had been asking the same thing since they left St.-Urbain three days ago and he was weary of it, if not of her.

They had had the Devil's own time when they reached the Seine downriver from Troyes. The river was not as powerful there as it would have been at the city, but it was dangerous enough. They were forced to rope themselves together to avoid being swept away by the angry current. Wide-eyed with fear, the horses had been most difficult to manage. Two nearly panicked when they were struck by small branches swirling downstream, and Richard and Poulengy had to pull on the bridles until the mounts' mouths were raw and bleeding before they were brought under control and urged to the opposite bank. And what were Jehanne's first words after they reached the steep bank on the other side? *I want to go to Mass.*

"Why?" she wondered now, sounding like a five-year-old.

"I've told you before," Metz said with labored patience, "it's not safe. Everyone around here knows who you are and what you plan to do. What do you think the Burgundians would do to you if they caught us? We'll just have to wait until we reach France."

"But we are in no danger, Jehan," she insisted. "My Counsel have assured me that we will reach Chinon safely."

With a groan, he turned his head from her in moonlit profile.

"God helps those who don't take foolish risks." Poulengy spoke up with a greater gentleness than he felt. "If we go into a town, we'll just be asking to be discovered. Jehan is right: We can't afford to take the chance."

But they did risk it when they reached the border town of Auxerre. By that time the men half-jested to Jehanne that they would prefer capture by the Burgundians to hearing her beg for Mass again.

The group was in full Bourgogne by now. They had ridden most of the night but stopped for a few hours' rest in a derelict barn an hour's ride from Auxerre, a cathedral town of four thousand situated on the River Yonne. Territory held by Bourgogne ended a few leagues to the west. Beyond it lay France, and safety. The weather was warmer than it had been all during their journey and a feeble sun illuminated the early morning winter sky.

Near midday, the weatherbeaten band took to the road again. At the bridge, they joined with other travelers and crossed into the city, concealed within the larger group. They found themselves in the company of tinkers with jangling carts of cups and iron pots. With eyes lowered to the ground, a small congregation of solemn monks walked in dual ranks, their hands folded inside the sleeves of roughly meshed habits. A squad of Burgundian soldiers on horseback passed them, impatiently scattering those on foot from their trotting horses. They paid no heed to the group from Vaucouleurs, but the sight of them made Jehanne's neck hairs stand on end. When at last their helmets receded, she relaxed again. Farmers from nearby towns and villages prodded along cattle and bleating sheep which they intended to sell at market. There were two or three wagons loaded with winter produce. A pair of haughty merchants, each armed to the teeth with two swords and a crossbow, rode through the crowd on well-fed horses.

Metz and Poulengy had decided that they, too, would play the role of merchants if anyone happened to ask their identities. Taking a cue from the men on the bridge, they flung their cloaks back to reveal their swords as dealers in goods for sale often did in these dangerous times. They told Jehanne that they feared her voice would betray her gender and forbade her to speak to anyone—even to them—unless wholly necessary. She knew it was just an excuse to silence her talk of God and Chinon. Her voice was low enough and her apparel sufficiently convincing that she could have passed for a boy even if she spoke.

She did not care. All that mattered was that there was a great cathedral in this town and soon she would hear Mass.

Her party did not have to ask for directions to the cathedral. A little way upriver past the bridge, the tall, square tower pointed toward Heaven as though holding up the sky. All they had to do to reach it was follow the congested alleys along the riverbank. They made their way slowly toward the grand spire facing the Yonne, through the jostling, noisy populace. When they reached the magnificent structure, Jehanne practically leaped from her horse before the others had a chance to rein in their own mounts.

Poulengy hissed her name, then put a warning finger to his lips. His normally congenial face wore a perturbed frown, and even Metz looked displeased with her. Sneering, Richard the Archer spat upon the ground.

Jehanne ignored them and ran up the steps into the cool darkness. She did not see, and would not find out until later, that the twins were posted outside with the horses during the Mass. The others followed her into the building.

People stood packed together in the nave and all along the aisles, and Jehanne had to worm her way through the throng of unwashed bodies to get a real look at the interior. She had never seen such a grand cathedral as this, not even in Vaucouleurs, and with an audible gasp she craned her neck to see, to inhale God's terrible Presence.

Pillars of stone, each larger than two men put together, supported the arched gallery at regular intervals, rising to a vaulted ceiling that dwarfed the people below. Tucked away in niches along the side aisles, sheltered stone-carved statues of saints gazed sightlessly from their chapels, and candles burned every twenty paces. Most dazzling of all, a giant round window executed in brilliant red and blue gleamed above the western portal, depicting the angels announcing Christe's birth to shepherds, and enthroning Him on high. Bathed in pools of colored sunlight, the people stood reverently as the bishop at the distant altar began the drama of the Mass before a massive oaken cross.

Jehanne was so overtaken by the majesty of the cathedral that she almost forgot why she was there. Jarred into penitence by the bishop's first words, she crossed herself and bowed her head, letting the musical cadence of the familiar Latin seep into her soul.

Surely God lived in this extraordinary edifice and in the moving ancient ritual that bound together His children. Jehanne felt all three Guides with her, bathing her in rosy-blue light as they whispered silently of God's Power and Love. The night terrors of her journey were extinguished, banished into an unreality where all was well and simply part of Heaven's great design. No longer staring in horror, the faces of the dead transformed into rays of resurrected light. Jehanne felt herself united with those present and with all who lived and were yet to be born, in a pulsating womb shimmering through the centuries until all time merged as one. She had felt this way before in another substantial house of God, in another time, but she could not recall where or when. It was just a feeling of remembrance that drifted into her awareness and then was gone.

An acolyte near the altar rang a tinkling handbell. The congregation knelt and averted their eyes as the Host was elevated and the bishop pronounced, "*Hoc est enim Corpus meum.*"

Jehanne knelt along with everyone else. Those who had been shriven made their way to the altar rail to receive Holy Communion. Rent by a feeling of deprivation, Jehanne ached to go with them, to partake of the blessed Sacrament. She would soon have to be washed clean in confession and have her conscience purged of her many imperfections. Lingering in her darkest places was a continuing hatred for the Burgundians and the demonic English. Out in the world, away from church, she often had to swallow the bad feelings her enemies provoked, and despite her confident words to Poulengy, she sometimes feared failure. She took comfort in knowing that Armagnac territory was only an hour away, with Gien only two days' ride from the unmarked border separating the two warring factions. When they reached Gien it would be safe for her to go again into a house of God as His reclaimed child.

The great bells began to ring in deep, solemn tones, signaling the end of Mass. Jehanne's heart pealed joyfully with every powerful clamor of the instruments. She did not want it to end, not ever. She could stand here always in the center of this vaulted Universe, not only listening to the bells but a part of them, almost one of them. Still raptly encased in the holy Moment, she held back as people began to file past her accompanied by the celestial music ringing high above their heads.

When Metz took her gently by the arm, she saw him initially as a stranger. In the next instant she wondered how long her friends had been standing there behind her. She had forgotten that they even existed.

Metz practically had to drag Jehanne from the cathedral. The men with her were uncomfortable at being in Auxerre at all, and when they made their way back into the street, their caution was instantly renewed. Leading the pack through the town toward the bridge, Poulengy smiled amiably but kept his sword within easy reach. Metz stuck to Jehanne's side as though joined to her hip, while Colet, on Metz's left, kept casting anxious looks over his shoulder and nervously licking his lips. The twins, Julian and Jehan, rode behind Jehanne but in front of Richard. Bringing up the rear, the archer rested a vigilant hand upon the weapon that hung from his saddle. An atmosphere of scarcely hidden menace glared from his stubbled, granite face.

Of all of them, Colet was the most uneasy. A young gentleman bred to poetry and music in the serene atmosphere of the Dauphin's court, he was unaccustomed to such dangerous enterprises as accompanying self-proclaimed visionaries through enemy territory. To travel alone with Richard for company was one thing; he had only himself and the taciturn soldier to be concerned with and could play the role of a traveling minstrel for protection. But this exuberant girl would give them all away if Metz and Poulengy found themselves unable to restrain her.

Most of the time the royal messenger was impressed by Jehanne's courage and her ability to endure hardship. He planned to give the Dauphin a good report when he returned to Chinon. Charles need not worry that he was being approached by another fraudulent mystic with an offer to ransom his wartorn realm for a price. This girl might or might not be sent by God, but she was entirely sincere. It could be that all the kingdom needed was someone like her to rally around.

When the group reached Gien early in the morning of the third day after Auxerre, they all breathed a little easier, for now they were out of reach of the Burgundians. There remained the possibility that they would encounter marauders, but at least they did not have to worry about being hanged as traitors if captured. And they were well armed.

After a brief consultation with Poulengy, Metz declared that as an added precaution against brigands, it would now be safer if they traveled by day. So they rented rooms for the night at a riverfront inn, where they ravenously sated their hunger. With her meal finished, Jehanne found her way up the hill to the church overlooking the town.

The village of Ste.-Cathérine-de-Fierbois lay fourteen leagues east of Chinon and ten south of Tours and the Loire. A chapel there was dedicated to the saint, a shrine venerated by all former prisoners of war, for Ste.-Catherine was their patron. In gratitude for their deliverance from captivity, French and Scottish soldiers made the pilgrimage to leave behind the chains that had bound them and the armor they had worn in battle. The illustrious knight, maréchal Boucicaut, had long ago built an almshouse next to the chapel, and it was here that Jehanne and her companions lodged.

They had been on the road for nine days since they had departed Vaucouleurs. The miraculous absence of highwaymen and the recently favorable weather had permitted a rapid sojourn into France and to Fierbois. Here, Jehanne dictated a letter, written by Colet de Vienne, to the Dauphin. She told her sovereign lord that she had traveled one hundred and fifty leagues to see him, and that as a messenger from God she had many important things to tell him about his kingdom. She added that God would let her know her Dauphin above all others in his court. She closed with a humble request for an audience with him. Then Colet mounted his horse and rode away with Jehanne's letter in his saddlebag.

As she watched him gallop down the road across a hill and out of sight into the trees, she thought, Well, that's done. There was nothing more to do but wait for the Dauphin's reply. She turned toward the shrine. She would hear Mass again, as she had done once already this day, and she would try her best to heed her Counsel's exhortations to patience.

The King of Bourges

March 6–19, 1429

harles de Valois, by the grace of God uncrowned and unanointed king of France, was trying to warm his long, slender hands over the brazier that stood on brass legs in the middle of his council chamber. Outside, the patter of sleet whipped in sporadic bursts against the shuttered windows, and he shivered as yet another wintry blast shook the small panes. He was so cold, was always cold in spite of the veritable bonfire raging in the cavernous fireplace and in every other room of the castle.

Of them all, this austere chamber was by far the most uncomfortable, for it kept a chill even during summer, and with spring still weeks away, the stone walls seemed to Charles to have been carved from blocks of ice. The stacked inferno raging near him was not adequate to heat the high-ceilinged space to the king's satisfaction, and he desperately wanted to leave this room and return to the warmer one he had grudgingly left. In that merry place his wife and courtiers were listening to the soothing *ballade* of a minstrel, and consuming good food and wine. There was nothing at all convivial about this council room, bare except for eight carved oaken stools arranged in a semicircle near the brazier. A chair, larger than the stools yet not a throne, faced them. The room's only adornment was an old bearskin lying open-mouthed with outstretched paws, its black fur glossy with firelight and the glow of many torches.

At a complacent distance from the brick-sheltered flames, three of the four ministers to the king were engaged in acrimonious debate. The Dauphin was only half-listening to them.

He was twenty-six but felt older. Indeed, he was unable to recall a time when it had not been so. For Charles, there had been no real childhood, as he understood that condition. From his earliest memories his mother was a distant icon, his father periodically deranged, and warfare between his parents was always there, lurking beneath the facade of domestic tranquility they presented to the people. Even as a boy, Charles had sensed their mutual antagonism. He also knew that he was homely and unloved, the least preferred of the three royal sons. As a result, his demeanor had from infancy been somber and withdrawn.

Charles had grown up surrounded by his brothers and sisters, with the occasional presence of his cousin, Jehan, known to the world as the Bastard of Orléans. Yet he had always felt alone. A scholar versed in Latin and Greek, he was not athletic like his older brother, Louis, nor did he possess the Bastard's gregarious charm. The solitary boy's only real friends were books, and in them and in God he felt momentary solace from the burdens that hunched like vultures about his rounded shoulders.

Louis, dead these thirteen years, was born to be king, but his doom lay in a twin curse of arrogance and impatience. Had he not taunted Henry of England with his impertinent "gift" of tennis balls, insinuating that Henry was equipped only to play games, perhaps the Plantagenet would have stayed on that miserable island and there would have been no humiliation at Agincourt, no disinheriting Treaty of Troyes. Preferring war to the lure of the intellect, Louis had never bothered to read history, unpardonable in a man groomed for the monarchy. Had he done so, he would have learned that Darius of Persis had made a similar fatal miscalculation by underestimating the fearsome Alisaundre. Perhaps Louis would even have lived to become King instead of going to an early grave after battling a wasting chill. In that event Charles could have lived out his life as the comte de Pontieu with his books, and his music, and the pleasant pastimes at his brother's court.

But Heaven had willed otherwise for the kingdom and for Charles. Unknown to England, God had made plans for Henry even as the interloper fashioned his greedy bid for the throne of France. *Take Catherine to wife,* God seemed to say, *and usurp your new brother-in-law's rightful place, and I shall exact from you the one price you do not wish to pay.* And so God had. The Welsh heir to Charles VI's realm had died even as his newborn son lay squalling in the arms of his wetnurse. With the mad king also called to God, there was now only civil war and a reluctant Charles struggling to hold it all together.

He did not look the part of king. His hair, cropped in the latest fashion but hidden by a dark blue velvet hat lined with fox fur, was light brown and appallingly thin, and the coif's wide-brimmed style contrasted unflatteringly with his sallow face, giving him the appearance of a skinned rabbit. He was aware that he was ridiculous in it, which was why he seldom wore hats at all; tonight, however, vanity had yielded to a need for warmth.

His forehead was decorated with brows as delicately sculpted as a woman's, arched above narrow, pale brown eyes that regarded the world with a melancholy suspicion. Between them, his long nose extended into an oily bulb overhanging a thick upper lip. He was so self-conscious about his crooked teeth that he rarely smiled even when he felt like it, which was infrequently.

But it was in his posture that his pedigree least asserted itself. He tried to redress the inadequate shoulders God had given him by wearing tunics padded to impart an illusion of virility and strength. That was effective most of the time, even though the tailor's skill could not hide the spindly legs on which he walked with such an awkward gait. The overall effect was that he looked like a rather short, ungainly man with abnormally large shoulders and a small head, when in fact the opposite was true.

The fur-lined boots he wore tonight, crafted in Spain, were not sufficient to prevent the chill from invading his feet. He drew his cloak about him more closely, then rubbed his hands together vigorously. The Dauphin tried to tune out the poisonously barbed exchange occurring between his ministers before the fireplace.

"My dear Raoul," Trémoïlle was saying in an unctuous endeavor to be placating, "we simply cannot allow any peasant who claims to be a God-sent visionary into His Majesty's presence. There are hundreds, perhaps thousands, of such people in the kingdom, none of whom are worth listening to. Surely you can see that."

Raoul de Gaucourt sneered at the obese, richly dressed Trémoïlle. "And surely you can see, seigneur Trémoïlle, that His Majesty's attempts at peaceful reconciliation with his cousin Bourgogne have been to no avail." The old soldier was breathing quickly, and it was with difficulty that he curbed his temper. "We stand to lose Orléans any day now, and if Orléans goes, the kingdom is lost!"

The two had long been enemies. De Gaucourt hated everything about Trémoïlle, from the dark mole encroaching upon the sensuous upper lip, and his self-indulgent, gross belly, to his venal ambition. During the reign of the mad Charles VI, Trémoïlle had insinuated himself into the office of Grand Chamberlain of France. Once there, he had treacherously betrayed and then defamed his former ally Arthur de Richemont, brother of the duc de Bretagne and former constable of France, to gain for himself that exalted station. And then there were his Burgundian connections, all the more reason to despise him.

Georges de la Trémoïlle was forty-four and had grown up in the court of the Burgundian duc Jehan, called "the Fearless." Through his marriage to the widow of the duc de Berri, Trémoïlle had acquired great wealth which he used to keep the ever near-bankrupt Valois on leash, lending Charles untold sums of money for who knew what purposes. Knowing the king's aversion to war, Trémoïlle played upon that, urging Charles into countless treaties with that miserable traitor and duc Jehan's heir, Philippe. The Burgundian was without honor, and in his confederation with England had broken every agreement Charles had proffered. That enraged de Gaucourt. He was a scrupulous knight of the old school, who favored fighting the English rather than trying to buy time through fruitless negotiations with their allies.

"So what are you saying, Raoul?" Trémoïlle goaded, his porcine eyes shining in the heavy folds of flesh. "That His Majesty should receive this girl, then give her leave to run off on a fool's errand to relieve Orléans?"

De Gaucourt was a moron in his opinion, a blundering soldier who would ruin the army through another defeat and bring about Charles'—and Trémoïlle's—necessary flight to Spain or Scotland. Didn't these idiot soldiers know that the war in the field was lost? The only way for the king to hold on to what he had left was through conciliation with his kinsman Bourgogne.

The chancellor hated the English as passionately as any man in France. They never paid when or how much they said they would, and were entirely untrustworthy. They wanted it all, the kingdom and Bourgogne as well. Philippe de Bourgogne was the real key to resolving this infernal mess. He was the richest lord in all of Europe and a patron of the arts. It was not for nothing that he was known to his subjects as "Philippe the Good." If anyone was worthy to be King of France, it was he, not this weak, cowardly Charles. The king had not even been able to prevent his cohorts from murdering Philippe's father, *right under his very nose!* What a muddle that had provoked! Now there was such animosity on Philippe's part toward Charles that if it happened to rain on the duc, he would suspect that the Dauphin had purchased the rain from the Devil. Only Trémoïlle's skillful negotiations with Bourgogne could vouchsafe an equitable outcome for all concerned.

He licked his thick lips in eager anticipation of de Gaucourt's response, thinking that he had the older man checkmated.

But de Gaucourt refused to be ensnared. "Your Majesty," he said to Charles, who remained standing with his back to them, hunched over the brazier, "you have nothing to lose by at least listening to the girl. I have heard from reputable sources in Vaucouleurs that she correctly predicted our recent losses before Orléans on the *very day* that the battle was lost. Perhaps she is a fraud"—he turned a baleful eye to Trémoïlle—"but it may be that God has at last heard our prayers and sent us a deliverer!"

"A girl?" Trémoïlle laughed with undisguised contempt. "And a peasant at that? Do you not think that God would send His Majesty another foreign ally if a deliverer was what he had in mind for France? But a girl," he snorted, "why, she knows nothing of warfare or strategy, I would wager half my fortune on that!"

"If God wills it," de Gaucourt countered through clenched teeth, "He may send a goat to lead the army and reclaim the kingdom! Or does the seigneur chancellor question the will of God now?"

"I do not question the will of God, nor do I feel adequate to speculate upon what His will might be. That is a subject best left to theologians, not the king's ministers," Trémoïlle said pointedly. "Excepting, of course, His Excellency." He gestured with a plump hand to the man in the purple robe who had heretofore been silent.

Charles lifted an eyebrow, but did not turn to look at them. "Quite right. What is the opinion of the archbishop of Reims?"

"Your Majesty." The archbishop gave him a small bow which he did not see. "I have no faith in self-declared visionaries, nor should you. Seigneur Trémoïlle is correct in saying that France is filled with such people, all of whom are at best deluded and, at worst, inspired by the Devil.

"As you well know, I was recently in that doomed city, until your combined forces were prevented from taking the English supply train and were forced to retreat with many losses. It was through God's grace that I was able to escape in the company of admiral de Culan and the comte de Clermont." His chin whiskers moved as he spoke, making him look like an old billy goat. The nose above his mouth was so long that he could have touched it with his tongue. "My prayers go up to Heaven daily for those poor wretches still inside her walls." He made the Sign of the Cross.

"Yes, yes, your point, Your Excellency?" Charles asked through gritted teeth, losing patience with the old man's affectations.

"It is my opinion, my lord, that the city is lost," he proclaimed. "Supplies into Orléans are a mere trickle; it is only a matter of time before the inhabitants are forced to submit to the enemy. I think it would be best for you to surrender it before further lives are lost, and seek refuge in Scotland, or perhaps Aragon, rather than continue this senseless war." Archbishop de Chartres' deep voice thundered dramatically with the authority of his office.

The Dauphin grimaced, throwing him a sour look over his shoulder. He returned to warming his hands. de Gaucourt snorted with scorn at the spineless suggestion.

"That is out of the question," Trémoïlle maintained, dismissing the man whose view he had sought. The full lips turned downward in a frown, and he shook his head so vehemently that his double chin jiggled. "I do think, however, that it is in the king's best interests to continue his negotiations with Philippe de Bourgogne and thereby break the duc's ties with the English." He glared at de Gaucourt. "We are not so desperate as to allow a lowborn girl to lead the army! His Majesty would become the laughingstock of Europe."

Charles wheeled from the brazier to confront Trémoïlle with his sad eyes. "We are already the laughingstock of Europe, are we not, seigneur chancellor?"

de Gaucourt smirked at the question. His stout adversary turned beet red as he groped for a response. Trémoïlle's forehead glistened with beads of perspiration beneath a fringe of short dark hair, making him look like a shiny apple with eyes.

Taking advantage of his temporary discomfiture, de Gaucourt interjected quickly, "Your Majesty, your past negotiations with Bourgogne have been unsuccessful, though"—he hastened to assure Charles—"not through any fault of yours. It was a very good idea to drive a wedge between him and the English, but he has betrayed your trust. I say that now we stop all this talking and muster the army into the field to fight them off.

"We *must* relieve Orléans, or your kingdom will be lost! I implore Your Majesty to receive the girl from Lorraine, just to see what she has to say. If she is an impostor or mad, then you can turn her away knowing that at the very least you tried all possibilities."

"Regarding further negotiations, I must disagree in the strongest possible terms," the archbishop insisted. "His Majesty courts a grave sin and God's wrath if he attempts to cling to a lost cause. It would also be sinful to grant an audience to one whose spiritual credentials are questionable. Surrender is his only recourse."

Charles allowed the statements to wash over him harmlessly. The king, accustomed to his archbishop's pious rantings, knew that de Chartres' statement about sin and Heaven's judgment was another calculated bid for power.

"What say you, seigneur de Trèves?" Charles inquired quietly of the small man whose voice had not been heard.

"I am uncertain, my king," the man stammered. Robert LeMaçon, duc de Trèves and former chancellor of France, was at sixty thin and frail. A prominent nose jutted out from his lemon-shaped head like the prow of a ship and his red, moon-shaped eyes shifted nervously. At his age, he had no stomach for disputes, and did not want to become mixed up in this argument, for he knew it had nothing at all to do with visionaries. He quickly looked away from the Dauphin's impatient stare.

Charles closed his eyes and put a hand to his brow. A headache was coming on, and he desired nothing better than to have this council finished. He looked at the men in disgust. God, how he despised these so-called advisers, actually little more than posturing whores. de Gaucourt cared only for war and glory and the privilege of adding more scars to those that already garnished his muscular arms. Forever scheming to increase his already bloated fortune, Trémoïlle was a pimp to whom loyalty meant nothing. The prelate's alarmist character, self-righteous and cowardly, never ceased to get on his nerves. As for LeMaçon, Charles could not have looked further to find a more worthless councillor. The decrepit man thought he could fool the king with his simpering, counterfeit humility, when in fact he was biding his time until one side or the other came into prominence, and then he would choose which to support.

Charles frowned at them. It was God's curse that he had no better than these to rely upon. "We will give our answer in the morning," he said, "after we have had time to consider our alternatives."

"My lord," Trémoïlle interrupted, "I must insist that you remember your position and turn the girl away at once!" He glowered at the young king, most often compliant and easily persuaded, and now so uncharacteristically recalcitrant. Trémoïlle feared that if Charles stumbled into some stupid mistake, it would ruin everything the chancellor had worked so hard to achieve, which would of course reflect badly on himself, not upon the king.

Charles turned a disdainful eye on Trémoïlle. "You forget yourself, seigneur chancellor. We have said that we will give our answer in the morning." He gave them a careless wave of his hand. "Leave us now."

The ministers bowed to him perfunctorily and turned to go. Charles noticed that as he waddled out the door, Trémoïlle cast a dark glance in his direction. The manipulative swine would no doubt remember his dismissal when the time came around again for Charles to ask for a loan, but for the moment he did not care.

He went to the high-backed, ornately carved wooden chair and sat down. A flaming log shifted in the fireplace, and as it fell sparks darted up the chimney. Charles' narrow eyes swept the empty chamber, scarcely seeing the ancient bear-skin that yawned before the fireplace. As he surveyed the ring of smaller vacant seats, in his imagination he asked the opinions of those who were not there. He knew that if they actually had been present he would have only half-listened to them.

Starting in his youth when his father was still alive and sometimes teetering on the brink of sanity, Charles had presided over many council meetings. He well knew the patterns they always took: the bickerings, the petty intrigues, the maneuvers for power. He had long since stopped trying to control his warring ministers. It was politic, though, to let them drone on as he observed their acid-tongued charades unfold, allowing the strongest to dominate the proceedings. Charles always did as he pleased anyway, but it did no harm to let them think that they had real influence with him. On the contrary, it gave him the opportunity to watch and wait while playing the fool.

He was fully aware that everyone thought him such. His courtiers might address him with respect to his face, but he knew that they mocked him behind his back, never realizing until too late that he had allowed them to rise in favor, all the while prepared to give them the boot. It was a strategy that had served him well, for it created no conspicuous unpleasantness and guaranteed that in the long run no one ruled but him. His actual aim was to buy time for himself by continuing his secret negotiations with Bourgogne. He hoped thereby to engender a concord sufficient to break Philippe's alliance with the English. And there was always the army to give bite to his pretty words.

Of course, he thought, Bourgogne was the weapon that would end this war and drive the English from his kingdom. Their forces in France were limited, and were it not for Philippe's purchased armies, they would have been expelled long ago. But Philippe had not forgiven Charles for what he supposed was the king's part in his father's murder. It was useless for Charles to maintain that he had not authorized the cowardly assassination of Jehan sans Peur, a murder that had been carried out in the royal presence by one of Charles' guard. Philippe did not know, and did not want to know, that although that had happened nine years past, Charles sometimes still relived the event in his nightmares.

de Gaucourt was also correct in his assessment, but only partially. Orléans was indeed the key to his survival on the throne, for it was the grand lady of the Loire, and if it fell, the English would swallow the entire valley and, with it, the kingdom. Fortunately, the city was not yet entirely surrounded and provisions were getting through a little at a time. And then there was his alliance with Scotland, whose king had promised fresh troops from the Highlands. Those uncivilized Celts were famed for their ferocity in battle and their long-suffering hatred of the English. To further ensure his fellowship with them, Charles had betrothed his young son and heir Louis to a Scottish princess. Orléans would hold, he was certain of that.

At least, he was certain some of the time. There were nights when he awoke in a cold sweat, his eyes red-rimmed with sleeplessness and fear. In those mad moments he would hasten to the oratory near his bedchamber and prostrate himself before the statue of Our Lord above the small altar. He had much to cause him trepidation. Assassination attempts, broken treaties, losses sustained in battles that he could ill afford, floors that collapsed while he held court—all of these had been visited upon him.

Worst of all was the suspicion that constantly nagged in his cold-hearted mother's voice that he was not the king but an unworthy bastard pretender. He knew that at least some of that was political policy. His German mother had no more love for France than she did for her youngest son, and her embrace of the English was driven by a lust for power and wealth. But if it were true that Charles was not really a Valois—Oh, merciful Heaven, let it not be!—then his rule was a sham and his kingdom doomed.

Taking a deep breath, he reminded himself that the royal astrologers had only recently assured him that he had nothing to fear and that he would live long as king. They told him that the tide would soon turn in his favor. However, cowards that they all were, they could not say exactly how that would happen. He snorted, remembering that those pedants who condescendingly read his stars and the fortunes contained therein were no better than his fawning courtiers. What he needed most was an assurance that he could not doubt, the sign from God for which he had prayed for such a long time.

Perhaps the girl from Lorraine had some answers for him after all. Years before Charles was born, his father had received at court a female mystic, Marie d'Avignon, who prophesied that one day a maiden would come, clothed in the armor of God, to rescue the kingdom from the war with England. Was this girl the one? He considered what de Gaucourt had said about her having known of his losses in battle before Orléans. Of course, that could be only a tale related by credulous imbeciles desperate enough to believe in anything hopeful.

Still, Robert de Baudricourt was no easily led fool. The man was a solid soldier with great reserves of common sense. Surely he would not have had the temerity to send the girl to his lord and king if she were not genuine. There was also the word of Colet de Vienne to consider. The courier had returned to Chinon with the girl's letter, which Charles read in amusement at first. His humor diminished when Colet assured him that whether or not she was truly sent by God, she was courageous and of good character.

On the other hand, it was possible that Trémoïlle was right and she really was merely an opportunistic charlatan. Continued diplomacy and peaceful overtures to Philippe might best serve him. And yet, given the minister's historic ties to the Burgundians, his absolute loyalty was questionable, though Charles was very careful to keep his suspicions to himself. He needed Trémoïlle for the time being, had use for the fat man's correspondingly plump purse to pay his army and to bribe those nobles whose loyalty was marginal.

Charles frowned, remembering de Gaucourt's argument. He had struck a nerve when he suggested that Charles owed it to the kingdom not to disavow any opportunity for assistance from Heaven, however feeble that possibility might be. The Dauphin was not deaf to his people's suffering. Try as he might to blot out the toll of war and his own tenuous fate through continuous, desperate revelries and divertissements, his imagination reeled at reports of semi-starvation brought on by anarchic raids, of the taking of innocent lives in all corners of his shrinking realm.

The Dauphin put his head in his hands and rubbed his eyes.

He would see her, this avowed prodigy who claimed that God had sent her to him. He had nothing to lose. If she was genuine, she would be able to pass any test he could devise. She had claimed in her letter that she would recognize him above all others at court. Charles would determine that for himself. If she failed, she would at the very least constitute an evening's entertainment for his jaded court, always on the lookout for new thrills to lure their attention from the destruction that threatened to sweep over all of them. Trémoïlle would not like it, but Charles was the king.

*　　*　　*

The Two Horses Inn was a favorite drinking establishment of the local population. As the sun descended behind the gray-tiled rooftops of Chinon, the tavern began to fill with merchants and shoemakers, with monks and glassblowers, with refugees from the plundered north and knights who had traveled great distances to seek audiences with their king. Every table was occupied, and the atmosphere thundered with the babble of twenty regional accents. The odor of seldom-bathed bodies salted the room through the tang of woodsmoke and roasting meats.

A drinking contest among a group of drunken soldiers climaxed with the participants banging their pewter tankards onto the solid table. Pleased with himself, the buck-toothed winner grinned as he accepted the back-slapping plaudits of his partisans, whose chorus of boisterous laughter ascended above the tavern's other voices. When a serving wench passed the table, one of their number made an inebriated swipe at her ample behind, but accustomed to the antics of a boisterous clientele, she deftly sidestepped his clumsy pass, causing him to fall onto the floor. His companions roared with mirth at the man's attempt to rise. No use; the wine pulled him down, and he leaned against a comrade's leg, laughing weakly.

Jehanne loosened her grip on the sword resting out of sight against her thigh. She was sitting alone in the far corner of the room, at a table small enough for one near the blazing fire. The cap Metz had given her was pulled down low over her face, and she clutched the black cloak about her closely lest it become obvious that she was a woman. Only the innkeeper knew her identity and, decent fellow that he was, had taken an oath of secrecy.

Her stomach was so knotted with a nervous hope that she had eaten very little that day. Rather than food, she nursed a goblet of wine diluted with water, drinking from it occasionally. She needed to keep her wits about her. Not only was there a potential for danger from the drunken warriors, but the Dauphin had not yet decided to see her. Tonight perhaps he would. She had been waiting for two whole days. Fidgety and a little worried, she drummed her fingers on the rough-planked table in an anxious rhythm.

Metz and Poulengy had been gone for over three hours. The Dauphin sent for them late in the afternoon, and they still had not returned from the castle dominating the ridge high above the town. Colet de Vienne was with the king as well, safe in his traditional residence. Richard the Archer was no doubt reunited with his compatriots among the king's guard. Jehanne smiled in memory of the gruff Scotsman whose trust she had not managed to acquire. The two companions to whom she felt closest had taken their servants with them to the Dauphin's fortress, and Jehanne felt cheated at having been the only one left behind. She would be safe here, they told her, as long as she kept out of the way and did not draw attention to herself.

The troop from Vaucouleurs had reached Chinon at noon on Sunday, March 6. Jehanne insisted that once they found rooms in this place, they depart immediately for the castle. No amount of pleading on the part of her comrades could dissuade her. But still the Dauphin had not seen her. Instead, she met reluctantly with a group of his ministers.

They received her in a somewhat large room of Chinon Castle. Poulengy and

Metz were stopped at the door by a burly, armored guard whose bladed spear was almost as thick as an average man's arm. To emphasize his authority and his means of upholding it, a heavy sword hung in a leather sheath from his belt.

Four of the Dauphin's advisers were waiting to see her, and since they did not bother to introduce themselves, she was unaware of their identities. They sat in a semicircle of grandly fashioned stools ringing a large, glowing brazier, its warmth augmented by the fireplace that burned near them.

A gray-bearded bishop, whose head and neck were completely covered by a round cap of black velvet, offered her a seat. When she started to sit in the prominent chair facing the men, their shocked faces told her that she had erred. She quickly moved to a place beside the bishop.

For a few moments they simply stared at her, saying nothing. The prelate had a large, hooked nose that ended in a mass of broken blood vessels. A corner of his crafty old eye twitched with misgiving as he examined her travel-worn apparel. His bishop's robe and the silver cross about his neck proclaimed his vocation, yet his face was icy and devoid of Christian compassion. Jehanne looked past him at the absurdly fat man in a splendidly wrought red velvet tunic. The hair on his head was cut far above his ears, giving it the appearance of a fringed apple. Outright malice burned behind the eyes enfolded in the heavy flesh of his face. To his right, a small old man who looked as though he could die any minute scrutinized her up and down, his lips pursed in distaste. The middle-aged warrior next to him had a faded scar across his chin, most likely the legacy of an archaic battle. They all stared at Jehanne with scarcely disguised contempt.

Finally, the obese man made an effort to give her a benign smile. "Well, now, Jehanne, we have heard that you desire an audience with His Majesty. Please tell us why you have come to Chinon."

"I cannot tell you that, sir," she answered, her jaw set firmly. "I can only tell the Dauphin."

She noted the glance the fat man and the bishop exchanged. Obviously, the man who had addressed her was displeased with her answer, for his sunken eyes grew colder and the full lips turned downward into a frown.

She did not care. These grand gentlemen had no right to interfere with her mission. She was resolved not to reveal any more to them than was necessary.

"But we are here in the king's name," said the old soldier. He had a powerful build, and another long scar lined his arm from the back of his hand to the elbow. "If you speak to us, it is as though you are speaking to His Majesty."

"That's right, you will just as well be speaking to His Majesty." The frail-looking man who said this reminded Jehanne of a little gray bird with shifty eyes. The heavyset man smirked at the redundancy. Clearly, he had no respect for the cringing old minister.

Jehanne flashed her most winning smile. "But where is the Dauphin?" She looked about the room innocently. "Can he hear what I say to you?"

"The king has other business at this time," the bishop answered, his black brows, like the wings of a raven, raised in haughty disdain. "We shall convey to him any message you might have for him. As you might expect, he is quite preoccupied with governing his kingdom."

She hesitated. If she gave them an answer, they might dismiss her as Baudricourt had first done and she would never see the Dauphin. What should I do? she asked her Guides.

There was no response. She chewed the inside of her mouth.

"Come, girl," the fat official prompted impatiently, "we are only slightly less busy than His Majesty. You are wasting our time."

"Very well." She lifted her head with dignity. "I have come with a message from my Lord, the King of Heaven. He bids me tell the Dauphin that I have been sent by God to raise the siege at Orléans, and after that is done I am to accompany the Dauphin to Reims, where he shall be anointed and crowned."

Jehanne bore the quiet that followed her words with a brazen look that challenged each of them in his turn. None reacted outwardly. Still, she had the definite impression that they were not surprised, that they had in fact known all along why she was there. Annoyed, she waited for one of them to speak, to say anything.

The bishop rose and the others followed suit. Grunting, the fat man strained to get to his feet.

"We shall inform the king of your message," the bishop said icily. "It will be for him to decide whether or not to receive you."

Jehanne stood, knowing that there would be no more for now. She bowed only as much as decorum dictated, then turned and left them.

That was two days past.

Taking a sip of the watered-down wine, she fretted miserably, going back over the fruitless conversation as though remembrance would change the way it had gone. She should have been firmer in her determination to hold her ground; she should have insisted that they take her to Charles at once. At the very least, it would have been better if she had refused to say anything at all about her mission. But if she had, they would perhaps have sent her away and her years of preparation would have been for nothing.

Help me, she implored the silence, untouched by the noisy inn. Tell me what to do.

You are doing what you are able for the time being. Patience, Little One.

Will he see me?

Just wait. See what happens next.

That's not an answer. She frowned.

It is all you need at this time.

Jehanne drank from her cup and stared sightlessly into the wine. A small breeze of inadequacy wafted through her heart and she sighed. She took no heed of the clamor of voices that rose and fell about her like faraway thunder.

A serving maid approached and made to fill her cup, but Jehanne stopped the flow of wine with an alarmed gesture. She knew that she would drink anything put before her. The last thing she wanted was to become intoxicated like those noisome soldiers who still hung about their table recounting past glories and boasting of those to come.

There was so much for her to do, and so little time. Hadn't Ste.-Catherine told her that she would have only a year and no more to accomplish her goal?

No, that wasn't it exactly. She had said that Jehanne would have a year from the time the Dauphin received her. Well, Charles had not done that yet. She chuckled softly. Her year had not begun. But when it did, she would shake the foundations of Heaven in the discharge of her duty. The earth would tremble with the stamping feet of the retreating *goddons*!

Sensing someone before her table, she looked up, startled.

Metz stood over her with his eyebrows lifted in the old joking manner. Next to him, Poulengy rested his hand casually on his sword. Both of them were smiling at her like fond parents.

"Well?" she asked. Her heart was hammering in her chest.

They looked at one another, then back to her, foolish grins creasing their faces.

"Don't jest with me!"

"He wants to see you, Jehanne," Poulengy answered gently.

"When?"

"Tonight," Metz said, "now in fact. So if you're finished with your wine. . . ."

Jehanne scrambled to her feet and bolted for the door, not bothering to look back to see if her friends were following. She pushed her way through the tavern's smelly denizens until she was outside at last. The cold wind blowing in from the river offered a bracing contrast with the inn's stuffiness. Jehanne drew her cloak about her more closely as her companions caught up with her and the three of them walked briskly toward the stable where they had left their horses.

"What did he want with you?" she inquired. A little puff of warm breath accompanied her question.

"He asked us about our journey and about you, how you conducted yourself, do we believe you, that sort of thing," Metz said.

"For all this time?"

"He didn't see us right away," responded Poulengy. She could see in his scowl that he was vexed by the treatment they had received. "He kept us waiting while he played a game of chess." A subtle contempt played through his voice.

Jehanne frowned. "Will he make me wait, too?"

"I don't know." Metz shrugged. "He only said, 'Bring her to me now,' so we are."

"There is one thing you should know," Poulengy volunteered matter-of-factly. "Do you remember the fellow who insulted you when we first got here, when we were riding to the castle?"

"Yes." She wrinkled her nose at the memory. How could she not recall the disgusting soldier they had encountered at the gatehouse leading to Charles' domain?

The man and three of his comrades had been slouching within a rounded niche in the wall before the portcullis. Jehanne would not have noticed him at all had he not said to a companion as they passed, "Is that the Maid? I swear to God, if I had her for a night, she would not be a maid by morning!" His friends had laughed like braying donkeys.

Jehanne had jerked her head in the direction of his voice, seeing him for the first time. He had not shaved in weeks, and his hair was stringy and unwashed. The leer on his ugly face was as revolting as a puddle of vomit. When he saw her looking at him, he gave his thigh a suggestive scratch.

Poulengy's hand had flown to the hilt of his sword. Jehanne reined in her horse and glared down at the man. He was still grinning at her in what he supposed was a seductive manner. She gasped as behind his right shoulder she saw a dark figure, incorporeal, with the wings of a giant bat.

"Man, how can you blaspheme God like that," she said in a soft, awed tone, "with you so near your death!"

The indecent grin disappeared from his face and he paled.

"Come on, Jehanne, pay him no mind," Metz had urged. In spite of the mildness in his voice, he was prepared to fight for her if necessary. Both of her companions were.

She had avoided a confrontation by spurring her horse. They continued through the gate and into the fortress without further unpleasantness.

Of course she remembered the incident. It was something she would never forget.

Metz said bluntly, "The fellow is dead. Drowned in the river. We heard it on our way back to the inn, and it's probably all over town by now."

Jehanne shuddered with a sudden violent spasm as she fully realized what she had seen looming over him. "God rest his poor lost soul," she muttered. "He probably died unshriven." She made a quick Sign of the Cross.

"It's not your fault." Metz put a reassuring hand on her shoulder and squeezed it. She could see even in the dim light that his normally jovial aspect was solemn.

She nodded. Having sinned, the man had been called to Judgment.

By now, they had reached the stable. Poulengy paid the owner and they mounted their horses. Then the three of them silently climbed the sloping road toward the citadel.

Longer than it was wide, the Great Hall of Chinon Castle was three times the size of the council chamber where Jehanne had been briefly questioned by the Dauphin's advisers. When she thought of the place later, she always would remember it as she first saw it, awash in an ocean of light created by the fifty or more torches that illuminated the ceiling-high windowpanes, revealing everything in a golden, breathtaking unreality. Near the door where she had entered, a fireplace the size of a small hut cast its own lively shadows upon the vast ceiling, its crisp smell of burning elm mingling with the torches' acrid odors. A raised dais at the far end held the unoccupied throne of France. Hanging on the wall behind it was a blue banner embossed with a multitude of golden fleurs-de-lys.

Jehanne had never seen so many people in one place; there must have been two or three hundred of them. Richly dressed gentlemen and their ladies thronged the hall in a dazzling sea of gold- and silver-threaded scarlets and blues and greens. Across masculine shoulders pinked-hemmed mantles, trimmed with otter and fox fur, draped casually and fell to the ends of tunics studded with glinting sapphires and fiery diamonds. Still others, some so long that they swept the floor, displayed long, satin-lined sleeves that drooped almost to their owners' knees. A few heads wore bowl-shaped fringes cut far above their ears, but most wore velvet hats that perched jauntily upon them or swirled to one side. The more daring among the men—one of whom sported a pointed beard that was dyed blue—were dressed in particolored hose and the absurdly long shoes called *poulaines* that curled at the toes, leading Jehanne to wonder idly how they ever managed to walk in them. The elegant ladies were clad in belted gowns whose necklines dropped to reveal the tops of creamy breasts ornamented by magnificently jeweled necklaces. All wore tall, conical hats, or elaborate winged headdresses of silks and brocades adorned with the feathers of exotic birds, and their foreheads were shaved in the latest fashion, their eyebrows plucked, then painted on again.

Their skirts whispered as they moved to observe the three strangers who had been admitted into their aristocratic presence. The jabber of conversation hushed.

Jehanne was still wearing the hooded leather doublet and black leggings from her journey, by now splattered with dried mud from the neck to the soles of her boots. Metz's cap sat atop her short hair. She had not had a bath in days, and when she moved, she discharged the smells of horse sweat and her own exertions. She felt more than a little self-conscious, and was glad that she had taken the time to wash her face and hands. She was also thankful to have her friends walking behind her, imbuing her with courage.

She entered the hall with her head raised and eyes unafraid, the clatter of her boots slapping the stone floor in the silence. She ignored the perfumed ladies who whispered to one another behind delicate hands, giggling at her appearance.

Jehanne returned their rudeness with an impudent stare. She was supposed to be here, had every right to be in this company. So what if they considered her a rough peasant from the farthest marches of the kingdom? They had not heard the Voices of God's emissaries, nor had they experienced the roaring visions of light and soundlessness that had directed her to this place.

Neither had the bishop who dominated the group of prelates, all of whose extravagant garments denied the vows of poverty they surely had taken when they were ordained. Most splendidly attired was the bishop himself, in a black silk gown lined in purple and a crimson-brimmed hat upon his head. The cross dangling from his neck looked to be cast from silver, and at its juncture there winked a large ruby. His wrinkled countenance smiled rigidly at Jehanne, who gave him a nod of recognition. When she inclined her head to the obese minister next to him, he acknowledged her greeting with a smirk that seemed to swallow the insectlike mole on his upper lip.

The room crackled with silent curiosity. Jehanne returned the probing gazes with her own as she ordered her features into what she hoped was a pleasant appearance. For what seemed an eternity she searched each masculine face, look-ing in vain for the man she had come so far to meet. No one said a word. In the stillness, she heard only the hiss of fire racing through the logs in the monstrous fireplace.

Suddenly, a door opened behind the throne at the far end of the room. Every-one's attention moved away from Jehanne to the group of six men striding con-fidently into the hall.

Even at this distance, she could see that one of them stood apart from the others. He was very handsome, more fashionably attired than the rest in a blazing orange velvet tunic embroidered with the crimson silhouette of a charging lion, and a sizable golden medallion hung from a thick chain of like metal around his neck. On his hands were black velvet gloves, each finger holding a sparkling ring. His great, jewel-encrusted hat bobbed gracefully as he acknowledged the courtiers with a dignified smile. There was a rustle as the assembled gentlemen bowed and the ladies curtsied.

Jehanne walked toward the smaller group, her head erect and her heart pounding deafeningly in her ears.

"So this is the Maid from Lorraine," the handsome man said, his voice a cultured purr. "Welcome to our court." The hand he held out for her to kiss had a large, clear blue stone on its middle finger.

There was something wrong here. This nobleman, although made to look like a prince, did not emit the sacred aura Jehanne had expected to find in her king. She gave him a sweet smile. "Thank you, sir. But you are not the Dauphin."

The man's mouth opened and he raised an astonished eyebrow. A murmur skittered through the hall.

Jehanne disregarded him and let her eyes pass over the faces of the other five. All were clearly noble knights, regal in their bearing, and like the courtiers, elegantly clad in silks and velvets. All but one looked at her with an inquisitive hauteur.

The fifth hung back behind the others, his dejected eyes fastened to the floor, and she observed that his garments, once no doubt splendid, were nearly threadbare. A large hooded hat covered his head entirely and swept into a broad band that hung down toward his right shoulder. Despite his hangdog demeanor, an exceptional radiance glowed about him, and when he lifted his face to her, she found in that cheerless countenance the burdens of the world.

His plain face bore no trace of nobility. The narrow eyes swam in sadness, cold and solitary, like a pool coated with a mossy residue. His nose was long and ended just above a short upper lip, as though he smelled something nauseating. The faded marks of old adolescent blemishes were visible in his pasty complexion. Jehanne had no doubt that this was the Dauphin Charles.

She sank to her knees before him and embraced his lower legs. They were thin and to her surprise, trembling. She looked up with a smile at his homely visage and gave him the little speech she had long rehearsed.

"Noble Dauphin, I am Jehanne the Maid from the village of Domrémy in the duchy of Lorraine. The King of Heaven sends me to you with the message that you shall be anointed and crowned in the city of Reims, and that you are the chosen lieutenant of God, Who is the King of France."

There was a general titter at her unrefined accent, mixed with gasps of wonder. She paid no attention to it.

Neither did Charles. "I am not the king, Jehanne," he said. "That is the king." He pointed to the good-looking courtier.

"In God's name, noble prince, it is you and no other." Her tone was as fond as that of a mother dispelling the pretensions of a naughty child.

A murmur, almost a sigh, raced through the packed room. Jehanne heard it only slightly. Her concentration was fixed entirely on the unattractive face look-ing at her, the mouth slightly ajar. She could see that his top front teeth were crooked.

He reached down and raised her to her feet. His eyes probed hers, almost, it seemed, in an effort to read her soul. Then he said, "Come with me."

Taking her arm, he led her to a far corner of the room, away from all ears. Poulengy and Metz, forgotten by their charge, stood uncomfortably amid the stunned, whispering crowd.

When they were out of earshot, Charles turned to Jehanne. His mien was no longer modest, but penetrating, searching. "Tell me what you came to say."

This was her moment, and she grasped it with conviction. "Sire, if I tell you something so secret that it can be known only to you and to God, will you believe that I have been sent by Him?"

The Dauphin hesitated. "Go on."

"My lord, God has instructed me to remind you of the prayer you sent Him a little over a week ago, when you knelt in the chapel next to your private chamber and begged Him to give you a sign that you are the lawful and the *only* king of France. You asked to be shown that you are the true son of your father, and if you are not, that you be allowed to find safety in Scotland or Spain."

Charles' eyes betrayed no emotion.

She took a deep breath as she felt herself move into the Power. "You also asked that your people not suffer any more on your account if you be not the rightful king, but that the war should end and peace come to us all.

"But this is what God has told me: You have nothing to fear, for you shall have a long life as king, and in your reign you shall accomplish what no one else has been able to. 'The last shall be first,' God says. There is no other king born to rule France but you, and God will give you the strength you need to expel the English from your kingdom and to bring about the peace. This is the true word of God, and His pledge to you."

Charles grew wan, and he licked his dry, heavy lips. "What of Henry of England and his claim?"

"God says that he is a thief," she replied with assurance. "Heaven's blessing is not upon him, for he is cursed with his father's sin, and his rule even over England shall be cut short. Your son will flourish as Louis XI of France when Henry has gone to his grave."

"And you?" he whispered.

"I am the messenger of God who has come to raise the siege at Orléans and lead you to your coronation." Jehanne paused, then said softly, "I am the answer for which you have prayed."

The Power surged from the core of her soul. Her ears rang with joy. An energy erupted between her eyes and shot from her into Charles, and in that moment there was no one else in the world but the two of them, bound together by a shimmering cord of silent light. She knew the Dauphin felt it too. She could see it in the way his face softened.

He burst into a smile and seemed in that instant to become boyishly handsome, indeed, a most comely prince. His grin was impossible to resist, and she returned it gratefully.

Charles turned toward the court. With a confidence that amazed even him, he announced in a loud voice, "My friends, we extend our heartiest welcome to Jehanne the Maid, who has traveled a great distance from the farthest outpost of our realm to be with us on this most auspicious night!"

A noisy outpouring of stupefaction erupted from the normally composed lords and ladies. They whispered together in little groups, twittering like birds.

Charles raised his hand in a command for silence. The chatter faded, then stopped.

"Where are you lodged?" he asked her.

"At an inn in the town."

"No longer." He grinned like a delighted youth. "Go, return to the inn and gather together your things. My servant will escort you to a room adjoining the royal apartments."

"My lord Dauphin, all that I possess is with me."

"Good," Charles responded decisively. "Then there will be no need for you to be separated from our company."

He offered her his arm and she put her hand through the crook of his elbow. They turned and walked together toward the door through which Charles had entered the room only a short time ago. The assembly bowed low as they passed.

When they were gone, a whirlwind of voices rose to a din as the congregation of France began its debate. Forgotten entirely, Metz and Poulengy looked at one another. Their duty was done; their time had come and gone.

The window from the Tour de Coudray, set back some distance from the curtain wall between the royal apartments and the Tour de Beffroy, offered a partial view of Chinon and the surrounding land far below Charles' castle. Jehanne would soon find that when the sun was shining, the rolling farmlands, brown and fallow in March, stretched as far as one could see beyond the narrow, musky Vienne River, yet on this gray and foggy day visibility was limited to a much shorter distance. On this side of the river the little town hugged the water like the random scattering of a child's toys, and from the castle, horses and wagons moved as insignificantly as insects down the muddied river road. Separating town and citadel but out of sight from her window, a thick copse of trees rose to meet the sheer drop beneath the turret where Jehanne was housed.

Her circular room was at the very top of the tower. A canopied bed of heavy dark wood crouched against one wall, and it had the most comfortable mattress Jehanne had ever known, although it was so high that she virtually had to vault into it. A tapestry depicting a hunting scene hung from the wall between the bed and the window, while a smaller one embroidered with a minstrel serenading his lady adorned the space above the cheerful, bricked fireplace. Near it was a small writing desk, and an unlit candle sat in a silver stick upon the polished wood. A bench, barely long enough for two, rested beneath the window.

The door to Jehanne's room took one down a spiral staircase to a parapet whose shorter hall to the left led outside to the Château du Milieu's courtyard and the small chapel where the Dauphin heard Mass. If at the bottom of the tower one walked straight ahead instead, one reached a stone bridge over a deep ravine proceeding to the defensive Tour de Beffroy where, veering sharply left again, one could follow the stone curtain wall to Charles' private lodgings.

Jehanne had not been invited to his chamber this morning. Last night, after they left his court gossiping about Jehanne and her extraordinary performance, the Dauphin had taken her there briefly. She had had only a few moments to gape at her liege's lavish quarters before he introduced a young page and instructed the boy to show Jehanne to the tower. Then Charles bade her good night. She had not seen him since.

She awoke early and went to the chapel to pray before the small marble altar. She sensed that her Guides were with her as usual, but They did not communicate with her when she summoned Them.

It did not matter. She was here in Chinon at last! It seemed dreamlike, unreal somehow, after all these years. Her Counsel had always given Their assurance that this time would come, and her faith in Them abounded a hundred-fold as she thanked Them for bringing her to within sight of accomplishing what God had charged her to do. She requested guidance in her venture, knowing that it was granted even before she asked.

Her thoughts turned to her family, so far away in Domrémy, and she visualized what they must be doing on this early spring morning. With the advent of the plowing season, Jacques would be in the fields behind his horse, gouging furrows into the sleeping earth. No doubt her brothers were there as well, or perhaps hunting rabbits or even wild boar in the murky thickets of the Bois Chenu. And Isabelle, having cleared the breakfast table, was doing housework alone, with no daughter to assist her.

Jehanne could not think of that, for the familiar sting of guilt would prick her if she did. That accomplished no good, only left her sick at heart.

Oh, please, she prayed, help my family now and always to understand why I had to leave them. Comfort them in my absence, and let them see that I am not wicked for having abandoned them. Show them that I will return when I have done Your Work. In return, I promise that I will plead for their forgiveness when I do.

She then beseeched God's help and solace for all of tormented France, and said a special prayer that Charles might be unafraid to take on the power God had given him. The night before, she had seen in his shambling demeanor the burdens that weighed upon him and the fear of failure that ate at his anguished spirit. She would teach him that he had nothing to fear. She had the Power and the support of God to awaken the Dauphin to his destiny. Her Counsel had pledged it. Charles, inspired by her, would reclaim his kingdom. She was confident that she would be at his side when he did. She did not need her Counsel's confirmation that it would be as she imagined it.

She was at prayer a long time. When she returned to her room, she found a breakfast tray carefully arranged on the writing table. There was fresh bread and cheese, dried apples and pears, and a large golden goblet brimming with milk. She suddenly remembered that she had not had a meal since midday yesterday, and her stomach rumbled with hunger as she sat to fill it.

She had just finished eating when there was a small rap on the door. Before she could answer, it opened and the page from last night entered, then stood to one side.

"His Majesty, Charles, King of France," the boy announced in a voice cracking with emerging manhood.

The Dauphin shuffled into Jehanne's room. He was wearing a magnificent green velvet tunic bound at the waist by a black leather belt, its shoulders enlarged to give him a stalwart guise. Near his ankles, the dark leggings wrinkled above emerald suede slippers that tapered to a point. He was hatless this morning and his hair was cut stylishly above his ears. Jehanne saw for the first time how fair he was, almost blond, and that his hair was thin and lusterless. The golden medallion, worn the night before by the noble impostor, hung from his neck. On closer inspection, Jehanne now noticed that it was embossed with the fleur-de-lys of France.

She got to her feet and, kneeling before him, bowed her head.

"Rise, Jehanne," he commanded.

She obeyed. Charles cast a glance over his shoulder at the page, who was staring at Jehanne. The Dauphin snapped his fingers. The flustered boy disappeared through the door, closing it behind him.

The prince turned his small brown eyes to her. "Have you rested and eaten well?" he asked.

"Yes, Sire."

"Come." He gestured toward the bench beneath the window. "Let us talk."

She waited until he sat, then she took a seat beside him. He was so close that she could feel the warmth from his thigh against her knee.

"Our servant informs us that you were not here when your meal was brought to you." He looked at her quizzically and it seemed to her with a definite lack of trust. His manner this morning was cool and contrasted sharply with the almost youthful animation he had displayed last night.

Her palms began to sweat and she wiped them furtively on her hose. Courage, Jehanne, she told herself. He is God's chosen king, but still only a man.

"That is correct, Sire," she answered in a steady voice. "I was at prayer in the chapel. I hope that you do not mind if I go there."

"Ah." Charles' arched eyebrows ascended further up his forehead than usual. "But you should not go anywhere unescorted. For what did you pray?" he questioned with a small smile.

"For you, my Dauphin. And for all of France." She returned his fixed look unflinchingly in a way that bespoke a calm she did not really feel.

"Do you often pray for us and our poor kingdom?" An ineffable sorrow settled upon him, giving him the look that she had seen when she picked him out in the Great Hall, and she felt an almost maternal tenderness for him.

"Every day, Sire." She smiled. "And I know that God hears my prayers."

"How do you know that?" he wondered, bemused.

"Because my"—she faltered, then recovered—"my Voices have told me that you shall be King and France healed."

"Voices?"

Shall I tell him?

HE WILL NOT TRUST YOU UNLESS YOU DO. YOU MUST GIVE BEFORE HE DOES.

"Yes, my lord. You see, my Voices first came to me when I was a child. They spoke to me in my father's garden, near noon on a summer's day." The truth, unuttered for so long, rushed to her mouth and she poured forth all that she had contained in her heart for four long years.

The Dauphin listened without interruption. His normally slitted eyes widened as she related every detail of her awakening and the subsequent communications she had shared with her Counsel. Somehow, she knew that her secret conversations were safe with him, and that he would never reveal them to anyone else, not even to his own confessor. She felt his openness, and, encouraged, even told him of her Dream.

"What does it mean?" His frown was perplexed, and she felt an element of suspicion return.

"I don't know," she admitted. "I have never received a full answer, though I've often asked. Ste.-Catherine once told me that it is my heritage, but I do not understand what she meant by that."

"Is it true that your saints told you about the battle our army lost to the English before Orléans?"

"Yes, Sire."

"And no one, no person, told you that before they did?"

She shook her head slowly, smiling.

Charles considered her response silently for a few moments. Then he asked, "How do you know that these voices of yours are from God and not from the Enemy?"

"Because They speak of love," she responded without hesitation, "and I do not believe that the Devil would do that. He would tempt me to sin, would he not?"

The prince smiled. "Are you a true maid, Jehanne?" he inquired abruptly, trying to catch her off guard.

"Yes, my lord." Her face colored, but she lifted her head with pride. "I vowed to remain a virgin as long as it pleases God, and I intend to keep that promise."

"Is that the source of your power?"

"I do not know," she confessed. "My Voices came to me before I took the vow, but I'm uncertain if they remain with me because of it."

"The love your saints speak of, it is not then the love of man and woman?" His expression was uncomprehending, and she knew he had misunderstood what she meant.

"It is the love of family, the love of God and of France. And the love of you, my Dauphin. You are the symbol of France, you are her caretaker, and God wills that you shall hold the kingdom in trust for Him Who is the true King of us all. That is what They have told me."

His smile was faintly morose. "I will tell you something, Jehanne, and I charge you never to repeat it: I would not choose to be king." He looked away from her, at the hunting tapestry upon the wall. "These are dangerous times to be a monarch, and I would like nothing more than to be left alone, perhaps to be a peasant like yourself."

"It is no less dangerous for peasants," she rejoined quickly. "My village of Domrémy was burned only last summer by the Burgundians, and my people have lived in fear of their return ever since."

An image of the massacred village from her journey came flooding into her memory. She closed her eyes against it, but could not shut it out.

"What is it?" he asked with a concerned frown.

Jehanne swallowed the bile threatening to choke her. Her nostrils were suddenly filled with the abhorrent stench of death. For a moment, she could not reply.

"I was just remembering something I saw on the way here, something terrible." She turned a look of anguish to his searching face. "People out there are suffering and dying in horrible ways, my lord. Believe me when I tell you that you would not want to be a peasant. They are helpless against the enemies of France." She smiled in apology. "And anyway, the choice is not yours, but God's, and His word is that you were born to be king."

"But why?" His moan was as pathetic as that of a child told he cannot have a favorite toy.

"They say it is for the good of your soul. They say that you need to learn courage and how to fight for what is rightfully yours. It is a lesson, They say." She looked at him tenderly.

He laughed without humor. "It is a lesson I would prefer to avoid."

"We all have our lessons from God, my lord." She grinned.

"And what are yours? Have your saints told you that?"

"No. I suppose they would not be lessons if I knew them in advance."

This time his mirth was genuine, and she thought, How good it is to see him happy. "But you have given me the significance of what God supposedly wants me to learn," he insisted, still smiling. "Why does He not tell you about yours?"

"Perhaps because you are more important to France than I am, Sire," she responded with frank sincerity. "People will remember Charles VII long after they have forgotten my name."

He grinned and wagged a finger at her. "That is a very good answer, Jehanne. You have the makings of a politician."

"Thank you, my lord." She laughed amiably, feeling at ease. "But I have no desire to be a politician."

"What do you wish, then?"

"Only to do the will of God."

"Do you not think it presumptuous to think you know His will?"

"I don't know it unless my Counsel tells me what it is. Truly, Sire, I know nothing without Their guidance."

Charles was mute for a few moments as he gazed off into empty space. "My enemies call me 'the King of Bourges' because of my reduced realm. But am I really the King?" he asked in the voice of a wistful little boy.

"You are not yet, my lord Dauphin."

He turned to her with a sharp frown.

"You must be anointed with the holy oil of kings and crowned in the cathedral at Reims before you can be King," she recovered quickly. "But what I told you last night is true. You are the son of your father, and there is no other who may sit upon the throne of France with the blessing of God."

He sighed heavily. "If only I could believe that," he whispered, more to himself than to her.

"Give me an army, Sire," she ventured, "and I will relieve Orléans, and then you will believe it."

"I cannot do that," he said, squirming uncomfortably under her unabashed scrutiny. "I have to consider the advice of my ministers, and frankly, they have doubts about you."

She frowned. "Doubts? But why?"

"Put yourself in their position—in my position—for a moment. Would you place your confidence in a girl who suddenly appeared with a promise to defeat the English in the field when no one has been able to do that?"

"I would if she were from God," Jehanne shot back, feeling his fragile trust falter again.

"But we have only your word that you come from God," he answered with an ironic smile.

"Unless you give me an army, I'm afraid that is all you will ever have."

"Then I suppose we are at a stalemate for the present."

"Will you at least consider it, Sire?" Her look was pleading and she willed him to swing back toward her.

Charles opened his mouth to reply, but before he could utter a word, a knock sounded at the door, startling them both. "Come!" he shouted with an angry impatience.

The door opened to reveal the most beautiful young man Jehanne had ever seen. A permanent blush adorned smooth cheeks beneath large brown eyes as guileless as a baby's. His hair was dark brown and, like the Dauphin's, cut above his ears, but in contrast to Charles, the bowl cut suited the shape of his head, complemented the handsome face with its perfectly chiseled nose. He was dressed in a tunic of golden velvet embroidered with scarlet thread, and the hose encasing his strong, well-proportioned legs were also red. A silver dagger hung from the belt around his narrow waist.

"Cousin!" Charles sprang to his feet, his eyes glowing with delight. Jehanne stood also as the Dauphin embraced the young man and the two of them laughingly clapped one another on the back.

"God give you health, Sire," the beautiful gentleman said with a broad smile, in a voice as sweet as his appearance.

"And you as well! I thought you were hunting quail. When did you return?" Their hands continued to clutch each other's shoulders. Charles and his cousin exchanged a look glowing with genuine affection.

"I have only just arrived. A messenger told me that a wonder has come to you, brought by God." His dancing eyes sought Jehanne over his kinsman's shoulder.

She returned his warm smile. The Dauphin said, "This is Jehanne, the Maid from Lorraine. And your servant is right; she truly is a wonder."

Jehanne, recalling his doubt of only a moment ago, was astounded by this assessment. But more than that, she was plagued by curiosity. "Who is this, Sire?" she asked, unable to check her inquisitiveness.

"We are pleased to present our cousin and loyal vassal, Jehan, the duc d'Alençon," Charles intoned formally, remembering his dignity.

"Oh!" Jehanne's face suddenly became radiant.

She certainly knew who he was; everyone did. The duc d'Alençon was the great-grandson of King Philippe III, and thus of the royal House. His father, a valiant knight, had been among the slain at Agincourt. More important to Jehanne, he was the son-in-law of the duc d'Orléans, held prisoner in the Tower of London ever since that terrible, disastrous battle.

"You are most welcome, sir," she said with a bow. "The more of you of the royal blood of France who are gathered together, the better."

D'Alençon's smile widened, revealing perfect, even teeth. "We of the royal blood have been together before, to no avail. It is you, Jehanne, who will make the difference."

Charles glanced at his cousin, then at Jehanne. "Not I, sir, but God," she said, holding the Dauphin's eye. A small, conspiratorial smile upturned the corners of her mouth.

"Perhaps," Charles murmured.

Conflicted in mind and heart, he remained unconvinced despite his evident admiration of her. But Jehanne also knew that God had answered her prayer. He had sent her the powerful ally who would tip the balance in her favor.

Jehanne was left alone for the rest of the day. After sundown a squire brought a meal to her room on a silver tray, but anxiety took away her appetite and she only nibbled at the food. Restless and bored, she opened the door, intent on finding her way to the chapel. At the bottom of the stairway two armed guards stood in the torch-lit corridor. They scowled at her appearance.

"Where are you going?" one of them snarled.

"To the chapel, sir." She pointed down the hallway.

"We have orders not to allow you to wander about."

"Then please accompany me." She stared the man fully in the face, daring him to refuse her.

The soldiers looked at one another, and the man who had asked her destination shrugged indifferently. "Follow me," he said.

She trailed behind him to the chapel. Kneeling before the golden crucifix, she crossed herself.

Why has he forgotten me?

HE HAS NOT. HE DOES NOT KNOW WHAT TO DO WITH YOU, FOR HE IS SUR-
ROUNDED BY FEARFUL MEN WHO ARE THREATENED BY YOUR POWER AND BY THE
PRESENCE OF GOD WITHIN THEMSELVES WHICH THEY CHOOSE NOT TO FEEL. BUT
BE OF GOOD CHEER. ALL WILL BE WELL.

I am uncomfortable with those guards. Why are they there?

CHARLES HAS BEEN TAUGHT BY HIS LIFE'S EXPERIENCES NOT TO GIVE HIS FAITH TO ANYONE, AND HE HAS NEVER MET ANYONE LIKE YOU. YOU HAVE NOTHING TO FEAR. YOU REMAIN UNDER HEAVEN'S PROTECTION.

She considered this new information, aghast at the poor Dauphin's isolation. *Will he turn me away?*

YOUR DESTINY IS WRITTEN AND CANNOT BE CHANGED UNLESS YOU ALTER IT YOURSELF. ENJOY THIS TIME OF PEACE. YOUR WORK HAS NOT YET BEGUN.

Will it begin soon?

There was only silence.

Shame warmed her face as she realized that Catherine had given her all the answer she needed. "Forgive me," she whispered aloud.

Jehanne prayed for wisdom and patience, the two virtues that persisted in eluding her. She closed the communication by making the Sign of the Cross.

Outside the chapel, the guard still awaited her. He looked at her disdainfully and indicated with a jerk of his head that she should return to her room. To make sure that she did so, he followed her, watching as she mounted the spiral steps to the tower.

The squire who had brought her meal was standing just within her doorway. He bowed to her with a curt nod. "His Majesty commands your presence at Mass in the chapel tomorrow morning. He has instructed me to add that he hopes you have a pleasant night's rest."

"Please thank the Dauphin for me," she responded, "and assure him that I will be most pleased to hear Mass with him."

The young man bowed again, and picking up the tray, left her.

She sighed. There was nothing more to do but sleep. She went to the fireplace and took the iron rod from its stand, then carefully turned over a log, which instantly burst into flames. As she watched it catch, a sudden apprehension made her shudder. She remembered Catherine's words: *Your destiny . . . cannot be changed unless you alter it yourself.*

I will not change it, I promise. I want what God wants.

She straightened up and walked to the writing table. She blew out the candle. By the light of the fire, she undressed and got into bed.

Sleep eluded her for some time as she contemplated the past few days. With a stab of unexpected guilt, she realized that she had barely bade Metz and Poulengy good-bye and had forgotten to thank them for seeing her safely to Chinon. She missed them terribly and longed for their advice. But they were gone now. There was nothing she could do but send up a hasty prayer for them.

She rolled over onto her stomach and fell asleep.

After Mass next morning Charles selected d'Alençon, Jehanne, and the fat councillor who had questioned her to accompany him to his private chambers, a magnificently furnished anteroom next to the oratory. Its walls were lined on three sides with bookcases of solid dark wood, their shelves filled with volumes bound in gilded and jeweled leather. A resplendent illuminated Bible lay open on a stand next to the bezeled, many-paned window, and from her seat Jehanne could see the vibrant colors upon the page. A fire crackled in the fireplace before the stools where they sat.

"Seigneur Trémoïlle, it is our understanding that you have spoken to the Maid on another occasion," Charles remarked with a sly smile, opening the interview.

"Indeed, Your Majesty," the chancellor replied, his eyes fastened on Jehanne, "I have had the pleasure." The last word carried a subtle bite that Jehanne did not miss.

She gritted her teeth angrily. She did not like this sinister man whose small, veiled eyes stared at her from the folds of fat swallowing his cheeks, his sensual mouth verging on a sneer. She would have to treat him carefully; he had the Dauphin's ear and might prove an obstacle to her plans.

But she had earned a portion of Charles' confidence as well, and she remembered her Guides' encouragement that he would accede to her will.

"Yes, my lord, we have met"—she smiled graciously—"although we were not introduced."

"Oh?" The Dauphin turned a surprised look to Trémoïlle.

"My apologies, Your Majesty," the official offered with a small bow, "but the interview was so brief that introductions were unfortunately overlooked." The red-lipped mouth twisted into a grimace that Jehanne supposed was meant to be a smile. "My apologies to the Maid as well. I am Georges de la Trémoïlle, the king's chancellor."

She nodded in acknowledgment.

"Well, that's settled," said Charles, rubbing his hands together. Addressing d'Alençon, he said, "You may have heard, Cousin, that Jehanne wants an army to raise the siege at Orléans."

"I have, Sire." The young man bestowed a warm look upon Jehanne. "I think that is a splendid idea."

She returned his smile, grateful for his alliance and his trust. She could see out of the corner of her eye that Trémoïlle shifted his substantial bulk.

"Would that be wise, Your Majesty?" he asked calmly. "I intend no offense to Jehanne"—he dipped his head in her general direction—"but all of us have longed for you to have your kingdom restored to such a degree that it might be easy for anyone to imagine that he—or she—has been called by God to defeat the English at Orléans. Does it not make more sense to continue our negotiations with seigneur Bourgogne to heal the realm?"

Jehanne clenched her fists until her knuckles whitened. It was an effort for her to maintain a neutral expression.

"What say you to that, Jehanne?" Charles asked, enjoying the drama he had provoked.

"How long have you been talking to the Burgundians, my lord, trying to sue for peace?" she asked.

"For as long as I can remember." He frowned. "Since before my father died."

"Then I think the time for talk has passed, Sire," she answered dauntlessly. "It seems that they do not wish peace unless they get their way and take all of France for themselves. But that would not be right because you are the true King of

France, not the duc de Bourgogne and not that little boy-king of England either. The only way they will leave the kingdom in peace is at the point of a sword.

"And excuse me, seigneur Trémoïlle," she ventured, resolution shining in her face, "but I do not 'imagine' that I have been sent by God; I *have* been sent by Him to raise the siege at Orléans and to accompany the Dauphin to Reims for his coronation."

She turned imploring eyes to Charles. "If you give your kingdom to the Lord of Heaven, He will uphold you as He has all the Kings of France before you, and will restore you to your rightful place as keeper of the kingdom. And then we shall drive the English out of France forever."

" 'We,' Jehanne?" Trémoïlle questioned quietly. A malicious smile played about his thick lips.

She remained steadfast in her resolve to withstand him. "Yes, sir, the Dauphin and myself. I have not told you yet, Sire, but my Counsel have told me that together we will send the English back to their own country, and that we will rescue the duc d'Orléans from his London prison." She glanced at d'Alençon with a gentle smile. "That is the word of God."

The three men sat stunned. Trémoïlle glowered at her, and she knew that it was he to whom Catherine had referred as a "fearful man." But he did not count. D'Alençon's admiring features showed understanding and faith in her.

Charles hid his amusement behind a slender hand. "One thing at a time, Jehanne." His eyes twinkled impishly. "Suppose that today we were to give you an army. What precisely would you do with it?"

"I would go to Orléans, Sire, to see for myself how the *god*—, the English have placed their fortifications, and then I would consult with your generals how to best lure them from their battlements. And we would defeat them and raise the siege."

"My dear girl," Trémoïlle said with feigned weariness, "that may seem simple to you, but I can assure you that once there you may not find it quite so easy."

"It would be easy," she retorted, irked at the condescension in his voice, "because we would have God on our side and He would give us His assistance in battle."

The minister yipped with a derisive laugh, casting a look at Charles to solicit the king's support. The scorn d'Alençon shot at him escaped neither Jehanne nor Charles.

"That may seem funny to you, sir, but I can assure you that the King of Heaven is more powerful than any army," Jehanne declared, no longer troubling to hide her anger. "And He has given His promise that we shall be victorious in liberating Orléans! The time has come for the Dauphin to regain his kingdom."

Charles' expression had changed in the last few moments. Instead of the guarded smile, there was now a look of quickening faith. He wanted very badly to believe in her; she could see it written across his pale face.

Jehanne stood abruptly, then knelt before the Dauphin. Placing her hands in his, she said, "Although you have not yet been crowned King and anointed with the holy oil, I beg you, Sire, give your kingdom to God as His fief and receive it from Him again, for He is your Overlord and you are His chosen vassal." Her voice dropped to an undertone. "Remember what I told you in the Great Hall, my lord."

He gazed at her in concentration, giving her that soul-reading look she had seen when they first met. The king's glance at his cousin asked an unspoken question. D'Alençon answered with an affirming smile.

Jehanne's eyes shone back at him with confidence and sincerity. Trust me, she pleaded silently.

His countenance softened a little. She could feel the struggle waging between his head and his heart as he tried to resist. Overcome by the unflagging spirit in her eyes, he fell into her Power and, for the present, into his own. A light blew across his face. "I give my kingdom to God," he whispered.

She bowed her head and kissed the ring that bore the royal seal. "Then receive it back from Him as His faithful steward, and know that now you cannot be defeated."

Charles smiled at her. "Thank you," he murmured, giving her hands a hearty squeeze.

With a great effort of will, he tore his gaze from hers and suddenly stood. The others got to their feet, an exertion that was difficult for Trémoïlle.

"We are hungry," Charles announced buoyantly, "and we invite you to join us for some refreshment."

They bowed in unison and followed their king as he strode with renewed confidence from the room.

"That girl is a menace and Charles is a drooling idiot, just like his cursed father, if indeed the King was his father!" Trémoïlle spat furiously. "She has flattered him like the shameless adventuress she is, with her talk of God's will and raising the siege at Orléans. And he apparently gives credence to her claims, can you believe that?"

He was pacing as quickly as his amplitude would allow, back and forth across the open flat battlement overlooking the Dauphin's well-tended garden.

Regnault de Chartres, archbishop of Reims, scratched a wizened cheek. "I believe anything that Charles does these days, but you know how he is, my dear Trémoïlle, one day taken with a new toy and the next. . . ." He shrugged. "I do not think he is so far gone as to seriously consider giving her an army."

"Oh, you misjudge the hold that she is beginning to gain over him," the chancellor insisted with scarcely contained wrath. His jowls shook with the force of his offense. "You weren't there, you haven't seen the witchery she uses with him, typical in a woman! Look at him." He nodded at the tiny figure below, who had paused in his stroll to examine a rosebush that was beginning to put forth tiny buds. "That frivolous, stupid fool!"

"You forget, Georges, that I interviewed her with you." The archbishop scowled. "I found nothing at all remarkable about her. Indeed, I thought her impudent and bothersome."

He had no patience for Trémoïlle and his constant, seething preoccupation with the Dauphin's follies. Everyone knew that Charles was fickle in his attachments and that the real powers behind the throne were Trémoïlle and himself.

"I tell you, Bishop, this is not just another of our little king of Bourges' momentary amusements," the minister hissed. "Over dinner he gave her leave to visit him at will and unlimited access to the castle and grounds. Do you realize what that will mean?"

Still not comprehending Trémoïlle's line of thought, the archbishop's brow furrowed, his rheumy old eyes empty.

"With uninterrupted access to the king, the girl may persuade the royal dolt to do whatever she wishes," the fat man prompted. "And there are others in the court who might listen to her. I've overheard some of the younger ones speaking quite favorably of her." Trémoïlle clenched his chubby hands into jeweled fists.

Understanding at last, Regnault's brows bent toward the sharp bridge of his nose. "Of course," he muttered. "This is very dangerous indeed. I had no idea."

"That's not all. He has ordered new clothes to be made for her. *Men's* clothes."

"No!"

Trémoïlle nodded, eyes ablaze with indignation. "Serious enough for you now, Your Excellency?"

"Men's clothes," the archbishop repeated in shocked amazement. "Why, that is an abomination, an encouragement to the sin of perversion!"

"She claims that God has instructed her to dress like a man, 'like a soldier,' she says, because she is a soldier of God. Filthy little peasant!"

"Blasphemy!" the archbishop swore. Alarm, mixed with righteous resentment, settled over him.

"Oh, yes, didn't you know?" Trémoïlle asked with heavy sarcasm. "She is God's agent on earth, who will deliver Orléans and accompany Charles to his coronation in Reims. In your cathedral, Bishop, and guess who will have the pleasure of performing the ceremony?"

"I have not been informed of this." The churchman frowned.

"You were there two nights ago when she knelt before him in the Great Hall and announced her intentions before the entire court. Didn't you hear what she said about his being crowned in Reims? *I* heard her, along with everyone else." The chancellor turned his back on the old man and pressed his hands to his massive hips. He glowered down at the man in the garden below.

"I did not take that seriously. She was an insignificant entertainment, like that green monkey he bought from the merchant who had been to Cathay. Charles has said nothing about a coronation to me," Regnault offered with a slim hope.

"Apparently, the Dauphin does not need to consult either of us any more, now that 'the Maid' has come to Chinon." Trémoïlle's anger was causing him to breathe in wheezing gasps, and his fat face was flushed.

De Chartres looked at him, disgusted. He loathed this bloated man whom heretofore he had considered a rival for Charles' attentions, but who was now his uneasy ally against a common threat. There must be a way out of this dilemma.

And suddenly there it was, certainly an insight from Above. "The Maid." He smiled. "Of course . . ."

"What is it?" the chancellor asked sharply.

"We are not as powerless as we might think, Georges," Chartres mused.

"Charles still needs us to save him from himself. The Maid just might hang herself under the right circumstances."

"What do you mean?"

"The girl claims to be sent by God, eh?"

"Yes. So?"

The archbishop's yellowed teeth spread into a vulpine grin. "Let us suggest to the Dauphin that she prove her claim before he assents to her requests. That would only be reasonable, would it not?"

Trémoïlle folded his hamlike arms over the broad belly in a gesture of labored patience as he waited for the cleric to continue.

"Charles would be well within his rights to have her tested. She says she is from God, so let him send her to Poitiers to appear before the best minds in Christendom, and they may ask what they will about her 'messages' from God. When she finds herself before professors of theology at Poitiers, she will be quaking in those men's boots of hers, and then Charles will see that she is nothing more than an opportunist."

Encouraged by the archbishop's scheme, Trémoïlle broke into an intrigued grin. "She also claims to be virtuous," he supplied, "so let us propose to Charles that she be examined by women, and not palace drudges either, but by noblewomen whose own virtue cannot be called into debate. As for her purported virginity"—he waved a hand in dismissal—"that should not be difficult to disprove."

"Why do you doubt that?"

"Do not be naïve, Bishop," the councillor admonished with a laugh. "She came here escorted by six men, *soldiers*. It took them eleven days and ten *nights*. You know what weak vessels women are. Do you honestly think that she did not work her wiles on those men?"

De Chartres chuckled in appreciation. "You are very subtle, Georges. Perhaps she is not a woman at all, but a youth of fifteen or sixteen. One cannot easily tell, dressed as she is. It may be advisable before she is taken to Poitiers for the Dauphin to appoint women to determine her gender."

"Very good, Bishop," Trémoïlle chortled.

"Do you think Charles can be persuaded?"

"Probably. After all, it makes sense that he would want to assure both himself and all of France of this girl's authenticity. He is starting to grow weary of being laughed at by his fellow monarchs, and would be most apprehensive of giving them another reason for scorning him. And we, his trusted councillors, have it as our duty to point out such a possibility.

"But there is another obstacle." Trémoïlle frowned suddenly. "D'Alençon. He is quite taken with her, and Charles trusts him. The king might listen to him instead of us."

"Yes," the archbishop slowly drew out the word. "But not even d'Alençon will support her when she falls flat on her face. In the meantime, we should play along with this charade. We should be courteous and even friendly to this lowborn little meddler, otherwise she might suspect a trap."

"Agreed."

De Chartres laughed in delight at his own cleverness. Trémoïlle joined him with a heartiness he had not known in days, ever since that miserable brat arrived. Their gladness rang out over the battlements like the barking of hounds after a scent.

Unaware of the plot taking shape upon the distant rampart, Jehanne was at that very moment with her new friend d'Alençon in the meadows where Charles' knights customarily exercised.

Spring would soon arrive. The afternoon was warmer than any had been for some time, and tiny buds seemed to have appeared overnight on the apple trees behind the castle. In another week or two the air would be fragrant with their blossoms, if the freakish warm weather held. New grass had already begun to sprout and dotted the heath with little pink flowers.

There were more than forty retainers in this spacious grassland, well over a third of whom were paired in swordplay. The sun gleamed brightly on the grunting, armored forms and light flashed from blades that rose, then struck in clanging, overlapping melodies. It was obvious that the blows looked more hazardous than they actually were, for the weapons were blunted and easily deflected off the heavy bucklers. Jehanne had never been this close to actual combat, even feigned. Watching them, she bit her lip in concentration, thrilled to see the might of France engaged in play that was not entirely recreational. She wondered how well they would fare in a real battle.

Nearby, a squad of marksmen discharged their crossbows at straw-stuffed targets roughly fashioned to resemble the human form. Every whizzing volley ended in a massed *thump!* as the bolts went home to their marks. Between shots the archers turned handles to crank the strings back to their maximum tension, then placed new arrows in the carved grooves.

In another section of the meadow men without armor were practicing on horseback with the lance. It was this activity that looked particularly difficult and that Jehanne instinctively knew required the most skill. Each rider was mounted on a giant charger bred through several generations to carry a steel-plated master. The knight had to not only manage his immense steed with one hand but also balance the thick eight-foot lance aimed straight ahead of him with the other. The very earth seemed to shudder as the rider charged a small round target set into a pivot atop a wooden post, and when he hit it dead center, it swung around rapidly in a circle. Between each attack a squire ran to the target and placed it back in its original position for the next contender.

"Would you like to try that?" d'Alençon asked Jehanne. In the sunlight his dark hair gave off auburn highlights. There was a small nick on his chin where his squire's razor had shaved too close this morning.

"Me?" Jehanne laughed in nervous surprise.

"Yes, of course." He chuckled. "If you're to be a soldier, don't you think it would be a good idea for you to accustom yourself to weaponry?"

"But I—I've never done that before," she sputtered, "and I've never ridden a warhorse."

"Come on, give it a try," the young duc encouraged. "Tell you what: I'll go first and you can see how easy it is."

He signaled to a squire, who brought a fierce-looking black stallion to where they stood. D'Alençon swung easily into the saddle designed with a high front and rear to steady its occupant. Then he took the lance the squire offered him.

"Now observe carefully," he instructed. "It's important to grip the lance closely against your body under your armpit, like this. That way, you can steady it toward the target. If your grasp is weak or if the lance is not close enough, then your aim will be wild and you'll lose it when you strike the target. You also need to lean forward in the saddle as you charge; that will help with your balance and will brace your weapon." He demonstrated what he meant in pantomime. "Watch me now.

"Hah!" He spurred the animal and it bolted toward the mark, tufts of grass and earth flying upward from its crushing hoofs. Rider and mount moved in such harmony that they appeared to be a single creature, powerful and lovely to see.

Upon impact the lance pierced the center of the target, which spun furiously in its socket. As d'Alençon reined the speeding horse, it obediently slowed its pace. He turned the reins with a deft motion. An alert squire ran toward the target and placed it back into position. The duc trotted back toward Jehanne with the weapon pointed toward the sky.

"See?" He approached her with a pleased smile. "It's actually quite simple." The young man tossed the lance to a waiting attendant and dismounted with a leap. "Now, let's see you try."

"All right," Jehanne replied, her heart pounding. She feared the humiliation of failure more than falling off her horse. At the same time, she did not want the duc to think her a coward if she refused.

She placed her foot firmly in the stirrup and swung up into the unfamiliar war saddle. The squire gave her the lance, and she took it under her right arm as d'Alençon had shown her, grasping it tightly under the conical shield. Some of the men had stopped to watch her. She saw one of them nudge another with an anticipatory grin.

I won't fall off, she told herself, I won't make a fool of myself. She leaned forward slightly and clenched her teeth, then dug her heels into the horse's side.

With a sudden jerk the steed lurched forward and thundered toward the target, snorting with every beat of its hooves. Jehanne gripped her knees tightly against the mighty animal as it soared toward the goal, making the wind whip against her face, and she narrowed her eyes, every nerve intent with total concentration. Her teeth rattled against the jarring impact of hooves upon earth.

When the lance struck the target, a vigorous shout went up from the men. Jehanne pulled on the reins and released her breath at the same time. The wind softened to a gentler breeze as the horse obeyed her command and slowed its pace.

Pointing the lance upward as d'Alençon had done, she turned the horse toward the left and spun it around, then cantered back toward d'Alençon and the others, who stood laughingly applauding. Her face was flushed with accomplishment.

"I thought you said you've never done that before." D'Alençon grinned.

She laughed. "I haven't. But I'd like to go again."

"Very well." Pride in her gleamed in the handsome face, and she saw that he was impressed.

By now nearly all the men had stopped their activities to watch her. When she performed again with the same result, an even louder cheer ushered her back to where the knights had gathered. Grinning broadly, she acknowledged their accolades with a self-deprecatory bow.

This was more fun than she had known in a long time! She could not distinguish which was better, the action itself or the surprised plaudits of these men. No one could have stopped her now had he tried.

She turned the horse back toward the target. This time the lance only struck the target's outer rim, but still it whirled in place and the cheers sounded louder than before.

The horse trotted back to the circle of men awaiting her and she dismounted. One man clapped her on the back; another shook her hand amid the exclamations of his fellows.

"Well done!"

"Good riding, Jehanne!"

She beamed at them proudly, riding the crest of their acclaim and acceptance. She recognized among them courtiers who just a few nights ago had sniggered at her appearance in the Great Hall. In their altered demeanors she felt something like equality flowering between them. Most important was the look that the duc gave her. She knew then that his faith in her, already substantial, had been sealed in a tie that would endure beyond this day, and that he would follow her regardless of what his royal cousin decided to do with her.

"That was wonderful!" he exclaimed, his large brown eyes shining with admiration. "Are you tired?"

"A little," she admitted. Then, noticing that the other men were staring at her, she felt an abrupt self-consciousness. "I did not mean to intrude upon your practice. Please, go back to what you were doing."

The men were slow to return to their exercises; some lingered to add further congratulations. Jehanne knew that tonight the court would hum with news that the visionary was also a born soldier.

D'Alençon said, "Come, let's take a stroll to the garden."

She wiped the beads of sweat from her brow and grinned. "Very well."

They turned toward the castle, which lounged like an armored giant high upon the ridge. For a few moments they walked in silence. A breeze cooled Jehanne's still flushed cheeks and moved her hair.

This had been a most unexpected day. First, the tense conversation with the Dauphin and that horrible man Trémoïlle, and afterward over dinner Charles' permission for her to explore his castle at will. That had taken her breath away after the sentinels who only last night had stood guard outside her door.

And now, this unplanned display of a prowess she had not known she possessed. Surely her Guides must have helped her, although They had never done anything but speak to her before. She marveled as it began to dawn on her that soldiering would come to her more easily than she had ever supposed. Her memory darted back to that day in the Bermont chapel when Michel had first told her that she would be a holy warrior, and her reply that she was only a poor girl who knew nothing of warfare. That day was long ago and that girl another.

"What?"

D'Alençon had said something to her that she had missed.

"I said, 'Surely you have ridden a great deal in your life to be able to handle a horse like that?' "

"Truly, sir, I have not."

He winced. "Please do not call me 'sir.' My name is Jehan and I want you to call me that."

She smiled broadly. "Very well, Jehan. In answer to your question, I sometimes rode my father's old farmhorse when I was a child, but that was very different because the horse was slow and was mainly used to pull the plow and the wagon. On my journey here I rode a better horse, the one that Bertrand de Poulengy and Jehan de Metz gave me; he's in the Dauphin's stable now. The duc de Lorraine gave me a horse, but I gave it away to a soldier in Vaucouleurs."

"Why did you do that?" D'Alençon's mouth was a perplexed bow.

"Because the duc is a traitor to the Dauphin, and I did not want anything of his." She frowned.

D'Alençon stopped walking and smiled at her curiously. "You really love the king, don't you, Jehanne?"

"Oh yes, he is the symbol of France and shall be her true King." All seriousness now, she turned a look of conviction up to the beautiful face. "Without him the kingdom would fall to the English, and if that happened we would all be lost."

"And that is what God has told you?"

She nodded soberly.

They walked on in slow silence. Then d'Alençon said brightly, "Charles likes you, you know. He is still uncertain that you are sent by God, but he respects your courage and he thinks you are well spoken."

"But, sir—I mean, Jehan—I am sent by God," she protested.

His look was gentle and almost reverent. "I know you are, I can see it in your face." He placed a warm hand against her cheek. "You shine, did you know that? Nobody but one touched by God could glow as you do. I feel certain that Charles sees it too, otherwise you would not still be here. But ever since he was a boy he has put his faith in people who have disappointed him sorely."

"Like his mother," she ventured.

"Yes, like his mother," d'Alençon confirmed grimly. "Now he doesn't trust anyone who really cares about him because he does not trust anyone at all. Not even me," he added sadly.

D'Alençon stopped and took her hand. "You must be careful, Jehanne. Do not take anything for granted when it comes to Charles. I have seen him turn on his favorites when he thought they might outshine him in the eyes of the people. It's not that he is a bad man; quite the contrary. If he were ordinary, he would probably be most kind, most generous, but because he is the king he has grown suspicious and fearful. For very good reasons, too. Everyone wants a piece of him, many care nothing about him except as a source of favors. Regardless of the reasons, for your own protection you must not confuse the King of France with the man."

"But when I deliver his kingdom and see him crowned, he will certainly believe in me then, won't he?" she asked.

"Perhaps. It may be that God will touch him then." D'Alençon's smile disappeared with the shadow that crossed his face. "There is something else, though. He is under the influence of seigneur Trémoïlle and the archbishop of Reims. He has other advisers, but those two hold the most power over him, and they are as treacherous as serpents. *They* do not believe in you, and if you fail, even slightly, they will take that opportunity to turn Charles against you. I do not say this to frighten you, just to warn you to be very, very careful."

"Thank you," she said with gratitude and affection. "But I am under God's protection and nothing can happen to me. He has given me His word and His faith, and I can only do His will. I shall not fail, rest assured of that."

"I have never met anyone like you," the young man responded with genuine astonishment.

She laughed merrily. "And I have never spoken like this with a duc before. You know, it's strange, but I feel that I have known you a long time."

"You too? I felt that I somehow recognized you when I first saw you with Charles. That is very odd, isn't it?"

"Perhaps we knew one another in Heaven before we were born," she answered buoyantly.

He laughed, revealing his healthy straight teeth. "Perhaps we did."

They had reached the garden beneath the castle walls. D'Alençon gestured that they should make themselves comfortable on a small stone bench, and to her surprise sat only after she did.

This was a beautiful spot, one of the loveliest Jehanne had ever seen. Long, rock-covered paths wound through hedges impeccably sculpted into shapes of diamonds and spheres, and rosebushes whose tiny buds portended the arrival of spring. A magnificent yellow butterfly flittered about one of the bushes. Birds, robins by the sound of them, chirped brightly as they glided between oaks speckled with emerging leaves. The sky was a cloudless, deep blue, like the royal banner of France.

"Would you like to meet my family?" d'Alençon asked abruptly. "I am certain that they would like to meet you."

"Oh yes, Jehan!"

"Excellent!" He gave his thigh a conclusive slap. "We'll leave tomorrow for St.-Florent. I have no doubt that I can persuade the king to allow you to go. But for the journey you must have a better horse than the one you brought with you."

"You haven't seen him, Jehan." She grinned. "He is a good traveler."

"Nevertheless, you must have another. Did you like the one you just rode?"

"Yes, he is a beauty."

"Then he's yours."

"Mine?" she gasped.

"Yes, yours. After all, a soldier of God should have a horse worthy of carrying such a holy burden."

He said this with no hint of mockery, but with forthrightness sparkling in his eyes. He was not the first to believe in her without reservation. But d'Alençon was of the blood royal, and Jehanne knew that he would protect her with his life.

She took his pale, aristocratic hand and squeezed it in fraternal affection. Unspeaking, they watched the sun descend through trees that whispered in the coming twilight.

When Jehanne returned to Chinon with d'Alençon after three agreeable days at St.-Florent, she was met with surprises, all but one unpleasant.

She had been almost apprehensive about meeting the duc's wife. Jehanne had half-anticipated that the young duchesse, daughter of the fabled duc d'Orléans, would be haughty, perhaps even forbidding. In this she was wrong. D'Alençon's bride of one year had heard of her even in the serene seclusion of St.-Florent, and unlike those at Chinon, offered Jehanne her faith and an eager hospitality. Relieved, Jehanne relaxed into a comfortable conviviality and the two of them became fast friends. Her stay with the duc's family was so informal and contented that she was lulled into a presumption of the whole world's goodwill. She found herself quite taken off guard by what awaited her at Chinon.

Informed at the castle gate that the Dauphin desired her presence in the courtyard near the chapel, she hurried there with d'Alençon at her side. Among the beautiful hedges and rosebushes now coming to flower, Charles was in conversation with Trémoïlle and the archbishop of Reims. With the men were two ladies whom Jehanne had not seen before. They were middle-aged and wore long elegant dresses of silk and taffeta. Their hair was hidden beneath tall hats, and their painted eyebrows regarded Jehanne with a contemptuous nonchalance.

"Welcome, Jehanne." The Dauphin smiled. Inclining his head toward d'Alençon, he murmured, "Cousin." They bowed low to their king. "Did you have a pleasant journey?"

"Yes, my lord, most pleasant." Jehanne obeyed the silent gesture the Dauphin made with his hand and stood up.

"We would like to present Madame de Gaucourt and Madame de Trèves, wives of two of our trusted advisers," Charles said with congenial formality.

The two women bowed stiffly to Jehanne. Hoping to disarm them, she acknowledged their acquaintance with a smile. The effort was wasted. They continued to look at her as though she were a beggar.

"For your convenience, Jehanne," the Dauphin continued, "seigneur de Gaucourt has most generously instructed one of his pages to attend to your needs. He will serve you during the daytime hours."

"Thank you, Sire." Turning to the minister's wife, she said, "And my thanks also to seigneur de Gaucourt."

The woman's only response was a frosty smile.

"We have decided that you should not be left alone at night, so while you are our guest you shall have the company of a good woman, Madame Bellier, to share your bed. This is a great honor, for her husband is our esteemed majordomo." Charles' amiable expression was concealing something; she sensed that more was to come.

"But naturally," the prince went on, "before we can entrust Madame Bellier to spend her nights with you, we must have the assurance that you are in fact the female you claim to be."

Jehanne burst into a disbelieving laugh. "Of course I'm a woman, my lord! Isn't that clear?"

"Not according to your dress," Trémoïlle contended, his lips pursed with satisfaction. "Is it natural for a woman to insist upon dressing as a man? Besides, if you are female, then you should not mind proving it."

The archbishop's drooping upper lip curled into a smile. He seemed quite content at the turn of events, and Jehanne wondered how this man of God could justify himself to his conscience.

D'Alençon's chest heaved in anger. "This is an outrage! You know very well, seigneur Trémoïlle, that she is a woman."

"I do not have firsthand knowledge of her sex, seigneur d'Alençon. Do you?" he asked with an insinuating smirk.

"Why, you . . . !" D'Alençon's mouth twisted into an angry snarl, and he reached instinctively for the dagger at his belt. Alarmed, Jehanne put a restraining hand on his sword arm. She saw Trémoïlle, raising his own, stumble backward a pace.

"You will control yourself, Cousin," the Dauphin reminded him sternly. His eyes narrowed into distrustful slits. "It is our wish that Jehanne remove herself forthwith to her room, where these good ladies will ascertain her gender for themselves. That should settle the matter once and for all."

"I will do as you command, Sire," Jehanne replied with a bow. Turning to the young duc, she said reassuringly, "It can do no harm, Jehan. I have nothing to fear from an examination." She glared defiance at the gloating Trémoïlle.

"Good," Charles remarked smoothly. "After these ladies have satisfied our curiosity, you will remain in your room. Some representatives of the Church"— he glanced at the archbishop—"have a few questions for you."

"Yes, my lord Dauphin." She set her jaw in a firm resolve, knowing that she had no choice but to obey.

"Then go. We shall see you at dinner."

Jehanne bowed low to the Dauphin and tossed a curt nod to his advisers. Turning to leave, she caught d'Alençon's eye and gave him a confident smile. Then she strode toward the castle, daring the ladies to keep up with her.

When they reached her room, Jehanne, wanting only to finish this humiliation as soon as possible, disrobed quickly while the ladies watched. She turned to them with a proud, insolent grin, hands on her naked hips. She raised a hand to scratch absently at a fleabite on her arm.

Expressionless, the women regarded her body. This is necessary, Jehanne reminded herself. The ladies turned without a word and left her alone, closing the door as they went.

The humor left her face at once, replaced by a thoughtful scowl. Those evil men were behind this, she was certain of that. Charles wanted to believe in her; she could feel his soul pulled in her direction, yet as d'Alençon had warned, he was under the power of his advisers. But she also remembered Catherine's words about them and took heart. The Dauphin would sooner or later align himself with her; she needed to fix her mind on that to the exclusion of all else.

She dressed again in the smelly clothes, grimacing at the musky odor. At St.-Florent, the duchesse d'Alençon had shyly suggested that she change into a woman's gown. The most Jehanne was willing to agree to was a much-needed bath. Now she almost regretted that she had not accepted the dress she had been offered.

Will I have to undergo more treatment of this sort before he believes me? she wondered, pulling the tunic over her head.

YES, BUT DO NOT BE DISMAYED. IT IS ONLY A NECESSARY PREPARATION FOR YOUR WORK, AND WILL CONVINCE CHARLES TO TRUST YOU. THERE ARE MEN OF THE CHURCH WHO ARE ON THEIR WAY TO YOU NOW. YOU MUST NOT FEAR THEIR QUESTIONS, BUT ANSWER THEM TRUTHFULLY. WE WILL HELP YOU.

She was surprised to see that the archbishop was not among the clerics. Instead, she found herself face to face with two of the Dauphin's personal chaplains and a third whom she knew to be Christophe d'Harcourt, bishop of Castres and the king's occasional confessor.

They asked her the same questions she had already answered for Charles, assailing her for more than two hours, and by the time they left her, Jehanne was impatient and angry. She was so full of wrath that when the young page who had been assigned to her arrived, she was brusque and demanded what he wanted from her.

Then, seeing his crestfallen face, she felt remorseful and asked more gently, "What is your name?"

"Louis de Coutes," the boy replied, "but everyone calls me Minguet."

He could not have been any older than fourteen and stood about two inches shorter than Jehanne. The hair hugging the top of his ears was a sandy blond, and his face bore the angry blemishes of late childhood.

"Tell me, Minguet, is it true that you are attached to sieur de Gaucourt?" she asked.

While he looked nothing like her younger brother Pierre, she was nevertheless reminded of him and she felt a small tug of home. His eyes, blue and very large, mirrored an awe of her that she had not foreseen.

"I am now assigned to you, Mademoiselle," he stammered. "I wanted very much to serve you."

"Why?" Jehanne wondered.

"Because you have come from God, Mademoiselle."

She put a hand on his shoulder and looked down into his nervous face, as smooth as a girl's. "Please, Minguet, call me Jehanne. And thank you for your faith. I don't seem to have much of that from others," she added sullenly.

"Oh, that is not true!" the boy exclaimed. "Everyone is talking about you and your mission to rescue Orléans. Down in the kitchens, that is all anyone talks about."

She laughed. "I hope that conviction travels upward a bit."

"It will, Jehanne, you'll see," Minguet replied eagerly in a voice that had not yet finished changing. "The king's faith grows stronger every day."

"How do you know that?"

He looked shyly at the floor and with a shrug kicked a diffident toe at a crack between the boards. "I don't know for certain, I just believe it. You must believe it too," he offered in an attempt to be helpful.

"I do, Minguet," she said with a confidence she had to summon. "Otherwise, I would not keep trying to persuade him; I would return home to my village." She regarded him for a moment, then asked, "Where is your home?"

His face darkened and he answered, "I have none. I am an orphan. My father was a knight of the House of Orléans, but he was killed in battle at Agincourt when I was three months old. My mother died when I was seven."

"And you have served sieur de Gaucourt ever since?" Her eyes filled with sympathy, and she felt doubly repentant for her curt greeting.

He nodded, still looking at the floor.

"Then I want you to know that I am honored that you wanted to serve me. I can think of no other page that I would rather have than one from Orléans, especially such a faithful one as yourself."

Blushing, Minguet raised his face to hers. A wide smile spread across the pockmarks. "Thank you, Jehanne," he replied, reddening such that all the blood in his body seemed to sweep into his face. "I will attend you steadfastly, you'll see."

He meant it with all his heart, she could tell by the look in his eyes. He would live to be an old man and would remember her with his last breath.

As Charles had instructed, Madame Bellier stayed the night with Jehanne. The older woman snored like a grunting pig and moaned so loudly in her sleep that Jehanne lay awake most of the night. She was grateful for the sunrise, when she got out of bed as soon as it was seemly. Then she went to the chapel and prayed that all the delays would soon cease.

She was summoned to breakfast with the Dauphin in his apartment's antechamber. D'Alençon and Trémoïlle were there as well. Though both behaved civilly, the tension between them was palpable. Charles informed Jehanne that he and members of the court—D'Alençon, Trémoïlle, the archbishop, and the other councillors—would be moving temporarily to Poitiers that very afternoon. Jehanne would go as well.

"Poitiers, my lord?" she inquired innocently. So here it was. Catherine had told her during prayers this morning that she would be taken to Poitiers for further examinations of a more searching nature.

"Yes," Charles answered, avoiding her eyes. "We spend some months every year at our castle in Poitiers."

D'Alençon glanced at him, then at his plate. Jehanne's spirit plummeted when he could not look at her either, for in their growing bond she had not expected that he would play false with her. Trémoïlle's response was predictable. His mouth formed a smile glowing with malicious triumph.

A wave of nausea took away Jehanne's appetite for the cheese and fruit that decorated her plate, reminding her that she was truly alone upon the earth.

"In God's name," she said with a sigh, "I know I shall have trouble at Poitiers." Her eyes burned into Trémoïlle's taunting pomposity. "But no matter, my Counsel will help me. So let us go."

It would be all right. She was ready for anything and would need no human allies.

CHAPTER FIVE

The Book of Poitiers

March 20–April 27, 1429

The most imposing house on the rue Notre-Dame-la-Petite dominated that district of Poitiers like a complacent *grande dame*. Built during the reign of Charles V, everything about it declared haughty affluence, from the stone facade enclosing four arched second-floor windows of geometric cut glass, to the perpetually fresh coat of whitewash. Its owner was Jehan Rabateau, advocate general to the Parlement-in-exile at Poitiers, an Armagnac partisan originally from Paris who in his youth had fled to sanctuary in the South. In this city, the Dauphin's capital since Paris had fallen to the English, he had flourished through God's grace and his own hard work.

His house was actually more than a dwelling place: the entire second floor was given over to a large council room where the Parlement often convened. Several compartments of smaller size, convenient to the conference chamber, were available for the many clerks employed there and their various *bureaux*. At all hours of the day and sometimes into the evening, the scratches of pens upon parchment beneath lighted candles gave evidence to the busy workings of the government.

When notified that Charles was coming to Poitiers, Rabateau informed his wife that she should make everything ready for the guest who would share their roof. For two whole days the servants scrubbed windows and hardwood floors, and at market the cooks selected plump vegetables and the finest hens for roasting. The spare room at the top of the house, not recently used, was opened to the spring air. The laundress fitted the bed with crisp sheets.

Charles and his retinue stopped there only briefly before continuing on to his château on the city's outskirts. One member of the party remained behind. While not confined to her room, Jehanne was forbidden to leave the house for any reason whatever, upon orders from the king.

The morning after her arrival, men of the Church began to fill the hall on the second floor where the Parlement met, coming in twos and threes until they had formed a sizable group. Once they were all assembled, Jehanne was brought into the chamber. Ignoring the massed strangers, she looked around for the duc d'Alençon. He had told her that he would be somewhere among the crowded gathering of clergy and curious civilians. She finally spotted him sitting to one side within a small group of laymen who looked to be soldiers. When he saw her, he gave her an encouraging smile. She nodded to him, then took her seat on a bench next to the table where a Dominican scribe waited with pen in hand.

Jehanne allowed her eyes to roam over the forest of faces that now turned to her. The men of the Church occupied places on the tiered benches, their tonsured domes shining like mushrooms in the windowlight. Some looked stern, others merely inquisitive; all ogled the rumpled, travel-stained black clothes from Vaucouleurs that she still wore. Apart from them was a conclave of well-dressed burghers and other officials of the *bourgeoisie*, including Monsieur Rabateau. The archbishop of Reims, majestic in his purple-brocaded robes and raven cap, held the seat of power elevated above the others. Not doubting the archbishop's hostility toward her, Jehanne had been chagrined when she learned that Charles had chosen him to preside over the council. Among the other Church officials were those she recognized. Charles' two confessors who had questioned her at Chinon were present, as well as the archbishop's assistant, Monseigneur de Montfort. But only much later would she learn the exact identities of the others.

Included in the commission of inquiry were masters from the universities of Orléans and Paris, a Carmelite, and four Dominicans, distinctive in their pristine habits cloaked with black mantles. She supposed that the bishop, younger than Regnault de Chartres but undoubtedly a high official, held the see of Poitiers. Unknown to Jehanne at that time, two famous theologians were also among the commission. Pierre de Versailles and Jourdain Morin, for the most part rendered inconspicuous by their silence, were here to act behind the scenes as advisers.

She mastered her misgivings and smiled at the predominantly nameless men with self-assurance. There was nothing to fear, she told herself. Her Teachers were wiser than these scholars, however educated they might be.

One of the prelates, whom she later discovered was a Master Lombart, professor of theology, looked questioningly at the others. When none spoke, he cleared his throat. "We have been sent here by the king," he told her.

"Then I suppose that you have come to question me." Jehanne lifted her chin in proud defiance. "Well, you should know that I don't recognize A from B."

"Why did you go to the king at Chinon?" the younger bishop asked. He was about forty, she guessed, and in spite of his seated position she could tell that he was tall and gangly. With those long arms, he looked like a crafty spider. The Dominican scribe at the far end of the table began to write in rapid strokes on a large piece of parchment.

"God spoke to me when I was thirteen and charged me to help the Dauphin to become King and to send the English back across the Narrow Sea."

"How did you come to find your way to Chinon?" The Dominican who asked this had a strong Limousin accent and Jehanne had a hard time understanding him.

"I went to sieur Robert de Baudricourt in Vaucouleurs and told him of my quest, and after much delay he sent me under escort to Chinon. The journey took eleven days and God protected us from harm while we traveled."

"How did God speak to you?"

"He sent me a messenger who spoke to me in a lovely voice, like that of an angel."

"How did this voice appear to you? Did it have a body?"

Jehanne bit her lower lip. May I?

YES, CHILD OF GOD, YOUR TIME HAS COME. BUT BE CAREFUL, FOR THEY ARE LIMITED TO WHAT THEY KNOW FROM BOOKS AND DO NOT HAVE THE CAPACITY FULLY TO UNDERSTAND.

"I was tending cattle at pasture with my friends on a summer's day and we decided to have a race. I ran the fastest and won. When I turned toward the shade of a great tree to rest, I saw a boy who told me to go home, my mother needed me. But when I got there, she told me that she had not sent for me. So I started back to pasture where my friends were waiting."

She paused and took a breath, uncertain if she could explain what happened next without giving away too much. She had not been afraid to tell the Dauphin the whole truth, but that was different. In his own way he was God's chosen one just as she was. But these men for whom God was a riddle to be deduced had never danced with angels, nor were they holy stewards of the kingdom.

Help me.

DO NOT BE AFRAID. WE ARE WITH YOU.

"A voice spoke to me through a roaring rush of wind and light in my father's garden. At first I was frightened because nothing of that sort had ever happened to me before, but the voice was so loving and so comforting that afterward I lost my fear, and it came to me again when I was at prayer in the chapel at Bermont Forest. It told me of the great compassion that God has for the people of France, and that He wills that the Dauphin shall become King and drive the English back to their own country. And it instructed me to go to the Dauphin and tell him that he is God's beloved guardian of the kingdom of France."

An amazed hum raced through the closely packed room. "How did this voice address you?"

"It called me 'Daughter of God.' "

"Did you ever see this voice with your eyes?"

"No." She hesitated, knowing that this would be difficult to explain. "I heard what it said to me in my mind, with my inner ear. I have actually seen him only in dreams. He is very beautiful," she added wistfully.

"Has it identified itself?" The monk who had initiated the interrogation smiled. His eyes did not.

A warning rang in Jehanne's ears. There were some things too sacred to reveal. "It told me that it is God's messenger and His servant." This was an evasion, she knew, yet not exactly a lie.

"Has it told you anything else?"

"It has taught me courage. It has taught me the love of God and of France, and that if I love God, then I must love all God's creatures, even the English. The voice comes and goes when I need it."

"So you do not see this apparition with your eyes?" asked a black-clad Carmelite.

"I do not see it. It is a"—she groped for words—"a presence who speaks in my head, but I feel it all around me."

"What dialect does your voice use?" asked the Dominican with the Limousin accent.

All of this was such nonsense. In God's name, how little vision these men possessed! Jehanne rubbed her hands on her hose, then clenched her fists in frustration. "A better one than yours," she retorted.

The assembly burst into laughter before they could stop themselves. When d'Alençon grinned at her, she could not resist responding in kind.

Séguin the Dominican colored slightly, but smiled in spite of the joke at his expense. Then he said affably, "Jehanne, God cannot wish us to believe you without your giving us some sign, and we cannot advise the king to entrust an army to you on your word alone."

"In God's name," she breathed irritably, "I did not come to Poitiers to give signs, but only take me to Orléans and I will show you the signs for which I *was* sent! There are four things that will come to pass, and these are God's promises.

"First," she ticked them off on her fingers, "the English will be destroyed in the field, and the siege of Orléans will be raised. Second, the Dauphin will be crowned and consecrated at Reims. Third, Paris will then return to the King's obedience. And finally, the duc d'Orléans will return from his captivity in England."

A murmur echoed within the chamber. She saw two monks cross themselves. Another raised an eyebrow and smiled at his neighbor.

"Why do you refer to His Majesty as 'the Dauphin'?" The Dominican who asked this did not look much older than Jehanne. Light from the window gleamed upon his broad, bald tonsure.

"Because I may not call him 'King' until he is anointed with the holy oil of kings and duly consecrated in Reims," she rejoined, irritated by the stupidity of his question. Certainly these men knew what every peasant held to be true. "It is the will of God that I take him there."

Renewed whispers buzzed among the robed men. "Tell us why you are dressed in men's clothing," the Carmelite requested. "Have you not heard the word of God as written in the Holy Scripture: 'The woman shall not wear that which pertaineth unto a man, neither shall a man put on a woman's garment, for all that do so are abomination unto the Lord thy God'?"

She waved an impatient hand. "I don't know anything about that. I only know that God has commanded me to be His soldier, and that to be a soldier, I must dress as one. How would it be if I were to try to lead an army in a woman's dress? The knights and other soldiers would not take my commands seriously, they would only think of me as a woman and not as a soldier."

She was growing tired and wanted this to be over. A headache had started to throb at her temples. With difficulty she conquered her rising temper and continued to gaze at them with aplomb.

"You say that your voice tells you that God wishes to free the people of France from their present calamities," a monk stated skeptically. "But if He wishes to free them, it is not necessary to have an army."

Had these men of the Church no common sense at all? "In God's name!" she cried, losing control at last, "if the soldiers fight, God will give them the victory!"

"You use the name of God freely," said Séguin. "Are you certain that you believe in God?"

"Yes, and better than you!"

"Jehanne, are you a good Catholic?" queried the younger bishop.

She nodded.

"And what do you know of your religion? Who taught you?"

"My mother taught me the *Pater*, the *Ave*, and the *Credo* when I was a child. I know that Lord Jhesus is the Son of God and that He died on the Cross for our sins and to keep us from the flames of Hell that we might see God in Heaven."

"Anything else?"

"I know that if we pray to the saints and to the Holy Mother in Paradise, they ask Lord Jhesus for His love and protection, and to keep us from sin."

"Are you familiar with Holy Scripture?"

"No, I cannot read. But I know the words of the Mass."

"Do you attend Mass and receive Holy Communion as is required for Christians?" questioned archbishop de Chartres.

She smiled. "As often as I am able, Your Excellency." He knew the answer to that very well, for he had seen her take the sacraments in the Dauphin's chapel.

"You call yourself 'Jehanne the Maid,' " the other bishop observed. "Is that what you truly are?"

"Yes." The muscles in her jaw twitched with resolve. "I swore to God that I shall remain a maid until such time as He gives me permission to change my status. I have taken this vow for love of Him, and because the voice has told me that I was born to be His warrior for France."

"Is your chastity the source of your power?" the Carmelite asked. "Is that how you knew of the king's defeat before Orléans?"

"I knew about that because God's messenger told me." She paused. "About the other, I do not know."

The murmur began again and a Dominican who had not yet spoken said, "Are you aware that the Devil can have no commerce with a virgin?"

"I have heard that said."

"And having heard that, what assurance have we that you are not lying about your purity, that you are not in fact in league with the King of Hell and all his demons?"

"I am Jehanne the Maid," she answered, staring him down. "So I am called, and so I am."

The conviction in her last words cut a swath through the stuffy chamber. Not a soul stirred until the monseigneur sitting next to archbishop de Chartres whispered something to him. Scowling, the president of the commission nodded, then stood.

"That will conclude the proceedings for now," he declared, "unless any of you have something further to add." He searched the faces of the theologians.

"Your Excellency, I do," Jehanne said, allowing her voice to rise above the returning babble.

Conversation ceased as the men turned to her expectantly. De Chartres nodded. "Very well, speak."

"Although I cannot read, I know that there is more in the Book of God than in any of yours," she asserted with a quiet fervor. "For I have felt His Presence in the fields and flowers. And here." She put a hand over her heart. Her Power tingled at the ends of her fingers. The very air crackled with it.

She could tell that at least some of the clerics felt it and were impressed by her. A reluctant admiration formed upon the younger bishop's lined face. His Dominican colleagues looked almost buoyant as, in whispers, they began filing out of the hall. With a benevolent smile at her, Séguin the Limousin went also, shaking his head in amusement. Monsieur Rabateau's bureaucrats departed with the theologians, but several men, civilians all, remained behind. They wore the simple clothes of working knights and men-at-arms. Led by a smiling d'Alençon, they approached her. She stood to greet them.

D'Alençon's beautiful face spread into a grin. He took her hand and grasped it as a brother would. "You comported yourself very well, Jehanne," he said, his eyes afire with pride. "I don't see how they can refuse you."

She laughed. "Too bad you're only a duc and not a theologian."

"Jehanne, my name is Gobert Thibault," interrupted a tall, wiry young man who had jostled his way into the forefront of the group clustered about her. "When you go into battle at Orléans, I give you my word that by the Holy Mother, I shall be in the van with you."

She clapped him smartly on the shoulder. "I wish I had several men of goodwill such as yourself, Gobert!"

"I will be there as well, Jehanne," swore another man.

"And I!"

The soldiers looked down at her with enthusiastic zeal, obviously as impatient to begin as she. What did she care if the churchmen did not believe her? In these war-worn, hardened faces was all the support she needed. By the grace of God they were gathering, if only a few at a time, her army.

The commission that had convened at the Dauphin's instigation deliberated into the night and through most of the following day. Detained at the home of the Rabateaux, Jehanne spent the morning in prayer in her hosts' oratory. She felt her Counsel's love all about her and took courage from Catherine's pledge that victory was at hand.

In the late afternoon d'Alençon came to her and informed her that the members of the commission had made their decision. A courier had by now already arrived at the castle with a detailed report for Charles. The clergy had based their findings not only on their interview with her, but also on the three-week-old account of two Franciscan monks whom Charles had secretly dispatched to Dom-rémy and Vaucouleurs to check into her background. The official record asserted that the prelates had found Jehanne to be a good Christian and a true Catholic, and that her past was beyond reproach. It stated further that the biblical injunction against a woman wearing men's dress applied only to indecent apparel, and, citing Esther and Judith, did not include military raiment.

Jehanne had no idea who Esther and Judith were, but her heart soared at the words that concluded the report: "In view of the imminent necessity and of the danger to Orléans, Your Majesty might allow the girl known as Jehanne the Maid to help you and might send her to Orléans."

Her eyes lit up and with a grin she flung her arms around d'Alençon's neck. They roared with laughter. "There's something else, though," he said.

She grew suddenly serious. "What?"

"Charles wants to take you to Tours," he answered, embarrassed. "Trémoïlle has been at him, suggesting that you are not a true maid. Though Charles believes in you more than he's willing to admit, he doesn't want there to be any question that you're what you claim to be."

"But I gave him my word!" she cried. "Why is that not enough for him?"

"Don't you remember what I told you at Chinon, that he trusts no one?" d'Alençon asked in a tone that was almost scolding. "At least, he trusts no one whom he should," the duc amended. "He does not want it bandied about by Bourgogne or the English that he accepted the aid of a sorceress. That would reflect badly on him and call into question—even more than there already is—his own legality as king. If he can prove your goodness and honesty to the world, no one can later accuse him of being in league with the Devil and having come into his inheritance through the Evil One."

She nodded thoughtfully, understanding Charles' design. A virgin could not possibly be in a compact with the Devil, for it was through the carnal act that Satan formed a pact with his prey. By the same logic, a wanton could not hear God's messengers. It made sense, after all.

"Why Tours?"

"Because Yolande, the king's mother-in-law, holds that city and has gone to her castle there. It is she who will examine you."

"I see." Jehanne paled. The Dauphine Marie's mother was said to be a most formidable lady.

"I'm sorry you have to endure all of this, Jehanne," d'Alençon apologized gently, "but with Yolande performing the examination, no one will ever be able to doubt you again."

She looked up at him with resignation. "Then I must do what the Dauphin commands. I will go to Tours and let them see for themselves that I am the Maid."

Early the next morning, Séguin and his brother monk Guillaume Aymerie paid her a visit at the home of Monsieur Rabateau. Her host's demeanor toward her had changed since her appearance before the commission. When they were first introduced, he looked her up and down with a barely disguised expression of disgust, and for a moment she had thought he would actually hold his nose. But now he practically tripped over himself to grant her slightest wish. Full of self-importance at having such an estimable visitor, he swelled with pride as together they greeted the theologians.

Like Séguin, Aymerie belonged to the Dominicans, also known as the Order of Friars Preachers. Jehanne recognized him as the man who had asked her why it was necessary to have an army if God would defeat the English. He had a round paunch of a belly and a florid face. A wooden cross hung between the arms he folded into the sleeves of his white habit. They had come, Séguin explained, to bid her Godspeed and to tell her in person that she had impressed them most favorably.

"Thank you," she responded, still a little resentful of the wearisome ordeal she had undergone at their hands. "If you truly mean what you say, there is something you can do for me."

"What is that, child?" Aymerie asked. With his large eyes and short lip, he reminded Jehanne of a curious owl.

"I have said that I cannot read nor write, yet I wish to send a letter to the English to warn them of my coming. I hope that they will leave Orléans of their own free will, for I do not wish for the Dauphin's army to kill any of them. If you write the words, I will dictate to you." The look she gave them was grim.

Aymerie reacted with a surprised gasp. Séguin's eyes danced and he smiled at her. Turning to Rabateau, who had been listening to the exchange, the monk asked, "Have you paper and ink?"

The adjutant general glanced at his valet, and with a jerk of his head ordered him to comply. The monk took up the quill and dipped it into the inkwell. "What do you wish to say?"

"Write this," Jehanne replied. While she talked, she paced. She knew the names of the faceless enemy, those sons of the Devil. D'Alençon had told her all about them.

†   J<small>HESUS</small> M<small>ARIA</small>   †

King of England, and you, Duke of Bedford, who call yourself Regent of the Kingdom of France; you, William de la Pole, Earl of Suffolk; John, Lord Talbot; and you, Thomas, Lord Scales; who call yourselves lieutenants of the said Duke of Bedford:

Do justice to the King of Heaven; surrender to the Maid—who is sent here from God, the King of Heaven—the keys of all the good towns you have taken and violated in France. She is come from God to uphold the blood royal. She is ready to make peace if you will do justice, relinquishing France and paying for what you have upheld.

As to you, you archers and men-at-arms, gentlemen and others, who are before the town of Orléans, go home to your own country in God's name; and if you do not so, expect to hear news of the Maid, who will shortly come to see you, to your very great injury.

King of England, if you do not do so: I am a commander, and in whatever place in France I come upon your men, I will make them leave it, whether or not they want; and if they will not yield obedience, I will have them all slain. I am sent here from God, the King of Heaven, to put you out of all France. Yet if they will yield obedience, I will grant them mercy.

And think not otherwise: For you shall not hold the Kingdom of France from God, the King of Heaven, Ste.-Marie's Son, but King Charles shall hold it, the true heir. For so God, the King of Heaven, wills it; and so this has been revealed to him by the Maid, and he shall enter Paris with a fair company.

If you will not believe this news from God and the Maid, wherever we find you, there we shall strike; and we shall raise such a battlecry as there has not been in France in a thousand years, if you will not do justice. And know surely that the King of Heaven will send more strength to the Maid than you can bring against her and her good soldiers in any assault. And when the blows begin, it shall be seen whose right is the better before the God of Heaven.

You, Duke of Bedford: The Maid prays and beseeches you not to bring on your own destruction. If you will do her justice, you may yet come in her company there where the French shall do the fairest deed that ever was done for Christendom. So answer if you will make peace in the city of Orléans. And if you do not so, consider your great danger speedily.

Written this Tuesday of Holy Week.

Jehanne considered whether there was more that she should add. But she could think of nothing else. She stopped pacing and said, "Read that back to me, Brother Séguin." While he complied, she resumed her gait with her hands clasped behind her back. At the letter's finish, she said, "That is good; it is what needs to be written."

"Is there anything else, Jehanne?" the friar asked with an ironic smile.

She thought for a moment. "Yes, this."

Séguin put aside the long letter and reached for a clean sheet of paper. He dipped the pen in the inkwell, then looked at her in expectation of her next words.

"To Bertrand de Poulengy and Jehan de Metz in Vaucouleurs: If you still believe in me and hold me in your esteem, and if you still desire to defeat the English at Orléans, them come to me in Tours where I am raising the army of God." She stopped her stride. "Have you got that?"

He nodded and read it back to her.

"That's right. Now, will you show me how to write my name? I want both to bear my signature."

"Yes. Come here," Séquin replied. His eyes twinkled with good humor.

She did as he requested, and he put the quill into her hand and covered it with his own. Then he dipped the instrument into the inkwell, and putting pen to paper, guided her hand in forming her name:

He put aside the letter to her friends and together they signed the one to the English. Jehanne looked at the first word she had ever written. Feeling most pleased with herself, she grinned at the monk.

But then her conscience pricked her, and abashed at the way she had ordered him about, she asked in a somewhat less commanding tone, "Brother Séguin, will you see that the one to Vaucouleurs is sent today?"

"Of course, my child." He nodded, patting her shoulder to indicate that he had taken no offense. He picked up the letter, folded it, then put it into his sleeve.

"I bid you Godspeed and safe journey, Jehanne. I know that Our Lord will watch over you." He made the Sign of the Cross above her head and muttered a Latin blessing.

Jehanne crossed herself and bowed her head while he prayed. Aymerie and the adjutant did likewise. When he was finished, the four of them made another Sign of the Cross. The monks nodded to Rabateau and left the house.

Heedless of her newly admiring host, Jehanne picked up the letter to the English and looked at the heavy black squiggles embossed on the parchment. Her eyes moved to the name she had signed at the bottom of the page. She would take the letter with her to Tours, and when she got there she would send it to the enemy in Orléans. It was a fair warning. She sat down on the chair at Monsieur Rabateau's desk.

The ring her father had given her caught the light and blinked at her. She rubbed it thoughtfully. Had the Franciscans spoken to her family when they sought information about her in Domrémy? Surely they must have. What had her parents thought when the strange friars appeared unannounced and told Jacques and Isabelle that they were there at the command of the king, seeking facts concerning their runaway daughter? Was her father angry with her, or proud? Had Isabelle wrung her hands in consternation?

She would not think of that now. There were other things to consider for the time being. Her eyes returned to the paper, and she frowned.

Oh, God, inspire them to take me seriously. Open their eyes so that they will see that we would be better allies against the heathen Turks than enemies against one another. Tell them, as You have told me, that they sin by trying to take a kingdom that does not belong to them.

Metz, Poulengy, come to me. I need you.

That afternoon the royal party arrived to take Jehanne to Tours. On the way they returned to Chinon, and after a night's rest in the castle a larger retinue set out for Tours shortly after dawn. Their number was increased with the addition of sixty armed knights, the Dauphine Marie, and Minguet the page. The queen went in order to spend time with her mother. Minguet went for Jehanne.

Charles took with him a good portion of what remained of the royal treasury, most of it borrowed anyway from Trémoïlle and others more monied than the Dauphin. He would need it to pay the army. At a rate of seven pounds, ten shillings Tournois per month for a crossbowman and fifteen pounds Tournois to hire a knight, the cost for an entire company was daunting, and the commanders usually insisted upon receiving their subordinates' wages in advance. Charles did not have quite enough silver but was confident that he could raise the balance in Tours. Renowned for its skilled armorers, the finest in Europe, the town was wealthy and had already contributed large amounts to its besieged sister city.

Riding in the royal coach surrounded by a phalanx of his Scots bodyguards, Charles congratulated himself for having had the foresight to begin raising funds three months before Jehanne appeared at his court. Sooner or later, he had told himself shortly after the siege of Orléans began, he would need to send an army to relieve it, and for that he would need ready silver.

He chuckled to himself in disregard of his wife, who sat across from him gazing distractedly out the window at the passing scenery. No one at court knew that he had redoubled his money-raising efforts the day he received word from Robert de Baudricourt that he was sending Charles a visionary who promised to relieve Orléans. It was not that he believed in her then, sight unseen. But somewhere in the back of his mind he had a notion that she could be used as a rallying mascot for the army if she were not a drooling idiot, or an obvious fraud, or a proven sorceress. That she had turned out to be intelligent, articulate, and absolutely sincere surprised him most agreeably. Never before in his life had he spoken to a peasant, and that one so lowborn could evince such courtly manners, reflecting an inner nobility of character, astounded him.

Most importantly, she had managed to pass all his tests. Only one remained, and he had no real reason to suppose that her honesty would be disproved. The physical examination was actually designed to quieten Trémoïlle's jealous insinuations rather than to try Jehanne. Of all his ministers, that fat pig was the only one who still held out that the girl could not be trusted. Even archbishop de Chartres had fallen into line now that the commission had produced its report. The archbishop testified that he had not personally interrogated her but had quietly observed the proceedings, and by the time it was over found himself, like others who had been there, moved by her straightforward manner and avowed spiritual devotion. It would be most imprudent of the king to reject God's gift, he said. She had promised to relieve Orléans, and to accomplish that miracle, it would be necessary to give her an army. Charles intended that she have the best-equipped army money could buy.

News of Jehanne's coming had preceded her such that when the royal entourage reached Tours and crossed the bridge into the town, they found Charles' jubilant subjects crowding the streets in wait. Hundreds of strangers, their individual voices lost in the pandemonium, called out an eager welcome. Above the passing cavalcade people hung out of windows, shouting and waving to Jehanne, their tributes also swallowed within the collective din. The royal carriage slowed nearly to a stop, and the Scots bodyguards found it necessary to urge their mounts carefully through the wall of onlookers while struggling to protect the Dauphin.

Jehanne was riding the black charger d'Alençon had given her, within the ring of soldiers but slightly behind the duc and Trémoïlle, mounted incongruously side by side. The flank of Minguet's horse was so close to Jehanne that it rubbed against her boot. The boy's mouth was open in bemusement, his blue eyes bulging at the spectacle. Jehanne pulled back a little further from Charles and his wife. She waved at the crowd.

That action touched the people off like a spark in a hayrick. In a flash, they surged toward her and broke through the guard.

"Get back!" the captain shouted, trying to wave them to the side. His teeth snarled through his thick russet beard. The roar of acclaim drowned him out so that he appeared to be merely mouthing the words. "Keep these people back!" His own soldiers were unable to hear his orders. They looked around helplessly at the lovestruck faces, torn between duty and an unwillingness to use their weapons against these civilians. A guardsman caught his commander's eye, and the captain shrugged in reply, surrendering to the situation against his better judgment.

He waved his men forward, gesturing that they should protect the king and leave Jehanne to her fate. D'Alençon turned in the saddle and looked back as the noble personages were surrounded by soldiers and cut off from Jehanne.

She and Minguet were now enclosed on all sides by clamoring humanity. The people pulled at her horse, clutching, straining to touch her. Mothers held up babies and young children for her to bless. Abandoned to the press of bodies that threatened to stop her horse and unable to avoid them, she could only watch in consternation as they grasped at her boots and tried to kiss her feet, hanging on to her saddle and pleading for her prayers. Minguet's blemished face was white, and he looked as though he would fall off his horse, if the people did not pull him off first. They were even mobbing *him*.

Jehanne replied to the ecstatic affection with a dazed movement of her hand. She had never expected anything like this. After weeks of skeptical scrutiny and only occasional acceptance, the scene was like an idly spun daydream bursting into actuality, and she was overwhelmed by the adulation.

"Jehanne the Maid! Jehanne the Maid! Jehanne the Maid!" chanted the people of Tours.

The words were like sweet music. She quivered at the sound of her name, shouted with such unquestioning faith. The people seemed determined to hold her to themselves, and would not stand aside that she might catch up to the Dauphin. On and on it went, down one congested, narrow street after another. Bakers and armorers, fearful of theft and themselves lured by Jehanne's presence, closed up shop and joined the parade. The company swelled to a huge, smothering multitude that cheered her all the way to the castle bridge. The drumbeat of her name thundered through her chest. Her ears ached at the tumult.

At the approach of the Dauphin, the palace guard rushed from the gate. Now joined by reinforcements, the mounted escort turned their horses toward the people and pushed them back, forming a protective wall that allowed Charles to pass across the moat. Brandishing their bladed *guisarmes*, they resolutely restrained the populace, securing passage for d'Alençon and the chancellor of France. Ten of them cantered forth to assist the last of the royal party.

Finally severed from the worshipful gathering, Jehanne and Minguet spurred their animals through the gate. The horse soldiers turned and galloped after them, leaving the footmen to contain the crowd. The castle wardens still within grounds quickly raised the drawbridge and lowered the portcullis.

Jehanne sprang from her horse and, grasping the bridle, grinned and waved to the crowd on the other side of the barriers.

They went wild at that. With a great shout of elation, the people hurled themselves toward the moat. It was with difficulty that the soldiers who had remained beyond the latticed barricade managed to keep back the mob and at the same time prevent themselves from being tumbled into the water.

The carriage came to a stop and a servant rushed forward to open the door. Stepping out, the Dauphine cast a perturbed eye at Jehanne. Charles disembarked after her, looking no less displeased than his wife.

"Well, Jehanne, it seems that Tours loves you already," he said caustically.

D'Alençon had already dismounted. He caught Jehanne's attention and put a warning finger to his lips as a servant came forward to lead his mount away. Trémoïlle was still attempting to heave his massive body from his horse.

"I have done nothing as yet to make them love me, my lord." Jehanne flushed, taken aback by the sardonic tone in the Dauphin's voice.

He looked toward the gate at the massed people screaming beyond the moat. "Indeed." His expression was cold, blank, and when he spoke it was without emotion. "Have you forgotten why you are here?"

"No, Sire." She smiled cheerfully, hoping to change his mood, if not his mind.

"Then go with this good lady." He gestured toward Madame de Trèves, who had come forward to greet them. "She will take you to your examination."

Jehanne looked to d'Alençon for support. He nodded, mouthing, "Yes, go."

Jehanne gave the Dauphin a contrite bow, then turned to follow the noblewoman. She did not see that Charles' eyes creased at the corners as she went, and was equally unaware of the chancellor's victorious smirk.

The women entered the cool darkness of a vast hall. To the left was a steep circular staircase. A guard wearing a steel breastplate stood at attention at the bottom, clutching a *guisarme*; two more were posted just inside the door. Madame de Trèves passed them without acknowledgment and mounted the steps with Jehanne at her heels.

Up and up, they ascended the narrow stairs until Jehanne's head swam. She did not dare look down for fear that she would experience a nauseating faintness. Out in the streets, embraced by all those people, she had felt charged by the theatrical outpouring of love, so much so that she really had forgotten her purpose for being here, despite what she told Charles. Now she could not hear the acclaim of Tours. Wending her way up the spare steps to the tower, she felt reality beckon to her.

She needed a bath most urgently, and the best thing she could have done to her rank clothes was burn them. On top of that, she was going to be intimately probed by a great lady, in fact *the* great lady of Europe, who had not only married royalty but, as the daughter of the King of Aragon, had been born into it. And who was she? Jhanette from Domrémy, that's all.

No, she admonished herself, I am Jehanne the Maid, Messenger of God. She forced herself to remember Michel's introduction to her Power. When all of this was finished and the king's pride satisfied, she would ride in glory and deliver Orléans from the Devil's clawed fist.

At last, they reached a landing so near the very top of the *donjon* that Jehanne could see the inside of its concave turret if she craned her neck a little. Madame de Trèves frowned and cleared her throat in a command for Jehanne to hurry along. She mumbled an apology as the older woman grasped the heavy iron handle of a door, pushed it open, then entered the room and stood aside. Jehanne crossed the threshold in trepidation.

Madame de Gaucourt, standing next to the window, turned unsmilingly toward her. Another woman, much older, about sixty-five as Jehanne reckoned, sat in an ornate carved chair, hands folded in her lap. Jehanne knew that this was the redoubtable Yolande of Aragon, Queen of Sicily and Naples, mother of the Dauphine.

Jehanne immediately went down on her knees and lowered her head. The fragile confidence she had conjured a few minutes earlier withered and turned into a tense knot that constricted her stomach.

"You may rise." The ancient aristocratic voice crackled with the barest trace of a foreign accent.

Jehanne got to her feet and looked bravely at the Queen. The muscles in her abdomen were like iron and her knees wobbled.

Charles' mother-in-law was dressed in a black gown of densely woven satin, and an intricate necklace of fine silver hung about her neck. Like the other ladies, she wore a grand headdress, an enormous *bourrelet* that resembled a dark gray moth's wings supported by shiny ebony ribbons, and in its middle twinkled a sun-colored jewel the size of an infant's fist. Her high forehead was shaven as was the fashion, which seemed to elongate the wrinkled face further. One painted eyebrow was cocked in haughty detachment above dark, penetrating eyes.

"So this is the Maid who has come to restore my son-in-law to his throne," she observed, taking in Jehanne's male apparel with evident repugnance.

"Yes, Your Highness," Jehanne mumbled.

"Well, let us see if that is true." Yolande gestured toward the high-canopied bed with a negligent movement of her withered hand.

I will not be afraid, Jehanne thought, as she crossed the room toward the bed. I am Jehanne the Maid, Messenger of God, and this is just one more step toward Orléans. Ste.-Catherine, Ste.-Marguerite, please be with me!

She could feel the ladies' patronizing stares as she removed her boots and placed them out of the way next to a large chest at the foot of the bed. With trembling fingers, she unlaced the sides of the doublet attached to the hose and pulled it over her head. She laid it across the wooden trunk. No one said a word. She removed the shirt and peeled off the hose, then folded them quickly and placed them on top of the doublet. The two ladies-in-waiting approached her and she climbed onto the bed and turned over onto her back. Madame de Trèves put a pillow under her hips.

The queen took her cane from its resting place against the chair, and leaning on it, rose from her seat and walked gingerly to where Jehanne waited with sweaty palms.

I am Jehanne the Maid, Messenger of God, I am Jehanne the Maid. She could smell the old woman's perfume. It haunted the funereal dress like lilacs in full bloom.

"Move your knees apart," the queen ordered coldly.

Jehanne did as she was commanded.

"Further." The voice, cracking with age, sounded impatient.

Jehanne allowed her knees to fall to either side of her body.

At the touch of the cold hand, the muscles in her midsection fluttered. A chill raced up her backbone. She wiped her dripping palms on the bedclothes and made herself focus on the silk canopy overhead.

It was springtime in Domrémy, and wildflowers grew in colorful random disarray in dewy pastures where children still took the cattle before sunrise. The fields would be coming alive now with newborn shoots of recently planted oats and barley. If she listened hard enough, she could hear the bells of St.-Rémy when the noon hour struck, and could kneel to prayer in the fresh green grass as crickets chirped and Michel called her Daughter of God.

An abrupt spark of pain shot between her legs.

She sucked in her breath between clenched teeth. Her face smarted at the affront to her humanity. Covering her eyes with the back of her arm, she tried to blot out the discomfort of the intrusive, probing fingers that explored her body where no one had ever touched her.

I am Jehanne the Maid, Messenger of God.

And then it was over. The hand withdrew; the pain ended. She lay motionless with her eyes still closed, her arm unmoved from her burning face.

The ladies continued to say nothing, but she could hear the rustle of their dresses and felt them shift away from her. Their footfalls as they made their way across the planked floor were punctuated by the *thump, thump* of the old queen's cane. The door opened, letting in a draft, then closed again, and she knew she was alone.

She took her arm away from her face and, opening her eyes, sat up. The smell of Yolande's perfume hung heavily in the air. She rolled over onto her side and got out of bed, knees shaking with outraged humiliation. Blinding tears splashed down her cheeks as she pulled the hose over her legs, and she wiped them away with the back of her hand. But the torrent was too insistent for her to halt. Still only half-dressed, she sat on the chest, buried her face in her hands, and sobbed.

It was not so much that she minded the examination itself; that was a distasteful necessity. What hurt was the way the ladies had treated her with no more regard than if she had been a sheep ready for shearing, without warmth or gentleness of spirit, without any sympathy at all. She knew that in their eyes she was only a peasant who had scandalized the court by daring to dress as a boy. She wanted her mother, longed to lay her head on Isabelle's cushioning breasts while Maman stroked her hair and whispered soothingly that it was all right.

The atmosphere around her began to throb with a subtle, tender glow that swelled in intensity until it was as though she were completely enfolded in Their arms. She knew that it was Marguerite, even though her potency was stronger than usual.

We are here, dear Child of God, we have been with you all along. You have done well.

A fresh onslaught of tears burst forth as Jehanne was flooded with the fathomless compassion and security for which she had yearned only a few moments ago. *They were unkind to me,* she complained, *I needed for them to be kind to me, and they weren't.*

Kindness does not come easily to them, for they live in a rarefied world of privilege and illusion and are unaware that each human soul is an aristocrat in the eyes of God. Had they vision, they would see what you truly are, and would know that your obedience and courage have earned you a place in Heaven higher than they imagine. In Paradise they shall bow to you and you will urge them to rise, for you will know what they do not.

Jehanne wiped her eyes and runny nose on the foul-smelling shirtsleeves. She sniffed to clear her sinuses, then swallowed. She breathed deeply a couple of times. Her eyes still smarted from weeping, and she rubbed them again with her hands.

How much more of this will I have to endure?

NONE. THEY WILL GIVE YOU EVERYTHING YOU HAVE REQUESTED NOW, AND MORE. YOUR WORK IS AT HAND. BUT REMEMBER, YOU HAVE ONLY A YEAR AND A LITTLE BESIDES TO SERVE THE WILL OF GOD. HAVE COURAGE, DEAR MAID OF FRANCE, AND DO NOT FORGET THE TRUST THAT GOD HAS PLACED IN YOU. WE ARE WITH YOU ALWAYS.

Their presence ebbed, but did not disappear altogether. She felt better now, much better. There would be no more of this disgraceful treatment. They had given Their promise and she believed Them.

She dragged the shirt over her head. Pulling the doublet over it, she laced the tunic to the hose. She was just putting on the second boot when a small knock tapped on the door. Steeling herself, she called out, "Come!"

Minguet peeked around the thick door and smiled at her. She was bathed in a happy relief. There was no one else she could have faced now.

"Are you well, Jehanne?" he asked. He came across the threshold and walked toward her. Noticing her still reddened eyes, he frowned with concern. "Have you been crying?"

"No, Minguet, I just had something in my eye, that's all."

He nodded, uncertain whether to believe her. "The king has sent you this." He held out a paper-wrapped bundle tied with a string.

"What is it?" she asked, taking it from him. Whatever was in the package was soft.

"New clothes," the boy offered. "He told me to tell you that he had them made for you before we left Chinon and he hopes they please you."

Jehanne sat down on the trunk and untied the string. The paper rustled as she opened the bundle. A fresh, new scent wafted pleasantly from the cloth within it. Standing again, she gave the package to Minguet for him to hold, and withdrew the warm azure hose in amazement. She plastered them against her to see how they would fit. The linen shirt was white and very fine, and laces hung through holes about the neck. There was a royal blue tunic, padded at the shoulders, along with a black leather belt meant to be fastened about the waist. At the bottom of the package lay a round blue velvet cap.

She grinned in delight at the surprise, sadness pushed to the back of her mind. "They're beautiful," she whispered.

"The king wanted me to tell you something else," Minguet said, his high voice cracking. "You are to leave immediately for the house of Monsieur du Puy, he's a rich merchant and his wife is lady-in-waiting to the queen. That's where you— where we—will stay while we are here in Tours. He told me to give you this as well." Minguet handed her a small, jingling sack.

She took it, incredulous at the clinking weight. When she opened the bag, a pile of silver coins winked at her. "My God," she said, stunned. This was surely a fortune!

"His Majesty says you are to buy some armor and weapons," Minguet babbled importantly, "and he says further that he's going to assign a squire to you whom he'll send to the house of Monsieur du Puy. He's also sending heralds to serve you. And a second page," the boy added with no small degree of resentment. "He says you may choose your own confessor."

"A confessor?" Her face lit up.

Minguet nodded.

Her own chaplain. Now she could hear Mass any time she wanted, even three times a day if she chose. The clothes were beautiful, the money grand, but her own confessor! That meant more to her than anything.

She reached into the bag and ran her fingers through the silver. She had no idea how much there was or what it could buy. But she would soon find out.

"Come, Jehanne," Minguet urged, "the king says we are to leave right now. There are soldiers waiting to escort you."

"How far is Monsieur du Puy's house from here?" she asked, remembering the horde beyond the moat. Once she was out in the streets, she would undoubtedly be mobbed again. It would take forever to reach her new lodgings. Forever until she could have a bath and change into these clean garments.

"Just a short way," the page replied, pointing in the general direction. "Do not be afraid," he encouraged, misinterpreting her frown. "The soldiers will protect you."

"I'm not afraid of the people, Minguet." She smiled. She folded her new clothes and retied the paper around them.

Then she thought the better of it and opened the package again. She laid the moneybag carefully within the cap and wrapped the whole thing once more, then tied the string around it tightly.

"Let's go." She grinned. She dreaded the commotion in the streets but could not wait to get out of this place.

136

The tub was in the anteroom next to Madame du Puy's kitchen, and it was here that Jehanne asked to be taken as soon as her introductions to her hostess had been made. Madame du Puy was a much-appreciated discovery. Jehanne had expected the lady-in-waiting to be like the others she had met at Chinon, aloof and condescending as a constant reminder that Jehanne was only an uncouth intruder. Instead, she found Dame Eleanor to be sweet-natured and friendly, with a plain, heart-shaped face and dark eyes. The lady was also young, just a few years older than Jehanne, although her husband was an old man of thirty-seven. Honored to have such a worthy guest, Eleanor du Puy immediately ordered the cooks to heat a large quantity of water. While Minguet waited in the parlor, Jehanne followed a serving woman to her bath.

This was the first that she had had since her visit to d'Alençon's family almost a month past, and she was determined to make herself as clean as possible. She did not want any of Yolande's perfumed touch to linger about her. She wanted an immaculate body for her spotless new clothes. She had changed her mind about having her old suit burned, though; the time might come when she would need it again. Rather than destroying it, she would ask Eleanor du Puy's washerwoman to launder it for her.

The door opened and a servant entered carrying a large bucket of steaming water that she intended to add to the cooling contents of the tub.

"Wait!" Jehanne said. "I want to wash my hair." She rubbed the soap briskly across her head and massaged the suds into her scalp. Just as her eyes started to burn from a trickle of soap, she raised her hand to signal the servant.

A cascade of freshly heated water washed carefully over her head, making her gasp. She wiped the water from her eyes and squeezed some from her hair which, although still short, had started to go a bit shaggy over the ears and had resumed its old habit of falling into her eyes. She would ask Minguet to cut it for her, this time with her temples and neck shaved in the style of a nobleman.

She stood up and the servant wrapped a towel about her shoulders. "There are men here to see you, Mademoiselle," said the girl matter-of-factly as she dried Jehanne's back.

"Oh? What manner of men?"

Dear God, let it not be another interrogation! She didn't want to be asked for the thousandth time to describe her Voices, or whether she was a good Christian, or the nature of her mission. At least they wouldn't ask her if she were a virgin any more, she thought ruefully.

"They look to be soldiers, and there's a friar with them," the girl answered.

Jehanne sighed, feeling a weight return to her spirit. "Very well, tell them I will be out in a moment."

The girl curtsied and left, taking the bucket with her. Jehanne opened the package that she had earlier placed on a stool next to the fire, and took out the new clothes. She dragged the shirt over her shoulders and scrambled into the hose and her old boots.

If they want to ask me more questions, she thought, this time I won't look like a travel-worn page when I appear before them; I'll go to them looking like a prince.

Wishing she had a mirror, she placed the cap on her head, then picked up the bag of coins. She would have to ask Dame Eleanor to put it somewhere safe. Knowing that she could not avoid this meeting, she went through the kitchen and beyond it into the parlor.

They all stood when she entered. Madame du Puy's sweet face smiled at her. In the firelight, she looked almost pretty.

And the men! Jehanne's vision exploded into light and she forgot all about her hostess.

Poulengy whistled in appreciation of her appearance. With a grin, Metz said in his old jesting manner, "Well, it seems your fortunes have improved since we last saw you, Jehanne."

She flung herself into their arms with a joyful cry. Laughing, they embraced her tightly. She inhaled their sweaty masculine odor as though it were the loveliest perfume. Metz's emerging beard scratched her cheek.

"You got my message?" she asked, her face aflame with elation.

"And just in time, too," said Poulengy. "We were preparing to be on our way to Le Puy-en-Velay to view the statue of the Black Virgin when your letter arrived. We went there anyway before we came here. It was there that we met these fellows, whom I believe you already know." His smile was a sly satisfaction.

She disengaged herself from their arms and looked toward the two who had been hanging back in subdued silence. Although only a few months since she had last seen them, it could have been a lifetime, but they had actually changed very little. The older was still dark and sturdy, a handsomer version of his father. A scheming mischievousness teased at the corners of the other's mouth in that old way that indicated that his mind was working toward something forbidden and perhaps a little wicked. They wore the plain farmers' pants and jackets that she knew so well.

"Oh!" Tears swelled up and spilled down her cheeks. Unable to speak for the homecoming she had not expected, she embraced her brothers, Jehan and Pierre.

She clung to them for a long time, her moist eyes closed. Since leaving home, she had made a few friends and certain enemies, but there were no others who knew her so well and whose blood flowed from the same source, as deep as the land of Lorraine. They squeezed her firmly and she felt their breaths on her neck. Jehan kissed the damp hair above her ear and tightened his grasp on her. She pressed ardent lips to his cheek and, turning, kissed Pierre with equal devotion. The three of them began to laugh.

"What—?" she stammered, pulling away from them. "How?—"

"Maman wanted to see the Black Virgin to plead for your safety," Jehan began, "so—"

"—so she had us take her there, and—"

"Shut up, Pierrolot, you're always interrupting!" his brother chided crossly.

In spite of their being practically men now, the old rivalry remained and they still seemed boys. Jehanne laughed, wiping away the tears. Some things never changed.

"Anyway," Jehan continued, "when we got there, we ran into these two"—he jerked a thumb at the beaming men from Vaucouleurs—"and they told us that they were the ones who'd brought you to Chinon to meet the king. We hadn't seen Poulengy in a long time, but Maman recognized him right away, and—"

"—and when he told her you had summoned them to Tours, she asked that we be allowed to come as well to keep an eye on you," Pierre finished, defiant of Jehan's rebuke. "Is it true that the king is sending you to Orléans?" he asked, wide-eyed.

"Yes, yes," she answered, eager for news of home. "Maman, is she well? And Papa?"

Jehan nodded. "They both send their love to you."

"They nearly lost their minds with worry when you left," Pierre volunteered with characteristic bluntness.

Jehan glowered at his younger brother and gave him a painful nudge in the ribs.

"I'm sorry," Jehanne said contritely. "But it couldn't be helped. I had to go."

"It's all right, Jhanette," her older brother assured her. "They understand that now. They're both very proud of you now that you're famous."

"I'm hardly that"—she laughed—"and besides, I haven't done anything to earn fame."

"But you will," Metz said with a confident smile. "You will when you take Orléans."

"And we'll be right alongside you," his comrade chimed in.

"All of us." Pleased with himself, Pierre's short face widened into a toothy grin.

She laughed again. "How can I lose with such a faithful band?"

"You can't, sweetheart," Metz deadpanned, using the nickname by which he had first greeted her. "Especially since we bring to you this good monk whom we also met in Le Puy." He held out his arm toward the friar who had been standing in the background next to Dame Eleanor.

The man came forward. He wore a habit that was familiar to Jehanne from her recent questioning at Poitiers. The long white gown, covered by a black mantle, proclaimed that he was a Dominican.

Metz went on, "Jehanne, this is Brother Pasquerel. When you get to know him, I'm sure you will like him very much."

Pasquerel smiled at her and she thought she had never seen a kinder face. His large, close-set eyes were the color of sapphires and seemed aglow with a tender inner light as constant as a hearth. He was about forty, only a little taller than she, about Pierre's height in fact, and though he was not handsome—his aquiline nose was too long for that—an inborn tranquility smoothed his features into serene beauty.

"I'm most pleased to meet you, Jehanne." The gentleness of his smile found equal measure in his voice. "I've heard much about you from these devoted friends of yours and from your mother. She's an exceptional woman."

"Yes, she is," Jehanne affirmed, melting as Isabelle's plump face appeared before her.

"If you have no confessor, I would be very honored if you chose me." There was a humility behind his words that she had rarely found in churchmen.

"Thank you, Brother," she replied. "Only this morning the Dauphin gave me permission to choose my confessor and I have none as yet." She surveyed the faces of those who loved her, knowing instinctively that she could consider him among them. "I am very happy that you want to be my chaplain."

"Well, that's settled," Metz intoned brightly, clapping the monk on the back. The little man stumbled forward a pace. "When do we start for Orléans?"

"That's not settled yet," Jehanne responded in a dry tone. "We have to be provisioned first, and the Dauphin has not told me when we will start the journey." She suddenly remembered the bag of money she still held. "But he did give me this." She opened the sack and ran her hand carelessly through the silver.

Poulengy gave a long, toneless whistle. Pierre's gray eyes widened in amazement.

"We could have quite a drinking party with that," Metz joked.

Jehanne laughed and punched him playfully. "It's for armor and weapons, silly." Then instantly sober, she asked, "How much do you think it will buy?"

"Let me see it."

She gave the bag to Metz. He opened the mouth and put his nose into it. They all laughed at his deliberate buffoonery. "Enough," he pronounced with mock solemnity.

"What, exactly, is 'enough'?" Jehanne wondered. "Seriously, Metz."

"Seriously?" He shrugged. "It depends on how fine you want the armor to be, and who you get to craft it for you; whether the fellow is honest or not; whether he can be bargained with to give you a good deal. It depends, Jehanne."

"You know weapons. And their value?" She was taken by an abrupt inspiration.

"Well, I've certainly bought my share over the years. Yes, I suppose I do—"

"Good," she said decisively. "Then I want you to be my steward. I want you to help me to get some armor and weapons for all of us, and I want you to keep the money safe." She beamed at his slack-jawed surprise. "Safe, Metz," she teased, "not for wine."

"Or women?" muttered Poulengy under his breath.

"What?"

"Nothing." The two men exchanged a confidential look. Metz raised his hand. "I promise, Jehanne, that your money will be safe with me," he swore with uncharacteristic sobriety. "May the Lord God strike me dead if I betray your trust."

"Watch out for lightning," said Poulengy.

"Thank you, Metz," Jehanne said, shooting an annoyed glance at Poulengy. He was jealous, she could feel it. In some respects these two were as bad as Jehan and Pierre.

"You, Bertrand . . ." she mused thoughtfully, turning to the tall, blond soldier, "you may be my squire. I'll need someone who'll know how to arm me and prepare me for battle."

A smile widened Poulengy's long face, and he regarded Metz with a triumphant lift of his eyebrows.

"What about me, Jhanette?" chirped her eager younger brother. "May I be your page?" He was not about to be excluded, particularly since Jehan had not yet volunteered for anything.

"I already have a page, Pierrolot." She smiled. "He's"—she looked about, searching the familiar faces—"where's Minguet?"

"Here," said a small voice.

He was standing against the wall, out of sight and apart from the circle. Jehanne's heart contracted with pain. In the midst of these people who knew one another, Minguet felt cast aside, excluded.

Jehanne smiled and held out her hand to him. When he came forward, she put her arm about his shoulder. "This is Louis de Coutes, also called Minguet, the son of a noble knight of the House of Orléans, and he has graciously offered to be my page." She bestowed a gentle smile upon him. "He is also from this moment forth my brother, as are these"—she gestured—"my brothers, Jehan and Pierre."

Minguet turned adoring eyes to her. She grinned at him and kissed his cheek. He blushed furiously, but returned her favor, and she found that his lips were moist and cool. He was no longer an orphan and would be a good companion for Pierre, who had always resented being the baby of the family.

Jehanne acquired for herself the best armor she could buy, crafted by the master armorer of Tours himself. She had never considered the many layers a knight wore and was dumbfounded when she arrived at the armory to be fitted.

First, she had to remove the tunic, followed by her boots. Over her shirt the workmen fitted a padded collar designed to cushion the armor's metal weight upon the shoulders, followed by a hooded, thigh-length hauberk, divided in front to make riding possible. A neckpiece of overlapping curved steel plates tapered to a point above a shiny metal corselet, and shoulder plates, to which steel sleeves hinged at the elbows were attached, concluded the upper body's defense. Protecting the hips was a series of terraced plates; a steel skirt guarded her thighs. Like the chainmail, it was divided to permit sitting astride a horse. Similar wear protected her legs: thigh pieces jointed at the knees, lower leg coverings, and steel shoes. Gauntlets extended the armor to her hands. The *basinet* enclosing her head featured a rounded chin cup and a movable visor. Even with the visor raised, the helmet was hot and stuffy, and she found hearing anything difficult.

Best of all was the ornamental silken *huque* worn on top of the contraption, a sleeveless surcoat split at the sides and secured at the waist by a belt. She could not choose between the scarlet cloak and the cloth of gold to wear over the armor—they were both so lovely—so in the end she bought both.

Jehanne knew from the admiring "ahhs" her comrades gave her that she looked grand. Unfortunately, walking in that thing was almost impossible, and she could not envision actually running in it. She was afraid that its weight would topple her. But the armorer guaranteed that she would grow accustomed to moving about in it if she practiced for a short time.

The price of her protection was one hundred *livres* Tournois, which Metz assured her was a bargain for work of such quality. She had similar suits designed for Metz and Poulengy to replace the rusted, battle-worn armor they had long owned. Because Minguet would invariably end up in the thick of things bearing Jehanne's standard, she ordered that he be every bit as safeguarded as she.

The poor little fellow was an immobile insect in his steel cocoon, and complained that he could not breathe. She was in secret sympathy with him, for she knew firsthand how he felt. But it did not matter that he didn't like it: this was for his own good. He calmed down after Jehanne persuaded him that the suit he hated so much might actually save his life. It was not so much this reasoning that soothed him as that Jehanne had voiced it. He was unable to refuse anything she requested of him.

For her brothers, there were lighter breastplates and bucklers reinforced with heavy hauberks. Both would receive solid *basinets* for their heads. Like her, they were not adapted to heavy armor, and she wanted them to get used to the lighter armor before she exposed them to the ordeal she had to undergo.

That explanation did not satisfy them. Jehan objected that he was at least as strong as she was. After all, she was only a girl and he a strapping man who could mow wheat for hours without getting tired. Besides, he was her older brother; it was not seemly that he take orders from her.

Thinking, erroneously, that Jehan was getting the upper hand, Pierre pushed himself forward and argued that if Jehan was going to have a full suit of armor, so should he. He was not a little boy any more and they could not treat him like one. On top of that, it was not right that Minguet, his junior, should have armor when he had to wear a simple buckler.

"In God's name! The King of Heaven did not order either of you to go to Orléans!" Jehanne shouted, losing her temper at their selfishness. "If you two don't want to accept the authority God has given me, then you can both go home!"

Her anger was not unfamiliar to them, but neither were they prepared for the Power that blazed from her eyes and crackled about her head. Sensing from their suddenly cowed expressions that they were about to back down, she snapped, "I know what I'm doing! You can accept that or not, and it's all the same to me."

They grumbled under their breaths and cast sidelong looks of distrust at one another.

In a few months, she promised, she would have stronger suits made for them. She made up for her loss of temper by seeing to it that each of her company was armed with a shiny new sword and a strong mace. That shut them up and ended the matter.

When it came time to arm herself, she set aside the sword that Baudricourt had given her in Vaucouleurs, for there was another she wanted. With his mentor's permission, she sent an apprentice of the master armorer of Tours to fetch it for her.

Catherine had told her in a dream that at her shrine of Ste.-Cathérine-de-Fierbois, buried in the ground behind the altar, was a sword with five crosses on it. God had placed it there for Jehanne. She asked Pasquerel to write to the chapel clergy requesting that they might let her have it. The priests did not know what sword she meant. But when the apprentice arrived and dug into the ground, he unearthed it exactly where she knew it would be. Although it was caked with rust and dirt, the earth's corruption fell away with bewildering ease when the monks polished it.

The clergy of Fierbois were so impressed with this miracle that they crafted a crimson velvet sheath for the sword. Not to be outdone, the people of Tours responded with one of their own made of a beautiful golden cloth. Jehanne expressed a guileless admiration for both, at the same time commissioning another on the quiet, this one of sturdy leather. The first two, however splendid, would not be sufficient to secure the divinely bestowed weapon.

There remained the standard. When Jehanne went looking for an artist to design it, she was referred to a Scotsman living in Tours and married to a lady of the town. The painter's real name was Hamish Power, but that was such a tongue-twister that no one could pronounce it, so he was known in French as Hauves Poulnoir. He was a tall, beefy man with wild red hair and beard and blue eyes. Jehanne liked him very much for his outspoken wit and for not arguing with her when she described the design her Counsel had revealed to her.

The standard was to be of fine white linen. Its silken fringe was sewn with heraldic fleurs-de-lys, and on it a painted Christe flanked by two kneeling angels sat enthroned with the world in His hand. To the right of this scene, as the standard began to taper to a point, were the words inscribed on Jehanne's ring: JHESUS MARIA.

She also ordered a smaller standard, a pennon, for her company. This one, made from the same cloth, depicted St.-Gabriel's annunciation to the Holy Mother, above which a dove carried a scroll in its beak inscribed—in French rather than Latin—ON BEHALF OF THE KING OF HEAVEN. The standards were mounted on staffs of ashwood topped by pointed iron lances. She ordered stout leather sheaths to protect both of them from dust and bad weather. When everything was finished, she paid Poulnoir a little more than she had contracted to pay, for she was most pleased with the beauty his labor had created.

Jehanne ran over the inventory in her mind. Very little remained of the Dauphin's money. It made no difference; there was nothing else to buy anyway, and all was in place now. She was ready for the battle to liberate the kingdom.

On Easter Sunday, Pasquerel sang the Mass for Jehanne and her three brothers in the home of the du Puys. Her hosts were present, along with d'Alençon and four men he had brought with him.

After Mass he introduced them to her. The Dauphin had sent all four. Two were heralds, Guyenne and Ambleville, and a third, a boy named Raymond, was to be her second page and would assist an unwilling Minguet. The heralds were older men, both in their thirties. Guyenne was short and slender, his dignified posture revealing the refined nobility of a gentleman. His sculpted hair glinted with silver strands, and he clutched a black hood that he would later wear as a jaunty hat. His colleague was taller than Metz but not as lean as Poulengy. Although Ambleville had disciplined himself to make his gray eyes unreadable, the thin smile he gave Jehanne made it clear that he had not requested this appointment. Because Jehanne possessed no heraldry of her own, both wore royal blue *huques* emblazoned with the Dauphin's fleurs-de-lys over their dark tunics.

D'Alençon had told her that heralds accorded a notable station upon those they served. Their functions were to act as messengers and to identify the arms of combatants engaged in the field. Arming them would not only be redundant but a violation of civilized law, for under the code of chivalry, their persons were considered sacrosanct and inviolable. No knight worthy of the title could take them prisoner, nor could they be held for ransom regardless of their master's identity and threat to an enemy. They were answerable only to God and their overlord.

They bowed to Jehanne with graceful courtesy, their feelings hidden behind faces long trained in the fine art of diplomacy.

Then Raymond came forward. Though young, only sixteen, he was already muscular and long of limb. His eyes were very close together and his mouth seemed small above a large, jutting chin trying desperately to sprout whiskers. The merry light in his face promised a sense of humor almost as outrageous as Metz's. When he grinned at Jehanne, she could have sworn he winked at her. Then it was gone, and she was not sure she had seen it at all.

There was one more man for her to meet. "Jehanne, this is Jehan d'Aulon," the duc said, "and he is to be your squire."

The shortish young man bowed to her. "I have seen you before, Jehanne, that day when the men of the Church questioned you at Poitiers, and afterward I came forward with the others intending to offer my support."

"Why didn't you speak to me?" she wondered, a puzzled smile playing about her lips.

"I don't know," he stammered. "There were others present whom I thought you might prefer." The embarrassed brown eyes looked at her out of a homely-handsome face. She could feel the solid practicality of the man.

"D'Aulon is being modest," said the duc. "He's actually the best man in the king's army."

"Well, then, I'm glad the Dauphin sent you to me," she assured him. "Because I have need for a good squire."

Out of the corner of her eye, she saw Poulengy flinch, and she knew that she would have to placate him somehow. Perhaps he would accept the position of personal bodyguard. God knew, she would need one to get her through the crowds that crammed the streets night and day, hoping to get a glimpse of her. She would have to get out of town somehow, when the time came.

There was an awkward pause in the conversation. D'Alençon saved them all from further discomfiture by saying, "Jehanne, I need to speak to you alone."

The others moved away from them and began speaking to Jehanne's brothers and hosts. Jehanne could hear them speculating excitedly about the coming journey to Orléans.

"What is it?" She turned her attention to d'Alençon, fearful of some new misfortune.

"Charles is sending me to Blois today to organize the troops and to see that the provisions are in order. He says that you and your companions are to go there tomorrow to meet with the commanders of the army." He smiled, looking down at her eager face. "He has given you the title 'Chief of War.' That is a very great honor, you know."

"Yes," she answered, incredulous at the news, "I know it is." Jehanne the Maid, Chief of War. She liked the sound of it. "So you'll be with us at Orléans?"

He shook his head. "Afraid not. I'm to be in charge of the stores for the army and for the relief of the city." Seeing her crestfallen face, he added, "Charles has invested a great deal of money in this, and he needs someone he can trust to oversee it."

"Of course. Then I'll see you after we take the city, Jehan."

He put a comforting hand on her arm and smiled consolingly. "Yes, you shall. And don't worry, you'll be in very good hands."

"The best." She grinned. She would have an army of angels to bear her into battle.

BOOK TWO

Lessons of Glory

No longer on Saint Denis will we cry,
But Joan la Pucelle shall be France's saint.

—WILLIAM SHAKESPEARE

CHAPTER SIX

𝕿𝖍𝖊 𝒜𝖗𝖒𝖞 𝖔𝖋 𝕲𝖔𝖉

April 23–28, 1429

A sprawling sunset colored the heavens and bobbed in golden-pink mirrors upon the surface of the Loire. Within another half-hour its fiery light would fade to indigo. There were a few stars visible overhead where daylight had already disappeared, and at the other end of the sky the half-moon crept toward encroaching night. A formation of geese, serenely indifferent to the city below, crossed a mass of violet clouds heading south. The man inhaled the night air and the effluvium of mud reeds and rotting fish drifting into Orléans upon a cool river breeze.

From the rampart, the Bastard of Orléans watched the English light their fires one by one within the bridge fort on the other side of the river. The faraway figures were moving back and forth around the firelight, behind the low wall they had constructed to face the bridge. They did not appear to be massing for an attack. Most likely they were preparing an evening meal, river trout perhaps. Not long ago a few of the bolder among them had been spotted in the shallows firing arrows attached to lines into the water.

The Bastard placed his hands on the stone battlement and leaned forward in order to get a better look. He could discern what experience told him were sentinels stationed beyond their wall. Every now and then one of them would move and send light flashing like a threat from his *guisarme*'s blade.

The Bastard was not alone. Within the last few minutes eighty of the garrison had climbed the steps to relieve the day watch. They would keep alert until dawn, when fresh pickets would arrive, allowing the night patrol to return to their billets for food and some sleep. In the meantime, the guard was divided into squads stationed at strategic distances between the city's broad, barricaded gates. Approximately half of them were walking a path which after many months was familiar to all. Back and forth they went, between upright torches and along the stone-toothed summits shielding the houses and churches and shops of Orléans. The others, cannon men and archers equipped with crossbows, held stationary positions. All wore armor and were ready for the battle they prayed would not come.

All but one, that is. The only man upon the wall not equipped for potential combat was their commander, the Bastard himself. In place of plate armor, he was dressed in a plain soldier's tunic and boots. His only concessions to protection were a light, visorless helmet that covered his short hair and the sword he never removed except at bedtime. Yet in spite of his simple attire, he was the most striking of all the lookouts.

An easy authority bred through generations of nobility distinguished him from the rest of the garrison. He was an attractive fellow, a little above average in height, and well built, with strong shoulders muscled by the weapons he had been hefting since he was a boy. His features were regular and pleasing to look at, though the mouth was somewhat small for his wide, square face. Dark brows arched above earnest brown eyes and pointed downward at the bridge of his strong nose. Whenever he smiled, which in these bleak times was more seldom than before the siege began, amiable dimples gave evidence of an essentially cheerful disposition.

But he felt no humor, no pleasure, and very little reason for optimism as he stared at the enemy encampment across the river. He had been there longer than the others upon the rampart, nearly six hours, but he was too restless for fatigue. His mind would not permit him a moment's leisure while there was any possibility of a night attack. He told himself that he would keep watch a little longer to ascertain what, if anything, Glasdale and Talbot would do tonight. If all remained quiet, he would go home for a few hours' sleep.

Thorough people, these English, he mused. They left nothing to chance. The earthern wall that faced the city at the Tourelles' entrance was unbreachable from this side of the Loire. When the enemy had overrun the bridge fort nearly five months earlier, the retreating garrison of Orléans had blasted a huge hole into the bridge, taking out almost an entire span, and the English had built their wall behind the chasm. Now the garrison could not cross the bridge without coming under a hail of English arrows, but neither could the enemy, for fear of the French cannon upon the city's wall. The hole simply yawned there, its ragged size defying both sides. And yet the English had not eased their vigilance for a single day. They waited within the twin towers of the Tourelles as though by some miracle they might be attacked.

The rear entry into the Tourelles faced the riverbank opposite Orléans. Nevertheless, the English controlled the avenue entirely, having stormed and then fortified the bridgehead at the Tourelles' gate. Positioned within the towers' highest places, their deadly archers could see an army's approach for more than half a league, for there were no longer any houses on the south bank of the Loire.

The Bastard almost regretted that he had ordered the structures on that side of the river razed before the English were able to unify their positions; his garrison could have used the buildings for cover during an assault upon the Tourelles. But they also would have provided the enemy with foundations for other temporary forts. The Bastard could not have allowed that, however disadvantageous the bare land was for an attack from his forces. As it was, the English already had too many of these *bastilles* ringing Orléans.

South of the Tourelles, they had converted the Augustinian monastery known as the Augustins into a mighty bulwark for the bridgehead, using beams ripped from the church's roof to build a sturdy, mud-daubed fence between the two structures. To the east, another *bastille*, formerly the church of St.-Jehan-le-Blanc, was similarly fortified and defended the road leading to the Tourelles. The French would certainly be stopped there before they could reach the bridge. The Bastille du Champ de St.-Privé west of the Tourelles, nearly as large as the Augustins, completed English dominance on the south bank of the Loire.

The nobleman turned his handsome profile toward the setting sun and the other English strongholds. While those across the river were a nuisance, the forts on this bank comprised the greatest threat to the city, for it was from them that the English periodically made their assaults upon the walls of Orléans. Sometimes at night, but most often during the day, they would rush at the defenders with scaling ladders, waving their lords' colors and yelling their fearsome battlecry. At the beginning of these incursions, churchbells within the walls sounded the alarm, and all able-bodied men, townsfolk as well as the garrison, mounted the battlements to fire their cannon and fling arrows and stones upon the invaders. So far, none of the English attacks had given them a breach, thank God. But one never knew when the next attempt would begin.

Talbot's men appeared quiet tonight, even subdued. Fires were now glimmering within the smaller citadel—like most of them, a makeshift construction of timber and mud—upon the Ile Charlemagne a little way downriver. To the west, the Bastille de St.-Laurent, a very large enemy encampment, swarmed with dark shapes whose movements looked more casual than belligerent. As usual, the smaller Bastille de la Croix Boissé straddling the western road into the city seemed peaceful. The enemy from that fort rarely attempted to force their way through the gate, the Porte Regnard. The Orléanais had sealed it shut at the very beginning of the siege, leaving little possibility that even the most determined attacker could breach the portcullis and heavy door, now blockaded from within by a solid wall of earth and upturned wagons.

The northern gates into Orléans were similarly girded against the three *bastilles* the English had established astride the Paris road. From this distance the Bastard could not clearly see their black contours in the coming nightfall, only the shafts of light burning upward through the top rims of the palisades. Squinting, he looked at them, imagining them as they appeared during daytime, when they were resolute, earth-encased wasp nests, dangerous and uncompromising.

There was a single route still passable into and out of Orléans: the Porte de Bourgogne, which opened to the eastern road to Chécy. Although the enemy's Bastille de St.-Loup was in reach of that road, it was more than half a league's distance from the gate, making it possible for provisions and messengers to enter the city without hindrance if they sailed downriver and thus avoided the English bulwark altogether. Thank Heaven that it was so! Had the Porte de Bourgogne been blocked, the city would have been starved into submission months ago.

The Bastard returned his attention to the shadowy activity within the Tour-elles. The English were too far away for him to hear their voices, which would have been swallowed anyway by the noises of Orléans settling down for the night. Somewhere in the distance, a dog howled at the rising moon. The steady *clip-clop* of a horse's hooves passed through a nearly deserted street. The clatter of armor below the Bastard's post indicated that the discharged watch were bound for their billets, or for the pleasant diversion of a tavern. But he was scarcely aware of any of it. His mind was on that towered fortress, the one the garrison had abandoned at the outset of the siege.

How long could they last in there? he wondered. Conditions within the *bastille* must be crude. He knew that some of the English had deserted; his sentries had seen them sneaking away under cover of night, probably to form a band of skin-ners eager to feast unopposed upon the unarmed rural populace. How long would the duke of Bedford persist in sending his army food and weapons from Paris? Through snow and rain the English had waited to take this city, their patience seemingly undiminished. He marveled at their determination, at the same time detesting their greed.

It made perfect sense for them to want Orléans. After all, it was the strongest and most important city of the Loire Valley. They had already captured Jargeau to the east, and Meung and Beaugency upriver. If Orléans were to fall, the English would be in a position to make a clean sweep of the region, taking Blois, Tours, and finally Chinon, effectively ending the war. Charles would have no choice but to flee to one of his allies' courts in Scotland or Spain, and Henry VI would sit upon the throne of France, ruled in fact by his uncle Bedford until the boy came of age.

The Bastard drew his cloak over his shoulder, wincing a little at the pain in his arm. The wound, although nearly healed, still ached when the weather was chill, as it was this evening. He had received the swordcut back in February, during the bungled attempt to overtake a supply train from Paris intended for the English. The French had suffered many casualties in that unfortunate sortie. Worst of all, they lost a most valuable ally, Sir John Stewart, constable of the kingdom of Scotland. The English taunted them for days afterward, calling out from their *bastilles* that the king's men were nothing but foppish cowards. As though to confirm their calumny, many notables had abandoned the city, among them the young comte de Clermont—the Bastard's own half brother—admiral de Culan, and that crafty old weasel, Regnault de Chartres, archbishop of Reims. While despising his compatriots' lack of courage, in his heart the Bastard regretted that he could not have gone with them.

But it was his duty to remain here. He had pledged his brother Charles, the duc d'Orléans, that he would defend the city with his last breath, and defend her he would. There was no one else willing to do so. Besides, he owed a debt of gratitude to Charles' late mother, who had raised him as part of her family.

The Bastard's official progenitor had been Aubert le Flamenc, the seigneur de Chauny and his mother's husband, but his true father was Louis d'Orléans, as-sassinated by Jehan Sans Peur in 1407, an event which provided a tragic denouement to the rivalry between the houses of Orléans and Bourgogne. The Bastard had been much aggrieved by his father's murder. Still only a boy at the time, he had scarcely known the duc. More familiar to him was the duchesse, Valentina Visconti, of the powerful Milanese family. Cultured and sophisticated, it was the duchesse who insisted that the lad be raised among his legitimate brothers and sisters as their equal. She was so kind to him that at the age of twelve he had renounced his established name and claims to property, declaring that henceforth he would be known simply as the Bastard of Orléans.

It was a name he wore with a defiant pride. In the exclusive *milieu* of the nobility, his illegitimacy did not detract from the fact that he was of the blood royal, and even though he could not inherit the title of duc, he was in a more fortunate position than his first cousin, Charles the king. If Charles were not in fact a Valois—which the Bastard doubted—his claim to the throne of France was without merit. But Charles *was* God's chosen king; the Bastard could feel it in his bones. That was the reason he had vowed to serve his royal cousin as his faithful vassal.

He had taken a similar oath before his half brother, imprisoned in London these thirteen years. Charles d'Orléans communicated with him frequently. His most recent letter informed the Bastard that he was well, and that life was not altogether unpleasant on that somewhat civilized island. He feasted regularly with little Henry of England and the king's uncle Humphrey, duke of Gloucester and Protector of the Realm. In his quiet moments he had taken to writing poetry in both French and English, and those at court insisted that he was becoming quite accomplished at that art. He finished the letter by sending greetings to the people of Orléans and commending the city into his half brother's care. He knew, he said, that the Bastard's military prowess would keep Orléans safe from the invaders.

The Bastard prayed that Charles was right. God knows, he had done his best. Upon assuming command of the city in November, he had taken the garrison in hand, much to the relief of the citizens, who had been troubled about the thousands of men-at-arms roaming the streets at will. He bombarded the outlying environs and reduced them to rubble, ignoring the protests of those who had lived there. Then he ordered jars of water to be placed at regular intervals upon the city walls; any disturbance in them would indicate that the English were burrowing like moles beneath the walls. He sent couriers from the Porte de Bourgogne to the king, asking for reinforcements and supplies.

Charles had not failed him. In early January, admiral de Culan sailed into the city with two hundred soldiers, and in February an additional thousand arrived. Then came that failed bid to seize the English supply train, filled with Lenten herring. That was the turning point. Admiral de Culan departed, taking with him most of the men he had brought in the first place, and the people, having lost some of their faith in the Bastard, began to grumble that their leadership had blundered. All of them, the Bastard included, needed something to restore their faith and sense of well-being. They needed a miracle.

One such had already occurred. Very recently, Burgundian forces allied with the English had abruptly furled their lord's banners and departed the *bastilles* in haste. The people were overjoyed, and for a day or so there was wild celebration in the streets. But to Orléans' dismay, the English did not follow Philippe de Bourgogne's men. The Bastard was curious as to what had taken place between Philippe and Bedford to arouse the Burgundian decampment, but not even his most skillful spies were able to find out. It hardly mattered. With the English still in place, the threat to his city remained.

Still, the Bastard had heard of one other who might provide yet another miracle.

Shortly after the debacle in which he received his wound, he had caught wind of a young woman from Lorraine who claimed that God had charged her to raise the siege at Orléans. To that end, she was en route to Chinon to seek an audience with the king. The Bastard immediately dispatched two couriers to Chinon to inquire into the rumor and the girl, if she existed. There was so much hearsay floating into and around his city that he could never be sure what to believe.

The messengers returned with the astounding news that not only was the girl real, she had made a most favorable impression upon Charles and others at court, notably the duc d'Alençon. Word quickly spread through Orléans, raising the atmosphere to a new level of excitement as the weather warmed. Three weeks ago, the Bastard had written to his cousin Charles, begging him to send the girl to him as she had requested. He continued to wait for a reply.

"Sir?"

The Bastard jumped, startled nearly out of his wits. He had been so deep in thought that he had not noticed young Georges Thibault standing behind him.

"I'm sorry, sir, I did not mean to alarm you." The guardsman's face, illuminated by two torch-bearing soldiers, was genuinely contrite. He had participated in this afternoon's defense of the city against an enemy raid, and there were circles of fatigue around his eyes. Yet beneath that was something else, an excitement he seemed barely able to contain.

"Yes, Georges? What is it?" the Bastard asked. His heartbeat resumed its normal pace, and he admonished himself that he would have to be more careful in the future. With his guard down, any disgruntled man-at-arms or civilian could sneak up on him, intent on doing him harm.

"A messenger, sir, from His Majesty!" The windswept torches frolicked in Thibault's tired eyes. He stepped aside, and another came forward.

A grin split the Bastard's princely face, deepening the dimples at the corners of his mouth. The man who stood before him was one he knew well. His short hair was plastered to his head with perspiration which ran in trickles down the temples and into his beard. His cheek was carved in half by an old battle cut that trailed from the bridge of his nose to his left ear. He wore no armor, just a thick buckler of beaten leather over his tunic. He grinned back at the Bastard, looking very pleased indeed.

"Poton!" the nobleman exclaimed, offering the soldier his hand. The man gave it a vigorous shake. "I did not expect to see you here. I thought you were with the army."

"I have been, sir," the man-at-arms replied in his gravelly voice. "In fact, I have just come from the king's main force at Blois."

"Blois? What is the army doing there?"

Poton de Xaintrailles bent over and pulled a piece of paper from the top inside of his boot. "Here you are, sir," he answered, holding it out to the Bastard. "That should explain everything, I think."

The Bastard snatched the folded paper. The wax seal bore a fleur-de-lys, emblem of the French monarchy. He ripped it open and saw the name at the bottom of the page, recognizing the grand flourish that always ended Charles' signature. Then he read the text of the letter.

Charles greeted his cousin in affectionate terms, adding that he valued the Bastard's continuing devotion and loyalty. It had taken several weeks to raise the silver necessary to pay an army's wages, but after much delay, a battalion of approximately three thousand was gathering at Blois under the supervision of Jehan, the duc d'Alençon. With them were the comte de Clermont, Raoul de Gaucourt, the maréchal de Sainte-Sévère, Ambroise de Loré, Gilles de Rais, and the battle captains La Hire and Florent d'Illiers. In a few days they would depart for Orléans with the intention of resupplying the city. The king sent his warmest greetings and those of the queen to the people of Orléans.

And, by the way, he was also sending Jehanne the Maid along with the army. He trusted that the Bastard would make her feel welcome in the city.

The Bastard threw back his head and laughed. He clapped Poton on the shoulder. "This is splendid news!" he cried. "Perhaps with the city resupplied, we can show those English that we have no intention of sacrificing Orléans to their ambition, and they just might give in and return to Paris."

"That's right, sir." Poton grinned. "The sons of bitches can't live in those dungheaps forever, can they?"

"Excuse me," Thibault intruded, a puzzled look kneading his brows. "But I thought that the king was sending the army to raise the siege."

The Bastard shook his head. "That would be impossible, lad. Look at them." He nodded toward the darkened *bastilles*, now pierced by glinting campfires. "They're too heavily fortified, especially the Tourelles. We would stand to lose too many men if we attempted to take them. The king is wise to send a supply train rather than a battalion bent on raising the siege. Our best chance is to sit it out until the English realize that *their* best move is to give up the attempt to starve us out."

"But, sir, my brother Gobert is with the army, and he told Poton here"—he jerked his head at the soldier—"that they all think that they're coming to Orléans to raise the siege." The young man's dust-caked countenance was the picture of disappointment. "The Maid had promised them that that is what God has told her."

The Bastard glanced at Poton, who shrugged. "Has your brother met her, then?"

"Yes, sir, at Poitiers, where she was examined by the masters from the universities of Paris and of Orléans. He says she is most remarkable, and certainly touched by God."

That was the assessment of the couriers the Bastard himself had sent to Chinon: both of them had been very impressed with her. He looked at Poton. "Have you met her, too?"

"Not yet." The soldier wiped his dripping face on the sleeve of his tunic.

"Hmm." The Bastard shrugged. "Well, the Orléanais have certainly heard of her, and these days all I get from them is that they look forward to seeing her for themselves." He smiled at the men. "Of course, I shall give her a hearty welcome. Her arrival may provide just the lift in spirit that everyone here needs. And let's hope that our friends in the *bastilles* have heard of her, too. Perhaps her presence will put the fear of God in them, and they'll decide on their own to return to Paris rather than mix with the Almighty."

He was not certain that they would. Still, there was always that chance. The English were well known for their superstitions. And maybe—just maybe—God had finally declared Himself for France after all.

"Rubbish!"

The duke's round face, crimson with wrath, appeared to Fastolf on the verge of exploding. His nose, so like the beak of an eagle, practically throbbed in indignation. Usually the most collected of men, at this moment he had forsaken all composure.

"I have never read such infamous, insolent, outrageous . . . !" He spluttered, groping for a word expressive enough to describe the offense he was feeling.

"Cheekiness?" provided the cardinal, with an amused twinkle in his eye.

Bedford turned on him, waving the letter in his hand. "This is more than 'cheekiness,' Uncle! The little strumpet has insulted the king and every man loyal to him, myself included! Who is this Jehanne who calls herself 'the Maid,' that she dare write such filth?"

"You know very well who she is," Beaufort reminded him. "Your own spies have returned from Tours—have they not?—with news that this girl is a mere cowmaid who has somehow persuaded the little king of Bourges that she is sent by God to raise the siege at Orléans." He pursed his lips in disgust. "And after that, so I'm given to understand, she intends to crown Charles King of France."

"Over my cold and lifeless body!" the duke spat. He began to crumple the page.

"Don't do that, John," warned his uncle, lifting a jeweled hand. "That is a most valuable document you are holding. We may have need of it in future."

"Need?" Bedford shouted, "What need? It belongs on the fire." He took a step toward the fireplace.

"Wouldn't you rather consign *her* to the flames, nephew?" The cardinal's mild-mannered voice flickered with malicious humor.

Bedford stopped in mid-stride. He flung a sharp look at the red-robed cleric. "What do you mean?"

Henry Beaufort, cardinal of Winchester, lifted his shoulders in a shrug, and as he did so, light glinted from the jewel-studded cross hanging from a heavy silver chain about his neck. "Just simply that the letter, which you are so foolishly prepared to destroy, may someday be put to good use. Suppose for a moment that this Jehanne is in fact a witch. She has without a doubt enchanted the so-called Dauphin, and others who support him. Is it not reasonable to conclude that she is guilty of sorcery?"

The duke frowned uncertainly. He often felt uncomfortable when confronted with the workings of the old man's labyrinthine mind. "Perhaps," he conceded.

"Let us suppose further that, through God's grace, she should fall into our hands. That document, in which she so outrageously claims to have the mandate of Heaven to taunt the king, might well be used against her in that event." Beaufort smiled, his wrinkled countenance smoothed with satisfaction. "Keep that letter safe, John. Keep it *quite* safe."

Bedford looked down at the page he still held. His mouth filled with a hot desire for vengeance. He swallowed the wish, knowing that his uncle was right, the sly old fox. He nodded. "Very well."

He walked to the desk and opened the carved ivory box upon it, then put the letter inside it and closed the lid. Raising his eyes, he glanced out the window, hardly seeing the spires of Notre-Dame in the distance. The loveliness of the Paris springtime washed over him without notice.

He turned to face the two men, one wearing a smug expression of triumph, the other silent and grim-mouthed. How different from one another they were, he thought.

His uncle, wealthy and learned, wore power as easily as his cardinal's resplendent scarlet robes. He had never wielded a weapon in his life, at least not anything so obvious as a sword. The cardinal preferred the more subtle blade: his tongue. And what use he had gotten from it over the years, swaying even Parliament in Bedford's absence! The regent's council Henry had created on his deathbed was solidly in his uncle's pocket now, something which in his wandering delirium Bedford's late brother had not foreseen. Together with his own brothers, the duke of Exeter and the earl of Dorset, Beaufort dominated the government as though *he* were king! Bedford detested the situation, but all he could do was show his uncles the respect they were due by virtue of their offices.

He had a greater esteem for Fastolf. First into the surf at Harfleur, the soldier had distinguished himself in battle after battle in these French wars. The man was simple and courageous, and his loyalty to Henry V—and now to his young son—without question. And although not even literate, his battle sense was flawless. He was one of the few men Bedford knew he could trust. But the duke did not have time to ruminate further.

"And now"—the cardinal clapped his hands together and rubbed them with evident relish—"I must be on my way. I left my escort waiting while I answered your summons to read the cowmaid's letter." His eyes shone mischievously. "I have much to do in England."

The duke banished dismay and arranged his face into a smile. "My thanks, Uncle, for your having taken time from the regency to come to France. I am gratified that you chose to bring the dispatches yourself rather than entrusting them to the usual couriers."

The prelate inclined his head. "It was my pleasure. One grows weary of life at court from time to time. However, one cannot stay away too long. I shall impart your affection to the king." He held out his hand toward Bedford.

The duke went to him and knelt to kiss the cardinal's ring. Smiling, Beaufort offered his hand to Fastolf, who also made his obeisance. Beaufort nodded briefly to both of them, then, with a sweep of his vermilion cloak, walked with assurance to the door.

Bedford continued to stare at the place where his uncle had vanished. *Much to do in England*, indeed. Like quarrel with my brother, he thought bleakly.

Ever since he had come to France, the periodic communiqués he received from Humphrey complained bitterly of the Beaufort brothers' continuing interferences with his role as Protector of the Realm. They—and the regent's council they controlled—were too damned tightfisted with their money, and allowed Humphrey small latitude for ruling the kingdom in Bedford's absence. In addition to that, they were all too willing to put their faith in Philippe of Burgundy's oily vows of loyalty. Humphrey, more insightful than they, knew that Burgundy was not to be trusted; it was plain that he cared nothing for the alliance but wanted the crown of France for his own miserable head. The day would come, he prophesied, when John would regret having entered into confederation with him.

Bedford sighed wearily and rubbed his pounding temples. No longer the youthful warrior who had fought so valiantly at his brother's side when Henry took Normandy, he was almost forty now, too old to play the role of intermediary between his relatives. But Humphrey, hot-headed and impetuous and given to outbursts of unprovoked violence, was right about one thing: Burgundy wanted France for himself.

Four weeks past, an Armagnac delegation had approached Philippe requesting that he put Orléans under his protection in the name of Charles of Orléans, and the acquisitive rascal had agreed. When Bedford flatly refused the proposition, Burgundy withdrew his battalion from that city, leaving England alone to forge onward with the siege. Bedford writhed at the position that put him in. He possessed neither the men nor the money to wage this war without assistance, yet his only ally was unreliable at best and treacherous in the worst of times. As it was, his forces were stretched to the breaking point, what with a tenuous hold on Jargeau, Beaugency, and Meung, not to mention the miserable wretches sitting it out at Orléans. And now there was the unfortunate news that the Dauphin was amassing an army at Blois with the intention of sending it on to Orléans.

Perhaps he had not heard Fastolf correctly. The old soldier had barely gotten the words out of his mouth when Beaufort arrived. As always, the cardinal had dominated the conversation. He turned a frown to Fastolf. "What is this about an Armagnac buildup at Blois?"

"It's true, my lord," growled the knight. "Our scouts've seen a huge Armagnac force gathering at Blois—men-at-arms, supply wagons, archers, knights. Even cannon. They're going to try to resupply the city."

Bedford lifted his receding chin, layered by rolls of flesh. "But not lift the siege?"

"Don't you go about fearing that, sir." Fastolf's smile showed stumps of mossy teeth. "You know how the French fight, if fighting you can call it. Every goddamned one of them is so bent on making a name for himself, wanting to be the first in battle, that they always end up in a rout. Why, when they tried to take the herrings from us, it was as easy as slapping a baby for us to put them in their place! You would think that they'd have learned better by now, the fools." He shook his woolly head. "They'll not lift the siege; you can bet your balls that they'll just sit it out in the city once they get there."

Bedford regarded the man before him with a searching eye. Sir John Fastolf, Knight of the Garter, was one of the best soldiers—no, *the* best—in the king's army. He had shown his mettle ever since Henry first introduced the might of England into this miserable kingdom, and they only a ragtag band. Ah, what a splendid string of triumphs that had been! Harfleur, Agincourt, Rouen, all had fallen like ripe apples to Henry, while the effete knights of France, decked out like ladies in their finery, were mowed down by good Welsh arrows as they deserved to be.

"What is it, sir?" asked Fastolf, taking note of the duke's dreamy smile.

"I was just thinking of my brother and all the plans he had for England."

"Aye, now there was a man!" The knight nodded his head with enthusiasm. "We'll not see his like again for a long time, if ever."

Bedford frowned. "No, I suppose we shan't." Henry evaporated before his eyes, replaced by the specter of Orléans. "What is it like there, at Orléans?" he asked. "Is it true that some of our men have deserted?"

"A few have, sir," Fastolf admitted. "But those are cowards anyway, and we're best rid of the filthy scum." He scratched at his beard. A louse was crawling down his cheek; when the soldier found it, he crushed it between his thumb and forefinger, then threw it carelessly upon the floor.

"But never you mind them," he continued, "for you've got the best commanders in the field at Orléans. Them Frenchies are no match for Talbot and Scales. And Glasdale's no slouch either, sir, that's damned certain."

"Pity we lost Salisbury, though." Bedford smiled sadly.

"Aye, sir, that was a dark day for England."

Thomas Montague, earl of Salisbury, had been Bedford's chief commander in the Loire campaign. It was he who had mustered the expeditionary force which landed in Normandy the year before, and he whose plan it was to take the unprotected towns surrounding Orléans before launching an attack upon that heavily fortified city. But God had willed that Salisbury not linger upon the earth, and shortly after the siege began, he was killed by a cannonball.

Yes, that was indeed a dark day. Bedford prayed every night that they would not have to see another. "Have we still men enough to maintain the siege?" he asked.

"That we have, sir," affirmed Fastolf. "We can sit there till Hell freezes over good and solid. There's still plenty of food and arms getting through the Armagnac lines, and not one of our supply trains has been taken. We taught the Frenchies a damned good lesson when they tried to get our herring, and they'll not be trying that again, I can tell you!"

"Can we take theirs? Stop them before they get to Orléans?" Bedford knew the answer already, but hoped that Fastolf had information that he did not.

As he feared, the soldier's ragged face darkened and he shook his head once more. "No, sir. The battalion they're sending is too big. We're already using every man we've got to hold Orléans and the other Loire towns. Even if we mustered them all, they wouldn't be enough."

The duke considered this assessment, knowing Fastolf's judgment to be correct. "Well, that's out of the question. There's no point in holding Orléans if the towns on either side of it return to the Armagnacs."

Bedford went to the window. Beyond Notre-Dame a heavy mass of iron-coated clouds had formed, growing larger with every second. A jagged tongue of light flicked toward the earth, followed a moment later by thunder. One could mistake it for cannon fire, if one closed one's eyes.

"Let them go, then," he said. "We'll just have to gamble that once there, they'll leave their supplies and return whence they came."

Jehanne awoke early after an agitated sleep, as excited as a child. Tomorrow the archbishop of Reims was to depart Tours bound for the army encamped at Blois, taking with him the old veteran of two kings' wars, Raoul de Gaucourt. Jehanne and her group would leave for Blois this afternoon, well ahead of the king's ministers.

She glowed with the knowledge that she had survived her testing period and finally won the respect and affection of the king and his court, and the veneration of the people. They especially—the shopkeepers and laborers, the minor clergy and farmers, the ordinary folk of France—had never doubted her, unlike the aristocracy. To them, her divine call was real from the first. Since Poitiers, they had starting calling her *L'Angélique*, a nickname that left her a little nervous, and "The Maid of the Banner," which pleased her. It seemed that everyone was behind her now; even seigneur Trémoïlle had smiled and wished her well. She knew that she would not fail.

From Blois, she would dispatch her other letter to the English at Orléans. The first, the one Séguin wrote for her, was delivered into Bedford's own hands by Ambleville the herald. The duke had given him a curt nod of thanks, then dismissed the messenger without reading the letter. Jehanne hoped that he had bothered to read it by now. The communication to the *goddons* holding Orléans was penned by her new confessor, Jehan Pasquerel, who copied it from the original. She fervently prayed that all of them would obey the terms she had dictated.

And today she would join the assembled armed might of France to engage in the final battle for the kingdom at Orléans!

Before she left Vaucouleurs, she had felt that her confidence in her Counsel could become no greater. Now, with all the obstacles having fallen away in so wondrous a fashion, she understood how fragile her questioning faith had actually been. A cloak of embarrassed chastisement fell about her when she recalled her petty importunities to her Counsel and beheld how lacking in wisdom she could be at times. They were all around her in the silence, and she knew beyond doubt that They forgave her lack of faith, even with a surprising touch of humor.

After breakfast Jehanne reinspected her armor for the fifteenth time. Minguet had polished it until it gleamed like a mirror, and Jehanne longed to put it on, although she was grudgingly aware that it was too early in the day to dress for war, since they would not start for Blois until the afternoon. So she had to content herself with running a loving finger along its seams, her eyes caressing the exquisite craftsmanship. Never had she worn beautiful things until now, and she loved the look and feel of all her newly acquired raiment, from the velvet tunics and silk shirts to the chainmail whose brightness encased her in an iridescence as fluid as water. She knew that she looked dashing in everything she wore. She had seen it in the faces of those who watched as she was fitted into the cumbersome but beautiful steel suit.

Given whatever she wanted by the townspeople, she seldom had to pay for anything, and instead gave generously to the poor from what remained of the Dauphin's money. People came to pay their respects to her: wealthy merchants, respected women of Tours, fine knights, and learned clergymen. The last did not come to interrogate her, but simply to converse and to gain an insight into her character, and the talks were for the most part serious in content but light in spirit.

The ladies of the court who had accompanied the Dauphine to Tours came to see her as well, flattering her with their eager attentions. Madame de Gaucourt and Madame de Trèves flaunted a newfound admiration for her. Jehanne sometimes was summoned to the castle, where she spent enjoyable afternoons in the Dauphine's company while musicians played soft music and ladies-in-waiting stood intrigued by the exchange between Jehanne and her queen. Although these soirées were pleasant, Jehanne nevertheless remembered the cool reception she had first received, and she remained skeptical of the genuineness of the ladies' advances into her company. She continued to feel uncomfortable in the presence of Queen Yolande. It was a great relief when the old woman went to Blois to haggle with d'Alençon over the cost of the supplies for which she was paying.

Jehanne was still staying at the home of the du Puys. Pasquerel was with her, as were the pages and the heralds. D'Aulon had joined Metz, Poulengy, and Jehanne's brothers at one of the inns, whose owner was recompensed from the Dauphin's coffers. Jehanne would have been appalled had she known about some of her companions' nocturnal activities, but her attention was elsewhere.

She was free to induce Pasquerel to recite the Mass for her as often as she wanted. While they waited through that day for their journey's start, she spent a long, confidential conversation with the man who was rapidly becoming the repository for her aspirations and misgivings. As Metz had foretold, she liked Brother Jehan very much. He was unlike any priest she had ever known. He neither judged nor condemned her frailties; he did not pretend to be loftier than she because he was a man of the cloth. Instead, he offered understanding and solace, intimating by his actions that a Christian was dutybound to love his or her fellow sinners. While her comrades prepared for the trip to Blois, the two of them knelt before the altar in the house's small second-floor oratory. The monk would soon say Mass for her, after she was confessed at her own insistence.

"One cannot purge one's conscience too often," she told him when he reminded her that she had done so only yesterday.

"And what weighs on your conscience, Jehanne?" He smiled with a degree of irony combined with amused affection.

She admitted her fears of being killed in battle. Her Guides had never mentioned that likelihood, but yet, what if something went wrong?

The priest answered that God would not let anything happen to His messenger.

She digested that slowly, with a careful frown. That was well enough, she said, but despite her best efforts to stop hating the English she had not been successful, so she feared not only being killed but killing. She knew she still had a terrible temper and was afraid that mixed with her hatred, it could reap dire consequences.

"Please, Brother, pray with me that I might learn forgiveness," she pleaded. "And pray with me also that God will put me where I cannot shed blood."

Pasquerel blessed her with the Sign of the Cross. Then he began the Mass, and when it was finished they prayed together for the rest of the morning.

After a midday meal that Jehanne was only able to nibble because of her nervous stomach, she removed her tunic and stood in her shirt and hose while Minguet armed her. Now that the moment to leave had come, the boy was so eager to please that his fingers fumbled with the straps, and at one point he let the breastplate slip from his hold and clatter to the floor with a loud bang. Jehanne winced at the noise, hoping that he had not dented her untouched armor before she had even been able to wear it. He picked up the piece and wiped it with his hand, then held it up for her to see that it was not damaged. But his labor proceeded with a maddening slowness, and she had to scold herself that he was new at this and would improve in time. It would be a sin to rebuke one so eager to help her.

She was still being fitted into the steel boots when her traveling party arrived. They were made to wait until Jehanne, bursting with impatience and frustrated that she could not bend over to help her page, looked down irritably at the flustered boy and said, "Enough, Minguet, fetch d'Aulon for me."

The boy flushed, but did as he was told. While d'Aulon quickly fastened the boot hinges, Minguet put the white silk *huque* over her head and belted it and Ste.-Catherine's sword around the breastplate. Then he handed her the small battleax. Bareheaded, Jehanne turned and walked uncomfortably in the heavy steel ensemble to the door and out into the street.

A sizable group of well-wishers was there to see them off. They clogged the street in front of the house, whispering among themselves at their first sight of Jehanne in her armor. Minguet went to the charger d'Alençon had given her and strung the shining helmet onto her saddle. Except for the pages, the others were mounted and ready to go.

When Raymond started to hand her horse's reins to her, the animal threw back its ears. The whites of his eyes bulged, and he reared and tried to bolt.

"Bring him to the church there." Jehanne pointed across the street.

Raymond led the still-protesting mount to the door of the church as Jehanne clanked noisily toward them, the crowd parting in her path. The horse calmed down long enough to allow Jehanne's older page to hold him firmly by the bit while he stroked his nose. Jehanne grabbed the high front of the saddle and tried to put her foot into the stirrup. But her horse, the one she rode every day without armor and never had trouble mounting, was too far from the ground dressed as she was now, with her agility hampered.

Seeing her dilemma, a young boy picked up a small stone block lying near the street and put it beneath the horse. Jehanne smiled her thanks at the boy, and, stepping upon the stone, hoisted herself into the saddle. Raymond continued whispering soothing words to the beast until Jehanne was comfortably mounted. Then she took the reins he offered her, grateful that her steed had finally been pacified. It would be an ill omen if her own horse gave her any prolonged difficulty, especially in front of all these people.

She turned toward the clergy assembled on the church steps. In a loud voice trenchant with authority, she cried, "You, priests and people of the Church, form yourselves into a procession and offer prayers to God."

She spun her horse around and turned him toward her companions, all horsed now and starting down the street. She looked back to see that the priests were still standing there, staring at her. They looked at her, then at one another, uncertain as to what they should do.

"Go on! Go on!" she shouted with a forward wave of her gauntleted hand.

Minguet rode past her. The beautiful unfurled standard he held flapped proudly in the April breeze. Compelled, the priests began to move. Jehanne nudged her horse forward, knowing that they would follow her down the choked streets of Tours, through the adoring, shouting, clinging mob.

The man who left the tent adjusting his clothing looked every inch the dandy he pretended to be, in a fine linen tunic trimmed with gold thread, open at the throat to reveal curling black chest hair. Long, shiny boots stretched up the muscled calves to hug his thighs. His face was lean and smooth-shaven but for the chin, which sported a pointed beard that he sometimes dyed blue when in attendance at court. It was there among the other lords that he set the standard for manly fashion, but however they tried, none could match his signature sense of elegance and style. Perhaps it was because an implicit dissoluteness hung about his handsome features, something elusive hinting at the mystery of a proscribed, hidden life.

He fixed the broad-brimmed hat at a rakish angle on his head so that the long feather pointed behind him. With a purposeful tempo, he stepped toward his destination, the black cloak about his shoulders billowing like a raven's wings.

It was not yet seven o'clock in the evening and already he had found for himself the kind of exercise he most preferred. What a delicious treat he had been, that beardless page from Brabant who had so willingly offered to prepare him for battle in his own fashion! Pity he had to slap the boy, though, when he asked for money afterward. That put him in his place, to be sure, and also gave the man an unexpected thrill at the sight of the boy's blood. He had not realized that another's pain could be so . . . arousing. That was something he would have to explore further, when the time came again. Barely mindful of his grin, his legs swept in a rapid gait across the camp as he envisioned enjoyments to be had later this night, after that damned meeting was finished.

His attendance was overdue and he knew it. But what could they do about it? he asked himself, quickening his footsteps almost to a run; after all, he was Gilles de Rais, a seigneur in Bretagne and a captain equal to any of them. It made no difference that he was only twenty-five years old; he had been a veteran from the age of sixteen. His presence was as important as any of theirs. Wasn't his experience the same and his knowledge of strategy as extensive? They would not dare start without him.

He found, however, when he reached the most impressive tent in the encampment—Clermont's own—that they had indeed already begun. That was apparent from the sober cadence of voices inside. He tossed a brief nod to the slouching warrior who stood guard at the entrance. Parting the flap, he entered.

They all stood in the center of the tent hunched over a table surrounded by four iron-held torches. "It will depend of course on favorable winds," Sainte-Sévère was saying. He had his back to the door and did not notice de Rais enter.

But the others did and turned to look at him. "Good evening, Gilles. Good of you to join us," Clermont said sarcastically. Sainte-Sévère swung around and glowered at the young man in the doorway.

Knowing his face was half-hidden in the dim light, de Rais grimaced. He detested the little worm who had spoken, yet did not dare openly challenge the Bastard's younger, legitimate brother. He bestowed a gracious bow upon the commanders. The grin affixed to his mouth was loaded with charm. "And good evening to you, gentlemen. My apologies for my tardiness. I was unfortunately detained elsewhere."

His eyes swiftly took in the group. Besides Clermont, there was the admiral de Culan, in command of the king's navy, and Ambroise de Loré, the grizzled, rough-spoken veteran of many battles. The maréchal de Sainte-Sévère, a large man in his fifties, was the eldest of the group and had the most thorough knowledge of the area surrounding Orléans. All of them were courageous warriors but not the best strategists.

"Well, I hope she—or he, perhaps?—was worth it," Clermont remarked. His upper lip curled with abhorrence. "Because I am afraid that we have already arrived at a plan without you." His gloat was indisputable in the set chin and upturned left eyebrow.

"Plan?" de Rais asked, suddenly suspicious, disregarding the comte's slur on his personal life. "What plan?" He took a few brisk strides to the table and made a space for himself between Clermont and admiral de Culan.

Spread out over the table was a map of the area surrounding Orléans and the city itself. Hastily written but legible words signified the locations of bogs and high ground, and the direction of the river's current. The parchment had been marked across in random strokes, detailing past battle plans that had been proposed and rejected.

"We will cross the river here, tomorrow," said Clermont haughtily, "and swing south through the Sologne." He pointed to the map, and de Rais, his brow furrowed in concentration, followed the comte's finger as it passed though the flat, wooded marshland.

"Then as we near Orléans we will swing far to the south, out of reach of the English *bastilles*. We'll take our position here"—he drew his finger to the southern bank of the river about a league east of the Bastille de St.-Jehan-le-Blanc—"and barges from the town will be sailed upriver to our location. We'll load the barges with supplies and float them down to the Porte de Bourgogne."

"Meanwhile," interjected Saint-Sévère, "we'll make a feint across the river at St.-Loup to keep the *goddons* busy while our escort sees the supplies safely through the gate."

"I suppose you've decided that the northern approach is too risky."

Ambroise de Loré nodded his shaggy head. "That's right. Those northern forts are swarming with *goddons*, and they would be all over us like flies on shit. The river's better."

"What about the rest of the men?" de Rais asked. "Where will the army cross?"

"The army will not cross," the maréchal pronounced. "We are not a relieving force, we are only bringing supplies to the city."

De Rais snorted in disgust. "We far outnumber the *goddons* at this point and could easily rouse them from their *bastilles*. What does the Bastard think of this scheme of yours?"

"This is the Bastard's strategy." Clermont emphasized the word. "The king feels, and the Bastard agrees, that it is too early for the army to assault the English, that we need to build up our numbers considerably before we try to raise the siege."

"But in the meantime they could acquire reinforcements," de Rais rejoined, "and we might again become outnumbered."

"That is a chance we will have to take," said admiral de Culan. His own aversion to the plan was obvious in the low grumble.

De Rais took off his hat and scratched his head. "What about La Hire and de Xaintrailles? They are not likely to consent to being simple baggage handlers." He knew those men well, having fought with them before. They were not the sorts to let an opportunity for action slip past them without protest.

"I will handle those hotheads when they arrive from Orléans," Clermont responded with a smooth smile. "After all, the plan is the Bastard's and it is his city in our brother's absence. Their assignment is to provision the town."

De Rais frowned at the self-assured young comte, wishing he could smack the pusillanimous face. "And when do 'those hotheads' arrive?" he asked in a voice purring with irony.

"Tomorrow," Clermont replied, determined to ignore de Rais' disdain. "Gaucourt is coming from Tours, and when he has been briefed we shall be able to depart."

"What about the girl, the miraculous visionary who has so charmed the king?" de Rais asked sardonically. "I've heard that he is sending her with us. What do you intend to do with her?"

Though he had already seen Jehanne once, at Chinon, he was not a man to credit the notion of God-sent maidens and, in fact, often wondered if there were a God at all. It was only when passion held him that he came anywhere close to approaching the Divine. On the other hand, he was most certain of the dark side of human nature, having seen it in long, vicious battles and in the random deaths of hundreds of innocents. And he well knew that there were very few virgins, male or female; he had personally seen to the former and shrank from the latter, that simpering daughter of Eve and the great Sin.

"She is indeed on her way here as we speak," answered Sainte-Sévère with a stern frown. "And word from the king is that she is to be treated with the utmost courtesy." He gave de Rais a warning look, for he was aware, as was everyone else who knew him, that young Bluebeard was no respecter of women.

"Do you intend to tell her of your plans?" the seigneur pressed, a cynical smile forming on his lips.

Clermont glanced at the others and did not answer. "There's no need for that," de Culan answered for the knight. "The girl is no soldier but a mascot, someone to rally the troops and to lift their spirits for battle."

"I have heard that the king has given her the title 'Chief of War,'" de Rais goaded. "Does that not authorize her to know battle plans?"

The men chuckled, and de Loré answered, "Come, Gilles, you know that is an empty rank with no authority whatever."

"Yes, I know it, but perhaps she does not." He could hear a sudden commotion outside the tent. "What will you do if she insists?" His question was eclipsed by the sound of indignant argument on the other side of the canvas.

The others turned their attention from him to the entrance.

The guard rushed in, letting the flap drop behind him. Not one to be easily cowed, he was nevertheless nonplussed. He licked his lips with a bemused tongue. "Excuse me, my lord, but the Maid is here with her brothers and she demands entrance. I told her that you are in a war council but she insists—"

"Never mind, André," Clermont interrupted. "Show her in."

"Now you'll get your answer, Gilles," whispered de Loré softly enough for Clermont not to hear him. The Breton chuckled in anticipation of the forthcoming departure from serious affairs that Clermont would have to deal with.

The tent flap lifted again and the girl came into the dim light with two somewhat attractive, very young men behind her. None was helmeted, and in the closely cropped hair and swarthy features was a clear bond of blood, especially between the girl and her dark brother. The smaller one was fair and had light eyes shaped like those of the other young man.

The girl was wearing shiny new armor which gleamed in the torchlight, its brilliance enlarged by a magnificent white *huque*. Shorter than her brothers, she looked sturdier and less feminine than de Rais' comrades had expected. Indeed, she did not resemble a girl at all but a youth of perhaps sixteen. An air of confident authority was as manifest as the sword hanging from her belt. In contrast to their sister, the young men were not in the least commanding in their hauberks and bucklers. It was not simply a matter of dress. They did not glow as she did.

She appraised the captains with a comfortable smile. "I am Jehanne the Maid, sent here from the Dauphin by the grace of God." Her voice was low in timbre but rang clearly above the hiss of the torches. "I was told by the soldiers outside that I could find a council of war here." She looked with congenial expectation at the rugged faces.

"Welcome, Jehanne. I am Charles de Bourbon, comte de Clermont." The comte smiled icily, surveying the armed peasants before him with overt distaste. He introduced his fellows, and the girl inclined her head to each, wearing her effortless look of goodwill.

"What have you decided?" she asked once the pleasantries were finished.

The men exchanged looks. Gilles de Rais appeared ready to laugh. Sainte-Sévère said, "We are still awaiting the arrival of chancellor de Gaucourt and other captains who are our comrades. So there has been no decision."

"Have you any suggestions, Jehanne?" asked de Rais. His gaunt face was roguish, taunting.

"Yes, I have," she responded in all seriousness, unaware both of the irony of his question and of the demonic spirit who voiced it. "While I was out there just now, walking through the camp with my brothers and our companions, I heard the foulest, most disgusting language issuing from the mouths of our soldiers that I have ever heard in my life."

"Such talk is common among the soldiers," said de Loré, trying not to laugh at her naïveté. "It is just one of the realities of army life."

"Well, it's going to have to stop." She frowned. "And the soldiers must send away all the loose women with them and be confessed and made to attend Mass and take Holy Communion."

The captains looked at her as dumbfounded as though she had suggested they all become monks.

"My girl, the men would never stand for that," de Rais said with a patronizing smile. "They need their leisure and the restoration of their spirits between battles."

"What they need is the presence of God and His assistance when they go into battle. It is He who will restore their spirits. If they go as sinners, they go without God, and how then are they any different from the godless enemy?" Vibrating with the Power, her voice rose with the vehemence of her convictions. "And if they go as sinners, God will turn away from them and not give us victory. Yet if they put aside their women and their swearing, and allow themselves to be confessed and receive Holy Communion, God will call them His own and will help us to raise the siege."

For several moments none of the men moved. Jehanne could feel the thoughts of each of them, could see their opinions proclaimed in the weathered faces and folded arms. Clermont was the way Charles' courtiers had been when she first came to Chinon: aloof and condescending, safely wrapped in his patent of nobility. The maréchal de Sainte-Sévère, professional warrior and strategist, regarded her warily, as did the admiral de Culan. But though he looked unnerving with his wild hair and beard, Ambroise de Loré alone seemed struck by her presence, and as she spoke his expression softened, changed to unfolding wonder. Jehanne could not quite read the dapper, fair-haired young man with the dancing blue eyes, but there was something dark about him that she could sense and from which all her instincts recoiled.

"I am sorry, Jehanne," said Sainte-Sévère finally, "but we cannot tell the army to change the habits of a lifetime on your orders. You must show us that there are practical reasons as well as godly ones for them to alter their behavior."

"Very well," she answered, her jaw set in determination, "what about this: There are divisions gathered here from all over the kingdom, no? You, seigneur de Rais"—she pointed to him—"you came here with troops from Anjou and Maine, did you not? And you, comte de Clermont, are here from Orléans. For days now, the army has been growing larger as the forces assemble at this place. We have the numbers, so how will we win?"

She paused, her gaze defying the skeptical faces. D'Alençon had told her back in Tours that the code of chivalry compelled each knight to exalt himself in battle through an unconstrained show of valor. When she asked if the English fought that way, the duc admitted that the enemy fought together, in united brotherhood.

"Well, small wonder that they always win!" she had exclaimed, aghast at the stupidity of the noble knights. "We must fight like that, too, unless we want to lose again."

The men were waiting for her answer. Lord God, help me to convince them, she appealed.

"We will win in battle only if we all fight together as one army of France instead of a collection of smaller armies loyal to single lords," she continued. "The only way that that can happen is if the soldiers are chastised and not allowed to do whatever they want. They need to know that you are their commanders, and that they are bound to follow your decrees, and that if you charge them to lay off swearing and to leave their women behind, it is for purposes of order. And if you then command them to be confessed and attend Mass, it is also for order's sake as well as for the good of their souls." She smiled. "Does that not make perfect sense, Maréchal?"

Sainte-Sévère smiled in return, and she could see that she was winning his respect. "It does indeed. However"—he glanced around the table at his cohorts— "the soldiers may not see it like that, Jehanne. They are accustomed to things as they are, and old habits are not easily put aside."

"Then I would like to propose a bargain," she said. "If I can convince them that what I ask is right, will you order them to obey the commands of God?"

An amused, condescending smirk formed on Clermont's face. "If you can convince them, we will order them to fly to the moon. But do not be disappointed when you fail." The smile faded into a haughty sneer.

She took up his challenge. "I shall not fail." She gazed with astounding confidence at each of the men, then bowed, her eyes still meeting theirs. "My lords."

She turned and strode from the tent. Her brothers followed. The captains were silent for a moment.

"Well, that was an event," said de Culan, laughing a little.

Clermont chuckled. "Can you imagine how La Hire will receive the news that he's to curb his tongue?"

In a society known for its creative use of profane language, La Hire stood head and shoulders above his comrades in his ability to contrive newer and ever more blasphemous idioms. He could not answer yes or no without throwing in an obscenity. Jehanne the Maid would have her hands full with him.

De Loré frowned at the comte. "Do not underestimate her, seigneur Clermont. She has a convincing way with her and is sure of herself. She may just win over the men after all."

"Has she won you over?" de Rais asked.

"Yes, but as a source of inspiration rather than as captain," the soldier replied. "Still, you must admit, her thinking is certainly sound."

"We shall see," Clermont said with a sly smile. "We shall see indeed."

La Hire and Poton de Xaintrailles traveled through enemy territory under a moonless sky and reached camp shortly after daybreak, but Jehanne did not meet them right away. Upon their arrival they were shown to Clermont's tent, where Sainte-Sévère and de Loré advised them in the matter of relieving Orléans.

The army spent much of the morning striking camp. As roiling clouds began to move in from the west, the squires finished fitting their captains into metal suits long since seasoned with blood and smoke. Then they dismantled the commanders' tents and loaded them onto the supply wagons alongside the crates of crossbow bolts and gunpowder casks. Around noon, just as the first strokes of lightning flashed overhead, Gaucourt's arrival from Tours in the company of the archbishop of Reims signaled that the time had come for the long-readied caravan to start across the bridge east of Blois.

The battalions trudged slowly through the rain and mud for most of the day and finally made camp in a field a few leagues southwest of Orléans. By that time, the storm's worst was over. However, the relentless downpour remained constant and there were no fires for the night. Like the regular soldiers, Jehanne and her party had no proper tent to shelter them from the elements. But before they left Blois, Metz had obtained from d'Alençon a moderately large measure of canvas with which he had intended to protect the armor against early morning dews. Instead, he used that to construct a leaky, makeshift refuge that was partly successful in keeping them dry.

Jehanne refused to take off her armor, despite d'Aulon's coaxings and the others' assurances of her safety. It was not that she feared their own soldiers, she replied. She wanted to be armed and ready in case the train was attacked by the English. No reasonable promises of the unlikelihood of that could change her mind. By sunup, with every muscle in her body bruised, she awoke sore, cranky, and fatigued from little sleep. Rising stiffly, she wished—although she would never have admitted it—that she had listened to her friends and disarmed along with them.

That stopped mattering once the army was on the move. Exhaustion discarded, she rode as she had yesterday near the front of the long column between the troops of knights loyal to de Gaucourt and de Loré. A procession of monks preceded the army on foot, Pasquerel among them. They carried a new standard that Jehanne had ordered for the priests before they departed Tours, this one portraying the Crucifixion. While the cowled figures walked, they sang *Veni Creator Spiritus* and other hymns to announce the coming of God's own legions.

At her side, Raymond gripped Jehanne's standard with his free hand, holding the ashwood staff in its notched place on his saddle. The pages had quarreled over who would have the honor of bearing it. Jehanne secured a truce in which Minguet agreed to carry her company's pennon, and now he rode on her other hand, clutching the Annunciation with pride.

D'Aulon, Metz, and Poulengy were right behind Jehanne. To their left cantered her brothers, as glorious as real knights in their new, modified armor. Aristocratically aloof on their dainty palfreys, the heralds continued to travel with the company, for Jehanne had decided not to send her letter to the English from Blois after all. It would be better to wait until she reached Orléans; then her words would be fresh in their minds, and with the army of God before them, they would be more willing to release the city.

But Orléans was still some distance away, and there was plenty of time to think about what she would do when she got there. In spite of the miserable weather and her stiff limbs, Jehanne's spirit climbed toward Heaven with the sacred music, and she thanked God for her newly purified army.

She had responded to Clermont's dare the instant she left his tent, two nights ago. With her brothers tromping after her in an ungraceful attempt to match her rapid gait, she made her way toward the largest campfire she could find. Thirty or so men-at-arms were gathered about it, and one of their number was telling a story to the agreeable laughter of his fellows. When Jehanne entered the circle, the tale ceased and the humor dwindled into silence.

The soldiers stared at her.

She smiled at them amicably, not at all afraid of the suddenly stony faces. There was a treetrunk on the edge of darkness that had very recently borne leaves but whose wood now provided light and heat for the company. Jehanne stepped up onto it.

"Men of France!" she called out in a loud voice, "I am Jehanne the Maid, from the village of Domrémy in the duchy of Lorraine. Some of you may have heard of me."

A murmur swept through the collection of rough countenances, and she knew that they were curious at least, if not welcoming. That would make her present task that much easier. They began to gather around her and she continued.

"All my life I have heard tales of this terrible war that has lasted so long that not even the oldest man in our village can remember a time of peace. And I have seen for myself how the war has destroyed families and sent young men to their graves when they should have lived to see their children grown. Several years ago, my own cousin's husband was killed in battle against the *goddons*, and I felt her grief then, child that I was.

"Like many in the countryside, I have also felt the pain of war even more personally than that. Only last summer Domrémy was burned, even the church, by the Burgundians. We were able to rebuild our village with God's help, and although we did not starve, there were nights when we went to bed hungry. But we were more fortunate than others, for as I traveled to Chinon to meet the Dauphin. . . ."

The pitiful, violated corpses of that unknown village materialized before her like an unbidden vapor, as they often did in her nightmares. A thick plug of emotion caught in her throat, and for a moment she could not go on.

She shook her head and put a hand to her brow. The present, Jehanne. This is the only moment that matters. The dead are dead; they're God's business now.

". . . As I traveled to Chinon," she went on in a trembling voice, "I passed through other villages that no longer exist thanks to our enemies, those cowards who have murdered our defenseless people, and destroyed our homes, and stolen our grain and animals! I have no doubt that you have seen such things for yourselves."

There was an angry mutter among the soldiers. More of them were approaching the fire to hear the small armored figure who glowed before them in the golden, flickering light.

Jehanne held her hands before her, palms out in a gesture requesting silence. They gave it to her.

"When I was thirteen, I heard the voice of God. He told me what you must surely know already, that France is bleeding and dying from this war, and that the *goddons* have no right to take the kingdom. But He also assured me"—the resentful buzz resumed, louder now, and she shouted above the commotion—"He also assured me that He has heard the prayers of our people, who have suffered so long and lost so much. He called me 'Daughter of God,' and instructed me to go to the Dauphin, who would give me an army to raise the siege at Orléans."

She had the full attention of the still-growing crowd. Her Counsel wrapped the Power around her in a warm glow, and she continued in a voice quivering with passion.

"You are all veterans of this long and costly struggle for our freedom, and I can see in your faces that you have suffered much over the years. Many of you have been wounded, some more than once, and you have lost comrades dear to you."

Her eyes searched the worn, scarred visages before her. "I know that you are all tired, as tired as the other people of France, the farmers who have seen their lives taken from them and burned in the fires of our enemies, and the townspeople who have undergone shortages of food. They are worn down with having to live in constant fear for their lives. Whatever the differences in our stations, whether we are peasants or nobility, farmers or townspeople, soldiers or civilians, we share two things: We are French, and we are all exhausted and yearn for peace!

"Do you want this war to end?" she shouted.

"Yes!" the men thundered.

"Do you want to raise the siege at Orléans to keep the Dauphin safe?"

"Yes!" Many of the men shook their fists in a gesture of vehement enthusiasm.

"Do you want to see our good Dauphin Charles anointed with the holy oil of St.-Clovis and crowned King of France?"

"Yes!!"

"Do you want to drive the *goddons* back across the sea to their own country, never to bother us again, and do you want to see Paris return her allegiance to Charles?"

There was another roar of consent, this one prolonged and so loud that it resounded throughout the camp. By this time, soldiers from all directions were approaching the firelight. Jehanne looked across the ocean of hardened faces stretching beyond the twinkling boundaries of the campfire and into the darkened field. She had them and she knew it. But there remained the possibility of failure, so she would have to be careful.

"God wants all of that too, and more besides. He has told me that in answer to my own prayers. He has told me that in the far future, long after all of us are dead, France will be a powerful kingdom equal to others in the world, a land of wealth and influence, and will not have to answer to the English or anyone else! But that shall not happen unless what we want and what God wants come about."

Her throat was going dry. She paused to swallow.

"The King of Heaven has made me His messenger and has given you to me to be His holy army that we might liberate our people. God has pledged His support in this, but He asks that we give Him something in return.

"If we are to be His holy soldiers, then we must, all of us, yield to His wishes that we lead full Christian lives, that we not go into battle burdened with the stink of mortal sin. Let the *goddons* rot in their sins, let them go to their arms without the support of God, while we, God's chosen warriors, fall upon them and send them from Orléans and from all of France!"

As with one voice the army bellowed its response and a good number of the soldiers, their appetites for conflict whetted, brandished weapons above their heads. "We are with you, Jehanne!"

"Lead us to Orléans now!"

"God for France and Jehanne the Maid!"

"Jehanne the Maid! Jehanne the Maid!" the chant began. As at Tours, the sound of it raised the short hairs on the back of her neck and filled her with potency. Once more she raised her hands in a plea for silence.

The chanting stopped.

"At God's instructions I had a standard made for the friars who accompanied me from Tours, and twice a day, once in the morning and again at night, we are to gather around this symbol of Our Lord's Crucifixion and there hear Mass and receive Holy Communion. It is what God demands of His army that we might be blessed with His assistance in battle. Of course, before we may receive Communion we all must be confessed and resolve not to lapse back into sin.

"This means that we must put away from us all temptation to mortal sin. For me, that means my fear of being wounded in battle, even though I know that God does not will that I die. Nevertheless, I am frightened, but I must put aside my fears because for me to be afraid is really a lack of faith that God will keep His word and spare my life.

"You, men of France, must cast away your own temptations to sin. First, the women who have followed you and lured you from God's love."

A rustle of voices began near her and spread toward the darkness. The atmosphere had changed abruptly, and she could feel their unspoken rebellion.

She lunged forward. "Those of you who are willing to be shriven and to obey the commands of the King of Heaven shall be admitted to the company of His sacred warriors beneath the banner of His Son! Any man who rejects the word of God will be outside the heavenly fold, and will put his soul in the greatest danger, for he shall no longer be a part of God's army and under His loving protection. And if that man should be killed in the state of mortal sin, his soul shall surely be lost to God forever."

Several of the men crossed themselves amid the low hum of warring emotions.

Jehanne waited until the rumble faded, then again raised her voice. "I want what God wants! I want to obey His commands and lead His army to victory in this sacred struggle to liberate the kingdom! And if He commands that I leave my fear of death behind me, here in camp, then I must do so or fall into mortal sin and thus lose the right to be a soldier of God.

"You are the bravest men in the kingdom! Are you willing to do what *I* do? Do you have the courage to leave your own temptations behind you?"

Their conflicting instincts flickered across their faces, and after a brief struggle were borne away with the drifting woodsmoke. At first moderate, like the rumble of far-off thunder, a shout of approval rose from the ranks, then another, the sound gradually increasing in volume until it was a roar.

She knew they were hers when they began to chant her name again. This time she did not attempt to silence them. Her victory sang in the burly cries of "Jehanne the Maid!" that echoed through the wind swaying the tall trees above the company.

When at long last they quieted down, she said in a voice that had become a hoarse croak, "Then go to, soldiers of God and of France. Send temptation from our camp this very night and rest instead in the arms of God, knowing that He will protect you at Orléans as He has promised."

Now, as the army drew near the besieged city, Jehanne rode full of hope among the other captains. The men had obeyed her, albeit reluctantly. Much to the astonishment of the commanders, a large throng gathered the next day beneath Pasquerel's banner. It was there in the steady drizzle before Mass that she declared that God also commanded them to curb their tongues in the use of profanity. They didn't like it, she knew, but she heard no obscenities as she subsequently walked through the camp.

Until she met La Hire.

The rain had only just stopped, and with Mass ended, she was with her little band on their way back to their campsite when just ahead of them a raspy baritone bellowed, shattering the spiritual calm where Jehanne was centered:

"Move that shit-eating animal, you fatherless son of a poxridden whore, or I'll tear his dick off with my bare hands and stuff it down your miserable, scum-sucking throat!"

Jehanne's mouth fell open. Her ears burned in disbelieving abhorrence. She had never even imagined that such slime could issue from the mouth of any Christian. She and her companions stopped dead in their tracks, gaping at the source of the disturbance.

The red-faced man who had said all this sat astride a dappled-gray charger of considerable size who stamped his right front hoof in the mud and restlessly threw back his massive head. The rider's only armor was a dented breastplate, and the sleeves of a thick leather jerkin underneath plate armor–covered limbs the size of a small, knotted tree. His shaggily cut head was bare and damp with sweat and rain. He glowered down at a hapless wagonmaster whose horse was rebelling against the harness he desperately tried to fit onto the beast.

Jehanne tramped toward the mounted man, her arms swinging with dogged wrath. She did not see that Metz, d'Aulon, and Poulengy looked at one another and rolled their eyes.

"Are you deaf, you witless bastard, or just stupid? I said, Get that God-cursed crap machine hitched up right now or I swear by Caesar's nuts I'll ram your head up his shit-smeared ass!"

The wagonmaster's horse, alarmed at the angry tone, became even more unruly and cried out in a high-pitched whinny. The animal tried to jerk away from its keeper, who was barely able to prevent it from running away altogether.

"Sonofacocksuckingbitch!" the soldier roared, banging his fist onto the high front of the saddle, an action that startled his own mount.

"Excuse me, sir."

He looked down toward his left at the boy in full armor who stood glaring at him with potent brown eyes. The lad couldn't be any more than sixteen, the man figured. He had thick black hair cut above his ears, and his face was so smooth that he had not even started shaving yet. A green one, thought the soldier with a grin.

"What do you want? Can't you see I'm busy here?"

"I can see that you're busy sending your soul to Hell with that filthy language of yours," the boy replied, his fists clenched at his side.

A small group of young men rushed forward to surround him protectively.

The horseman reasoned that, with that splendid, obviously new armor and those attendants, he must be the son of an unknown lord. Well, lord or no lord, no one spoke to him like that. "And who the bleeding fuck are you, you little fart?"

"I am Jehanne the Maid, Messenger of God and Chief of War, and I would very much esteem it if you would dismount when you speak to me."

"Well, I am La Hire, the best mother-fucking soldier in the king's whore-humping army, and I do not take orders from women!"

For several moments they glowered at one another, each obstinately determined not to yield to the other.

Finally, Jehanne's face softened and she said, "You are right, La Hire, I have no command over you and no right to order you to do anything. But I really would like to speak with you, and I feel uncomfortable with you way up there on that horse and me down here on the ground." She smiled at him sweetly.

A smirk divided his beard, revealing a wide gap between yellowed front teeth. "I'm still busy."

"But look"—she pointed toward the conveyance and its half-harnessed beast of burden—"all is well now and the wagon will soon join the others. Please talk to me. It won't take more than a few minutes."

He could not resist her earnest smile. He dismounted. "Well," he said, leaning his right arm against his horse, "what do you want to talk about?"

Jehanne instantly took his measure. A long scar ran from above his right ear to the chin, and its trace cut a path through the fresh outgrowth of graying facial hair. In his fiery green eyes Jehanne saw the anguish that fueled an angry soul. He had lost everything he had ever cared about, she was certain of that. He howled his pain with every blasphemous oath.

She looked at him gently and said, "I want us to get along, La Hire. I think that's very important if we're to fight together against the *goddons*. We can't fight them if we're fighting among ourselves, can we?"

"That is so." He nodded soberly.

"It seems to me," she mused, "that the only way we can get along is if we respect one another and are careful not to offend one another. I certainly did not mean to offend you by issuing orders to you. I hope that you will accept my apology."

He grinned at her, surprised by the change in her demeanor. "I do."

"I'm very glad of that. It's important to me that I keep to my end of a bargain. And it's equally important to me that he with whom I've bargained keeps to his agreement to give me respect and not offend me."

"That is fair." He was aware of her manipulation but was enjoying it so much that he did not want to stop her.

What an amusing little prig she was! Still, he had to admit that there was also something uncommon about her. It was not just that she had had the impudence to challenge him, nor the fact that she skillfully reversed her position when she saw she wouldn't get her way by a frontal assault. And her distinctiveness really had nothing to do with the fact that she was here in the first place, a lone woman amidst all these earthy men who lived as though each day would be his last. There was something that hung about her as intangibly as a dream, something powerful, something irresistible.

He decided to play along with her for now. "How do you propose that I keep my part of our bargain?"

"By showing me respect and by not offending me with your language," she responded simply. "It is very rough and I am not accustomed to it. Even if I were, I would still know that it offends God, Who is our sovereign Lord."

"I believe in God," La Hire said with mock solemnity. He hawked, then spat on the ground. "I pray on my knees before every battle."

"Really?" Her eyes widened and the serious young face brightened. "What do you pray?"

"It is always the same prayer." He shrugged. "I say, 'God, I pray that You will do for La Hire what La Hire would do for You, if You were a soldier and La Hire God.' "

Jehanne frowned. "That does not sound like a proper prayer."

"Nevertheless"—he beamed—"it never fails me. God always responds just as I ask Him to, by protecting my hide in battle. It must be that He loves me, don't you think?"

She laughed, unable to maintain sobriety in the face of such an unyielding, unrepentant opponent. "Of course He loves you, La Hire, even if He hates the words you use. But even though He loves you, He will not save you if you should die in mortal sin."

He gave her a long, cautious look. A dubious smile curled the whiskered corners of his mouth as though he were trying to decide something.

At length he asked, "What is it you really want, Jehanne the Maid?"

"I want to lift the siege at Orléans," she answered. "I want to drive the English from France and see the Dauphin crowned king at last. Most of all, I want peace." Her eyes filled with frustration and sadness and she brushed the sudden tears away.

"Very well." La Hire nodded. "I want that too, so does everyone. What has that got to do with my speech?"

She took a deep breath and told him what she had told the army, that God had appointed her His messenger and had pledged His assistance in the deliverance of the kingdom. As she explained in a pleading manner that this army of France was not just the Dauphin's army but God's own, and that its sanctity depended on its being in a state of grace, incredulity faded from La Hire's face and in his eyes she saw him struggling with comprehension. For the mortal sins of a single man, she cautioned him, God would bring defeat and ruin to the army. Had they not experienced more than their share of reverses, living as they did in sin?

"Please, La Hire, this is more important than words. Our sins could condemn all of France, don't you see?"

"I was told you banished the whores from camp," he replied drily. "And now we're to leave off speaking normally?"

"Please," she repeated.

He threw his hands up in the air. "Well, what the f—, what am I supposed to do? I don't know how to talk any other way!"

"You can say what I say when I feel disheartened. You can say, 'In God's name.' Or you could also say, 'By my sword'—that one would suit a soldier like yourself."

"By my sword?" He grimaced in disgust. "What the Hell kind of oath is that?"

Jehanne smiled. "It is one that God does not mind."

Riding now at the head of the army, she thought of La Hire and prayed that God would keep him safe on his journey back to Orléans. He had left early this morning, though on what business she was not told.

There was much that was not being disclosed to her; she could sense it in the evasive answers the captains gave her when she asked about their plan of battle. Even her Guides would not relate any information, but continued to counsel patience and to promise that all would be well. With reluctance, she released her troublesome suspicions and plodded along in the rain with the rest of the column.

By mid-afternoon the storm had resumed in earnest. The wind blew great watery sheets across the Dauphin's army, and men and animals alike struggled ponderously against the stinging rain. Every now and then the gray figures of knights and horses were illuminated for an instant by sudden cracks of lightning, followed a split-second later by bone-jarring thunder which crashed over them, spooking the mounts. When the wagons and cannon became mired in ankle-deep mud, the captains pulled entire divisions from their ranks to push the stuck conveyances back onto what passed for solid ground. The trip seemed to last forever, what with the army's tortoiselike crawl.

De Gaucourt had sent ahead scouts, who returned with news that by now they were close to Orléans. Fearing a possible English attack, the host stopped for the knights to don their armor, and henceforth all of them rode with increased alertness. Apprehension pervaded the columns, giving a sense of urgency to the irritable commanders' orders.

Jehanne had untied the thong holding her *basinet* to the saddle and was wearing it, partly for protection against ambush, partly in a useless attempt to keep the rain off her head. Massed pinpricks of water smacked against her armor; she could hear them and little else through the helmet. With the visor lowered, her breath heated the inside so that she found it difficult to take in anything but stale air, and she also felt confounded, unable to see where she was going for the rain that fell before the narrow slits. She had little choice but to lift it if she did not want to suffocate. But with it open, the downpour drenched her face and streamed down her neck and into her suit. It blasted through the joints until her clothes beneath the steel skin were wringing wet.

She had worn this suit continuously for three days and nights, and it had long since ceased being comfortable, if indeed it ever had been. Every muscle in her body pulsed in pain, and as the journey lengthened, so did her bad mood. She had had very little sleep and was bone-tired. In mind and heart she hummed with impatience to get there and prepare for battle so they could finally defeat the *goddons* and return to the Dauphin. She also daydreamed about going to sleep in some warm, dry bed.

The tempest had not subsided when a couple of hours before nightfall the army halted on the southern bank of the Loire, nearly half a league east of Orléans and across the river from the English-held *Bastille* de St.-Loup. Through the blinding torrent, Jehanne could barely distinguish the English fort silhouetted on the other side of the river. It was only when the sky flashed that she momentarily saw it as it truly was, looming like a gigantic anthill astride the Chécy road. Nor was she able to see clearly the thick, high walls of Orléans west of the *bastille*, though she knew they were there. The great hulking shapes, ornamented by intermittent lights from faraway torches, hovered like structures from a dream beyond the pall of water. Unreachable goals, they teased her, singing a silent, alluring summons that she ford the swollen river and broach their remoteness. She could have screamed the frustration she was feeling. The Loire was an impassable barrier racing in swift currents past the French position, the thick brown water carrying tree limbs and other debris in its swirling, angry path.

The army halted abruptly. As though responding to a secret signal that Jehanne alone could not hear, the knights began to lower themselves to the marshy ground.

"Why have we stopped here?" Jehanne demanded of de Gaucourt as he dismounted stiffly from his horse. "Why aren't we going on, into the city?"

He pretended that she had not spoken.

The rest of the horsemen were on foot now. A battalion of men-at-arms began to make camp, while civilian quartermasters drove the laden wagons toward the river. Shouted instructions from company commanders rang through the rain as everyone hurried to his assigned tasks. Jehanne looked behind her to see that even her companions had dismounted. Metz was unrolling the provisional canvas tent. Stupefied, Jehanne watched the others lead their horses toward a hitching rope stretched between two staked posts that someone had already pounded into the soggy ground.

She swung down from the horse, her stiffened limbs creaking within the muddy armor. Having gotten no answer from the old warrior, Jehanne grabbed a hurried Gilles de Rais by the arm and repeated her question.

The menacing young man regarded her impatiently. "Please release me, I have much to do." Then, seeing her distressed face, he said, "Very well, I suppose there's no keeping it from you. The plan is for the Orléanais to sail barges upstream to where we are now. We'll load the barges and sail them back downstream to the Porte de Bourgogne, which is the only open road into the city." He expelled a dark look at the fort directly across from them. "A detachment from the garrison will skirmish against the English over there"—he jerked his head in the direction of St.-Loup—"while the provisions are being brought into Orléans."

"Well, what about us, what about the army? When do we cross?"

"We don't." De Rais spat, frowning in grim disapproval of the others' idea. "We've done our job, my girl. We're to return to Blois after Orléans is provisioned."

"What!"

He nodded. "I'm afraid so. I don't like it either, but then no one asked me what I thought any more than they did you." His sharp features exposed the bitterness gripping him. "Now, if you don't mind, I really have work to do." He pulled her clutched fingers from his arm and walked away.

They deceived me, she thought, dumbstruck at the betrayal. They made me think that they were ready to lift the siege, and all along they only intended to escort supplies. They've probably been laughing at me, at how stupid I am and how easy it was to fool me!

A steaming brew of anger in her midsection began to boil toward her brain, and when it got there she exploded.

She stormed over to Metz, who was staking the last corner of the shelter parallel to the soggy ground. He smiled at her approach, but seeing the now familiar anger in her red face, his expression changed to alarm.

"What's wrong?"

"They lied to me!" she shouted. "We're not here to raise the siege, we're just a supply convoy!"

"How do you know that?"

"Gilles de Rais told me himself." She briefly related what the seigneur had said, fighting back tears of rage and disappointment.

Metz frowned and said, "I'm sorry, Jehanne."

She looked across the camp. "Well, I'm not going to give up!"

She started walking. Her aching muscles groaned with each indignant swing of her arms.

"Where are you going?" he called after her.

"To change their minds!"

She did not have far to go. The comte de Clermont's imposing tent was already pitched near the riverbank, about a hundred yards downriver from the miserable covering that Metz had raised. Oblivious to the fresh, steaming horse droppings ground into the mud by hooves and many human feet, she tromped through the muck and past the cloaked archers huddling in groups against the deluge. All around her the camp whirred with the activity of men-at-arms rushing to unload the wagons. Jehanne made straight for the closed tent flap, thankful that at least there was no guard posted outside.

With her foot barely into the tent, she blurted, "Why did you lie to me?"

The captains looked up at her from the table. Clermont raised a contemptuous eyebrow at her dripping, mud-splattered appearance. "What are you doing here?" he asked. "You were not invited to join us."

"Of course not!" she raged. "I have never been invited to take part in your discussions, even though the Dauphin made me a captain too! Why did you lie to me, why did you make me think that we were coming here to lift the siege?"

"Jehanne, Jehanne," de Loré said soothingly, "we did not purposefully lie to you. But you are inexperienced in war and know nothing of strategy, while we have long years of practical training behind us."

"Training? Strategy?" she shouted, incredulous at the blindness of these craven men. They were worse than little old ladies; at least the elderly had a strong faith in Heaven's wisdom. "In God's name, none of that matters! God has promised that if we attack the English in their forts, He will give us victory over them and the siege will be lifted. How could you throw away this Heavenly opportunity?"

The men glanced at one another, and in that look Jehanne saw that they thought her promise of small importance.

"Be that as it may," intoned Clermont, "the plan has been ready for some time now, and as it is actually the Bastard's idea, you should take that up with him, not us." He turned back to the table, trying to dismiss her.

She became even angrier. A furious rebuttal sprang to her tongue, but before she could say another word, her brother Pierre burst into the tent.

"Jhanette! La Hire is crossing the river with the Bastard of Orléans!" He was gasping for breath, having run to Clermont's tent in the armor to which he was not yet accustomed. Water dripped from the ends of his hair and ran in little rivulets down his muddy face. His eyes shone with excitement. "Poulengy says for you to come right away."

Casting a victorious glare at the captains, Jehanne darted out of the tent and back into the downpour. She ran across the deeply mucked field after Pierre, dodging soldiers and horses, until she reached her encampment.

All of her companions were there, including Pasquerel, who had left the monks to join her. He was turned toward the river with both hands cupped above the bridge of his nose. The dark cowl, streaked with filth, clung to his head, covering his face. Even though Jehanne could not see his features, she recognized the soiled white habit.

Metz, Jehan, and Poulengy stood next to their pathetic little tent on the slippery bank sloping down to the Loire, while Raymond leaned against the pole that held Jehanne's leather-encased standard. Their gazes were fastened on the Loire. D'Aulon rested an affectionate arm around Minguet's shoulder as he shielded his eyes against the rain with his free hand. Both of them and the elegant heralds, Guyenne and Ambleville, were also looking at the indistinct shape on the river that grew closer with every pull of the oars.

At first, given the distance and the rain, Jehanne could make out only the craft and not its occupants, but as it neared the shore, silently except for the splash of oars carving through the water, she saw the flag that hung at its stern. The wind caught it for a moment and it fluttered proudly, as though it aspired in defiance of nature to announce its master's arrival. The emblem was just as d'Alençon had described it: a triple golden fleur-de-lys on a blue field, bordered along the top by a downturned, three-pronged bar, with the white bar sinister of bastardy drawn across the map at a diagonal, from the top right corner to the bottom left.

The boat emerged from the thick mist. Its passengers were clearly distinguishable now. At the prow a helmeted La Hire sat next to a man enshrouded in a wine-colored cloak. The hood was lowered and hid his face except for the strong nose. Behind them twenty armed figures, ten on either side, rowed with powerful strokes. A soldier knelt at the stern, guiding the rudder.

When the vessel reached the shallows, La Hire and the other soldiers sprang out of it into water that reached their thighs. Metz, Jehan, Poulengy, and Pierre helped to pull it up onto the shore while the soldiers pushed from behind. The boat rammed the muddy shore with a smack and rested there.

The man got out of the boat and waded toward Jehanne. He flung back the hood and smiled at her through the rain.

"Are you the Bastard of Orléans?" she fumed.

"I am, and I rejoice in your arrival," he answered with a gracious nod. He was tall, and though drenched, bore himself with dignity. His forehead was wide above intelligent brown eyes, and dimples dented the corners of a mouth too small for the face. He sparkled with an inner nobility that had nothing to do with bloodlines.

"Was it you who advised them to bring me here by this bank of the river instead of sending me straight to Talbot and his English?" Jehanne's ire was stronger than ever and she did not care whom she addressed. She was tired and sore, she was disappointed, and so infuriated that her companions cringed at her words.

Hit by this unexpected bolt of peasant wrath, the Bastard's expression changed to consternation, and he instinctively stepped back a pace. "Not only I, but others wiser than myself made the decision, believing it to be more prudent than any other plan."

"In God's name!" she cried, insensible to the captains' arrival, "the Counsel of Our Lord is wiser and better than yours! You thought to deceive me, but you have really defeated yourselves, for I bring you the finest help that anyone ever brought to knight or to city, since it is the help of the King of Heaven!"

"I have no doubt of that, Jehanne, but we must be practical," the Bastard answered, looking to de Gaucourt for support. "The other side of the river is heavily fortified by the English, and it would have been foolish for the army to attempt to resupply the city by a northern approach."

"Resupply!" she shouted above the thunder. "Why are we not going to fight? We are an *army*, we could lift the siege!"

"The English have the advantage, girl," Sainte-Sévère interrupted sternly, "and we'd be better off not risking the lives of all these men in a senseless attack."

"Or does the Maid think that God's love for her will be enough to raise the siege?" Clermont's sarcastic tone incensed her even further, and she could have slapped him.

Instead, she answered, "This mission does not come from God's love of me, but from the pleas of St.-Louis and St.-Charlemagne. Through their prayers God has taken pity on the town of Orléans, and will not suffer that enemies hold both the seigneur d'Orléans *and* his city!"

She breathed rapidly, glaring at the men who by now encircled her. "You think your plan is so good; well, the barges cannot sail to where we are because the wind is blowing in the wrong direction!" she seethed in caustic triumph. Strategy indeed!

The Bastard looked somewhat embarrassed. "Yes, well, that is something that we were unfortunately not able to foresee. We may be forced to wait here for some time before it changes in our favor. In the meantime"—he smiled in a conciliatory manner—"why don't you sit down and rest? You must certainly be tired after your journey."

Jehanne was gazing off into space and heard only half of what he had said. After her last expression of anger, she seemed purged of some perplexing force that had held her since the army left Blois. To her amazement, she had simply spit it out, all of it. The wrath she had felt only moments ago had somehow vanished as though it had never been there in the first place. There was no rain, no wind, nothing but that calm breeze that always blew a silence through her soul when They spoke to her. And she heard Catherine now.

DO NOT BE DISCOURAGED. THE WIND SHALL SOON CHANGE, AND THE SIEGE LIFT AS GOD HAS PROMISED. YOU WERE NOT BROUGHT HERE TO RESUPPLY THE CITY. FAITH, JEHANNE.

"All will be well," she mumbled, staring with a rapt frown at the dark, swirling Loire. "The wind is going to change now."

"What, Jehanne?" Poulengy asked. "What did you say?"

"The wind," she answered. Her consciousness returned to the men clustered around her. It was not raining any more. "The wind's going to change. Now."

At that a mighty gust swept across them. Its touch was cool, reassuring. Far above their heads the iron gray clouds began to move in the opposite direction.

There was an audible gasp of astonishment from the men. Their tongues froze into stillness as the worthy captains of France looked in wonder from the sky to her. Pasquerel crossed himself. So did de Loré. Metz put a sturdy hand on Jehanne's shoulder and beamed at her solemn, dirty face.

"Well, now," de Gaucourt harrumphed, half in denial of what he had witnessed, "we all have work to do. Those barges will be here soon, and we'll have to get them loaded. Everybody back to work!" he shouted to the small crowd that had gathered about the boat.

The men dispersed except for Jehanne's friends and brothers, and La Hire, who stood grinning gap-toothed at her in frank, awed admiration. The Bastard was likewise impressed, to judge by his widened eyes and the small O that his mouth had become.

"Well, Jehanne, it seems that Heaven is indeed on your side," he said softly.

"On *our* side," she corrected him. Although still mildly irked that she had not been consulted, she felt somewhat vindicated. Yet she remained disappointed with his unnecessary strategy.

"Come with me, tonight," he urged, "back across the river to Orléans. The people are most anxious to see you."

"What about the army?"

"They will return to Blois, of course, to await further instructions and to gather reinforcements."

"And not to fight? Not to lift the siege?"

The Bastard made no reply but looked at her with benign patience.

"Then I shall return to Blois with them," she said.

"What?" the men chorused.

"Jehanne, you've come all this way," Metz reminded her. "Why would you want to leave now?"

"I will not be separated from the army." She frowned stubbornly. "If I am not with them, they might fall back into sin, and then that would be on my head."

"Please, Jehanne, come with me into the city where you can rest," the Bastard pleaded, his eyes registering concern for her. "The army will be safe without you, and the people of Orléans need to see you; it would greatly lift their spirits."

She gave him an even look. "If I go with you, will you promise that the army will return to raise the siege?"

"I swear to you by Our Lady," he said seriously, "that the army will return to battle the English after gathering its reinforcements. I shall pass that word to the commanders."

"Just a minute, Bastard," La Hire intruded in his gruff, raspy voice. "Jehanne doesn't want to leave the army, and you can bet your ba—, your head that they surely don't want her to go to Orléans without them. They have a great affection for her, and besides, they came here to fight, same as she did, same as I did!"

"I understand that, La Hire, but the army must be reinforced before we attempt an assault." The Bastard's normally congenial eyes bore into the captain's as he wielded his authority. He raised his right hand. "I pledge before you all that the army shall return from Blois within three days and will engage the enemy in his *bastilles*. That is my word."

"But what about the men? Who will keep them from sin?"

"I will, Jehanne." Brother Pasquerel stood behind and to her right. He had been so quiet that she forgot he was there.

She was glad to see his gentle countenance, and she smiled in return. "Thank you, Brother. You will make them attend Mass, and keep the women away from them?"

"Yes, I promise."

"I promise as well, Jehanne," said d'Aulon.

She smiled and clapped him on the shoulder. "Thanks. I know that you will keep them in line."

"Well, we're not going," Pierre rebelled, drawing his brows into a straight line across his nose. "Jehan and I promised Maman that we wouldn't leave you."

"That's right, Jhanette, we're not going," echoed Jehan.

"Very well." She frowned, bothered by his big-brother watchfulness and use of her old name. She would have to speak to both of them about how they addressed her in public. She turned to the Bastard. "I'll want my pages and my heralds with me as well. I have a message to deliver to the English."

"Of course." He smiled, relieved. "Anything you want."

"We'll return with the army," said Poulengy, meaning himself and Metz. "Are you sure?"

He nodded, and Metz said with his usual good humor, "Somebody's got to help d'Aulon keep order." He put a playful arm around d'Aulon's neck and the shy man beamed, pleased with the camaraderie.

"All right." She nodded. Metz and Poulengy would not lie to her, and if the captains refused to return with the army, her friends would let her know about it right away. So although she would miss them and would fret for their safety, it was good that they were going.

Two hours later, as the loaded barges began to drift back toward Orléans, Jehanne and her reduced company rode across the river in the Bastard's boat. Four other craft filled with armed men flanked their passage. From their place on the river, they witnessed the fiery skirmish occurring at St.-Loup and could hear the distant shouts of men and the heavy pulse of cannon from both sides. The closer they drew to land, the stronger the acrid smell of cannon smoke became. They passed St.-Loup still in the middle of the Loire, and made their way upriver to the east.

When they reached Chécy on the opposite shore, some three leagues east of Orléans, they disembarked and La Hire took the soldiers back across the river to the army. The Bastard suggested that the rest of them spend the night in the village of Reuilly, at the home of his friend, Guy de Cailly. Too tired to argue any more and well aware of the fighting around St.-Loup, Jehanne agreed. It had been a long day, full of exhausting hindrances, and she knew she would need her strength for whatever came tomorrow. She had thought all day of resting in a good bed. Tonight she would do so.

A mighty crash of thunder shook the house near dawn. Jehanne struggled to waken, but curiosity lost out to her weary body and she tumbled back into a deep place. She was aware in passing of the warmth of Madame de Cailly as the older woman shifted to the edge of the bed, then was gone. Somewhere far away a window closed in her mind and the droning sound of rainfall became fainter. Then the heavy presence was next to her once more, its weight bending the mattress. But Jehanne had gone back to where she was before the heavens tried to rouse her.

The steed she rode was a great charger that was sometimes black but then changed to white, and back again. Whatever the color, his coat unfailingly shone with a luster that sparkled in minuscule pricks of light. He snorted and shook his head, and when he reared, she fused with him so that rider and mount were one.

Vitality rippled through the powerful flanks as he pranced with confidence toward his destiny.

They turned and cantered down an open road which ran through a fair green meadow. A day in Heaven would look like this, she thought. The sun drenched the landscape and coated the grass and flowers with a preternatural brilliance. Their colors, more dazzlingly green and red and yellow than any she had ever seen, hurt her eyes to look at them. When they trotted under a tree, she noticed the sweet songs of robins and larks coming from the boughs above her head. Their melodies filled her spirit with well-being. She smiled, knowing that everything was favorable in this beautiful land.

From out of nowhere an audience of happy people emerged to cheer Jehanne on her way. She caught without effort the bouquets they threw to her, so many that after a time she felt a mild worry that she might drop them into the dust.

Her concern became anxiety when the people began to urge her to juggle them. She looked aghast at the hundreds of bunched flowers.

"But I don't know how to juggle," she protested, "I never learned!"

They began to exhort her with clapping hands. "Juggle them, juggle them, juggle them—"

She looked in dismay at the crowd, and begged them to release her from the assignment. They did not appear to have heard her. They became more insistent and their faces changed, twisting into distorted leers. They chanted the impossible order so loudly that her pleas were drowned out.

She knew she had no choice, so she threw the flowers into the air. Most slipped through her desperately grasping fingers and fell onto the ground, where they were trampled underfoot by her horse. The only thing she was able to hold on to was a single red rose.

The crowd muttered angrily despite her trying to tell them, But look, I still have this rose, I caught it and it is the most beautiful of them all.

They would not listen to her. Picking up the rocks that the flowers had become, they began to pelt her with them. Her mount neighed in terror and reared upon his hind legs. She spurred him away, fearful for their safety. He galloped down the road and through a field that grew ever darker with each passing step.

All of a sudden, she saw that they were no longer on a road at all. As they raced across the land that stretched ahead, increasingly forbidding, she found herself engulfed in a dreadful, choking mist as malignant as smoke. She could not see where she was going, nor was she able to make her horse turn around, no matter how hard she pulled on the reins. She knew without doubt that he would take her to the edge of death that lay ahead.

She awoke very frightened yet not entirely conscious. Madame de Cailly's cozy shape was gone, but the bed was still warm where she had lain.

It had only been a dream, she told herself. Half-asleep, her heart nonetheless thumped with terror. Jehanne turned over and smacked her pillow. Fright drifted away from her and she floated down into herself.

A silver orb appeared and as she watched, it swirled within itself and took on the shape of Michel's reassuring features. All the love that had ever existed smiled through his awful essence and she was home where she belonged.

You are God's special one, who was born for glory on earth and in Heaven.

He had said that before, long ago, and at the time it had filled her with confusion. But now it did not. She was filled with glory.

You do not understand us. You are our instrument on whom we play for the Glory of God.

The Glory of God

The only Glory that can ever endure.

The Glory of God.

With her assent, he released her and she plunged, featherlike, into nothingness.

When her mind began to stir in her body, she became aware of the comfortable bed and the feel of the dry, clean sheets. She ran a hand across her pillow and felt the cloth beneath its warmth. She opened her eyes and looked at the closed window. It was still raining very hard. Thunder pounded faintly, far away. Jehanne stretched her arms over her head and yawned. She sat up, wondering what time it was.

There was much to do today. After breakfast she would send her letter to the English to give them a gallant warning of her presence and of her intention to drive them away from Orléans unless they surrendered. And when the army returned, she would attack the enemies of France if they did not obey her command. She would lift the siege as her Counsel had directed.

She threw back the blankets and rolled out of bed. Her clothes were where she had left them last night, piled carelessly upon the trunk at the foot of the bed. As she picked up the hose and started dragging them over her legs, a tiny thrill darted up her spine.

Orléans was practically within hailing distance of this place. Soon it would all be over.

CHAPTER SEVEN

The Maid of Orléans

April 29–May 7, 1429

The troop moved at a cautious pace through the soggy, wooded terrain and the night. All around them the clutch of overhanging trees dripped darkness and exhaled a woodsy odor pregnant with decay. Every now and then branches burdened with rain slapped unwary faces, startling them into wide-awake vigilance. The horses, attuned like their masters to every sound, moved with ears pricked up and snorted anxious vapors from their broad noses. No one spoke. Near every sword, a hand was on guard against perils skulking just out of sight within the thickets, stalking them on invisible feet. Here in moonless, unfamiliar territory a surprise attack was wholly possible, even likely, for somewhere through the dense foliage Orléans, and the enemy, waited for them on the Loire, and all knew that the land was probably teeming with *goddons*.

Jehanne rode at the front of the troop with the Bastard on her left. Dead ahead of her Minguet's small, dim form perched in childlike expectation upon the horse that was too big for him. In his right hand he held her standard, furled now and encased in its sheath to protect it from the rain. Occasionally, he turned his head to gape at the glistening bushes, and although Jehanne could not see the face beneath the helmet, his erect posture showed that he was as attentive to the night sounds as she was. Her brothers were somewhere to the rear. Even though she did not turn to look, it gave her comfort to know that they were there.

The Bastard had decided not to travel by boat to enter Orléans from Reuilly after all. It would be wiser, he said, to elude the English altogether by making a wide circle around St.-Loup through the northern forest, for given the vagaries of the prevailing winds and the inconstancy of the Loire at this time of year, if they went by boat they could be washed ashore onto one of the more-or-less-permanent islands in the river. That made the land route less risky, he explained to Jehanne. He could not chance their falling into enemy hands. He especially did not want to hazard anything happening to her.

She disliked the idea of sneaking into Orléans. Her heart shouted that it was dishonorable, that they should enter the city from the Chécy road in bold defiance of the English. She had expressed her disagreement in strong terms, and it was only after a lengthy and patient explanation from him that she gave in, at first in a spirit of resistance.

But as she rode next to him now, she had to admit that in this instance his stratagem was right. It would not do to encounter the treacherous *goddons* in this damp darkness, for they had no honor, no sense of chivalry, and would perhaps spring a trap for which God's army was unprepared. She had heard that that was one of their favorite tactics. So she discarded her regret for this necessary, inglorious stealth and gave herself permission to tingle in expectation of what this night would bring.

By this time the forest was not as dense as it had been. In the fragment of sky above their heads a faint, unnatural hue glowed within the clouds, burning brighter toward the south where its strongest light could be seen through and just above the thin copse of beeches. The thought that the forest must be on fire drifted into Jehanne's head, but when she noticed no smell of smoke it floated out again.

The woods parted ahead of the column and they came upon a small clearing. Before Jehanne had an opportunity to enjoy the liberation into open space, they were once again entering the all-embracing press of trees.

Now the light in the heavens floated over the treeline, enticing the silent patrol to come closer, closer, soon surrounding them in a rose pink radiance that glistened upon the treetrunks in their path. It was easy to see the shiny armor and the small puffs of breath emitting from the mouths of men and horses. The small detachment gleamed with the light of impending victory, and Jehanne's pulse began to race as they drew nearer to the source.

Without warning the walls of Orléans emerged through the trees. It shone golden beyond the thinning forest, an enormous stone vision bathed in the light of hundreds of torches ascending from within its walls. There came from it a steadfast humming sound like that around a great beehive. As the soldiers trotted toward the city, the sound became recognizable as the murmur of thousands of voices.

The forest abruptly ended, and the party disconnected from its darkened embrace. Blinking, they rode into the light pouring through the Porte de Bourgogne. Jehanne held her hand in front of her face to avert the unexpected brightness. Minguet's horse took a few aimless steps as the boy bowed his head and rubbed his own assaulted eyes.

A squad of knights sat ahorse before the great latticed portcullis. Now raised, its teeth yawned at the top of the archway through which the lights from Orléans washed over the escort's steel in particles of fine rain, making them almost painful to behold. They shifted to look in Jehanne's direction; shadows flitted through the half-light within their open visors. Four of them held the blue and red banners of Charles d'Orléans, made limp by long exposure to the night's moist air. Their horses pawed the hard-packed mud impatiently, as though they had been there for quite a while, waiting.

The Bastard waved to them in salutation, and recognizing him, they lowered their swords. Jehanne removed her helmet and lashed it to her saddle. There was no longer any reason to fear an attack. Besides, she wanted the people of Orléans to see her.

Minguet quickly stripped the sheath from Jehanne's standard and unfurled it. He then moved into position in front of her, making sure over his shoulder that he gave her enough room to maneuver her own mount. Without a word, the soldiers melted into an advance guard before their comrades and escorted them to the gate.

Jehanne was astride a magnificent white horse the lord of Orléans had given her. Thick plates of steel protected his rump, chest, and face, while his mane was covered by a shimmering cascade of chainmail. It did not matter that both Jehanne and her horse were by now splattered with forest mud; together they were a vision of triumphant virtue in their rain-glistened armor. As she watched the portcullis swallow the escort ahead of her, she thought that she was ready for anything. But the crowds in Tours had been trifling compared to the scene that now awaited them.

The instant Jehanne passed under the high archway, the hum of humanity broke out into a tremendous cheer that took her breath away like a punch in the stomach. An incoherent multitude rushed at her wielding that ear-exploding yell and all its hopes for liberation.

She was suddenly at a virtual standstill, hemmed in on all sides, enclosed suffocatingly within a quicksand of yelling, overjoyed faces. Their heat smelled of wine and old perfume and neglected hygiene of every sort, so mixed together that they congealed into a single rank, overpowering odor. Jehanne sucked in her breath and waved at them. She could feel the emotions of every one. The force of their souls assailed her with a desperate faith, frightening in its terrible extremity. They would not allow her to fail them. She was their last hope. They would yell her to victory through the night and for as long after that as it took for God to deliver them.

Overtaken by their expectations, Jehanne felt herself reel slightly in the saddle. Her hands itched to untie the straps holding the *basinet* in place. With her helmet on again she would have time to collect herself while she shut out the pandemonium.

The wish was stillborn. Its fulfillment would be rude when they had waited for her so long, and she could not bring herself to wound these expectant masses. She would just have to see this procession through to the end.

Resistance to sin loosened the tightness in her stomach, and the Power sparked at the base of her spine. Serpentlike, its radiance climbed toward her head, eating through the dying vestiges of weakness. Her posture became more erect and she lifted her chin. When the Bastard nudged his mount to a walk with a gracious smile at his people, Jehanne imitated him and coaxed hers forward, careful not to step on anyone but determined to get through this.

The chant of "Jehanne the Maid!" was pounding through her head. The people had abandoned restraint and were screaming their jubilation as loudly as they could, waving hats and kerchiefs above their heads. Random atonal trumpet blasts screeched in competition with the voices. The music, the ecstatic faces, the compelling hope were more than she could resist, and with a smile she lifted a hand to acknowledge their rapture.

There were so *many* of them here! Shopkeepers and craftsmen, matrons and monks, children and graybeards, they engorged the street in the colorful gowns and mantles that were their best clothes. Splashes of vivid silks and coarse linens flamed amidst the drab shades of beggars as a common humanity, forgetful this night of class, pressed forward and craned its neck for a glimpse of Jehanne. People lifted children upon their shoulders that they might see her and remember. Packed eight and ten deep along the street and clogging the riders' path, people held aloft hundreds of torches to light their way, making everything shine as though coated in gold dust. From windows high above the street, the flag of Orléans flew next to the lilies of France. Members of the garrison were there in sword-scarred leather, hollow-eyed from sleeplessness and the prolonged deadlock of siege, all of them hungry for victory and waving *guisarmes* and maces in the air. Behind their ranks, windows in every half-timbered building were stuffed with eager, shouting people who rained damp flowers upon the procession and toasted Jehanne with wine, everyone ecstatic at the sight of the miraculous Maid who had come to rescue them from the English.

Their graceful enthusiasm made her feel that she could fly and she began to quiver with an elation nearly equal to theirs. She waved up at them gaily. A young girl, no older than eleven, shot out of the crowd and snatched a lilac from the deeply rutted mud, and with a smile at Jehanne, stuck the stem through the bridle of her horse just below the ear. Her hand caressed Jehanne's steel-covered leg and then she was gone, enveloped within the masses.

The entire population, it seemed, followed her company through the city as though bewitched by the sight of her. They pressed forward to touch her, to stroke her horse's mirrored flanks. Appalled, she watched helplessly as they kissed her boots and the end of her *huque*. Townsfolk called to her from every direction, pleading for her prayers. Old women wept with joy as though they gazed upon the face of God. Mothers, husbands, even small children seemed transported to another realm, forgetful that the siege had not yet been lifted.

All of a sudden, the silken fringe of Jehanne's standard caught fire from a too-near torch. Minguet was looking away and did not notice the tiny flame eating through the virginal linen.

Jehanne's brain screamed an alarm. She immediately spurred her horse ahead.

People staggered backward out of her way. A middle-aged woman fell into the arms of a soldier. Careful not to trample anyone, Jehanne deftly turned the animal and crushed the flame between her gauntlets. To her relief, the torch had done little damage.

A great "Ahh" sighed from the crowd, followed a moment later by a cheer that hurt her ears, so loud that Jehanne wondered if the English heard it. The people applauded her as they would an acrobat who had just performed a feat requiring the greatest possible skill. Grinning broadly, she accepted their approval with a hearty wave.

The entranced population of Orléans accompanied her across the entire city, east to west, from the Porte de Bourgogne to the densely fortified Porte Regnard facing the English *bastilles*. The tumult of voices and musical instruments was so great that when this journey eventually ended, Jehanne's ears would thump for hours afterward.

Sir William Glasdale was in the middle of a dream. He knew himself to be at Portsmouth, standing at the edge of the seashore. Across the tossing, white-capped Channel in the direction of Harfleur, a thick bank of dark clouds was rolling in from France. Flashes of light pulsed like cannonades upon the horizon. Then came the sound.

It was as though God had clapped His mighty hands together. The terrific boom rattled his teeth, and, quaking with a fear that resounded to the depths of his soul, Glasdale watched the cloudbank spread with an alarming swiftness across the sky, coming directly toward him, tumbling like a titanic stone down a pre-ordained slope. Ragged lightning shot from the blackness overhead, followed in the next instant by another crash of thunder, this one louder and more menacing than the first. His feet seemed embedded in the wet sand and when he tried to lift them, he was unable to move.

Horrified, he watched the great swirling ocean rise like a grinning monster released from the deepest pit of Hell until it was surely more than a hundred feet high. It started to bear down upon him with relentless speed, the ghastly, drab wall of water rushing straight at him—

He jerked awake.

In his fright he had kicked off the blanket he had wrapped around himself when he first lay down upon the floor to catch some sleep. It lay next to him, twisted and abandoned. His hands grasped the wooden planks beneath him to stop his downward spin. He felt like sobbing with gratitude.

He gasped, panting. Everything is well, he told himself as his breathing slowed down and began to resume its normal pattern. It was only a nightmare, that's all. He was safe in his room within the tower nearest the riverbank. But he could still hear that roar of thunder from his dream.

He rolled over onto his side and looked toward the stone chink of a window. Sir William de Moleyns was turned in profile, staring at the walls of Orléans across the river. His smooth-shaven face, with that blunt nose that looked as though someone had smashed it in, was lit by an orange glow and his hair seemed afire. The rest of him was in the half-shadows.

He turned toward Glasdale, cleaving his face into dark and light. Something like a smile twitched his mouth. "Are you all right? You were having quite a dream, Will."

Glasdale nodded, trying to shake the cobwebs from his mind. "Quite a dream," he murmured. It was a dream that had not yet ended. There was still that constant drone of thunder.

He heaved his stocky frame to a standing position and walked on unsteady feet to the window. Orléans was brighter than he had ever seen it, and in fact appeared to be on fire. A great conflagration of golden light originating from within those battlements soared into the night sky, illuminating rooftops and church spires.

The city thundered in the glow of its immolation, and where it was reflected, even the Loire seemed ablaze.

Glasdale suddenly understood. His nightmare really had ended, and that sound was not thunder. It was the roar of thousands of human voices, giddy with joy.

"What the devil is that bloody racket?" he asked, displeasure compensating for the spasms of fear that still trembled in his bandy legs.

De Moleyns leaned his elbow upon the sill and gazed toward the city. "I'm not certain," he admitted, without looking at his commander. "But I think it must be the girl the Armagnacs brought with the supply train. Somehow, the Bastard must have managed to sneak her into the city."

"Why do you think that's what it is?"

The knight shrugged. "What else would make them go wild like that? They haven't much else to give them hope now, what with the so-called Dauphin's army having dumped their supplies and then fled back to Blois. They all think that the cowmaid has brought some kind of miracle with her." He laughed woodenly, almost against his will, as it seemed. "Poor bastards! I almost feel sorry for them. They were chanting something a little while ago, but I couldn't hear what it was. A prayer, perhaps."

"Well, they can pray all they like, and it won't help them a bit." Glasdale's smile was grim. "Poor buggers, indeed. The fools are too daft to see that God would not send a whore to do His bidding and that that girl is a damned sorceress besides. Their bad fortune, not knowing that God is for England and St. George."

He shrugged, actually not giving a bag of shit what consequence the Orléanais faced in the next world as a result of their present bad faith. If those frog-eaters burned in Hell, it was no concern of his. The only important thing was his own situation. It was vital that he hold on militarily until his exhausted men were relieved. It was almost too late; there was an ending coming, of that he was quite certain, and he trembled at the prospect.

"We shall force them to submit in the end," he recited, with an unwitting glance across the Loire.

"Do you really think so?" A subtle smile curved de Moleyns' lips, and his eyes twinkled sardonically.

Glasdale knew that the knight saw through his halfhearted bluster. He could not deceive this man with whom he had fought in countless campaigns for more than five years. Even so, de Moleyns had no inkling just how bad things really were, otherwise he would not be smiling.

"Perhaps." Glasdale's mood tumbled into reality. "I don't know; I doubt it." He sighed through his nose, blowing out a thin stream of mucus. "You know how stubborn these bleeding French are, and now that they've gotten fresh provisions, they're likely to hold on until their supplies run out again, which could mean months more of this. At least they haven't been reinforced, thank God."

"And what of us? What was in my lord Bedford's response to Talbot's request for reinforcements from Paris? You still haven't told me."

Glasdale turned his back to the window and the roar of French merriment. "He agreed that we need reinforcements."

He hesitated. De Moleyns was a man of discretion, but it always seemed that once a secret was uttered, it spread like the wind despite its guardian's caution. How many more men would desert once word got out that they had to hold this city on their own?

"And?" The knight wrinkled his flattened nose impatiently.

The commander of the Tourelles had no choice but to answer. Deserters be damned, the truth was the truth.

"He says that he has no men to send us." Glasdale gave his boot an absent kick, aimed at an empty spot on the floor. "It seems that he needs every man to hold the other Loire towns. His brother Gloucester is trying to raise the money to send us more from England." He sighed again. "That is the proper story, as written by the duke. But the courier who brought his letter told me that hearsay is that the cardinal is delaying an audience with my lord Gloucester and refuses to release the necessary silver."

"Goddammit!" De Moleyns crashed his fist against the windowsill.

"Indeed," his friend commented wryly. "We are left to dangle in the wind."

His entanglement was almost funny when one considered the idiotic dance occurring at this very moment in the little king's court. Having seen their intrigues up close, he found it tragically predictable and thus unsurprising. Nevertheless, the stark infirmities of the royal house were sharper than ever when seen from France.

It really was not at all amusing. What it meant was that England's disheartened manhood in the field was bleeding to death while the lords played games with one another, each faction maneuvering and amassing their power behind Henry VI, at seven too young to understand any of it.

No longer caring to pretend, he was taken by a righteous anger aimed at the true source of his plight.

"By the blood of Christ, I hate politics! And I hate politicians even more. God damn them all to Hell! How in blue blazes do they expect us to hold on here without sufficient forces to carry on? If that son of a bitch Burgundy hadn't furled his colors for God-only-knows-what reason, we'd still have his detachments here with us, and we wouldn't be in this predicament!"

His friend's dismay settled into a resigned frown. "Well, he did and we are."

"That we are, lad."

The men were silent for a moment. What else was there to say?

Glasdale turned around again. The tumult across the river showed no sign of diminishing. Those God-cursed French would probably keep this up all night, and he and his men would be robbed of much needed rest. And there was not a single bloody thing he could do about it.

"Do we still have a priest with us?" he asked de Moleyns. "Or have they all deserted along with the rest of those miserable traitors?" His voice growled with the bitterness of a man who felt power he could no longer hold slipping away from him.

His subordinate nodded. "Brother Thomas the Franciscan is still here. Last I saw of him, he was downstairs giving Last Rites to an archer with an infected ratbite."

"Well, fetch him. Tell him to say a Mass, right here, tonight, and he is to dedicate it to Our Lady. God knows, we need her help. Go on." He frowned when de Moleyns did not move. "Hurry!"

The knight left him. His footsteps pounded all the way downstairs.

Glasdale looked up at the pinkish-gray mass of clouds, then at the lustrous jewel that was Orléans. He could not remember ever having been so frightened. The city's very foreignness and beauty mocked him, and he felt as much at its mercy as though he were an infant abandoned in an alley.

More than half of his men were ill, stricken with a fever that seeped up from the river's foul mud. It did not help that the bulk of their provisions consisted of leather-hard dried beef and moldy flour crawling with weevils. But at least they were right here on the river and could still catch fish, a boon not open to the other besiegers. According to the couriers who scuttled back and forth between him and Talbot, conditions were actually worse in the other forts. The doctors had their hands full, what with the sick and those poor bastards wounded in the fighting. As disgusting as it was, Glasdale was thankful for the food, and especially for the arms, that Bedford's men still managed to bring in from Paris.

But, oh, what he would not give to wake up one fine morning to see a battalion of stout Welsh bowmen and men-at-arms marching toward the city, fresh from the training fields of Kent and Surrey!

He was not by nature a praying man, but he prayed now. He beseeched Heaven with every scrap of desperation in his soul.

Oh, God, do not let us perish in this place! Send us an army as stouthearted as the one You once gave King Harry, for all our sakes.

"You're going where?" Jehanne could scarcely believe what the Bastard had said.

"I am going to Blois to fetch the army," he repeated in a firm, masterful tone. Daylight from an open window glinted auburn in his hair and shone through his eyes, making them look like jewels. He had not shaved this morning, and dark stubble peppered his square chin. "I feel that it is important that I attend the gathering of reinforcements and bring them here as quickly as possible."

They were in a council room in the Bastard's house, converted from a parlor at the outset of the siege and used ever since as headquarters. It was here that the joint command planned the city's defenses, for although the Bastard ruled Orléans, it was his custom to seek the counsel of the captains in military matters. This morning he was standing over the large table where he sometimes took his meals, or ignored them altogether when necessity demanded unceasing labor and no food. A map of the city was spread before him, illuminated both by natural light and by the candle which dripped heavy streams of wax down its holder. Shoved out of the way to make room for the map, last night's half-eaten supper sat on a tray, covered by a napkin. Two or three flies buzzed around it.

In the room with them were the sieur de Gamaches, a Scottish captain named John Campbell, and three other officers of the garrison. The men were staring at Jehanne, and she could feel their intolerance crawling upon her skin. Campbell, bearded and foreign-looking with the gray and black tartan slung across his shoulder, deplored her being there at all. Actually, none of them thought she belonged in their company. Even the Bastard considered her in the way. She wanted to weep with exasperation because they did not know or understand the cause of her outrage.

"But we could attack the English today!" she cried. "After last night, the garrison and the people are eager for an assault, and after I send my summons to Talbot we can drive them away!"

"We need the army for an absolute victory, Jehanne," the Bastard said with a patient smile. "If we try to attack the English with only the garrison, we could suffer many losses to no avail. We might even give them the opportunity to breach our walls." He sounded like a parent explaining something complex to a small child.

"But the King of Heaven is on our side," she protested, vexed by his condescension and the smiles of the other captains. "I know we could win! If we wait for the army's return, the *goddons* might get reinforcements of their own, and then where will we be? Right back at the beginning, that's where!"

The sieur de Gamaches' fierce blue eyes regarded Jehanne with aristocratic disdain. An officer of the garrison, he was one of the Bastard's oldest friends, tall, strongly built, and passably good-looking, his appearance marred by a long hooked nose that had been broken in battle by an English mace. He snorted ridicule through it now.

"Since our spies report no movement on the part of the English toward Orléans, that is not likely to happen. The Bastard is right when he says that we need further reinforcements."

He did not understand; none of them did. She could see that in their stony faces. They thought that they had time without limit, and perhaps they did. But God had given her only a year. A year in which to raise the siege, have Charles crowned at Reims, take Paris, banish the English from the kingdom, and rescue Charles d'Orléans from the Tower of London. Each day was precious and not to be squandered. Already the Dauphin had nibbled away at her time with his determination that she be tested first, and there was still so much to do!

"In God's name," she responded, "the garrison is ready to fight now, and the people are behind them. If we hesitate, we may lose our chance!"

"If we fight now, when we are ill-prepared, we will lose men unnecessarily!" the seigneur shouted back at her.

The Bastard's forehead creased in a thoughtful frown. Jehanne could see that he was torn between a wish to appease his friend and the more trying need to control the young visionary who stood before him with her fists clenched combatively. "What exactly would you suggest we do, Jehanne?"

She had no chance to respond.

"Since you pay more attention to the advice of a little magpie of low birth than to a knight such as myself, I will say nothing more." Gamaches flung a baleful glower at Jehanne.

He snatched his standard from his startled squire and began to furl it. "Henceforth, I am lowering my banner and no longer wish to be anything more than a simple squire," Gamaches said. "When the proper time and the place come, I'll do my duty and let my sword speak for me as the king and my honor demand. I prefer to have a nobleman as my master rather than a hussy who may once have been God knows what!" He thrust his banner toward the Bastard, who put up his hands in refusal.

"Hussy, am I?" Jehanne shouted, furious at the insults to her virtue and her family. "Lowborn I may be, but God has entrusted me with the sacred task of driving the *goddons* from the kingdom, since none of you 'noble knights' has been able to do it!"

"We noble knights have been in this war since you were in swaddling, you little baggage, and I can assure you that defeating the English is not as easy as it seems to you, who have no experience in war and no sense of strategy!" His face was very close to Jehanne's; his breath burned her nose with onion and wine.

For one calamitous moment it appeared that he might strike her, or her him.

"Please, friends, let us not fight among ourselves!" the Bastard intervened. "If we are divided, we'll become easy targets for the English and they will surely defeat us. Together, we can save this city."

John Campbell quickly stepped forward and put his arm across Gamaches' shoulder. "The Bastard speaks like a wise man," he said in his badly accented French. "We should save our hatreds for our common enemy."

Assent babbled from the other captains. Constrained by his equals, Gamaches loosened his stance, though he continued to glare at Jehanne.

"Come, Gamaches, you and the Maid should conclude your quarrel," the Bastard said with a smooth smile. "Kiss one another on the cheek in true Christian charity. We are all on the same side here."

Gamaches frowned at his friend in reply and made no move to do as the Bastard had requested.

"Please, Gamaches."

The nobleman hesitated, then said, "Very well." He bent forward and gave Jehanne a swift peck on the cheek. She returned the gesture with a reluctance as plain as his.

The Bastard sighed with relief. "And now, my friends, please leave me alone with Jehanne. I have a most urgent need to speak to her in private."

The men began to file out of the room. Gamaches nodded to the Bastard but did not even glance at Jehanne as he closed the door behind him.

When they were alone, the Bastard said to her gently, "Really, Jehanne, you must be careful not to offend the officers. I know you are impatient to have this matter concluded"—he went on when she opened her mouth to protest—"but you must not discredit their wisdom. Gamaches was correct in saying that they have long years of seasoning that you do not."

"And where has their seasoning gotten them? We are still at war and the *goddons* are still in France. They are all fools!" she stated bluntly.

"That they are not. They are merely cautious, as I am."

She made a contemptuous face in reply.

"Please try to understand my obligation," the Bastard entreated. "My brother gave me command of this city, and I must do what I think is best for it. I want to lift the siege as badly as you do, perhaps even more, but I want to make certain that it is done without an unnecessary loss of life. When I return from Blois with the army, our position will be much stronger than it is now, and our chances of winning will be greater than they are at present. I am keeping my promise to you. I will order the army to attack when it arrives."

She gave him a sudden sharp look. "Very well. Why do *you* have to go to Blois? The army will return anyway, they gave their word. We need you here."

A slow smile brought forth the dimples in his handsome face. "I must go because I want to raise the siege, just as you do. I know that the army promised to return, and many of them surely will, but there are some among them who need prodding, otherwise they lose their forbearance. I said I want to raise the siege." He put his hands on her shoulders and smiled deeply into her eyes. "We can only do that if we have a large enough complement to *defeat* the English, not just wound them a little. That solitary event will force them to leave Orléans. And that is why I must go to Blois. No one else has enough authority to bully those who are irresolute into returning, for I shall do it in my brother's name."

She knew he was right. The stubborn frown was there to defend her pride and to hide her fear of time running out. "We already have the Army of God with us. His Power is mightier than any numbers the English could throw against us."

" 'If the soldiers fight, God will give us the victory.' " He smiled. "Did you not say something to that effect to a churchman at Poitiers?"

Her eyes widened in astonishment. "How do you know about that?"

"The king sent me a copy of their report," the Bastard answered, amused by her surprise. "Don't you know that I have been following your venture since you went to Chinon? It was I who advised my cousin Charles to send you here."

"I did not know that," she mumbled.

"Oh, yes." He grinned. "I have believed since I first heard about you that you are exactly what you claim to be: God's emissary. But faith alone is not enough to accomplish what you have been charged to do. You must balance your faith with good sense."

"But God has told me that I have only a year and a little more to do my Work!" she exploded, no longer able to hold the truth in her heart. She was close to tears now, and genuinely afraid. "Every day that is wasted is time lost. If we dilly-dally and become mired in our choices, *my* time will run out and I will fail to do God's will! Please, Bastard, let us attack without further delay, after I send my letter to the *goddons*."

He shook his head. "I am going to Blois to muster the army. La Hire shall command while I am gone. And in my absence, you are to do nothing to worsen the situation," he ordered decisively, tired of arguing with her. A frown replaced his genial dimples. "Do you understand me?"

He sounded like her father, she thought. She felt her anger return. "My first duty is to God. I will do as *He* commands, not you!" she answered. Turning on her heel, she marched from the room and out into the street without a backward look.

Her foot was hardly out the door when she was mobbed by the Orléanais, whom she had forgotten were there in the street, waiting for her with their mad love. Their mood was only a little less spirited than it was last night. They continued to shout for victory and God's blessing; they begged for her prayers; they called her *L'Angélique*, which made her cringe. They were crammed around her horse, and she had to shove her way through them to reach the mob's center where Raymond stood, smiling broadly and holding her animal's reins along with those of his own. Jehanne clambered up into the saddle and as she took the reins from the young man, she waved to them with an uncertain smile. Spellbound, they followed her as they ceaselessly had since she entered Orléans the night before. It took a long time for her to return to the lodgings the Bastard had arranged for her.

Her temporary home in Orléans was the house of Jacques Boucher, treasurer to Charles d'Orléans. He, his wife Françoise, and their eight-year-old daughter Charlotte lived in a spacious domicile within hailing distance of the Porte Regnard on the westernmost edge of the city. Modest in style when seen from the street, the house was not unlike the other timber-and-plaster buildings in the area. But once inside, the visitor found its walls hung with beautiful tapestries and its rooms decorated with fine oaken furniture crafted in Spain. A staff of servants ran the household as befitted the expectations and position of a great man.

Jacques Boucher was in his fifties, a hearty, pot-bellied fellow much given to laughter and the delights of the table. His wife, twenty years younger than he, had almond-shaped eyes in an oval face, and a small mouth, traits that she had passed on to Charlotte. The little girl was so excited to have Jehanne sharing her room that last night she had chattered all the way up the stairs. Her prattling continued nonstop while they undressed for bed, and then she tossed restlessly in her sleep, unwittingly keeping her illustrious guest awake until very late. As a result, Jehanne slept later than she had intended and arrived at the Bastard's house after the council had begun, feeling a little bleary-eyed.

But she was fully awake now, thanks to her contretemps with the Bastard and his captains. She was still seething with indignation when she sprang from her horse and flung the reins to Raymond, who in turn passed them to Monsieur Boucher's stableman. The page was right behind her as she swept through the crowd and bolted into her lodgings.

How civilized they all looked sitting there on benches before the parlor's cozy fireplace, their laps spread with napkins, dainty pastries in their hands. Madame Boucher was deep in a trivial conversation with Jehan and Pierre, all about the rivalry between Tours and Orléans to determine which would be the trading center of the Loire. Gentlemen that they were, the heralds inclined their heads politely while they listened to their hostess' misinformed chitchat about the glories of Orléans and its professed supremacy over Tours. Charlotte had heard it all before; uninterested in armorers and life anywhere but in Orléans, she was showing Minguet her doll.

They looked up at Jehanne's entrance wearing a common bland smile. Their calm unconcern was irritating after the ordeal she had been forced to suffer, alone, this morning. While they had spent their time eating little cakes and chatting about absolutely nothing, she was wrangling with powerful men over life-and-

197

death issues and the fate of the kingdom. It was unfair that they were not as distressed about lifting the siege as she was and not in the least enraged at the delays. It was all she could do to address them without conspicuous anger.

She urged her mouth into a pleasant smile. "Good morning, Madame. Would you please excuse my brothers? I have need of them in council."

"Oh?" Françoise Boucher looked from Jehanne to the young men and back again, distinctly unwilling to release her audience. "Of course, Jehanne," she replied, her own smile as false as her guest's.

"Thank you."

To her stupefaction, none of Jehanne's party moved. Pierre took another bite of cake, then licked his fingers as though his sister were not even in the room. Minguet and Charlotte were whispering together and giggling.

"*Now!*" she thundered, her wrath finally unrestrained.

Everyone gaped at her. Pierre's next bite of cake hung suspended between his napkin and his mouth. Minguet's blue eyes were as large as the moon. Embarrassed by her outburst, Guyenne creased his lips and cast his eyes down to the floor.

Jehanne shrugged and gave Madame Boucher a weak smile. The woman would clearly prefer to continue entertaining her visitors. She who had sworn last night to give Jehanne anything she wanted was not being at all helpful, and Jehanne was sorely tempted to point that out. At the same time she did not want to offend the Bouchers. After all, they had welcomed her into their home.

So, without waiting for her comrades and afraid to say another word lest her temper run away with her, she trounced upstairs to the second-floor bedroom that Jacques Boucher had released for her use as a council room. Brothers, heralds, and pages leaped to their feet and followed her, now really alarmed. Despite her somewhat cordial discourse with her hostess, they knew her well enough to see that she was very angry indeed and they dreaded this council.

She threw her helmet across the room. It smacked against the wall, then landed on the high bed. She began to pace back and forth, her dark brows drawn into a heavy frown, hands clasped behind her back. Jehan had barely closed the door when she rasped angrily, "The Bastard says we can't attack! He's going back to Blois to fetch the army, he says, and meanwhile we just have to sit here doing nothing when we could vanquish the *goddons*!"

None of them dared speak, not when she was like this.

"Well, I'm not going to wait." She stomped to the table and picked up the letter to the English that she had put there earlier. "Guyenne, you and Ambleville ride over to the English *bastille* and give this message to Talbot. I mean to give them fair warning before we attack."

"Jehanne, what are you saying?" her older brother asked with a lift of his thick eyebrows. "Are you going to order an attack even though the Bastard says to wait for the army? That could be dangerous, you know. He's the lord of Orléans—"

"Yes, yes, Jehan, I *do* know." She ran a hand through her short, dense hair. "No, I don't have the power to do that. The captains would never let me." Her voice sang bitterness. "But I can send the letter to the English." She thrust it toward Guyenne. "Here, take this to them. Do you know which *bastille* Talbot commands?"

"I do." The herald's lean face was grave now that he was embarking upon the work he was trained to perform. "Is there to be a spoken message as well?"

Jehanne pondered for a moment. "Yes. Tell them that they have until sundown tomorrow to make their ruling. After that, we shall attack."

"But, Jehanne," Jehan protested again, taking a step toward her, "we can't promise to attack them if the Bastard says we can't use the garrison. And the army probably won't be back here by then."

"I didn't say how soon after sundown we'll attack, just that we shall. If it comes a day or so later, I'll still make good on my threat. The Bastard gave me his word that he'll order the army to go against them." She turned to Guyenne. "Do *you* understand the message?" she added, tossing a barb at Jehan.

"Yes." Ambleville nodded.

"Good. Then may God be with you and send you back with a favorable reply."

Looking like elegant twins in their *huques* adorned with Charles' lilies, the heralds bowed to her in unison.

They were gone for nearly three hours. In the meantime none of Jehanne's company ventured a resumption of their pleasant gossip with Madame Boucher. While Pierre and Jehan fidgeted idly, the pages polished and repolished her armor and Ste.-Catherine's sword. Jehanne paced the floor for some time. Then she went to the oratory next to her conference room and prayed.

Will they do as I have asked?

There was no answer.

She tried to listen harder. It was possible that They were trying to tell her something, but that she was simply too nervous to hear Them.

They were silent.

She bowed her head and said a fervent *Credo*, followed by a *Pater Noster*. She had already finished more than half the rosary when she heard: "Jehanne!" It was Pierre's voice. "Come quickly!"

She made a hasty Sign of the Cross and shot down the stairs.

To Jehanne's surprise, the Bastard of Orléans was there with Ambleville, whose normally unruffled countenance was a few shades paler than usual. There was nothing courtly about the herald now. He had lost his hat, and his *huque* was torn and dirty. One of the fleurs-de-lys on it was smeared with what smelled like excrement, but he was so frightened that he appeared not to notice. The poor man was trembling with terror, and when Madame Boucher handed him a goblet of wine, he drained it in one gulp.

"What happened?" Jehanne demanded. "Where's Guyenne?"

"They're going to burn him!" the herald gasped, wide-eyed. "They laughed at your letter, some of them did, Talbot did, but others were very angry." He accepted another cup from Madame Boucher and slammed its contents down his throat. "They said to tell you that you are just a whore and that you should go back to minding your cows."

Jehanne's eyes narrowed grimly and her nostrils flared. "They have no right to keep a herald against his will," she said in quiet fury. Then, with a look at the Bastard, "That is against the code of chivalry, is it not?"

"Yes, it is," he replied somberly.

"Barbarians!" swore Jehan.

"You must go back to them, Ambleville," Jehanne ordered. "You must tell them that no matter what they think of me, they have no right to hold Guyenne. Tell them that by doing so they reveal themselves to be cowards and worse: men who have turned against God."

Ambleville became even paler and looked as though he would faint.

"Tell them also," said the Bastard, "that under the rules of chivalry, they are violating what is defined as lawful military conduct. If they can do that with impunity, so can I. Therefore, if they do not release Guyenne, I will kill every English prisoner held in Orléans as well as their own emissaries."

The courier, his face as stolid as one who has accepted his death, bowed to the Bastard. Ambleville departed with his shoulders rounded in resignation.

He returned an hour later.

"They said to tell you again that you are a wanton whore and a milkmaid, and that they are not bound by the code of chivalry to respect your envoys because you are just a peasant and not a true commander." Ambleville paused at the harsh look on her face.

"What else?" she asked quietly.

"They said—they said that if they catch you, they will burn you as they are going to burn Guyenne. Then they repeated that you should go home to your cows."

She said nothing.

"You are a brave man and have done well, Ambleville." The Bastard put a reassuring hand on his shoulder. "Have no fear." He smiled. "You do not need to go back to them again." The look he gave Jehanne was a command.

The others glanced at one another in nervous anticipation of a storm, but none came. Jehanne turned and walked slowly up the stairs, then made her way to the oratory. She knelt before the shrine and crossed herself.

Help me. Tell me what to do now.

There was only the sound of muffled voices and footsteps downstairs.

The English will not listen to me. I don't want to kill them, but we must drive them away if we are to lift the siege! Please help me, please don't leave me hanging like this.

IT IS NOT OUR CHOICE, JEHANNE, AS TO HOW YOU ARE TO ACCOMPLISH THIS TASK. YOU ARE FREE TO CHOOSE ANY SOLUTION YOU WISH. THE KEY IS BALANCE.

That does not help me. I don't understand you.

YOU SHALL SOON HAVE EVERYTHING YOU NEED.

She pondered the enigmatic words, thwarted by her inability to understand what Catherine meant.

No matter what happens, will you keep me from killing anyone in battle?

THAT SHALL BE YOUR DECISION ALONE. YOU WILL DO WHAT YOU MUST WHEN THE TIME COMES.

What of Guyenne? What will become of him? Will they kill him?

Her unspoken thoughts taunted her, bounced back toward her in the silence. It was her choice, Catherine had said.

Very well. She would go to the English herself, to those who held the Tourelles, so that she could shout to them across the hole in the bridge. She would show them that she was not going to be frightened by their threats. She would warn them of the Power of God.

She went to them at dusk, escorted by seven soldiers the Bastard had selected from the garrison. As they rode onto the bridge toward the Tourelles at the other end of the span, a large crowd of townspeople hung back, waiting to see what would happen when the Maid addressed the commander of the *goddons* who had usurped the bridge fort, known in Orléans as "Clasidas."

They trotted across the Loire, Jehanne carrying her standard and flanked by the grim men-at-arms. The towering old fortress with its dual twin spires loomed ahead like a man-made mountain. Drawing closer, she could see that the English had fashioned a low wall, an interwoven timber-and-earth structure surmounted by a pointed wooden palisade, to face the bridge and its absent span. A fire glowed eerily behind this desecration, casting long-armed shadows of moving figures upon the inner bricks of the bridge's raised gate.

When her party came to within fifty yards of the wide cavity the French had blasted into the span, they halted.

"Clasidas!" yelled Jehanne, "Clasidas, can you hear me? I am Jehanne the Maid, sent by the King of Heaven to command that you surrender this place and return to your own country. In the name of God, if you do not give up yourself and your men, you will face your destruction, for God has given me the Power to drive you from this city!"

"Cow-wench! Poxy slut!"

"When we catch you, we shall burn you!"

"Has Charles run out of real men to send against us now, that all he has left is his court jester?" While the words were heavily accented, there was no mistaking their meaning.

She glowered in the coming darkness. "You respond in peril of your lives and your souls! For God has promised that you shall be driven from this kingdom of France, and He will give us the means to do so!"

"Do you expect us to surrender to a woman, and a whore at that? You faithless pimps! Take this milkmaid back to where she belongs, back to your barracks for the night where she will do you the most good."

"The *only* good!" The fortress roared with scornful, bawdy laughter.

Jehanne's ears burned with humiliation. "You are all liars!" she shouted, "and you will surely pay for your blasphemy!"

She wheeled her horse around suddenly and started back across the bridge, accompanied by catcalls and hoots of derision. Her escort, surprised by her abrupt turnabout, quickly followed. The clatter of horses' hooves sounded against the pavement in the early evening stillness.

She had tried her best to warn them of what was coming. It was not her fault that they refused to listen. When the army returned from Blois, the *goddons* would reap the fruits of their dirty-minded vanity and their blasphemous disregard of God's promise. She had performed her duty as a true Christian.

The three days between the Bastard's departure and his return with the army would pass with a maddening slowness, made all the more wearisome by the dull pattern of their events. During this interval it seemed to Jehanne that God Himself had stopped the hands of the great Universal Clock.

La Hire reappeared in Orléans sometime after midnight. The next morning he and Jehanne, with a sizable troop from the garrison, ushered the Bastard and his men out of the city through the Porte de Bourgogne and down to the Loire. From the riverbank Jehanne watched the boats and their inestimable cargo sail upwind to the other side. As the crafts touched dry land and their passengers disembarked, she prayed for the Bastard's safety and for the hasty return of the army. Then, miraculously unchallenged by the English, the troop cantered their horses back toward the city's one open gate. La Hire took his men to their billets, while Jehanne returned to the Bouchers' tall house.

It was Sunday, May 1, and she yearned to hear Mass. She knew, however, that the worshipful Orléanais would never allow her to reach the cathedral in a timely manner, much less let her pray peacefully in public. So she had to content herself with solitary prayer in her host's oratory.

She had been on her knees before the altar only a short time when she heard a loud disturbance downstairs, so noisy that it broke her concentration. It was useless to try to ignore it, for it sounded as though a herd of mighty warhorses were trying to kick their way through the door. Jehanne crossed herself and went down to see what the trouble was.

People in the street were pounding on the door, clamoring to see her. They were pressed up against the windows, peering in at the startled family, at the child with frightened eyes who ran to her mother's side for comfort and protection. It made no difference to the people that they were disturbing one of their wealthiest and most powerful neighbors; to see the Maid and to have her favor them with her allure, they would have broken down the duc's door had he been her host. The familiar chant, punctuated by heavy fists banging on the very walls of the house, was no longer friendly but demanding, hungry, desperate for Jehanne's presence. It was the first time she had ever heard her name uttered as a threat.

Jacques Boucher, fearful for his property and perhaps even the safety of his family, begged her to go out to the street. She was the only one who could calm them, he said.

Leaving the house was the last thing she wished to do; it was Sunday, God's own day, and she wanted to return to the oratory and her prayers. She longed for peace and reflection, not the chaos of the streets. She was also somewhat less than happy at the prospect of dressing again in the uncomfortable armor. But faced with the destructive power of the crowd and concerned for the Bouchers, she finally agreed. She had no set destination in mind, yet was compelled to show herself. While Pierre went to the stables and ordered her horse saddled and brought around to the front of the house, Minguet and Raymond armed her. When she was ready, she took a deep breath and went outside, huddled within an enclosure composed of her brothers and Raymond.

The people immediately set upon her. As always when she went out, they clutched at her with frantic, revering hands. Her household tried valiantly to surround her, but four against this multitude was impossible. Minguet especially was almost trampled at one point, and his foot would later be bruised and swollen from having been stepped on so many times. Jehanne scolded herself for having sent Metz, Poulengy, and d'Aulon away with the army, for their commanding skill and experience with handling numbers of people would have been most useful. As it was she had to struggle to her horse, which was being held by one of Monsieur Boucher's burlier stablemen. Not even his strength could contend with the horde's determination, and they jostled the man so much that it took all his willpower not to lose the animal's reins.

It was all so unreal and dreamlike. She had expected to be greeted warmly in Orléans, though to be honest she had not foreseen that it would be so *deranged*. There was something almost obscene about it. This was not just love, not just hope. It was a command, and she felt helpless to resist it. The people cheered her so raucously that her head pounded and she felt lightheaded from the adoration. They held on to her legs, kissing them and her feet, clinging to her horse with a mindless fervor. Their devotion, far from lessening, had indeed increased with her continuing presence in the city, and dazed, she rode through their congested ranks, trailing the Power in her wake.

As much from boredom as from resolve, she decided to challenge the English once more. This time the townsfolk followed her to within safe distance of a hostile post at the Croix Morin on the western outskirts of the city. When she was close enough for the enemy to hear her, she again demanded that they yield to the King of Heaven and surrender what they had unlawfully taken. She received vulgar responses similar to those that had come from the Tourelles the previous night, and when it was clear that all she would get was insults, she reluctantly turned her horse and went back into Orléans.

The next day she was again on horseback, this time for the purpose of reconnoitering the English defenses. She soon became aware that the ever-present mass of onlookers no doubt made her efforts absurdly clear to the enemy, and she felt like a fool for trying to gather information surrounded by half the city. She gave that up after a few minutes and took advantage of the situation by asking the civilians gathered around her about the English *bastilles*. How long had this one been occupied by the enemy? How many defenders were inside? What weapons did they have, and how many? How often did they come out to engage the garrison? When she was satisfied that she knew enough, she returned to the city.

By eveningtide she had had enough of the Orléanais' despotic adoration, and heard Vespers in the cathedral in defiance of those swarming about her in the streets and inside the building.

On Tuesday, garrisons from Gien, Châteaudun, Montargis, and Château Reynard began streaming into the city. For a few hours the people forgot about *L'Angélique* and greeted the garrisons with the same kind of delirious tumult they always inflicted upon Jehanne. The soldiers said that the army was on the march from Blois and would reach Orléans the next day via the northern road through La Beauce. La Hire posted sentries in the belfries of St.-Paul and St.-Pierre Empont in case the English decided to attack the approaching battalions. But the enemy made no move to emerge from their *bastilles*, and the people wondered, awestruck at their inaction. Surely it was the hand of God that paralyzed the *goddons* in their forts! All because of the Maid. To her dismay, Jehanne's fame tripled, something she had not thought possible twelve hours earlier.

At dawn the next morning, in the company of La Hire and other captains, she went with a force of five hundred to meet the returning army. She was most eager to see her friends again, and as she rode surrounded by the garrison, her heart throbbed with excitement. The waiting, the ennui were over. The army was here at last, and she had no doubt that Orléans would soon be delivered and France free for the first time in almost a century.

When all of them had attained safety within the city walls, the fresh troops went to their billets, and the garrison, under orders from the Bastard, took control of the distribution of the food and weapons the army had brought with them. Jehanne had a happy reunion with her confessor and her friends, then returned to the Bouchers' for a midday meal. Not all of her company went with her. Metz and Poulengy were lodged nearby in another private home. Pasquerel chose to remain for a few hours with the monks who had followed the army from Tours; he promised to join her later. But d'Aulon was there now, and he and the other members of her household shared the Bouchers' meal in high spirits.

They had finished eating but were still at table when the Bastard arrived. "I have received word within the last hour that the English knight sieur Jehan Fastolphe is on his way here with reinforcements for their *bastilles*," he informed them. "They are already at Janville, roughly a day's march from here."

Madame Boucher gasped and looked to her husband for reassurance. He did not seem to notice her. Like the rest of them, his attention was fixed upon the Bastard.

Jehanne got up from the table and walked to him, her eyes troubled. "You're not going to use the army to overtake them, are you?"

He raised his brows in surprise. "No, of course not. That would mean dividing our battalions, and our chances for victory are stronger if they remain in one place. Besides"—he shrugged—"the king's army would be more exposed out in the open. Why do you ask?"

"I was afraid—I just thought you might be thinking that." Thank God he did not intend to do something to weaken their resistance to the siege from within these walls! Her Counsel had told her that they would be triumphant here in Orléans, and she did not want to have to argue with him again. Still, with more English on their way to the city . . .

The *goddons* had a reputation for invincibility won through many years of success in the battlefield, and Jehanne well knew that despite their brave swagger, the Armagnacs were frightened to death of them. She had finally realized that that was the real reason the captains had been so insistent that the army be reinforced when they first brought in the supplies a week ago. Now, with English support coming toward Orléans, she feared that the Bastard's men might again refuse to raise the siege without additional troops of their own. If they could have their way, they would not be satisfied until every soldier in France was with them!

But all they really needed was a reminder that God had promised them victory, and that was why He had sent her here.

"Bastard, I order you to let me know as soon as you hear of Fastolphe's arrival, for if he passes without my knowledge, I promise you that I will have your head!"

"You need have no fear, Jehanne," the Bastard replied, trying not to smile at the incensed boyish figure. He was becoming accustomed now to her pugnacity and realized that much of it stemmed from frustration. "I will indeed inform you when the English army reaches Orléans." With that, he nodded to those assembled around the table and departed.

When he was gone, a furor of conversation broke out. Jehan was all for rousing the army from their billets this very minute and dispatching them toward Janville. In a typically challenging bid to surpass his brother, Pierre pointed out that the Bastard himself had just said that he did not want to break up the army, and since he was commanding them, they should listen to him, for he was a real captain and knew more than they did about warfare. D'Aulon supported Pierre's opinion, but for a different reason. The army had been on the road throughout the night, and he could vouch firsthand that every man was exhausted. Better to let them rest for the real battle that was marching toward the city.

Jehanne uncharacteristically said very little. Her eyelids were drooping despite her best efforts to stay awake, and she suddenly realized how tired she was. She had tossed sleeplessly through much of the night, her mind whirling with all that remained to be accomplished, and then she had risen before the sun to meet the legions returning from Blois. She had the Bastard's promise; now she could give in to fatigue.

No longer able to hold her eyes open, she stood up from the bench she had been sharing with Minguet and Ambleville. "I need to take a nap. I want to be well rested when we go against the *goddons*."

"I will go with you, Jehanne," offered Madame Boucher, ready to get away from all the war talk. Turning to her daughter, she said, "Charlotte, you stay here, and do not go out into the street. There are too many people about."

"Yes, Maman," the child mumbled.

"Do not worry about her," Minguet offered with an obliging smile. "She will be safe with us, Madame."

"I need some sleep, too," yawned d'Aulon. "Would you mind if I lie down in your room as well, Jehanne?"

She smiled at him. Poor fellow, he must be very tired. She knew how little rest one got by sleeping on the hard ground, as he had done for over two weeks. Even soldiers needed a real bed or something like it every now and then.

"Very well," she said. "Come."

The three of them trudged up the stairs to the third floor. Fully clothed, Jehanne and Madame Boucher spread out on the bed Jehanne normally shared with Charlotte. D'Aulon flopped down wearily onto the small couch beneath the open window.

Jehanne found it even easier to summon sleep than she had expected. As she floated toward oblivion, random pictures of the last few days' events began to drift in and out of her awareness. She saw individual faces within the crowds, faces she thought she had forgotten. They were banging on the door, demanding to be let in, heedless of Monsieur Boucher's fear for his family. Nothing could stop them. They were everywhere all at once, in the windows, in the street, in the nasty laughter of the English soldiers.

Suddenly, the people were gone, replaced by swords flashing across her vision in a panorama of blood and fire. She could hear the screams of the dying.

Your moment has arrived, Little One. Arise.

Jehanne snapped awake, as alert as though she had never dozed. Outside, there were confused cries and hoofbeats pounding in the street. She leaped out of bed and dashed over to the snoring d'Aulon.

"Wake up!" she commanded, shaking him.

He raised his disheveled head and sat up, trying to look at her with unfocusing eyes. "What—?"

"In God's name, my Counsel has told me to go against the English!" she cried, her face alight with bemused exhilaration. "But I don't know whether I should go against the *bastilles* or against Fastolphe, who's on his way here with supplies. Hurry," she shook the dumbfounded man, "we need to arm ourselves and be out of here!"

Still only half-awake, d'Aulon struggled to his feet. Jehanne bolted down the stairs, taking two at a time, with Madame Boucher right behind her.

Raymond, Pierre, and Jehan stood clustered around the front door, babbling excitedly at the commotion in the street. Charlotte was watching the knights ride past on their warhorses, and as the troop dashed by in a cloud of dust, Monsieur Boucher pulled his daughter back into the room.

"Jehanne, people outside are saying there's a battle going on!" cried Pierre. Her brother's wide face was spread in a toothy grin and his eyes bulged with euphoria.

"I know. Raymond, you saddle my horse. Jehan, you and Pierre get into your armor. Now!" she shouted when they did not move.

The entire household was in tumult as the men darted to their tasks. Charlotte stood with her father's arm around her shoulders, watching the scene. "Where's my armor?" Jehanne demanded. "And where is Minguet?"

Madame Boucher collected her daughter, and together they quickly fetched Jehanne's armor from her council room upstairs and began fitting her into it. It was something they had never done before, and their hands fumbled with the cumbersome plates. They were only half-finished when Pasquerel arrived with four other priests whom he hoped to introduce to Jehanne.

He walked in the open door just in time to hear her say angrily, "Where are they who are *supposed* to be arming me? The blood of our people is reddening the ground!"

At that moment Minguet dashed through the door, squeezing between Pasquerel and another monk. His face was flushed and there was sweat streaming into his eyes. "Jehanne," he shouted, pointing to the street, "there's—"

"There you are, you good-for-nothing boy! Why didn't you tell me that we are suffering losses? Off with you, go out back and help Raymond with my horse."

Minguet flinched at her angry tone and his face turned apple red. Without a word he melted back into the street.

While the Bouchers finished arming Jehanne, the noise outside became louder and people could be clearly heard, wailing that the French were coming to great harm at the hands of the English. Jehanne was so frustrated by the slowness with which she was being fitted that she wanted to scream. It was stupid of her to have sent Minguet away when he knew how to fasten her into this thing, but it was too late to call him back.

She had to be on her way before it was all over and the English victorious! Her head raged with indignation at the Bastard for not having kept his promise.

Minguet returned as she was belting her sword about her waist. "Where's my standard?" she asked him.

He pointed upstairs.

"Well, don't just stand there, get it!"

She ran out the door, nearly knocking over one of the priests. Raymond was there, holding her white horse, and while he steadied it, she scrambled up into the saddle as quickly as her armor would allow. Everywhere in the street was a flurry of confusion and near panic. Civilians were running about waving pikes and heirloom swords in the air, all bound in the same direction. Another detachment of soldiers galloped furiously past Jehanne toward the east.

The second-story window opened and Minguet looked down at her. "Here it is, Jehanne, catch!" He let the standard fall through the opening.

Raymond caught it deftly with one hand. Jehanne snatched the flag from her page and took off down the street in pursuit of the soldiers with sparks flying from her horse's hooves.

Oh dear God, she begged, let me not be too late!

She hurried past the running townspeople aimed in the direction of the city's one open gate. Men and women alike, they carried weapons of every sort and implements that could be used as such, from swords to brooms to rolling pins. This battle, whatever it was, signaled to them that it was time to reclaim their city. Hundreds of them were converging upon the wider avenue from the side streets where they worked and lived. The closer Jehanne drew to the Porte de Bourgogne, the more swollen with Orléanais the street became, until she was forced to slow her pace to a tortuous plod.

"Out of my way!" she shouted, trying to coax her horse through the wall of humanity, "I must get through!"

People shifted out of her path as best they could but there were too many of them to permit quick movement and no place for them to go. For what seemed an eternity, she could only flow with the masses intent upon reaching the gate.

Finally, she saw the Porte de Bourgogne just ahead, and through it, dust rising from the distant fort. Even from this position, well behind the gate and with the throng obstructing it, she could see the brilliant banners beneath the tower, a flash of swords at its top, and men falling as they were hit by English arrows. A number of them lay motionless upon the ground. She had to get to them, she had to rally them before they faltered! But she was frozen within the choking crowd, which by now had stopped moving forward and was bunched about the gate's opening.

"Let me pass!" she shouted above the din. "I must get through!"

"Jehanne!"

"Please, let me pass!" The tastes of dust and distress took the moisture from her tongue so that she hardly heard her own words. She swallowed the dryness at the back of her throat, then shouted again even louder, "Let me through!"

"Jehanne, wait for us!"

She turned halfway in the saddle, as much as she could manage because of the confining armor. D'Aulon, Minguet, and Pierre were attempting to prod their horses through the human barrier, ten or so deep, separating them from her. All three were fully armed. A little further back, sunlight reflected off Jehan's *basinet* and Raymond's steel-plated shoulder. A large contingent of the city militia was forcing its way up behind them through the impenetrable crowd, and Jehanne recognized the maréchal de Sainte-Sévère at their head. The old soldier was flailing his mace over heads in the crowd in a somewhat successful endeavor to work his way through them.

"Jehanne!" d'Aulon called again. "Wait for us!"

She looked around at the unmoving populace and threw her hands up help-lessly. She did not exactly have a choice. "These people won't let me by!" she yelled at him.

After their great show of aggression, the townsfolk were unresolved to go fur-ther now that they had reached the gate and the battle at St.-Loup raged less than half a league before them. In no apparent hurry to rush toward the fray with their homemade weaponry, they hung back, creating a static wedge within the Porte de Bourgogne which backed up all the way down the street.

"Move out of my way!" Jehanne shouted, now really angry. If these cowards did not intend to fight, they should let pass those who did!

She looked back over her shoulder. Sainte-Sévère's men were hemmed in on all sides and could not budge. The maréchal was soundly cursing the people, whose best efforts to get out of his way were thwarted by the sheer numbers packed so densely into the meager space. D'Aulon and Minguet were closer to her now, having forced their way through the multitude by a supreme act of will. Red-faced from exertion, Pierre struggled to keep up with them.

Jehanne might have been stuck there all day had she not received a stroke of good fortune from a macabre ally.

At the foot of the *bastille* a contingent of men-at-arms and archers separated from the battle and began limping toward the gate. Worried at this development, Jehanne put her hand up to her visor to shade her face from the sun, squinting to see better.

The wounded were being brought to the city by their comrades. As they came nearer, stumbling forward with fatigued steps, Jehanne saw that all were caked in dusty sweat. Two wearied soldiers strained to drag a third who had an arrow sticking out of his hose just above the knee. A bloody torrent gushed over his boot, leaving a trail in the dirt, and his steel-covered head was slumped insensibly upon his chest. Behind them another carried an unconscious man-at-arms whose arm dangled at his side. One of the stricken, carried on a stretcher, held blood-soaked hands over a gash in his gut as he writhed in agony. Others, outwardly unhurt, lurched toward Orléans like walking dead, their faces blank, mouths gasping for air. A few dragged the poles of their *guisarmes* behind them in the dirt. Here and there, a bloodied hand limply held a sword.

Jehanne's anger at the impasse climbed to her throat and lodged there in a lump. Desperate to get through, she nudged her horse forward using her spurs. The animal brought her to the front of the crowd, who mercifully parted ranks to allow the wounded into the gate.

"Who is he?" Jehanne asked one of the stretcher bearers with a nod at the moaning soldier.

"Jacques Licher, of the garrison," the man panted. His tongue licked cracked, dry lips and lapped at the sweat streaming down the sides of his face.

It was the first time she had seen wounded and dying men fresh from a battle-field. She felt like vomiting. There was no glory in this, no billowing banner to see them home, nothing but useless suffering, and her heart raged with hatred for the invaders who had inflicted it. The nearly disemboweled soldier tugged at her compassion, sending a trickle down her cheek. The life force in his eyes was very faint and burned with a terrible fear. Gore squirted from the rip in his abdomen with every shallow, rapid breath. The stretcher was soaked in it; it dropped into the dirt in brown clumps.

Jehanne was taken by a vehement shudder. "I don't think I could ever see French blood spilled without my hair rising in horror," she said to d'Aulon, who by now had forced his way to her side. Just behind him, Minguet gaped at the exhausted ghosts staggering through the gate with their grisly burdens.

Taking advantage of the cleared path ahead of her, Jehanne impelled her horse through the Porte de Bourgogne and trotted a short distance toward the mêlée. Her companions followed her. She knew they were there without looking, and while they caught up to her, she focused her attention on the battle. It was clear that the Armagnacs attacking the fort were getting the worst of it.

At the bottom of the tower a colorful array of standards designating regional battalions fluttered amidst the shining hereditary armor of knights. Men-at-arms had propped long scaling ladders against the beehive-shaped citadel on all sides, and hundreds of French soldiers, those who had gotten through the Porte de Bourgogne before the townsfolk blocked it, were struggling to climb them while the crossbowmen in their ranks aimed their bows at the English and fired. But weapons that should have given the attackers additional cover did little good, for the staunchly mud-bricked redoubt was an effective shield and most of the bolts failed to connect with the targets.

The English, on the other hand, were pushing the ladders to the ground almost effortlessly, and from their aerie archers shot back at the assailants, some of whom fell, screaming, from the ladders to their deaths below. Another swarm of Welsh arrows mowed down men-at-arms who did not have a chance to mount the ladders. Impaled where they stood, they sank to the ground, clutching their in-juries; others, fatally wounded, toppled onto their faces or their backs without making a sound. Those who made it over the top were engaged in a desperate hand-to-hand struggle, and from Jehanne's location their weapons could be seen slicing through the spring sky. The cries of the wounded and dying were like wolves baying in a wintertime Bois Chenu.

An immense *Boom!* sounded from the city wall, followed an instant later by a cannonball that ripped through the top of the *bastille*, raising further shouts of pain from those inside and flinging ladders to the earth. Jehanne saw men who had nearly reached the summit jump clear as their ladders clattered into the dust.

Her attention was caught by d'Aulon's tap on her shoulder. "Here they come," he said, pointing.

There was a noisy dustcloud blowing at great speed from the direction of the English fort of St.-Pouair north of the city. Jehanne was unable to see the English as such, but it was plain from the size of that cloud that large numbers of the enemy were racing on horseback toward St.-Loup, no doubt to succor their comrades with an attack upon the nearly spent Armagnacs.

Jehanne dug her spurs into her horse's side and with d'Aulon, Pierre, and Minguet at her heels, headed for the conflict at St.-Loup. When she was close enough to be heard, yet still out of range of English arrows, she yanked on the reins and came to a stop. She held her standard up so that all could see it.

"Onward, men of France!" she yelled above the uproar, gripping the banner's pole tightly. "Do not be afraid, for God is on our side!"

At the sound of her voice a tremendous "Hurrah!" burst from the discouraged Armagnac troops at St.-Loup.

At precisely that moment Saint-Sévère, having finally attained the gate, raised his sword, and the militia, yelling and waving their weapons, sent up an impassioned howl and charged the English who were dashing toward St.-Loup from the northwest. When they saw the screaming Frenchmen bearing down upon them, too many for them to engage successfully, the enemy wheeled their horses about sharply and started hurrying back toward the security of their fort. The militia tore after them, urging their horses forward with their spurs, growling their anger and slashing weapons through the dust swirling above their heads. The stragglers turned to defend themselves, and there was a sickening crash as the militia collided with them and began hacking at them without mercy.

Jehan and Raymond had been expelled from the gate along with the militia, and now they cantered toward Jehanne and the others who were watching the battle from a safe distance at the bottom of the fort.

Heartened by Jehanne's arrival and the militia's successful repulsion of English reinforcements, the soldiers at St.-Loup gave a boisterous yell, and shaking off the aura of defeat that had hung about them only minutes ago, began scrambling up the tall ladders. The big gun from Orléans had struck the center of its mark, and where the top of the *bastille* had been a briarpatch of English archers, now there were fewer left to rain death upon the Armagnacs, who were pouring into the fort, flailing their swords and *guisarmes* and snarling as savagely as demons.

Someone or something—perhaps the cannonball connecting with a barrel of gunpowder—must have set fire to the structure because there was the unexpected smell of burning wood. A long black dragon of smoke began to rise from St.-Loup, followed by waves of heat shimmering into the sky. From her horse Jehanne witnessed the onslaught of enemy arrows become more infrequent as the stream of Armagnac soldiers moved steadily up the ladders. Soon the entire top of the structure was a forest of busily engaged weapons, visible through the thick curtain of smoke.

The wind picked up, parting the smoke, and a man-at-arms at the crest could be seen waving his lord's standard back and forth in triumph. St.-Loup was theirs. The English had surrendered the fort.

The long hours of frustration burst from Jehanne's lungs. Oh, thank You, God, she sang. Thank You, thank You!

Now the fire was clearly visible, licking at the edifice with its great crackling tongue. The soldiers started hastening out of the fort, lowering their wounded and dead to the ground. Jehanne watched the English prisoners, forty or so in all, being forced to descend the ladders. When they reached the bottom, they were made to kneel with their hands clasped behind their heads. The victors still at the summit hurled the confiscated weapons to the bloody earth below.

Jehanne and her companions waited on their horses until the living had quit the *bastille*, and all the dead with them. To ensure that none of the enemy from the other forts could retake St.-Loup and use it again, the French armies finished burning it. Theirs was a great victory. With no further obstacle to block the Porte de Bourgogne, fresh troops and supply trains could enter the city unmolested by the English.

The battle concluded and their triumph assured, the army gathered about Jehanne and turned dusty, blood-smeared faces up at her. They split the skies with an emphatic bellow, brandishing their weapons over their heads.

"Jehanne the Maid! Jehanne the Maid! Jehanne the Maid!" they shouted.

She smiled at them through her tears and waved in acknowledgment of their acclamation. She was so very, very proud of them! They cheered her on for quite some time, chanting her name until they were hoarse. Then the weary soldiers began moving back into Orléans with their wounded and their prisoners.

Jehanne looked around at her jubilant companions. Brother Pasquerel was there with his knowing smile, and she wondered at what point during the battle he had joined them. She climbed down from her horse and sank to her knees in the gruesome dirt. Lifting a contrite face up to the monk, she asked him to confess her on the spot. In silence, her household turned their horses away and moved to a discreet distance.

Now that it was all over, her soul was constricted in pain at the thought of the unshriven English dead. She was responsible, she said, for the ruin they had brought upon themselves. She had wished for this victory, had prayed for it. Even when her confessor reminded her that the state of their souls was not in her hands, she twisted with guilt and insisted that he give her a much-deserved penance, for her hatred of the English had not lessened despite her prayers that she might learn forgiveness.

After Pasquerel prayed with her for a little while, Jehanne and her companions returned from whence they had come, straggling behind the army. They were met at the Porte de Bourgogne by the Bastard, who escorted them to a spontaneous Mass of thanksgiving in the cathedral. All through the streets Jehanne rode enveloped within the celebration of the worshipful, adoring city, accompanied by the peals of the great bells issuing from every church in Orléans. This time she did not mind so much when the people screamed her name.

Later, she issued a proclamation that whatever remained of the church of St.-Loup was not to be plundered, on pain of mortal sin. She also insisted that the army be confessed and that they give thanks to God for their victory. If they did not do as she instructed, she would leave them. A few of the English survivors had frantically attempted to disguise themselves as churchmen by donning vestments from the former church-turned-fortress, and the French soldiers were all for killing them. But Jehanne forbade their murder, saying that they should be allowed to enter Orléans in peace. Every one of them looked half-starved and some were ill. In Orléans they would find food and medicines.

She would be obeyed in all that she had commanded.

The next day, Thursday, was the Feast of the Ascension of Our Lord into Heaven. Jehanne was confessed again and attended another glorious Mass in the cathedral. Before she entered the building, she positioned herself at the great entranceway and addressed the crowd standing at the bottom of the steps. In a loud, clear voice she declared that no fighting should occur on this holy day, and that any man who intended to go into battle on Friday should attend confession and receive the sacraments. She further announced that the soldiers should dismiss the harlots who had sneaked back into their society, otherwise "God would bring defeat to them because of their sins." Again, she was heeded.

While she was at Mass, the Bastard brought a number of commanders and city burgesses to the Boucher house without Jehanne's knowledge and held a war council in the very room that Jacques Boucher had appointed hers. Upon her return, she was infuriated at the deception and further perturbed that none of her household except her confessor was there. She paced the parlor floor until Ambroise de Loré came downstairs to fetch her.

They were all standing around the table on which the always present, worn map of Orléans had been unfolded. La Hire and his friend Poton de Xaintrailles were there with the Bastard, as well as Gilles de Rais, the maréchal de Sainte-Sévère, sieur de Gaucourt, Jacques Boucher, and others—soldiers and civilians—whom she did not know.

"What have you decided without me?" she demanded, skipping past petty pleasantries. Sainte-Sévère exchanged a pained look with de Gaucourt which she chose to ignore.

The mayor Cousinot came forward, smiling. A strutting bantam rooster of a man, his simper dripped self-importance. When he spoke, the high-pitched nasal whine immediately raised Jehanne's defiance. "We are going to engage the English tomorrow, Jehanne, and we want you to take a troop to attack the *Bastille* de St.-Laurent beyond the western gate. Does that not please you?"

She frowned, undeceived by his pacifying manner. There was more to all of this than was apparent, and she resented their having banned her from this council and their attempts to trick her. "No."

The men looked at one another. La Hire grinned at her and shook his head.

One of the burgesses rolled his eyes in dismay. Gilles de Rais fidgeted with his chin whiskers and peeled her with a cynical smirk.

"Please sit, Jehanne," said the Bastard, gesturing to a stool.

She began to pace, her glower undiminished. "Tell me what you have really decided. I assure you, I know how to keep a secret far greater than any you could think of."

Taken aback, the others shifted their feet awkwardly. "Jehanne, do not be angry," the Bastard said in a soft voice. "We cannot tell you everything at once. What the mayor has told you has indeed been decided, but we have also agreed that if the English who are on the Sologne side of the river come to the assistance of those who are in the fort, we shall cross the river to do whatever we can against them there. We consider this plan good and profitable."

She looked at them, still frowning, trying to decide if she could believe them. It really made no difference whether or not she did, for they would fulfill their scheme regardless of what she said. Besides, she had no other choice to offer them.

She breathed heavily through her nose and nodded. "Very well. I will carry out your plan."

Gilles de Rais took the map from the table and began to roll it up. It was plain that the meeting was adjourned.

Jehanne turned abruptly and left them. She still had a great deal left to do this day. Somehow, she had to convince the English to surrender before another battle killed more of them. She also needed to persuade them to release her herald, Guyenne. She went downstairs and sought out Pasquerel, who was waiting for her in the parlor where she had left him with Madame Boucher and Charlotte.

"Come," she told him, "I want to write again to the English."

Jehanne and Pasquerel slipped through the parlor into Monsieur Boucher's office and she closed the door behind them. She could hear the muffled voices of the council, though their words were indistinct, followed by heavy masculine footsteps upon the stairs. She made herself comfortable on a stool in front of the fireplace. The monk sat down at the desk and spread a fresh sheet of parchment across the polished rosewood. Then he opened the inkwell and dipped the quill into it.

"What do you wish to say, Jehanne?"

She ran her hands through her hair. Head lowered, she pinched the bridge of her nose as her thoughts took form. After a few moments she said, "Write this."

The brief letter repeated that the English had no right to the kingdom, and that God, through Jehanne, commanded them to abandon the siege. If they did not, she would drive them out. She pledged not to write again.

Then, as an afterthought, she said, "And this to it, Brother."

I would have sent you my letter in a more honorable manner, but you detain my heralds, you have detained my herald called Guyenne. Please send him back to me, and I will send back some of your people captured at St.-Loup, for they are not all dead.

When Pasquerel had read it back to her, she got up and walked over to the desk. He gave her the pen, then covering her hand with his, helped her to sign her name. Without waiting for the ink to dry, she snatched the page from the table and bolted out the door with the monk after her.

She did not bother to stop to put on her armor, for she would not need it. Instead, she ran through the busy kitchen, unmindful of the startled reactions of the cooks and scullery maids, and departed the house through the back door. Charging into the stable, she ordered Monsieur Boucher's groomsman to saddle her horse.

When the stableboy brought her horse around, Jehanne heaved herself into the saddle. She stretched out her hand to Pasquerel, who took it and climbed upon the animal behind her. She nudged the mount and he brought them to the street. Grabbing the first mounted archer she saw, she dragged him with her and Pasquerel to within shouting distance of the Tourelles.

As the crossbowman tied her letter to an arrow with a bit of string, Jehanne cupped her hands around her mouth and yelled toward the fort, "Here is news for you, read it!"

The man shot the arrow across the chasm in the bridge. It pierced a log near the top of the palisade with a *Thump!* and quivered there briefly. A brimmed helmet appeared above it, then the arrow was quickly snatched by a steel gauntlet and the helmet vanished.

After a few moments they heard, "Ah, news from the Armagnac whore!" followed by ribald laughter.

"Return to your cows, you filthy French slut!"

"Go spread your legs in some whorehouse!"

"But she likes bulls, lads, and as we all know, there are no *bulls* what go to *French* whorehouses! Come over here and we'll show you what real men are like!" Someone in the *bastille* made mooing sounds, and there was further hilarity.

"Please listen to me!" she pleaded, feeling an aching sorrow climb to her throat. "I am not what you think I am, for God has truly sent me to deliver this city and send you back to your own kingdom. Do not do this. You are endangering both your lives and your souls!"

"To Hell with you, you bloody whore!"

"God-cursed witch!"

"I mean you no harm, you must believe that!" Her voice broke under the weight of her emotions. "But you must give up Orléans and return to your own country! The King of Heaven—"

"This is our country as much as yours, you miserable cunt! And when we catch you, we'll burn you for England and St. George!"

"Three cheers for our good sovereign, Henry VI!" A chorus of hurrahs mocked her from the other side of the low mud wall.

She burst into furious tears, frustrated by her useless attempt to convince the doomed men. "Oh God, forgive them!"

They would not listen to her; they had scorned God's messenger, when all she wanted was for them to return home to their families and leave France in peace.

They refused to accept that it was as much for their good as the kingdom's that God demanded their surrender. And now they would certainly force the army's hand.

Pasquerel put a hand upon her shoulder and said softly into her ear, "Come, Jehanne, let us return to the city."

With a grave foreboding, she turned her horse and walked him away from the Tourelles. The archer who had come with her spat contemptuously at the fort.

"I know that God is nearby, comforting me." She wiped her eyes with her free hand. "I'll want you up early tomorrow, Brother, to confess me again."

"Of course," he said. They rode slowly back into the city and the solace of her acclaim.

Pasquerel kept his promise. The next morning, Friday, May 6, he again confessed his truculent charge, and because the oratory was too small to hold all of them, said Mass for her and her comrades in the Bouchers' parlor. Jehanne murmured a special prayer for the Englishmen who she knew would die today in a state of mortal sin. Then she asked God to watch over the brave men of France when they went into battle. Most of all, she prayed that all of this would soon be over. She was thankful that her entire household was safe, reunited, and here with her now to share in this Mass.

Early on, Metz and Poulengy had knocked on the Bouchers' door, bringing with them two loaves of fresh bread, a cheese, and a jug of wine for Jehanne's hosts. She was very glad to see them again. They had been with the army when they took St.-Loup, they told her, and although they saw her then, she had not noticed them among the other grimy, exhausted men.

After they finished breaking their fast, La Hire and a large number of soldiers came to fetch her. "The Bastard has changed his mind about attacking St.-Laurent," he snarled, obviously disliking this change in strategy. "He's crossing the river right now with a large force. They're going to attack St.-Jehan-le-Blanc instead."

"He did not tell me about that," she said, distrust of the Bastard's purposes taking hold of her. "Why did he change his mind?"

La Hire grinned down at her from his horse. "Don't you know by now that the seigneurs have him in their pocket? He doesn't want to get their butts—that is, make any of them feel slighted, so he always gives in to them, no matter how stupid their ideas are. This particular change in strategy was that little sh–, his brother Clermont's notion." He practically belched the name.

She looked at the drying mud beneath his horse's dancing hooves, anger flushing her face. "He did not tell me," she repeated.

"Nor me." La Hire's own outrage crackled in the black brows. "I found out by accident," he explained, "when a man-at-arms who's a friend of mine came to me with the news."

"Then we must hurry, or we won't catch up to them!"

This time she did not need to order her pages to procure her armor. At the sight of La Hire, both boys had dashed upstairs to fetch it. It took only a few minutes for them to fit her into the metal pieces. When they were armed too, all of them, including Pasquerel, mounted the horses Monsieur's stablemen had saddled and waiting. No more than twenty minutes had passed.

They raced through the city, scattering alarmed townsfolk in their path, and out the Porte de Bourgogne. By the time they reached the riverbank, the main body of the French army had already crossed the Loire over a hastily built pontoon bridge that stretched to the Grande Ile-Aux-Boeufs, then resumed on the other side of the island. An advance group had detached from this larger battalion and was rapidly closing in on the little church of St.-Jehan-le-Blanc, whose walls the English had plundered to raise a surrounding palisade. It was apparent that the enemy had spotted this troop bearing down on them, for they could be seen in the distance, abandoning the less important *bastille* and rushing toward the safety of the Augustins, a few hundred yards south of the Tourelles.

The old monastery, usurped by the English at the start of the siege, had long been protected by its own wall, enclosing the inner archways of the cloister on three sides. To secure the area further, the English had ripped planking from the chapel's steeple and roof, and used the wood both to surround the churchyard and to build a fence against the northern face of the chapel. Beyond it was a shallow dry moat that stretched two hundred feet or so to the awesome *boulevard* bridgehead leading into the Tourelles.

This monster was a man-made plateau, forty feet high and three hundred feet across, with sloping bricked sides leaning slightly toward the center, and a drawbridge on its eastern face. During peacetime it could be lowered to allow traffic from the river road access to the bridge, but now it was raised against the Armagnacs. Another drawbridge connected the *boulevard* to the Tourelles proper, which actually sat in the water, its four giant towers hulking over one hundred feet above the Loire. This second drawbridge could be raised or lowered from the Tourelles; now it was down to give the English admission to and from the bridgehead.

But Jehanne's concentration was not yet fixed upon the Tourelles. From the northern bank of the river, the enemy and their pursuers looked like desperate insects scrambling toward the desecrated St.-Jehan-le-Blanc.

She prodded her horse with her spurs, and with La Hire and the others tore across the unsteady pontoon that creaked and bobbed beneath the horses' clattering hooves. Even if the infernal thing collapsed, she promised herself that she would keep riding; she would swim the Loire if she had to!

As though in obedience to her will, the bridge held up, and she breathed a little easier when her mount jumped the short distance onto the sandy, brush-covered island. It took no time at all for them to traverse it and the shorter pontoon linking the island to the other side of the Loire. Just as they reached the south bank and the army's rear, de Gaucourt gave the order to retire.

"Fall back!" yelled the seigneur de Villars with a broad sweep of his arm. The trumpeter sounded retreat, and the order was shouted toward the Loire from first one captain to the next down the line.

Ignoring the command, Jehanne, La Hire, and the men following them dashed past the bemused infantry to the front of the column, now just a hundred yards from St.-Jehan-le-Blanc. Jehanne halted her horse within a few inches of the constable.

"What are you doing?" she asked in alarm.

"We could take the smaller *bastille*, but not the Augustins," de Gaucourt huffed, wiping the sweat from his wide forehead. Jehanne shifted her attention to the armored man in the familiar blue and white *huque* trotting toward her, and barely heard the old soldier say, "It is better that we withdraw."

The Bastard stopped his horse and raised his visor. "What are you doing here, Jehanne?" The friendly dimples were gone. He looked most displeased to see her.

"I am where I belong," she fumed, "here with the army. Why are you breaking off the attack?"

"As the constable has said, they are too many for us."

"But—"

"Look!" A man-at-arms in front of the Bastard's horse suddenly pointed toward the enemy. His gaunt face had lost all color.

The English were streaming from the Augustins a quarter of a league to the west, charging toward the now-retiring French army, shouting their feared battlecry at the top of their lungs. The sunlight sparked dangerously from their weapons and upon the wide-brimmed helmets of their infantrymen.

A wail of dismay rose from the Armagnacs in the advance guard. Already falling back, the men-at-arms among them picked up their pace and began running toward their commanders and the rest of the army. The horsemen in their ranks wheeled about and spurred their animals to retreat. All bluster was gone from their faces, and they resembled frightened children running home to their maman.

Jehanne looked at La Hire and he at her. "Are you ready?" he asked. His hand grabbed the hilt of his sword and pulled it free of its scabbard. The foot soldiers had reached them and were speeding past, bound for their rear and the security of the river.

"I am." She looked back over her shoulder at the army.

Now in near rout at the sound of the massed "*Hurrah!*" from the oncoming English, they were fleeing in the direction of the pontoon bridge. Some of them had already reached it, but Jehanne's own comrades were still with her. Poulengy drew his sword and licked his lips. Metz and d'Aulon slapped their visors shut.

"Let's go forward boldly in the name of the Lord!" Jehanne yelled.

Together, she and the captain lowered their lances and spurred their horses toward the attacking English. She heard Minguet's voice break as he cried her name.

Even as she surged ahead, Jehanne sensed the retreating French knights slow their flight to watch the tiny company charge the enemy, defended by little more than the soiled white standard flapping from one of the leading horses. Somehow she knew that, to a man, they were shamed at the sight of this reckless disregard for danger displayed by a girl. Honor would certainly demand that they ignore the order to return to the river, even as their leaders continued shouting for them to do so. She looked back over her shoulder to find that they were not going to disappoint her.

With an abrupt, ear-splitting howl, they raised their weapons and flung themselves after Jehanne and La Hire. The foot soldiers raced past a protesting constable de Gaucourt in pursuit of the horses, brandishing their *guisarmes* and swords.

Now it was the enemy's turn to be afraid. Hundreds of howling soldiers were bearing down upon them at full speed. Banners from Picardy, Anjou, Bretagne, Champagne, Limousin, and Orléans hurled their brilliant colors at the defenders of the Augustins, daring them in their lords' names to fight for their lives, with the white standard inscribed "JHESUS-MARIA" carried by the figure in burnished steel in front of them all.

The English turned about and sped back toward the Augustins with the Armagnacs close enough to taste the dust they raised. Caught at the end of the column, a few were slashed to the ground by the advancing French cavalry. Here and there, the odd English archer turned and shot at the horses. A well-placed arrow penetrated one horse's chest armor, and screaming, the beast skidded on its knees, tripping the mounted knight behind it. Both horsemen jumped clear. The master of the stricken horse did not even slow down but continued to run toward the *bastille*. The second, dazed animal struggled to its feet and wandered directionless for a few moments. Dodging the other oncoming soldiers, his master sprang forward, grabbed the bridle, then vaulted into the saddle as the rest of the army tore past him.

Among the first to reach the ravaged monastery, Jehanne leaped from her horse. She was immediately encircled by her comrades. A wave of horsemen dashed by her and quickly dismounted. She tossed the reins to Minguet, then ran after the soldiers toward the palisade at the southern end of the churchyard, wielding her standard in both hands. She stopped a few feet from the opening to deploy those behind her.

"Onward men of God, men of France!" she urged above the turmoil. "Have courage, for God is with us this day!"

Her efforts finally had support from the Bastard and two other captains, who had also dismounted and were motioning the running men into the Augustins with exhortations of their own. Gilles de Rais dashed by with his visor shut, but Jehanne recognized him by his armor. He drew his broadsword and led a contingent of men into the churchyard, and presently she could hear the contending swords and maces and the cries of pain from the other side of the wall. When the Bastard led a detachment around the corner to the western end of the church, Jehanne picked up her standard and ran after them with d'Aulon and her brothers on her heels.

Ahead of them lay a stretch of land that was once the monastery's garden, dotted with a few trees sprouting the first leaves of spring, and straight ahead, the roofless remains of the kitchen, now burned to the ground. Only a wall remained, its doorway open to the space before the chapel's westernmost portal, and beyond that the fence the English had constructed before the moat. The men ahead of Jehanne were running across the lawn, past the trees, intent upon taking the chapel on the other side of that gaping doorway.

A giant red-haired Englishman stood blocking it with a broadsword. His confederates behind him were racing to the fence, fright giving them the strength to leap the redoubt they had built, then down the other side and across the waterless moat facing the *boulevard*. As she sprinted after the leaders, Jehanne could see Englishmen atop the bridgehead hastily lowering ladders to their escaping comrades, who started scrambling upward. By now the Armagnacs had reached the Goliath's position, and he began to mow down his approaching adversaries with broad swipes of the monstrous weapon. Hacked nearly in half, men screamed in agony and crumpled to the ground.

D'Aulon, coming to a halt just in front of Jehanne, ordered a gunner known as the Lorrainer to fire his culverin at the enormous man. A noisy blast of sulfur and fire from the hand cannon ripped a hole in the *goddon*'s chest, and he toppled backward like a felled tree.

The oncoming Armagnacs unleashed a mighty cheer and flooded through the doorway and into the churchyard. Now insane with fear, the dozen or more desperate English still on this side of the fence threw themselves at the attackers and engaged them in fierce battle. The clang of their striking weapons, interspersed with grunts of exertion and anguished cries, rang through the May sunshine. The grass became slippery as bodies dropped to the ground, and in order to press on, the relentless wave had to step over fallen men.

There were too many of them for the English to withstand. Covered by whistling arrows from their comrades high upon the *boulevard*, the survivors leaped the fence and darted across the moat to the larger fortress, dragging their least wounded with them. The few who remained behind sacrificed their lives; within moments all were dead.

Jehanne started to run after the others who were already trying to make their way over the fence. A sudden sharp stab of pain pierced her left foot behind the big toe. She howled in surprise and dropped to one knee.

She had stepped on a *chausse-trappe*, a spiked iron ball used to hobble cavalry. It was still stuck to the bottom of her boot. Enraged and wincing in pain, she pulled it out and slung the hateful thing out of harm's way, grateful that at least it had not caught her horse. She hefted herself onto her good foot and limped into the courtyard as remnants of the army raced past her.

The last of the surviving enemy had escaped to safety upon the Tourelles' breastwork. With the Augustins now theirs, the exhausted French ended the chase. They would not attempt to assault the impregnable bridge fortress, not tonight with the sun setting. They paused instead to rest against the outwork and to see to their wounded.

For an hour or more the two armies shouted insults at each other across the short unbroachable distance separating them. But with nightfall taking away what little light there was, an uncanny hush came over the battlefield, disturbed only by the moans of the hurt and dying. The French dragged their dead and those of their enemies out of the monastery's grounds and arranged them in a row behind the far wall on the other side of the kitchen. The buzz of flies droned in the stench-filled air.

Jehanne hobbled painfully to the chapel door and, falling into a sitting position, leaned against the outer wall. After determining that her injury was not serious, Pasquerel began to administer the Last Rites to those who needed them. His ivory-clad form could be seen walking among the prostrate figures within the courtyard, stooping every so often to tend to a dying man. When he had finished seeing to the men on this side of the ruined kitchen, he made his way to the garden, where Jehanne lost sight of him.

She could feel her foot swelling within the boot until she thought it would burst its hinges. Turning her head a little, she took a deep breath of the dusk air and tried not to faint. She inwardly chided herself for being such a baby; this was only a little hurt compared to what many of the men had suffered. Beside her, Minguet rested a comforting hand on her other knee. Raymond sat across from her, leaning against a tree. He had removed his helmet and sweat glistened from his temples to his neck. He swatted absently at a fly that circled his damply matted head.

D'Aulon emerged from somewhere within the chapel's dark interior and offered Jehanne a flask of water. She gave him an exhausted, grateful smile and drank deeply.

"You should go back to the city, Jehanne," he said gravely. "You need to have your foot bandaged."

"That's what I told her," muttered a rueful Minguet.

She took another long drink and shook her head. "I can't do that. I'm not leaving the army."

A few steps away, the Bastard heard the exchange and came over to her. He hunkered down and looked at her with a tired smile. In the waning light she could see that his face was smeared with dirty perspiration, and there was a small swordcut on his cheekbone.

"The army will be all right without you," he said in a voice so gentle that it surprised her. "You led them bravely today, Jehanne, but now you need to rest."

"Am I to abandon our people just because I'm hurt and tired?" She looked around her in the darkness at the wearied soldiers. "Some of them are also wounded, and all are tired. You too."

"That's true," said La Hire. He was standing over her, grimy hands on his hips. "But you cannot help them. I will see you back into the city, and you can return here tomorrow after you have rested."

"Listen to them, Jehanne." Raymond smiled. "This is no place to watch the sun rise." The other four looked at her earnestly, concern etched in their drawn faces.

"You will do nothing more tonight?" she asked the Bastard warily. By now she was unwilling to believe anything he said. She still felt indignant about the lies he had told her.

He shook his head. "On my oath as a son of Orléans, I will not. I shall send word into the city that the people should ferry food and horses for us across the river. But I swear to you, I will not order an attack until tomorrow."

"The army needs rest, too," said La Hire. He spat onto the ground. "Besides, it would be foolish to attack the *goddons* in the dark."

Jehanne hesitated. The temptation to leave was stronger than the desire to stay. It was not only for her own sake that she should leave. If she went, Minguet and Raymond could go with her. They were not really soldiers, she told herself, and it would serve no useful purpose to keep them here.

"Very well." She looked at her pages. "I want you two to go with me."

She tried to stand, but the unexpectedly cumbersome armor and her swollen foot dragged her back to the ground. La Hire and d'Aulon each took an arm and hoisted her to her feet.

"Jehanne, wait!" cried Pasquerel from the other side of the fort. The monk's white robe bobbed ghostlike in the dimness as he stepped over the wounded and made his way to her. "I want to go with you," he announced.

"What about the men?"

"I've done all I can here." He looked about the darkness. "I've ministered to them as well as I can tonight, and the dying are in God's hands now. My first duty is to you."

His plain face was somber in the moonlight. Weary circles underlined his eyes. Dark droplets of other men's blood were splattered across the skirt of his habit, and a smear stained his sleeve where a soldier in his death throes had grabbed his arm.

She nodded.

They helped her to her horse. D'Aulon gave her a leg up into the saddle as La Hire barked orders to some of the men to help him accompany the Maid back into Orléans. Two familiar shapes approached her from the direction of the garden, the one tall and lanky, and the other with his walk still bouncy despite his tiredness.

"Where are you going, sweetheart, on such a lovely night?" Metz joked. The light from the moon made his teeth gleam like chalk.

She gave him a wan smile. "Back into the city. Do you want to come too?"

Metz looked at his friend. Poulengy shrugged as though to say, It's all the same to me.

"It looks as though you have a strong enough escort," Metz said, sweeping his eyes over La Hire and the other mounted men. "We're having such a good time here, I guess we'll stay. If the *goddons* decide to get frisky in the middle of the night, the army will need us. After all"—he grinned—"we're the best and they can't win without us."

Jehanne laughed in spite of herself. "Are you sure?"

"Yes, Jehanne, go." Poulengy nodded. "Don't worry about us; we'll be safe enough."

She suddenly thought of something. "Have you seen my brothers? I haven't since the attack started and I—"

"It's all right, Jehanne," Poulengy assured her. He looked around at the men resting upon the ground. "They were here a few minutes ago, and neither of them is wounded. I don't see them now, though."

"They've probably straggled off into the bushes to relieve themselves, or something like that." Metz rubbed his nose with the back of his hand.

"If you see them again, will you tell them I've gone back into Orléans and that they can come, too, if they want?"

Her friends assured her that they would deliver her message. Then they bade her good night and settled back down upon the ground among their comrades. They were really in their element here, she realized. That was a mild surprise. For some reason, she did not often think of them as soldiers. In many ways it was easier to regard them as gentlemen.

She was bone-tired by now. Every muscle in her body ached, and her foot throbbed so that she again thought she would faint. She remembered a prediction that Catherine had made yesterday when Jehanne knelt in the Bouchers' oratory for her morning prayers.

Now she asked, Is this it, is this the wound you told me about? It hurts, but it's not what I expected.

YOUR TEST WILL COME TOMORROW IN BATTLE. DO NOT BE SURPRISED TO FIND BLOOD FLOWING FROM A PLACE ABOVE YOUR BREAST.

Is it really necessary? she pleaded.

IT IS THE ANSWER TO YOUR PRAYER.

What do you mean?

Catherine faded away without giving Jehanne an answer.

Oh God, I do not understand, but please help me to accept Your will! Her eyes filled, misting over the darkened landscape before her and the silent men-at-arms riding stoically at her side. Feeling increasingly lightheaded, she clung to the saddle.

She had to take herself in hand before they reentered Orléans. It would not do for the people to see that she was wounded and sad and just a little afraid of tomorrow. They expected strength from her, and courage. It occurred to her now, as they crossed the river the way they had come and headed back to the eastern gate, that God had sent her not only to raise the siege but to give the people hope. She straightened her posture and coaxed her face into a smile.

The ever-present crowds greeted them at the Porte de Bourgogne. While still ardent, the people had begun to murmur in concerned curiosity, for they had had no news since the army left the city. "What has happened over there?" boomed a masculine voice.

"Never fear," Jehanne shouted, "we have taken the Augustins, and tomorrow we shall overrun the Tourelles and lift the siege!"

A joyful whoop blared forth as from one voice. The inhabitants danced up and down and embraced one another. They surrounded Jehanne's party and began trolling her name for the thousandth time. She smiled and waved to them again. Tonight, with victory on the horizon, she too felt buoyed and encouraged, and exhaustion and her injury were almost forgotten. The Orléanais followed her all the way to the Bouchers' door.

The family and household made a big fuss over her when she reached her lodgings. While Raymond and Minguet quickly peeled away her armor, Madame Boucher went to the kitchen and instructed the cook to heat some water. Jehanne sank down wearily onto a stool. Pasquerel knelt before her and unfastened her metal boot. The blood had dried into a thick cake that glued the bottom of her foot to the boot, and the sticky skin pulled painfully as it came off. Very carefully, Pasquerel stripped away the brownish-red sock. Jehanne inhaled sharply and her back stiffened.

Madame Boucher carefully cleaned and then wrapped Jehanne's aching foot in white bandages. A sip of wine from the cup Charlotte offered her made her feel much better. She had to admit that she was glad that the Bastard and La Hire had talked her into returning here. Unlike all of those still at the river, she would get to sleep in a real bed tonight, a fact that made her feel a bit guilty. She mentally whispered a quick prayer for their safety and another that the Bastard would keep his word.

With her wound dressed, the pages helped her to her feet and she limped to the table where the evening meal was spread. They were still eating when a battle-stained knight knocked on the door. A servant admitted him, and he sought out Jehanne.

"I have come to tell you that the Bastard's council of war has decided that we are still too few in numbers to take the Tourelles. Therefore, we are going to wait for reinforcements from the king before we attempt it. The townsfolk are bringing food across the river to the army, so we are well supplied and can afford to wait."

Those fools! she thought angrily, I knew it! Once again the Bastard had disappointed her, if not exactly broken his word. If the captains were not such cowards, this siege could have been lifted a week ago.

Forgetting her foot, she tried to stand. An abrupt sting made her sink back onto the bench.

"You have been in your council and I in mine," she retorted. "And believe me, my Counsel will hold fast while yours will come to nothing!" She looked across the table at Pasquerel. "Get up early tomorrow, Brother Pasquerel, even earlier than you did today, and stick by me as closely as you can. I'll have a lot to do, more than I've had yet, and I'll be wounded here"—she touched her left shoulder—"above my breast."

All eyes were on her. Minguet went pale. She returned her attention to the exhausted knight. A shamed look crossed his face, and he found himself unable to meet her insolent gaze.

He did not believe her, none of the captains believed her. But the people did, and more importantly, the army did. The Orléanais demonstrated that with a genuine affection every time she went out of the house. Today, for her, the army had turned retreat into a magnificent triumph. They would follow her anywhere she chose to lead them. If the captains were such imbeciles as to turn and run like sheep every time they were threatened, that was their lookout. But the people and the army were hers.

She stared silently at the messenger the council had sent in such a spineless fashion. And she knew that he understood her. Bowing, he turned and left the house.

Madame Boucher shook her awake before dawn. The city's burgesses were there, Jehanne's hostess whispered, and desired most urgently to speak with her. She was sorry to have to turn Jehanne from her bed, what with her injury, but the gentlemen were quite importunate.

Jehanne tumbled out of bed, careful not to disturb Charlotte. Her emotions were still in the grip of a dream, something frightening about riding a horse across a hellish landscape. She pulled on her clothes in the half-darkness, then went downstairs, the dream forgotten.

There were five of them sitting in the parlor, their worried features dimly illuminated by candlelight. They stood as Jehanne limped into the room. She recognized them from the council meeting of two days ago. All were dressed in fine tunics of satin and damask and rich velvet mantles. Silver pins adorned their swept-back hats. Their mien was almost humble this morning, unlike the air of haughty judgment they had last displayed.

Robert de Valcourt, their leader, glanced quickly at the others and cleared his throat. He informed Jehanne that the captains had decided to wait for reinforcements before attacking the enemy. Jehanne groaned. She almost wished that they had not roused her for this. It was old news and most unwelcome to hear again.

"But we have been in our own council," the burgess continued earnestly, "and we have come to ask you to rise to the obligation that God and the king have entrusted to you. We want you to disregard the captains, we are begging you to rally the army to lift the siege as you promised."

She looked at them intently. So this was what it had come to. At long last, they had seen the commanders' true mettle. And hers. She was filled with a sense of exculpation and sweet satisfaction as she answered, "In God's name, I will do as you ask."

Turning away from them, she staggered up the stairs. Her foot still hurt but she was resolved to put discomfort aside. There was too much to do; enough time had already been wasted without allowing herself to be slowed by a minor injury. She knocked on the door to the room that Pasquerel shared with Ambleville. Then she went to the converted council room where the pages slept and woke both of them. Returning to Pasquerel's room, she induced him to say a hasty Mass for her. After Minguet had prepared her for war, they hurried downstairs.

The burgesses had gone. D'Aulon and Ambleville were waiting for her. Jacques Boucher stood at the table next to his wife. When he saw Jehanne, he proudly held up an enormous trout still lying on the damp brown paper in which it had only recently been wrapped. "See what someone has brought for you, Jehanne." He beamed with undisguised delight. "Let us eat this fish before you leave."

"Keep it until tonight"—she grinned—"and I will bring back a *goddon* to eat his share after we have taken the Tourelles and returned by the bridge."

She did not feel comfortable voicing it, but she meant Clasidas. She had fallen asleep the night before thinking about how, when the battle was won and he had surrendered the Tourelles and the siege was lifted, she would bring the English nobleman home with her. They would sit down to eat something together, and then he would know that she was not as he had feared. She would tell him that she forgave him and his men for the verbal filth they had flung at her, then she would explain to him in a civilized manner why God had decreed that his little king had no right to France.

But in the meantime, there was work to be done.

Outside, the sun was just rising and the faintly pink sky promised a clear, sunny day, a good day for victory. The stablemen held the company's horses before the door. Jehanne's, armored and magnificent in his glittering chainmail, stamped his foot impatiently. Even at this early hour a large crowd was gathered, an armed sea of pikes and swords, some wielded by women. They gave Jehanne a loud cheer.

D'Aulon bent over next to her horse and cupped his hands together. She stepped into this support, grimacing at the sudden pang, then up into the saddle. When she waved to the crowd, they applauded her again. Her companions clambered upon their own mounts. She surveyed the assembly and shouted, "Let all who love God follow me!"

The roar from the people was a tonic that warmed her all the way down to her swollen foot. They proceeded through the city toward the east, and as they rode, other Orléanais, tired of being imprisoned within their own city, joined them. There were no soldiers in the crowd. Jehanne assumed that all of them except the militia, under orders from the Bastard to remain in their billets for the time being, were on the southern bank of the river. As usual, it was a stupid strategy. Had the English wished, they could have taken the city with little effort.

When they reached the Porte de Bourgogne, they found that the portcullis was down. Constable de Gaucourt stood in front of it with six or seven of his guard. All were heavily armed. It was apparent from their belligerent stance that they had heard the clamorous parade approaching even before it entered their sight. But when he saw the horde of townsfolk approaching, led by Jehanne and her companions, the elderly minister's jaw dropped and he gasped. As Jehanne drew rein, he raised his hand.

"I am sorry, Jehanne," he said, frowning sternly, "but I have orders not to allow anyone to leave or to enter the city."

The multitude exhaled an angry mutter. De Gaucourt looked around at their numbers with some anxiety. Secure in her support, Jehanne smiled. "And who orders you, sieur Constable? You are the most powerful man here aside from the Bastard, are you not?"

"The captains have decided—"

"The captains are fools who have let this thing drag on for too long!" she shouted. A terrible light shone in her eyes. "And you are indeed a wicked man. How many soldiers do we need to defeat the *goddons*? Must we wait until every man-at-arms and knight in France is here with us?"

There was another rumble from the crowd, louder this time. Some of them raised their crude weapons in an unvoiced threat.

"I have said again and again that God is with us and with His help we will lift the siege, for that is His solemn promise." Her intense brown eyes defied him.

The glower creasing his forehead deepened.

"If your faith and that of the captains is weak, the army believes and so do the people." She pulled on the reins to steady her restless mount. "Whether you like it or not, or believe it or not, the army will win this day as they won yesterday and the day before that!"

"That's right!" someone shouted.

"Move out of our way, old man!"

"Death to de Gaucourt if he will not let us pass!"

There was a roar of approval from the throng. De Gaucourt's wrinkled jowls went pasty and his eyes became larger. He was shaking visibly. The guard behind him tightened their grips on their weapons.

"No!" Jehanne raised her hand. The people grew silent. She turned halfway in her saddle and looked around her.

"There is no need for violence among ourselves. The enemy is over there!" She pointed toward the river. "Sieur de Gaucourt shall let us through." She directed an unflinching smile to the constable. "Won't you, my lord?"

He hesitated for a moment. Jehanne's horse reared his head nervously. The soldiers in de Gaucourt's guard looked at one another and tensed, their weapons ready.

The old warrior glanced over his shoulder at them. "Raise the gate," he ordered.

A yell of triumph resounded from the Orléanais. Jehanne and de Gaucourt continued to stare at one another, now with perfect understanding.

Two soldiers rushed to the wheel beside the gate and turned it. The giant portcullis creaked upward, opening its mouth. When it was high enough to allow those on horseback to pass, Jehanne ripped her eyes from the constable and spurred her mount. Her companions trotted briskly after her, followed on foot by the howling populace.

The sun was peeking over the city wall now, and its golden light twinkled brightly upon the Loire. The pale blue sky already burned with a severity that portended a hot day, and as they tore down to the riverbank and trotted across the shaky pontoon bridge, Jehanne felt the sweat dripping down her back beneath her armor. From the bridge she could see tiny figures running the distance between the Augustins and the *boulevard* connected to the Tourelles, the winking flashes from their weapons and the seigneurs' colors flying in the midst of armor and beaten leather, visible through a cloud of dust. The battle was already under way.

Urgency goaded her across the pontoon bridge, and when her party reached the southern shore, she spurred her horse to a fierce gallop. They passed the deserted St.-Jehan-le-Blanc with the warm wind whipping through her helmet and whistling in her ears. Even so, she could hear the conflict dead ahead. The shouts of encouragement from the commanders and screams of pain were unmistakable, increasing in volume the closer she came.

She drew rein at almost the exact spot where she had dismounted last night. Leaping from her horse, she dashed toward the action without looking back to see who followed.

The French had torn down the Augustins' rear wall which the retreating English had leaped last night and were assaulting the even larger earthen redoubt leading into the Tourelles. Hundreds of Armagnac soldiers were in the dry moat, attempting to scale the long ladders made from the now dismantled fence and propped rung-to-rung against the wall. With their shields on their backs and their helmeted heads, the climbers looked like determined beetles. Flying arrows zipped from the *boulevard*, cutting through the steaming sunlight, followed in the next moment by screams and shouts from wounded men. Jehanne saw men fall back into the ditch as they were hit. The English upon the wall pushed the ladders backward, flinging Armagnacs to the ground. Another volley of arrows whistled from the outwork, skewering those below, but the French pushed ahead, scrambling over their fallen comrades to reach the wall.

Meanwhile, archers in the moat were returning the *goddons'* fire; here and there, enemy men-at-arms plummeted to earth; others of their company lurched back into the fort. In return the English hurled heavy stones at French heads, and while some bounced harmlessly off the sturdy armor, others crashed onto their targets, cracking skulls. Those few Armagnacs who made it to the top were cut down with swords and maces before they could use their own. A blast from an English culverin killed two men simultaneously. Jehanne watched in anguish, intuition whispering that the exhausted army of God was beginning to falter.

"Be hopeful, men, and do not give up," she shouted, "for today God will give us victory!"

The army had not known until they heard that unmistakable voice that she was among them again. Now they sent up a mighty "Hoorah!" They renewed their attack as though crazed by a disregard for their mortality.

With her standard fluttering from her hands, Jehanne ran from one end of the ditch to another, urging on the determined warriors while arrows whizzed around her. Pasquerel and Minguet followed her with their hearts in their throats, for they had not forgotten her prediction.

With the battle raging through the morning and on toward afternoon, the pile of corpses in the moat grew deeper. By now the garrison had brought two cannon from Orléans, which they positioned in the moat behind thick wooden shields, and the bellow of the guns rent the air. From the redoubt, the English returned the cannon fire with their own, and men in the moat choked upon dust and smoke and death. Unable to reach the fortress itself, the mammoth stationary cannon upon the city's ramparts across the river blasted into the low wall protecting English access to the bridge, but the breastwork was too heavily defended and did not give. As the hours passed with the enemy still in control of the battle, French resolve began to slacken. Many of the men, their strength depleted, fell back and stumbled across the moat into the Augustins. Jehanne felt dismay begin to nibble at her confidence in them.

She could not let them give up, not now when victory could be theirs if only they persisted! It was up to her. For the last two days her words alone had been enough to inspire them to victory. Now, if she led by her example, they were sure to follow.

Thrusting her standard into the hands of a grimy man-at-arms, she placed her foot on the bottom rung of a ladder. "Follow me, men!" she yelled. "The day is ours!"

An unexpected punch in her left shoulder knocked her backward. She fell onto her side with a bone-rattling thump and stared stupidly at the arrow sticking out through her armor.

"We've killed the witch!"

The exultant cry came from gleeful figures above her whom she sensed, rather than saw, dancing up and down. With her entire arm beginning to go numb, she looked up and saw three or four Englishmen on the high wall prepared to leap down to where she lay. Their faces were contorted in hatred.

Almost casually, she thought she was certainly dead. Before fear could really manifest, she was surrounded by a defensive ring of armor-plated legs. Through a mist of gnawing pain, she was aware of the panting grunts of her comrades as they slashed ferociously at the enemy who had jumped to the ground to finish her. More knights rushed forward to help, and in a short time the English were cut to pieces. One of Jehanne's saviours turned to look down at her and lifted his visor.

It was sieur de Gamaches, the same man who had argued with her over tactics a few days earlier. Sweat streamed down his brow and trickled across his prominent, scarred nose. He raised a gauntleted hand and beckoned testily to a squire on the other side of the moat.

"Are you all right?" he panted.

She could only whimper in pain and fright.

"Here," he said as his squire reached them, leading a sturdy warhorse, "take my horse to safety." He helped her to her feet, and she swayed dizzily. "Let us not have any more bad feeling between us," the nobleman said with an apologetic smile. "I confess that I was wrong about you." His image blurred before her but she heard his words.

"I'd be in sin to hold a grudge," she gasped, obligated to say something. Even moving her tongue in speech was painful, and her next words were a mumble: "I see you truly are a noble knight."

The Bastard was there now with Pasquerel. They boosted her, half-swooning, into the saddle. She grasped the high pommel frantically as Pasquerel led the mount at a trot across the ditch and up the other side to the ridge. By now the initial numbed shock had worn off and the pain was excruciating. Every jolt of the animal provoked a fresh stab in her shoulder. She could no longer feel anything at all from her elbow to her wrist. The hand within her gauntlet was wet and sticky.

I'm going to die here, she thought desperately. Her breathing had changed to quick, shallow bursts.

Pasquerel and Minguet helped her down from the horse and into a sitting position. The monk pulled the helmet from her head and laid it beside her on the ground. Minguet's face was white, but he unbuckled and removed her breastplate without hesitation. A small puddle of blood stained her shirt.

"Has it gone through to the back?" she whispered. Her confessor nodded. His face was as ashen as though he were the one injured. "Then break off the point," she muttered through clenched teeth. Oh God, she had never imagined that anything could hurt so much!

Pasquerel did as he was told and snapped the rounded iron point from the shaft, but even the careful movement of his hand jarred the wound and evoked a more profound agony. She cried out. Sweat streamed into her glazed eyes, mixing with tears.

"It must come out, Jehanne," her confessor said.

She looked up into his distressed face. "I know."

"Do you want me to do it?"

"No," she groaned, "I will." She grabbed the shaft with her right hand. Please, Lord Jhesus, give me courage!

She counted to three and pulled out the arrow with a quick motion. Someone screamed. From far away, she realized that it was herself. Blood and bits of tissue gushed from the hole in her shoulder, flooding her shirt in a crimson stream. She collapsed onto her back and finished falling into faintness.

Why was this necessary?

All in good time.

Why?

Do not be afraid, Child of God. It is a little pain that will soon be healed. You are our beloved one, our brave one. You shall not die. You can never die. Rest awhile in the arms of God.

Although the voice was Michel's, all three of Them were with her. Their sparkling essences glowed soothingly through the pain, and the radiance surrounding Them hummed a healing tune, single-toned and powerful. Someplace within that lovely light was a realm where all had meaning and everything made perfect, elegant sense. It was, as Michel had said, only a little pain.

"We should charm her wound," she thought she heard someone say.

"No!" she cried, instantly alert. She opened her eyes.

Several dirty-faced soldiers stood behind Minguet and Pasquerel. One of the warriors held out a crude charm of horsehair and feathers. The monk was holding her blood-stained right hand, and when he saw that she was conscious, he squeezed it to comfort her.

"Get that thing away from me!" she gasped, glaring at the crude talisman as though it would bite her. "I would rather die. I shall not use magic; God will heal me instead."

D'Aulon broke through the circle of anxious, pale-faced men, holding a wooden cup. He knelt beside her and handed the vessel to Minguet. Then he ripped her shirt above the bleeding wound. Jehanne was aware that the top of her breast was exposed for all to see, but she did not care. Her squire dipped two dirty fingers into the cup Minguet still held and lifted out a glob of thick, whitish paste.

"What is that?" she whispered.

"Bacon grease and olive oil. It will stop the bleeding." D'Aulon wiped away as much blood as he could with a rag and spread the mixture across the oozing hole in her shoulder.

Jehanne let her head fall back onto the ground and smiled through her tears at the worried masculine faces. "It's all right," she said, "God is with me." She turned her head to Pasquerel. "Will you confess me, Brother?"

"Of course, dear child." He was still holding her hand.

The soldiers and Minguet stood reluctantly and moved away from her. Pasquerel made the Sign of the Cross in the air and mumbled some words in Latin.

"Bless me, Father, for I have sinned," she whispered. "My Counsel have assured me that I shall not die, yet my faith is so puny that I still doubt Them sometimes." A barb of pain pierced her shoulder and she grimaced. "They told me this would happen, but in my heart I would not let myself believe Them. I did not want to believe Them. I wanted to choose my own fate instead of relying on God's will for me. I ask His forgiveness for my double sin of disbelief and fear. I know that I shall die someday; everyone does. Yet I am so afraid of death, even though my Counsel have promised that when I die I shall go home to my Heavenly Father."

The monk smiled and wiped the clammy sweat from her brow with his hand. "Do not trouble yourself, Jehanne," he said quietly. "God forgives you your weakness, and in His mercy will give you strength and courage." He made another Sign of the Cross over her. "For your penance, say a *Pater*."

"Will you pray with me?"

He nodded. Together, they intoned the sacred words. As the tears streamed down her sunburned cheeks, a sense of peace settled over her. With the prayer finished, she crossed herself with a shaking, bloody hand.

She tried to sit up. Her head was pounding and the earth tilted at a crazy angle as nausea grabbed her throat.

"Stay still," Pasquerel said. "Sleep a little."

"I can't. The army needs me."

Her confessor looked toward the Tourelles and shielded his eyes from the sun. "The battle is still going on." He smiled down at her. "The soldiers know that you are hurt. They are fighting for you and will not give up until they have won. Sleep, Jehanne."

She closed her eyes. It would do no harm to rest a little, to wait for the ground to stop swaying before she returned to the fight. She slid down a long tunnel, away from the battle.

From far and away a trumpet blared the call to retreat.

Jehanne's eyes popped open and this time she did sit up, quickly, exiling the ache in her shoulder to a place of irrelevance. The sun was lower on the horizon now and with barely three hours of daylight remaining, it cast an orange-golden light onto the clouds above Orléans. She had been unconscious longer than she had intended. The soldiers had turned away from battle and were stumbling across the ditch toward her.

"Help me up," she ordered Pasquerel. He put his arm around her waist and lifted her to her feet. "My armor, Minguet, hurry!"

The boy picked up her punctured breastplate and secured it in place with hurried fingers. Then he put the helmet on her head. There was still no sensation in her arm, but the nap really had made her feel better.

Jehanne stumbled down into the moat toward the oncoming army. She swallowed the bile tempting her to throw up. The Bastard came toward her with a fatigued smile. Before he could say anything, she grabbed his arm with her free hand.

"Why are you retreating?" she asked.

"It's no use," he replied wearily. "The army is spent, Jehanne, they cannot fight any more today. The fortress is too strong for us to take. I'm going to have to call upon the king for more men."

"Give me a little more time," she begged. Out of the corner of her eye, she could see La Hire and Poulengy coming toward them. "God has promised that we'll have a victory today, so we must not give up!"

The men exchanged a doubtful glance.

"Tell the army to rest for a little while," she implored. "There's plenty for them to eat and drink. When I return, we can renew the assault." Without waiting for an answer she turned and started back toward the Augustins.

"Where are you going?" Poulengy called after her.

"I'll be back soon!"

She climbed the ridge, grunting painfully, and mounted the horse that d'Aulon held in wait for her. Spurring the animal, she rode toward the vineyard a few hundred yards south of the monastery. When she reached the isolated spot, she eased her aching body down from her mount and knelt on the ground. She crossed herself and clasped her hands together.

Help me. The army does not believe they can win. Give me the Power to persuade them.

THE POWER IS YOURS AS IT HAS ALWAYS BEEN. IT IS THE WILL OF GOD THAT THE CITY SHALL BE FREE. FOLLOW THE DESTINY YOU HAVE CREATED, AND DO NOT BE AFRAID OF FAILURE. RETURN NOW TO THE ARMY; THEY HAVE NEED OF YOU.

She said a *Credo* and a *Pater*, then quickly crossed herself. She mounted the horse and hastened back toward the ridge.

The army had collapsed to a state of rest within the Augustins' churchyard, at a safe distance from the fort and its lethal inhabitants. Jehanne looked down into the moat and saw d'Aulon running toward the *boulevard*. Behind him a Spanish soldier known to everyone only as the Basque was holding her standard in his left hand and a broadsword in the other, and from the tension in his body it looked as though he was preparing to join her squire.

Furious, she jumped down from the horse and ran to the Basque just as he started after d'Aulon. Grabbing the staff, she stopped him in mid-stride.

"What are you doing?" she demanded in outrage. She pulled it toward her. "Give me my standard!" She tried to yank it out of his hand.

But he jerked it back toward him. The black eyes were dull, uncomprehending, almost stupid.

She clung to the pole, unwilling to relinquish it. "I said, Give that to me; it's mine!"

He tugged it back toward him, grinning now as though this were a game.

The other soldiers must have thought that it was an intentional signal to attack, because suddenly they bolted to their feet, and with a powerful yell surged toward the Tourelles. Taken by surprise, the Basque let his attention slip from Jehanne to the army.

She wrenched her standard free from his hands and tore into the ditch after the soldiers. "The day is yours!" she shouted above the assault. "God has promised that you shall enter!"

The army flung itself against the breastwork, this time refusing to be repulsed despite the renewed hail of English arrows and stones. Imbued now with an implacable determination, they scaled the tall ladders in great numbers and began streaming to the top of the wall. On and on they went, heedless of the defenders' attempts to stop them, and surrounded by the thunder of voices alternately barking orders and yelling in agony. Nothing would turn them back, not arrows nor stones nor the blades flashing from the desperate *goddons'* swords and battleaxes. They were hacked and gouged and more took their places, exhorted upward by the short, wounded shape in gleaming armor. There were so many on the ladders now that those still in the moat growled impatiently for their turns to scale the wall. As the Armagnacs poured into the *boulevard*, they met with little further resistance from the English.

The defenders broke and began running across the top of the bridgehead, toward the drawbridge and into the fortress. The Armagnacs howled in triumph and continued scaling the breastwork unimpeded.

Jehanne climbed a ladder propped next to the raised drawbridge, standard in hand. She had to move slowly since her left arm was useless and her right occupied. First a step up, then a grip to the ladder and the banner's staff simultaneously, then another step. Already dizzy, she did not dare look down. It was all right if she took her time. She had filled the army with the decisive yearning for victory, and if they took the Tourelles ahead of her, it would be God's will. A step up, and another; she would get there eventually.

She reached the top of the *boulevard* well behind the rest of the army. Looking down at the fortress ahead of her, she saw that a burning barge had come to rest beneath the thirty-feet-long drawbridge, its heat shimmering through the dense cloud of black smoke rising toward the coned towers. The boat had been fired and floated toward the Tourelles in order to prevent the English from raising it and to block their retreat. Now the confounded enemy were densely packed into the fort with no means of escape. French knights and men-at-arms continued to fling themselves onto the bridgehead, and soon the narrow space where the drawbridge met the *boulevard* was crowded shoulder-to-armored-shoulder with snarling men bent on carving the English to pieces if they tried to brave the flaming drawbridge and return to the redoubt.

Jehanne was standing near the northeastern corner of the *boulevard*, her position elevated above the drawbridge and well to the right of the Tourelles. When she became aware of the sudden noise from Orléans—like the angry drone surrounding a beehive—she limped all the way into the corner to determine the source of the commotion. Leaning out over the water as far as she dared in order to see past the Tourelles, she gasped at what was coming from the city, across the bridge leading to the fortress.

The Orléanais who had followed her through the Porte de Bourgogne had at some point in time returned to the city without having crossed the river. Now a vast, armed host crammed the bridge north of the missing span in wait for the English. In front of them, carpenters had nailed planks together to traverse the blasted hole, and the city's militia were crossing the makeshift link to engage the enemy.

With a new threat from the other side of the Tourelles, the surrounded English were in panic. Desperate to escape, they darted toward the drawbridge, which was now in flames. Leading them was the man whose eagle-embossed arms had been described to Jehanne by the Bastard so precisely that she recognized him without having ever laid eyes on him before.

"Clasidas!" Jehanne yelled, "Surrender to the King of Heaven! You called me a harlot, but I have great pity on your soul and those of your men!"

She would never know whether he heard her. More willing to face the Armagnacs than the population they had so terrified all through the winter, Glasdale and several of his knights started across the drawbridge toward the *boulevard* bristling with French arms.

There was an abrupt groan from the wood, followed by a loud *Crraaack!* and the burning timbers collapsed beneath the weight of their armor. The combined might of England fell screaming into the river and was immediately pulled to the bottom.

A jubilant yell from the French burst through the twilight, and they waved their weapons in triumph and clapped one another on the back. Some of them embraced, laughing. They began to shout, "Agincourt! Agincourt!", their weapons piercing the air with every cry of that hated word.

But Jehanne felt only horror at the thought of the unrepentant enemy dead. They had gone to their Judgment cursing her name, still disbelieving that she was God's agent and that it was His will that they leave France. Her lovely daydream sank to the bottom of the Loire with Clasidas. He would not go back to Orléans with her; they would not share that fish.

She bowed her head. A profound sorrow seized her and she was overcome with tears. Pasquerel put his arm around her shoulder and she wept against his shoulder.

"It could not be helped," he whispered, "you could not have saved them."

After a few moments she raised her head and looked down at the fortress. The remaining English had surrendered and thrown their weapons onto the floor of the Tourelles. Now overrun and seized by the militia, they were being taken from the fort with their hands above their heads, across the planks that now connected the Tourelles to the northern bridge.

It was over. With the Tourelles again in French hands and only the northern *bastilles* left in English control, the siege of Orléans was ended.

As she had predicted to the Bouchers that morning, Jehanne returned to the city by way of the bridge, after the Armagnacs spent three hours constructing a new link between the *boulevard* and the Tourelles. Every bell in every church exploded in joy, and there was wild, drunken dancing in the streets, for the taverns had opened their wine barrels to the public to commemorate this magnificent, liberating victory. Jehanne rode through the streets flanked by the Bastard and La Hire. She had temporarily put aside grief and her soul pealed like the giant instruments as it never had before tonight. She had managed to find her brothers with God's help, and they rode behind her, next to her confessor and her pages. D'Aulon was there as well, along with Poulengy, Metz, and the elegant Ambleville. She thanked God for sparing them, and prayed for the soul of her lost herald, Guyenne.

The city was ecstatic beyond belief. Her inhabitants had been captive for seven long months, and now with their liberation no longer a dream, they were deranged with gladness. In the coming night the Orléanais screamed Jehanne's name until their throats were sore; indeed, they shouted until they lost their voices. The streets were as brightly lit as though it were day, for not a torch in Orléans was unlit. Smoke from a potent cloud of incense rose toward Heaven like the massed prayer of thanksgiving, and accompanied the procession of monks who walked in solemn steps before Jehanne, singing *Te Deum laudamus*.

Jehanne grinned at the people hanging onto her saddle, clutching at her. She clung to her horse with her knees and waved her uninjured hand at the worshipping, raucous crowd. There was still no feeling in her left arm, but her agony and dizziness had diminished enough for her to remain in the saddle. She was determined not to allow the pain to show in her face. This was Orléans' own glorious night, and she would not ruin it by succumbing to her wound. Soon enough she would have it treated and fall into bed. It had been the longest day of her life.

In a scene reflecting her arrival over a week earlier, massive crowds followed her across the entire city. The longer it went on, the more her fortitude began to weaken. It got to the point where with every sluggish moment, Jehanne thought she would faint. She found herself wishing when they were halfway there that Jacques Boucher had had the foresight to buy a house near the Porte de Bourgogne. Then, stung by remorse, she reminded herself again that this was the townsfolk's night, the army's time of victory, and more important than her selfish desire for rest.

But respite did come, finally.

Only when the door was shut did she allow herself to lean heavily against d'Aulon. Jehan held her up while the squire and Minguet quickly stripped away her armor. She was near fainting when the Bastard picked her up like a child and carried her to Charlotte's room. She was only half aware of Madame Boucher's quick yet gentle hands as the woman cut away Jehanne's bloody shirt and began ministering to her wound. They were alone but for Charlotte, who held the bowl of warm water while her mother cleaned the puncture and applied an herbal ointment. The warm concoction felt good, restorative; it penetrated her shoulder and soothed the wound. When it was bandaged and her arm slung at a comfortable angle, Madame Boucher smiled at her.

"You should eat something, Jehanne. We have a meal prepared for you."

She blanched at the thought of the fish. It reminded her of Clasidas and made her stomach turn. "Water," she rasped. "I'm so thirsty."

"Charlotte, bring Jehanne something to eat and drink." The little girl ran from the room.

Jehanne dozed.

Before she knew it, the child had returned with a tray laden with the unwelcome portion of baked fish, and bread, and cheese. There were also two cups, one filled to the brim with water. The second contained wine.

Jehanne sat up groggily and reached with her right hand for the water. She drank noisily until forced to breathe. There was still some left and she poured a little of the wine into it. Then she dipped a piece of bread into the mixture and ate it, then another.

It was all she could ingest. She would eat something more substantial tomorrow when no longer in the grip of nausea and fatigue. She pushed away the tray and her head flopped down onto the soft pillow. She slept.

CHAPTER EIGHT

Shadow Wars

May 8–June 10, 1429

y five o'clock in the morning a large crowd of torch-bearing Orléanais had turned out to wait upon the city wall, eager to see what would happen next. Even in the gray half-darkness the battalions below were so close to the ramparts that the crowd had no difficulty seeing them. If they engaged one another today, the resulting spectacle would give the people a sweet satisfaction, for the wheel of Fortune had turned and there was no doubt in their minds who would win.

The sky began to pale, and a silence as thick as cannon smoke drifted over the two armies facing one another between the western English strongholds and the walls of Orléans. The light of the coming day shone blood-crimson upon helmets and the prickly forest of swords and *guisarmes* pointing toward the violet, still starry sky. A warm breeze blew in from the river, lifting in silent challenges the brightly colored banners scattered among both sides' infantry and steel-coated horsemen. The men, roused long before sunup, covered yawns with their hands and uneasily shifted stiffened limbs. Well over two hours had they faced one another in the lifting darkness, yet neither side moved to attack.

La Hire's great hairy hand gripped the hilt of his broadsword as he stared straight ahead at the enemy lines and the obscene flag of the English king quartered with the golden, red-fielded lions of that kingdom and the fleurs-de-lys they hoped to make their own by force. The captain's eager grin made it clear to his comrades that he had not had enough of battle, not yet. Perhaps today would give him a chance to cover himself in further glory by killing many more *goddons*. He had prayed that it would be so during the two Masses his little friend ordered sung before the sun began to rise. And after he prayed he was reassured that today God would surely do for La Hire what La Hire would do for God, if only the King of Heaven were a man-at-arms and he God.

In the line next to him, maréchal de Sainte-Sévère's horse stamped its enormous foot and snorted. The old man nodded an acknowledgment to the Bastard of Orléans, who was riding back and forth in front of the assembled knights, inspecting the battalions headed by his comrades and equals, Gilles de Rais, Ambroise de Loré, Poton de Xaintrailles, and Florent d'Illiers. His brother Charles de Bourbon, the comte de Clermont, smiled at him as he passed and raised his sword in a salute to the city's victor.

The Bastard smiled back at him, filled with pride in the younger man who had so distinguished himself in yesterday's triumph at the Tourelles. In truth, he was pleased with all of them, every battle-stained one, from the lowest archer under his command to constable de Gaucourt. How contented the duc d'Orléans would be when he received the Bastard's letter announcing the wonderful tidings! For the Bastard would proclaim that the dishonorable curse which had haunted the armies of France for some seventy years had finally been lifted along with the siege. Never again could the English say that theirs was the most skilled army on earth. Never again would a king of France have to hang his head in shame and despair at his forces' defeats. God had given them their chance at last, and they had proved themselves masterful battle knights all. But even as he favored them with his handsome smile, the army knew, if the Bastard and his captains did not, who was really in charge and to whom they owed their victory.

Because her still raw wound would not permit the weight of her breastplate, Jehanne was wearing a long tunic of chainmail over her steel leggings. The hauberk reflected the late spring dawn in tiny shimmering mirrors, and a pale rose aureole glinted from her helmet. To her right, Minguet rested the shaft of her standard in the leather socket attached to his horse's saddle. When a brisk wind caught the banner and unfurled it for all to see, some of the men crossed themselves.

She had been summoned from her bed by Madame Boucher in the very early predawn hours. Sentries posted on the battlements of the city's western wall had spotted the English emerging from their *bastilles* and ordering their companies into military formation. By this time, bells all over Orléans were tolling their warning. The hastily awakened city was in chaos, said Madame Boucher in a voice trembling not with fear but with excitement.

Raymond and Minguet had quickly armed Jehanne with the fluid coordination that was beginning to characterize their partnership. Then, together with her brothers and Pasquerel, they all mounted up and rode in the company of the captains through the Porte Regnard to the west.

Still full of yesterday's victory, the army had wanted to press their advantage and finish off the heathen *goddons*, but Jehanne held them back. Because today was Lord Jhesus' day, Sunday, May 8, it would not be permissible to attack them, she said. But if they were assaulted first, then of course God would allow them to defend themselves. Before the sun came up she had ordered two Masses said there in the open field. The bishop of Orléans, accustomed to praising God in the cathedral of St.-Croix, felt himself honored on this special Sunday to perform the ceremonies on a crude wooden chest. With yesterday's certainly God-bestowed triumph fresh in their minds, the army had knelt and received Holy Communion in a spirit of reverential awe foreign to most of them.

Now, with both observances finished, they were all back in the saddle and waiting for the English to make a move. The enemy remained still for a long time.

Finally, when the sun had crested the horizon and the stars disappeared, a trumpet sounded from the enemy lines, two high notes followed by a lower tone, then another high note. The sequence was repeated. The Armagnacs tensed, ready for battle, and pointed their weapons toward their adversaries.

Like a sluggish giant rising from a deep sleep, the English stirred. The well-trained ranks reversed their colorful flags, and turning their backs on Orléans, began to march away toward the west.

A cheer thundered from the ramparts above the city. Civilians were waving their hats and jumping up and down upon the wall.

"Come on, men, after them!" shouted La Hire, aiming his sword forward.

"Let them go!" Jehanne yelled. "It is not the Lord's wish that you should fight them today. You will get them another time!"

Most of the army obeyed her order and fell reluctantly back into line, but La Hire and Ambroise de Loré were determined to do battle and were already racing with the men under their commands after the fleeing English.

Jehanne watched them go with mixed emotions. On the one hand, she was vexed that the two commanders would not listen to her. It was unchivalrous and against God's teachings to harass a retreating enemy. They would certainly have to be confessed and do penance when they returned. Yet, the other half of her heart did not mind if they disobeyed her. She was still very tired despite her night's rest, and lightheaded from lack of food and the loss of blood she had sustained in yesterday's battle. Besides, the truant knights just might return with valuable arms and information about English intentions, if they could capture a *goddon*.

The Bastard raised his hand. "Into the forts!" he shouted, loudly enough for the army to hear. "Let us see what the enemy has left behind!"

A cry of approval rose from the ranks. The captains spurred their horses ahead. Jehanne did likewise, and accompanied by Sainte-Sévère and de Rais, galloped toward the former church of St.-Laurent southwest of the city. Jehanne's household chased her white horse in a useless attempt to keep up with her.

St.-Laurent dominated the western road into Orléans and was the largest of the remaining enemy forts. From a distance there was little evidence of its earlier role; it looked like a massive, baked-mud lump. But as they came closer, Jehanne saw that the original structure had been surrounded by a planked wooden fence which stretched almost to the roof. Like the Augustins', it had been partially ripped apart for its lumber so that the beams nearest the steeple—and the front of the steeple itself—were open to the elements. The base of the palisade was planted in the earth, and over the frame, spread not quite all the way to the top, the English had plastered a thick wall of mud mixed with generous portions of grass. One did not have to look far to determine the wall's source: a shallow dry moat ringed the *bastille*.

The party made its way down into the moat and up the other side. They dismounted at the only visible opening in the wall, a crude portal six or seven yards east of the church door. The fort was very quiet but for the muffled moans of the wounded echoing eerily from somewhere inside, like indistinct conversation coming from a room in another part of one's house. Jehanne removed her helmet and gave it to Minguet for him to tie to her saddle. De Rais and Sainte-Sévère drew their swords and entered the palisade. Jehanne and the others followed the warlords through the opening.

Approximately ten feet separated the fence from the church in the middle of the fortress. Though small, it no doubt had once been grand when its sturdy stone walls were new and the stained-glass windows clean enough to permit the light to shine through them like colorful rays from God. But now St.-Laurent reminded Jehanne of a despoiled woman, what with its broken windows and torn-away roof, and at the sight of this sacrilege resentment and anger again began to race through her blood and tighten her throat.

What remained of the churchyard's lawn had long ago been gnawed to stubble by English horses, and a veritable army of flies swarmed about the droppings that lay everywhere in both fresh and old piles. A defensive catwalk circled the fence about four feet from the ground, high enough for the English soldiers to have shot their arrows at attackers, and wide enough for a man to stand upon it without fear of losing his balance and falling to the ground. There were a few old barrels against the fence; all empty, reported Sainte-Sévère's men. Splintered arrows, cracked shields, and one or two bloody bandages further contaminated the sacred ground. But there was no sight of anyone except the Armagnac men-at-arms, who were walking cautiously about the area with their swords drawn. They could hear the enemy, though. The ghostly groans originating from the church were louder now, as though those inside knew that succor or a quick death had come for them, and the sound of it shuddered in the fine hairs at the base of Jehanne's scalp.

His own weapon still unsheathed, Sainte-Sévère went to the church door and entered. Jehanne followed him, knowing without really looking that her comrades were at her side.

For a few moments the knight blocked the doorway, so she smelled it even before she could see anything, and the stench nearly knocked her over. The combined odor of human waste, blood, and death attacked Jehanne's nostrils and she gasped, the gorge rising in her throat. She swallowed but could not force back the salty nausea.

Sainte-Sévère moved forward several steps and Jehanne saw the men, English and captured French, who covered the church's dirty floor, groaning. Many were mortally wounded. In their delirium they were babbling of battles long past and speaking to families whose faces they had not seen in months. Here and there arms stiffened by death's rigor stretched upward as though beckoning pitifully to God. A boy about Pierre's age, whose stump of a right arm ended at the elbow and was wrapped in a blood-encrusted rag, lay against the ruined altar whimpering in pain and fright of the death he knew was at hand. The plaster crucifix behind him was turned at an odd angle on the wall. There were no statues of any kind, and but for the cross, one would never have known that this was once a church. A heavy drone of flies buzzed in the oppressive interior. The ill, victims of malnutrition and rotten food, lay in reeking puddles of their own filth. They were surrounded by the litter of war. Battered shields and broken swords lay haphazardly among forgotten crossbows and maces, and there were even a few unopened barrels of gunpowder stacked in one corner next to a dead man.

"My God!" Pasquerel gasped. He made the Sign of the Cross. Brushing past Jehanne, he went to administer the Last Rites to those who still lived.

She started after the monk, intent on helping him. A weak hand grabbed her foot, and surprised, she looked down.

A bearded Englishman lay white-faced on his back, one filthy hand tightly gripping a rip in his stomach from which his entrails protruded. The other was wrapped, clawlike, around Jehanne's boot. His breathing made a ghastly, rattling sound, and there was a froth of bloody bubbles at the corners of his mouth. He seemed unaware of the lice crawling through his matted beard, one of which was meandering toward his nose.

"Kill me," he croaked, beseeching Jehanne with those terrible, desperate eyes, "for the love of God, have mercy on me. Kill me!"

The pool of blood beneath him was black, puddinglike, and Jehanne was appalled to see that she was standing in it. She pulled her foot free of his feeble grasp and lurched back a pace. It took everything she had to keep from vomiting.

Her eyes filled, and she breathed, "I can't."

"Please." The whisper sounded like that of a child, lost and helpless.

She shook her head. "Brother Pasquerel!" she called urgently. "Over here!"

The monk raised his head and rose from his crouched position. He pulled the skirt of his habit up to keep it out of a puddle of combined feces and blood, and stumbled over a dead man to where Jehanne stood white-faced, pointing down at the fading English life. Pasquerel knelt as best he could beside the man and began to murmur the Latin rite of death.

Jehanne's tears spilled down her cheeks and dropped from her chin onto an abandoned boot. Oh dear God, be with them at this time of their deaths. Forgive their sins and grant them entry into Your Kingdom!

"Jehanne, come quickly!" D'Aulon's shadow was framed in the narrow doorway, the morning glowing behind him. "There is something you must see."

She limped toward him and out into daylight where the stench was weaker and she could breathe again. The pain in her shoulder throbbed beneath her hauberk.

Gilles de Rais, his curiosity piqued, pursued with his sword still in hand. Pierre nudged his brother and the two of them ran from the charnelhouse after Jehanne. It was a signal for the rest of her household to follow. Sainte-Sévère and his men did not bother; they were too busy collecting the abandoned arms and gunpowder.

D'Aulon took them to the rear of the *bastille* and pointed to the stake the English had pounded into the earth. A man was bound with chains to the evil instrument, and a large pile of unlit wood lay stacked around his feet. His head slumped forward limply on his chest. The once grand heraldic clothes were torn and caked with dried mud.

"Guyenne," Jehanne whispered. She ran toward him, her sore foot forgotten. "Guyenne!"

Taking care not to slip, she climbed the sticky, pitch-smeared woodpile. She grasped his face and lifted his head.

He had been beaten savagely. The entire left side of his face was swollen and discolored, and a large purple bruise closed his eye. Dried brownish blood formed a crust around a large cut over his cheekbone. His breathing was faint and shallow, his lips cracked by violence and lack of water. Jehanne wiped away her tears and swatted angrily at the insistent flies swarming about his head.

"Is he dead?" asked de Rais, his voice detached, no more concerned for Guyenne than he would be for a wounded deer.

"No." She shook her head. "Help me to get him down."

While Pierre and his sister held up Guyenne, the seigneur and d'Aulon untangled the heavy chains. Then they carefully lifted him from the unignited pyre and laid him on the ground.

Jehanne sat down next to him and cradled his wounded head in her lap. She accepted the open flask of water that Jehan gave her and poured a little onto the herald's parched lips. His tongue licked at it uncertainly. Raising his head a little, she put the container to his mouth. He drank slowly at first, then in deep gulps as some of the water spilled down the sides of his newly bearded chin. His one good eye opened and he tried to smile.

"Thank you," he rasped.

A heavy sob pounced from her throat. "I'm sorry," she whispered. Forgive me, Lord, she begged. This is all my fault.

She turned anguished eyes to those around her. Minguet was wiping away his own tears with a grimy hand. Confronted by the treatment that might have been his, Ambleville stood next to the boy, pale and shaking. Jehan knelt down in the dirt beside his sister and squeezed her shoulder. Pierre, to de Rais' left, stared grimly at the half-conscious herald. Jehanne could feel Raymond standing behind her though she did not see his face.

"We need to get him to a doctor." D'Aulon frowned.

Jehanne nodded, unable to speak for the tightness in her throat. She gently lifted Guyenne's head and placed it on the ground. Then she stood up.

D'Aulon and Jehan stooped and put the courier's arms around their shoulders and lifted him to his feet. They half-carried, half-dragged him to the entrance of the fort and put him on a horse. He was too weak to hold on, so they laid him across it and Jehan mounted the animal behind him. The rest of the party climbed upon their own horses and they started slowly back toward the city.

At the junction in the road linking the *bastille* de la Croix Boissé and the Porte Regnard, they came upon a comical yet shocking sight.

Approaching them from the west was a soldier riding on the back of an aged monk. The knight wore a broad grin and his long legs hung ludicrously almost to the ground. Beneath him, the monk stumbled and nearly fell. The strain of his burden made the friar's face look as though it would explode; sweat poured from his temples. The group halted as the soldier and his peculiar mount reached them.

"Good morning," said the warrior. "Lovely day for a ride, don't you think?"

"Who are you, sir knight?" de Rais asked, trying not to laugh.

The man got down from the monk's back, then kicked his backside. The friar fell forward onto his face with a grunt. "I am Bourg de Bar of the garrison, and I have been held captive by the *goddons* for almost three months. They thought to ransom me, but now we can turn the tables and ransom this"—he pointed to the prone monk—"instead. Tell them who you are, priest."

The elderly monk sat up and looked at them, eyes bulging in terror. "Please don't kill me," he implored.

Tossing a disgusted glare at Bourg de Bar, Jehanne jumped down from her horse and helped the friar to his feet. De Rais also dismounted and swaggered toward the Englishman, scowling ominously at the frightened man. "Who are you?" he barked.

"My name is Thomas Warren," the monk stammered. "I am confessor to Lord Talbot."

"Do you see that man there?" de Rais pointed to the unconscious Guyenne. The monk nodded. "Your master had him tied to a stake. Why did he not burn him?"

Brother Thomas hesitated for a moment and looked at the others. Then, prodded by de Rais' sinister frown, he answered, "He could not without permission from the University of Paris. The theologians there are the only judges who may condemn a man to death in that fashion. Sir John did not have the authority."

"Nor did he have the right to burn a *herald*!" De Rais swung his arm and struck the monk across the face.

Warren fell backward into the dust. The seigneur took a step toward him and raised his foot. But before he could kick the whimpering priest, Jehanne put herself between them.

"No!" she shouted. "He is a man of God!"

"He's a filthy *goddon*."

"He is a man of God," she repeated, "and you commit a grave sin by doing him violence."

De Rais' lips contorted into a sardonic smile. Abruptly, he turned his back to her and stepped up into the saddle. He gave each of them a derisive look, then turned his pale, malicious eyes back to Jehanne.

"You feel sorry for these English? Well, Jehanne the Maid," he said with a sarcastic sneer, "we'll see how much charity you have left for them when they chain you to the stake and decide that they need no one's permission to light the fire."

A fragment of her recent nightmare flashed beneath her mind and she shivered. She had no chance to retort. De Rais had already whipped his horse around and was pressing it toward Orléans.

Good riddance, she thought. She had never liked him. Of all the captains in the Dauphin's army, he alone made her tremble with an indefinable apprehension. There was something malignant about the young lord, in spite of his pedigree and his courtly charm. A presentiment told her that he would come to a bad end. She frowned as she watched his horse canter down the road.

"Hey, look!"

She turned to see Pierre pointing at a large cloud of dust hanging over the highway to the west. Jehanne shielded her eyes from the sun to watch the troop nearing them at a brisk trot. La Hire and de Loré were returning from their adventure. In their train was a captured wagon piled high with canvas-covered booty. Two horsemen were dragging a middling-sized cannon behind them. But Jehanne was not impressed.

"Why did you disobey me?" she glowered as La Hire drew rein.

He pointed to his chest with pretended innocence, then looked over his shoulder and back at her as though she surely meant someone else. "Me? How did I do that?"

"You know very well, La Hire." She ignored his jest and continued to glare at him. "It is a sin to provoke battle on Sunday."

"But we have done no battle. We found all this sh–, this stuff by the side of the road. The *goddons* did not have the strength left to bring it with them. Surely that was the will of God."

Her nostrils flared angrily. "That is a blasphemous lie! You stole those things from an enemy in retreat, and for your sins and the ill use of His Name, God will certainly punish you!"

"Not I?" La Hire pointed to himself again, grinning like a mischievous little boy.

"Forget it, Jehanne," intruded d'Aulon before she could respond. "We must return to the city. Guyenne needs a doctor." The normally mild man was frowning at her impatiently. His petition was repeated in her brothers' faces.

She nodded. He was right to rebuke her. Because of her, Guyenne might still die, and her first duty was to him. She could argue with La Hire later.

With a glare at the uncontrollable captain, Jehanne climbed back onto her horse. They took Brother Thomas with them into Orléans.

Pasquerel stayed on at St.-Laurent into the early afternoon. Soon after Jehanne and her companions left the fort, townsfolk readied by the Bastard began arriving to take away the wounded and bury the dead. With the last of the stricken survivors of the battle for Orléans confessed and prepared for Judgment, the dusty, blood-stained monk rose stiffly to his feet and stumbled, blinking numbly, out into the sunlight. Florent d'Illiers gave him a ride into the city on the back of his warhorse. As he held on to the captain, it occurred to Pasquerel that his work as a confessor was not done. He had seen Jehanne's face when they entered the *bastille*. His experience told him that she would seek absolution for what she supposed was her accountability in all of this.

Instead, when he reached the Boucher house, Pierre Darc informed the friar that his sister was asleep. He said that after the doctor had come to tend Guyenne, and Jehanne was assured that her herald would live, she had seen to it that the English monk was given food and wine. She forbade anyone to bother him. She told them that she would give him into the custody of the Church, later. Then she had retired to Charlotte's room for a nap.

Her shoulder wound still bothered her, added Minguet, and not even the noisy celebrations in the streets could keep her awake. It was all Madame Boucher could do to persuade Jehanne to eat something before she dropped into bed.

But Jehanne did not sleep for a long time. She lay on her back with her good arm under her head, staring at the wooden beams crisscrossing the ceiling.

She could not remove the tableaux of death from her mind's eye. War was not as she had imagined it would be. Truth be told, she had not known what to expect. For all this time leading up to her arrival in Orléans, she had been fixed solely upon lifting the siege and had not foreseen men hacked to pieces, limbs missing, eyes shot out with arrows. Her Counsel had never prepared her for the pathetic moans of the wounded and the panic of the dying when they knew at last that the end was near. And, truth be told, she had not *wanted* to see such things.

It had also shaken her to her foundation to find that she, too, could be wounded, that she was as much at risk in battle as any other soldier. The Guides had not told her in the beginning that something like an arrow wound could happen to her. Indeed, They always promised that she was under God's protection. They still refused to address her confusion directly.

She curled up onto her side and bit her fist, fighting back tears. Her memory took her back to her first real conversation with the Dauphin at Chinon, when she had told him that they all had their lessons from God. How innocent that sounded now. She had been so confident then, so unaware of the import of what she had said. But here in this shuttered room, in the aftermath of dreadful suffering, she heard her words with new ears, mocking her.

What were her lessons? Charles had asked that, and full of her own importance, she had given him a careless reply. Now she made the same inquiry of her Counsel with a chastened, guilty heart.

I do not like this. Something is very wrong. Please speak to me, please.

The answer came in the faintest trace of a whisper. THERE ARE THINGS WE MAY NOT TELL YOU. THESE "LESSONS," AS YOU CALL THEM, MUST BE ANSWERED ONLY BY YOURSELF. And then, as though she had been nothing more than a fantasy, Catherine was gone. Jehanne could not feel any of Them.

She put her hand over her face as frustration and remorse filled her eyes. Perhaps They had abandoned her because she had somehow failed.

No, not "somehow." There was no use lying to herself. She had failed, and her greatest failure had a name.

Poor Guyenne! That noble man, bred to the pleasant life at court, had found himself in the service of one not wise enough to consider what would happen to him when she used him to send her message to the English. She should never have appointed her heralds to undertake that mission. She should have done it herself, or shot it into the *goddon* fortress as she was finally forced to do. If she had only done anything else but risk a life other than her own!

Well, she had certainly learned that lesson and would never do it or anything like it again. Now that he was recovered from the stake, Guyenne would live, thanks to God's mercy. But how could she possibly protect the rest of the army?

They were soldiers and therefore prepared to take chances, that was true, but this was *her* mission, *her* war.

That is not so. Take yourself in hand, Jehanne.

This is not your war. The English have been here for longer than even the oldest Frenchman or woman can recall. They started it, not you. Agincourt happened when you were three years old, and it was an ancient hatred even then. It is they who maintain it, they and the Burgundian traitors. You are seeking to end it.

But how to end it by fighting? Is that possible? A tiny suspicion bubbled into her brain that perhaps God did not countenance the war either. After all, the English were also Christians. They worshipped Lord Jhesus just as she did. They probably loved and laughed and feared and hated just as any Frenchman. She had seen for herself that they bled to death in the dust and the indignity of their own excrement, and in their last throes were much the same as their Gallic counterparts.

Stop this!

You have been sent by God to defeat the English and to drive them from France. They have shown by their treatment of Guyenne and their hatred of you and of all things French that they will not make peace until they are defeated. Has not this great victory shown you that God holds you in His tenderest mercy and confidence? You should feel cleansed by His forgiveness. If your Guides are silent, now when you most need them to explain why you feel so let down and miserable, then that must be your fault. There is surely something you have left unfinished.

Her eyes blinked open and she tried to sit up, but the ache in her shoulder pushed her back into the pillow.

The Dauphin had not yet been crowned! That must be the reason for her low spirits. The Work was only half done. Tomorrow, she would leave Orléans and go to Charles. She would tell him that in liberating the city she had given him the sign he had requested. She would remind her liege that now it was time for him to take on his share of the burden for France's future. Surely now that he had a solid victory to his army's credit, he would be joyously eager to drop everything and hasten to Reims. Even as she thought this, she somehow knew not only that the war was not yet over for her but that it had scarcely begun.

A yawn seized her. She was so very tired. Her mind needed to be clear if she was to go on. It would be all right to think about all of this later, after she was rested.

She closed her eyes again and drew the blanket up to her chin. The world receded and she tumbled into a quiet place.

She awakened from her nap still haunted by scenes of death and a dreadful, blurred premonition stirring somewhere in her mind. Feeling a need to unburden herself to Pasquerel, she eased herself gingerly into a sitting position, then to her feet. Her wound, although stiff, did not ache as severely as it had before she slept, and she was able to walk downstairs without feeling that she would faint.

The house was unusually quiet. Jehanne found Madame Boucher and Charlotte in the parlor, spinning flax on Madame's wheel. When Jehanne asked where her companions were, she was informed that none of them was in the house.

Not even her confessor?

No one, Madame told her.

Where did they go?

Madame did not know. Was Jehanne hungry? she wondered. Supper was not yet ready, but her hostess was sure that the cook could find something in the kitchen for her to eat while the evening meal was being prepared.

Jehanne frowned and replied that she was not hungry. In fact, she was piqued that they who claimed to love her were off who-knew-where while she was feeling so downcast. She wanted to go back upstairs and just sleep through the night.

Since she did not want to eat, Madame asked if perhaps Jehanne would like a bath.

After a moment's reflection, Jehanne accepted the offer. The warm water would be a balm for her shoulder, and besides, she had been too busy for the past few days to bathe properly but had only washed her feet and the sweat from her face. So Madame ordered the cook to ready Jehanne's bath in the pantry. She soaked for a long while and emerged clean, water-wrinkled, and in somewhat better spirits. Madame applied fresh bandages to her shoulder and foot, which lifted Jehanne's mood a little further.

Poulengy and Metz, dressed in handsome tunics she had never seen them wear, came for her as the sun began to set. Both men were newly shaved and their hair was cut short, Poulengy's for the first time since Jehanne had acquainted herself with him again in Vaucouleurs. They were on their way to a tavern and wanted her to go with them. At first she demurred, pleading fatigue, but they reminded her that she had not spent any time with them since the army left Blois well over two weeks ago, and they missed her company.

"Come on, sweetheart," Metz prodded with his familiar grin. "Remember back in Vaucouleurs, when you went drinking with us? We paid for the wine that night, and now that you're rich with the Dauphin's silver, you owe us at least one tankard."

She laughed. "I thought you said there's none left! You told me that I spent the last of it in Tours."

"He lied," Poulengy offered, cupping his hand to his mouth in a mock whisper. "He held back a little because he knew that we would raise the siege, and he's been looking forward to your buying him a drink."

"Or two." Metz held up two fingers, then three.

She was really in no mood to leave the house. The streets were still raucous and lively from the victory celebrations, and she did not think that she could countenance the crowds, not tonight. But her friends' faces were so eager and joyful that she could not in good conscience refuse the invitation. And they were right. It had been a long time since she had spent any time with them. Although they said they missed her in a joking manner, she knew that they really did.

So she dressed in her finest clothes, without armor. She put on the blue tunic and hose that the Dauphin had given her in Tours, and around the doublet she belted Ste.-Catherine's sword. She also wore a grand hat, a gift from an Orléanais admirer. It was made of gray felt, and had a large brim that turned up in front and was fastened by a gilt pin in the shape of a long fleur-de-lys. On its top was another flowered pin from which a waterfall of small chains flopped against the brim in tiny, tinkling lilies. The hat was, she knew, a perfect complement to her princely garments. It also made her appear a little taller.

Normal business still had not resumed. Everywhere was rapturous merrymaking, and Orléans was alive with the looks and sounds of a citywide street fair. The familiar banners emblazoned with the coat-of-arms of the duc d'Orléans and the king's golden lilies hung from windows and balconies much as they had when Jehanne first came here. Wearing a satisfied look which proclaimed the profit he was making this night, a baker was selling pastries from his cart, little tarts and sweetmeats decorated with sugary fleurs-de-lys. He was not alone in his pursuit of ready money: craftsmen who customarily plied their wares behind residential shopfronts—glassblowers and cheesemakers, silversmiths, clothiers, and wood-carvers—had placed small tables with samples of their goods before their shops, and were competing with one another for Orléans' patronage in a babble of urgent entreaties.

In front of a wineshop a group of musicians added to the din, playing a sprightly tune on their pipes and lutes and vieles, accompanied by the dull rhythm of drums. Drunken civilians and militiamen quaffed from the stored wine barrels which again had been opened to the public, and they were singing and dancing to the music with women who, in tribute to springtime, wore wreaths of bright flowers in their hair. Children were chasing one another between the baker's cart and his patrons. When two of them stumbled into a juggler, nearly causing him to drop the blue and yellow balls he seemed to have suspended in the air, the baker grabbed them and boxed their ears.

A little further down the narrow thoroughfare, a street magician was swallowing fire from the end of a long stick, and a team of acrobats tumbled and frolicked near him. In contrast to all the liveliness, a long dual column of Franciscan monks filed down the littered street toward the cathedral, their cowls lowered over unknown faces. With great solemnity they walked along, chanting their song of thanksgiving, seemingly heedless of the festival going on about them.

The people recognized Jehanne at once and, abandoning their singing and dancing, massed upon her. Metz and Poulengy found it necessary to push some of the more eager away, threatening them with their swords, otherwise she would have been dragged from her horse and suffocated with love.

Jehanne waved to the people, smiling but with remorse clogging her throat. This had long since stopped being exciting; in this moment it took great willpower for her not to spur her horse and flee Orléans forever. It was not only that she missed her privacy, the right to walk about freely. Far more important was the blasphemy she felt in their attempts to kiss her hands and feet, as though she alone had given them this liberation. It was God Who had spared Orléans, though no one but Jehanne seemed to realize it. She did not deserve to be praised for following God's commands. Indeed, she had failed so miserably to protect even her own household from harm that she hardly merited any honor at all.

She did not feel like going to a noisy tavern. She wanted to shut herself away and be alone with her grief; but it was too late for that.

Her friends took her to an inn known as the Wandering Goose on a quieter little street off the main route. She was much surprised to see that there were five armed knights in full armor standing guard under the swaying painted sign. When they saw her, they pointed their swords toward the townspeople who had followed her and stepped forward to shield her horse from the crowd.

"Get back, you people!" one of them growled. "Return to your revelries. This tavern is closed to the public tonight."

Jehanne raised her eyebrows and stared at him in surprise.

"It's all right," Poulengy said to her with a mysterious smile. "He doesn't mean us." He swung down from his horse and beckoned, indicating that she should do the same.

The knights moved in front of her with their weapons aimed at the muttering crowd, who were already starting to disperse. Jehanne and Metz slowly dismounted.

She gave her smiling friends a suspicious look. "What's happening? Why did he say that the inn is closed?"

"Never you mind," Metz answered, grinning like a boy with a secret.

"Come, Jehanne." Poulengy opened the door and held out his hand in a gesture indicating that she should enter before him.

Jehanne walked across the threshold, then froze.

They were all there, dressed in their best clothes and bathed in a many-candled, golden light. Constable de Gaucourt, Gilles de Rais, Poton de Xaintrailles, Boussac de Sainte-Sévère, the sieur de Gamaches, the comte de Clermont, and all the rest—even the Scotsmen in their plaid cloaks—stood behind two long trestles crowded with platters of food and large winejugs. Chains of bright flowers festooned the rafters above their heads. From the table of honor connecting the trestles at the room's far end, the Bastard of Orléans, shaved and clad in the deep green and scarlet colors of his House, favored Jehanne with a dimpled grin. The space to his right was empty, waiting. Jehanne's proud, smiling household stood near it. Like the battle lords, they were immaculately groomed and beautifully dressed.

For a moment Jehanne did not know the man on the Bastard's other hand. Then with a start, she recognized La Hire. He had shaved off his beard and cut his hair above his ears. His muscled torso bulged beneath a splendid crimson tunic.

Her eyes filled with tears as she understood.

"Gentlemen!" Smiling, the Bastard picked up the cup in front of him and raised it. The men quickly lifted their own goblets. "I give you the messenger of God, the liberator of Orléans: Jehanne the Maid!"

"*Jehanne the Maid!*" They raised their cups and drank deeply.

La Hire and Poton de Xaintrailles ran to her and pulled her into the open space in the center of the tables. One on each side, they picked her up and tossed her above their heads. "The Maid!" the captains shouted.

When she landed, they flung her above them again, toward the flowered rafters, once more shouting her name.

Muscular arms caught her. "The Maid!" they cried with the next upward thrust.

She was laughing when they put her down at last. The ritual was the same as they performed when any of their number rendered an exalted deed. It was an act of comradeship bespeaking equality, a show of respect for her captaincy and her contribution.

De Xaintrailles shoved a full tankard of wine into her hands. "Drink!" he instructed. He had obviously been at it for some time. His eyes were glazed and a thick river of wine trickled darkly from his chin. He wiped the sweat from his brow with a meaty hand. "Go on!" he exhorted. "You've earned it."

She smiled back at his eagerness and at the happy, leathery faces of her comrades. Raising the cup, she cried in a voice quavering with emotion, "To you, men of France, who with God's help have sent the *goddons* from Orléans!"

She put the tankard to her lips and drank. The wine burned all the way down her throat as she drained the vessel without stopping to breathe.

A robust manly sigh rose from those about her, followed by gruff, hearty laughter. When La Hire, intending to be friendly, thumped her injured shoulder, she flinched. Metz offered her his arm. She accepted it, and he escorted her to her place at the Bastard's side. Then the party got under way in earnest.

The Bastard had hired three acrobats who, while the meal was in progress, tumbled and executed splits in the central space between the tables. The innkeeper and his family hovered in the background, fetching platter after platter heaped with fruit, or roast capons, or bread, or leg of lamb, or cheese. Accompanied by an ensemble of musicians, a troubadour took the place of the acrobats, and in a hearty voice sang of great deeds of valor performed in battle by courageous, honorable men. Not to be outdone, a Scotsman produced his bagpipes and played a jaunty tune—which sounded to Jehanne like someone torturing a cat—while his fellows whooped and danced to attendant hand-clapping from the French.

More food appeared: rabbit stew, swimming with onions; pike seasoned with rosemary and ginger; buttered greens and turnips with chestnuts. The celebrants rapidly drained the first wine barrel, then another. They began on a third just as a jester took the floor. The man had a funny, rubbery face that he could twist into any shape, and he was a master of puns and marginally lewd *double entendres* that made Jehanne squirm a little.

But on the whole she found him exceptionally entertaining, and laughed heartily along with the others. Her merriment increased when a tipsy La Hire and Florent d'Illiers stepped into the focal spot and lampooned what was actually a serious love song, a dialogue between a knight and his lady. To see La Hire singing the part of a timid noblewoman, accompanied by suitable simpering and eyelash-batting, was truly uproarious, and Jehanne laughed so hard and so loudly that her sides ached. She was enjoying herself a great deal and had to admit that she was very glad that Metz and Poulengy had appeared to spirit her away to this place.

That night she got sick on wine for the first and last time in her life. She rarely had more than one cup a day with meals and then irregularly, and so was not accustomed to drink. And despite the wealth of food, she had actually eaten very little. When she felt nausea coming on, she excused herself and left the tavern through the kitchen. Almost no one noticed; most of the men were well into their own cups.

Everything came up in an alley behind the inn. She hunched over onto her hands and knees above the shallow gutter and let the poisons gush from her mouth. Vomit splattered onto her face and her tunic. Her eyes watered profusely as she heaved and heaved and then discovered that her stomach was empty. For several moments she gagged in shuddering spasms.

She was finally able to lie back against the rear wall of a house. The passageway pitched up and down, then sideways. She laughed weakly, wiping the moisture from her eyes, the spittle from her mouth.

What would they say, those blasphemous, adoring people, if they could see Jehanne the Maid now? What would they think of their *L'Angélique*? She wanted to go to them, to tell them that she was not worthy, that God's servant had failed His trust, and in so doing had nearly brought about a brave, gentle man's death. The war was the war, there was nothing she could do but obey her Lord. But Guyenne was a different matter. What would they think of her then, when she confessed her miserable failings? Would they hate her?

Anger rose from its well and clutched her sick stomach. She had not asked that this fate be visited upon her. She was minding her own business in Domrémy when God had decreed that somebody should save France, and He had chosen her, unworthy creature that she was. She did not want to be a messenger at first, but her Counsel had brought her along so gradually that she had not noticed it. First one step and then another. Until she found herself here, in torment.

Why have you forgotten me? What have I left unfinished? I have done everything you told me to do, so why are you punishing me? Speak to me!

Please.

She heard the sharp laughter and drunken voices of her friends. A dog's bark echoed nearby. Several streets away, the piping of faint music attested to the ongoing carnival that would continue throughout the city all night. But she heard nothing at all from her Teachers. She buried her befouled face in her arms and sobbed loudly.

Pierre and Jehan found her a little later. Together with Pasquerel, they helped her onto her horse and took her home through deserted alleyways and back streets. Madame Boucher met them at the door, candle in hand. Her husband was at a dinner of fellow assemblymen, and Charlotte was asleep.

They carried Jehanne upstairs to the council room. Madame Boucher washed her face with a wet rag, as gently as though she were tending to her daughter. When she was cleaned up, they brought her to the sleeping child's room and laid her on the bed. The men left the room, and Jehanne's hostess undressed her and took the vomit-splattered clothes away.

It was an incident none of them would ever mention, either among themselves or to anyone else. Pasquerel said a special prayer for her. He knew that she would want to be confessed tomorrow. He beseeched God to give him the wisdom to heal Jehanne with the right words.

With the day's first meal digesting in his stomach, the Dauphin had been in a pleasant mood. It was his plan to read some of his correspondence in the shade of the ancient oak commanding a peaceful corner of Château Loches' garden. Perhaps later he would amuse himself in a game of chess with one of his retainers, or read from Plato's musings regarding statecraft. But his ministers claimed to have urgent concerns that could not wait, so with the greatest reluctance, the Dauphin permitted them to lead him to the anteroom of his private quarters where they could speak without intrusion. It did not take long for them to reveal their purposes.

"Might I ask if Your Majesty has decided to consent to the Maid's request that you dispatch yourself to Reims Cathedral for a formal coronation?" The archbishop's near-sighted eyes peered at the young man seated before him. The forehead beneath his velvet cap was beaded with perspiration and the end of his nose glistened in the morning heat.

"You may ask, Your Grace," Charles smiled cagily. "We have not yet made up our mind."

The two councillors traded a worried glance. De Chartres cleared his throat. The wrinkled skin beneath his chin jiggled like a rooster's beard as he said, "In that case, Sire, my sacred duty compels me to remind you that the girl is, in the recent words of our most renowned theologians, Masters Gélu and Gerson, 'a flea bred on a dunghill,' a lowly peasant who basks in the adoration of the people and who thereby tempts God to withdraw His support from her for her sin of pride."

"So we have heard," Charles replied in a smooth, calm voice, already noting where the conversation was leading. "Yet within the past month God has quite to the contrary given her a magnificent, surprising victory, has He not?"

"That is true, my lord, but will He continue to maintain her if she persists in her sins?" The old man drew his winglike eyebrows into a dark scowl.

"Do you not remember the rest of what Masters Gélu and Gerson said regarding the Maid?" the Dauphin wondered. "They declared that our cause is just, our predecessors virtuous; the populace has suffered unremittingly in these wars; and the enemies of France have proven themselves cruel beyond description. If God in His infinite love and wisdom has chosen this girl as His instrument to inspire the army and to have us crowned, then perhaps it is because God has created this 'flea' to humble the mighty, which of course refers to us." He gave the archbishop a wry, knowing smile.

"In any event, she is chaste, as we discovered when we had her tested, and moreover, she has succeeded where commanders with many years' experience in the field have not."

That could not be denied. Charles glared at the two of them, daring them to contradict him. "The learned doctors have further warned us that, should we turn her away, we run the risk of refuting God's wisdom and of thereby committing a grave sin ourselves. We may perhaps also cause even greater suffering for our people.

"We may, of course rely upon our own good sense and the advice of you gentlemen"—he inclined his head slightly—"when it comes to the particulars of equipping and mustering the army, but in matters of faith, we must listen to the Maid. And we must all of us—king and court, knights and vassals—continue to live piously and attend upon God. As a result of our upholding His will, God will give us further victories." Charles ended his recitation with an ironic smile.

Archbishop de Chartres turned helplessly to his confederate.

"All of us must indeed live upright lives, Sire," said Trémoïlle. "But let us put aside these 'matters of faith' for the moment and discuss the particulars to which the learned doctors referred." He scratched idly at the mole above his upper lip. "If Jehanne the Maid were to content herself with prayer and the will of God. . . ." He shrugged. "But, as you know, she continues to give military advice where it is neither sought nor welcomed."

Charles' eyes narrowed and he drew his face into a serious mask. The chancellor was beginning to tread into an unsettling domain.

"You may recall, my lord, how pitifully she wept when you informed her that you were disbanding the army immediately after its glorious triumph at Orléans, even when you most patiently explained to her that you had already spent one hundred and ten thousand *livres* Tournois to liberate the city. And what was her response? That you will need to follow your great victory by risking another venture against the English, lest they regroup."

"The Maid's actual words reminded us that the land surrounding Reims is in enemy hands"—Charles frowned—"and that before we go there to be crowned, our armies must be kept intact to safeguard the way."

"Bah!" Trémoïlle waved a dismissive hand. "Why, everyone knows that the English are established in the cities surrounding Orléans and do not have men in sufficient numbers to challenge Your Majesty further. Yet, the Maid claims to know better because God has spoken to her! And naïf that she is, she insists that the army will fight your battles whether or not they are paid!"

Discomfited, Charles squirmed in his seat. "What she said, seigneur chancellor, is that the army would come for us because we will be the true King of France and the people now know it."

"That is absolute poppycock, Sire! The only loyalty those ruffians ever evince is to silver. Don't her words suggest that she is misguided, if not addled?"

"Seigneur Trémoïlle is quite right, Your Majesty," said the archbishop, sensing that Charles' stubborn resistance was weakening. "It may be that in reality the girl believes that your knights would fight not for you, but for herself. As I have already told Your Majesty, there are rumors—and more than rumors—that the common folk have begun calling her *L'Angélique*, and that their adoration of her borders on outright idolatry!"

"And what would happen," Trémoïlle hammered, "if in following the Maid the people decided that they could manage quite well without their king? Where would she dare lead them? Why, I shudder to think of that prospect!"

The Dauphin shook his head in vehement denial. "We do not believe that.

She has steadfastly proven her honesty, and when she says that she desires nothing for herself but wishes only to serve us and see us crowned at Reims, we cannot but believe her. You are wrong, gentlemen. The Maid has no wish to challenge our primacy."

Trémoïlle shifted his considerable bulk and gritted his teeth. "Then consider the cost, Sire. A coronation at this time would require the disbursement of vast sums of money which the royal coffers no longer contain for such a frivolous symbol of power. Your best strategy is the same as it has always been: to husband the resources you still have for future military defensives, *if and when* the English find themselves reinforced. In the meantime, you must continue your negotiations with Philippe de Bourgogne."

That was the final point, the one that hit the target dead center, piercing the Dauphin's fragile defiance of his ministers. Without uttering it outright, Trémoïlle had reminded Charles that he controlled the treasury, at the same time raising the sensitive matter of his estrangement from Philippe. Thus, the minister pricked Charles' two greatest weaknesses such that by the time Jehanne caught up with him at Loches, the Dauphin still had not made up his mind to become King.

Jehanne watched d'Alençon walk away from her across the lawn at the rear of the castle. He had promised that he would give earnest thought to what she had said and that he would pray for guidance. She did not doubt his word. She only hoped that God would answer the duc as He had counseled her, and most of all that the young man would listen.

This morning was the first time since they had known one another that she had quarreled with her friend. For several days now, a tension had existed between them that neither had the courage to address. Jehanne knew he was holding something back, and she had a good idea what it was. But she avoided broaching it because she did not want the closeness they had always enjoyed to be damaged by the disenchantment that opposing wishes could bring upon them. He was her beautiful duc, her best friend apart from her Guides, and she needed his support as much as she needed Theirs. He was the only human who really understood her.

On this lovely morning they had strolled together to a large tree at the southern end of the garden. It was a peaceful spot, and since she had been at Loches, Jehanne often came here to pray. In the near distance the castle rose above the landscape like a regal, ornate cake, its turrets gleaming in the late spring sunlight. Within the flawlessly crafted garden, even more beautiful than that at Chinon, vivid flowers of every conceivable color grew in neat, well-tended beds. The tiny voices of insects buzzed through the warm air.

Jehanne and the duc sat a few inches from one another on the carved stone bench beneath the tree. Neither felt like saying anything. Pleasantries and stories about the siege had been long since exhausted, as well as the playful repartee that had marked their reunion, and now there remained something real, something serious to be introduced.

Finally, d'Alençon sighed and looked at her profile. Her eyes were on a hawk flying above the tallest turret, and she watched it swoop to a tree.

"Jehanne?"

She turned her head to him. "What?"

"I've been thinking very seriously about your wish that Charles should decide to be crowned now. I'm sorry," he tried to smile, "but I think the king should send what remains of the army to Normandie. The people there are sick to death of living under English tyranny, and if Charles' forces march on them, they will rise up and expel their masters."

She shook her head. "That is not what my Counsel have told me. It is the will of God that the Dauphin be crowned in Reims before he does anything else. They have made that very clear to me."

"But Jehanne, a march on Reims would require the king's traveling through Bourgogne and Champagne. The risk of something happening to him would be too great to venture, especially now that he has released the armies."

"Nothing shall happen to him," she answered firmly, "because he is under God's protection."

"Perhaps. But doesn't God want him to take every precaution? If the Burgundians, or, God forbid, the English should capture him—"

"That is why what is left of the army should escort him to Reims! I'm sorry, Jehan, but that is more important now than saving Normandie. Later, when Charles has become King, then he can send the army north."

"Not so! When Normandie falls, the lords who have supported England will change their allegiance, for that is the *first* English duchy, and it is *they* who will make Charles King!"

She gave the handsome young man a long, even look that made him squirm. "You have been speaking to seigneur Trémoïlle, haven't you? And the archbishop?"

He tore his eyes away from her angry stare.

"They are poisoning your mind, Jehan. They know how much you desire to regain your lands in Normandie, and they are using that to take your support from me."

D'Alençon stood abruptly and turned his back to her. He stooped down and plucked a blade of grass from the earth, then chewed on it thoughtfully. When he looked at her again, his eyes were filled with confusion.

"I know what they are," he said quietly, "but in some respects they are absolutely right." The duc spread his hands in a gesture that pleaded for her assent. "If Charles goes to Reims now, with only a portion of his kingdom having been restored to him, he goes as a pretender in the eyes of the world—"

"But Jehan—"

"I'm not finished!" he said with finality. "But if he wins more territory through conquest, the people of France will certainly support his claim to the throne, and that will make his coronation genuine to them. Can't you see that?"

"You have it backward," she responded, her dark brows drawn together in a determined line. "God has told me that it is most important that the Dauphin be anointed with the holy oil of St.-Clovis before Heaven will support him. It is a holy sacrament that will bind Charles to God forever, and the people with him, and then all of France will accept him as the true King. And when that happens, *then* the cities and towns that have pledged their faith to England will rebel and throw in their lot with the King.

"I give you my word, Jehan, that is what God wants. Please believe me." She looked up at him almost desperately. "You are my most trusted friend. I need you to help me to convince the Dauphin."

D'Alençon's pensive face mirrored his dilemma, and she felt a wave of pity for him. He looked absently at the bit of grass that he had tied into a knot. "I told you once before that you do not know Charles as I do. With the prize in his grasp, it is likely, given his nature, that he will just sit back and expect his true kingship to be enough to rally the people behind him."

His frown deepened. "But the people expect leadership from their King, they want him to use the army to take back what the English have stolen. It is not enough to have a king who will not use the army because he is afraid of defeat and because he has a personal distaste for war."

She shook her head again. "That shall not happen, Jehan. We will not let it happen. *I* will not let it happen. I promise you, I will remind him daily that he needs to be King once he wears the crown. I will push and push and push until he agrees to give me the army necessary to win the war. But he must be King first. You are a duc, you do not know the people."

He gave her a pointed look.

"It is not your fault," she assured him, crestfallen at his wounded expression. "Because of your position, you have not spent much time among them." She put her hand to her heart. "But I do know the people and how they think, because I come from them. Charles will never conquer those whose loyalties move back and forth with whatever army happens to occupy their town at the moment, until the other side takes it back again. He must be God's anointed King first, and then they will know that if they break faith with the King, they break faith with God. Even those loyal to Bourgogne will reflect upon what they're doing once he has gone through the ceremony."

D'Alençon toyed idly with the chewed, knotted blade of grass and did not look at her. After a few moments he met her steadfast gaze. "Very well." He sighed, "I shall pray that God will direct me." With that, he walked away from her.

When he was gone, she knelt on the ground before the bench and crossed herself, then clasped her hands tightly. She prayed that her friend would come back to her in spirit as he had first found her. She begged God that He would reveal Himself and His wishes to the Dauphin.

They no longer believe, she complained. God has made the kingdom a gift to Charles, and yet he rejects it.

HE DOUBTS THAT HE IS WORTHY OF GOD'S SUPPORT. HE IS AFRAID THAT HE IS NOT STRONG ENOUGH TO RULE. HAD HE FAITH, HE WOULD KNOW THAT GOD WILL GIVE HIM THE COURAGE AND SKILL TO BE A TRUE KING AND NOT A PUPPET OF MEN WHO FEAR THEIR OWN DIVINE ORIGIN.

How may I convince him?

BY NOT WAVERING IN WHAT GOD HAS CHARGED YOU TO DO. YOU MUST REMIND HIM DAILY OF YOUR MISSION. YOU MUST LET HIM SEE THAT GOD IS STRONGER THAN HIS FEARS. YOU HAVE DONE WELL, CHILD OF GOD, AS YOU HAVE BEEN

COMMANDED. BE AT PEACE AND ATTEND UPON GOD, AND HE WILL NOT FAIL TO ARM YOU IN THIS STRUGGLE. GO FORWARD, AND YOU WILL FIND THAT WE ARE WITH YOU.

The warm summer air purred with Their old familiar love. Their energy throbbed around and within her. A bolt of faith struck her to the core of her soul, and she felt dejection fade. She became one with Them again, as she had after she fled the celebrations in Orléans.

The turmoil in her soul that she now knew to have been the voice of the Devil, tempting her to abandon her duty to God, had settled under the onslaught of her constant prayers. Back in Orléans, her Counsel had returned to her after her head cleared, when despair had run its course.

At prayer the morning after her self-inflicted penance, Their love had suddenly washed into the room, bathing her in its piercing, overpowering Light. So keen and unexpected was Their return that it threw the raw abandonment she had felt into sharp relief, and she wept with joy and dread.

I am not worthy, she cried, but please forgive my anger and my loss of faith! I need you.

DO NOT FEAR OUR LOSS, LITTLE ONE, FOR WE HAVE BEEN WITH YOU ALL ALONG. WE ARE ALWAYS WITH YOU, ESPECIALLY WHEN YOU CANNOT FEEL US, FOR THAT IS WHEN YOU NEED US MOST. IT IS DURING THOSE TIMES WHEN YOUR FAITH WAVERS THAT YOU BEGIN TO LISTEN TO THE DARK ONE WITHIN YOU. THAT IS THE VOICE OF FEAR, NOT OF GOD.

But does God forgive me, really forgive me, for my great sin? I was responsible for Guyenne and he almost died.

YOUR SIN WAS NOT IN WHAT HAPPENED TO GUYENNE. THE ENGLISH LORD MUST ACCOUNT FOR THAT. YOUR SIN LAY IN YOUR HATRED OF THE ENGLISH, AND IN YOUR IMPATIENCE TO DELIVER YOUR MESSAGE. BECAUSE HE WAS WITHOUT INIQUITY, GUYENNE WAS ALWAYS IN GOD'S CARE. IT WAS HE WHO PREVENTED THE MAN'S DEATH.

Am I forgiven?

Do you forgive yourself? God loves you most tenderly, and would never condemn you. You are the only one who judges yourself unworthy. But you are God's chosen one, His messenger, and in His unfathomable wisdom He would never have selected one who was undeserving. When you doubt yourself, you doubt God, and it is then that you suffer.

Now at Loches she no longer wrestled with the anguish that war had visited upon her. The battle for the kingdom was a just one, and the Dauphin's eventual victory ordained by the Lord of Heaven. In her terrible dark struggle with the Evil One, that very conflict had served to deepen her faith and her confidence in herself and in God. She knew with a reborn sense of purpose that she was God's instrument. She was responsible only for her own actions, not those of anyone else. It was a certainty she swore she would never again forsake, even if no one else around her understood or accepted it.

She wished that others could know God as she did, could feel His compassion for them and His limitless Love, the fatherly caring that had brought her back from the chasm and was there for all of them. But they turned deaf ears to Him and listened instead to the temptations that the Devil whispered to them. In spite of their love for His messenger, even the army had not heard.

That is not quite right, she thought. Not the army, but the captains.

No sooner had she departed Orléans bound for Blois in search of the Dauphin—within a few days of raising the siege—than the Bastard, de Xaintrailles, and Sainte-Sévère had taken a too-small force to Jargeau in a vain attempt to wrest the town from the English. They skirmished with the *goddon* defenders under the command of the recently defeated Suffolk, only to retire after a three-hour assault. The moat was too deep to permit success, they said.

Jehanne snorted contemptuously when she thought of their stupidity and cowardice. It was something she would never have advised, not with so few men. Had they bothered to ask her, she would have told them that with Orléans safe at last, it was the wish of God that they rest for a short while, until they were needed again in greater numbers to clear the way to Reims of the enemy.

Yet they had not dared ask what she thought. Plaudits for her notwithstanding, their pride had been bruised because a woman did what they had failed to do. She smiled bitterly. Well, they had discovered that *this* woman, in alliance with God, was more powerful than an army without Him. The captains might not ever admit it, but that was the truth.

It was the people who still believed in her, who indeed had never wavered in their faith. When she entered Loches in the company of Pierre de Versailles, one of the masters who had questioned her at Poitiers, a large crowd had greeted her with an enthusiasm similar to that she had received at Orléans. The prelate watched in horrified fascination as they grasped at her saddle and tried to kiss her feet. Some of the women knelt as she passed and crossed themselves as though in the presence of God.

"It is wrong of you to permit this," Versailles said in stern admonishment. "You must beware, Jehanne, that you do not lead these people into idolatry."

As the memory of his rebuke returned to chastise her, she bowed her head and said a *Pater*. If she could not ultimately rely upon the captains, she could not put her faith in the people either, for they had the beguiling power to lead her into temptation.

"*Sed libera nos a malo.*" The words made her shudder, but she knew that God would help her to keep faith. She made the Sign of the Cross and got to her feet.

The magnificently tiered castle loomed beyond the hedges. It was time for her to return to Charles and remind him of her assignment, and his. She would summon her Power and ignore the two evil ministers who were sure to be with him. Her Counsel would speak through her. She was not afraid.

When Jehanne later looked back on that summer, she found that events had passed with remarkable speed.

Assured once more by her that God willed him to become King, Charles cast off the doubts raised by his ministers and agreed to go to Reims. But first, he said, he wanted the Loire towns which the English had seized retaken, and to that end, he appointed the duc d'Alençon to lead the armies. As she had hoped, he gave Jehanne permission to collect the scattered battalions together again. It would be vital that they move with all dispatch, for upon being driven from Orléans the defeated English had regrouped at the already captured towns of Jargeau and Meung on the Loire east and west, respectively, of Orléans. Informants reported that sieur Jehan Fastolphe had been sighted on his way to Jargeau with an even larger force, bringing with him arms, heavy artillery, and an army of two thousand. Jargeau therefore must be the first target of the Dauphin's assault.

Half-healed, but having recovered well enough to return to the field, Jehanne went to Selles, south of Blois, where she was reunited with veterans of Orléans, many of whom had been fighting in minor engagements elsewhere. They brought with them not only their experience but, in some cases, captured armaments. The Maid's banner also drew provincial nobility who thus far had only been tested in skirmishes. These sons of the far-flung lands of France approached her respectfully, eagerly, hoping that some of the Divine blessing would fall upon them. Their conviction wavered when news of Fastolphe's march reached them, sending dismay racing through the French ranks, and some of the soldiers of fortune, those who cared only for booty and had no genuine faith, deserted. But many more remained, heartened by Jehanne's words of hope.

The armies gathered at Orléans, where the people received Jehanne once again as their great deliverer and gave d'Alençon a large fund of money for military wages and food. The Orléanais also contributed the large cannon nicknamed *La Bergère* which had been key in fighting for their city. The duc brought with him almost two thousand men, and an equal number came with the Bastard of Orléans and Florent d'Illiers.

When all were ready, the army departed Orléans for Jargeau, which they hoped to reach before nightfall. They sent no scouts to seek out enemy movements. La Hire and d'Illiers were all for doing so, but were held on leash by d'Alençon, who did not want to waste the army in a minor skirmish. Jehanne's audience with Charles and the Dauphin's resulting decree had cleared his mind. Now, full of a reborn faith in Jehanne and in God, he reminded the captains that they were in the Lord's hands.

The army was ambushed near the outskirts of Jargeau by a battalion under the earl of Suffolk. Some of the men began to panic as Jehanne had feared they would, but she took the situation in hand and yelled above the tumult that God willed their victory and would succor them as He had at Orléans. So they held their ground, then took the offensive and chased the English back into the walls of Jargeau.

They spent the night busily placing the big guns for the attack. The next day would be Sunday, and Jehanne nursed a grain of remorse that they would have to fight on Lord Jhesus' day. But she also knew that the English would start the battle, and that God would forgive her and Charles' army for defending themselves. So she bodily commanded the placement of artillery, and the captains marveled at the inborn shrewdness that told her where the city's walls were weakest.

With preparations nearly finished, Jehanne called to the *goddon* garrison to yield to the King of Heaven and to the noble Dauphin Charles, otherwise she would smoke them out. There was no response at all from the silent darkened walls, not even curses. It was plain that nothing more could be done until the sun rose, so Jehanne went to her tent for a few hours' rest.

She no longer had to sleep on the ground under a tattered piece of burlap. The Dauphin had given her a beautiful white tent for this campaign. A torch burned at its entrance, where two guards were always on duty when the army was not on the move. Within the main room, four stools encircled a table on which burned a candle, and the interior was further illuminated by torches in low iron stands. The small cot where Jehanne slept was behind a partition at the rear of the tent.

When the cannon were in place and everything was ready for the next day's battle, her household conducted her from the field. Her brothers disarmed and Raymond rolled her standard for storage in its sheath, while d'Aulon and Minguet freed her of the steel weights that she now wore with ease. Dressing and undressing for war had become as commonplace as it had once been for her to slip in and out of her red dress.

Her older page had become her standard-bearer, to Minguet's distress. Jehanne explained to the boy that Raymond was only her battle page, while he, Minguet, was her personal page and thus closer to her every day. The truth was that she was more afraid for Minguet's life than for those of her strong, farm-bred brothers and Raymond, who was almost a man. Minguet had grown a little during the past few months but was still small for his age and barely acquainted with weapons. She doubted that she would be able to protect him during the thick of battle.

She accepted the cup of wine that he now offered her and, remembering her vow of temperance, sipped from it. She gave the goblet back to the boy and padded tiredly to her bed. Lying down on the cot with a groan, she closed her eyes, confident that all would be well and none of them harmed. God would be the next player in the game.

Bedford plucked an arrow from the stand next to him and fitted its notch into the bowstring. Lifting the long ashwood bow to eye level, he pulled the string back and took careful aim at the straw dummy two hundred feet in front of him. He let the arrow fly. It zipped across the distance and impaled the dummy in the center of its forehead, dead between the eyes the effigy would have had if it were human.

"Excellent shot, my lord."

Warwick's comment was without much enthusiasm. Archery, in his opinion, was an avocation for one from the lower classes, usually Welshmen, not a skill for a nobleman to boast about. Not that Bedford looked anything like a nobleman today, much less the uncrowned king of England. Clad as he was in a simple soldier's tunic with bowmen lined up on either side of him, one could easily have mistaken him for just another hired archer practicing his skills upon the real duke's lawn.

He wiped perspiration from his receding chin and gave his second in command a mischievous smile. "Would you like to have a go at it, Richard? It's not too far distant, and the wind is most favorable this afternoon." He licked the end of his forefinger and held it up. "That's right, it's still blowing from our backs."

"No, thank you, sir. As you know, hawking is my game. And swordplay, of course."

"Of course." Bedford raised his left eyebrow and the right corner of his mouth sympathetically.

He was well aware of Warwick's disapproval of his sport, but to Hell with what he thought. It did his heart much good to be out here among the men with whom he had fought and it did them good to see that he could match them, if necessary. Besides, the bow and arrow relaxed him as no other pastime did, particularly when he needed to focus his mind on important subjects, and today he had much on his mind. And much to avoid thinking about.

He took another arrow from the wooden quiver and set it in its place on the string. Then he took careful aim at the figure on the other side of the lawn, beneath the high wall encircling the Louvre Palace. He released the missile. When it struck this time, it pierced the dummy's throat.

"How are our affairs in Rouen?" he asked Warwick, forcing his voice to sound casual.

The earl frowned. "I'm not certain what you mean. The populace is subdued and show no signs of rebelling."

He knew that Bedford was fishing for something. A few days earlier, the duke had quite unexpectedly sent for him from the Norman capital where he was military governor. He had arrived last night and this morning had breakfasted with Bedford, expecting the king's uncle to explain straightaway why he had summoned him. But the duke had spoken of trivial things, of stag hunting and literary matters, rather than getting to the point. Warwick's curiosity felt on the verge of exploding, but he had known Bedford long enough to be certain that sooner or later he would tell him his purpose for being here.

Bedford seemed in no hurry, however. He took another arrow and held it up. But this time he hesitated before placing it upon the bow. "How secure is Rouen Castle?" he asked.

"As secure as it could be, sir, given that I have only five hundred men to garrison it."

"Hmm." The duke raised the bow and drew back the string. The arrow struck the straw man's chest.

Bedford lowered the bow and stood it on its end in the grass. "I am writing to my nephew today, or rather, I am writing to my brother and to the Regent's Council." He looked at the dark-haired man beside him. There was a little gray in Warwick's temples and lines at the corners of his eyes that he had not noticed the last time he saw him, eight months ago. Yet he was still handsome and lean.

We are all getting older, Bedford thought emotionlessly. How truly short life is.

"I shall ask the king for further reinforcements, and the lion's share shall be used to reinforce Rouen," he continued. He paused at Warwick's bewildered expression. "After they arrive, I want you to make everything at the castle ready for a guest. A very *special* guest."

Warwick responded by inclining his head a little to the side.

"When the time is right," Bedford went on, "and I hope that time is soon, I plan to propose to the Council that they approve the king's passage across the Channel. When he reaches France, he shall reside in Rouen until . . ."

"Until?"

"Until I have completed arrangements for him to be crowned King of France. In Reims."

The earl's jaw dropped and his eyes widened. In that moment he looked almost stupid.

"That's right," Bedford smiled. He placed another arrow upon the bow and lifted the weapon again. The dummy took the projectile in its left lung.

"We are in a race, Richard, did you know that?" He looked at the earl with narrowed eyes. "It is a race we cannot afford to lose. My spies in the Loire Valley have reported that Charles de Valois is at this moment besieging Jargeau with the intention of expelling the king's army from the Loire. After that, so I'm told, he plans to get himself to Reims for his own coronation."

Warwick burst into a disbelieving laugh. "Charles? That weak-minded fool? Why, he cannot find his way to the latrine without assistance, much less his way to Reims! Who told you this?"

"That does not matter." Bedford frowned, shaking his head. "What does matter is that now—ever since Orléans fell—he is fired with renewed purpose, given to him by that black demon from Hell who calls herself 'the Maid.' With witchcraft on his side, who knows how far he'll go?"

"Straight to the Devil, may God damn him!" The end of Warwick's nose quivered in indignation.

"May He indeed." The duke crossed himself quickly. "Most assuredly, the state of Charles' soul is in the hands of the Almighty. The condition of this miserable kingdom is in ours. That is why I intend to make Rouen as secure as possible before I permit His Majesty to come here. For even if the Loire should fall to Charles, Normandy must be safeguarded at all costs." He smiled. "I promised my brother on his deathbed that I would hold Normandy before all other duchies, did you know that?"

Warwick nodded. "Yes. He fought so hard for it. We all did. But what did you mean by 'if the Loire should fall?' I heard that Fastolf is on his way to Jargeau with reinforcements. Surely with his battalions there, we'll be able to hold it."

"Perhaps. I pray so. However, I have been a soldier long enough to know that if God's will is a thing of mystery, it is nowhere more confounding than in war."

He beckoned to a squire, who immediately trotted over to where the two nobles were standing. Giving the bow to the man, Bedford wiped the sweat from his forehead with his hand.

"Come, Richard," he said, "walk with me." He touched Warwick's padded shoulder.

The men began strolling slowly toward the palace. Ahead of them, the Louvre's stone facade hung over the crisp green lawn like a canker on otherwise smooth skin. Bedford detested the place. Oppressively hot in summer, freezing in winter, its dark, drafty rooms were never comfortable, no matter how many doors and windows were left open and regardless of the bonfires that were left burning in the fireplaces day and night. God's curse belonged on those who had built it.

"I would like to request, my lord, that you allow me to take the field against the Armagnacs," Warwick said. "With my experience—"

"No, Richard. I need you exactly where you are. Or to be more precise, the king needs you where you are. Besides"—Bedford shrugged—"we have good men in the field. Suffolk, Fastolf, Talbot. An embarrassment of riches, eh?" he smiled. "You would only be wasted at the head of an army, for you have the administrative skills that they do not. Could you imagine Fastolf trying to govern Rouen?"

Warwick laughed in spite of himself. "I see what you mean. But the Loire . . . Just suppose for a moment that it cannot be held. What then?"

Bedford stopped walking. "Then we reinforce Paris and push through to Reims with what forces we have available to us. It is most pressing that Henry be crowned there, because that is where kings of France have traditionally received their crowns. The God-cursed population will be more devoted to a legally anointed King crowned in their customary manner than one who is not."

"What difference does it make whether the people are satisfied or not?" Warwick sniffed. "The King rules at God's pleasure, not the people's."

"True enough." Bedford scratched the gnatbite on the side of his beak. "But do we really want to have to garrison all of France for the rest of our lives? Believe me, it would be infinitely more politic for us to have the people's consent and their acceptance of Henry as their true King than for us to have to fight them into the next generation and the one after that."

Clasping his hands behind his back, the duke resumed his walk. Warwick's long legs effortlessly matched the shorter man's stride. He glanced at Bedford's hawk-nosed profile, at the familiar grim mouth that seemed to hang above the fleshy throat unsupported by any chin at all.

"Can we take Champagne? That is still in Armagnac control, is it not?"

"It is. And yes, we can take it. With Burgundy's help."

"I thought Philippe had turned against us," Warwick responded, knitting his brows.

"He did. But I have recently made advances to mend our rift with him, and if all goes according to plan, I should be meeting with him no later than July. I shall remind him that he is, after all, my brother-in-law. I pray to God that he will see that he gains no advantage by remaining estranged from us."

"And if he is not responsive to Divine inspiration?"

They had reached the entrance to the palace. Bedford peered into the darkness within the walls. He was weary of this conversation and the questions that could not be answered for the time being.

"In that case," he replied, "we shall just have to see what choices are available to us then." He made an attempt to smile at the earl. God, how unimaginative the fellow was, like most men of war who did not have to trouble themselves with larger issues.

"And now," he said, "I must take myself to my quarters. It is time that I let the Council—and the king—know that Orléans has fallen."

"Have you not told them already?" Warwick looked puzzled. "That was weeks ago."

"I know exactly how long ago it was," the duke growled. "I have been waiting for the right time. Certainly you can imagine what an unpleasant task I have before me?"

"Yes, sir, I can. Please excuse me. I did not mean to imply that you are remiss in your obligations to the king." Warwick's face had gone a little pale. His superior was so genial most of the time that it was easy to forget how much power he wielded and how angry he could become if provoked.

"Very well, you are forgiven." With the threat of a storm having passed, Bedford smiled at him again. "May I look forward to having your company at dinner?"

Warwick bowed to him. "Of course, sir, it will be my pleasure."

"Until then."

Bedford turned away and went into the palace's dim interior. He passed the immobile, helmeted guards at the entrance to the corridor on the right and walked purposefully toward the end of the hall. Reaching it, he made a left turn down another passageway. His bootheels clattered loudly, echoing upon the flagstones. At the end he nodded briefly to the guards, who pulled their halbards toward themselves and stiffened their backs. One of them opened the door for Bedford, and he entered the room that served as his office.

"Leave the door open," he ordered. "It's bloody hot in here."

The men bowed, then turned away from him and extended their arms, holding the weapons so that the blades pointed outward. Bedford crossed the floor, not noticing the loaded bookshelves and the empty fireplace, or the tapesty hanging above it. He went to the desk before the open window and sat down. Pushing away the documents scattered across its surface, he reached for a clean sheet of parchment, then spread it before him. He uncorked the inkwell and reached for a quill.

But the words did not come. The noises of Paris on the other side of the palace walls—of passing wagons, and vendors selling their wares, of crying children and scolding women—interfered with his concentration as much as the insect buzzing about his head. The rank stench from the sewers combined with the odors of cooking food nauseated him.

He put down the pen and rubbed his eyes. This was going to be every bit as difficult as he had feared it would be, but he had to do it. His duty to the king compelled him. Lord Jesus, give me words! he thought.

He picked up the pen again. After a moment's hesitation, he began to write.

Bedford greeted the king in affectionate terms, then recounted a long description of the siege of Orléans, including the sad death of Salisbury. The more he wrote, the angrier he became. His hand was trembling with rage as it delivered the news of shameful defeat.

> There fell, by the hand of God, as it seems, a great stroke upon your people
> that was assembled there in great number, caused in great part, as I suppose,
> by lack of sad belief and unlawful doubt that they had of a disciple and limb
> of the Fiend, called the Maid, that used false enchantments and sorcery.
> The said stroke and discomfiture not only lessened in great part the number
> of your people there, but as well withdrew the courage from the remnant in

marvellous wise, and encouraged your adverse party and enemies to assem-
ble forthwith in great number.

Bedford read back over what he had written thus far. His eye stopped at the name of the Devil's own tool that he had written, watching as the vile word seemed to leap up at him from the page. With a frown, he put down his pen.

The Maid. God curse her blackened soul!

When he first received the insolent letter she had dared write him, he never envisioned that she would actually make good on her boastful threats. He had underestimated the strength of the pact she had undoubtedly made with the Evil One, taking her for another of the fraudulent mystics that this accursed land seemed to breed like rabbits. How very foolish of him not to have hastened to Notre-Dame straightaway and offered a series of novenas to plead for St. George's and Our Lady's intercession against the forces of Darkness. Because of his blithe disregard of the Devil's hand against him, this evil woman had triumphed and brought ruin to the king's men. He would not make the same mistake again.

His eyes fell upon the little ivory box sitting at the corner of his desk. He drew it toward him and lifting the hinged lid, took out the folded bit of paper which he had put there some time ago. He had almost forgotten it. Now, as he read it once more, he was filled with a rage that seemed likely to burst from his lungs, and again he was tempted to consign it to the fire.

But his uncle the cardinal's advice sounded in his brain, and controlling an impulse to destroy it, he refolded it and returned it to the casket. Winchester had been right: Perhaps the time would come when this document would prove most useful, if the witch could be captured.

Bedford suddenly knew what he would do. His face broke into a smile and he chuckled.

Men who distinguished themselves in battle were often rewarded for their valor by being given entrance into exclusive knightly societies. Both Warwick and Fastolf had earned admission into the Order of the Garter through their heroics. For men of lesser stature, there always existed the possibility that they could be raised to knighthood, or even to the peerage, through a dedicated show of arms. Still, where other, more elusive favors were required, nothing constituted a greater lure than silver.

He pushed aside the unfinished letter to Henry and took another fresh sheet of paper. This time, his pen sped across the page.

Bedford did not doubt that he could convince Winchester to release the money necessary to pay for the Maid's capture. After all, it had nearly been his idea in the first place. Nothing would please the old man more than the chance to strike a blow for God through a trial designed to bring to justice a witch and a heretic.

264

CHAPTER NINE

Victories of Summer

June 11–July 1, 1429

oon after dawn the earl of Suffolk, commander of the English garrison holding Jargeau, met with La Hire in hope of striking a bargain with the besiegers. He would be willing to come to terms, he said, if the Armagnacs delayed their assault for a fortnight; in the event that Fastolf had not arrived with reinforcements by the end of that time, Suffolk would surrender. When La Hire delivered Suffolk's message to d'Alençon and the other battle lords, they first laughed, then responded by attacking the walls of Jargeau. By sunset the town was theirs, just as Jehanne had promised.

She would come to hear that over a thousand Englishmen had been slaughtered in the battle and nearly five hundred taken prisoner, while Armagnac casualties were considerably fewer, less than a hundred slain. Rumor insisted that the earl of Suffolk had been so frightened that he'd surrendered to a squire; the act was true, said an archer who claimed to have been present, but it was not from dread of the French that Suffolk had surrendered. Knowing that he was outnumbered and overcome, the Englishman had called upon common sense and bowed to reality. But because he would not have his enemies swear that he had yielded to someone of a lesser social rank, the squire to whom he relinquished his sword first knelt before him to become a knight. In the aftermath of battle the townsfolk, uninterested in and unaware of the downfall of great men, cowered within their houses, fearful that the Armagnacs would inflict an appalling vengeance upon them for their earlier submission to the English. They did not know that d'Alençon had already forbidden the army to harm them.

When the last of the regular army's prisoners were aboard the barges that would sail them to Orléans, the duc ordered horses sent from camp for Jehanne and himself. Moments ago his squire had brought news that the city's garrison were holding a number of captives before the church whom they refused to yield into La Hire's custody. If either of them doubted the captain's response to this challenge, it was dispelled even before the church came into sight; well above the other shouts that fiery, unmistakable voice was raging in a veritable litany of obscenities. Already tired, and steaming within her armor so that she had been able to think of little else since the battle ended, Jehanne was further irritated that he had forgotten his promise to master his tongue.

But the instant they rounded the corner, she forgot her anger and discomfort, and stared, horrified, at the scene before the churchyard.

Fifteen or more English prisoners had been put to the sword, and from the haphazard heap of decapitated corpses darkened streams oozed thickly, meandering between the paving stones. Severed heads looked with bloody, half-closed eyes at the clouds riding across the summer sky. Unbelievably, one headless torso was still twitching. In this heat, the bodies had already started to stiffen, and the sickly-sweet death odor had attracted a swarm of hungry flies.

La Hire and de Gaucourt were just inches from Pierre Mouton, commander of the same garrison which until an hour ago had been prisoners of the English, and the three of them were yelling into one another's faces. Behind the two Armagnac captains a group of men-at-arms pointed their unsheathed swords at the militiamen, themselves in a contentious mood and poised for conflict. Fifty or so frightened prisoners, a number of whom looked young enough to be boys away from home for the first time, were kneeling in docile resignation with their hands clasped behind their heads.

"What is the meaning of this?" d'Alençon shouted, leaping from his horse.

Jehanne dismounted slowly, unable to tear her eyes from the abominable pile. Her mouth watered with an evil taste; she spat upon the ground and commanded her sight elsewhere.

The antagonists did not appear to have noticed the duc. They were still shouting incoherently, their mutual enmity defiling the churchyard with the threat of further violence.

D'Alençon forced himself between them. "Stop it!" he ordered. La Hire and Mouton continued to glare at each other. "What's going on here?" d'Alençon barked at La Hire.

"The militia"—he said sarcastically—"want to kill the *goddons*, but we say that they should be taken to Orléans and held for ransom!"

"These are not worth ransoming," sneered Mouton, a bloated ogre of a man with thinning hair smeared across his melon-shaped head. Sweat dripped down the sides of his face, streaked onto a scar dividing his left ear like an apple that had been halved then carelessly put back together.

He rubbed the graying bristles on his cheek. "Look at them; they're just shit-eaters, not worth anything. We can't feed them all, and we don't want them running back to some other fatass *goddon* lord, like that Fastolphe who's supposed to be coming this way. We should kill them and be done with them."

"This is wrong!" Jehanne intervened, no longer able to stay out of it. Her face was red with outrage. "God has appointed and blessed the army, and He condemns the senseless murder of unarmed men!" Her voice trembled with the approach of furious tears. "I can promise you, sir, that He will withdraw His support from any army, even one fighting for a noble cause such as ours, if it resorts to this—this"—she gestured helplessly at the pathetic, bloody carcasses, the terrified prisoners. "You shall not have any more of them killed, do you hear me?"

Mouton grinned at her, revealing half-rotted teeth. "The Maid," he mused, his eyes searching her up and down. "So you have come to give orders to the militia as well as to Charles' regulars, eh?" He laughed scornfully. "Tell me, little girl, do you want to keep fighting these same bastards over and over again? Because that will surely happen if we let them go!"

Jehanne could feel her comrades tense around her. She took a step closer until she could practically see up his nose. He reeked of sweat and woodsmoke, and it was obvious from his breath that he had already embarked upon a successful quest for a wine barrel.

Her eyes fastened upon his, and mustering all her self-control, she said, very softly, "First, I am not a little girl, I am Jehanne the Maid, sent by God to deliver His kingdom to the Dauphin, and as such I do not 'give orders.' I reveal messages that come from God." She could feel a cold fury rising up her spine, and as it shot to her hands, she shivered and clenched her fists.

"Secondly, whether or not we fight these men tomorrow or next week or next year is no concern of yours, or of ours for that matter. Their lives are in God's hands, and you do not have the right to make God's choices for Him. If you murder them, you put yourself against God, and you damn yourself and all who follow you."

Jehanne had used all her willpower to keep her voice under control, knowing that if he thought her shrill, he would continue to laugh at her no matter what she said. She did not care what he thought of her, but she did want his submission, and as she watched a frown appear above his eyes in a tremor acknowledging her Power, she knew she had it.

She turned to La Hire. "Have our men round up the prisoners and escort them to the river." She glared at Mouton. "We're taking them to Orléans."

La Hire nodded somberly and glanced at d'Alençon for confirmation. The duc waved his hand, and the captains began ordering their men to bring the English to their feet. Turning away from the militia, Jehanne got back on her horse.

At the riverbank she saw that her companions, even Poulengy and Metz, were waiting for her to board the Bastard's personal barge. They stood holding their horses' reins as the vessels glided away from Jargeau, and watched the black smoke of battle spread like gauze across the summer sun.

D'Alençon removed his helmet and smiled at Jehanne. His hair clung wetly to his skull; a bloody smear from a dead enemy streaked across the flawless cheekbone. "Charles will be pleased."

"I hope so." She grinned tiredly. "God has been most generous to him today."

The noise from the city became fainter, then ceased altogether as the boat drifted around a bend in the river.

Within the week, Jehanne received news of the massacre that finished the liberation of Jargeau. Once the army had gone, the militia vented their rage upon the terrified population, slaughtering citizens regardless of age or gender. Jehanne ordered three Masses said for the souls of those innocents who had perished at the hands of Pierre Mouton and his savages, and when the last one was over she bade her companions take their suppers without her, then knelt again before the altar. She was at prayer a long time.

In Orléans, the Bastard presented her with a crimson cloak and a tunic in the green and white colors of his House, gifts from his half brother, Charles d'Orléans. In his faraway English prison, the lord of the city had heard of Jehanne's triumph and sent word by courier to his treasurer—Jehanne's old host, Jacques Boucher—commissioning the finery. Jehanne accepted the gift graciously, astonished at the unforeseen honor. She had never stopped dreaming that she would meet that great man. Someday she would cross the Narrow Sea with an army and set him free.

But for now she did not intend to linger in Orléans. After Vespers the night of their arrival, she told d'Alençon that she wanted to go to Meung, where battalions of the English army were holding the town. Shortly after noon the next day, June 15, they departed.

The English were waiting for them behind the fortifications they had built on the bridge leading into the town. D'Alençon sent the famous Lorrainer—hero at the Augustins—and his equally renowned culverin to the steeple of a nearby church, and on the duc's signal, the Lorrainer's shot began the skirmish for possession of the bridge. It lasted no more than an hour. The French overran the clumsy bulwark and the enemy retreated with their wounded into the town. It was growing dark, so d'Alençon decided to wait until morning to take Meung. He went with a squad to the church, where they could guard the bridge through the night. As was customary, Jehanne's household pitched her tent in the center of the encampment.

D'Alençon's scouts woke him in the early hours with news that Talbot had retired to Janville, ten leagues north of Orléans, leaving Beaugency almost undefended. Armed with this new information, d'Alençon decided that tomorrow they would leave a garrison at the bridge and instead attack the enemy at Beaugency.

By dawn the army was once more on the move. The English garrison at Beaugency saw their approach and withdrew into the large rectangular *donjon* dominating the bridge, leaving behind a few men within the town to lurk in ambush. De Gaucourt's division wiped them out while the rest of the army bombarded the *donjon*. But the English held their ground and would not yield the bridge.

D'Alençon was now undecided about what to do next. At Meung, the army possessed the bridge but not the town; here at Beaugency, circumstances were reversed. He did not know where he should center his forces. He broke off the attack for his soldiers to rest, and the captains, Jehanne included, went with him to his tent for a council. Shortly thereafter, messengers arrived with news that made the ruling for him.

They said that long-expected English relieving forces under Fastolphe had finally reached Janville from Paris, increasing Talbot's army by three thousand. Now they were certain to move on Beaugency. To confound matters further, couriers sent by Arthur de Richemont, former constable of France, came to say that he was approaching from the west, bringing with him a strong Breton company, and requested d'Alençon's hospitality.

The duc became livid, angrier than Jehanne had ever imagined he could be. The couriers listened politely as he raged against their master, and when he was finished, they bowed and left d'Alençon's tent without saying another word.

"I don't understand," Jehanne said when they had gone. "If this sieur de Richemont is offering to help us, why would you refuse him when we need as many soldiers as we can get?"

"He's a traitor, that's why." D'Alençon's look was cold, foreign, very unlike him.

"Jehanne, Arthur de Bretagne is the comte de Richemont, which is actually an English title," explained the Bastard in a tone more contained than d'Alençon's. "When his father the duc de Bretagne died, his mother married Henry IV of England, and he became the ward of Jehan sans Peur. He spent part of his childhood with Charles and the other Valois children, but that was before the quarrel between Bourgogne and our late king. When he got older, he married Philippe de Bourgogne's sister."

De Gaucourt picked up the tale, describing the weblike intrigues in which Richemont had taken part over the years. After a drunken fight with Bedford, Richemont had renounced his allegiance with England and thrown in his lot with the Dauphin, who then appointed him constable of France. Richemont lost no time in rooting out those at court who threatened his power, and together with Trémoïlle, had some of them assassinated. Then he proceeded to turn against Trémoïlle, which proved to be a serious error.

"That same year," continued the Bastard, "his brother, the duc de Bretagne, met with Charles and essentially asked the king to abdicate in favor of his vassals, namely, himself and Philippe de Bourgogne. That not only angered Charles but turned his suspicions of treachery toward Richemont, who then made a fatal move: He approached my brother Clermont and the comte de la Marche with a plan of rebellion, and when Charles discovered the plot, he revoked Richemont's office and banished him from court."

"Naturally," said de Gaucourt with a wry smile, "Trémoïlle's appetite for vengeance was whetted at that, and ever since he has whispered to Charles about Richemont's other plots, which may or may not be real."

"And now after wasting his time engaging in countless petty intrigues against Trémoïlle, Richemont is offering his 'services' to Charles! Well, I won't have it!" D'Alençon turned steely eyes to the captains. "I swear before God, if that traitor comes, I go!"

The Bastard smiled at the furious young duc. "I agree, Jehan, that of course Richemont is a snake whom it would be fatal for us to trust very far. But Jehanne has a point when she says that he has the numbers that could turn the tide in our favor, and—"

"Excuse me, Bastard," d'Alençon said testily, "but even if he had a million men-at-arms, we would still be under orders from Charles to shun him. If we let him join us, we disobey the king, and *we* become traitors along with Richemont! We cannot let his stink become attached to us."

"It won't if he swears his loyalty to the king on oath, before God. That must be our condition to letting him join us."

All eyes darted to Jehanne. She was standing a little apart from the men, a thumb hooked into the belt encircling her armored waist. Her hair was longer than it had been for some time and fell in a thick shock over her eyes. Raising her hand, she flipped it to the side without being aware of what she was doing. She smiled cannily at the captains.

"If he repents of his sins against the Dauphin, then he will not mind swearing before God that he will henceforth loyally serve the true King of France. That is an oath that he could not take without damning his soul if he broke it."

D'Alençon was frowning thoughtfully at her, his wrath gone.

"Since he has come to us *now*, at the very moment when we most need him for us to win, and since we have no doubt that God is supporting us, then it is reasonable to believe that Richemont is the help sent from God. If we refuse him, it may be that we refuse God's help." She fixed upon d'Alençon, her eyes entreating him. "I know that he has been a traitor in the past, but it is possible that he truly repents of it—"

"You don't know him, Jehanne," interjected de Gaucourt. His mouth was drawn into a downward bow, his brows bristling above his eyes.

"That's right, you don't," the Bastard confirmed kindly, the dimples once again deepening his cheeks. "True repentance is not in his nature." The other men laughed bitterly.

She could feel her eagerness turning into temper. They had lined up against her, and it stung after the recent camaraderie.

"What they mean, Jehanne"—d'Alençon smiled—"is that Richemont is truly a detestable man. Not only is he a traitor, he is also unrestrained in war and has no mercy for enemies, particularly the English. If we accept his help, we may not be able to stop him from massacring any prisoners we take."

"Nevertheless"—she pouted, only slightly pacified—"what I said is sound. It is possible that God has sent him to us, even if he doesn't know it. God sometimes uses evil men to accomplish His will, and who are we to question that?"

The captains pondered the situation silently, each haunted by what a refusal might bring. It was decided in the end that they would meet Richemont at the leper hospice on the outskirts of Beaugency. He came to them within the hour in the company of his squire and thirty armed retainers.

Despite his noble birth, there was nothing at all patrician about the comte. A dark, stocky man, shorter than average, with a neck the size of a small tree, he had a face filled with bitter cruelty and untrustworthiness. His clothes and his person bore longstanding filth, and he scratched his crotch while he walked. But he did take the oath of loyalty to Charles, finally, after he had used it to bargain for Jehanne's help in restoring him to court. He swore the words as though they were the dirtiest blasphemy he knew.

Jehanne would have crossed herself but refrained because she knew he would think it a sign of weakness, and she was not weak. She was Jehanne the Maid, liberator of Orléans, winner of battles great and small, inner and outer, and she would not be browbeaten by any man, however powerful the darkness in his soul.

But the oath satisfied her. If he went back on it, he would be condemning himself. She would keep her word whether or not he was true to his.

Richemont asked for the privilege of attacking the English. In part to satisfy him, and in order to keep his Bretons busy and away from the rest of the army, the captains agreed.

When the English in the *donjon* saw Richemont's division approaching from the west, they thought it was part of a larger reinforcement and surrendered without further fighting. D'Alençon gave them terms, allowing them to retire fully armed. Then he left two battalions in Beaugency to secure the town against their return. The French army was returning to Meung, where spies reported they would find Talbot. By late afternoon they had ranged themselves along the spine of a low ridge between Meung and Beaugency, and there they waited, battle-ready, for the English.

They did not have to be patient for long. The great adversary could be seen in the distance, coming toward them in a cloud of dust with blue and red banners floating ghostlike on the horizon. When they were still several hundred yards away, the English dismounted and began to cut down saplings which they carved into pointed stakes and planted into the earth, sharp ends facing the expectant French. It was an old tactic, one they had used successfully at Agincourt when they lured the army of Charles VI into a whirlwind of arrows.

While d'Alençon's men made no move to attack, they stirred restlessly, hands grasped tightly at their swords and around the handles of their maces. La Hire spat in the enemy's direction. Jehanne stole a glance at Richemont. The Satanic face was twisted in hatred of the English, and she recalled what de Gaucourt had said about the seigneur's bitter quarrel with Bedford. Perhaps he would remain faithful to Charles after all.

A horseman was cantering toward the army, a herald to judge by his grand clothes and lack of arms. As he came closer, Jehanne remembered Guyenne with a sharp jab of conscience. The ranks parted and the herald rode through them to the captains upon the ridge. He dismounted and bowed to the Bastard uncertainly, not knowing who was in command.

"My lord Talbot sends his compliments to the noble army of the Dauphin Charles." His voice was refined and musical, his French excellent.

D'Alençon acknowledged him with a graceful nod. "I am Jehan, the duc d'Alençon, lieutenant general of His Majesty's armies. Have you a message from seigneur Talbot?"

"Yes, Your Excellency." The man bowed to the duc, lower this time. "My lord suggests that we settle our differences with a tournament, three of your best knights against three of ours."

D'Alençon's handsome visage broke into a boyish smile. The other captains laughed out loud. "Tell your master," the young man replied, the smile losing its humor, "that we are not here to play games. Tell him to go and find lodgings tonight, for it is getting late. But tomorrow, if it pleases God and Our Lady, we shall see you at close quarters."

The herald inclined his head curtly, then, mounting his horse, rode back through the parting sea of men-at-arms and archers toward the English lines.

D'Alençon still did not move. He and the army sat there until the enemy turned his back on them and started marching away toward Meung. That would be the duc's goal as well. The English would try to take the bridge at Meung where d'Alençon had left two divisions, and he would have to hurry if the army was to relieve the bridge and take the town. First they would rest for the night, as no doubt would the enemy.

Early the next morning, June 18, scouts reported that the English under Fastolphe had assaulted the garrison at the Meung bridge, but the garrison stubbornly refused to yield. Without delay d'Alençon called a war council.

La Hire, his sword hand itching for blood, counseled that they ride like the wind to Meung and attack the *goddons* before they could know what hit them. The Bastard pointed out that there were in effect two English armies, one under Fastolphe and the other commanded by Talbot, and they did not know where to find either. They must be careful that they did not ride into a trap.

"What do you say?" d'Alençon asked Jehanne.

"Do you have good spurs?" She grinned.

"What do you mean?"

"Are we to turn our backs on them!" de Gaucourt roared.

Jehanne laughed. "No, it is the English who will not be able to defend themselves, and you will need good spurs to catch them! You will defeat them, and with hardly any French blood shed." She grinned at La Hire. "Let's go get them."

"Yes, let's get them!" His laughter reminded her of a roaring bull. "My horsemen will lead the attack, and you, Mademoiselle, shall bring up the rearguard."

"No." Her humor was instantly gone, replaced by the resolute frown they knew so well. "I want to be in the van so my standard can be seen by all."

"Jehanne, be reasonable," the Bastard urged. "You would be exposed to the greatest possible danger if you were to ride in front of the army. Your presence is too important to all of us to risk something happening to you. Please think over this."

"Not only that," said de Gaucourt, his voice for once barren of harshness, "but we need for you to guard our rear in case we're attacked from behind."

"If I'm put in back with the rearguard, the men won't be able to see me. What if they become afraid and lose heart altogether?" They were ordering themselves against her once more, and she burned with rancor.

"Jehanne." D'Alençon's voice was gentler than she had heard it in a long time, and the sad look in his eyes touched her hair, her face. "I cannot allow you to put yourself in danger. You saved my life at Jargeau when you warned me away from the cannon that surely would have killed me. And now I give you back yours."

She started to protest, but he put both hands on her shoulders and she became lost in his warm eyes. "For Reims," he said softly.

She could not answer right away. A thousand images darted in and out of her awareness: the men in the ruined church at Orléans; her mother's embraces when she was little; Guyenne, recuperating in bed at Orléans; the way d'Alençon looked when she first saw him at Chinon, then the gallant nobleman. So much had happened since then.

She explored his fatigued countenance for some remnant of her beautiful duc. But that man was temporarily asleep in some back room of his character; this now was simply her commander and her friend, and she knew she would obey him.

"For Reims," she said with a smile.

They had gone only a few leagues when a band of scouts brought news that Talbot had broken off the attack at Meung and fled north toward Janville. The English whereabouts were presently unknown, as they had split their forces and vanished into the thick woods. D'Alençon summoned the other captains for a quick conference. Because she was tucked safely in the rear with her companions, Jehanne was the last to arrive. The weather was unbearably hot, and as she drew rein she removed the potlike helmet and wiped the glistening sweat from her brow. The breeze cooled her face most pleasantly.

The duc quickly explained the situation and asked their opinions. Sainte-Sévère advised that they return to Beaugency and, once there, send for reinforcements; the Bastard agreed. With his usual forthrightness La Hire rejected the idea, saying that they should finish the English now, when they had the chance. Equally outspoken, Jehanne urged the captains not to withdraw.

"But, Jehanne, we don't know where they are."

She felt her hackles rise at the Bastard's indulgent tone. "In God's name," she swore, "even if they took refuge in the *clouds*, we would still defeat them, for God has sent them to us that we might punish them! My Counsel have told me that today they will be all ours, and the Dauphin will have the greatest victory he has ever had. We must attack them!"

That was enough for d'Alençon. Above the captains' protests, he ordered them back to their positions and sent La Hire's cavalry in advance of the rest of the army. Sixty or so mounted scouts had already moved out of sight toward the enemy. In the far distance the cavalry, closely pursued by Richemont's men, dashed rapidly down the slope and disappeared into the shadowy line of trees where the English had abandoned their sharpened fortifications.

Jehanne had to wait for some time before her rearguard could proceed, while the hundreds of foot soldiers aligned between the knights and her troop poured across the sloping plain and into the woods. As the rearguard finally began their forward movement, she seethed with impatience, knowing that stuck back here she would miss it all.

That night an exuberant La Hire would describe to an equally spirited audience what passed on that auspicious day, and Jehanne would then learn how truly her Counsel had spoken.

The patrol had led the army to the vicinity of Patay, where they lost sight of the English. As they moved through the forest, the pounding of their horses' hooves startled a stag, which ran away from them straight into the nearby English camp. The enemy, always open to anything sporting, sent up a "hoorah" that gave away their location to the French outriders, who raced back to La Hire. The cavalry spurred forward waving their swords, while the main body of the French army ran after them.

Clearly visible atop a small ridge beyond the forest, the English commanded by Fastolphe waited as bait. Talbot's men, between Fastolphe and the oncoming Armagnacs, were preparing their ambush along a row of hedges that bordered a narrow road wending its way to the ridge. It was apparently their plan that, once in place, their archers would stand at some distance behind the crude palisade and skewer the French as they rode into the trap. Then the men-at-arms would fall upon them and finish them.

But it did not turn out that way, not at all.

When the stag burst out of the woods, the English were still sharpening their customary stakes to line the road. Before they could finish their preparations, La Hire's cavalry descended upon them and savagely struck down the astonished, unready English. In a frenzy of longstanding hatred, the horsemen led by Richemont's Bretons put the Englishmen to the sword, and chased the onrushing reinforcements sent too late by Fastolphe back toward the enemy upon the ridge. Fastolphe, seeing his advance guard pursued by the Armagnacs, rallied his army and retreated north toward Paris, abandoning Talbot.

By two o'clock in the afternoon, the battle was already won. More than a thousand enemy lay dead, with another two hundred taken prisoner. Among those captured were Lord Talbot, Sir Thomas Scales, Sir Thomas Ramston, and Lord Hungerford, all veterans of Orléans. Incredibly, only three Armagnacs were slain, one of whom lost his life when his horse reared and threw him upon the spiked end of a stake. It had all happened so quickly that by the time she reached the battleground, it was, as Jehanne had feared, all over. And she had not been there to stop its savagery.

Scores of enemy dead lay between the hedgerows. Their blackened blood covered the grass in slippery, stinking pools and dripped thickly into the bushes, for many had been pushed onto their own pikes by the charging horses, and they hung there with the sharp, bloody ends sticking out of their backs. The bodies of archers littered the nearby field where they had been hit before they could get off a shot. Several had been struck so quickly that they were beheaded, and disembodied faces stared sightlessly at the ground and at the palisade they had not finished making. Nearby, a severed arm still grasped its longbow. Broken arrows, splintered beneath horses' hooves, were scattered across the ground.

Richemont's men were riding slowly through the macabre field, and once in a while they dismounted to finish off wounded Englishmen with their swords. Soldiers from the main army were collecting enemy weapons that could still be useful. The familiar nauseating smell of death emanated from the blood-soaked bodies, which had begun to cook in the heat of the day, and everywhere was the buzz of flies. Vultures circled lazily overhead, then swooped to feast on the recently slaughtered carrion. A soldier who was not quite dead was feebly trying to fight off one of the filthy scavengers, which was tearing at his wounded shoulder with its beak. From all over the field there were infrequent cries as the wounded were put to death by Richemont's men. A squad of soldiers was dragging corpses from the road to clear a path, and they plopped them into a stiffening, grisly pile.

Jehanne's mouth was ajar at the sight of the appalling scene. Her companions, as dazed as she, took it all in wordlessly. Pasquerel made the Sign of the Cross as though entranced.

"I must go to the dying," he said to Jehanne. She nodded, pale-faced and silent. The monk nudged his heels into his horse's ribs and headed for the field, where Richemont's soldiers were still busily slitting enemy throats.

Near the end of the hedgerows a dual column of prisoners, their hands clasped behind their heads, was being escorted in Jehanne's direction by mounted guards.

All of a sudden, for no apparent reason, one of the Breton soldiers raised his mace and struck a prisoner on his bare head. The man crumpled into the dust. The rest of the captives simply stepped over him until he was left alone in the road. Jehanne could not take her eyes off him, even as the columns passed her, and she guided her mount to where he lay. She jumped down and rolled him over onto his back.

He was only a boy, no more than fifteen or sixteen. Freckles dotted a face whose chin had not yet sprouted whiskers, and above his pug nose startled blue eyes strained to see her.

Jehanne sat down beside him and took the boy's auburn head onto her lap. It was cracked near the top like a broken egg, and blood and brainy matter oozed from the fracture. A thin stream of spittle leaked from a corner of his mouth through which breaths came in sharp bursts. His left eye filled with a translucent film of blood.

Jehanne gently touched his cheek and whispered through her tears, "Do you repent of your sins before God? Do you beg His forgiveness?"

He did not appear to have heard her. His eyes started to close; he was drifting away.

"Fetch a priest," she ordered those standing above her without looking up. Her full attention was on the boy, and she was only half aware when someone left the circle to do as she asked.

"Do not be afraid," she whispered softly, "today you shall be with God in Heaven."

She could have sworn that he almost smiled, but in the next instant his eyes rolled back in his head and he did not move again. His spirit had gone to God as Jehanne had promised.

Unable to see him for the tears, she rubbed a bloody hand across his brow and bent to kiss his lifeless cheek. She imagined that somewhere in a province of that faraway, mysterious island, a mother would receive news that the boy she had watched march away with his comrades to claim France for their king would never return. A father would not see his son's sons grow to strong manhood. And in that distant village, perhaps a young girl waited with the memory of her first kiss prophesying those that would never be again.

Jehanne threw back her head and howled, the sound a long, wordless note of primal rage and grief, wrenching to hear and as old as feeling itself.

"Oh God, they do not belong here!" she cried loudly at the burning sky. She looked at the dead youth, barely able to see him for the tears. "Tell them to go home so we don't have to do this any more."

Her brother Jehan knelt beside her and put an arm around her shoulder, then kissed the thick sweaty hair. He held her for a few minutes while she cried and cried against his chest. She was weeping not only for the English boy but for all the fine men who never should have been slaughtered like so many cattle in this war. Her grief was for the ravaged village she had passed through on the way to Chinon and all those like it, and for the generations on both sides of the sea who had been driven beneath the earth by the greed of English kings.

When she was finally spent, she lifted her head and rubbed her eyes with the back of her hands. D'Aulon stooped and took her hand. "Are you all right now, Jehanne?" Concern wrinkled the corners of his eyes.

"Yes," she nodded. She pulled her hand from d'Aulon's grasp and wiped eyes that instantly flooded once more.

Pasquerel suddenly burst out of breath into the group. He gasped when he saw the dead boy in Jehanne's lap, and quickly knelt in the dirt beside them. The monk made the Sign of the Cross and began murmuring the ritual of Extreme Unction. The others silently bowed their heads in prayer. When he finished, he made another cross in the air above the corpse.

It was then that he saw Jehanne's face for the first time. The unearthly brown eyes looked at him across the dead Englishman, red-rimmed from weeping and fatigue. There was the sorrow that he had seen at Orléans, but it was changed now, somehow different. He was struck with the realization that somewhere along the line she had lost the quality of confident innocence he had first seen at Tours. His heart tugged with remembrance of the childlike faith in herself and in God that she had had then. But that was before she knew firsthand what war was actually like.

After that terrible scene in the Bastille de St.-Laurent at Orléans, she had been heard moaning in her sleep, and the child Charlotte told him that once Jehanne cried out so frightfully that thereafter Charlotte had fallen into a nightmare of her own. From that time on, he watched her carefully and noticed that although she tried to put on the same old certain manner for the rest of the world, she could not altogether hide from him a spark of sadness that oftentimes consumed her when they were alone together.

She did not, perhaps could not, express in words the depth of her suffering. She had simply surrendered to remorse and punished herself, as God would not, in the only way she could. Yet Pasquerel knew without her uttering it that from that night in the alley at Orléans had come a strength that no longer accepted personal blame for the wages of war. That was what he saw now, the new element he sensed as she wiped away her tears and tenderly placed the dead boy's head upon the ground.

Pasquerel wondered what the conflict between duty and charity would do to her. After today, would she have the fortitude necessary to withstand the promptings of the Devil and hold on to her faith?

The monk did not have to wait long for his answer.

That night, when La Hire had told his story and was making ready to relate it again, Jehanne sought out her confessor and they retired together to a secluded spot under the benevolent illumination of the full moon. She knelt in the tall grass and he blessed her. The ghostly light shone like a cap onto her hair and made her seem to glow from within the armor she had not yet taken the time to remove. Her drawn face caught the shadows such that she appeared as fragile as a plaster statue, but when she spoke her voice was strong and confident.

"I do not hate the English any more, I feel sorry for them. God has condemned their coming into France because it is a plan created by the Devil and will bring them only death and defeat. Today I saw in that dying soldier that God loves the English as tenderly as He loves the French, and I know in my heart that in spite of their sins He will welcome them into His Kingdom. I pray that God will lift the darkness from their vision and they will come to understand that their place is in their own country. And then they will stop sending their young men here to die."

Because die they would, she said, at the hands of God's anointed army of France. If they did not listen, she would have no choice, the army would have no choice but to kill them. She regretted with all her soul that it must be so. She asked for strength to carry out her mission, and requested also that God continue to protect the French army.

"Will you say a special Mass for me and another for the Dauphin's men?" She turned her gaunt face, spectral in the cool light, toward Pasquerel.

His soul throbbed with a tender love for her. He smiled. "Of course, my child. Is there anything else?"

She shook her head.

He made the Sign of the Cross over her. "*In nomine Patris, et Filii, et Spiritus Sancti.*"

She prayed silently with him while he recited the prayer of absolution, though she had not actually confessed anything. When he finished, she crossed herself and got to her feet.

As he watched her walk away from him toward the camp, he realized that she had said nothing to blame herself as she had once been wont to do. Much relieved, he uttered thanks to God for helping Jehanne to absolve herself and asked that she have the strength never to punish herself again. She was on the right path now, and knew at last that she was Heaven's own Soldier.

The heat moderated after the sun went down but did not disappear altogether, and the countryside was sultry under the clear night sky. Most of the archers, knights, and men-at-arms pitched camp in the fields downwind from the battlefield and its recently dug mass graves. A select troop from the Dauphin's army was chosen to occupy the town of Patay, just enough to keep order among the already frightened civilian population.

D'Alençon forbade Richemont and his Bretons to set foot in Patay. Because they had fomented the worst of the afternoon's massacre, the duc would not chance their having a free rein within the town. Richemont pretended not to mind having to remain in camp, surrounded by distrustful, nearly hostile companies, but d'Alençon was not fooled by the comte's agreeable words. He secretly ordered sentries to ring the Breton enclave, just in case Richemont decided to challenge his authority in his absence.

After she left Pasquerel, Jehanne got onto her horse and went with d'Alençon to an inn in the town where, the duc told her, they would receive Talbot's official surrender. She took none of her entourage with her, despite their strenuous objections. She needed time alone, away from them and their hovering protectiveness. Tonight she would sleep in a room that d'Alençon had rented for her at the inn. She would be quite safe there.

The inn was bristling with soldiers. De Gaucourt, the Bastard, and Gilles de Rais were already there and waiting when Jehanne and d'Alençon arrived. Their men had moved the tables away from the center of the main room and placed a seat conspicuously in front of the empty fireplace. D'Alençon took his seat as commander of the king's army, with the captains beside him.

Jehanne stood at his right hand. Her armor was in her tent back in camp. Tonight, she was handsomely dressed in the clothes from the duc d'Orléans. Although it was a hot, humid evening, the red cloak fastened at her throat was casually flung back across her shoulder, revealing the dark green tunic and hose. Ste.-Catherine's sword hung from the leather belt about her hips. Instead of boots she wore crimson slippers, and a similarly shaded cap perched on the back of her head.

Bound at the wrists, Lord Talbot was brought into the inn by guards, who shoved him roughly toward d'Alençon. He staggered briefly, then regained his balance.

Given his reputation, Jehanne had expected his appearance to be at least as loathsome as Richemont's, but such was not the case. In any country he would have been considered a handsome man. Not even the dust covering his torn *huque* could cloud the air of dignity that he surely wore even when naked. He was medium tall and strongly built, with broad shoulders, a narrow waist, and muscled, slightly bowed legs. His short, dark brown hair, though disordered, was neatly cut. A manicured beard covered his chin and circled his thin-lipped mouth. He looked at the duc seated before him with intelligent hazel eyes, glanced quickly at Jehanne, then back again at d'Alençon.

"Well, seigneur Talbot," the young man said amiably, barely able to contain his delight, "it seems that we finally meet. I would wager that you did not expect to find yourself in this position this morning."

Talbot raised his chin and said stoically in a clipped voice, "Such are the fortunes of war."

"Indeed." The duc's smile was bitter. "I well know the fortunes of war, having spent three years in a Burgundian prison tower at Le Crotoy. Not such a bad place, really, if one does not regret not only the loss of one's freedom, but knowing full well that the ransom demanded by the enemy will plunge one's family into poverty. Are you a wealthy man, seigneur Talbot?"

The Englishman lifted his chin in reply.

"No matter. Perhaps we shall set you free one day, after we have won the war and restored Charles to his throne."

278

"Then I shall be a prisoner for a long, long time, sir," Talbot said with a touch of proud irony, "because, you see, France already has a king, agreed upon legally in the Treaty of Troyes."

"Agreed upon perhaps by the enemies of France, but not by her people." The Bastard's silky voice floated above the venom in his words.

Talbot's laugh was mirthless. "Her people? What hypocrites you all are! You are not 'her people'! You pretend to support Charles for the people's sake, yet how in the name of God do you know what 'the people' want? All of you have lives far removed from the common masses who populate this God-forsaken kingdom!"

De Gaucourt snarled and drew his dagger, but before he could take a step, the Bastard and de Rais had grabbed him. "It's all right," said d'Alençon to the old soldier. "Let seigneur Talbot have his say. It's the last chance he'll get for a while." He gave the Englishman another narrow-eyed smile.

Talbot sneered at the men. "What does it matter anyway? A kingdom is ruled by its monarch, not by its people. And not by its lords either," he added pointedly. "That privilege is bestowed upon the King and ordained by Heaven, through bloodlines and by treaty. Under those criteria, Henry VI is the King of England *and* of France!"

"Is he? I recall no coronation having taken place, granting the child that title and its attendant privileges." The Bastard's tone was pleasantly disingenuous. "I do not know how these matters are conducted in England, but here in France the King partakes of an ancient ceremony going back nearly a thousand years, one that binds him to God, and yes, to his people. As Henry has not been crowned King of France, he is *not* King of France, but a pretender."

"You are mistaken, Bastard. Your late King made Henry's father his heir, which means that it is Charles who is the pretender." Talbot snorted. "Why, even Charles' own mother disavowed his suitability to inherit the throne on the grounds that his father was someone other than the King, and his mother should know. As to Henry's not having been crowned yet"—he smiled, tight-lipped, at d'Alençon—"we shall shortly take care of that."

Enraged hatred from the guards rumbled through the candlelit room. Gilles de Rais crossed his arms and glared at the Englishman, sending daggers of dark malice toward the rigidly bound knight. A wordless growl purred through de Gaucourt's chest.

D'Alençon grasped the arms of his chair and slowly rose to his feet, nostrils flaring angrily. "Your little king's only direct descent from the dawn of French Kings through St.-Clovis comes through his mother, and therefore his kingship is not ordained according to Salic Law! Charles VII, the *true* son of Charles VI, son of Charles V, is the rightful lord of this realm, and God will proclaim him so.

"And make no mistake: Though you may be right in saying that most of us here do not know the people of France, there is one among us who does, and it is she whom God has sent to recover the crown that you have stolen. Is there anything you wish to say to him, Jehanne?" He did not turn to look at her but kept his exquisite profile pointed toward the famous captive.

The English lord's emotionless eyes took in her manly garb and proud stance. "Yes," she found herself saying. "I am Jehanne the Maid—"

"I know who and what you are," Talbot's precise voice intruded. "You are a reeking peasant, a cowmaid who has seduced these 'noble lords' with rubbish about being sent by God and ill-conceived dreams of glory. You are the limb of the Fiend who has brought about our defeats through the use of sorcery forged in your agreement with the Evil One. One day we shall catch you without your army of traitors, and when we do, we shall burn you." His eyes calmly touched a cold place within her, and she shivered even as she felt her anger rise.

"That is a lie," she stated flatly. "I am God's messenger, sent to liberate the kingdom of France from your king's greedy clutches. Mark me well, seigneur Talbot: God has told me that no English king shall ever rule France. All who try to take it will meet with defeat after defeat until you understand that He will not let you take it. Heaven's blessing will be withheld from your king until he quits his evil venture and returns all of you to your own land."

A sneer twisted Talbot's mustached lip, and he looked at her as though she were offal. She felt the Power charge her, negating his threat. I will fear no evil, she told herself.

Aloud she said, "You doubt my words, I know. Nevertheless, I speak the truth as God has revealed it to me. I pray that you will realize it before it is too late."

"And I pray daily for your death. I only hope that I am there to watch you burn." The stately voice was deadly cold.

"What you shall have instead is a French prison," d'Alençon said harshly. "Take him away." The guards grabbed Talbot's arms and dragged him out the door.

Later that night, as she drifted into sleep under the guarded security of the inn, Jehanne prayed that the uneasy dread he had prodded would leave her. There had been something almost convincing in the confident dignity Talbot had displayed in spite of his captivity, in the words that sounded so compelling. Jehanne knew that he was wrong, yet had felt herself pulled toward him against her will.

I will fear no evil, I will not lose faith again. I am God's agent and under His loving protection.

Talbot hated her, she had seen that in his face, and no mistake. That bewildered her. She had spoken to him most truly, in a gentle voice, about God's wishes for the kingdom, without malice or desires for vengeance. And yet he hated her, wanted her dead.

She would relive the encounter in her head many times during the coming months, and not even the merciful assurances of her Counsel could entirely erase it from her memory. The poison in his threat did not depart until the first snows fell.

With Pasquerel's help, Jehanne wrote to the "loyal and gentle Frenchmen of the city of Tournai." She told them that within the space of a week she had chased the English from the Loire, killing many and taking a number prisoner. She ended the letter by inviting them to Charles' coronation. Without waiting for her to ask, Pasquerel read the letter back to her. While she listened to the mild voice recite her words, she paced back and forth across the tent floor, hands clasped behind her back.

"That is good," she said when he was finished. "Now I wish to write to the duc de Bourgogne."

Pasquerel dipped the quill into the inkwell and waited. Since Patay he had put aside his monk's robes, and now wore a plain tunic and hose that bunched up around his ankles. He had told Jehanne that because he was now virtually a member of the army, he should dress like a soldier. The truth was that his habits were so bloodstained that even strong soap had been unable to restore them to their original condition. But he did not speak of it to her. She did not need to be reminded of the carnage they had witnessed together.

Jehanne was so tired that she could barely think. She forced her eyes to focus on the candle flickering beside the clean sheet of parchment while she gathered her thoughts. They were as disorderly as cattle on their way to pasture, and she strained to round them up. Finally, she rubbed her forehead, sighed through her nose, then began dictating.

She conveyed her greetings to the duc, then told him that she hoped that with God's grace he was well. The King of Heaven had commanded her to attend the Dauphin on his journey to Reims, where he would soon be anointed and crowned as the true King of France. The murder of the duc's father Jehan sans Peur had been a great tragedy for France, but if the duc could find it within himself to reconcile with the Dauphin, there would be great rejoicing throughout the realm and France would be healed. She invited him to join the journey to Reims and thereafter to take his place in the ancient ceremony that would make Charles King. She prayed that God would touch the duc's heart with charity, and that he would remember his former allegiance to the Valois dynasty.

When he saw that she had nothing more to add, the confessor read this letter to her also. She nodded her approval, then said, "Give the first letter to Guyenne, and have him deliver it to the burgesses of Tournai." She smiled dreamily. "They will receive him favorably, since they are loyal to the Dauphin."

Perhaps they would even hold a modest feast for him, she thought, and give him a real bed on which he could rest after his journey. He would certainly savor that after having slept on the hard ground since his convalescence in Orléans.

"Please ask Metz to give him a little money for his journey, will you, Brother?"

"Of course." Pasquerel sensed that she had sworn to herself and to God never to endanger the lives of her heralds as she had done at Orléans. The duc de Bourgogne was not as ruthlessly dedicated an adversary as were the English and was certainly more civilized, but still the monk wondered how she planned to send the second letter.

As though she read his mind, she then said, "I do not wish to use Ambleville for the other. Tell La Hire to assemble a guard to take it to seigneur Bourgogne."

"Yes, Jehanne."

As he folded and sealed the pages, the monk studied her exhausted face. There were times, as now, when she looked touchingly young. Her eyes were circled in dark rims of fatigue, and she was slightly hunched, as though the burdens of her mission were almost too much for her to bear. She was wearing an old tunic and homespun leggings that covered her calves to her boots. Minguet had cut her hair just a few days earlier, and dressed as she was she had the look of a common soldier.

"I wish to sleep now," she said, rubbing her eyes. She sat down on a stool and with a grunt slowly pulled off one boot.

"Do you want me to summon Minguet with some food?" he asked. "You have not eaten since this morning."

"No, thank you." She smiled tiredly.

None of her entourage except Pasquerel was in the tent. Jehan, Pierre, and Raymond were with d'Aulon somewhere in camp. The whereabouts of the heralds was unknown, but she deduced that they must not be far away; dutiful men, they made it their business to stay near her tent in case she needed them. She could hear Poulengy and Metz outside, and knew from their words and the clangs of ringing steel that they were instructing Minguet in swordplay. That pleased her very much. The boy's shyness and his worshipful attachment to Jehanne made him an easy target for the others' jealousy, especially Raymond's. The older page was a gregarious joker who loved to tease the gullible Minguet, and there had been occasions when the animosity between them exploded into heated arguments.

Once, Raymond bought a live pig at market and placed it in Minguet's bedroll before dawn. When Minguet awoke, he found himself lying next to the muddy, perturbed animal. Jehan and Pierre had laughed at Minguet's frightened reaction, but no one laughed louder than Raymond, who called the boy a sissy and a crybaby. Jehanne's irritated rebuke had only made Raymond feel further distanced from her and more inclined to pester his smaller rival.

Jehanne's friends from Vaucouleurs had developed a special affection for the orphaned boy, particularly Metz, whose jests were harmless and designed to make Minguet feel more at ease with himself. Knowing how vulnerable he was during battle because he had entered Jehanne's service before he could finish the military training a page customarily underwent on his way to becoming a squire, the older men had taken it upon themselves—without Jehanne's having to ask—to train him in the use of arms. Minguet loved them for it. He was also starting to develop a more confident bearing.

"Don't interrupt him just now," Jehanne replied to Pasquerel's question. "He needs to be doing what he is doing. Anyway, I am not very hungry."

"Jehanne, you must eat, you must keep up your strength."

"I'm just tired. I will eat tomorrow after I've had a chance to sleep." She tugged at the other boot. "I haven't had more than a few hours' sleep over the past few days."

"I know that," he remarked with an edge in his gentle voice. "You are trying to do too much and will wear yourself out. In the past week alone, you have acted as liaison between the army and the burgesses of Orléans, you have resupplied the army, you have been to see the Dauphin, you have brought the army from Orléans here to Gien. You are trying to do too much all by yourself. You must slow down."

For a few moments she did not answer but sat looking at the floor, her hands absently holding the boot. She raised her eyes to Pasquerel's concerned, ascetic face. "No one can do it but me," she almost whispered, "and if I don't do it, it won't get done." There was a flicker of her old grin. "You know how hard it is to get people moving in the right direction."

He could not answer. She was right as usual.

She picked up her other boot and stood. "I'm going to bed. Please ask Minguet to wake me early. I must be ready in case the Dauphin decides that we proceed to Reims tomorrow."

Pasquerel noted the bitterness in her words, just the barest trace, but there nevertheless. "Sleep well, dear child."

She smiled her thanks and walked sluggishly to the rear of the tent. Parting the flap, she plopped down wearily upon her little cot. Jehanne rolled over onto her back and closed her eyes. She was so tired that she doubted that she would be able to sleep. Her shoulders ached and a dull pain throbbed in her lower back.

Attempting to move the Dauphin to Reims was more difficult than she had envisioned. Not only were Trémoïlle and the archbishop always there, goading Charles with lies and half-truths, but the Dauphin himself seemed reluctant to hasten toward his destiny. Instead, he made constant excuses about his lack of money to pay the army. By now he certainly knew as well as she did that the knights and men-at-arms no longer cared whether or not they were paid. They were winning at last, and from all over France they converged upon Orléans and Patay and Gien to fight with the Maid for God and for Charles. Her discontentment with the Dauphin had boiled over three days ago after he joined her and the other soldiers at St.-Benoît-sur-Loire.

While they were watching the troops and artillery move past them, bound from Orléans to this place on the outskirts of Gien, Charles had suddenly turned to her and said with affected concern, "Jehanne, we fear that what you most need at this time is rest."

She had been up half the previous night, helping to ready the army for its journey. It seemed a long time since she had had a proper meal and sound sleep. To add to her fatigue, Charles kept stalling, moving in babysteps—now here to enter this loyal town, now there to court that local seigneur—so that she felt as if she was trying to roll a large stone uphill.

He was doing so again with this sham regard for her welfare. She knew that he was only frightened of his future role as King and was hoping that if she did stop to rest, he could delay his fate. It saddened her that he was not genuinely concerned for the weight he was placing upon her. It also made her feel firmer than ever that she would have a hand in everything leading to Reims.

She burst into tears of frustration. "Oh, Sire, please do not doubt. Your whole kingdom will indeed be restored to you, and you shall be crowned!"

Taken by surprise, he had gasped at her insight and made no response.

Just thinking about that now made her eyes fill again, and she wiped away the tears that leaked into her hair. Charles was not the noble man, the dashing prince that she had imagined from childhood. He was weak-willed and indecisive and afraid. She could see that at last, though she would never speak a word against him and would always uphold him. Yet she could not help but wonder why God had chosen him to be King.

GOD DOES NOT ERR. CHARLES SHALL ONE DAY BE A STRONG KING AND SHALL REDEEM HIS KINGDOM FOR GOD AND HIS PEOPLE.

But why is it so hard?

FOR THE GOOD OF HIS SOUL, AND YOURS. SLEEP, CHILD OF GOD, REST IN HIS LOVING EMBRACE.

After much tossing about on the little bed, she did. She awoke in the middle of the night in the grip of her recurring nightmare. It was almost sunup before she wearily fell back to sleep.

CHAPTER TEN

Reunion at Reims

July 2–18, 1429

rother Richard? Who is he?" Jehanne's brows knit together above her sunburned, peeling nose. Droplets of perspiration glistened in a mustache above her lip, and she wiped her forehead with her sleeve.

"A Franciscan monk recently come from Paris," Pasquerel replied. "And before that he came, or says he came, from Jerusalem, where his order guards the Holy Sepulchre against the Infidels."

"You sound as though you don't believe that, Brother Pasquerel." She smiled.

Her confessor shrugged. "It is possible that what he says is true. I have never been to the Holy Land. But I heard him speak about six months ago in Paris, and let me tell you, I can vouch for the power in his words."

The blistering late afternoon light shone through the tent like the sun itself, steaming the inhabitants into puddles of discomfort. Jehanne was wearing a white linen tunic that stuck to her back between her shoulders. Yellowish circles discolored the shirt's underarms, and she was aware that she smelled. The lightness of her clothes made her seem swarthier than ever as she sat with crossed legs upon a camp stool. Every now and then she scratched the prickling hose. Because the Dauphin had not yet decided to besiege Troyes, her armor was neatly stacked in a corner. It was unlikely that there would be a battle today with darkness coming on in a couple of hours.

All her household and d'Alençon were with her. D'Aulon, Raymond, Jehanne's brothers, and even Minguet had discarded their shirts and were sitting on the floor with sweaty streamlets inching down their backs. D'Alençon wore a pearl gray gossamer shirt whose loose, open collar revealed a small patch of black hair at his throat. His cheeks were flushed through dark stubble that thickened as it neared his chin, and his tall frame occupied the only other stool, as befitted his rank. To Jehanne's right, Poulengy lay on his side with his head propped upon a bedroll, while Metz sat cross-legged beside him, fully dressed but for his long wiggling toes.

"They say he can preach for hours at a time without tiring," d'Alençon mused. "Is that true?"

"Oh, yes, the man never seems to grow weary," Pasquerel answered from his place at Jehanne's feet. "I witnessed him speak from near noon until eight o'clock at night, and his message was so convincing that when he finished, the Parisians threw their dice and gaming boards onto a fire they had built. The women even burned their tall hats and trains as a sacrifice of their vanities."

Jehanne digested the information thoughtfully. So many people came to see her these days, local lords and their ambitious sons, women who pleaded with her to heal their children, retainers trying to curry her favor with the Dauphin. She had never imagined the burdens her mission would bring.

The army was encamped on the outskirts of Troyes near the village of St.-Phal, deep in territory loyal to the Burgundians. Jehanne had been dismayed to find that the people of Troyes were unyieldingly opposed to the Dauphin's entering their city; dismayed but not surprised, for it made sense. Troyes was the site of the late mad King's despicable treaty of alliance with Henry V wherein the Dauphin had been disinherited. There was a small Anglo-Burgundian garrison within those strongly fortified walls, and they had many prisoners of war taken in past skirmishes and held for whatever ransoms the English hoped they would bring. Yesterday Jehanne had written a letter to the city burgesses which she had not yet sent, informing them that if they accepted Charles as their true King, the army would spare their town; if not, they would be attacked. She knew very well that their cannon could not blast through the mighty walls of Troyes, but her Counsel had promised victory and she did not doubt that they would have it.

And now, even without Jehanne's ultimatum, the city had responded to the presence of Charles' army at their gates by sending a delegation, headed by the dubious Brother Richard, not to the Dauphin, but to Jehanne. She kept him waiting outside her tent while she conferred with her family.

"I want to see him," Pierre stated impatiently. "Please, Jehanne, let's hear what he has to say."

"I wager that will be quite a lot." D'Alençon chuckled, his dark eyes dancing mischievously. "It's said that he exhorted the people to sow beans for the Deliverer he prophesied would come to oppose the Antichriste and defeat him, and the people did. Now Troyes is rumored to be full of the stuff, which would certainly benefit our army if we could get our hands on it!"

Jehanne's ears perked up. "Deliverer?" She grinned. "Did he happen to say who this might be?"

D'Alençon, knowing what was on her mind, laughed. "Don't jump to conclusions. Brother Richard referred to his 'Deliverer' as 'he.' The man is very popular with the peasants, and I doubt that he would welcome a rival for their affections."

"But I am not a rival, Jehan," she said with wide-eyed sweetness, "I am God's messenger."

"So is Brother Richard," Poulengy remarked sleepily. Metz and d'Aulon snickered.

286

"Do you think he's a trickster?" Jehanne asked no one in particular. Her Guides were silent on the subject and she had no idea what she should do.

"Who knows?" Metz shrugged. "You won't unless you receive him."

She glanced at d'Alençon, who lifted his shoulders with a smile. The others looked at her expectantly, and she found no answer in any of them.

A pensive scowl creased her sopping forehead; she wiped it away with a shirt-sleeve. "I need to pray for a bit." She got to her feet. "I'll be back soon."

She walked to her alcove at the rear of the tent and dropped the flap behind her, then knelt beside the cot. The weather had been so hot that she had recently taken to sleeping outside on a bedroll and came into this room only when she needed something from her satchel, such as a change of clothes. Now it was the one private place, stifling though it was. She dragged her shirttail across her streaming brow, then crossed herself and clasped her hands. She could hear her comrades debating the merits of Brother Richard beyond the thin muslin separating them.

For several moments she could feel Them only dimly. She directed her gaze to a spot on the canvas wall made by a drop of dried mud, and as her focus tightened, it seemed to gape open and she slid rapidly through immeasurable caverns into the sheltering cool, where the light was most silent and she was always safe. Their presence began to pulsate with a soft brilliance, slowly filling her vision until she was unconscious of anything else.

Who is this Brother Richard? she asked. Is he truly from God?

ALL ARE FROM GOD, JEHANNE, SURELY YOU KNOW THAT.

That is not what I mean. Please do not jest with me. This is too important.

HIS WORK IS NOT THE SAME AS YOURS. IN THAT SENSE HE IS NOT GOD'S MESSENGER. HE SPEAKS OF THE END TIMES, WHICH ONLY FRIGHTENS PEOPLE. BUT GOD SO LOVES THEM THAT HE WILL NOT BRING ABOUT THE DESTRUCTION THEY FEAR.

Should I receive him?

HE BRINGS WITHIN HIS COMPANY AN OFFER OF PEACE FOR THE CITY. IT IS AN OFFER YOU WOULD DO WELL TO ACCEPT. BUT YOU MUST MAKE YOUR OWN DECISIONS AS REGARDS HIS STATURE. RELY ON THE SENSE THAT GOD GAVE YOU, AND YOU SHALL CHOOSE WISELY.

There was to be no more for now. Catherine's airy vibration began to dissolve steadily like vapors under summer sunlight. Jehanne felt herself gently pulled upward from the grotto where They resided with her, the emptiness before her gradually expanding into a sense of the present place and time. Before she knew it, she had returned to her aloneness on her knees next to her bed.

She lingered over a *Pater Noster*, then made the Sign of the Cross. She propped her hands on the cot and pushed herself to her feet; parting the flap, she ducked under it.

Her household stopped their exchange about the enigmatic friar and turned to look at her. "Let's see what Brother Richard has to say," she said, smiling.

Her brothers sat up and applauded, laughing with approval. D'Alençon rose sluggishly from his seat and straightened his tunic. Pasquerel muttered, "Let's see indeed," and stood up stiffly.

Jehanne loped to the front of the tent. "Come on, boys, put your shirts on," she demanded good-naturedly, "let's show some respect for these men from Troyes."

She waited for Minguet to scramble into his shirt and part the hanging, tightly woven burlap. He went before Jehanne into the startlingly brilliant heat and held open the aperture for her.

Thirty or so fairly well-dressed men were milling about, speaking to one another in timorous whispers. At a slight distance to Jehanne's left, five or six soldiers whispered among themselves, visibly contemptuous of the townspeople who had come to see the feared Maid, rumored to be either full of God or a witch from Hell. To the soldiers Jehanne was simply their own comrade, their Maid, as down-to-earth and approachable as a sister.

The men of Troyes froze in their tracks at the sight of her. They looked so much like frightened rabbits that she wanted to laugh. Conspicuous among their prosperous but modest dress was a slovenly monk in crudely woven sackcloth alive with lice, and Jehanne knew at once that he was Brother Richard.

She had not expected him to be so tall and thin. His long arms hung below dark brown sleeves that were much too short. The blazing eyes of a fanatic burned in a long, horsey face made even more equine by teeth that appeared fashioned for a larger mouth. A mop of dull gray hair, as tightly curled as lamb's fleece, hugged his ovoid head. He made no move toward her but hung back with the frightened burgesses, muttering prayers beneath his breath and sprinkling holy water in her direction from a cannister.

Without warning, a spidery hand flew up into a dramatic gesture that peasants made against the evil eye.

She looped her thumbs into her woven white belt and grinned. "Approach me boldly. I promise that I shall not fly away," she said with mock reassurance. Her household laughed, their camaraderie embracing her in its love.

Brother Richard slowly lowered his arms a little and warily narrowed his stare. "Be you from the Devil, or God?"

"The church says I'm from God," she responded brightly. "The Dauphin says I'm from God. Most of all my Counsel tells me They're from God, and since They speak only of God and not of the Devil, then I say I'm from God. What do you say, Brother Richard?"

He inched forward in suspicious steps. His clothes were soiled with the remnants of meals long since eaten, and he smelled of perspiration, old and new. He made the Sign of the Cross in the space separating them, then knelt before her.

With a naughty grin curving her mouth, she likewise went down on her knees. For several moments they investigated one another's eyes, probing for quality of soul.

"Now that we're both like this, what are we going to do?"

The jest was more than he could bear. His lips parted and the huge teeth escaped into a raucous laugh that sounded like a donkey braying. He was such a funny man, so unlike his reputation, that relief flooded Jehanne and she joined in his mirth. Her companions were laughing, too, not very kindly, and she knew without looking that they were nudging one another.

In plumbing the monk's essence she intuited that some of his ideas were nonsense, but he was a sincere believer in Christe and in the things he said. He was no threat to her personally or to her mission. Without waiting for him to respond, she bounced to her feet.

He stood slowly, then looked down at her from his unexpected height. "I have a message for you from Troyes." He spoke with a slightly effeminate smirk.

"So I've heard," she answered, smiling wryly. Minguet tittered. Jocularity erupted through Pierre's nose.

Brother Richard's smirk spread suggestively as though he brought with him a great secret and was demanding that she ask what it was.

She spread her hands and smiled. "Well?"

He took a step toward her and put a filthy arm around her shoulder, breathing rankly in a whisper, "Beans. God has instructed me to tell the people to plant beans for their Deliverer. If you are from God, then you must be that saviour, and the food for you. But before we give it to you, all of Troyes wishes to know how God speaks to you. Do you stare into pools of water or anything like that; do you throw sticks upon the ground? Is that how your messengers come to you?"

A finger of caution tapped her shoulder and in that instant she knew that he had no message from the city. He lacked a genuine contact with his soul and was curious about hers. He envied her, she could feel that; there was no longer any dread in him. But it was that covetousness, far more hazardous than fear, that she had to guard against.

Frowning, she disengaged herself from his spurious familiarity. "I was examined in Poitiers by a commission of churchmen at the Dauphin's request," she parried, her smile dignified and somewhat aloof, "and in their report they stated that I am from God." Her eyes shadowed and the humor vanished. "As to how God makes His will known to me, that is between me and Him."

"They say you communicate with angels," Brother Richard insisted, undaunted by her Power. "Is that true?" He was trying to invade her soul; she could feel his mind probing her resolve.

"That is my concern, not yours," she answered briskly. "Have you an actual message from the city? Will they yield their resistance to the good Dauphin Charles, the *true* Deliverer of France, or will they force our army to attack them?"

"I don't know," he stammered, taken aback by her composure, finally feeling her Power. "I'm—I'm not authorized to surrender Troyes." He stepped back a pace.

Darting a look of disgust at the monk, one of the delegation came forward to present himself. "Jehanne, I am Pierre de Sologne," the man said, elbowing Brother Richard out of the way. He wore a wide puffed hood that swept around his head and ended across his right shoulder. His face wore the long, narrow aspect of a sensible merchant. "We were not sent to settle terms with the Dauphin, only to see you."

"To test me, you mean, as the Devil tested Our Lord," she retorted. "Well, you have seen me. Now go back to Troyes and decide which it shall be, siege and conquest, or peaceful submission. Here"—she reached into her shirt and withdrew a soggy piece of paper—"give this to the aldermen and tell them to make their choice quickly. In God's name, the Dauphin shall be crowned in Reims before month's end!"

With that she turned her back on them and reentered her tent before anyone knew what was happening.

The interior was oppressive after the fresh air. She crossed the floor and sat down on one of the stools. She was not really as angry as she had pretended to be. The townsmen were fools, but it was certain that they did not want their city besieged and sacked, and were only stalling for time.

As for Brother Richard, he had a certain greasy charm that might work on the frightened peasants. Unlike Jehanne, however, he lacked true revelation and sought a glory she abhorred. All the same, she would have to treat him carefully. She could not afford his turning popular approval from her, at least not until the Dauphin was crowned. They would make better allies than enemies, for all their sakes. She would summon him later, after the Dauphin had entered Troyes, and at that time she would grant him a more extended audience. But she knew she would have to watch her back.

Minguet stuck his head through the door, then came into the tent. "Is everything all right?" He had grown a bit during the past two months, and his voice was straining to deepen.

"Yes, Minguet." She laughed. "Come on in." She waved her arm, encouraging him to join her. "What's happening out there?"

He came forward and sat down next to her. "The duc is talking to the men from Troyes. He told them that you have his support and that of the army, and that if they do not accept your decision, we will defeat them. Then that man— what's his name?"

"Pierre de Sologne."

"Yes, that's it. Anyway, he answered that the townsfolk still think you might be a witch, or some of them do, only a witch would support the king since he's such a bumbleton, and the duc said the king is not a bumbleton and anyway the army knows you're from God and not a witch because you pray to God and He answers you, and our victories have been miracles from Heaven." Minguet stopped, out of breath.

"What else?" she asked with a smile.

"Then the duc reminded Brother Richard that God would not have instructed him to tell the peasants to plant beans for their Deliverer if the Deliverer's vassal was a witch, and that he should not have questioned you about your private matters. Now the king is here, and his army is running low on food. So the beans are God's sign that the Deliverer really is the king. And he said you are the one who was sent by God to bear God's message to the king. So you cannot possibly be a witch."

"Then what?"

Minguet shrugged. "I came in here then—"

The burlap flipped open and the rest of her household began filing in, d'Alençon last. He was grinning as he walked toward Jehanne. Minguet quickly vacated his seat and the duc took the boy's place.

"I think we gave them something to think about," he said, crossing his legs.

"Yes, Minguet told me some of it. How did it end?"

"Oh, they made some bother about your being a witch"—d'Alençon waved a slender hand negligently—"and I told them that they have become bewitched themselves by the English, who can't admit that they've been defeated in battle and so must blame it on your supposed sorcery. They asked if I believe you're from God, and I told them yes, of course, the entire army believes it. I told them that they're blind to the very signs God puts before their eyes."

"Will they yield to Charles?" All this talk of witchcraft made her uneasy. It reminded her of Talbot's threats and the cold place he had touched.

"That remains to be seen. But I cannot imagine how they could possibly refuse now."

The company argued the answer to Jehanne's question all through the setting of the sun and the meager evening meal of stale bread and old cheese. They were tired, but the mood was festive. Everyone had an opinion whether Troyes would surrender or face destruction, yet all knew the outcome. Troyes would yield, Charles would be King and France saved.

Finally, with her head reeling from the continuous discussion that produced no clearcut answer, Jehanne took her blanket outside and spread it on the grass. She lay down on her back and folded her hands behind her head, which she rested on her satchel. Thousands of stars spread across the clear black heavens as far as she could see, and she watched one of them dart across the sky. She smiled at God's great wonder. What would it be like to fly up and up and up and reach one of those forbidden lights? Could she still see France from so far away, and how would it look if she could? Is that Heaven way up there? she wondered.

Suddenly seized by a yawn, she closed her eyes. All about her the army rested and prepared for sleep. Men were singing a plaintive old folksong several hundred feet away, the off-key voices nevertheless pure in their emotional fervor. Just a short walk from her, a tethered horse snorted and a couple of its fellows rustled their hooves in reply. Conversation within the tent had died down, and she heard footsteps leave the shelter and their owners come toward her. Someone, actually two or three someones were spreading their blankets upon the ground near her, in silence so as not to awake her. Jehanne did not stir but let them think she was asleep. She wanted no further talk tonight. At least, not with them.

Her breathing gradually deepened and her consciousness started to float into genuine drowsiness. The world receded as she drifted into the outskirts of dreamtime.

Please make Troyes surrender without bloodshed. I will fight them if I must, but you know I do not want to.

GOD CANNOT FORCE HIS WILL UPON THE PEOPLE. THEIR FATE SHALL BE THE PRODUCT OF THEIR CHOICES, FREELY MADE.

Do not worry so, Ste.-Marguerite whispered. Be merciful toward yourself and toward others, and you shall not sin. Leave everything to God.

"Everything to God," Jehanne mumbled.

Pasquerel smiled at the sleeping girl beside him. He raised his hand and blessed her before he drifted away himself.

*   *   *

The men-at-arms took Brother Richard's beans anyway, above the bawling protests of the city's ministers, who could not do anything to stop the army, since the beanfields were outside the city wall where the forces were massed. Brother Richard seemed not to mind. He returned to Troyes bearing Jehanne's letter, impressed that she had withstood him, and mysteriously generous in his praises of her. Declaring her to be a messenger from God as powerful as himself, he eagerly sanctioned their acceptance of her terms.

The burgesses ignored him and burned her letter. She was no agent of God; she was a madwoman in the grip of the Devil. Still, the men of Troyes did not dare disregard the import of the communication brought by the Dauphin's heralds, even though they did not respond to him either.

Charles had written that they should forget the past—that is, the Treaty of Troyes—and he would spare them the anguish that a siege would bring to their helpless people. They had only to consider his forces' victories if they doubted the outcome of any resistance. He would await their reply before he attacked them.

The aldermen sent a secret dispatch to the people of Châlons and Reims. They advised their allies that the ignoble pretender to the throne was prepared to besiege Troyes, and desperately beseeched these cities' aid in repulsing the invader and his terrible Maid sent from Hell. There was the hint that they would do what was fitting to save their town from pillage and ruin, and that if Troyes fell to the Dauphin, they could not be held accountable.

Troyes received no reply from the towns to the east.

Charles allowed one day to pass, then ordered the advance guard of the army to position itself closer to Troyes. The garrison sallied forth and skirmished with the besiegers, but was beaten back after a short time and returned to the safety of the towering fortifications. Charles' soldiers, unable to be repulsed, quickly ringed the city. It was then that they found the beanfields that Brother Richard had accidentally grown for them. They were very hungry. Food was quickly becoming scarcer: something would have to be done soon or they would not be able to hold out.

No one knew that better than Charles. Still, he wanted opinions other than his own so that the blame would be not solely his if they failed. To that end, he summoned the princes of the blood royal—d'Alençon, Clermont, and the Bastard of Orléans—and his ministers and generals, to his temporary residential château in nearby St.-Phal. He included Jehanne in his invitation, but kept her waiting in the anteroom while he sought the counsel of the others. Wearing an anxious frown, she helplessly paced the floor, wondering what, in God's name, they would do.

An hour or more may have passed before the Dauphin sent for her. At last, the door opened and the page gestured with his hand that she should enter.

Jehanne bolted through the door and went down upon one knee to the Dauphin. He told her to rise, then related the gist of the discussion. The council had decided, he said, that unless Jehanne could present them with a sound reason for besieging Troyes, they would withdraw the army until reinforcements could be assembled and sent to them. She listened without interrupting, her face serious but otherwise not betraying her emotions. She was insulted that they had not asked her to join them from the start. They still did not take her seriously, at least the Dauphin's ministers did not. These old men were fools whose ambitions would demand the sacrifice of Charles' birthright.

"And now we invite your opinion, Jehanne," Charles said loftily, but with a twinkle in his icy smile.

"Will what I say be believed, Sire?" Jehanne remembered his constant dithering and was steeling herself for further arguments. She was becoming quite exhausted by them.

"I do not know," he admitted, and she felt her heart plunge. "If what you say is reasonable, then we shall support it."

"Will *you* believe me, my lord?" she insisted through gritted teeth.

"That depends upon what you say." The Dauphin would not yield a pace.

"Then, noble Dauphin, do not debate this matter any longer, but order the army to assault this city of Troyes immediately. For in God's name, I shall deliver this town to you within three days, by agreement or by force, and the Burgundians will be filled with dismay."

"Jehanne," the archbishop broke in, his tone one of hypocritical kindness, "rest assured that the army can wait for ten days, but we have no guarantee that your words are true."

She pretended not to hear him. Taking a few steps closer to Charles, she looked him straight in the eye and said, "Sire, have no doubt that tomorrow you shall be master of Troyes."

"Thank you for your advice, Jehanne," the king responded blandly. "We have decided to wait here for three days, and if after that time the army has not seized the town, then we shall leave it and continue our journey."

He stood, and the rest of them leaped out of their seats. Charles abruptly left the room through a door behind the throne.

Jehanne turned at once and made straight for a passage out the same way she had entered. But someone grabbed her arm, and d'Alençon asked with a smile, "Where are you going so quickly?"

"We don't have time to lose, Jehan! I have to rally the army."

"Now?"

"Naturally! Come with me." She withdrew her arm and began pulling him toward the door. The older men had already left the room in vigorous pursuit of the Dauphin, no doubt in hope of changing his mind. But the captains were still there, and the younger men. "Come on, all of you," she urged, "let's return to Troyes and get to work."

When she did not linger for their reply but dashed from the room, the Bastard remarked to d'Alençon, "Well, Cousin, we have another battle ahead."

La Hire, d'Illiers, and the others pushed past them. The duc grinned. "Another battle? Of course. There will always be another battle where she's concerned." They were alone now. The rest had already sprinted after Jehanne like hounds chasing a stag.

"She is something, isn't she?" The Bastard chuckled. "When Charles gives the word, the men would follow her anywhere, like César or Alisaundre."

"She's neither; she's not in all this for personal glory. In fact, I think there are times when she almost hates it, though naturally she does not express what she's really thinking most of the time."

"Indeed?" The Bastard raised his eyebrows in surprise. "I have always found her to be most straightforward and honest, insufferably so at times if the truth be told."

"Oh, she is honest. Yet sometimes I get a sense of depths within her that, when she catches someone looking at her, quickly disappear as though they were never there at all." D'Alençon mused for a moment.

"But you know the thing that worries me most about her, Bastard?" Something had just occurred to d'Alençon. "What will become of her once Charles is crowned? When he is officially King, he is likely to forbid any further military adventures, and what will she do then? Frankly, I have a hard time envisioning her returning to her village after all this."

"You know her better than I, Jehan. What do you think she'll do?"

Apprehension bit d'Alençon like a rat, and the short hairs on the back of his neck stood on end. "I don't know. I honestly do not know." He considered for a moment. "I just remembered something else. She has often spoken of taking Paris and of freeing duc Charles from his prison, and—"

"But that's absurd, Jehan. The Dauphin does not have the ransoms to redeem my brother! How does Jehanne propose to raise the money?"

"She doesn't. What she has in mind is to cross the Narrow Sea and set him free."

"What?" The Bastard was stunned. A suspicion began to form that perhaps she was fallible after all. The dimples disappeared into his downturned mouth.

"That's right," d'Alençon confirmed. "I've asked her if her voices have commanded that of her, but she always evades the question. Somehow I think that the notion may be hers alone."

"Well, the men wouldn't follow her!"

"They would follow her into the very maw of Hell if she asked." He smiled tiredly at his solemn kinsman. "So would I. And so would you, if you're honest enough to admit it."

"You're wrong, Jehan," the Bastard replied with a determined shake of his head. "I would not follow her on a fool's mission, and I doubt the army would either, especially if God does not sanction it in advance. I shudder to think of some of the risks we've taken on her word, and if God had not been with us, we could not have made things turn out all right. If she should recommend something as outrageously perilous as invading England, and she lacks Heaven's support, then God help us all." He shook his head again. "I love her, God knows, but I would not follow her to destruction and I know the army wouldn't either."

"I would follow her anywhere she chose to go," d'Alençon insisted, the muscles working in his sculpted jaw.

"If Charles allowed you," rejoined his cousin. "My guess is that, once King, our royal kinsman will resume his former habits of dice, books, parties, and fruitless negotiations, and will disband the army as he has in the past. He will move on to another favorite, another astrologer, and will still be in Trémoïlle's and the archbishop's pockets, will still owe them embarrassing sums of money, and they will set him against the Maid. He has never fully accepted her in the first place." He looked down at the flagstone floor and sighed. "If Jehanne should strike out on her own and try to lead an army without Charles' support, she will be doomed."

"I shall protect her."

"Don't be a moron, Jehan!"

D'Alençon stepped back a pace, shocked by the Bastard's sudden peevishness.

"You know as well as I do that you don't have the power to protect her," the Bastard stated. "Oh yes, yes"—he waved a dismissive hand—"you would perhaps prevail against the chancellor and the archbishop, but you don't have the power to protect her from Charles' envy. You have seen how he treats those he considers rivals for popular affection. The minute he leaves Reims Cathedral and the shouts for her are louder than those for him, she will begin her descent at court, and when she takes an army that he has forbidden her out of spitefulness—even if it means that he's only harming his own interests—when she does that, she will be signing her name to certain annihilation."

"Oh, my God." The young man's face stiffened in sudden understanding. "How can we save her?" he asked, anxiously grabbing the older man's arm. "There must be something we can do."

"Talk to her," the Bastard said simply. "Reason with her, if that can be done. It would perhaps not be prudent to mention any of Charles' weaknesses to her, so try instead to get her to agree that she will admit it if her saints no longer speak to her, or if they forbid her to move any further. If you can do that, it will be easier for you to convince her of any folly."

"Yes." D'Alençon nodded slowly. "I see what you mean. But you know how stubborn she is once she gets something into her head. I know you've seen her temper."

"Everyone has seen her temper." The Bastard laughed. Then he grew serious again. "But we're talking about her life, perhaps literally, perhaps not, but her life nonetheless, and I tell you this, you must convince her no matter how much it angers her. Wouldn't you rather have her shout at you than find that you can no longer hear her voice at all?"

"Of course. But you know, we really should be listening to the sound of her voice now as she readies the army." D'Alençon grinned.

He was so unsettled by the turn the conversation had taken that his hands were trembling. He needed to put it aside for now. Tonight he would sift all his cousin's words through his reason and his faith. But for now, he needed to be doing something real—anything—to protect him from the unwanted images that soared above him, then swooped into his mind.

The Bastard understood and smiled at the wan young man. "Yes, indeed we should." He clapped d'Alençon on the back and put a fraternal arm around his shoulder. "Let's help her."

The sun was starting to go down when they left St.-Phal, and by the time they rode into camp the noblemen found that Jehanne had already assembled the captains and given her orders. They could see her in the dusk, an unarmed figure in white helping the soldiers to cut and bind brush, twigs, and vine shoots. She laughed in response to a marksman's jest, breaking the pace of her labors. She waved at him playfully and then picked up the fascine she had made and tossed it onto an ever-increasing pile.

D'Alençon nudged his horse and they trotted toward her, past the furiously toiling men. Night would come soon, and the rays of the waning moon would be of little use.

"Jehan! Bastard!" She threw a loose collection of brush onto a larger heap, then wiped the sweat from her throat with the back of her sleeve. Bits of grass and leaves stuck to her face in heavy beads of perspiration and there was a dirty smear across her nose. Her clothes hung wetly to the stalwart body.

She came toward them and they dismounted, tossing the reins of their mounts to alert pages. D'Alençon waved and said, "My, my, Jehanne, you certainly fashion a well-tied bundle."

She grinned at the joke. "I used to help my father with the harvest, and this is no harder than that. Matter-of-fact, that was harder. We didn't have all this help!"

The men laughed and the Bastard said, "What is it you've planned here?"

"Those men there"—she pointed—"are binding fascines, and those over there are using whatever wood they can find—planks, faggots, beams, even tables—to build assault towers and covered walkways to the walls." She swung her arm to the bare-chested crowd who grunted and pushed in their struggle with the cannon. "They will blast a hole in the wall so the army can enter."

"You're not going to try this tonight!" The Bastard's expression in the lowering twilight was only half-joking.

"Of course not, silly." A grin creased the grimy face. "We'll wait until morning. Who knows? They might even surrender."

"Do your Counsel say they'll do that?" d'Alençon asked, the memory of his recent conversation fresh in his mind. He was glad that the Bastard was with them to bolster his resolve and give him a silent encouragement to ask the right questions.

"No." She pushed the sheaf of damp hair from her forehead and smiled. "They have promised that Troyes shall acknowledge the Dauphin, but They say that the people of Troyes shall have to decide whether or not it's done peacefully. They say that we all have free will, that God will not stop us from sin."

D'Alençon glanced in pleased triumph at the Bastard. Out of the corner of his eye, he saw Jehanne's sudden frown, and he knew that she had divined that something was amiss. But to the duc's relief, she said nothing about it.

"That sounds like a sensible plan, Jehanne." The Bastard nodded. "Well"—he clapped his hands together and looked around at the busy camp—"I suppose I must see to my Orléanais, so if you'll excuse me, I'll see the two of you later."

Jehanne waved as he walked into the near darkness. He turned to raise his hand.

D'Alençon removed his shirt and threw it upon the ground. A page instantly picked it up and flapped it to remove the grass. Then he folded it over his arm and disappeared in the direction of the duc's tent.

Jehanne and d'Alençon went back to the work his arrival had interrupted. They kept at it steadily as night descended and the moon sailed in a sliver across the ebony sky. D'Alençon eventually tired and decided to rest. He sat down on a tree stump and wiped his dripping torso with a towel his page had brought him, marveling at Jehanne's endurance. Here she was, working unflaggingly, encouraging the exhausted men to finish their labors, and she showed little sign of fatigue. Oh, she was tired, he could see that her pace had slackened from what it was, but she would not cease until the work was completed.

He remembered what the Bastard had said and a chill shot up his backbone. He would protect her, he swore to God he would. Whatever she did, he would share in it with her. Until the very end.

He stood up and returned to his work.

D'Aulon had already saddled her horse by the time Minguet finished arming her. She stepped into the saddle quickly, and rode toward the lines.

By eight-thirty, Jehanne had the army poised for the attack before the moat and the high walls of disobedient Troyes. With her was a bemused Dauphin, looking absurdly out of place—and generally comical—in his sparkling, unused armor. But Jehanne was entirely at ease, and now she would show Charles what it meant to lead an army into battle. She was surrounded by her friends. Ever since she was wounded at Orléans, Pasquerel and Minguet had stuck to her like second skins, and now they were practically breathing down her neck. She loved them for their worry but knew it was wasted. She would not be wounded, not today. The Counsel had promised.

Jehanne lifted her hand and the trumpeters let loose a shrieking blast. As from one throat, the troops yelled their challenge, and the woodmen began flinging the bundles into the moat. The captains, or rather Jehanne, had learned from the losses before Jargeau that they could spare French lives by throwing the fascines into the moat instead of wading across with them. The first wave of attackers would then wedge the stacks beside the wall in wait for the ladders.

Now the sheaves, weighted with stones, soared through the air like straw birds in flight, then plunked into the water. The resultant spray was so thick and pervasive that for a while it was difficult to see the walls. Behind the ranks, eager laddermen waited with their instruments, while off to the side the gunners watched for Jehanne's signal to fire. The carpenters stood ready with the walkways they had fastened under the cover of night.

A white flag suddenly beckoned through the mists from high atop the battlement, and at first Jehanne thought she was seeing things. But there it was, moving sluggishly left then right. They were surrendering.

God be praised, You have touched their souls and we shall not have to fight them! "Stop!" she yelled, waving her standard in a reflection of the flag above them. "They are renouncing their struggle!"

The soldiers, at first stunned by this abrupt outcome, grew silent. When they realized that it was all over, to a man they burst into an exuberant bellow, waving their weapons above their heads. Pasquerel made the Sign of the Cross, and Jehanne turned to the astonished Dauphin.

"Isn't it wonderful, my lord, they are giving up!" Her joy could not have been this great even in victory, had there been further loss of life.

"I suppose so," he sighed, "but I really wanted to see you lead the army."

"I'm just thankful I don't have to." She frowned irritably.

Charles was disillusioning her steadily. Not only did he dilly-dally to a degree unbecoming to a king, but now she perceived that he was selfish and a bit shallow as well. She had already seen that in his refusal to grant clemency to Richemont, even after Jehanne assured her Dauphin that the seigneur had fought bravely at Patay and that she believed that his vow of loyalty to Charles was genuine. But God had a use for Charles, else He would not want him to be King. She was certain of that, although she did not understand it.

An abrupt noise of metal scraping on wood shifted her attention to the wall. The townsfolk were lowering the drawbridge. It creaked forward rustily and finally settled into the dust on the Armagnac side of the moat. Through the cloud several figures emerged from the gate, walking in a sluggish line toward the army. At their head a mitred bishop dressed in full episcopal robes carried a long pole crested by a cross of silver. A small group of somber, prosperous-looking men crossed the bridge behind him with their hands clasped behind their backs. Pierre de Sologne was among them. Every one wore a knotted rope around his neck. When they came to within a few feet of Charles, they knelt and lowered their heads.

An astounded, pleased smile lit the Dauphin's sallow face.

"Your Highness," said the bishop, "I am Léon de Bourges, bishop of Troyes, and this is the chief magistrate, Robert de Montépilloy." A middle-aged man, dignified in his large hat and linen tunic, bowed to Charles. "The city of Troyes yields to Your Highness, and invites you and your captains to enter the gate. We submit ourselves to your mercy."

"You may rise," Charles allowed with a benevolent smile. The men obeyed. "We thank you for your hospitality, and assure you that we shall continue to grant your fair city the same privileges that you have enjoyed in the past. Your charter and liberties shall also be preserved and secured."

The men looked at one another. "Sire?" asked de Montépilloy. "Do you not want our lives?"

Charles' eyes darted to the rope around the man's neck. He shook his head. "We only request in return that you pledge your faithfulness to us."

"We do pledge it, my lord." De Montépilloy's lower lip trembled, and he appeared near tears.

"Good." Charles nodded with satisfaction.

"Excuse me, Your Highness," ventured the bishop, "but may I ask, what should we tell the garrison who are here?"

"Haven't they surrendered, too?" Charles' magnanimous goodwill evaporated and his face suddenly paled.

"Oh, yes, my lord," the magistrate responded quickly, "it is just that we do not know what we should tell them your intentions are."

"They are free to go on their way," the Dauphin answered, his own relief evident in the way his color returned. "And, of course, they may take their belongings with them."

"Thank you, Your Highness, you are most kind." The men bowed even lower than before.

"Now we shall cross the bridge and enter your city." Charles raised his hand and beckoned to a squire, who responded by bringing the Dauphin's horse to him. "Jehanne, you shall come with us." He climbed into the saddle with difficulty, unaccustomed to the weight of the armor.

"Yes, my lord." She smiled. She had forgotten all about her annoyance at his spiritual stinginess and saw now only the wise and merciful King that he could become.

A mounted bodyguard closed about the Dauphin, but he waved them on as a sign that they should precede him. Jehanne hoisted herself onto the horse a soldier brought to her, and Charles gave her a look of affection. She was at his right hand as they clattered loudly across the wooden bridge.

That evening, Jehanne put on her clothes from the duc d'Orléans and dined with the Dauphin and d'Alençon. The magistrate de Montépilloy was so overwhelmed with gratitude to the king for having spared their lives that he offered his three-story house to Charles for the Valois' stay in Troyes. The Dauphin's bodyguard were posted in the street outside and within the house itself. De Montépilloy had left behind his awestruck servants to attend Charles, with strict orders that there was to be no chicanery among them. He need not have bothered with an admonition. They were terrified of the soldiers and of that fearsome Maid, and were so attentive that it was comical. The cooks went out of their way to prepare a sumptuous meal for their master's guests.

Jehanne had not seen, let alone tasted, such food for a long time, since Loches. The table groaned with quail marinated in wine and cunningly prepared in thick, deep-dished pastries, and shiny apples fresh from the nearby fields, and a large, juicy ham, and little loaves of bread so fluffy that it was like eating a cloud. There were turnips cooked in a gleaming, buttery glaze that dripped down one's fingers, a large pink salmon on a silver platter, two kinds of cheese, and a bowl of boiled walnuts. Both men partook of a flagon of wine which Jehanne declined in favor of water. Charles chattered away as he sawed happily at a fat roast goose.

"Isn't it marvelous," he exclaimed, his face aglow with bright-eyed euphoria, "isn't it just too wonderful! They have relented, they have finally recognized the blood of Kings, and in *me*, Jehan!"

Charles grabbed d'Alençon's wrist with a greasy hand, and in that instant he was no longer a prince wrapped in studied dignity, just a man who was at ease enough with his dinner partners to reveal his insecure delight. Jehanne and the duc smiled at him warmly.

"I *never* thought this would happen. You know I did not believe you, Jehanne, but here we are, and they have accepted me; once they disinherited me, and now they accept me!"

Jehanne and d'Alençon laughed. "Yes, my lord"—she chuckled—"I know you have not always believed in me, but do you really now, Sire? I hope that you see that God really does want you to be King."

Charles nodded, unable to speak for the mouthful of meat. He swallowed and washed it down with a deep draught of wine. "I have recently come to believe it, and now I want to be King. I'm tired of people laughing at me—oh, I don't mean you just now, that's different—but all the others, those other kings and ducs and barons." He glowered resentfully, and Jehanne wondered at his revealing manner.

He was only a man after all, not a bad man but a fearful one, and she saw with her own eyes now to what extent her Guides had been right about him. There was a part of him that had long been hidden but would surface when he accepted the challenge of being King. She had seen it today in his courtly acceptance of the town's submission and in his absolute lack of vengeance.

"You shall be King, Sire," Jehanne confirmed, "and a wise and good King at that. And in your reign the war will end and the English will leave France forever."

"Have your angels told you that?" Charles had heard it a hundred times yet only now was it really starting to take root.

"Yes, my lord." She smiled. "That is God's promise to you."

A grin widened the Dauphin's face and he looked as pleased as a boy. But his delight suddenly changed to solemnity, and he said, "I'm afraid the coronation will not be as it should. Not all of the peers will be present."

"Peers, my lord?"

"What His Majesty means, Jehanne," d'Alençon said, smiling, "is that officially, there are supposed to be twelve peers who take part in the coronation ceremony, six great nobles and six prelates. The duc de Bourgogne is one, and he—"

"But I wrote to him, Jehan, I invited him to the coronation."

"What?" the two men chimed together. Charles did not look pleased.

She nodded, reaching nervously for her cup. "Yes, I wrote to him, but I do not think he will go to Reims."

"That's a safe bet," the Dauphin said wryly. "He would rather die than yield to me."

"It does not matter, Sire," d'Alençon reassured him, "I shall take his place in the ceremony."

"Who else should be there and will not?" Jehanne asked. This was something that had not occurred to her.

"The duc de Guyenne, the comte de Flandres, the comte de Toulouse, and the comte de Champagne," Charles recited morosely, "and the duc de Normandie, which of course is now a vacant duchy in the hands of the English."

"You can also bet that the bishops of Langres and Noyon won't be there," said d'Alençon. "And Cauchon wouldn't set foot in Reims Cathedral."

"Cauchon?" Jehanne laughed at the name. "Is the man a pig then?"

"Very nearly." The duc laughed. "He is the bishop of Beauvais, a dedicated partisan of the English, he really kisses their asses—oh, excuse me, Jehanne."

"A detestable man, really," Charles complained, his voice rising to a whine, "and very like a swine. He is as ambitious as Lucifer and twice as deadly. He was a leader of the Burgundian faction at the University of Paris and a tireless opponent of my father and my older brother, Louis. He helped to negotiate that evil treaty that questioned my legitimacy and effectively disinherited me!" The Dauphin's nostrils flared and his eyes widened wrathfully.

"It's all right, my lord," d'Alençon soothed, "we do not need him, nor any of the others. There are nobles and prelates loyal to you who I'm sure will be greatly honored to participate in the ceremony. I shall represent Bourgogne," he repeated, "if it pleases Your Majesty."

Charles smiled. "It pleases me well, Cousin. I would almost rather have you there than that traitor. But what about Charlemagne's sword, and the crown, and the golden spurs and scepter?" he wondered, suddenly anxious. "They are all in the abbey of St.-Denis near Paris, and still well out of our reach."

D'Alençon shrugged. "We shall have to find substitutes. Surely the treasury of Reims Cathedral has suitable replacements."

"Isn't the sacred oil at Reims?" Jehanne asked. "Well, then," she continued, in response to the duc's affirmative nod, "as long as you are anointed with the sacred oil of St.-Clovis, you shall be the true King, Sire, and it does not matter who attends and whether or not you have St.-Charlemagne's sword."

"Do you really think so?" the Dauphin asked with no small degree of apprehension.

She smiled. How like a young child he could be at times, touchingly so, and it was in those rare moments, as now, that she found him most human and lovable. "The oil is the most important thing, Sire, for its holy essence binds you to God, and since God has promised that you shall be King, you need not worry. You—"

Jehanne was interrupted by a sudden scuffle that could be heard outside the door. Charles turned pale and put a slender hand to his throat. D'Alençon stood, automatically reaching for the dagger at his belt.

"I tell you, I am the Maid's brother, and I have urgent news for her!" Jehan's familiar cry was mixed with the sounds of heavy footsteps and a body being hurled against a wall. "Let me go, I must speak to my sister!"

The door flung open and a burly soldier stepped across the threshold and knelt upon the floor. In the doorway, two fierce-looking guards held Jehan's arms. He was drenched with perspiration and out of breath, and outrage reddened his swarthy face.

"Sire," said the kneeling man, "this fellow claims to be the Maid's brother, and—"

"Yes, yes," Charles answered impatiently, "let him go."

The men released Jehan with wary reluctance, and he bolted through the door and past the guard. Remembering in whose presence he was, he went down upon one knee. "Excuse me, Sire, for this interruption, but I must speak to Jehanne."

"What is it, Jehan?" she asked, dismay racing in her chest.

"The garrison is leaving town, and they are taking their prisoners of war with them!" he exclaimed excitedly. "They claim that His Majesty said they could take their belongings with them and they count the hostages among their possessions. We tried to stop them, but they won't listen."

"What!" She leaped up from the table, aghast at the news. "Sire, please come with me, we cannot allow them to take their hostages with them!"

Charles frowned at the waiting guards and said, "Saddle our horses and bring them around to the front of the house." The men bowed low and dashed out of view. Then to Jehan, "Have they left the city yet?"

"No, Sire, not yet."

"Then we should not tarry here. Come"—he turned to Jehanne and d'Alençon—"we must hurry."

Night had fallen by now and the Dauphin's guard, illuminated by the torches they carried, sped through the streets past the long column of retreating Burgundians, scattering them out of their way. By the time they reached the city's gate, the enemy stretched a quarter of a league beyond the walls, bound north for Paris, their lights flickering ahead like fireflies. Near the front of the train, just behind the supply line, a crowd of feeble men were chained together at their hands and feet. Even in the torchlight they looked underfed and some of them had been beaten.

Jehanne snarled with rage at the sight of them and spurred her horse to the head of the retiring troops. D'Alençon stayed right with her as though it were a race. The guard tore after them. But Charles struggled only halfheartedly to keep up, afraid that he would fall off his mount and make a terrible fool of himself.

From out of nowhere it seemed, a battalion of Armagnac horsemen came at the column, yelling their ferocious warcry. Vigilant sentries from camp had seen Jehanne and the king's bodyguard leave the gate in pursuit of the retreating garrison. Reacting according to instinct, La Hire ordered what men were even half-armed into their saddles. Now eager for bloodletting, they emerged from the shadows and descended upon their enemies with swords drawn.

Jehanne knew it, and as she and the duc drew rein in front of the halted procession, she raised her hand and shouted with all her might, "Stop! Men of France, do not do any violence here, upon pain of mortal sin!"

Obediently, the cavalrymen reined their horses but slowly continued to advance. La Hire, de Rais, and the Bastard, their path lit by squires, cantered to the caravan's leaders. Charles had caught up to them and was trotting into the ranks.

A whisper ran through the cavalry, "The king." There was little enthusiasm and no awe. D'Alençon glanced at the Bastard, who pretended not to notice the Dauphin's lukewarm reception.

"Your Majesty." De Rais' respectful bow was repeated by the other captains.

"La Hire, what is the meaning of this?" Charles asked loftily.

"Excuse me, Sire," he rumbled, "but we could ask the same of you. We saw you coming from Troyes in one hell of a hurry, and we thought there might be something wrong." He turned to Jehanne. "What have these sons of—excuse me, Sire, Jehanne—what have these cowards done now?"

"They are trying to take French hostages with them!" she stormed. She wheeled her horse around and for the first time turned her famous stare upon the Burgundians. So terrible was her fury that one of the men in front of the line cringed.

"Who are you?" she demanded, daring him to refuse to answer.

"I am Jacques Langois, captain of the guard." He was young, no more than twenty. On his head was a brimmed, hatlike helmet in the English fashion, and he was dressed like a man-of-arms in a battered leather breastplate and high boots. There was a mace strung by leather thongs to the front of his saddle; from his belt dangled a broadsword. The face was not remarkable. He looked like any one of a thousand such young men who had joined the army for adventure, or for politics, or for profit. Perhaps he had fled a domineering father, or was an orphan disinherited by war.

At any rate, his eyes wore an aspect of unease as Jehanne bore upon him, a violated sense of honor crackling about her. "Who gave you leave to take your prisoners with you?" she shouted at him.

"The Dauphin"—he looked to Charles for support—"said we might take our possessions with us," he stammered, "and we took that to mean our hostages as well."

"They are *not* your possessions, they are free men loyal to the Dauphin, and in God's name, you shall not have them!" She was trembling with outrage, and there was no one present who did not feel the heat of her implied threat.

"Who are you to call upon the name of God, you Armagnac whore?"

Clearly an Englishman to judge by his accent, the man who addressed her was some years older than Langois and sat ahorse at the captain's right. Jehanne had not noticed him before, so intent had she been upon browbeating Langois with her Power. But now that he had spoken, she took a good look at him.

He was of the rough soldiering type, thick in the chest and legs, with heavily muscled arms bulging through his soiled shirt. Like Langois, he wore leather armor. Long, greasy brown hair hung down his neck, partially obscured by his helmet, and two hardened eyes defied her between a once broken flat nose. His face was covered with shaggy black hair.

Jehanne felt her partisans tense at the man's insult to her, and there was the sound of swords rattling in their scabbards.

"I am Jehanne the Maid, and I order you to release these men into the custody of the king's army."

Two hundred or more men were fixed on him, eager for his refusal so that they might string him from the nearest tree, but he did not seem to care. He spat upon the ground, then gave Jehanne a nasty smile.

"I remember you, you are the Witch of Orléans. I was there; I saw the way our men trembled before your sorcery and lost the will to fight." He looked around him defiantly, and when he turned to her again he was quaking with hatred. "Well, I will not yield to you now, you poxy slut, you cow-wench, even if it means my life. Under the code of chivalry, we own these prisoners; they are ours to ransom, and we shall not yield them to you who are the creature of the Devil!"

"They are not yours, and chivalry or no, we shall fight you for them!"

As though to back up her words, the cavalry drew their swords and turned them toward the column. The very air hissed with an enmity that all knew would soon explode.

"We are the king here, and *we* decide if our army fights!"

The masterful voice was startling, and the antagonists turned toward its owner, who had been jostled aside and forgotten. His posture was unexpectedly erect, and an aura of grandeur wafted like perfume from his detached person. The group around Jehanne silently moved their horses to allow Charles to inch his way through them. He stopped at her side and looked with patronizing insolence at the Englishman.

"Who are you, fellow?" he asked frostily.

The man did not answer.

"Come, come, we do not intend to sit here all night. What is your name?"

"Thomas Larkin, captain in the army of my sovereign lord, Henry VI, king of England." His yellowed teeth spread maliciously. "And of France."

A unified gasp burst from the Armagnacs, and they poised again for an attack.

But Charles laughed in lighthearted dismissal of the man's importance and of his words. "You are quite mistaken; you see, your master can hardly be the king of France, for I am he, and a kingdom cannot have two monarchs, now can it?" The Dauphin's mien was as pleasant as though he were discussing a tennis match or the latest court gossip.

Larkin refused to be cowed. "You are just the pretender, you are not the king."

"Quite right, we have not yet been crowned, but we shall be, and soon." Amiability vanished, and he abruptly stood up in his saddle.

Let no one doubt that we are the true and only King of France!

Several horses whinnied and tried to bolt. "And because we will be King," he went on, "we shall observe all the proper tenets of chivalry!" He sat down again and looked disdainfully at Larkin. "We shall pay your ransom for these prisoners at the rate of one mark per head."

"Two," the man bid.

"We said one. Take it or leave it; if you leave it, we shall take your prisoners and you shall have gained nothing." He smiled. "You might lose even more than that, yes?"

Larkin looked at the overwhelming odds surrounding him and did not reply.

"Just so," Charles said with a wry lift of his brow. "D'Alençon!"

"Yes, Sire?"

"See to it that these men are properly paid, no more, no less."

"Yes, my lord."

"We shall now return to Troyes to finish our supper." There was a dry humor in his voice. "Jehanne, will you join us?"

"If you don't mind, Sire, I think I'll remain here with the army."

"Very well." His response was cool, and she sensed that she had accidentally hurt his feelings.

Without another word, he dug his spurs into his horse's flanks and cantered into the night back toward the city with the torch-bearing guard at his heels.

Jehanne watched him go, feeling pride in him ringing through her ears. Again, he had surprised her by behaving like a true king. Very soon he would become the master of France instead of his ministers' dupe; he certainly had not needed them here to advise him as to the proper course of action. She could see in the

304

firelit faces of her comrades that Charles had earned a greater measure of their respect as well.

La Hire caught the Bastard's eye, and in the smile they shared was the same thought: The little king of Bourges was growing up at last.

Châlons, long an Armagnac island in an otherwise Burgundian locality, opened its gates to Charles with enthusiasm. Once more Jehanne rode at his side, this time into a welcoming city. As at Orléans, people of all ages and classes choked the streets: beggars, craftsmen, clergymen, mothers, merchants, knights, and always, children. They followed the illustrious riders as best they could, but were unable to get close enough to Jehanne to touch her as the Orléanais had. Nowadays, the Dauphin's guard formed an enclosure to protect the king front, rear, and on the sides. Within the entourage rode the Bastard, d'Alençon, Trémoïlle, de Chartres, the comte de Clermont, and René d'Anjou, duc de Bar, the same René whose services Jehanne had requested from his father-in-law, the duc de Lorraine, five months earlier.

Riding well behind her, René chided himself for not having joined the army before Patay. He would have given anything to have known her from the beginning, but now it was too late for that. Too late because she had already established her circle of intimates by the time he met her. She kept glancing over her shoulder at them, that small band of young men who rode outside Charles' enclave, right behind the bodyguards.

It was not that she was worried about them back there, but they were in every sense her family and she felt unprotected without them, as though something might happen to snatch them from her. She tried to dismiss her unease, but every time she made up her mind that she would and waved to the crowd, a spasm of dread hit her in the stomach, forcing her again to look behind her to make sure they were still there. At one point, after she had turned around for the fifth or sixth time, Metz and Poulengy made funny faces at her, and Metz waved in mockery of her own greeting to the people. Feeling much better, she laughed out loud, unmindful of the quizzical look the Dauphin gave her.

Although d'Alençon was within the shield with her, just behind the Dauphin, his handsome, smiling presence was of little comfort to her. She had had words with him the previous night and they stung her even now.

After the last mark had been paid to the Anglo-Burgundians and the prisoners' chains opened, Jehanne and d'Alençon returned to the main army. Instead of going straight to her tent, Jehanne consented to walk with d'Alençon for a bit through the camp. He took her past the fires ringed by storytellers and singers to a more remote spot on the outer fringes of the encampment. The moon would soon be full, and it cast the light of its quarter-face upon them. Crickets were chirping a duet with the bullfrogs that dwelt within the Seine. Jehanne took a deep breath and smiled at the silent, shimmering stars.

"Jehanne?"

"Hmm?"

"Do you have any idea at all how much I love you?"

She jerked her head from the heavens to him. He had his back to the moon and even though his face was in shadow, what she could see of it startled her. A profound sadness marked the beautiful features, making him appear much older, and she could suddenly feel the grief that threatened to crush him. It was like a melancholy cloak that he could not remove, and her heart ached with pity for him. But it also frightened her.

"Of course," she responded with forced cheer, "and I love you too, Jehan."

He took a step toward her and gently seized her damp hands. "I'm serious. It's me, Jehan, and you don't have to make light of this." She turned away from him, but he put a callused hand on her chin and guided her face back toward him until she was looking directly into his dark eyes. "I love you more than I love anyone else except my mother and my wife, even more than I love the king, and I need for you to listen to what I have to say and to know that when I say it, it's because I love you."

"What is it?" She frowned, overcome with a fear such as she never known in battle.

"First," he said, placing both hands upon her shoulders, "I need to ask: What are your intentions after Charles is crowned?"

"That we take Paris, of course," she responded with instant certainty. "That has been the plan all along."

"Your plan?"

"Yes, my plan." Displeased at his tone, she pulled free of his grasp. "What is this all about?"

"I've asked you this before, but you always avoid it: Have your saints told you to take Paris, or is that only your notion?"

"You sound like a priest," she said angrily, "like one of those theologians at Poitiers." Her rapid pace through the high grass swished like the furious tail of a cat, and she clasped her hands behind her. "What do you want from me, Jehan?"

"I simply want you to tell me the truth!" The duc groaned. "You've just parried my question again, as you have before. But I have to know what you mean by all of this."

He opened his hands in a gesture of appeal. "Please, Jehanne, if you really know that I treasure you, you must also surely know that I am not your enemy, and that if I ask difficult questions it is because I would not want any harm to come to you."

"Harm?" The word dripped scorn. "What harm can possibly befall me except in battle, and that is in the hands of God, not me. I have the love of the people, the support of the army, and the protection of the Dauphin, and when he becomes King, I shall still have his protection. Together, we will drive the *goddons* back to their own land and the war will end. Your fears are foolish."

"You are the fool, because you don't understand that just because you have Charles' patronage now, you may not always have it!" Really angry now, he put his hands on his hips. "Don't you remember what I told you the day I met you, that you should not confuse Charles the man with the King of France?"

Jehanne's eyes narrowed and the muscles in her jaw jerked.

"Don't you?"

"Yes, so?" she sulked.

"The advice still holds. Have you thought of what could happen if Charles wants one thing and you another?"

"We want the same thing," she insisted.

"Are you sure enough of that to gamble your life on it?"

"What do you mean?"

"You do not know Charles as well as you think you do, as well as I do," d'Alençon warned. "You do not know, for instance, that one reason he has been so indecisive in reaching for the crown is because his way is to avoid strife and to settle things through diplomacy and treaty. That is not something he merely says; he means it. He's actually very fussy and abhors violence, not because he is a particularly peaceful man but because he so dreads that he might be bested in war. He really, truly feels that in the long run it is diplomacy that will secure his kingdom. But in the meantime, if he has to compromise his ambition, he's willing to do it."

"Well, that's stupid," Jehanne said with a bluntness handed down through a hundred generations of peasants. "His treaties have never gotten him anything but broken promises."

"Nevertheless, that is the way he has always preferred, and there is no reason to suppose that he will change at this point in his life."

She cast her eyes upon the ground. Finally, she looked at d'Alençon and said in a quiet voice, "What are you trying to tell me?"

"That because the English hold Paris at the pleasure of Philippe de Bourgogne, with whom Charles is trying to reconcile, it is very likely that he will oppose your march on Paris," the young man said, his manner gentler now. "That is, unless you can persuade him that it is God's will that you do." He paused to let his statement sink in. "I ask you again: Have your saints told you to take the capital, or is that your own idea?"

"They told me long ago when I was still in Domrémy that I should relieve Orléans and afterward escort the Dauphin to his coronation." She turned her face up to the friendly moon. "They told me that Paris will return its loyalty to the King once he is crowned, and that the English will return to their own land."

"Did they say that it's you who'll take Paris?" d'Alençon pressed.

"No."

The duc sighed with relief. It was banished by her next words.

"But They did not say that I wouldn't either." Her eyes filled with tears of confusion. "They have not answered me when I've asked that same question." D'Alençon lifted his brows in surprise. "Oh, yes, I've asked, of course I have," she said bitterly. "Do you really think that I'm such a fool as to not ask about something so important when I've always sought Their counsel in lesser things?" She glared at him, feeling alone and abysmally misunderstood.

For some time neither of them spoke. Jehanne was wounded into speechlessness by his betrayal; her throat actually hurt. Since Loches she had felt a division beginning to threaten their friendship, and now it was in full bloom. He did not believe in her, after all. It had all been a lie and the love he spoke of a dream, as immaterial as a morning fog.

"I'm sorry," he murmured. "I did not mean to hurt you."

She wiped away a tear trickling thinly down her cheek. She could not answer for the lump in her throat.

"I do love you, Jehanne."

"Stop saying that!"

"It's true."

"Then prove it."

"How?"

"Help me to take Paris," she said evenly. "And after that, Amiens and Rouen and Calais."

"Ask your saints again whether or not you should, and if they say yes, then I'll follow you anywhere, as far as you want to go."

"I've asked and asked and asked." She was tired to the bone and wanted this conversation to end. "Why don't you leave me alone?"

"There's too much at risk, that's why." He would not yield. "If you oppose Charles, you give Trémoïlle and the archbishop the very weapon they need to finish you. Charles now has the power to disband the army, and once he is officially King, that power will only increase in the minds of the soldiers and they'll obey him, not you. So, what will you do when they all refuse to fight with you because their King has forbidden them? Who do you think will support you then?"

"The men will follow me"—she lifted her chin—"for the glory of God!"

"For the glory of God or the glory of Jehanne?"

She stepped back a pace as though she had been slapped.

The look on his face said that he knew he had gone too far. She started stalking away from him, but he ran to her and grabbed her arm. "Jehanne, listen to me—"

"Let me go!" Jehanne struggled against the strong hands that pinned her arms to her side. "I said, let me *go!*" Her foot crashed into his shin and he yelled. She wrenched herself free and staggered backward a couple of steps.

"Keep away from me," she ordered, now blinded by the tears that would not stop. "You are not my friend! You never were."

"That's not true!" he shouted. "I am your best friend, better than you know, or else I would not have spoken to you as I have tonight. Do you think I want to see you destroyed, whether by your own stubbornness or by the ministers? Because that's what will surely happen if you defy him!" D'Alençon's emotions had exhausted him, and he paused to take a breath. "Ask your saints again, Jehanne, and I give you my word that if they command you to conquer Cathay, I'll follow you there."

"And if They don't answer, what then?" She wiped a grubby hand across her wet face.

"Then I'll take that as a yes and follow you anyway," he smiled wanly, "but only if the King sanctions it."

"So your love is limited after all." Before she turned away she saw the miserable wince that wrinkled the corners of his eyes, but she did not care.

She turned her back on him and walked quickly toward the glowing campfires and the security of her army. She didn't care! Her pain was worse than his, and there was an elusive, wicked satisfaction in knowing that she had gotten in a stab at him. But she could not deny the guilty sensation that dogged her all the way back to her tent and prevented her from sleeping soundly.

"Jehanne the Maid! Jehanne the Maid! Jehanne the Maid!"

The old singsong refrain jarred her back into the present, and she waved to the throng with a grin. These were her people, the lifeblood of the kingdom, and she was one of them. They were not like the snobbish nobles with whom she rode, so remote from the populace that they did not comprehend that the people would never fail her. D'Alençon did not grasp them any more than he did her, or he would have known that they would be her army when and if all others deserted her. The people would fight for the King and for their Maid.

She raised her hand again, unaware of the cold, narrow-eyed glance that Charles shot at her and the way he stiffened in his saddle at the sound of her name.

On Sunday morning, July 17, 1429, horses bearing a small group of lords in shining steel trotted to the abbey of St.-Rémi on the outskirts of Reims. The riders were identified by the heralds who went before them, carrying the proud banners of their stations: Gilles de Rais, admiral de Culan, the sieur de Graville, and the maréchal de Sainte-Sévère. The men were introducing the first step in the coronation ceremony.

A very special vial, perpetually housed in the ancient monastery, elevated the burial site of St.-Rémi to a position of holiness transcending all others in France but one. For it was here that nine hundred years earlier the pious monk had converted, then baptized Clovis, king of the Franks, making him the first Christian lord of the kingdom. Legend had it that at the moment of Clovis' immersion, a dove bearing the chrism in its beak had descended from Heaven. The oil it contained had been used to anoint every succeeding King, as commanded by Scripture. Its divine origin and the sacred bond between God and sovereign pledged that its contents could not be diminished, no matter how many came after Clovis to wear the crown of France, for without it the realm would not have a true King however closely the ritual otherwise followed custom.

Upon their arrival at the abbey the lords swore a ceremonial oath, administered by the caretaker abbé, that they would safely conduct the sanctified relic to Reims. Then the abbé, dressed in his finest clerical robes and sheltered beneath a golden canopy supported by his brother monks, bore his sacred trust on the back of a white mule into the city and through streets bursting with onlookers to the steps of the cathedral of Notre-Dame. The vast crowd, silently sober overall, had been awaiting their arrival since dawn, and now those surrounding the cathedral stirred with expectation as the procession halted.

Prepared to greet them and to receive the ampulla, Regnault de Chartres, for twenty years archbishop of Reims without having ever set foot in his diocese, stood solemnly in front of the high arched doorway of the cathedral's western face. On his head was the white fish-shaped mitre of his office, and in his right hand he held a silver shepherd's crook. His silken robe of gold covered a pristine, long-sleeved undertunic spun from the finest linen. But despite his grandeur, the archbishop was dwarfed by the surroundings which had come into being long before his birth and would endure centuries after he had turned to dust.

Above him, an arched embrasure soared grandly between two smaller gables, all of it supported by confident, worthy angels and the rapturous souls of the Blessed. The rose window—depicting the Holy Mother surrounded by the Apostles and angelic musicians—stared like the eye of God above the central gable's pointed spire.

Closer yet to Heaven, Kings of France shepherded their city beneath the rectangular twin belltowers that seemed so high as to stroke the sky, today as clear and blue as the royal standard of France. The cathedral's entire exterior was a mass of filigrees and gargoyles and buttresses designed to support the awe-inspiring bulk, the Holy Scriptures in marvelous stone.

The rector of St.-Rémi dismounted and bore the ampulla with stately grace up the steps to the archbishop, who blessed it slowly, murmuring Latin words written more than a millennium past. The abbé then returned to his mule, still bearing the vial in his soft, pale hands. De Chartres turned and entered the portal, preceded by two columns of dignified, cowled monks, at whose head walked a priest carrying a long-staffed crucifix. The heavy perfume of incense announced them, steaming from the censer which another monk at the procession's head began to swing back and forth as he walked.

The masses congesting the outer steps had likewise spilled into the porch and beyond that, to the nave, the ambulatories, and the galleries high above the floor, and now they craned their necks eagerly to see the archbishop's entrance over the shoulders of the Dauphin's guards, who lined the aisle with crossed *guisarmes* all the way to the transept. All at once, the organ's mighty song burst forth like a command from Heaven, ushering the archbishop through the porch, swirling through the slow, formal steps he took down Notre-Dame's central aisle toward the altar. As he passed them, the multitude crowding the nave and the side aisles, shoulder-to-shoulder, genuflected behind the impassive, sober-faced soldiers.

Now the lords coaxed their gaily frocked horses into the cathedral, turning at the porch to approach the choir by way of the side aisles behind the enormous pillars. At the same time, the abbé of St.-Rémi rode his little white mule down the nave's center, toward the archbishop waiting at the altar. A hymn, as sweet as the song of angels, rose from the throats of the acolytes positioned behind the altar at the transept crossing. When the lords reached the choir, they left their mounts in the ambulatory and took their places on either side of the altar. The abbé dismounted and knelt before the archbishop, then proffered the sacred vial to him. De Chartres mounted the altar steps, reverently placed the chrism before the Holy of Holies, and made the Sign of the Cross. Then he turned, and leading with his silver shepherd's crook, descended the steps and walked to the opening in the altar rail, where he awaited the Dauphin's arrival.

The coronation procession was still wending its way on foot through the narrow streets. The gold-on-blue lilies of France hung from every window along the route, proclaiming the city's loyalty to Charles in a fluttering forest of azure. Those lining the way waved miniatures of the King's banner and cheered the royal cavalcade until they were hoarse. The very air sizzled with joy and goodwill and thanksgiving. People from all over France who had come to see their Dauphin become King stood on tiptoe, straining for a glimpse of the participating dignitaries, waving their ardent best wishes as the royal train floated past them.

The twelve peers of the kingdom, or their substitutes, headed the procession, marching with earnest majesty, hands folded in front of their chests. The coats-of-arms of the titles they represented flew at their right hands, borne by elegant standard-bearers.

After them came Charles, his royal person shielded from the sun under a pure white canopy supported by four servants. The unanointed king wore a simple, long golden robe belted loosely at the waist by a silken cord. It reached past his ankles, and as he walked, white slippers peeked through the shimmering cloth that billowed with his movements. He was hatless and the sunlight shining through the canopy cast a reddish tint to the bowl-cropped, mousy brown hair. Like those preceding him he looked straight ahead, his fragile face expressionless and aloof, and he appeared unaware that he was the focus of all eyes, as he secretly knew himself to be.

He was wrong. The peasants and jongleurs, silversmiths and ladies had not come all this way from the remote areas of the kingdom solely to see Charles anointed and crowned. They were also there for the boylike shape in the green colors of Orléans overlaid with a scarlet cloak, the gift from a faraway, captive lord, who walked several steps behind him with her dark head bowed over folded hands. A tall, fleecy-haired monk, as lean as a scarecrow, carried the renowned standard at her side. A corner of it was charred, and all the careful cleaning to which it had been subjected had not been enough to remove the battle stains that had birthed the victories of summer.

Behind her walked the generals who had helped to bring the Dauphin to his golden moment: the Bastard of Orléans, La Hire, de Gaucourt, and the others. Somewhere in back of them, as decorum insisted, marched Jehanne's household and the army of liberation.

She could feel the worshipful stares bearing upon her as forcibly as the hot July sunshine, but was resolved that she would not acknowledge them. This was her sovereign's day, not hers. The second step in her Great Work was all but finished, accomplished. By sundown, France would have a King again to shepherd the realm, and together he and his Maid would establish a kingdom free from the tyranny of war.

On the heels of this came the bitter recollection of her moonlit dispute with d'Alençon. Could he have been right? His face had been so pained and—her pride made her reluctant to admit it—so full of loving concern that she could not doubt his sincerity. But was he wrong? Try as she might, she could not escape the fact that Charles had been a cross for her to carry, what with his indecisiveness and self-doubts.

Yet she had succeeded despite great odds. She had no reason to suspect that King Charles would snatch away his support now that he could see for himself that she had indeed been sent by God. Of course d'Alençon was right in stressing that Charles preferred diplomacy to conflict; she had heard the Dauphin voice that on many occasions. She was also aware of the value of delicacy in these matters.

Had she not only this morning dictated a letter once again to the duc de Bourgogne, pleading that he make peace with the King? In her message she said that if he must make war, he could fight the Saracens who held the Holy City, but that France belonged to God, and He would surely give the King's army victory as He had done in the past. She begged him "with clasped hands," and assured him that his alliance with the English would come to nothing but pain and death for his people.

What about Paris? she wondered for the hundredth time. Is that truly the next step? She asked the same old question again as she walked with eyes fastened to the dusty ground that met her feet: Am I really meant to drive the English from France?

Even as she looked at the Dauphin's slippered feet walking before her, they suddenly disappeared behind a great burst of light like an exploding sun, blinding her so that she gasped with a sharp intake of breath and nearly stumbled.

Alarm sent its rhythm racing through her chest, clutching her lungs and wringing them empty. Just when she thought that she would not be able to continue, that she would tumble into that awful, searing Radiance, that she would lose consciousness altogether, the Light's severity ceased, and a soft rose ambience began to swirl around her in a sweetness she had not felt since that other, long-gone July day in her father's garden.

Through the delicately spinning vortex she saw the domain where she most desired to be, ageless, loving; and a serenity overcame her, all at once expelling fear and reducing everything human to the level of a child's game. In the center of that eternal Moment nothing else mattered; the only thing real was that blinding, singing warmth that pulsed in her ears and whistled through her like a wind from Forever. This time, between the distant tolling of the cathedral bells, came Michel's answer, clear and reassuring.

Do not doubt, Daughter of God. The people could never have been delivered without you. Those not yet upon the earth shall remember until it exists no more that you redeemed this land for the Lord of Heaven. Do not break faith, for you shall come to dwell in the Kingdom that He has promised you.

Her vision blurred with tears of gratitude and joy. In spite of her unworthiness and her wavering faith, God had never abandoned her and never would. If she were left alone, she would have God for her Companion.

She looked up, shaken from her vision. The procession had arrived at the cathedral, where there were so many of Charles' gaping subjects that soldiers had to hold them back for the peers to ascend the steps. Music from the mammoth pipe organ poured through the archway into the street, a stalwart reminder of God's own summons. On the outer rim of vision, Jehanne saw the people kneel and cross themselves at the Dauphin's passage. Her heart pulsed with excitement as she followed Charles up and up, into the cool expanse.

The cathedral's vaulted ceiling towered a hundred feet toward Heaven, supported by gigantic columns of sculpted marble, each greater than the largest tree Jehanne had ever seen. Shafts of colored light streamed through the windows high above the crowded galleries and fell in sharp pools onto the hundreds of people cramming the nave. The cathedral vibrated with the music, so sweet and pure and encompassing that it brought tears to the eye.

The masses dropped to their knees like falling wheat as Charles walked down the nave's center, through the variegated reflections from the windows proclaiming the Annunciation and birth of the Son of God. Within the high, faraway apse beckoned a luminous rose window of Christe enthroned and championed by St.-Gabriel and St.-Michel, and it seemed to Jehanne that the soul-shaking music issued from those same angelic throats. A clump of elation stuck in her throat and she had to defy the desire to sob her gratitude to God for delivering Charles to his capital moment.

The twelve peers of France parted before the archbishop to allow Charles a clear path to the altar. With a grave stateliness they ordered themselves on either side, the nobles to his right and the bishops opposite them.

Jehanne stopped and received her standard from Brother Richard, who stepped back several paces and knelt upon the stone floor. Jehanne did not kneel but stood with upright pride behind her sovereign prince. He had commanded it. She was, he avowed in a rare emotional moment, the sole agent for his journey to Reims, and not even her protests that God had worked the miracle, not she, had been enough to alter his decision. She would stand behind him throughout the ceremony as he had commanded. Her standard was the only one present in the cathedral. No one, no peer of France, had ever been accorded such an honor.

The thunderous hymn died away, making her ears ring with its absence. The Dauphin fell gracefully to his knees and prostrated himself before the archbishop. Behind her, Jehanne felt the people kneel also, heard the rustle of their gowns and the scrape of their boots as they dropped to the floor. The priests at the altar began the litanies, beseeching the blessings of God and of all the saints in holy plainsong, the familiar names and the singular response, *Ora pro nobis*, chanted in their echoing, three-noted voices. The prayers rang through the cathedral for a long time.

Then, as suddenly as they had begun, the euphonies halted. The archbishop stepped forward and made the Sign of the Cross, slowly, ritualistically, over the Dauphin's bare head. There was a flutter as the throng crossed themselves. The archbishop recited a long prayer in Latin.

Then he said loudly enough for all to hear, "Do you Charles de Valois, son of Charles VI, King of France, and Dauphin by the grace of God, swear before the King of Heaven, His Holy Son, His Blessed Mother and all the saints to sustain the faith of your ancestors; to defend Holy Mother Church against all adversaries; and to uphold the justice of Kings in ruling the kingdom that God has entrusted upon you?"

The response was strong and firm. "I do swear to all these things before God."

Jehanne wiped her cheeks with the back of her free hand. Through her tears she saw the archbishop step aside and d'Alençon come forward to his place before Charles, who did not look up from his folded hands. An attending priest offered the duc a silken pillow on which rested a sword of jeweled gold. D'Alençon took the ceremonial weapon from the pillow and grasped it lightly in his right hand. The handsome face was solemn.

"By the grace of God, I dub you Charles de Valois, Knight of the Most High, in the name of the Father"—he touched Charles' shoulder delicately with the sword—"and of the Son"—then the other—"and of the Holy Spirit"—and again the first—"Amen." D'Alençon returned the sword to the pillow and went back to where the other nobles were standing.

Charles rose to his feet again. Two of the ecclesiastical peers approached him and untied the belt around his waist. They removed his robe to expose a tunic of white silk fastened by silver cords at the throat and back of the neck. Charles knelt once more, this time before the archbishop, who took the sacred ampulla from a priest and dipped a golden needle into the oil. Very carefully, de Chartres withdrew a drop and mixed it with other consecrated unguents upon a paten from the abbey of St.-Rémi. One of the peers untied the cords of Charles' tunic. The archbishop gracefully anointed the top of the Dauphin's bowed head with the Sign of the Cross, and then his chest, back, shoulders, and elbows. The choir burst into song again, this time proclaiming "They Are Anointing King Solomon." Jehanne drew her hand across her eyes, barely able to see the archbishop fasten the cords of the royal undergarment.

Two priests in shining robes stepped forward and put a violet tunic over Charles' head. They then accepted from attending acolytes a long royal blue cape lined in ermine and scattered with small golden fleurs-de-lys, like stars across a night sky. Together with the archbishop, they draped it around Charles' shoulders. The priests gave the implements of kingship to the archbishop, and the old man who had so resisted his role and Charles' journey to this place put the baton in Charles' left hand and the scepter in his right.

In response to this agreed-upon signal, the twelve peers stirred and came forward to take their places around Charles. At the same moment, another acolyte approached de Chartres carrying a pillow on which waited the crown, four large golden fleurs-de-lys joined together by a wide band. The archbishop picked it up and raised it high above the royal head. Each of the peers placed a finger upon the crown, symbolic of their support of the new monarch.

With deliberate grace, de Chartres lowered it.

A sob exploded from Jehanne's soul. She was standing at the center of the Universe, and felt God clap His hands as fantasy and fact, promise and reality, merged to become one Holy Instant. After seven long, leaderless years the monarchy and the people had reunited with God in this most sacred place.

"Rise, King of France," the archbishop commanded loudly. "Charles, the seventh of that name!"

Jehanne wanted to wail for joy, like the voice of the organ which now blared into rhapsodic song. Her shoulders shook with the unleashing of the exclamatory music, her spirit trumpeted toward the highest belltower. She could hear the masses cheering behind her.

Accompanied by the peers, Charles moved majestically up the steps, turned, and sat upon the throne. The nobles descended the steps and moved to their positions before the altar. Then Regnault de Chartres, archbishop of Reims, took off his mitre and knelt before his King. He took Charles' hand and kissed it, then both cheeks. Rising, he took his place at the King's side. One by one the peers came to the throne and made their obeisances.

When the last of them had finished, the archbishop made the Sign of the Cross in the air, blessing the new monarch and his people. All present crossed themselves as the prelate recited the concluding prayers that the kingdom might enjoy a reign of peace, justice, and plenty, and then once more he blessed the people of France.

As was customary, Charles ended the ceremony by bestowing honors upon those who had served him so faithfully. Georges de la Trémoïlle and Guy de Laval were given the title of comte, and Gilles de Rais received the office of maréchal. The comte de Clermont knighted the damoiseau de Commercy, the former robber baron who had once wrangled with Jacques Darc over Domrémy's taxes. René d'Anjou was made a knight by d'Alençon, who gave the same honor to Jehan de Metz. Jehanne was elated at this particular ritual, for she knew that her old friend from Vaucouleurs was being knighted for having believed in her from the first. It was d'Alençon's way of apologizing to her for his part in their quarrel. He had already done so the night before.

He had accompanied her and the Dauphin to the castle of Sept-Saulx, stronghold of archbishop de Chartres. As soon as he could, he made an excuse to draw her apart from her entourage.

Taking her to a quiet corner, he smiled sadly at her and said, "Jehanne, let's make peace between us. You probably don't realize how much I've regretted my harsh words to you. I know how much I must have hurt you and I'm terribly sorry."

She looked up at his remorseful face and put a hand to his cheek. "I'm sorry too, Jehan." Her words shook with the tears that lay beneath the surface of her nearly mastered calm. "I know you meant well, and I understand your concerns, honestly I do. But you must believe me when I say that I am under God's protection, I always have been. He has given me His promise, and if I doubt that even for a moment, I'll lose faith and fall into sin." Her eyes wrinkled at the corners and she pleaded silently for his understanding. "Do you believe me?"

He nodded. "Yes." But in spite of the affirmation, she saw that he looked away from her quickly as he answered.

It did not matter. He was her beautiful duc once more, and whatever his misgivings, he would follow her again.

"Noël!" The congregation of thousands shouted as though from a single throat, their joy supported by a trumpet blast that seemed to shake the cathedral and rattle the magnificent windows.

The King stood up and carefully stepped down from the throne. When he reached the spot where Jehanne was standing, she fell to her knees before him and embraced his legs. The bronzed face she raised to him was wet with joy.

"Noble King," she said softly, "now the will of God is fulfilled. He Who desired that Orléans should be delivered, and Who has brought you to this city of Reims to be crowned, has shown that you are the true King, and that this land of France belongs to you alone."

Charles smiled down at her. "Thank you, Jehanne."

"Thank God, Sire." Unable to contain the ecstasy that had been swelling within her since the procession began that morning, she burst into wracking sobs and clung to his feet. He did not stop her for several moments.

At last he handed the scepter and baton to d'Alençon and gently raised her. His smile appeared to illuminate him from within, making him appear almost as handsome as the duc. He wiped her wet face with his slender fingers. "Come, Jehanne, let us greet the people."

D'Alençon gave the instruments of monarchy back to his royal cousin. After he had passed, Jehanne followed his prolonged tread back down the center of the nave, between the masses who were shouting, "Noël!" over and over, their elation thundering through the cathedral. Far above them all the great bells sounded Charles' triumph over his former, uncelebrated fortune.

A great cry sprang from the population waiting outside the cathedral when the new King emerged into the startling afternoon. "Noël!"

"God save King Charles!"

"God save France!"

Then they saw Jehanne appear from the shadows. The people's blessings for their King became lost in the roar of an all-enveloping excitement, furious in its enthusiasm and gratitude and love.

"*Jehanne the Maid! Jehanne the Maid! Jehanne the Maid . . . !*"

She groaned inwardly, and for an instant she considered fleeing back into the cool safety of the cathedral. But not wanting to disappoint the people, she remained where she was, and tossed them a small wave and a smile. An expression of frozen happiness turned Charles' pale mouth upward, and he waved impassively at his subjects.

Jehanne had her back to them, so she did not see the raised eyebrow that the Bastard turned to d'Alençon, nor the exultant sneer that passed between the archbishop and Georges de la Trémoïlle.

Four cloaked figures, one much smaller than the others, rode as quickly as the crowds would let them down the narrow street toward the cathedral. Although darkness had fallen, people were still dancing and singing by torchlight throughout the celebrating town. The revelries had started in the afternoon upon completion of the coronation, and every few steps inert bodies lay by the roadside, stupefied with drink, barely noticed amidst the jongleurs and acrobats and musicians entertaining the crowd. In spite of the late hour, they continued to quaff the barreled wine the new ruler had provided for their festival, all mindful that dawn was still some hours distant.

The horsemen passed a performance of puppeteers and laughing children. To the distracted populace they were just a small band of nameless monks, no more out of place than the butchers selling sausages and chickens and the peddlers who hawked their goods in loud, competitive voices. But even with the nighttime carnival as their ally, the riders kept the hoods drawn carefully over their faces, and so that their horses would not bolt, they went out of their way to avoid a dancing bear held on leash by its trainer. It was necessary that they not be recognized. This mission was personal and so secret that only the King and d'Alençon knew of it.

When they reached the darkened cathedral where Charles had received his destiny that morning, they turned the mounts toward a row of densely packed old buildings opposite it. They halted beneath a swaying sign that proclaimed the inn called the Golden Donkey.

The riders dismounted, and the taller one said to the youngest member of their party, "Stay with the horses, and for God's sake try not to let anyone notice you."

"I won't," he responded in a voice recently deepened into manhood.

Scarcely had he spoken when they were forced back into the shadows by two brawling soldiers who were being pushed through the door by the innkeeper's husband.

"Stay out of here, you bastards!" roared the man in a dirty apron. "This is a respectable place, and I won't have any of your mischief here. Get back to your billets where you belong and sleep it off!"

As he turned to go back into the inn, he caught sight of the disguised group. His stubbled face grew pale, and he stammered, "Oh, it's you, I'm sorry for the fuss, these men-at-arms have been drinking all night and—"

"Never mind them," the tallest one said testily, "are they here?"

The innkeeper nodded. "Come with me."

They entered the sultry, boisterous tavern, passing tables that serving girls were busily rushing to stack with food and wine tankards. The large chamber was full of soldiers and travelers from a hundred districts of France, and the atmosphere was heavy with laughter and animated conversation. But the hooded figures took no notice.

They followed the innkeeper up a short flight of stairs, which turned before resuming to the third floor. The noise from below receded into a muffled clatter of indistinct sounds. The man led them down a short hallway.

He stopped before a door. "They're here."

"Thank you, sir," said the shortest of the three, giving him a coin.

The innkeeper bowed and disappeared down the corridor. One of the cloaked men opened the door.

A small man was sitting on the sagging bed, whittling an apple-sized block of wood which had grown the head of a bear. Small flecks of the blond stuff littered the floor before his farmer's boots. When he saw the three walk through the doorway, he grinned and sprang to his feet. The other fellow, who had been looking out the window at the tall spires facing the inn, ripped his gaze toward them.

He seemed much changed after all these months. His shoulders were slightly more stooped than they had been last winter, and the black hair was awash in strands of gray. He had grown a beard to keep the bushy mustache company, and through both silver bristles gleamed like frost on stubbled wheatfields in early autumn. He was wearing his best clothes, a homespun tunic that came to mid-thigh above clean brown pants. The new boots had been polished until they shone.

The trio threw back the cloaks shrouding them. Jehanne flung herself into the large man's arms with a whimper filled with gladness and repentance.

"Papa!"

Jacques crushed her to him and covered her face and hair with desperate kisses. "Jhanette, oh my dearest Jhanette, my darling child!"

She could feel his massive chest heave with emotion as he gripped her in a strangling embrace. She sobbed against his shirt, loving the smell of him that she thought she had forgotten, the aroma of manly sweat and earth.

He released her and held her at arm's length, his swollen eyes touching the beautifully clad, boylike vision that was his lost daughter. Then he kissed her face again and again until it hurt and pulled her back into his grinding arms. Her fingers clasped his tunic as a drowning person clutches at a raft, and she felt her lungs collapsing with the force that sought to merge her into his very being.

"Please, Papa," she gasped, "I can't breathe."

He released her and seized her face in his huge hands. "You little sausage!" He laughed through his tears. "I ought to thrash you within an inch of your life for giving your mother and me such a scare."

"I'm sorry, Papa," she said contritely, no longer Jehanne the Maid but simply Jhanette from Domrémy. No one else on earth had the power to restore her to her rightful place as he had in those few moments, and she wept for joy at this make-believe reclamation of her old life.

"How grand you look—if like a boy." He grimaced with distaste. "Why did you cut off all your hair?"

"I had to, Papa." She smiled, smearing the tears across her face. Leave it to him to think of something like that before all else.

As though he had not heard her, Jacques found his sons over her shoulder, and he enfolded both of them in his arms. The shy man was smiling hesitantly at Jehanne, and she knew that he was uncertain if he should embrace this boy-girl who had risen to such exalted heights.

"Uncle Durand!" she exclaimed, a wide smile splitting her face. She threw her arms about his neck and kissed his thin cheek. "I am so glad to see you." She wheeled her head around to her father. "Both of you. But why didn't Maman come, too?" Glad as she was to see her father, Jehanne would have given half her remaining years to see Isabelle again.

Jacques drew a rag from his tunic and honked loudly. He shook his head. "She couldn't come, Jhanette. You see, Marguerite has been ill, and—"

"Oh, that's what Jehan Morel told us," Jehanne intruded, alarmed. "Is she still sick, is she all right?"

"Jehan Morel? You saw him?" asked Durand.

"We certainly did," Pierre stated importantly, "in Châlons. He came to see us there, with Gérardin d'Epinal, and he said—"

"Just a minute, Pierrolot." Jehanne grabbed her father's arm. "Is Marguerite really sick, Papa?" Marguerite was the wife of Jacquemin, the oldest of the Darc children. Jehanne had not been concerned when Morel, her godfather, had relayed the family news, thinking at the time that Marguerite's illness was not serious. But if Maman was caring for her instead of coming with Papa—

"Not too bad." He smiled, dispelling her apprehension. "But you know how your maman is, she tries to take care of everybody. She said to tell you that she loves you and that she hopes you'll be home soon."

Jehanne slowly dropped to her knees and looked up at the big man whose love had called her into being. She took his heavy veined hands and said, "I ask your forgiveness, Papa, for leaving the way I did. I had no choice, though, because God called me and I had to obey Him." A tear slid toward her mouth.

"Get up, Jhanette," he said quietly, pulling her to a standing position. He put a thick arm around her shoulder and drawing her to him squeezed her painfully in a fierce hug. She lay her head against the heart hammering beneath his scratchy tunic, her arm slipping around his waist.

"I need to ask your forgiveness as well," he whispered into her hair. "I should not have suspected you of—that is, I should have known that you'd never do anything wrong."

His rasping breath smelled of garlic and wine. She looked up at him and smiled.

"And we are all so proud of you!" Jacques announced in the booming voice she knew from infancy. "For months all we've heard from travelers passing through the village was Jehanne the Maid this, Jehanne the Maid that. You should have seen their faces when we told them you were ours!"

The company erupted into laughter. A loving glow wrapped itself around them and within Jehanne's soul a breeze from the Bois Chenu floated just out of sight. If she closed her eyes for only a moment, she could swear that she was home again where Jhanette still carried baskets of millet into her father's stone cottage.

Pierre and Jehan made themselves comfortable upon the floor. Jacques gestured for his daughter to sit on the room's one stool, then he settled onto a corner of the bed next to Durand. "Come, Jhanette"—he grinned—"tell your old father all that has happened to you since you left Domrémy, and mind you, don't leave out anything!"

"Did you go to the coronation, Papa?" Jehan asked.

"Yes, yes, Jehan," he responded with the old gruff impatience, "I was near the front and I saw your sister standing there behind the King." He turned to Durand and said with confidential glee, "Just wait until Zabillet hears what she missed." He prodded the small man with his elbow. "She'll be sorry she did not let Marguerite's mother nurse her instead, eh?"

Jehanne smiled sadly as Maman's face floated before her, then vanished. Oh, Maman! She shuddered at the unwelcome premonition that took her mother's place.

"But Jhanette was about to tell us of her adventures, so let's be quiet for now." Jacques sat forward expectantly, and in that instant he became the boy Jehanne had never known.

"I don't know where to begin." She ran a hand through her thick, short hair. "In Vaucouleurs, I met with sieur de Baudricourt—you remember him, Papa?"

He nodded.

"He did not believe me at first. And then I met a man called Jehan de Metz, he was knighted today by my friend"—a stab of pain—"my friend the duc d'Alençon, anyway he's a friend of Bertrand de Poulengy. I know you know him."

Jacques nodded again, his expression fixed on her words.

"Anyway, the two of them helped me convince sieur de Baudricourt that he should send me to Chinon to meet the Dauphin."

She talked and talked for a long time. She told them about meeting Charles and then d'Alençon. She recounted her adoption of Minguet—"he's in the street right now with the horses, Papa, you can meet him if you want"—and spoke of her journey to Poitiers to be questioned by the churchmen. But she left out any mention of the humiliating physical examinations and of her loneliness, and when she reached the battles at Orléans, she leaped over the part about her being wounded. She prayed silently that her brothers would keep their mouths shut about that. She need not have fretted. The children of Jacques Darc had learned from the time they could speak that there were some things best kept hidden from the old man.

But otherwise she told the truth. She showed them Ste.-Catherine's sword, and the two men from Lorraine touched the crosses on it with reverential awe. And then came the inevitable question that she had been dreading all evening.

"When will you come home, Jhanette?" A gleam of fear reflected back at her from her father's black eyes.

"I don't know. How are Hauviette and Mengette? Do they speak of me?"

"Hauviette wept bitterly when you left," he stated bluntly, trying to punish her for avoiding his query. "She was torn to the heart that you did not tell her good-bye."

Jehanne flinched at the specter of her old guilt.

"She is engaged now, to a prosperous man from Neufchâteau," he concluded. He did not add, "as you should be," but Jehanne knew him well enough to gather that, his pride in her notwithstanding, a part of him still resented her refusal to marry the man he had chosen for her.

"And Mengette?" she asked with feigned eagerness.

Jacques shrugged. "She is still at home."

An uneasy silence settled over the small room. Jehan wiped his boot absently, and even Pierre kept his peace. Knife in hand, Durand moved the instrument in careful strokes across the wooden bear's emerging shoulders. Jehanne looked away from her father's stare and crossed her legs.

The fragile tension was shattered by the question she knew he would eventually ask again. "When will you come home, Jhanette?"

She sighed and looked at him. "I do not know. When God gives me leave." Even as she spoke, her recurring nightmare that had no end raced between her ears and she shivered.

"When will that be?" he insisted. "You have delivered Orléans, you have restored the King, what more does God want of you?"

"There is still Paris. The *goddons* are still in France." Her tiny smile was apologetic. "My work is unfinished, Papa."

Confusion flitted through the stare that he continued to fix on her. "Can you not let the King do all that now? Why must it be you?"

"Because God wants me to. I don't know why, Papa, only that He does. He told me that it's what I was born for." A wall, higher and more insurmountable than the Tourelles, loomed between them, and she helplessly tried to scale it. "Didn't you and Maman always tell us children that we must obey God above all others?"

"We did not understand what we said then, Jhanette." The old man's eyes closed with the sorrow he could not express, and a drop fell into his silver-veined beard.

Jehanne got up and, kneeling at his feet, placed her hands on his trousers. She took his hands and looked up at him. "Let me go, Papa," she whispered, "give me your blessing to follow God's will."

He reached out and put a hand to her damp cheek. He did not see Jehanne the Maid but his heart's greatest treasure. She did not know what he was unable to bring himself to tell her, that he had recently dreamed that she was on fire, and screaming.

"I can do nothing else," he sighed.

She released his hands and hugged him. Her father's embrace, desperate with love and fear, bent back her neck uncomfortably, but even so she did not wish him to disengage from her. She wanted him to summon his old authority, to order her to return home with him, to drag her back to Domrémy if necessary rather than grant her request. But she knew he would not. Times had changed.

He let go of her and she stood. When she returned to her seat, she quickly pointed the conversation toward the doings of their village. What was the latest news? she wondered. She told him of the things Jehan Morel had said and asked Jacques to add to them. He answered, knowing that the subject of her return was closed and could not be mentioned again.

As he spoke the mood lightened, and the group talked for a few more hours. At long last, when the late night made it difficult for them to ward off sleep, Jehanne gave her father a small, jingling sack, sixty *livres* Tournois from the King himself, a present to the Maid's forebear. Like a delighted child, he accepted the money and told Jehanne to thank the King for him.

There was nothing more to be said. Pierre's eyes were closing with encroaching sleep, and his brother pulled him to his feet. The three children donned their cloaks. Jehanne entered her papa's outstretched arms and clung to him for several moments before he released her unwillingly, then hugged and kissed his sons.

"Take care of Jhanette, you two," he ordered.

"We will, Papa," Jehan replied. "Don't worry, she'll be all right."

The youngsters bade farewell to their uncle Durand and went to the door. Jehanne, the last to leave, gave her father a lingering look of love and regret. Then she closed the door behind her.

Their footsteps tromped down the stairs. Jacques went to the window and looked out into the street. The sky, propped up by the cathedral spires, had turned lavender with the coming dawn, and pigeons were soaring between the towers of the old building. He could see the horses below his window and the boy who sprang to his feet as the three monkish shapes appeared from the inn. They climbed tiredly aboard their mounts, then turned them away.

Jacques listened to the slow, clopping hoofbeats for what seemed too brief a time. No longer forced to hold back his emotions, he buried his face in his hands and the broad shoulders began to shake. Durand could not console him.

BOOK THREE

The Road to Eternity

Put not your faith in princes, in man, in whom there is no salvation.

PSALMS 146:3

CHAPTER ELEVEN

The Wolf on the Ice

July 19–September 11, 1429

J uggle them, juggle them, juggle them—!"

She tried frantically to catch the descending flowers, but there were too many, and they slipped through her desperately grasping fingers into the dust. Her horse threw back his head with a loud, wild-eyed whinny, at the same time crushing the delicate colors beneath his hooves. Looking down, she saw that the once fragrant bouquets had become transformed into stones.

The mood of the crowd turned surly and she was enveloped within a loud "Boo-o!"

"But look, I still have this rose!" She held up the perfect flower for all to see.

The people were unappeased and jeered even louder. Their faces, misshapen with hatred, shouted angrily at her. They picked up the rocks and began pelting her with them. Her horse reared in terror and she turned him away with a jab of her spurs.

He galloped and galloped, and the pleasant green countryside unexpectedly changed into a bleak, forbidding wilderness. He was taking her across the threshold into nightmare. She pulled on the reins with all her might, but the beast's strength was beyond her control now and she could not stop his mad flight.

The air filled with a thick, blinding blizzard, and as the cold fury of the wind lashed at her face, stiffening her hands, she thought, I am not dressed for this, I will certainly freeze to death. Desperation hammered in her chest and she pulled harder at the bit; the horse hastened to the top of a hill. Looking down, she saw ahead of them a large, frozen pond. She had to stop the horse before they reached it, no matter the cost, for she knew that there was something terrifying on that ice, something beyond imagining. Now near panic, she yanked upon his bridle until he screamed in pain, but he did not slow his insane dash toward the glassy lake.

A jolt hit her spine when his hooves collided with the ice. For a moment the clattering hoofbeats pounded in her brain, and then, with a sudden, almost graceful movement, the horse's legs buckled beneath him and they fell against the hard surface with a sickening *Whap!* The air in her lungs exploded into a white vapor and she could not move.

Slowly, she struggled to her feet and looked back over her shoulder. All at once, her blood turned as icy as the lake.

The horse was gone. In his place a gigantic wolf leered at her, its long fangs dripping wickedly. Two coals like the Devil's own eyes burned within the black fur, compelling in their evil, silently declaring the creature's undiluted hatred. A low snarl began in its gut and rose to the lolling tongue, where it issued forth in a shriek.

Slipping unsteadily, she started to run on feet quickened by terror. She knew that somehow she would be safe if she could reach the other bank, for there, beyond the invisible barrier on the distant, snow-covered slope, the monster could not harm her.

But it was so far away—and she was nearly unable to move her feet, for they were encased in caskets of lead; her total will struggled to pry them from the ice. She found that no matter how fast she ran, she was always in the same place, with the slathering jaws of the fiend nipping at those barely moving feet.

A loud crack rang out like a cannonade. Looking down in dismay, she saw the ice fracture beneath her and streak outward in all directions.

There was that moment's hesitation between the first splinter of the ice and its collapse when she thought she might still get away. Even as she plunged into the freezing water, she grappled in mindless despair at the thin ice, which crumbled into liquid the instant she touched it.

The weight of her clothes pulled her down into cold, numbing darkness; terrified, she fought to wriggle her way to the surface before her lungs burst.

When she hit the frigid air, she gasped noisily for breath. Her face was a mass of frosty beads, so thick it almost sealed her eyes. She grabbed blindly at the ice in front of her, trying to grab onto a support solid enough for her to climb out of the paralyzing water.

She touched wet fur, thick and cold. Its breath burned her hand. She opened her eyes to see the malevolent, growling snout of the demon gloating upon the ice—

Jehanne leaped from the water into wakefulness.

The thunderstorm which had begun after she fell asleep was still flashing through the sky, its startling illumination followed a few seconds later by a tremendous blast of noise. The rain must have been blinding to judge by its relentless rhythm, but that was nothing compared to the gale raging within her, galloping in her heart in a furious rhythm.

Between the cracks of thunder she could hear Poulengy's deep snores coming from the tent's other room. She had been with these men for so long that she could sort his from d'Aulon's. Her squire breathed in a high-pitched wheeze when he slept, while Poulengy always sounded like a sow rummaging in mud.

I'm safe, it was only a dream, she thought desperately. I'm here in my tent and all around us are the dear soldiers of the King's army. We're still at Reims where we've been waiting for three days for our sovereign lord to give the word that we might continue to Paris. This is the reality; that was only a dream.

She sank back into her pillow. The thumping in her chest slowed, and she took a deep breath. It was just a dream.

No, not *only* a dream, but the same cursed nightmare that had come to claim her at random intervals ever since Orléans. Except that now it had an ending whereas before she had never reached the ice. In previous encounters with the dark journey, she had not seen the Beast that her horse became. She had always wakened herself, and now she recalled that immediately after rejecting the scene, she always knew that she had avoided something unspeakably horrible.

She sat up in her cot and rubbed the clammy sweat from her brow. Take a deep breath, Jehanne, it is only a dream, nothing more.

She lay down again and clasped her hands together. The words of the *Pater Noster* rattled through the corners of her brain as the terror returned, and for once the prayer did not comfort her.

Oh, dear God, keep me safe, she begged, let this dream slip away from me. Have I not done all that You have commanded? She forced her breathing to a slower pace, and her heart began to thump accordingly. Have I not done as You asked?

YOU HAVE NOTHING TO FEAR, LITTLE ONE, FOR NO HARM CAN COME TO YOU IN THIS LIFE NOR IN THE NEXT. BEAR ALL THINGS PATIENTLY AND ATTEND UPON GOD WHO LOVES YOU MOST TENDERLY. SLEEP AGAIN. DO NOT BE AFRAID.

Will the King give me leave to take Paris? Despite what she had told d'Alençon, a sense of foreboding had always prevented her asking this with a fully open heart, until now. But she had to know.

YOU HAVE DONE AS THE KING OF HEAVEN HAS COMMANDED. IT IS TIME NOW FOR YOUR EARTHLY KING TO ACCEPT HIS SHARE OF THE BURDEN. GOD HAS PROMISED THAT PARIS WILL YIELD TO CHARLES THAT HE MIGHT SHEPHERD GOD'S LAND.

Will we take Paris, though?

Your King is the King of Peace. Do all things with charity, and you shall follow His will.

But the English hold the city, and they will not yield without a fight.

PARIS SHALL KNEEL TO CHARLES OF ITS OWN FREE WILL, IN GOD'S OWN TIME.

The premonition that lay like a bubble in her stomach ascended to the surface, and when it reached her mouth she asked, Will I live to see that happen?

Do you doubt God's love for you, dear child? You cannot ever die except through fear. Rest now; hold to your courage. One day you shall walk the streets of Paris and marvel at its beauty, and you shall see then how changed it has become. Do not burden yourself with the darkness of your thoughts. We are with you through Eternity. Sleep now.

They are with me. God will protect me from harm. Oh please God, look out for my brothers, too, all of them.

She closed her eyes and descended again into the misty realm of sleep and, mercifully, did not dream. It rained throughout the night.

A lone rider paused at the top of the hill. No more than a quarter of a league from his position, the royal army was snaking northward through the rolling green valley. Leading the host was the cavalry, and the courier could clearly see the flags of maréchal Gilles de Rais and Raoul de Gaucourt amidst the brilliantly colored banners of the other captains. A vast company of men-at-arms perhaps three thousand strong came after the horsemen, their motley armor glittering beneath the summer sun. Ahead of the infantry and the lumbering supply wagons, the golden fleur-de-lys floated on the King's standard next to the battle-damaged emblem of the Maid.

The messenger was one of La Hire's own men and had been sent ahead to scout territory that might be hostile to the new King. Wearing a cheerful smile, he touched spurs to his horse's flanks, and they cantered down the grassy slope, toward the center of the broad column. He would have glad tidings to announce this day.

The King saw him coming and raised his hand. From one company commander to another the order to halt was shouted up and down the line as the courier sped across the high grass. When he was close enough he yanked on the reins, and his horse came to a stop just inches from the King.

Charles looked every inch the virgin warrior, clad as he was in the steel suit that had never been worn in a real battle. The end of his sallow nose had begun to burn red from the sun, and he looked hot and uncomfortable. At His Majesty's right hand an armored Jehanne the Maid sat ahorse, gleaming under the July sky. A battered helmet dangled from her saddle, held in place by a leather thong. Her brows drew together thoughtfully as she pushed a thick shock of black hair from those startling eyes.

The messenger recognized the Bastard of Orléans and the duc d'Alençon in the mounted company surrounding the King. He did not know the portly, glowering fellow to the King's left, but he reasoned that this must be Georges de la Trémoïlle, said to be the slyest fox in the kingdom.

"Your Majesty." The man bowed low over his saddle. "I bring you wonderful news from Château-Thierry. Bourgogne's garrison has abandoned the town and is headed toward Paris!"

"What?" The narrow, ale-colored eyes widened in astonishment. "Why have they done that?"

"The burgesses demanded it, Sire." He wiped a thin stream of sweat from his shaven cheek. "It seems the people have grown tired of those Burgundian ruffians and are ready now to give Your Majesty their fidelity."

"You see?" Charles looked around him, a satisfied smile appearing beneath the bulbous nose. "What did I tell you? Again, we shall not have to fight another town that is prepared to give us its faith!" He turned to Trémoïlle and said with the blunt privilege of his rank, "Jehanne was right, sieur Chancellor, and once more you were wrong!" The King laughed, wallowing in satisfaction.

Ever since his coronation a week earlier, the towns of Champagne had fallen to him without protest. On the heels of his private meetings with Bourgogne's envoys, during which he had reluctantly agreed to a temporary delay of hostilities,

Charles had completed his ceremonial duties as King by embarking on the cus-tomary royal pilgrimage to the abbey of St.-Marcoul, where he had touched the scrofulous wretches who sought the miraculous healing power of their sovereign. It was not a duty he performed with any pleasure, but it was his royal obligation.

He had departed the monastery as soon as it was seemly and headed north again, to the village of Vailly. There he received ambassadors from Laon and Soissons, who knelt to him and handed over the keys to their cities. In Soissons he learned in the wake of his triumphant entry, and much to his delight, that Coulommiers, Provins, and their neighboring towns were also willing to kneel to the royal will.

Now Château-Thierry had acceded as well! This was a fine day indeed. With any luck, Paris itself would not resist either, as Philippe de Bourgogne had prom-ised, and very soon he could enter the capital unimpeded. Meanwhile, he could travel from town to town, gathering them to his regal bosom like bouquets of spring flowers while he waited for the truce to expire.

Trémoïlle was a pessimistic idiot lacking any vision. If Charles had listened to him after the coronation, he would be cowering in Chinon Castle instead of claiming the destiny that Jehanne continued to promise him. He told himself that it did not matter that the people now called her name louder than his. Once he had Paris in his grasp, the Norman cities would be deserted by the English and he could negotiate a permanent peace with Philippe. The war ended, Jehanne the Maid could return to her village or reside at court if she liked, and the people would soon forget her.

"May I remind Your Majesty," Trémoïlle said, his tone one of chilly offense, "that just because a few barely defended towns have yielded to the blood royal, it does not mean that the capital will be so easily dismayed. If you draw any closer to Paris, it may be that the seigneur de Bourgogne will interpret that as an act of aggression and any future treaties with him will be endangered."

"So what if he does?" Jehanne insisted. She was sitting forward in her saddle with a rigid eagerness that demanded Charles' attention. "Your Majesty is the true King of France now, and the seigneur de Bourgogne is only your vassal, however powerful he may be. He does not have the right to tell you what to do with what is yours. And Paris is your city, Sire. If it will not yield of its own accord, then it is your right to take it!"

La Hire, de Gaucourt, and de Rais trotted to them as she finished speaking. Their arrival prevented a tart reply from the chancellor. "Is something wrong, Sire?" de Gaucourt rasped suspiciously. "Why have we stopped?"

"Another town has fallen to us!" Charles beamed. "Château-Thierry. Our loyal chancellor," he sneered, "suggests that we retire now to await further treachery from Bourgogne, but fortunately, we have the Maid to remind us that God's support is still with us."

"I did not say that, Sire, and neither did she," Trémoïlle countered, his rotund face scarlet with indignation. He looked defiantly at the adversaries encircling him. "I simply reminded His Majesty that although the towns of Champagne have given him their loyalty, he should not expect that Paris will follow. If His Majesty should attempt to besiege the capital, he may find that it is a great deal more dogged than he presently supposes." The chancellor imparted a disdainful glance at Jehanne. "The Maid, with a woman's rashness, would have the King attack the city and risk the army's ruin."

"Rashness?!" Jehanne exploded. "Rashness? It is just plain common sense, that's all! We should have followed up our victories after the coronation with a direct assault on Paris while we still had the advantage in numbers. Who knows what has happened since then? For all we know, the *goddons* might have reinforced their army within the city, and by the time we get there, they may outnumber us!"

"She's right, Sire, as usual." La Hire glared at Trémoïlle as though eager to wring his fat neck. "I say to hell with any more waiting around, let's march on Paris today!"

De Gaucourt growled in assent. D'Alençon and de Rais nodded grimly.

"We have not ruled against the plan to take Paris, we simply feel it best to protect the army by surrounding the capital with loyal towns before we make the attempt," Charles said smoothly. "We thank you all for your advice, and now we will renew our journey." He chuckled. "We do not wish to keep our loyal Château-Thierry waiting for our arrival any longer than is necessary."

The cavalry commanders glanced at one another uncertainly. They bowed to the King, then turned their horses toward the front of the column. The order to resume the march rang out along the column, and they were soon on the move again.

Charles smiled at the sky, admiring the beautiful weather. His heart filled with an unaccustomed affection for the girl who rode beside him. "Are you pleased, Jehanne, at the way things are working out?"

She bit her lower lip. "Somewhat, Sire."

"Somewhat?" he raised his brows.

"It is wonderful that the towns are falling to you, Sire, but I still think you should commence with all haste to Paris."

"Oh, we shall get there, never fear," he replied, determined that she not spoil his good mood. "But tell me, what may we do to show our appreciation for all that you have done for us?"

"My lord?"

"Is there nothing you want that you do not have? Another horse, or a new suit of armor, perhaps?" Charles gave her a rare impish smile. "That one is so badly dented that it looks like an old pot!"

She laughed at his joke. "It serves me well enough, my lord. Besides," she ventured with an air of unconcern, "when we take Paris a new one will only become dented, too, so I may as well keep this one since it is already damaged."

"Oh, come now," he insisted, "is there nothing that we may give you?"

She frowned thoughtfully for a few moments as they plodded along the rough road. And then her face lit up, and she said, "I don't want anything for myself, Sire, but there is something you could do that would please me."

"And what is that?"

"My lord, the village I come from—Domrémy, it's called—is quite poor," she said, now all eagerness, "and although the people there work very hard, they have a difficult time paying the war tax every winter, especially during those years when God does not grant them a good harvest. If you would do something for me, then I ask in all humility that you release my village from any more taxes."

The air exploded from Charles' lungs in amazement. What an extraordinary girl she was to think of something like that! "You never cease to astound us, Jehanne," he replied, a look of surprised awe written on the homely features. "Of course, it shall be as you desire."

She beamed at him, disregarding Trémoïlle's haughty profile and the dark disapproval wafting from him. "And for Greux as well, Sire?"

"Greux?"

"That is the neighboring village, Sire. The people there would be most envious if Domrémy had a liberty they did not share."

Charles burst into laughter. "Very well, Greux shall be spared as well, but stop with that, I beg you. We cannot afford to pardon the whole of Lorraine!"

"That's all, my lord." She grinned. "I am most grateful, and I know the people of Domrémy and Greux will be too."

"Is there nothing you want for yourself, nothing at all?"

"No, Sire, just that we take Paris."

"Well, let's just see what happens when the time comes," the King urged with a smile. "After all, we are not yet at Château-Thierry, and we do not know what lies beyond it."

Charles was true to his word. After they reached that welcoming town, he dictated an order to the bailiff of Chaumont, seat of Jehanne's village, ordering a remission of taxes on Domrémy and Greux in perpetuity. Jacques Darc would never again be forced to wrangle with a local lord over money his village could not afford to pay.

The King's army circled Paris from town to town like a wrestler unsure of what grip to use on his opponent. Jehanne could have screamed her impatience, and she tried on more than one occasion to goad Charles into making a determined feint against the capital. But always Trémoïlle was present, hovering about the King like a wary, lunatic mother, and his hold over him was such that Charles continued to forbid an immediate attack on Paris. Instead, he paraded his meandering army to Provins, ready to bow to him as its neighbors had done. Heady with his bloodless victories, Charles happily accepted the news from his spies that Bedford's battalions had been spotted near Melun, a mere ten leagues southeast of Paris.

On August 5 he brought the army to the vicinity of Nanglis Castle, midway between Provins and Melun, and waited for English forces which did not appear. The King's soldiers sat in battle formation throughout the day in the steaming heat, and their impatient grumbles became louder as the sun wandered into the afternoon hours.

Finally, messengers were seen dismounting at the King's position under a large, shady oak, and it was at that point that La Hire and de Gaucourt were sent by the company commanders to the tree to ask for an audience with Charles.

His personal bodyguard, not members of the regular army but handpicked palace sentinels from Scotland, stood in a ring some twenty feet from the shade, protecting the King, his guests, and his favorites, Trémoïlle and de Chartres. When de Gaucourt demanded entry, one of the guards told him that he was not allowed to pass. De Gaucourt insisted. The guard left his station, walked over to Charles, and whispered in his ear. The King spoke to him briefly, and although the two commanders could hear his voice, they were unable to grasp his words. The sentry returned and informed them that the King forbade them entry. The two captains, incensed that their presence had been denied, mounted up and returned to where Jehanne, d'Alençon, the Bastard, and the others were posted at the front of the army.

"Well, who are they anyway?" Jehanne demanded. Although she had removed her helmet hours ago, she was nevertheless sweltering underneath her armor and like all of them was tired and angry at these infernal delays. The tone in her voice was not amiable, and the other captains understood that her wrath was directed more at Charles than at them.

"I don't know who the f—, who the hell they are," groused de Gaucourt, his aged face crimson with indignation, "but they must be awfully damned important for the King to have turned us away. It's those cursed ministers of his, they're up to something!"

"What do you think is going on?" d'Alençon asked. His hair was a mass of wet ringlets plastered to his forehead, and the bloom in his smooth cheeks had spread to the rest of his face in the heat.

"Rumor has it that he received a delegation of Burgundians while he was still in Reims," de Rais offered maliciously, "and that that's the reason he wasted four days before he started this pointless march. It may be that those men have something to do with whatever happened there."

"If that's true, then it has Trémoïlle written all over it," said Sainte-Sévère. "He's always been half-Burgundian anyway, and who knows what he's put Charles up to now! I've never trusted that son of a bitch." The old warrior glanced at Jehanne's black scowl, misinterpreting its cause. "Excuse me."

"Well, what are we going to do about it?" asked René, duc de Bar. "We can't just sit here waiting for God knows what to happen."

"I'm not going to wait," swore Jehanne. "I'm going over there right now to find out what's going on."

Without pausing for any further discussion, she snatched her horse's reins around and quickly urged him toward the tree. The Bastard and d'Alençon followed her. She leaped from the mount and stalked over to the circle of bodyguards.

"Let me pass, I have urgent matters with the King." She felt her friends dismount behind her.

"I'm sorry, Jehanne, but I cannot let you by," one of the soldiers said. He was a large fellow with a countenance that seemed carved from solid rock.

"I tell you, this is urgent!" she contended. She fixed her stare on him as she felt the Power pulse through her. "If you do not allow us an audience, the King will certainly be most displeased with you."

His eyes hardened with a determination to resist her. "It is by the King's orders that we must turn you away. He would have our heads if we were to disobey him."

"Fellow, do you know who I am, and who this man is?"

"Yes, sir, you are the Bastard of Orléans and that is the duc d'Alençon."

"That's right!" the Bastard barked, frustration supplanting his natural amiability. "You must also know that we are the King's kinsmen, and because we are the King's kinsmen, we have leave to speak to him whenever we want. Jehanne the Maid also has that liberty. You may turn away the other captains, but I assure you that if you deny us admittance into His Majesty's presence, he will make you regret the day your mother met your father! Now let us through."

The hapless guard glanced at his fellows uncertainly. One of them shrugged as though to say, Let it be on their heads, not ours.

"Very well," the large man muttered, "you may pass." Without wasting another second, Jehanne charged into the circle, followed in close order by her comrades.

Charles was sitting on a stool at the base of the sheltering oak. De Chartres and Trémoïlle rested comfortably next to him. The mysterious horsemen had gone. The King frowned when he saw Jehanne and his cousins, and as they bowed to him, he asked coldly, "What is the meaning of this? We did not give any of you leave to approach us."

"Excuse us, Sire," said Jehanne, "but the army is growing restless. They have come to this place expecting to fight, although to be honest, they would rather be on the road to Paris." She glanced at d'Alençon for support, and his look told her that she had it.

"I'm sorry, my lord, but we all feel that we're wasting precious time while the *goddons* and the Burgundians sit back and laugh at us." She was tired of being polite to this man of frail character whom she had made King. Her nerves were frayed to the breaking point, and at this moment she did not care how he reacted.

Charles said nothing, simply looked at her with stern disapproval. Yet she saw something else behind his eyes which she could not quite grasp.

"Jehanne speaks for all of us, Sire," said d'Alençon. "We may not have the claim of knowing your intentions, but I urge you to consider that we are all your most loyal vassals and have fought hard to prove that devotion. Why, Jehanne was seriously wounded at Orléans and has sacrificed much to come with you this far when she is not a soldier by birth or training. She could have remained safely at home in her village, yet she followed God's instructions to bring you to your rightful throne."

"What do you want, Cousin?" Charles asked, so quietly that it almost seemed that he had not spoken at all. His rounded shoulders slumped forward a little.

"What I think Jehan is trying to say is that the entire army has come all this way hoping for a solid victory," said the Bastard. "What should we tell them, Sire? As Jehan pointed out, they may not have the right to know, but they do hope that their King would be generous enough to consider their stake in this war."

Charles glanced uncertainly at his ministers. Trémoïlle did not look at him, only at the Bastard. A smirk curved his mouth, while behind the small eyes there smoldered a passionate hatred. The old archbishop could not meet any of their gazes but stared at the ground in front of him.

The King raised his chin. "We may as well tell you, then. Following our coronation, we met with envoys of Philippe de Bourgogne and after prayerful reflection agreed to a fifteen-day truce, during which time we shall not attack Paris. At the end of that period, he has sworn to turn over the city to us."

"Since when has the duc ever kept his word to the King?" Jehanne blurted. "This truce he has proposed is a lie for him to buy time. We should go to Paris now, my lord, and take it from him!"

"That is not for a peasant to decide," Trémoïlle scoffed, "much less a woman who knows nothing of the subtleties of royal diplomacy. How dare you speak to the King like that?"

"Sire, may I speak?" the Bastard broke in, licking his upper lip uneasily.

"Of course, Bastard." Charles smiled at his kinsman.

"It may be that both are right," the Bastard stated, his dimples deepening the clean-shaven corners of his mouth. "On the one hand, honor does demand that you hold to any agreements that you have made, whether with the duc or with Satan himself. However, should Bourgogne break his word and refuse to give Paris to you, you would indeed have the right as the offended party to seize the city. I confess"—he smiled apologetically at Jehanne—"that I did not think a month ago that it would be possible to take the capital, but much has changed since the coronation, and the army is willing to attempt it if necessary. I recommend that you continue your march toward Paris just in case you are indeed betrayed."

"I agree completely, Cousin," said d'Alençon. "Your Majesty must be most cautious if you are not to allow Philippe to trick you." He shrugged. "And who knows? This time he might actually keep his word."

"Keep his word?" snorted Jehanne. "That would be a first."

D'Alençon winced. The Bastard looked as though he wished he could stuff a gag into her mouth. He inquired quickly, "If I may ask, Sire, who were those messengers who were here earlier?"

Charles turned his vexed attention from Jehanne. "They were emissaries from Reims," he admitted. "They are fearful that we shall abandon our purpose to march on Paris, and that in that event they will be left defenseless."

"What did you tell them?"

Charles hesitated. "We have decided to return to the security of Orléans for now."

Jehanne and d'Alençon groaned aloud, their worst fears realized. Although he must have felt the same way, the Bastard kept his expression neutral.

"We have always thought that our best course of action was to divorce Philippe from the English," Charles said peevishly. "If we can make a separate peace with him, then he will withdraw his support from them, and if that happens, their strength in France will be greatly reduced. And together, we shall be able to drive them out at last. He will never give us his fealty, though, if we offend him by fighting against him."

Jehanne moved across the short distance separating them and knelt in the grass before him. She took his thin hands and placed hers between them in a centuries-old gesture of loyalty.

"Sire, I beg you, please do not return to Orléans. We are so close to Paris now, and if we retreat, it may be that the towns that have swung toward you since the coronation will withdraw their support, and then all of this will have been for nothing. The army will wait out the terms of your truce with the seigneur de Bourgogne, but they can do that on the outskirts of Paris as easily as they could at Orléans. Again, my lord, I beg you as your most humble servant, do not do this."

Her mind throbbed with a desperate sense of futility. What a coward he was, this pitiful man God had chosen to steward the kingdom! In his imploring glance at Trémoïlle she saw that no matter what she said, Charles would do as his puppetmaster commanded.

"We must return to Orléans, Jehanne," he said. "We cannot chance insulting our cousin Philippe, not now when there is the possibility of bringing about a real peace."

Jehanne bowed her head. "Very well, my lord."

She got to her feet slowly and turned away from him, but remembered to bow to her King again before she walked with her head down past the guards and out of the circle. The Bastard and d'Alençon, likewise aware that there was nothing more to say, followed her lead and returned to their horses.

Jehanne did not go with them to tell the other commanders that the King had ordered the army to retreat to the Loire. Instead, she went looking for Pasquerel, and when she found him, dictated a letter for him to write to the people of Reims.

She greeted her loyal and good friends, and assured them that a truce had been made with the duc de Bourgogne to last for two weeks. But the Remois should not be surprised, she said, if she entered Paris before that time, because she was not pleased with the cease-fire's terms. If she did keep them, it would only be to preserve the King's honor. She swore to keep the army together, ready to fight at the end of the fortnight if the peace were not maintained. She promised her dear and perfect friends that they should not worry while she lived but must guard the King's city, and if anyone tried to harm them, they must let her know and she would come immediately to their aid.

When the letter was finished, she allowed Pasquerel to guide her hand in the formation of her signature. Then she sent Ambleville to Reims with the dispatch, penned at "a stop on the road to Paris."

Shortly before nightfall, Charles received a courier from the town of Bray, whose burgesses promised him safe passage down the Seine, away from Paris. As the news spread throughout the camp, a pall of dejection passed from man to man, and finally from man to Maid.

There was nothing more that could be done. She had made a pledge to Reims, and would have to defy her liege lord openly. That likelihood produced a rancid taste in her mouth and the dinner she had barely eaten churned uneasily in her stomach. She did not feel any better when it came up behind her tent near the tethered horses. The King would retreat tomorrow to Orléans, and she would have to make the most difficult choice of her life. Nothing could change Charles' mind.

She did not reckon on the English.

"Jehanne!"

Someone was shaking her shoulder, exhorting her to consciousness, but she did not want to wake. It was so comfortable here on the blanket beneath the still cool dawn sky. She had tossed restlessly until the early morning hours, unable to sleep, and now having finally dropped off into the world of vague shadows, someone was trying to rouse her.

"Jehanne, come on, wake up," a voice insisted. "There's good news."

She pushed herself to the surface and opened one red-rimmed eye. D'Alençon was kneeling beside her. His stubbled face shone with glee and light danced excitedly in his eyes. The Bastard was stooped over her with his hands on his knees, a beautiful grin plastered across his face.

Jehanne sat up and rubbed the crusts from the corners of her eyes. A tear had dried on her cheek, and she wiped away its residue. "What is it?" she asked, suddenly wide awake.

"The English have taken the bridge just outside Bray!" the duc exclaimed. "The army cannot cross it to board the boats that would have taken us down the Seine."

"Charles has once more changed his mind," said the Bastard, his dimples working at the corners of his mouth. "We are to return to Château-Thierry. From there the King has decided that we shall turn northwest, toward La Ferté and then on to Crépy-en-Valois, which are both prepared to receive him."

"Crépy is only twenty-five leagues from Paris, Jehanne!" D'Alençon was as excited as a child.

"With any luck, the King will allow us to attack Paris after all," declared the Bastard. He gave a short laugh. "I never thought I'd say this, but thank God for the English!"

Jehanne stared at them mutely, uncertain that she was actually awake and hearing all of this. She looked around her to find that her companions had stirred in their blankets and were getting to their feet. Everywhere, the camp quickened with a bustle of activity as men-at-arms and knights rushed to pack up the roused bivouac. D'Aulon, his hair rumpled lopsidedly to one side of his head, walked over to where Jehanne still sat.

"Did you say we're going to Paris?" he asked. The others gathered around, as dumbstruck as Jehanne.

"We cannot assume that yet," the Bastard cautioned, "because our first destination is to be La Ferté. At the very least, we'll have to stay north of the Seine since there's no way to cross it. But don't be surprised if we end up at the walls of Paris yet!"

This was no joke, nor was it a dream. God, in His enigmatic way, had inspired the English to the very act that would assure their eventual defeat at the hands of God's own army!

A rush of exaltation surged through the half-asleep men. Jehan Darc whooped with joy, and he and his brother danced up and down, then laughingly embraced. Pasquerel made the Sign of the Cross and with a smile murmured a prayer of thanksgiving. His rivalry with Minguet set aside, Raymond put his arms around the younger boy and squeezed him so hard that he farted. Sieur de Metz grinned down at Jehanne and said, "Come on, get up, do you want to sit there all day?"

Jehanne scrambled to her feet. She was full of vigor now and impatient to be on the road. "When are we leaving?"

"As soon as we can strike camp"—d'Alençon grinned—"so we should get started, eh?"

After three months of soldiering they all knew their duties so thoroughly that it did not take more than a quarter of an hour to bring down the tent and ready the horses.

The army reached Château-Thierry by noon. After a brief respite within sight of the town's wall, Charles marched his army northwest to La Ferté. It was here that they encamped and the King received the expected delegation from Crépy-en-Valois. Jehanne deliberately stayed away from the meeting. This was Charles' hour of recognition, and she did not want her presence to detract from it. The King was most generous, having shared his coronation with her as he had, but she sensed that his pride was wounded when the people gave her the acclaim that should have gone to him. So she kept her distance from his magnificently appointed tent and instead celebrated with her companions an actual meal of roasted chicken, cheese, and bread, courtesy of the citizens of La Ferté.

She followed the same tactful policy the next morning on the road to Crépy. Charles did not seem particularly disappointed that she chose to ride between the Bastard and archbishop de Chartres rather than at his side. Back here, behind d'Alençon and de Rais and de Gaucourt, she could simply be one of the captains, and those who had come from their villages and farms to stand in the heat could see Charles, and Charles alone, without his having to vie with her for his subjects' attention. To ensure that that would be the case, she had discarded her armor and ordered Minguet to furl her banner. To an uninformed observer she was just another young soldier in a plain tunic and hose, actually a suit she had borrowed from Pierre.

People from miles around lined the road, cheering their new King. Most were peasants whose best clothes, the homespun dresses and tunics and handmade shoes, were scarcely identifiable as such. The curés among them held crudely painted pictures of the Holy Virgin and St.-Michel, Charles' personal patron, and they knelt and made the Sign of the Cross when the King rode past them. The people placed flowers in his path, covering the road with the lilacs and tuberoses they had picked from their gardens, along with the wild daisies their cattle would have grazed upon had Charles not chosen to ride this way.

"Noël!"

"God save our good King Charles!"

"God save France!"

Their good wishes resounded in a chorus, and Jehanne knew that what governed their thoughts was the knowledge that they would soon be free of Anglo-Burgundian bondage now that the King was marching on Paris.

"These are certainly good people." She smiled. "I've never seen people rejoice so much at the coming of such a noble king. I hope that I'll be lucky enough, when my life is over, to be buried here."

The archbishop lifted a bushy eyebrow. "Where do you hope to die, Jehanne?"

"Wherever it pleases God." She shrugged. "I don't know the time or the place any more than you do yourself." She looked at the clear sky and thought of her own people back in Domrémy. "I wish sometimes that now God might let me withdraw, so that I could take my brothers and return home to my parents."

She remembered her father's face when she said good-bye to him back in Reims. During the time she had been away from home, Jacques had become an old man. Had Maman changed so drastically as well, aged by the grief of separation?

"Noël!"

"God give you victory, King Charles!"

The praise warmed the King's ears. He raised a benevolent hand and waved to his subjects with a smile. No matter that the English had disrupted his return to Orléans. He was confident that the sieur Trémoïlle, riding at the King's side and therefore directly confronted with the adoring populace, could now see for himself that God intended Charles to gather his loyal towns to his breast. And perhaps this time Bourgogne would honor his agreement.

Things were going well. Very well indeed.

This supposition was fortified in Crépy, where Charles was yet again hailed by his worshipful subjects. As he rode through the gate, the crowds greeted him with an ardor that echoed his own exultation. The army of foot soldiers marching in his train waved to the people and brandished their swords and *guisarmes* above their heads triumphantly. The King received the keys to the city from smiling aldermen, who led him to the mayor's house for a bath and a sumptuous meal.

In the late afternoon he received an English herald bearing a most unexpected letter from the duke of Bedford. Certain that it was good news, he did not break the seal but summoned the captains to hear it read. The mayor's second-story office was too small to hold all of them. The junior commanders had to content themselves with standing in the doorway. When they were all assembled, Charles took his seat on the room's most prominent stool. Favoring them with a gracious smile, he ordered the Bastard to read Bedford's letter aloud.

The letter was not at all the peace offering Charles had expected. Bedford began with a denunciation of Charles' coronation, followed by a pointed nod at the Treaty of Troyes. He charged that the King had stolen through violence vast tracts of the realm belonging to Henry of England, aided by "a woman of a disorderly and infamous life and dissolute manners, dressed in the clothes of a man." He derided the King for a coward, and calling upon Heaven's succor, challenged him to timely battle.

At first dejected by the letter's tone, Charles was furious by the time his cousin finished reading it, so much so that he urged his shouting, angry captains to take the field against the English wherever they could be found. Royal honor demanded satisfaction.

Charles went first to Dammartin, where he left an advance guard to shield their rear, and then to Lagny-sur-Marne, six leagues from Paris. Near a small tributary of the Seine called the Biberonne their patrols came upon and skirmished with the English, but the encounter was fought to an impasse, and by nightfall Bedford had rolled back his battalions to Paris.

With nothing for the army to accomplish in that place, Charles brought them back to Crépy. He was in council with his commanders when the King's heralds returned with the news that Compiègne had obeyed his summons to surrender. Beauvais had likewise knelt to the royal couriers and its townsfolk had shouted, "Long live Charles, King of France!" The messengers reported that some of the Burgundian sponsors, including Pierre Cauchon, bishop of Beauvais, had left the town to the joyous Armagnac citizens rather than acclaim the King.

It did not matter, replied Charles. He was content to have a completely loyal Beauvais rather than one that nurtured traitors among those who loved him. A devoted city so close to Paris would join the others to shield his army's flanks.

The enemy were spotted a few days later on the Paris road, coming toward Senlis in a great cloud of dust. The King's spirits had been lifted after Bedford's letter by the royal heralds' receptions at Compiègne and Beauvais, and now he was bent more than ever on avenging the insult to his honor. When he learned that they were approaching, he deployed his army in a flat field between Montépilloy and the Nonette. It was a fortunate position. Nearby, an old ruin of a castle topped a small, wooded hill, and the view from the tower made it a perfect place to observe troop movements once they crossed the water. Hidden within the thick treeline, the Nonette passed the King's loyal Senlis further downstream.

As expected, the English did arrive with a strong company of the Paris garrison and Picards loyal to Bourgogne. After they had sharpened and positioned their stakes, the Armagnacs hurled insults at them into the coming night. For all Bedford's heroic words, he was not ready to engage in full battle against the King's army. When conflict came the next morning, it was in a disappointing series of mêlées which produced no conclusion.

Many on both sides were killed in hand-to-hand combat and the hail of arrows. At one point Trémoïlle fell off his horse and would have been taken prisoner had it not been for the rapid intercession of a squire. The Scotsmen fighting for France proved themselves in a teeth-gritting feast of hatred against the Picards led by Bedford. After they joined the day, there were no more prisoners taken on either side, and bloodlust stained the dusty ground that lay between them.

When the sun began to set for the second time in that spot, the enemy settled back into his fortification and lit fires behind the pointed bulwark that glowed eerily into the trees. The French shifted their positions so that a detachment of armor and crossbows guarded their front. Jehanne and the skirmishers pulled back behind them with the advance guard. The army made camp for the night and lit their own fires, and although Jehanne did not remove her armor, she lay on the ground with her head on a saddle. She slept, on and off.

The next morning, Charles returned to Crépy while his army remained behind to see what Bedford would do. At noon the English lord packed up his forces and marched them back across the Nonette, toward Paris. With the enemy gone, the armies of France followed their King to Crépy.

* * *

Jehanne shouldered her way through the tent's open entranceway and clattered toward the horse that d'Aulon was holding for her. Minguet had just finished arming her, and except for the helmet that she carried under one arm, she was ready to leave the field outside Compiègne's walls for St.-Denis. With the army saddled, d'Alençon and the Bastard were waiting for her to mount. Her household would strike her tent and catch up to the advance guard once they were on the road.

She had been much distracted and was not in a good mood. This morning in prayer she had asked for guidance, but her Counsel had been mute. She could not feel Them at all, even when she pleaded for some contact. That worried her. They had always been present before other battles, and a sense of unease had taken root while her page strapped the metal plates to her body. She tried to shake the loneliness and sense of defenselessness swarming like bats about her. Dread nevertheless lingered in the back of her mind even as she put a foot into the stirrup.

"Excuse me, Jehanne."

She stopped in mid-motion and brought her lifted foot back to the earth. A handsomely dressed man in a pale green linen tunic was standing next to her horse. A large hat perched above his long, narrow face, and the end of its hood hung over one eye. He smiled, offering her a piece of paper.

"Yes?" She was peeved at this intrusion which threatened to delay the entire army.

"I am Richard de Clermont," the man said with a small bow, "and I bring you a message from seigneur Jehan d'Armagnac."

Jehanne gave him an impatient grimace. This d'Armagnac, unlike his esteemed father, was no upholder of the Valois cause but a traitor whose own battalions were comprised of Bedford's veterans. She was irked to see his herald here.

"What do you want?" she demanded. "Can't you see that I'm leaving this place?"

"It will only take a moment for you to read this letter, will it not?" De Clermont's smile was a polite request.

"Very well," she sighed, "but you will have to read it to me as I cannot read myself."

The messenger broke the seal and unfolded the paper. D'Armagnac sent her his greetings in embarrassingly flowery terms, then explained that he was asking her opinion on a matter of utmost importance. Which Pope now living—Clement VII, Martin V, or Benedict XIV—was the true heir to St.-Pierre?

Jehanne was taken aback and for a moment could only stare at the man. She did not understand why d'Armagnac wanted her opinion. Although the question had long been under bitter debate when contrary claimants emerged to challenge the pontiff in Rome, the question had for some time now been settled in favor of Martin. This was a trivial matter.

She turned from de Clermont and swung up into the saddle. "When you hear that I'm in Paris," she said, looking down at him, "send another messenger to me and I'll give your master his answer. But I cannot think about that now." She looked at the young men who had followed her over the months as they began to dismantle her billowing tent. "The King's army is marching to Paris now, and I must go with them. When I get to the capital, I'll give seigneur d'Armagnac's question up to God for Him to answer."

Without a backward look she dug her heels into her horse's flank and he began to canter along with the rest of the cavalry across the abandoned field. It was a fine day for a journey. The weather was mild and the sun not too bright but partially hidden by large, fluffy clouds. God willing, it would not rain until after they had won their next and greatest victory.

They moved all afternoon through the grassy countryside, occasionally met by avid civilians who gathered to watch the mighty host pass and whose cheers filled the warriors with confident power. They reached St.-Denis within sight of the very walls of Paris just as night was beginning to fall and made camp near the holiest place in all of France, more sacred even than Reims.

It was there, in the earliest days of Christianity, that the Roman emperor had ordered Denis, bishop of Paris, beheaded. Through the grace of God, and as a mark of his sanctity, Denis picked up his own head, washed it in the Seine, then walked six thousand steps to the north, where he expired. The abbey of St.-Denis was established on the site of his death. In 639, Dagobert I was buried within its vaults, as was every subsequent French king. The monastery's hallowed walls housed the remains of those whose pact with God had created the great kings of France, from Pepin to St.-Louis to Charles the Wise.

Its loss to the English—and with it the sacred *Oriflamme*, the golden-dragoned banner that proclaimed the battlecry of France, "Montjoie Saint-Denis!"—had been a serious blow to the French soul. St.-Denis had sprung from them, was one of them, and his death tied them all to God through history. It was therefore most vital for the army to recover his sacred resting place before the kingdom could be healed.

Charles' army liberated the abbey on August 27. Jehanne ordered the soldiers to be confessed and then to attend the Mass that archbishop de Chartres celebrated in the cathedral of St.-Denis. She thanked the King of Heaven for having brought them so close to victory, and devoutly received Communion. But throughout the ceremony that should have filled her with the greatest exultation of her life, the feeling of dread clung to her and would not be banished. It dogged her even as she watched d'Alençon ride to Senlis to fetch the King.

The duc returned alone except for the guard he had taken with him. Charles would be along shortly, he said.

But two days lapsed before the King joined them. Two days, during which the army fretted and Jehanne practically lived on her knees before the statue of Our Lady that stood in majestic serenity before the cathedral altar. She neither ate nor drank anything throughout the first day. Instead, she prayed frantically for Their return.

Please, I beg you, do not desert me. I feel that I am as helpless as someone without eyes. If I have sinned, then tell me, but do not let me go forward without you.

They did not answer.

So she went to the abbey in search for Pasquerel. When she finally found him, he was deep in conversation with two abbés, in the middle of a long walkway bordered on one side by many rounded arches. He did not notice her at first because she approached him from the rear. But the friars saw the miserable-looking figure in light armor and broke off their sentences. She was only dimly aware of them.

Pasquerel turned to her, surprised. She had been so occupied with the army and her meetings with Charles that he seldom had an opportunity to speak to her lately. He smiled fondly. "Jehanne, how are you? What's wrong, my dear?" His graying eyebrows lifted in concern.

"May I speak to you alone, Brother?" There were circles beneath her eyes and she looked as though she would cry at any minute.

The monks bowed graciously and glided away from them. "What is it, Jehanne?" Pasquerel asked. "Has something happened to Jehan or Pierre?"

"No." She shook her head forlornly. "Oh, Brother Jehan, my Counsel have left me, I can't feel them any more!" Grief broke through the dam guarding her control and gushed from her eyes and nose. She shook with impassioned sorrow. "I don't know what to do, I don't know why I'm here. I don't know what I've done wrong that They would punish me like this!" She broke down and put her face into her hands. The wailing sobs echoed down the long, arched corridor.

Pasquerel put a tender arm around her shoulder and she wept into his chest. The monk patted the thick hair as though she were a kitten.

She began to hiccup, and he released himself from her grasp. He put a warm hand to her face. "Do you feel a little better now?"

She started to say, "Yes," but another hiccup grabbed her throat and made her swallow the word. She nodded.

"Have you prayed for guidance, Jehanne?"

The question took her off guard. "Yes!" she answered, frustrated and angry again. "I've prayed and I've prayed, but They're gone, I tell you!"

"Dear Jehanne," the monk said softly, "don't you know how fortunate you have been to have heard them at all? Don't you realize that most people go throughout their lives and do not ever hear them?"

She stared at him, stunned.

"I have never heard them," he admitted, sounding almost bitter. "I have spent my life hoping that I would, but God has not blessed me with that gift." He touched her cheek again and wiped away an emerging tear. "He did bless you with it, Child of God, and it may yet return. Did you not say that they told you that they would be with you always?"

She nodded. "That's what They said. But I must have offended Them, or God, or They would not have left me!"

"Perhaps they have not left you. Perhaps you just simply cannot hear them?"

Her head shook emphatically. "If They were with me, I would feel Them; I can always feel Them when They're with me."

"Very well, let's assume that is true," he allowed, fully aware that it would be useless to argue with her. Once she had something in her mind, she would never let go of it. "It does not necessarily mean that they have gone because you have sinned."

"What else could it mean?" she demanded. She was once more becoming angry—angry at him for not understanding the depths of her distress, angry at herself for having committed some elusive sin.

"Listen to me, Jehanne," Pasquerel said gravely, taking both her hands in his. "The most important thing I have learned during my years as a monk I have learned here." He put a hand over his heart. "And it is this: God sometimes tests us by bringing upon us misfortunes that we do not deserve and that are not the results of our sins. If you search your soul to its deepest levels and can honestly say that you have not sinned, then you must surely know that God is testing you for some great purpose of His own." The light that bound his eyes to hers and the even-tempered, simple voice hummed comfortingly.

"I do not believe that your saints have abandoned you"—he smiled—"but even if they have, it does not mean that God has deserted you as well. Perhaps this is a test of faith that God has devised for you, to see if you will hold to what they have told you before."

"I see," she responded, as slowly as a sleepwalker. "They have told me many hopeful things. They said Paris shall be free and give its loyalty to the King. They said that he will drive the English back across the sea."

"Then you must believe them. God's messengers would not lie to you. You must hold to your faith."

She tried to smile at him. "Thank you, Brother. I feel much better now."

He embraced her and patted her shoulder. "Do not worry so."

She continued to feel better as she went to her horse. She needed to see to the army before the sun went down.

But once released from the peaceful atmosphere of the abbey, Jehanne's unease flamed into a shortened temper. When she returned to the bivouac at La Chapelle, a hundred little things seemed to plot against her. Although they were near enough to Paris for them to see its spires and rooftops on the other side of the overwhelmingly monstrous wall, Charles' enthusiasm had been only lukewarm since his arrival from Senlis, and Jehanne was very angry that he did not show greater leadership and appreciation for his position. A further nuisance was his turning over command of the entire army to Trémoïlle. She could not yell at the King for having appointed Trémoïlle constable, so she lit into a hapless Raymond for not polishing her armor as she wanted it done.

Worst of all, she finally lost her temper altogether when she spotted a prostitute from Compiègne trying to importune her men-at-arms. For the first and only time, Jehanne drew Ste.-Catherine's sword and ran at the painted woman with a yell. She could hear the men laughing as the woman looked up in alarm to see Jehanne charging toward her. The campfollower turned to run but was not fast enough to avoid the blow that the flat of the sword gave to her backside.

The soldiers' loud amusement became suddenly hushed, and they found themselves gazing in horror at the ground.

Well over half of the long blade lay glinting in the dust. It had broken slightly above the handle that Jehanne held in her stunned fist. She stared at it stupidly, unable to believe that she was actually seeing the unevenly shattered weapon.

This was unthinkable. Ste.-Catherine's sword could not break! A cold wind whistled through her soul and seemed to blow Catherine away from her to some unreachable place.

It was an evil omen. Jehanne could see in the faces of the soldiers that they knew it, too. They muttered among themselves, then slowly dispersed.

Charles was distressed when she related to him what had happened. He crossed himself, then told her that she should have used a stick instead of the sword. It was something she had already told herself, but his bad-tempered reproof stung nevertheless. Yet nothing was as profoundly disturbing as the loss of the sword itself. Catherine had given it to her at the start of her mission as a mark of God's trust and His blessing. She could not feel Them any more, and now the sword was gone.

Jehanne returned to the basilica and flung herself at the altar rail.

What have I done wrong? she cried, tearfully desperate. Why have you withdrawn from me when you promised time and again that you would always be with me? How have I offended you, or God?

Panic raced through her stomach and pulsed in her folded hands, so tightly squeezed together that her knuckles whitened and fingernails dug into her palms. She propped her forehead against her fist. These portents were the very worst that could have occurred, and for an instant she considered abandoning the attack. She would ride back to camp and tell the King and his captains that they must postpone taking Paris. Until when? She did not know. What could she possibly tell them? Her Counsel had left her, but she did not dare reveal that. There was a chance that They would return if she was patient. In the meantime she had to persuade the army to withdraw.

When she did rejoin the company a few hours later, however, and was back to the affairs of war, she felt her resolve wear away around the edges until it blinked out of sight. She would go forward and take Paris. Her fear was only an illusion. Brother Pasquerel, the wisest man she knew, was certainly correct; it was a test from God. The army of Charles was the army of God, the King of Heaven, and she could not yield to fears created by the Devil to distract her from her mission. She would lead God's hosts to victory once more.

As the sun descended to the horizon, scouting parties ringed the walls of Paris in preparation for the war council. Jehanne reconnoitered the city with d'Alençon, while the Bastard, the comtes de Verdôme and de Bourbon, and Sainte-Sévère took a troop to explore the other side of the capital across the river.

It was a squad commanded by the brothers Laval, Gilles de Rais, and La Hire who found what they determined was the weakest spot, at the Swine Market near the Porte de St.-Honoré. The army positioned their horses and guns where the dawn would find them ready for the assault. In the dim light made brighter by campfires, archers toned their bows and squires sharpened and polished countless swords. Men-at-arms stripped to the waist and cut down trees and bundled them into the fascines that would be hurled into the moats. Darkness had settled upon them by the time the commanders aimed the cannon at the place they hoped to breach when morning came again.

When she was satisfied that everything was readied for battle, Jehanne returned to the abbey of St.-Denis. She kept vigil before the many-candled altar until dawn, as became a soldier on the eve of momentous conflict.

BOOM!!!

The explosion shook the ground beneath the huge cannon and an instant later a smattering of bricks blasted from a place just above the Porte de St.-Honoré, causing debris and dust to rain down before the barricade the Parisians had constructed. But Jehanne could see, when the smoke cleared a little, that the damage was slight and the barricade still held.

She was not at all surprised. The gate at the bottom of the city wall could easily allow the passage of three very large wagons, or twenty men marching shoulder-to-shoulder. St.-Honoré was thickly fortified by reinforced brickwork and two portcullises, between which were recently built earthworks. The wall that ascended above it was at least fifty-five or so feet high, and on its ramparts men swarmed like ants in great numbers.

Jehanne turned her attention to the area separating the army from Paris. In front of their position was a system of moats. The closest was a dry gully perhaps eight feet deep that gradually rose to a high embankment known as the Donkey's Back. On the other side of that a pool of standing water soaked the mossy feet of the citywall. It was of formidable construction, more than sixty feet across, and its unknown depth summoned a pang of concern to Jehanne's mind. If the water was over a man's head, they would have to work very hard for three days or more to fill that monster with enough fascines to hold the scaling ladders. Still, it could be done. She did not doubt that in God's time Paris would fall.

But in her time there was an alternative to the ladders. She looked back over her shoulder toward the big cannon positioned upon the hill above her battalion. Behind it, the knoll descended to a level plain, and it was there that d'Alençon and the comte de Bourbon were waiting with the advance guard. A similar detachment was deployed at the Porte de St.-Denis. Because both gates were lightly defended, compared to others, and guarded permanent roads rather than drawbridges, it was possible that the army could enter the city by destroying the portals' fortifications, making the ladders unnecessary. The cannon would first blast through the portcullises and earthworks, then the regularly paced waves of skirmishers would attack the garrison. If all went as planned, the attackers would draw the *goddons* toward the advance guard, who would fall upon them in the trap.

Jehanne signaled the artillerymen with her banner. Another ground-shaking blast rang in her ears, this time shattering the first portcullis into hundreds of wooden pieces. A cheer went up from the skirmishers as the artillerymen began the reloading process. When they were ready, they sent another missile at the gate and the blast evoked a hail of earthern clumps together with screams of pain.

"Now is the time," Jehanne shouted to the mounted men under her command. "Go, go!" She accompanied her instructions with a broad wave of her arm.

A squad of forty detached themselves from the other soldiers and took off down the ridge. When they reached the road, they swung to the left and galloped, howling, across the wide moats, their weapons glinting in the sunlight. They dashed through St.-Honoré and Jehanne lost sight of them, though she could hear the ringing of engaged weapons and cries from the stricken.

She could tell that the fighting was heavy and regretted that she could not be there to give them heart. Against her will and her better judgment, Pasquerel, d'Alençon, the Bastard, and all the others had persuaded her to swear before God that she would not skirmish at the gate but would instead direct the attack from a safe distance. Her household, all of them, including Metz and Poulengy, were now clustered about her, and as she strained to watch the first assault she chafed at the promise made in a moment of weakness. Her men needed her encouragement while they fought hand-to-hand with the English devils.

The horsemen were being pushed back through the gate, and their swords flashed in furious, desperate swipes as they strained to stay mounted. Jehanne yelled to the trumpeter, "Blow retreat!"

The horn's three-note shriek was repeated twice in rapid succession, and the remaining warriors, fifteen or twenty of them, cantered wearily back across the bridge, bearing their wounded. Although the defenders high upon the wall shouted in triumph, those behind the gate made no attempt to pursue them.

Jehanne waved her standard to signal the next wave of riders. They dashed pellmell toward the city as the first had done and like their comrades met with savage obstinacy from the English. They fought for some time before they were beaten back.

When the survivors returned to their battalion, Jehanne rested all of them for about half an hour before she sent in the next troop. As she watched her fresh knights pushed a third of the way back across the bridge, she knew that the direct path would be useless. The attempt to breach the St.-Honoré and enter the city by road was having little effect. Nor would the enemy take the bait and follow the skirmishers into d'Alençon's trap. They would have to cross the moat after all. It was fortunate that the army had cut so many trees into fascines.

She turned to look at the wood-laden wagons upon the hill above her position and saw Trémoïlle riding toward them. She groaned. He was formally in command of the army, and she knew that he had come to harry her.

"Here he comes," Metz murmured, "right on time."

Jehanne had told them all that he would show up sooner or later, probably sooner, to hold her to accounts if Paris did not fall without delay. He surely knew that it would take time, but his enmity was so potent that he would use any excuse to halt the attack.

Trémoïlle's horse picked his way down the slope with careful steps. Ever since he was unhorsed at the Nonette, the constable had taken pains not to hurry anywhere. The animal jumped to level ground and started toward Jehanne, its obese rider bouncing heavily upon the saddle with every trot. Trémoïlle was outfitted in an old suit of plain armor, and his swollen face poked up through it.

He drew rein and smiled pleasantly enough but did not dismount. "How is the attack proceeding here?"

346

"We have sent three assaults across and are preparing another," Jehanne responded calmly.

"Have the enemy attempted to pursue the lure?"

"No."

"How many men have you lost?" Trémoïlle's smile was no longer friendly, and she knew what was coming.

Even so, she would not lie. "About thirty-five, I think."

He shook his head, clicking his tongue. "That will not do, not at all." He sighed as though filled with genuine regret. "Things are going no better at the Porte de St.-Denis, I'm afraid. They have lost more than fifty men. This city is impregnable"—he gazed at the wall in frank admiration—"and so I am going to counsel the King that he break off the endeavor to take it."

"There is still the moat," Jehanne insisted. "What we are going to do next is bring the faggots to the water and throw them in. When the moat is filled with them, we'll bring across the scaling ladders and climb the walls."

"I see," the constable smirked, looking down from his horse disdainfully, "and how deep is the water?"

"We don't know that yet," she admitted. "We'll find out when we get there."

Trémoïlle's cheeks jiggled as he shook his head. "I cannot sanction that. It would take a long time even if it were possible, and the King is in a hurry to have this done or abandoned. Why, you don't know how deep the moat is, it could be very deep indeed, so deep that it would take a forest to fill it! How many months do you think it would take just to get the ladders to the walls? Even if you can fill it, don't you see how many men there are up there?" He pointed a stubby finger toward the battlement. "I can assure you that they are ready to rain hot oil upon us and heavy stones and so many arrows that our losses would be inestimable." His last few words came out in a wheeze.

"And if the moat is shallow, we can ford it in no time at all," Jehanne parried. "As for the wall, our cannon can blow a breach into it if we endure. We have plenty of gunpowder and cannonballs. When the breach is large enough, the army can pour into it as they did at Jargeau." Her jaw jutted with conviction and she fixed him in a resolute stare. "We can take Paris if we do it right."

The skirmishers had noticed the heated discussion and now all of them surrounded Jehanne's household and the constable. He glanced at their frowning, exhausted faces contemptuously, as though they were cattle.

"That plan will take too long," he said. "I am calling off the attack."

An angry rumble from the men startled his horse, and Trémoïlle caught the front of his saddle in an instinctive clutch.

"We're here to fight, Chancellor!" someone shouted.

"That's right!"

"We want to try it!" Their voices rose in a hostile wave and in a moment they were all shouting at once.

Trémoïlle had not counted upon a defiance of his authority, that was apparent by the way his eyes bulged. But then he held up his hands in a command for silence, and their forceful protests died down and, at length, stopped. A slow smile spread across the pie-shaped face. "Very well," he said. "You may commence your attack of the wall."

The soldiers cheered and waved their swords. The constable looked down at Jehanne. "But if your attempt is not successful, I will break it off. Do you understand?"

"Perfectly." She smiled. We shall succeed, my lord constable, she thought grimly. Just give us enough time.

He turned his horse around and trotted back to the footpath up the hill. Jehanne waved her standard to the loaded wagons, and they began their descent to the edge of the first moat.

"I'm going to the water," she told her household. "I want to see how deep it is."

"Then we're going with you," d'Aulon insisted.

"No. I want all of you to stay back here."

"Jehanne, you promised before the Holy Virgin," reminded Pasquerel.

She grinned, a glimmer of her old self returning. "No, I didn't. I only promised to stay away from the gates. None of you mentioned the moat."

"This is insane!" Poulengy swore. "I'll go test the water, you stay back here."

"No," she repeated more forcefully than before. "If you want to make yourselves useful, then help the men-at-arms unload the wagons and pass the fascines across this dry ditch. I'm going to the water alone."

"At least take one of us," d'Aulon begged.

"Very well." She looked at each of them. "I'll take Raymond to carry my standard." She snatched the lance from Pierre's grasp.

"Hey!"

"You won't need it, Pierrolot, but I might." She had to have a weapon of some sort. This one would do now that she no longer had Catherine's sword. "Come on, get to it," she urged, "these men need help." She pointed to the infantry who were busily emptying the wagons.

Her companions grumbled but obeyed and moved toward the wagons. Minguet looked wistfully at her over his shoulder as he went.

"Come on," she said to Raymond.

The boy took her standard and followed her into the dry moat, past the men who were ferrying the bundles of bound wood above their heads to the receivers on the Donkey's Back. Although the ditch was deep, its slope was at an incline that made it possible for one to scale it without too much difficulty. Jehanne dug her boots into the grassy soil and, leaning forward, grabbed at the earth that angled above her. It was a slow climb, but she reached the summit on her hands and knees, and stood up between two men who were stacking the fascines into handy piles. She reached down and took the banner that Raymond held up to her, then extended her free hand for him to grab. She pulled him from the ditch's mouth, and when he was standing beside her, she gave the standard back to him.

She saw, now that she was here at the water's edge, that it did not change gradually from dry land to water as other moats sometimes did. There was hardly any bank at all, just a sharp drop into water. If it were deep, over a man's head, the weight of his armor would pull him to the bottom, drowning him. She would have to test it with her lance. First things first, she thought.

The wood bearers were not moving very quickly or with much zeal, and there were not enough men on this bank to hurl the fascines. Their motions were almost clocklike and wanting of the high-spirited rage they had shown at Orléans. They had defied Trémoïlle for love of her, but their hearts were not in it. For a moment, she faltered as the realization hit her. She remembered their horrified, slack-jawed responses to her broken sword. She remembered their fear and felt her own return.

You will not do this, she told herself. "Come on, men of France and of God, put some strength into it!" she yelled. "God has promised that Paris shall be free of the English and shall return to our good King's rule! Be of good cheer and know that God is with us in this holy struggle!"

She swung around and looked at the small figures clumped together upon the wall. "In God's name, surrender this place to the true King of France!"

"Slut!"

"Armagnac whore!"

She did not hear them because she was half-turned toward the fascine stacks. But in the next instant a sharp jab struck her right thigh, and she lost her balance.

She fell onto her side and stared unbelieving at the arrow protruding through her armor. She was slightly aware of the jubilant whirlwind coming from the wall. And something else. Someone other than herself was screaming.

She looked up at Raymond. He still held the banner but his right foot was fastened to the ground by a crossbow bolt. He could feel but not see the arrow from the confines of his helmet, so he lifted his visor and reached down to pull it out.

He was in a semi-crouched position when he was hit between the eyes. The backward motion of his body yanked his foot free from the earth, and he fell with a heavy crash.

"Raymond!"

Jehanne pushed herself to him. He had landed with his head twisted beside a stack of wood now bristling with arrows. The bolt had struck him just above his nose, and a river of blood ran into eyes that stared sightlessly at the cannon smoke. His lips were parted slightly. He looked astonished.

"Raymond," she moaned tearfully. She touched his bloody chin.

He could not be dead, it was not supposed to be this way! She always prayed that her intimate band should come to no harm, and her Counsel had never even hinted that any of them could perish. This was not possible. The bolt that she saw with her own eyes could not be real. None of this could be real, not even the arrow digging deep into her flesh, numbing her foot. It was a nightmare like the others and soon she would wake up.

She made the Sign of the Cross over him. "Pater Noster, qui es in Coelis . . ."

Strong hands suddenly grabbed her arms and began to drag her away from him. "Let me go!" she yelled, "I wasn't finished!"

Five or six of the woodbearers lifted her over the Donkey's Back and passed her to the many others who had been working in the dry ditch. No one was left alive on the other side. The unexpected onslaught of arrows had killed seven men besides Raymond, and the others had scrambled down into the safety of the first moat.

They laid her on her back against the bottom slope. One of the men removed her helmet and put it on the ground next to her. "Give her some air, now," a large fellow said. He was shirtless, and his stout torso glistened with dirt and sweat. He pushed the men back, then grinned at her with brown teeth. "Hey, that wound's not so bad, Jehanne. I've seen worse."

He went down next to her on one knee, and she was overwhelmed by the sickening odor he exuded. She was going to faint or throw up and her mind could not feel.

"Jehanne!"

Pasquerel was running down the moat toward her and behind him her other companions. The monk reached her first and knelt beside her. "Jehanne, we saw you fall! How bad is it?"

"I don't know," she answered through gritted teeth. It was really hurting now and would have to come out soon before it had a chance to fester. If that happened, she could lose her leg.

The others arrived and at once Metz and Poulengy pushed the soldiers back away from her. D'Aulon hunched down across from Pasquerel. "Let me see it," he ordered capably. "Come, Minguet, help me."

She looked up at the sky. Thick black smoke was moving like a dragon across the heavens, parting every now and then for a glimpse of fluffy clouds. Jehanne knew that it was still a hot day, but she was suddenly cold.

They unbuckled the plate at her hip and knee. D'Aulon lifted it very slowly over the arrow and gave it to Minguet. The boy was ashen; even his lips were pale. He was staring at the bloody legging and the arrow that seemed sprung from her thigh like a dark tree. D'Aulon ripped the soaked garment apart to examine her pierced flesh. He probed the angry red area gently, frowning all the while in concentration. He quickly removed his belt and wrapped it around her hip, then yanked hard on it to slow the bloody torrent.

He bent toward her and said, "Jehanne, I must remove the bolt. It's in there pretty deep, so it's going to hurt. Do you hear me?"

She nodded. His voice seemed far away and as dreamlike as the rest of it.

"Here." He shoved a bit of wood at her, part of a branch that someone had ripped from a bundle. "Put this between your teeth."

She opened her mouth and took it. The clouds were more visible now and they glided far above in the silence in a place where there was no fighting, and she felt that she could drift up to them, forever and ever.

She was wrenched back to earth by an almost unbearable agony. She screamed, biting down hard on the stick.

D'Aulon's fist was wrapped around the gruesome missile. It was nearly eight inches long, and well over half of it was soaked in blood.

"It's a clean wound," he reassured her. "The arrowhead is rounded, not barbed, so it did not take any flesh with it."

She could no longer control her nausea and rolled over onto her side to purge her stomach. She felt a little better and collapsed onto her back.

Metz leaned over her. "How is she?" he asked d'Aulon.

"She's lost a lot of blood. We need to get her to the abbey."

"No!" she shouted, outraged that they were talking about her as though she were not even there. "I won't go anywhere. I'm going to stay here and rally the men."

"Jehanne, the battle is lost," Poulengy said softly. He hunkered down and stroked her hair. "They haven't had any better luck at the Porte de St.-Denis, and you can bet that Trémoïlle will call it off now." He hesitated and looked around him at the others for support. "And the men are afraid. They look at the size and strength of those walls and they know they cannot take it."

She tried to sit up but could not. "That's why I need to stay here, to give them the will to fight. We *can* take it, I know we can! We just need time, that's all."

They argued with her for a long time, past sunset, but she was adamant. She would not be moved. If they worked through the coming darkness, she said, the English would not be able to see well enough to shoot at them and they could fill the moat. And if they worked all night, they could surprise the enemy before dawn.

She fainted in the middle of a sentence and did not revive until she felt herself being lifted from the ground. When she opened her eyes, she saw that she was being carried like a child by seigneur de Gaucourt. She tried to struggle but was too weak to resist his muscled arms.

"Let me go," she pleaded, "you don't understand, we could take it, we could take it."

They hoisted her from the ditch and placed her into waiting arms that carried her to a wagon. Her confessor, squire, and remaining page got into it with her. Metz and Poulengy mounted their horses and together with her brothers brought her back to the holy abbey of St.-Denis.

They took her to the guesthouse and the monks summoned women from the town to wash her. Off came the grimy, blood-crusted armor, then her tunic, rancid with perspiration and the crimson waste of war. They spoke in low whispers and she did not catch most of what they said. "So young," "What a shame," and little more.

The room spun around, boiling in her brain, chilling her limbs, and she was hardly aware of the bed. She fell into a deep hole where d'Alençon shouted at her, but she passed him and glided through a tunnel that never seemed to stop.

Without warning she felt the surface of the room come at her, and there was a babble of voices and a cool damp cloth to quench the fire in her head. A loving hand touched her brow, but she could not see far enough up the arm to tell who it was. The image washed right through her and she plummeted back into the underground vault where darkness waited like a womb.

It was comfortable down here in the land of spectral memories and half-wished choices. Maman was kneading a large loaf of bread with vigorous punches, and every now and then Jhanette added flour to the growing mound. At the end of the room the hearth radiated an early, monotonous peace.

Suddenly, flags and trumpets flew across her vision and stole her mother away. Jehanne wept, desperately straining to find her, but she was lost in a bewildering mist and could only hear herself saying, "Noble Dauphin, I am Jehanne the Maid from the village of Domrémy in the duchy of Lorraine. . . ."

"Jehanne? Jehanne, are you awake?" She could feel consciousness in the shallows, telling her that she was not able to remain down here. The images were receding, merging into the world that it was time for her to leave.

She opened her eyes to morning and saw shapes standing over her. She blinked the fog away until she was able to see them clearly.

Her brother Jehan was sitting on a stool next to her bed. His face was unshaven and gaunt, and beneath his eyes bulged large circles. Sadness clung to his mouth, but his look was one of relief. Pierre knelt next to him, and she saw that he was holding her hand. The others bunched around her, d'Aulon seated to her right, across from Jehan. Minguet's eyes were as red from weeping as two raging coals.

Poor boy, she thought, he quarreled often with Raymond and now he's haunted by guilt. "Raymond is dead," she tried to whisper.

The import of her words climbed to her throat in a lump, then spilled down her cheeks. Raymond is dead, she repeated to herself, Raymond is dead.

Jehan nodded. "We know," he said, pushing a strand of hair from her forehead. "We were able to recover his body and bring him here. The monks gave him a Christian burial with a High Mass. He was very brave, Jehanne. He died well."

She put a hand over her face and began to sob. No one said anything, but let her feel her grief. The gash in her leg bit her and she wailed in remembrance of her night terrors.

Jehan moved to a place beside her on the bed and folded his arms around her. His embrace was strong and comforting; she could feel his devotion in his knotted muscles. But it was not enough. Something had ended, and neither his gentle, rocking arms nor the careful kiss that brushed across her hair could bring it back.

She pulled away from him and as she lay down the room began to sway again. "I'm sorry, I'm very tired," she sniffed, wiping her nose on the bedsheet.

"We'll go now, Jehanne; you get some rest." Pasquerel lifted a scholarly hand and blessed her from the end of the bed.

D'Aulon kissed her hand and smiled at her. Then he bent over her and put warm lips to her cheek. "We'll be back later, when you're stronger," he whispered. He moved away from her and Minguet came forward shyly. He touched her hair, then swiftly stooped and kissed her, and she felt a warm tear drop onto her brow.

They all approached her, one by one. Metz was last, and Jehanne knew even through her pain that he had put himself at the end on purpose. He put on his old joking posture and leaning over her, nibbled her earlobe in a kiss. His breath warmed her skin, and the next thing she heard was, "You know you're the only woman I'll ever worship." His voice was so low that she thought she had imagined it.

She must have. Because now he was grinning at her from his careless height. "Now, don't give these monks any trouble, Jehanne," he said with mock sternness. "They have enough to do without chasing you all over the place."

She gave him a sad smile and reached out toward him. He extended his hand and she put her lips to the hairy knuckles. "God keep you safe, dear Metz."

"And you." He turned away quickly and she knew he was no longer grinning.

All of them were gone now except Jehan. He was still sitting on the bed, and his arm lay casually across her shoulder. "Do you want me to go, or would you rather I stay with you while you sleep?"

"What's happening on the battlefield?"

"When we left, the captains were in council."

"Have they started leaving yet?"

"No."

That meant it didn't have to end, there was still hope! She had been taken from the field too early; if she had stayed, she could have rallied the army. They could have filled the moat before the sun came up, then pounded the stubborn wall until they drove a breach into it. It could still be done. She just needed to rest a little first.

"Then stay for a bit. I want you to wake me in a couple of hours."

He looked at her, mildly surprised. "Why?"

"Because I want to go back down there."

"You can't do that!" he cried. "You're wounded."

"I was wounded at Orléans and I was back in the saddle the next day!" She was fully conscious now and able to see the way he recoiled from her anger. "Wake me in a couple of hours, no more."

"But I promised Maman and Papa that I'd look after you!"

"They're not here, Jehan." She rolled over with her back to him and went to sleep.

When the coming autumn darkness began to creep over the roof of the abbey, the monks of St.-Denis sat down to their stark supper of fish and hard bread. As was customary, the abbé went to the end of the trestle where they were eating and took his place behind a low rostrum. He opened the large, leather-bound Holy Book in front of him and began to read the beautifully crafted Latin.

He had been abbé of this sacred place for a long time and a mere friar for longer than that, and he knew by heart vast portions of what he was reading. It gave him pleasure nonetheless to be able to caress with his failing eyes the Divine Word made manifest in the even, black markings whose neat order was illuminated by the flights of angels. He loved the delicate vellum, as silky as the voice of God. It was a Voice he felt flow through him when he read aloud for his fellow monks and for the frequent guests who came here on pilgrimage.

His cowled brother friars ate in disciplined silence, just as they did every night throughout their lives. They did not look at one another, nor did they smile, or nudge one another under the table. None of them let their eyes roam to the rounded ceiling, only half-hearing what he read. The friars knew what was expected of them and behaved within those limits. The abbé had not known until the Maid and her young men arrived how colorless his evening meals had been.

When she first came here, Jehanne was always attentive when he started reading, but soon enough one of the youths would goad her into losing her concentration. Although none of the young people dared speak aloud, they used hand gestures and facial expressions to communicate—to an unfortunate degree for the abbé, who found his own diligence lapse. He quickly recovered, smiling inside at the guilelessness of youth.

But that was before the unfortunate attempt to take Paris. Now, Jehanne's household took their meals apart from their hosts and at an earlier time. The boy Raymond's death had aged and numbed all of them, but the abbé knew that there was more to the funereal solitude into which they had fled than their comrade's passing. Hearsay had it that the King had called off the assault on the capital, ruling that the Parisians were too committed to Philippe de Bourgogne to surrender. Wild rumors raged that Charles would order his army to burn and pillage the city if he captured it. The people, raving with fear, had fought like minions from Hell and the invader had withdrawn.

So Jehanne stayed in her room most of the time now, and the abbé rarely saw her. He prayed that she would overcome her blackness of spirit. Having so faithfully served Him, she deserved the peace of God.

At that moment she was in the basilica, stacking her armor before the statue of Our Lady to the left of the high altar. She took the battered helmet from Minguet and rubbed her thumb across a scratch. How beautiful the armor had once been, long ago when everything was new. She could still see her rounded reflection in the helmet, but now a dent halved it and the scarred veteran who looked back at her was a stranger.

She put it on top of the disassembled pile and stepped back a couple of paces. She raised her sights to the haughty, vacant-eyed stare of the Virgin, and the Holy Child who sat on His mother's lap with his right arm outstretched. Behind the rail to the left of the statue, Pepin le Bref and his wife Berte, and Charles Martel and Clovis II, had slept peacefully through the centuries. They were all there, those departed Kings of France and their families: Clovis II and Philippe le Hardi and Charles V, the last attended in death, as he had been on earth, by his loyal constable Bertrand du Guesclin, whose effigy lay at his feet. Their ghosts flitted through the silence, unmindful of both the delicately lovely curtain of stained glass which bathed the choir in colored light, and of the condition of their former, bleeding kingdom.

Jehanne knelt slowly. Crossing herself, she stretched out her arms in tribute to the Holy One on the crucifix above the altar. Her companions were at the rail behind her, lost in the depths of their own desolation. A sunbath of colors from the transept's round window, depicting the Signs of the Zodiac with God in the center, fell upon them as though in a blessing, but none noticed.

It had failed. Even after Jehanne dragged herself from her bed and returned to rally d'Alençon to a renewed fight; even after Montmorency, the primary baron of Paris, arrived with sixty of his knights to give Charles' army aid; even after all that, the King had sent Trémoïlle to the battle site with an order to retreat. The baron protested, claiming that he had risked his life by bringing his gentlemen to fight for the King. His opinion was supported by the others, most eagerly by Jehanne and d'Alençon. Outnumbered, Trémoïlle had yielded.

They were still positioning the cannon when young René d'Anjou and the comte de Clermont arrived to tell them they must stop the assault, upon orders of the King. Bleeding again from her freshly opened wound, Jehanne had banished her pain and ridden to the King's encampment to plead with him.

He stood steadfast. He was withdrawing his army and, furthermore, would disband it now. He was tired of war, he complained; he wanted to end it peacefully. None of Jehanne's reminders of his destiny nor her tears could dissuade him.

Outside the King's tent, d'Alençon had taken Jehanne aside and in a whispered conference they agreed that the next day they would return to the city on their own and attack it one last time. To that end, d'Alençon had ordered his men to construct a crude bridge to span the Seine; it would be their way into Paris.

But someone must have overheard them and talked. Somehow, Trémoïlle must have gotten wind of the coming battlefield rebellion. Because when Jehanne and the duc, hopeful for battle, arrived the following morning at the place where the bridge should have been, they found that it had been disassembled during the night at the King's command. He had turned Paris over to the Burgundians and the *goddons* after destroying the bridge that could have given him back his capital.

That was the end of it. Charles was ordering Jehanne to return immediately to St.-Denis, and the next morning she was to accompany him to Senlis.

D'Alençon had told her that she must not lose heart. He swore that she was not to blame as some in the army were muttering. But now, as she held her rigid arms toward Heaven, she blamed herself. She offered this small penance up to Lord Jhesus and all the saints for her wicked sins. Her Counsel had not consented to her attack on Paris, and she should never have ignored Their silence. Had They not told her from the first that the Devil would come to her through her own impatience? They had tried to pound that into her head from the time she was thirteen, and now in the most crucial time of her life she had forgotten it. Because of her unwillingness to wait until she could persuade the King to renew the conflict, the chance to take Paris was lost forever. Paris was lost, and Raymond and all the others had died for nothing. All because of her.

Her arms stiffened and began to ache. She looked up at Him whose death had redeemed the world, unmoved by the beautiful stained glass that arched toward the vault above the crucifix.

Forgive me, my Lord, I have failed. You sent me to save this kingdom for You, and I have failed. I can never forgive myself for my weakness and stupidity. I cannot forgive myself for having been unworthy for such a holy mission. Oh, God, Whose love will save the world, help me to make atonement!

Tears cascaded once more down her sunburned skin and dropped onto the stone beneath her knees. She would hold her arms out in disregard of the agony until she fainted. She deserved nothing less.

Her armor gleamed on the floor in vanquished splendor. It would remain here always as her renunciation of arms, something knights did when they were wounded in battle. The sacrifice gave thanks to God for having spared them to fight again another day, and also signified that they had offered their lives for this kingdom of France. It was the most precious thing she had ever owned, but she would not need it again.

CHAPTER TWELVE

In the Company of Women

September 12–December 31, 1429

ate afternoon sunlight fell in an airy blanket upon the stone floor of the King's chapel, unfolding steadily until Jehanne's knees grew warm. She could feel it through her hose, a hot tingle upon her thigh gradually spreading to her waist. But her mind was upon the crucifix above her head, and she was for the most part unaware of her body. Had she been less intent, she might have heard laughter from the courtiers drifting upward through the chapel window, for down in the courtyard Charles had told a joke to a lighthearted audience and now was the pleased center of attention. He had chosen not to linger at St.-Denis but hurried here to his castle at Gien a week ago.

On the heels of her defeat, Jehanne's heart had raged against Trémoïlle for his treachery. If he had not run to Charles with news of d'Alençon's bridge, they still could have taken the city and the losses would not have been in vain. For a little while that was all Jehanne could think about, and in the time following their retreat from Paris she nursed a bitter hatred. But a change had come over her during the past two days, almost without her knowing it and without her consent.

Where at first she had fallen to sleep angry and wakened just as angry, more recently she noticed that her wrath did not hang about through her days no matter how hard she tried to hold it to her. It had come to her only this morning that she must cease her struggles against those things that she did not have the power to alter. Raymond was dead. Paris was lost. The King's ministers detested her. Those were inescapable facts, and there was nothing that she could do to change any of them. The only thing she could do was accept the will of God. She knew that now.

In the first few days after Paris the constant questions she had flung to her Counsel simply sped past her, remaining unanswered. That threw her into a whirlpool of dismay and she had blamed herself.

That did not last. After wallowing in self-reproach for an agonizing day and night during which she could neither eat nor sleep, she had become angry at

Them for Their disavowal, every bit as angry as she was with Trémoïlle. Why had They brought her this far only to snatch away Their support when she needed Them most? Had she not done everything as They had commanded?

Finding only a taunting silence in answer to her anguish, she had railed against Them for Their betrayal of her faith. They were playing games with her and in the loneliness of Their abandonment she had despised Them for it. When she remembered Pasquerel's words that perhaps Their silence was a test of faith, she quarreled with that in her head, scornfully rejecting it. God would have no cause to so torment one who had proven her faith time and time again and had served Him with such steadfastness. *She* had not failed; *They* had failed her. God had failed her.

But now she was exhausted by her questions and by the blackness into which she had fallen. She felt emptied, drained, depleted, and full of an uncomprehending, budding remorse. She lifted her eyes to the small wooden crucifix. Help me, my Lord, she pleaded, I have nothing left but You.

A breeze from the window whispered through her hair. The surroundings softened and began to throb with the scent of love, as sweet as honey, and all at once she knew that They had returned. Contrition sent a tear to the corner of her mouth.

Why did you leave me?

WE DID NOT LEAVE YOU. WE HAVE BEEN WITH YOU ALL ALONG.

Then why didn't you speak to me? I needed you to tell me what to do.

WE WERE SPEAKING TO YOU BUT YOU DID NOT HEAR US. YOU CHOSE NOT TO HEAR US.

But I *did* want to hear you! I listened as hard as I could for any sound of your Voices, yet you were not there.

YOU WERE LISTENING TO THE VOICE OF YOUR OWN DESIRES, NOT TO US. YOU WERE SO INTENT UPON FOLLOWING JEHANNE'S WILL THAT YOU DID NOT HEED THE WILL OF GOD, AND SO YOU HEARD NOTHING THAT WE SAID.

Shame crept across her face to the roots of her hair. The Power that had so long sustained her receded into a lashing repentance, and she was as small as the thirteen-year-old who had first heard Them on that dead summer's day.

Forgive me. I am nothing without you. I have been unworthy of your trust. I have failed you, and God.

There is nothing to forgive. It is human to make mistakes, Jehanne; only God does not err, and He did not make a mistake by choosing you for His work. You have done well, and so must not scold yourself as you are doing now.

The knowledge that she did not deserve Marguerite's gentleness flooded her eyes and fell in warm droplets onto her folded hands.

What about Paris? God commanded me to take it from the English for my King, and I failed.

WHERE IS YOUR FAITH, LITTLE ONE? DO YOU NOT BELIEVE GOD'S PROMISE THAT THE CITY WILL BOW TO CHARLES?

But he has turned away from it! He has decided that it is too much trouble, she complained with no small degree of bitterness.

NEVERTHELESS, IT SHALL FALL TO HIM AS WE HAVE SAID. IT SHALL COME TO

HIM IN GOD'S OWN TIME AND UNDER THE CIRCUMSTANCES THAT HE CHOOSES. DO NOT PRESUME UPON THE KING OF HEAVEN, JEHANNE, FOR WHEN YOU DO, YOU FOLLOW THE DARKNESS OF YOUR DESIRES AND NOT HIS WILL.

She let the chastisement sink in for a bit, and again remorse chattered in her brain. Catherine was right to rebuke her. However much she wanted to blame Charles, or Trémoïlle, Jehanne was forced to admit that she had tried to capture Paris without Their sanction and had gone into battle alone. In so doing, she had led the King's valiant men to their deaths.

What must I do now? How can I atone for my sin?

God asks no atonement of you, for you have not sinned. All He requires is that you learn from your mistakes and that you allow your faith to renew itself. He loves you more than it is possible for you to imagine. He is never as far from you as you sometimes believe. It is for this reason that He sent us to guide you, and as His servants we are always with you. If you would not err, you must still your heart and your wishes, and then you will always be able to hear us.

I understand you. But please tell me, what does God want of me now? Am I to continue my part in the war?

BE FAITHFUL TO THE COMMANDS OF THE KING WHOM GOD HAS CHOSEN TO HAVE DOMINION OVER YOU.

I asked him to let me return home to my parents, but he has refused. He said he wants me near him. Yet I do not understand what he wants from me, since he will not let me fight. I am useless here.

OBEY HIM. CHARLES DOES NOT KNOW IT, BUT GOD STILL HAS NEED OF YOU. AND IN GOD'S TIME, YOU WILL AGAIN BE A WARRIOR FOR FRANCE.

When will that happen?

AS WE HAVE SAID, IN GOD'S TIME. YOU WILL KNOW WHEN THE MOMENT ARRIVES.

In the meantime, purify yourself by dismissing your desires. Keep faith with your king, and do not judge him for what you consider his weaknesses, for in his own way he is guided by God just as you are.

He is surrounded by evil men who hate me, she said grimly. They hate me and would have me killed if they could.

You must not hate them in return, for if you do, you lose sight of God, Who is in everyone. As we have told you before, it is not that they are evil. It is more that they are unaware of their own Divine origin and so are blind to God's love. They have never felt His love and therefore have that void as an excuse. But you have known it, and because you have known it you must not forget it.

Brother Pasquerel said that your silence was a test of faith from God. Is that so?

Someone cleared his throat, and she jerked around, startled.

"I'm sorry to disturb you at prayer, Jehanne," said d'Aulon, "but I knocked and you did not hear me. I'm afraid that I have some bad news for you that couldn't wait."

She had neither seen nor felt her squire enter the room. He was only a foot or so behind her, and as she stood he took a step forward. He wore no armor, just a simple homespun tunic over the hose extending to his worn boots. The light from the window shone like a halo on his short brown hair.

"What is it?" she asked, filled suddenly with a nameless fear.

He glanced at the summer hills outside and for a moment did not answer. "Bedford has retaken St.-Denis. He has punished the people there for their acceptance of Charles by demanding that they pay what he calls 'fines.' He also allowed his soldiers to sack the monastery." D'Aulon frowned bitterly. "They stripped the gold and silver ornaments from the tombs of our Kings and forced the monks to hand over all the money they had. The abbé refused at first, until they threatened to burn the place over his head and those of his monks. Then of course he had no choice but to do as they commanded."

"What?" she asked, disbelieving what she had heard. "St.-Denis is the holiest place in the kingdom! Did they kill anyone?"

D'Aulon shook his head. "No, but they roughed up some of the monks who tried to resist them."

Jehanne could only stare at him speechlessly. The *goddons* were animals, worse than animals to defile that sacred hill! Surely God would punish them for their blasphemy. She took heart from Catherine's assurances that He still intended that they lose possession of France.

"There's more, I'm afraid," d'Aulon admitted, trying not to look at her. "They took your armor, too. The messenger who brought the news to the King said that the *goddons* gave it to Bedford as a trophy to mark your defeat." He smiled sadly. "I'm sorry, Jehanne."

"My armor? That cannot be! I offered it to God in sacrifice for His having spared me in battle."

"I know, I was there." His voice was soft and very gentle. "But they did take it."

Jehanne was dumbfounded. She could feel the coals of her hatred starting to ignite, and she knew that the spark would consume her if she allowed it. She remembered Marguerite's most recent words and swallowed the nasty lump in her throat.

She looked at d'Aulon. His eyes were on the ground and he shifted his feet nervously. "What else?" she asked.

He did not, could not answer.

"What else?"

"The King is disbanding the army for good. He says that he cannot pay them any longer." He hesitated, looking at her as though to say, There's more and you won't like it.

"And?"

"The duc d'Alençon is with Charles right now in the King's private chamber. I heard them speaking through the door," he admitted sheepishly. "The duc asked for permission to return home. He wants to raise an army to take back his fiefdom, and the King agreed." The squire took a breath to steel himself to continue. "He asked that you be allowed to go with him, but the King refused. When I left they were arguing."

Jehanne bolted past him. D'Aulon had no doubt where she was going.

Indifferent to her aching, half-healed leg, she ran down the hall to the end of the corridor, then turned right and dashed up a narrow flight of stairs. Her heart pounded in her head and its rhythm yelled, *No! No! No!* She paid no attention to the guards outside Charles' chamber, and the suddenness of her arrival took them so much by surprise that they did not have a chance to stop her.

Bursting through the door, she found that d'Alençon was still there. He was standing at the window, looking out, and when she came in he turned toward her. Charles was also on his feet, with his back to d'Alençon. Discord hung in the air like an unsheathed sword that neither of them had ventured to use.

The King gave Jehanne a sharp frown. She went to him and dropped to her knees. "My lord, is it true? Is Jehan going away?" Her voice broke, and the glance that she gave d'Alençon begged him to deny it.

"Who told you that?" Charles demanded.

"It does not matter, is it true?"

The narrow brown eyes studied her as though trying to read her soul. "Yes."

"Please, Sire, let me go with him!"

He turned away from her tears. "I cannot allow that, Jehanne. The duc has duties to attend to." He swung around and looked at her. "It is time he returned to his wife," he added pointedly.

"But, Sire—"

"We have made our decision," the King stated with cool finality. "Jehan will return to his estates, and you shall remain with the court."

"But why?" she pleaded. Her mind whirled in space and plummeted toward darkness as she struggled to understand. "You do not need me, my lord, now that you have disbanded the army. I cannot be of any use to you at court."

"*I* decide where you are needed," Charles said, becoming angry. "And I do not need you to run all over the countryside. You shall remain with the court. I will say nothing more about it." With that, he stalked to the door and swept out of the room, scattering the guards who waited for him.

The tears came in earnest now and her shoulders shook with sadness. She felt d'Alençon's hand caress her hair. He knelt next to her and she flung her arms around him.

"He cannot send you away," she cried, "you are my only friend. Oh, Jehan, what will I ever do without you?"

"I must go." He kissed the top of her head. "I have no choice, I have to obey him. So must you. He's our liege lord. And he is correct in saying that I have concerns at home."

She pulled away from his arms and looked at him with swollen eyes. "I want to go with you; please take me with you."

He sighed heavily and stood up. "I can't. You heard what Charles said; he forbids it."

She got to her feet. "Why is he doing this?"

"Trémoïlle," he answered simply. "And the archbishop. I can't prove it, but it's a reasonable conclusion. I think that they've probably convinced Charles that

unless they separate us, we'll somehow rally the army again and try to take Paris."
He smiled at her. "They're afraid of you, you know that, don't you?"

"Afraid of me? Why should they be afraid of me?" Even as she asked, she knew,
and his answer did not surprise her.

"They fear your power. They would never admit it in a thousand years, but
they know you're from God, and being little men who do not know God, they
fear you." His smile returned. "They know that you have the ability to inspire
men to heights they can never hope to attain."

He took her hands in his and kissed them. His look was deadly serious. "Do
not misjudge them, Jehanne. There is nothing they would not do to keep their
hold over the King. Be very cautious around them, do nothing to outrage them
further. I am sometimes quite afraid for you, so promise me that you'll be careful."

"I don't have to do anything," she said resentfully, "just the fact that I exist is
enough for them." She turned her face up to him. "Will you pray for me?"

He put a hand to her wet cheek. "Of course. Every day."

"When do you have to leave?"

He could not look at her. "Today. Now, in fact. If you had not come here, I
would have sought you out to say good-bye."

"I don't want you to go," she whispered. "I know you must, but I don't want
you to."

"Believe me, I would rather stay." He smiled. "But my first duty is to my
fiefdom. The Armagnacs had liberated it, but in the past few days it has been
overrun again by the English. The people there have suffered much at their hands,
Jehanne, not just recently but for some time. I must help them."

"I know."

She saw him shudder. He embraced her again, very tightly, and her fingers
entwined around the seams of his tunic. "I'll send you word from time to time,"
he mumbled into her hair, "and you'll do the same, eh?"

She nodded, then gently pushed him away.

"I have to go now. My escort is waiting."

"You'll be careful, won't you? On the road and in battle?"

He smiled. "Yes. I won't take the kinds of chances that you always did."

They laughed together without real humor. He took her hand and kissed it.
Then, noticing the ring, he rubbed it thoughtfully and said, "I always meant to
ask you: Where did this come from?"

"My father gave it to me a long time ago. He bought it after a harvest, in a
market at Neufchâteau."

D'Alençon nodded. "I've always wondered why you look at it sometimes before
you go into battle."

She rubbed her eyes, fighting back tears. "It reminds me of where I came from.
It reminds me of my home."

"Go home if you can, Jehanne." The duc's beautiful face was solemn. "If
Charles will not let you leave, take your brothers in the dark of night and go
anyway. I doubt that the King would bother to pursue you. But you must get away
from him as soon as you can."

"Why?"

He looked at a spot on the floor. "It's just a feeling I have. You are no longer safe at court."

"Because of the sieur Trémoïlle?"

"Yes."

She sighed. "I cannot go, and not just for the sake of the King. My Counsel have told me that God has more work for me to do. I could perhaps disobey Charles, but I am bound in love to God. Do you understand?"

He did not answer for a moment but simply looked at her, and she thought she saw him shiver again. "I understand," he said.

There was nothing more to say, and they both knew it. He put a warm hand against the side of her face. "God keep you safe, Jehanne."

"And you." She choked on the words.

He turned away from her and went to the door. He hesitated and looked back at her. "Good-bye."

And then he was gone. His boots clattered against the stone floor, and she could tell by the change in his steps when he reached the end of the hall and began his descent.

A hawk cried outside the window, and its mournful, solitary voice was like death in her heart. She wiped her face and sniffed loudly. There was nothing more for her to do in the King's room, so she went to the door and limped slowly down the corridor. She needed to breathe fresh air and would go to the garden. Surely there was some quiet place under a tree where she could pray for her beautiful duc.

Morning found the ladies of Bourges beginning to fill the women's section of the public bathhouse. They brought with them their daughters and elderly mothers. A few steps behind them, household servants carried bundles of clean towels and fresh clothing. Although early, the large tubs were already prepared for them, and while the ladies disrobed the last of the attendants emptied the torrid contents of her bucket. Their salutations drifted toward the ceiling like the clouds of thick steam partially shrouding the gleaming white, rounded bodies, and the cackle of female voices overlapped through the mist in a round of gossip that had nothing to do with the war.

Elise Théraud was pregnant again, and wasn't it a shame that she would be having another one so soon after she almost died from the last? And had they not heard that Madame de Soissons had caught her kitchen girl stealing silver from a casket on the master's desk?

When a small child did not want to get into the hot water, a maternal hand smacked against the little bottom. Her cry dissolved into a resigned whimper that floated above the steam and then was gone. The women settled into the sleepy comfort of their tubs as more of them arrived in twos and threes, searching the wall for empty pegs onto which to hang their clothes.

Madame d'Auvergne suddenly grabbed her tubmate by the arm and pointed with an excited whisper, "Héloïse, look! The Maid."

A dignified woman of near forty had just crossed the tiled threshold. She glided

362

toward a bench against the wall, bobbing her head in casual greeting to her envious neighbors and relations.

"Good morning, Joyette, Pauline." The smile she deigned to give them dripped with complacency and the sweet taste of victory.

But the women she knew so well looked altogether past her at the young woman who walked with such confidence behind their matronly friend. She was dressed like the son of a merchant, in a pearl gray tunic with puffed shoulders whose sleeves tapered gracefully to her wrists. The ladies could see the leg muscles bulging through the dusky hose that ran down to her surprisingly small, slippered feet.

She removed a cap from the back of her cropped head and nodded at the gawking women, then gave them a nervous little wave. "Good morning." She smiled and looked at a grandmother. "Good morning."

A timorous acknowledgment mumbled back at her. They did not turn shyly back to their baths, however. Curiosity was stronger than any reverence they may have felt because of her fame. Twenty-seven pairs of eyes, all agog at the living legend, were plastered to her even as she turned toward the wall and began to undress.

She could feel their combined curiosity upon her bare back, and her fingers shook as she loosed the lacings that held the hose to her waist. Even after conversation resumed she still sensed their furtive inspection. To them she was *L'Angélique*, and it embarrassed her to be thought of in that way. They were looking for a saint to intercede with God for them. Well, they would not find one in her. She just wanted to have a bath in peace, that's all.

She did not want to talk about the war, not with them, nor did she want to be asked to be godmother to their babies. She had so many godchildren now that she would never be able to remember them all, but she also had a hard time saying no. They were sure to ask about her Counsel, people usually did get around to that, and here she had a customary answer: God has not given me permission to talk about that. It always satisfied them, but she dreaded the question nonetheless. Most of all she did not want to be asked to bless anything. That was for God to do.

Three of them had come to her hostess' home to ask her to do His work. They approached her with an unsettling homage and requested that she bless their rosaries.

Madame la Touroulde was the midwife of their request, Jehanne was sure of it. The wife of the King's Collector of Taxes, she belonged to one of Bourges' most prominent families, near but not at the top of the court's inner circle. Marguerite la Touroulde loved her husband and quite naturally wanted to see him advance in rank. To that end, she busied herself with seeking the friendship of anyone at court who held the King's ear, sometimes pretending to intimacies that did not exist. Jehanne knew that her hostess valued being seen in the company of notable people. But the falseness of her frequent "Jehanne, dear," particularly in the presence of others, made her skin prickle.

The older woman did not know the inner Jehanne. All she knew was that Jehanne hated gambling and prostitution, and other surface things. Jehanne had told her about her examination before the churchmen at Poitiers and her useless meeting with the duc de Lorraine before she went to Chinon. However, sensing that her hostess, although not a malicious person, held a place of power in the echelons of local gossip, Jehanne kept her real self to herself. At the same time, she was irked that Marguerite would so misunderstand Jehanne's mission that she would invite her friends for a visit as a ruse, that they might witness a miraculous event. She was a soldier, not a magician, and certainly not *L'Angélique*.

So rather than play Marguerite's game, she had laughed and looked at the women and their rosaries with a good-natured grin. "Touch them yourselves, they would benefit as much from your hands as from mine."

The women shrank with disappointment, and their astonishment at her response secretly pleased her. She was Jehanne from Domrémy, and two years earlier they would not even have noticed her. Indeed, she would have been just a peasant from the country and the subject of their scorn.

She could feel the same expectations from those here at the bath. Their veneration searched her as she folded her hose and stepped gingerly across the wet floor and into the tub where Madame la Touroulde had comfortably established herself.

Jehanne's feet recoiled at their first contact with the scalding contents, and she winced at the delicious sting. Slowly, she lowered her body into the water and as it covered her she gasped at the severity of its heat. But she found very gradually that it was not as pungent as it had first seemed; as a matter of fact, it felt wonderful. The receptacle was large enough for her to stretch out her legs without troubling Madame la Touroulde, so she sank a little further until only her head was sticking up out of the water. She rested it against the rim, and with steam moistening her face, looked up at the rain-spotted ceiling.

Her companion was babbling on in a self-important way, making certain that all could hear the familiar remarks she tossed to Jehanne. She was unaware that her renowned guest did not hear a word she said. Jehanne was actually very far away, despite her occasional "Oh, really?" and "Yes," and the more frequent "Hmm."

She bore no rancor toward Marguerite la Touroulde. Actually, she was grateful to her hostess for having rescued her from the rigid formality of the court. There she was an oddity, the boy-girl deliverer of Orléans who had been unaware of correct conduct at table before she first went to Chinon and who had to be instructed in it. At home they had usually relied upon their fingers, and the soldiers in camp ate what food they had any way they could get it into their mouths. It was a shock to learn that those more gently born than she were accustomed to following a ritualistic etiquette when dining.

One did not slurp one's soup directly from the bowl; one used a spoon. It was not proper to rip away a large hunk from bread or meat and then tear at the portion with one's teeth; using a knife, the diner cut small bites and chewed them delicately. During her months in the field, Jehanne had forgotten the lessons she had learned at Chinon, and although she quickly came into a recollection of her manners, a mortified pang stabbed at her under the vigilant, wordless censure.

As a result, her discomfort only made her even more open to the commission of social *faux pas*. At games and during hired entertainments she often seemed to laugh or speak at the wrong times, and the courtiers' discomfiture at her accumulated mistakes only increased her feeling of isolation.

True, her brothers were still with her, along with Minguet, d'Aulon, and Pasquerel, but none of them had the kind of power that counted in the rarefied milieu. They were just her household, little more than retainers in the eyes of the lords and ladies who followed Charles, while to the King's servants, the stablemen and kitchen workers and gardeners, they were heroes. All but Pasquerel at one time or another had succumbed to the temptation to boast of their exploits in war. Far away from any battlefield, they were as bored and out of place as she was, and for amusement frequently squabbled among themselves. Jehan picked on Pierre as relentlessly as he had when they were children. On one occasion Jehanne had wearily intervened, reminding them that conflict between brothers was a sin.

The men in her entourage at least had each other in a bond forged by the masculine camaraderie of war. Without the army, without a purpose, and lacking something to do besides hawking or other pointless recreations, she had no friendly counterpart at court. In the three weeks since Paris, she had been in the middle of people all day every day and known the greatest loneliness of her life.

And then, miraculously, Madame la Touroulde had asked the King for permission to bring Jehanne into Bourges. Jehanne accepted at once. She needed to get away from the stiffness of Bourges Castle and badly required a respite from those closest to her. They tried to convince her to stay; she was unyielding. Charles expressed regret at her leaving, but she knew him well enough by now to see that he was actually relieved. With her gone, he would not have to listen to anyone's pleas that he reassemble the army. The war was very distant from his croquet lawn, just as he preferred it.

So she packed her satchel and went into Bourges. Life in the town was different but brought challenges of its own. Here she was fêted in a constant round of parties and dinners and was rarely alone, even at night, when she shared her hostess' bed as was customary. Influential people, aldermen and the wives of wealthy merchants, competed with one another for her time, all hailing her as their cherished friend. They asked her about the siege at Orléans and she was so often compelled to recount the taking of the Tourelles that her recitations finally became rote and, to her at least, monotonous. She drew upon the skill she had always possessed after They first spoke to her, to experience an outer life while at the same time holding to her inner core. There was the Jehanne who bought new clothes and another fine horse with Charles' gold, who gave lavishly to the destitute and the infirm, and the other who journeyed where no one could follow.

The only time she was really happy was in the cathedral. She went there often in the afternoons, and Madame la Touroulde's constant presence notwithstanding, Jehanne entered into the silence the moment she crossed the high arches into the sacred, cool shadows. It became habitual for her to pad on tiptoe past the immense columns to a spot in the choir and there to kneel upon the stone floor facing the altar. She prayed often for those she loved who were far away: her mother and father; Poulengy and Metz, now with La Hire and the remnants of the army; the Bastard, safe at his beloved Orléans; and d'Alençon. Her most heartfelt prayers were for him.

And always she felt her Counsel. It did not take long for Them to come after she said her prayers, and she never had to summon Them. The light from the beautiful windows would change into an otherworldly brilliance, mocking the meager hand of man who had built the cathedral, and as it swirled around her, cleansing her spirit, she was inevitably overcome by Their dauntless, perpetual love. They were her oldest and most profound Friends. Each time she remembered that was like the first. No one, not even her beloved duc, could ever breathe across her soul as They did, and by contrast the fragile constancy and limited reach of human devotion seemed as meaningless to her as the busy labor of ants. To her troubled questions about her destiny, They responded with unswerving forbearance that she should attend upon the will of God in all things, no matter how difficult. When They spoke to her, the angelic music They sang took her away from her surroundings so that time stopped and she soared into that land where They were the only certainty.

One afternoon They gave her a vision whose terrible beauty she never forgot and would not ever come to comprehend. In the center of Their love a many-colored, swirling mist that had started as a seed grew and grew until she could see nothing else but its tiny, winking specks. Rapt, transfixed, unable to move, she watched the spinning vortex slowly part a space and move toward the edges of her sight, and in the place where it had been most concentrated she saw herself from both within and outside her body.

She was not Jehanne at all but a man dressed in a short gown that ended at her knees. A tall-pillared ceiling towered high above the grand chamber whose open walls surrounded her in an airy spaciousness. Before her stood a dignified, bearded man who had the most tranquil human eyes she had ever seen. But instead of being moved by him, a dark anger flooded her soul and throbbed in her temples, and when she addressed him, disdain gushed from her mouth.

"You know, Master Pythagoras, that I could become the most gifted of all your students, and therefore should not be required to endure the capricious demands you have placed upon those who would study with you." Her words rang through the unusual, columned hall in haughty scorn.

The man simply smiled and his lips barely moved as he said, "It is the Law."

"I do not need the law!" she shouted, annoyed at the teacher's calm. "The hand of God is upon me and that raises me above your law."

"It is the Law." That was the only answer he would give, the man of the ceaseless smile.

"May God condemn your pointless law and send you to the Void for rejecting his worthiest!" Jehanne roared.

"It is God's Law, Kylon. The time will come when you will make amends for the wrong that is in your heart." The man's seamless face was full of compassion and his words fell upon her in a blessing. "The time will come when you will uphold the Law you now condemn."

The window suddenly closed across the scene and the mist was as it had been before the startling apparitions appeared. Her Guides quickened in the whirlwind of light and she could feel Them waiting for her certain question.

What was that? What does it mean? Dread peppered the ecstasy she had felt in a scattering of hard, black nuggets, and she trembled.

IT IS THE LEGACY YOU HAVE BROUGHT WITH YOU FROM HEAVEN AND THE GATEWAY TO YOUR SALVATION.

Who was that man? He looked like Michel.

HE IS NOT MICHEL BUT THE PROGENITOR OF YOUR FUTURE.

I do not understand, she whimpered, close to tears of frustration. You speak to me in riddles that I cannot understand.

YOUR MIND MAY NOT UNDERSTAND, BUT YOUR SOUL DOES. LOOK THERE, FOR IT HOLDS THE ANSWER. YOU DO NOT NEED FOR US TO TELL YOU WHAT YOU ALREADY KNOW.

That was all. She catapulted back to earth with an abruptness that made her dizzy. For a moment she thought she would swoon.

Her hostess was standing next to her, whispering that they must hurry home. The mayor's wife was expected there at any time. Surely Jehanne did not want to disappoint her?

Marguerite la Touroulde was speaking to her now from the other side of the tub. Jehanne had not heard what she said.

"Excuse me?"

"I wondered, what is that scar just beneath your shoulder, Jehanne dear?" The older woman knew very well what it was; she had seen it before when Jehanne undressed for bed. Even so, she asked the question in an unnecessarily loud voice, smiling sweetly and looking around her in a way that confirmed that she had everyone's notice.

"It is from the arrow I took at Orléans," Jehanne replied. She put an unwitting finger to the pale pink, ragged indentation. The Tourelles flashed before her, and for a moment she could hear the agonized screams of contending warriors.

"Oh, my goodness, that must have hurt a great deal!" Marguerite exclaimed, the picture of exaggerated distress.

Jehanne smiled in spite of herself. "It did, a bit," she admitted. Sometimes it still did, when the weather was cold.

The other women had ceased their chatter and were carefully straining to hear without actually going so far as to gather around her. "But I knew that God was with me and I would not die." She did not look at the women, only at Madame la Touroulde. Still, she could feel them hanging on her words and suddenly she found herself welcoming their attentions. She had been brave at Orléans.

"I know why you take part so fearlessly in assaults," Marguerite half-teased, "it is because you know that you will not be killed."

"That is not true," Jehanne denied with a solemn frown. "In battle, I have no more assurance of that than any other soldier." She raised her left foot from the water and pointed to the crease across its dripping, water-wrinkled sole. "Do you see this? I stepped on a *chausse-trappe* at Orléans, and I had no idea it was there because God did not tell me."

The women had grown bolder, and four of them left their baths and crept toward her. She looked around at their curious, clammy faces. "I have another on my thigh"—she put a hand under the water and touched her leg—"that I got recently, and I did not know that I would be wounded that day either." She did not say, "at Paris." There was no need to remind them, or herself, of the failed attempt to take the capital. She smiled almost apologetically. "I don't know when or where I'll die any more than any of you. That is in God's hands."

"We are praying for you, Jehanne," said an old woman whose sagging breasts had nursed many children.

There was a murmur of feminine accord, and as she smiled up at them she felt the bashful affection that they had been too restrained to voice. She was a little ashamed of herself for having wished them away when she first arrived at this place.

These were good and simple women whose lives were determined by the daily routines of work and church and familiar social exchange. They were not like the sophisticates at court in whose esteem she had unjustly fallen after Paris. The ladies who now openly gathered around her tub were not living for the latest amusement, for the next rising luminary to distract them from jaded, empty lives. Jehanne saw with a surprising clarity that it was for these women that she had fought, for it was they and thousands like them who were the real France. Not the silk-clad lords and ladies around Charles, and in a mysterious way that she found difficult to understand, not even the King. She sensed that his faith in her, never really strong, was teetering away from her now toward the black mutterings of his ministers. As for the courtiers, in their smug disbelief they did not really credit anything.

But these women did. They knew that she had come from God. She was overwhelmed by a wave of affection, and silently asked their forgiveness for her erstwhile disregard of their faith. She vowed that she would not consider them nuisances again.

"Thank you all," she said, flicking away a tear. "Please pray for the kingdom as well, and for all the people of France."

"We will, Jehanne," a young girl of about thirteen promised.

Someone put a reassuring hand on her shoulder, and she raised her eyes to the young mother of two small children who smiled down at her. Jehanne covered the woman's hand with her own and squeezed it in thanks. In a most surprising way and in this most common of places, God had shown her that she was not alone after all.

As he walked quickly through the nearly empty marketplace, a sudden gust of brisk air struck the monk's face and he clutched the cloak more tightly about his bony shoulders. In prophecy of an early winter a cold wind from the north had been howling through the city since mid-morning, and it sliced through the feeble, long-shadowed daylight like a sharp knife. The man's feet, scantily shod in crude sandals, were turning blue from the chill, but he did not mind. He was accustomed to hardship, having been a member of a mendicant Order for some years now. But the woman who struggled to keep up with him was more gently bred than he, and although she did not complain, her small body trembled visibly.

"How much further?" she asked, glancing up at his long, equine face. She was wrapped so thoroughly in her woolen cape and the scarf covering her head that her question was a mumble. Only her eyes, one brown, the other green, were visible, and they were watering in the frigid draught.

"Not far. We need to turn here, down this street." A long skeletal hand gestured to the left. They entered a narrow alleyway that carved the ancient houses into rows.

This was the old section of Jargeau where the buildings were more than two hundred years old. All the windows were tightly closed against the elements in anticipation of the coming storm. It would not snow tonight, but Brother Richard's experienced eye told him that the thick, iron gray clouds certainly proclaimed the approach of rain. He smelled it coming through the heavy odor of woodsmoke spewing from many chimneys. They hurried past shops and private houses where the heat from fireplaces cast warm vapors upon the windows, calling to the travelers, inviting them to enter.

He put temptation behind him and walked on past an inn. The woman was panting breathlessly as she tried to match his long strides. For every one of his steps she had to take two.

Poor Catherine, he thought. She may have been touched by God, but austerity was not in her nature. That was not her fault. The daughter of a tailor, she had made a comfortable marriage to a prosperous man of the town, a wineseller by profession whose commerce required his frequent travels to many regions of France. Catherine was the mother of three children, and until the last year when God had called her, she had spent much of her life in quiet, matronly pursuits as befitted a woman of her class. Things were different now, though, and if she wanted to meet the King, she would have to endure whatever small nuisances Heaven tossed her way.

She was very unlike Brother Richard's other protégeé, the acclaimed female soldier whom God had summoned to save France for King Charles. Now, there was someone who knew how to sacrifice comfort for the sake of achieving a goal! Although he had not personally witnessed her in action, for he did not like the company of soldiers and had no stomach for battle, the friar had been told that Jehanne could stay in the saddle, fully armed, for three days and nights. He shook his head in admiration. How fortunate she had been to have met him when she did. After he practically gave her Troyes, the road to Reims had been a level one free of obstacles, and she had conceded his importance by giving him a place of honor at her side during Charles' coronation. She recognized that he, like herself, was one of God's own messengers.

And now here he was with yet another. Soon there would be three of them to do God's work to restore the kingdom. The King, contented by their performances in his service, would no doubt retain him and Catherine as royal spiritual adviser just as he maintained Jehanne. Perhaps he would give grand appointments to Brother Richard that he might embark upon a crusade against the Bohemian

Hussites, or against the infidel Turks. It was therefore seemly that he should be taking Catherine to meet Jehanne. Everyone knew that she had the King's ear as no other, and Catherine bore important news for Charles. This time was the beginning of their rise. Catherine's White Lady had foretold it.

The end of the alley intersected with a much wider street. Here, where trades-men normally sold their goods from open-shuttered shopfronts, several establish-ments remained closed, bolted against the bitter north wind. Those that were still open had curtains drawn behind tables laden with wares, and the owners looked up cautiously from their worktables as Brother Richard and Catherine pressed past them. The untimely cold snap was a major nuisance to the craftsmen of Jargeau, who had not counted on the early arrival of winter. It was like that, some years.

The two walked on until the shops and taverns receded, replaced by prosperous homes. At last Brother Richard stopped before a three-story stone domicile whose Romanesque windows looked out over the cobbled street, its sloping roof newly pitched as protection against the coming snows.

The monk pulled back his sleeve and rapped loudly on the door. After a mo-ment footsteps could be heard on the other side and the iron handle turned. A young serving girl peeked out at them from a narrow crack. Her auburn hair framed a thickly freckled, somewhat mischievous face. She smiled and opened the door just enough for them to enter.

"We are here to see the Maid," Brother Richard said, surveying the room.

This was the home of a burgher, and they were standing in an anteroom that boasted a small friendly fireplace. To their left a partially closed door offered a limited view of the master's counting room. A shuffle of papers and the flicker of a candle indicated that the room was in use.

The girl curtsied, then, picking up a candle from a small table, opened the door in front of them to reveal a flight of stairs. When she began to climb, the guests followed in silence. Their breaths made small clouds in this unheated part of the house.

The stairway ended at the second floor, where it veered sharply in the opposite direction toward the top of the structure. The servant rapped lightly on a door.

They heard a low-pitched woman's voice say, "Come."

The girl held the door open for them and stood aside before vanishing back down the stairs.

Jehanne was sitting on a bench a few feet in front of the fireplace. She wore a dark tunic of thick velvet belted at the waist and boots that reached almost to her knees. Next to her sat Pasquerel. One would not have taken him for a monk. His tonsure had grown out so that a bowl of dark hair covered his formerly bare scalp, and he was dressed like a soldier in a heavy surcoat and woolen hose. He smiled pleasantly at the new arrivals, secure in his position as the Maid's confes-sor, a station from which Brother Richard had found it impossible to dislodge him.

A middle-aged woman, apparently the mistress of the house, occupied a stool to Jehanne's left. Her face was as open as sunshine, and the eyes that greeted her guests swam in grayish-green pools. She stood up, smoothing the folds of her skirt. The other two followed her example and got to their feet.

"Welcome, Brother Richard." Jehanne smiled. "This is Madame Paulette de Barneville, my hostess. You remember Brother Pasquerel, I'm sure." A corner of her mouth curved slyly.

"Of course," the lanky friar replied, drawing his lips back from horsy teeth. He looked at the older woman. "Madame." He inclined his head toward her and she nodded in response.

As though suddenly remembering his friend, he said, "May I present Madame Catherine de la Rochelle." He held a spidery hand toward the small woman who stood beside him.

She was a full foot shorter than Brother Richard. Her hair was pulled back into a blond bun and fastened at the nape of her neck. She had a long nose and high cheekbones which gave her face the appearance of severe sharpness, and her eyes were strangely mismatched, like different colors of cut glass. She was wearing a long dress of deep scarlet wool that ascended past her throat to her chin.

"I am most honored to meet you at last, Jehanne," she said with a brittle smile. "One hears so much of the Maid these days."

"The pleasure is mine, Madame." Jehanne grinned, ignoring the implied barb in Catherine's words. "Please"—she gestured toward two vacant stools—"be seated."

Catherine glanced at Brother Richard. "I have come with urgent news for the King," she said haughtily, "and I must speak to you alone." Her odd eyes darted to Paulette de Barneville, then to Pasquerel.

"I can assure you that you may speak freely here," Jehanne answered with a smoothness that belied her displeasure. "Brother Pasquerel is my personal confessor, and Madame de Barneville is my good friend. Whatever you have to say shall be safe with them."

"I am sorry, but I must insist," the woman said. "There is a matter of great secrecy which I must discuss with you and only you."

Pasquerel gave Jehanne a wry smile, then looked at her hostess. "Madame de Barneville, I believe that you wanted to show me that portrait of your husband."

"Indeed, Brother." She drew herself up into a dignified posture and accepted Pasquerel's arm. "Dinner in one hour, Jehanne."

"I'll be there."

The soldier-monk and the lady of the house left the room, and Paulette closed the door behind them.

"Please," Jehanne said with a gracious wave toward the stools. She sat down again on the bench. "Now, what is it you have to tell me?"

They made themselves comfortable, Catherine leaning forward slightly in the seat. Her eyes widened, and she nearly whispered, "Recently, a most wondrous thing has happened to me, a thing which I'm sure you will understand." She paused dramatically before continuing.

"I have had a vision of a marvelous White Lady dressed in gold who appears to me every night. She tells me that I must go through the good towns of France to proclaim that everyone who possesses silver and gold should bring it forth at once, so that the King may renew his treasury and use it to equip his army. To that end, the King is to give me heralds and trumpets to announce my coming, and if the people do not do as I ask, I shall know those who have hidden their treasures and will seek them out." As she finished her tale, Catherine gave Jehanne a triumphant smile.

Jehanne pursed her lips and nodded thoughtfully. A warning whispered in her ear. There was something about this that was not right. "Is that all?"

"No." Catherine shook her head. "I am also to go to the duc de Bourgogne to make peace between him and the King."

Jehanne looked at Brother Richard, whose large teeth were drawn back in a rapt smile. She wondered whatever in the world he could be up to now, bringing this creature to her. Ever since Troyes he had clung to her side, even talking himself into the coronation ceremony. He was a forceful preacher, no doubt about that. When he had scolded the army with his sermons against gambling, the soldiers listened and cast away their dice. It was for their sakes and at their urging that she had suffered his presence. But she never really trusted him, and she was suspicious of this woman who followed him.

"Do you have children, Madame Catherine?" Jehanne wondered.

"I do, three of them, fine boys." She lifted her pointed chin with pride.

"Then I think that they probably miss their maman," said Jehanne bluntly, "and you should return to them. It is my opinion that the only peace that can be gained with Bourgogne will be at the end of a lance."

Brother Richard's brows drew together in an acrid frown. Catherine exhaled a sharp burst of air, and the color drained from her face. "But the White Lady has commanded me to do as I have said," she insisted. "Surely you cannot turn me away! You, of all people, who have heard the voices of angels will not refuse to speak to the King for me."

Jehanne stared at both of them for a moment, humor playing at her mouth. Finally, she asked, "You say that your White Lady comes to you every night?"

"That is correct."

"Then she will come again tonight?"

"Most assuredly."

"I should like very much to see her." Jehanne smiled. "What time should I be at your house?"

"I—I"—Catherine looked nervously at the monk—"I do not know if you will be able to see her."

"As you pointed out, Madame, I speak regularly with messengers from God. If anyone can see her, I can." The smile disappeared from Jehanne's mouth.

She stood up so quickly that Catherine flinched. "I shall be at your house after I have had my dinner here. Please give directions to Madame de Barneville's servant before you leave."

The other two rose on unsteady feet. Jehanne could see that Brother Richard was angry, but there was nothing that he could say.

"Very well, Jehanne," Catherine replied. "We shall meet later." She turned her back to Jehanne and dragged the fragments of her dignity to the door. The monk hesitated for a moment before he followed her. He did not look back at Jehanne.

She was alone. A horse *clip-clopped* outside past the window. There was a shift in the fireplace and sparks shot up the chimney. Jehanne knelt upon the floor and closed her eyes in concentration.

She could feel Them very near, and she asked, Is this woman to be believed? Is there really a White Lady?

WHAT DO YOU THINK, JEHANNE?

I think that there is not. Her story does not sound right somehow.

THEN YOU MUST TRUST THE GOOD SENSE THAT GOD GAVE YOU, AND YOU WILL DISCOVER THAT YOUR INSTINCTS ARE CORRECT.

Why then has she come to me? What is it she wants?

HER LIFE IS EMPTY AND UNFULFILLED, AS ARE THE LIVES OF MANY WOMEN. SHE FEELS IGNORED BY HER HUSBAND AND LONGS FOR RECOGNITION.

So she is a liar?

NOT EXACTLY. WHEN SHE FIRST HEARD OF YOU, THE YEARNING IN HER HEART DEEPENED INTO ENVY, SO STRONG THAT SHE HAS CONVINCED HERSELF THAT HER DELUSIONS ARE REAL. SHE DESERVES YOUR COMPASSION AND YOUR UNDERSTAND-ING.

Emotions she had not fully known were there battled within Jehanne's head. Part of herself was gladdened that her intuition had proven correct, that her rejection of the story of the miraculous lady was not founded in the sin of pride. But she realized that another side of her secret self had been joyful when Madame de la Rochelle first began speaking of her mythical lady. There was no one with whom she felt complete, not a soul who understood the burden she carried nor the exaltation that communication with her Guides brought to her. She had long since been aware that Brother Richard was not such a one. Now, a spark of hope that she had at long last found someone who shared her visions sputtered before its fragile flame died.

DO NOT BE SAD, DEAR ONE. IN A SHORT TIME YOU WILL MEET ANOTHER WHO IS LIKE YOU, SOMEONE WHOM GOD HAS CALLED TO HIS SERVICE.

Who is it? When will we meet?

YOU WILL KNOW HER THE INSTANT YOU LOOK INTO HER EYES. SHE SHALL BE REVEALED TO YOU VERY SOON. YOU MUST HAVE FAITH. AND PATIENCE.

I have told Madame de la Rochelle that I wish to see her lady. She will be expecting me.

THEN YOU MUST GO, IF ONLY TO SATISFY ANY DOUBTS THAT YOU MAY YET HARBOR. BUT DEAL WITH HER GENTLY, WITH LOVE, OR YOU WILL CERTAINLY REGRET IT.

Jehanne thought of her conversation with Ste.-Catherine as she sat up with her Counsel's namesake through the evening and into the night. As she had expected, nothing happened.

"When will she come?" she asked, more than once.

"Soon," Madame de la Rochelle repeatedly answered, "very soon."

Finally, Jehanne could no longer hold her eyes open and drifted into sleep. When she awoke the next morning, Catherine told her that the Lady had come while Jehanne slumbered, but that she had been unable to wake Jehanne, no matter how hard she tried. Jehanne asked if the lady would come again that night, and Catherine affirmed that the White Lady came every night.

In the house where she was lodged Jehanne took a nap, a long one, that lasted from late morning until four o'clock in the afternoon. It was difficult for her to sleep that long, but every time her mind struggled for wakefulness, she forced it back into a dream.

She returned to Catherine's house after darkness fell. Again, no lady appeared, and Catherine slept at last. Every time she dozed, Jehanne shook her shoulder and asked, "Will she come?"

"Yes," Catherine mumbled, "soon."

Jehanne continued the routine until dawn, and did not allow the woman to sleep. At last, when the sun appeared above the rooftops of Jargeau, Jehanne bade Catherine a pleasant farewell and returned to the home of Paulette and Gustave de Barneville.

"You may rise, Jehanne."

The King's command was as cool as the dim October sunshine, his face an unreadable mask. The dark yellow tunic he was wearing was unflattering and made his complexion appear more sallow than usual. He sat on a stone bench beneath a tree whose turning leaves floated to the earth like tears, unaware that one of them perched ridiculously on the corner of his wide-brimmed velvet hat. Near him stood the ever-present councillors, de Chartres, splendid in his new, violet clerical robe, and the rotund Trémoïlle. Jehanne immediately recognized the third man as sieur Charles d'Albret, the chancellor's half brother.

She remembered him as one of the many courtiers she had met in Reims before the coronation. He was younger than Trémoïlle, in about his mid-thirties if Jehanne's guess was correct. He looked nothing like his powerful relative. A bowl-shaped cap of dark brown hair crowned his head, and he stared at her with mildly curious green eyes. He was taller than the other three, with muscular shoulders and thick arms that testified to his occasional military experience.

She got to her feet. Something was going to happen; she could feel it, could see it in the stony countenance of the archbishop and in Trémoïlle's satisfied smirk. Whatever it was, she welcomed it after all these weeks of galling inaction. Charles, restless in the peace that he had purchased, had rambled from one château to another along the Loire, and Jehanne had been forced to accompany him. Now they were at Mehun-sur-Yèvre. For the last couple of days, she sensed some coming event, but her Guides would not tell her what it was. As always, They counseled patience, that endlessly elusive virtue. And now it was here, whatever "it" was.

As though he could read her mind, Charles said, "You have perhaps wondered why we have summoned you."

She nodded. "Yes, Sire."

"We have decided on the advice of our council"—he glanced at Trémoïlle— "that it is time that we reclaim La Charité. You may not know this, but that town has for some time been in the hands of Perrinet Gressart, a common mason whom the English king made governor several years ago."

"I have heard of him, my lord."

It was common knowledge that five years earlier this Gressart had welcomed the sieur Trémoïlle in his role as ambassador to Philippe de Bourgogne, then without warning thrown him into prison. The fat man was held for several months in a castle *donjon* while his family collected a ransom. Jehanne smiled slightly, able now to see why Charles had sent for her.

The King turned toward Trémoïlle's kinsman. "This is the sieur d'Albret, brother of our chancellor."

"Yes, Sire, I know. I remember you, sir, from His Majesty's coronation." She assembled her features into a congenial smile.

D'Albret's lips parted, showing even white teeth. "And of course, who could forget the illustrious Maid? The last time I recall seeing you, shortly before the coronation, you were wearing armor and a magnificent cloth of gold."

Jehanne recoiled at the memory of her lost armor. She would have to find another suit if she was to go into battle again.

"It is well that you have met before," Charles said, "because we intend that you be joint commanders of the army in its assault upon La Charité. You will take a force of three hundred and lay siege to it before winter comes. It is almost alone among the Loire towns south of Orléans still in the hands of Bourgogne."

"Thank you, my lord," Jehanne replied, relieved that she was going to be of use again. "But would it not be better to send the army north, to try once more for Paris?"

The ensuing silence screamed at her; her ears burned as she waited for Charles to speak.

The King's eyes grew cold and he said, "We thought you understood that that subject is closed, Jehanne. You know very well that we cannot afford to pay a large force any longer. In fact, we are barely able to pay this smaller one. The only reason we are sending a battalion against Gressart in the first place is because he has been harrying what remains of our army from the rear, and we also expect a spring offensive from Paris. If that happens, the bulk of our forces could be caught between Gressart's Burgundians and the English. Do you understand?"

"Yes, Sire." She frowned at his question. She had taken part in more battles than the King, who had never seen action in the field. He was talking to her as though she were a dimwitted child.

"Do you want the assignment?" he asked tersely. Trémoïlle's upper lip twisted into an ugly smile.

Jehanne nodded. La Charité was not Paris, but it was better than the irksome idleness of the court.

"Good." Charles looked briefly at d'Albret. "Before you attack La Charité, we want you to go against St.-Pierre-le-Moustier."

"Where is that, my lord?"

The King's three intimates chuckled at her ignorance. Even Charles permitted himself to smile. Anger rumbled in Jehanne's head and her gritted teeth flexed the muscles in her jaw.

"It is on the River Alliers, between La Charité and Moulins," the King replied. "It also threatens Bourges to the north, and that is why you must take it. We cannot have a buildup of Burgundian forces that may eventually threaten our loyal Loire towns. With St.-Pierre-le-Moustier and La Charité once again returned to our domain, then perhaps—I say, *perhaps*—we can turn our attention to the north. Do you have any questions?"

Jehanne looked at the leaf-strewn ground. Winter would be here sooner than any of them wanted, making warfare difficult. If the army were to reclaim any territory for the King, they would have to do it quickly.

"No, Sire," she answered, giving him an even look, "I understand."

"Very well. Go now, both of you. Return to Bourges and begin gathering together the army."

The assault began an hour after dawn. For three hours cannon hammered at a portion of the wall surrounding St.-Pierre-le-Moustier, but when they tried to take it, the Armagnacs were beaten back. Jehanne yelled above the fray that God intended that the King's men enter the town, and a short time later, the royal troops renewed the attack. This time they did not allow themselves to be repulsed. St.-Pierre-le-Moustier fell to the army of God.

The King was pleased with her latest victory, he said, and looked forward to her besieging La Charité. Regrettably, he had no money to pay for any further arms, or food, and could spare no additional men-at-arms for the task. Jehanne would have to make do with what she had.

So she went to Moulins, ten leagues south of the town she had just reclaimed for France, and from there wrote letters to Riom, Clermont, and Orléans, asking for their assistance. The first pledged sixty crowns which were never sent. Clermont responded with saltpeter and sulfur for the artillery, along with two cases of crossbow bolts. For Jehanne's personal use in the upcoming battle, the magistrates sent armor, a new sword, two daggers, and an awesome battleax that she could barely lift. She gave the latter to Pierre.

Of the three, the Orléanais proved most generous: The city provided enough warm clothing to see Jehanne's force, now swelled to five hundred, through the coming winter, and money with which to pay them. The men-at-arms they sent to their saviour toted behind their train all the cannon and a few culverins that the town had retained from previous battles. They also brought her an affectionate letter from the Bastard, who explained with regret that urgent matters in the city he ruled prohibited him from joining her, but that he knew that God would be with her.

While she waited for the men and materiel to catch up with her in Moulins, she stayed at the home of Charles Cordier and his wife, on the corner of the rue d'Allier and the rue de la Flèche. Her room was on the first floor, facing the street. Monsieur Cordier had made his fortune as a goldsmith, and now employed several craftsmen who labored long hours in the workroom next to Jehanne's alcove. When they adjourned for meals, she often spent time with them. Their original awe of her was soon worn down by her dogged affability, and before long she had them laughing at her impressions of those she had met at court. But inevitably, they had to return to their work, leaving her with very little to do while she waited for responses to her letters.

Sometimes she helped Madame Cordier spin wool, returning easily to the vocation she had learned as a child. Antoinette was an attentive and kind woman who had none of the wearisome ostentatiousness of Madame la Touroulde, back in Bourges. Jehanne found it easy to talk to her, and readily shared stories of her childhood; she did not feel comfortable talking about the war or past glories. On occasion, the two of them went to market together, where they purchased winter vegetables and salted meat. But on the whole, Jehanne found the lag between battles nervewracking. She wanted to get on with it, to finish with La Charité so that Charles might keep his word and send her north to the real fighting.

On a chilly afternoon she wandered alone to the convent of the Reformed Order of the Poor Claires. Several nuns were at prayer in the small chapel when Jehanne stole to a quiet corner and knelt discreetly upon the floor. She crossed herself, then slipped into the familiar silence.

As always she asked God to protect her loved ones, near and far away. Madame Cordier's spinning wheel had reminded her of Isabelle, and she wondered if she would ever see her mother again. After all that had happened, she knew that she could never return to Domrémy, at least not permanently. When the war was over she would go to Orléans where she had experienced her greatest triumph. She would buy a house there for her parents. They would all live together, Maman and Papa, and Jehan and Pierre, and even her oldest brother Jacquemin, if his wife agreed. Maman could have servants to help her in running the house, and Papa would be given the respect he deserved as a good man and the father of Orléans' Maid.

She suddenly sensed a presence nearby, human not angelic, and turned her head.

A nun was standing a few feet behind her, silhouetted against the light from the chapel door. All the others had gone, as quietly as ghosts, although when they departed Jehanne could not say. She stood up slowly.

"Welcome, Jehanne. I have been expecting you."

The voice was the sweetest music Jehanne had ever heard this side of Heaven. But its owner was a shadow outlined in daylight and Jehanne could not see her face. She put her hand up to block the light, yet the figure remained in darkness.

"Expecting me? How did you know I was coming?"

"God told me." The nun took two steps toward her and became visible in the shifting light. "Is that better? Can you see me now?"

She was an inch or two taller than Jehanne and could have been any age between thirty and fifty. Her face, framed by a stiff wimple, was round and unlined, and accented by a strong, aquiline nose. An impish smile danced at the corners of her mouth. Most remarkable were the eyes. They shone with an ethereal light whose source was a soul in harmony with itself and with the world, in a flawless accord with God. With a start, Jehanne remembered Ste.-Catherine's prediction.

"Come, let us walk," the nun said. She took Jehanne's arm and crooked it around her own. Together they strolled across the floor into daylight.

"You do not know me, do you?" asked the nun. She gestured to a stone bench just outside the chapel door. Jehanne sat down, then the nun took a seat next to her.

Jehanne frowned, trying to place the woman who was smiling at her with a gentleness that was both tranquil and knowing. Her habit was woven from coarse brown wool, and a white veil covered her head. It hung past her shoulders like the wing of an angel.

"I am sorry, Madame, but I do not—"

The nun's laugh was as merry as a little bell. "It's all right, Jehanne, I would not expect you to know me. When I saw you last, you were only seven years old. That was a long time ago, no?" A waggish dimple creased her cheek.

"I don't understand. I don't—"

"—remember me? As I said, that was long ago." The nun gave Jehanne's hand a reassuring squeeze.

"I was traveling with two of my fellow sisters through Lorraine when we stopped to rest in a little out-of-the-way village called Domrémy. A kind couple gave us a meal, and we spent the night in their cottage. *Your* cottage, Jehanne. I can still recall you sitting at your father's feet. I saw even then that you were not an ordinary child. I told my sisters, 'There is a most unusual girl,' and they agreed that there was something special about you." She smiled again. "Do you remember me now?"

Jehanne's brow wrinkled in an effort to recollect the moon-shaped face and those incredible eyes that shone like blue flames from Heaven. So many travelers had stopped through her village when she was a child that they mingled all together in her remembrance, a panoply of forgotten faces. She shook her head uncertainly. "Excuse me, Madame, but . . . who are you?"

"I am Colette de Corbie."

Jehanne's face brightened. "Oh, yes, of course! I have heard of you."

Madame Colette's reputation was known throughout the kingdom. Her father had been a carpenter in Picardy, and upon his death and that of her mother she had taken the veil, first joining the Order of the Poor Claires. But the Rule of the Order had become lax in the two centuries since it was founded, departing drastically from the intentions of its originating saint. For three years Colette fasted in seclusion, during which time she experienced visions of St.-François and Ste.-Claire, who told her that she must reform the Order. Granted a charter by Pope Benedict XIII, she spent the intervening years founding the Reformed Order of Poor Claires in convents throughout France and Flandres. The simplicity of the Rule attracted many who had come to abhor the departure from piety that Ste.-Claire's community of women had begun to embrace.

Of Colette herself, it was said that she had witnessed many wondrous things while in the rapturous state. God had instructed her to make peace between the then twenty-two-year-old Dauphin and Philippe de Bourgogne, and while Charles had been willing, the duc resisted her. Rumor had it that he ordered his guard to seize her, intending to detain her in prison, but the man was rooted to the spot and could not obey the command. Philippe, fearful of God's retribution, had released her.

There was a story that on one memorable occasion she had caused the sun to rise three hours too early and clocks to go three hours later than they should have. Rumor was that she had taught lambs to kneel at the moment of the elevation of the Eucharist. The English and the House of Bourgogne accused her of being in collusion with the Devil, and it was only through the Pope's intervention that she had escaped the clutches of the Inquisition. The common people believed her to be a living saint.

"So this is your convent," Jehanne said, looking around at the simple buildings nestled within their protective wall. "You are the abbess here."

"It is God's convent, Jehanne." The melodious voice embraced her name. "I am only His servant, as you are."

"Oh, I am not at all like you, Madame," Jehanne replied, blushing to the roots of her hair. "I'm a simple soldier, that's all."

"France is filled with 'simple soldiers,' but there is only one Jehanne." Colette's marvelous eyes beamed at her with a teasing humor. "You do realize that?"

Jehanne hesitated, then, lowering her head, gave a small laugh. "Yes." She suddenly became serious. "But it is nearly always a burden, you know, to have people calling my name, asking me to bless them or their children. They call me *L'Angélique* and I hate that. They do not understand that I do what I do only because I have no other choice. It is God they should be praising, not me."

"Oh, yes, I know." Colette sighed. "It is not easy to keep one's conviction when serving God. Especially when one knows only too well the temptations to sin within oneself. The Devil is not always easy to resist, is he?"

"That is true. I . . . ," she hesitated, uncertain whether she should continue. She bit her lower lip and looked at the serene, wise woman who waited for her confession with such patience. "I do not always understand my Counsel when They speak to me, and there have been times when I've become angry with Them. But They always forgive me. And when They do, I feel so small and unimportant and unworthy. Do you know what I mean?"

"Indeed." The nun laughed. "I am a very stubborn soul, Jehanne, and I often quarrel with mine. Fortunately, They are more obstinate than I. Once, when I balked at Their commands, They struck me dumb, then blind, until I finally surrendered and gave Them the faith They were asking of me. Another time They pulled my stool out from under me!" She chuckled at the memory of her willfulness.

"Really?" Jehanne exclaimed. "Mine have never done anything like that, thank God."

" 'Thank God' is right." Colette's brows drew together in an ironic frown, but her dimples indicated an underlying jocularity. "I think you are perhaps not as unworthy as you think you are."

"Unworthy enough." Sadness floated through her. "I lost Paris, Madame. I did not listen to Them, and because of that many brave men lost their lives." Sorrow for Raymond fell in a tear she did not trouble to wipe away. "I should have waited until the King was more fully committed to battle, but I was impatient and wanted to have my own way instead of listening to what God wanted. I failed," she whispered.

" 'Should have done' is a useless set of words, my dear." Colette's sweet voice throbbed with compassion. "Did your Counsel tell you that you had failed?"

Jehanne shook her head. Wiping her eyes with the back of her hand, she admitted, "They told me that God forgave me and that I must forgive myself."

"Good advice. If you have not forgiven yourself, then perhaps you would do well to ask yourself, who knows better, you or God? I think that sometimes we are much harder on ourselves than our Heavenly Father could ever be. That is the sin of presumption, is it not?"

"I suppose so," Jehanne mumbled.

Colette put an affectionate arm around her shoulder and kissed her temple. "None of us is perfect, Jehanne. Try to become so, try as hard as you can, but do not blame yourself when you find that you are not. It just means that you have further to grow in your understanding and in your faith. And never forget that you are in league with the Almighty, Who is always there to help you."

Jehanne sniffed, then rubbed her runny nose. The comforting words seemed to seep into her suffering conscience. She realized that there was a wound within her that had never really healed, not since the carnage at Orléans. Clasidas, Guyenne, the nameless English boy at Patay, Raymond, and all the others had festered like a black disease in her soul. But Colette's wise understanding was like a release for her and for all those who had silently accused her of blame, and she felt an overflowing gratitude toward this sympathetic nun.

"Did you really know that I was coming here today?" asked Jehanne.

"Oh, yes. Actually, I have known since I first met you in Domrémy that we would meet again. At that time I thought that you would perhaps join our Order, because I saw even then that God had His hand upon you. Later, when I began to hear that you were seeking an audience with Charles, I knew that your destiny did not lie within the contemplative life, but that God had other plans for you. So, to answer your question, yes, I knew that you were coming here. My Counsel told me a few days ago that you were very near."

Jehanne laughed. "And mine told me that I would meet you! Though They did not give your name, They told me that I would soon meet someone like me who would understand the things that I feel." Her eyes filled again. "I have not had anyone in my life who really understands, not since They first came to me. I have been very lonely."

Colette closed her eyes and smiled. "It is a lonely life, the way of those to whom God speaks. There was a time when I found it nearly unbearable, until I came to see that it is because I was born to give my life to Him and only Him. Lord Jhesus said that one cannot serve two masters. If one's attention is fixed on the world, we cannot listen for the voice of God."

"But we are in the world, Madame Colette." Jehanne frowned. "There are always other people around us, needing our attention."

"That is true, even in a convent. However, Our Lord also said that we must be in the world but not of it." Her smooth brow wrinkled with concern. "Do you understand what that means?"

Jehanne frowned, afraid to admit that she did not.

"It means," Colette said quietly, "that although we can never entirely escape the world and its snares, we should resist the temptation to embrace what it esteems, because that is quite often at odds with what God treasures. Those of us whom He has called to His service must know—really *know*—that His way is the only way to true happiness. Only then can we live outwardly in the world while holding to the stillness within us where only God dwells. And yes, my dear, it is a very lonely life."

Jehanne smiled through her tears. "I am glad that I came here today. I am glad that I met you."

"So am I." Colette reached out and with a careful stroke of her finger dried a tear trickling down Jehanne's cheekbone toward the crease in her nostril. "Try not to take things so seriously, Jehanne. Don't you know that God laughs sometimes?"

"Do you ever regret it, that He called you?"

"There have been moments, of course," the nun responded with a tender smile. "But they disappear when I hear the voices of His messengers. The joy I experience then more than redresses any difficulties I must otherwise bear. Is it not the same for you?"

"Yes." Jehanne nodded soberly. "I forget everything else when They speak to me. Nothing seems important or even real but Them. They have shown me some wonderful things." Suddenly remembering the wolf who lurked within her nightmare, she shuddered. "And some terrible things."

Colette's eyes softened with comprehension, and encouraged, Jehanne asked, "Do yours ever send you dreams that . . . that make no sense?"

The nun gave a short laugh. "Dreams often make no sense, Jehanne, to a great many people." She hesitated, then raised her sights to Jehanne's thoughtful frown. "But you speak of a special kind of dream, do you not?"

While her mouth still curved upward in a pretty bow, the lightness of spirit she wore as assuredly as she did her abbess' robes had suddenly vanished, and in its place a quiet expectancy willed a reply, those extraordinary eyes all the while searching Jehanne for a glimmer of concealment. A tremor skittered up Jehanne's spine and she shuddered again, this time in recognition that here was not just a kindly nun of good fame but someone whose Power equaled her own.

Yet . . . would she understand? Jehanne's heart began to race with a certainty that she had gone too far to turn back now, even if it meant that Colette would think her mad or a coward, even if she were alone upon the earth after all. It could not be helped; she would have to gamble.

"I am plagued by a nightmare that comes to me often," she admitted. "At first it troubled me only a little, but now I feel its darkness for days after I see it. It's almost as though it is stalking me."

"Would you like to tell me about it?" Colette asked gently.

"Yes," Jehanne whispered. With a sigh, she began to speak haltingly of the horse who rode into her sleep and carried her to the frozen lake, where the wolf waited for her upon the ice. As she spoke, she seemed to feel the cold terror, as real as a memory, seep into her bones, and before she knew it she was trembling.

Colette rubbed Jehanne's hands, then put an arm around her shoulder. "I fear that the Devil is following me," Jehanne said miserably, now feeling close to tears again, "that he has decided to wage war against God for my soul. I try as hard as I can to be brave, to resist the Evil One and to hold on to God, but I am frightened."

"And your Counsel?" wondered Colette. "What do They tell you?"

"That I should attend upon God, and He will help me in all things, however difficult." She had heard this so many times that her recitation was mechanical, without understanding.

She did not feel any better when Colette smiled and said, "Then that is what you must do, is it not?"

"Yes. It is what I must do." She knew that she should take comfort from Colette's words, imparted with such sympathy and compassion, but she felt no better for having confessed her dark dream.

"What is wrong, Jehanne? You look very sad, my dear." Colette looked as though she already knew the answer.

"It's just that . . . I pray every day that I might be faithful to God, and for a little while afterward all is well, but just when I begin to think that I have conquered fear, that dream comes again to shake my faith, and I am afraid once more!"

Jehanne ran her hand through her short hair. "Brother Pasquerel, my confessor, says that it is a test from God, nothing more, but that does not comfort me." She sighed. "Brother Pasquerel means well, I know he does. But he has not had such a dream and does not know its power."

"Then as long as you remain afraid, the Devil is already winning his battle for your soul."

Jehanne tore her eyes from the ground to Colette's face. A corner of the nun's mouth was turned upward, but her look was kind. "If you allow the dream to frighten you into believing that God will abandon you, then to whom have you turned, God or the Devil? I think that you are braver than that, Jehanne, and more worthy of God's protection than you know. He called you to His service, did He not? Well, then"—she continued, acknowledging Jehanne's nod—"He will not allow any harm to befall you."

This peaceful response touched Jehanne as nothing else had in a long time. Tears spilled down her face, and she put her head on the nun's shoulder. Colette gently stroked her hair, reminding Jehanne of Isabelle.

Jehanne was taken by an abrupt desire to relinquish her part in the war, to return home and let Charles do what he would. At the same time, she knew that that road was closed to her forever. A sob assaulted her and she wept for the life she could have lived, far away from the Power that had shaped her destiny.

Colette turned slightly and embraced her as Jehanne released sorrow into the nun's scratchy woven garment. "It's all right," Colette whispered. "You have kept much bottled up for a long time, haven't you?"

Jehanne nodded, then looked at her companion in God through a swimming vision. "Thank you, Madame. You are very kind to trouble about me."

A bell began to toll in the chapel tower. "I must go now, Jehanne. I am very sorry that I cannot stay with you longer, but I have duties to attend to."

"I understand." Time had slipped away as it did when she was with Them, and she wondered what the hour was. "Thank you for talking with me."

They stood up together. Colette took Jehanne's hands and kissed her knuckles. "God keep you safe, Jehanne. Perhaps we may meet again."

Jehanne nodded, then smiled suddenly. "I'm sure we'll see one another in Heaven."

A little laugh gurgled from somewhere in the depths of Colette's soul. Her jolly, clear eyes frolicked with good-natured humor. "You may count on that." She hugged Jehanne to her tightly.

Jehanne kissed the nun's cheek. "Farewell, Madame Colette. God be with you."

"*Et cum tu, carissima.*"

Jehanne clung for a moment to the nun's hand, their fingers intertwining. Reluctantly, she turned away and walked rapidly toward the gate, wiping her eyes as she went.

When she reached the street, she looked back and waved. Colette acknowledged her good-bye with a hand raised in silent benediction.

Minguet stuck his head through the closed tent flap. "Jehanne, Brother Richard is here," he whispered loudly. "He has that strange woman with him."

She groaned, looking across the candlelit table at Pasquerel. When she rolled her eyes, the monk laughed.

For the last hour he had been there to watch while she practiced signing her name. He was very patient with the slow strokes that she made across the parchment. She was getting better at it and soon would not need him any more at all, he joked. Jehanne laughed, reminding him that even if she learned her signature, she could not be her own confessor.

The pastime was a good way for her to dismiss her disquiet. The army had returned north, to Montfaucon-en-Berry just a few leagues south of Bourges. Jehanne and d'Albret had decided that tomorrow they would attack La Charité from the west. The King, when consulted, agreed with their plan. But despite warmer weather, Jehanne felt an unease that she could not shake, for her Guides were silent about the outcome, always an ominous sign. Nevertheless, she was committed to seeing the strategy to its end. The army, bolstered by their victory at St.-Pierre-le-Moustier, still believed in her, as did her household.

She could hear them singing outside, and Jehan's deep voice, roaring off-key above the rest, reminded her of the way Jacques used to lead his children in song while they worked in the fields. The old folksong about a lovesick *trouvère* and his indifferent lady had only just a moment ago lifted her spirits.

Now Brother Richard was here to mar her mood, no doubt with Catherine de la Rochelle in tow. "Very well, Minguet," she sighed, "show them in." She looked at Pasquerel's ironic, faintly illuminated face. "This time I want you to stay," she whispered.

He put a finger to his upper lip and nodded.

Minguet held the flap open for Brother Richard and the woman to enter. Jehanne turned toward them, arranging her face into a pleasant expression. "Good evening, Brother Richard, Madame."

She found it difficult not to chortle at the absurd disparity in their statures. The friar was slovenly as usual, the tight curls clinging to his head in a greasy mass. It was not warm enough for him to be wandering around without a cloak, yet here he was in only the soiled habit that she was certain he never washed. In contrast, Madame de la Rochelle was bundled in her fur-lined mantle as though she had come in from a blizzard.

"Good evening." Brother Richard grinned, seeming all teeth. "We've heard that you're going to attack La Charité, so we came to wish you Godspeed and another victory."

"Thank you," she replied. "Please sit down"—she waved her palm toward the tent floor—"I regret that I have no stools to offer you."

The tall monk immediately did as she asked. Catherine looked at the ground uncertainly before she too sat. Madame de la Rochelle glanced at Pasquerel as though she wanted him to leave. Jehanne's confessor made no effort to obey, but leaned an elbow upon the table and rested his chin on a pale fist.

"We are also here to ask whether you have decided to speak to the King for me." Catherine was determined to come to the point.

"I have considered it, Madame, but I regret that I cannot." Jehanne's face remained impassive, but inside she was grinning.

A dark look crossed Brother Richard's long face as he scratched idly at his fleabitten chest. "Why not?" he demanded.

"I am sorry, Madame Catherine," Jehanne answered, her eyes never leaving the woman. "I consulted with my Counsel, and they told me that your place is with your husband and your children. It is not God's wish that you trouble the King."

" 'Trouble!' " the lanky friar snorted irritably. "Since when is it 'trouble' to give Heavenly assistance to the King? If someone had not 'troubled' to support you, you would not be where you are now!"

Jehanne fastened a defiant gaze on him, trying to control the bile rising to her throat. "I was not speaking to you, but to Madame de la Rochelle." She swung her penetrating brown eyes to the woman. "Your place is not at court; it is with your family. The King of Heaven has given another to serve King Charles, and— pardon my plain language—He has sent no 'white lady' to you, Madame. I regret that you are unhappy with your life, but it is the one you have and you must make peace with it."

The two of them sat speechless at the blunt words they had not expected from her. "Of course," Jehanne continued, feeling a devilish impulse creep upon her, "you are free to join me in battle tomorrow if you wish."

"I cannot do that," Catherine spluttered, "and you should not either."

One corner of Jehanne's mouth turned up in concert with her eyebrows. "Why not?"

"Because it is too cold there." The woman tossed the response back at her as though it were a triumph.

This time Jehanne could not help but laugh. "Go home, Madame. Your sons have need of you."

Catherine leaped to her feet, not an easy task in the long skirt that clung to her legs. "I shall not stay here and be insulted. You are jealous of anyone else who has heard God speak to her. You are infected with the sin of pride, and may Our Lord punish you justly for your arrogance!"

She flounced out of the tent, nearly knocking over Minguet, who was eaves-dropping outside the door. Brother Richard stood up, clenching his hands in passionate indignation.

"Who do you think you are to speak to her like that? 'Jehanne the Maid, chosen of God,'" he mimicked with a sarcastic smirk. "Catherine has spoken the truth, and you turn her away. She is correct in saying that you are arrogant, and fur-thermore, you are a spoiled brat who wants all the glory for herself! You are in love with your fame, L'Angélique, and you would not share it with anyone, no matter how deserving that person might be."

"There is no white lady," Jehanne answered with a calmness that denied her rising temper. "Your friend there is a fraud."

"How do you know that?" he roared. "Do you think you know everything just because God has given you a few victories?"

Jehanne stood up. The Power struck into him with her reply. "I know because I spent two nights with her, waiting for something that never came. I know because my Counsel, whom I trust with my life, whom I trust more than any human being, have told me that Madame de la Rochelle sees no visions from God nor from anywhere else!" Jehanne's chest was heaving now in righteous anger.

"It is she who longs for glory. *I* never asked for it, *I* never wanted it, I wish I could go home to *my* family, and let me tell you something else, Brother: You are just as deceitful as she is, with your long sermons that drag on for hours and say nothing of any import!" She lowered her voice to a hiss, "Your speeches are painful to listen to, because you beat people over the head with what you have to say. You are not a man of God, you are a bully who seeks only power over people that they might acclaim you!"

His face was beet red, and fire leaped from his eyes so that he looked like the Devil himself. She knew he wanted to strike her. Instead, he turned on his heel and strode wrathfully from the tent.

When he was safely gone, Jehanne kicked the stool on which she had been sitting. It flew several inches and fell over onto its side. She was still very angry, so she kicked it again.

"Careful, Jehanne, you will damage a fine stool," Pasquerel drawled.

"He makes me so mad, I could—!" She pummeled the stool with her boot one more time.

Pasquerel was looking at her in mock consternation.

The humor in the situation suddenly caught up with her, and she started to laugh. The more she laughed, the funnier it became, until she finally collapsed upon the floor with tears streaming down her face. Pasquerel was laughing, too. The two of them howled with mirth.

It was just beginning to subside when they caught one another's eye. That sent them both into a renewed gale of comedy, and Jehanne cackled so much that her sides ached.

At last, she lay on her back, exhausted. Their titters petered out after a few minutes.

"You know, you probably shouldn't have spoken to them that way," Pasquerel remarked when he could talk again.

"Oh, they can't do anything to me. Besides, I needed to tell them the truth."

She scrambled to a standing position and walked over to the stricken stool. She brought it back to the table and sat on it. "Come now, I want you to help me write a letter to the people of Tours. Héliote Poulnois, whose father designed my standard, is getting married soon. I want to ask the men of Tours to provide a dowry for her in my name."

She forgot all about Brother Richard and his misguided acolyte. But Catherine de la Rochelle's warning to stay away from La Charité came back to her in the days and weeks ahead as the siege dragged on. Regardless of how hard the big cannon from Orléans pounded at the city walls, they could not break the resolve of their elusive objective. After almost a month, Charles ordered them to raise the siege, and the army was forced to abandon the cannon the Orléanais had entrusted to them. By the beginning of December, Jehanne was back with the King at Mehun-sur-Yèvre.

CHAPTER THIRTEEN

The End of War

December 10, 1429–May 23, 1430

he King was in a jovial mood at supper. As he entered the hall, those courtiers whom he addressed by name bowed to him from their dining places, smugly glancing about to make certain that his regard was noted by their less favored fellows.

Jehanne eyed the King sadly from her bench, wondering if she would ever have another opportunity to speak to him alone. There was a time when she had dined at his right hand and had leave to converse with Charles whenever she wanted. But ever since her latest defeat at La Charité he had avoided her except when in the company of his retainers.

It was not that he was ever outwardly censuring. On the contrary, he had made light of the lost siege with a careless toss of his hand, assuring her that she would soon have another day in the field. He graciously included her in games, and admired her skill with a horse when his company hunted quail in those last days before the snows came. He insisted that she accompany him to Mass in his private chapel. Nonetheless, he did not have to voice his disappointment in her, for she could feel his unuttered displeasure. Occasionally, something akin to reproach crossed his plain face when he looked at her, and he never let her get close to him.

But she discovered that evening that he still had the power to surprise her.

When the meal was finished and everyone was expecting the entertainments to begin, Charles' majordomo walked to the central space between the trestles and announced that the family Darc were summoned to His Majesty's table forthwith. Jehanne and her brothers rose uncertainly to their feet and knelt before the King.

Bowing, the majordomo gave Charles an official-looking ribbon-bedecked parchment. The King cleared his throat and in a strong voice read that hereby he was issuing letters-patent of nobility to Jehanne and to everyone in her family, in both the male and the female line, forever. He gave the males the right to bear arms and a heraldic emblem, thus inscribed: Azure, a sword argent hilted and supporting on its points a crown of gold between two fleurs-de-lys. Their name henceforth would be the family du Lys.

Jehanne and her brothers returned unsteadily to their places at table. Her eyes swept the room and she saw to her astonishment that nearly all the courtiers were smiling broadly. To them, she was no longer an upstart peasant out of place in this company. She had become Jehanne du Lys, noble of France.

She sat in numbed silence through the rest of the evening's entertainment, insensible to the jugglers and acrobats who frolicked in the open space before the table. Her brothers, having recovered from their shock, were now in high good spirits and laughed loudly at the antics of Charles' jester, a silly man who ridiculed the duc de Bourgogne's coming marriage to his third, much younger wife. Almost everyone became a little drunk from the limitless wine that appeared every time a cup was emptied. Indeed, Jehanne could tell by their slurred words that Pierre and Jehan were quite inebriated.

She drank very little. Isolated in the wake of the King's generosity, she felt herself to be nothing more than a numbed observer, without a body, nameless. In less than a heartbeat, her identity as she had always known it had become transformed, and truly, she did not know how she should be feeling. She tried on her new name as though it were a strange, ill-fitting suit.

Jehanne du Lys.

She did not like it. Oh, she was grateful to Charles for the unforeseen honor; it was not thanklessness that made her ill at ease. She could not precisely mark the source of her dissatisfaction.

Perhaps it was due to the fact that she could not forget that she was peasant-born, that the girl to whom Michel first spoke had seen him fresh from pasture where she had been tending the village's cattle. But that girl had vanished long ago. Or maybe, she reasoned, it was because an acceptance of her new name would mean a disavowal of her parents. Yet that was not it. They were now as ennobled as she.

And then she knew.

Jehanne the Maid was her right name, given to her by God rather than by man. If Charles had really wanted to please her, he should have given her the army she needed to finish the war. She was not, nor could she ever be, of the nobility of the earth. For her to assume that rank would mean that she had given up all hope of saving the kingdom, for it was Jehanne the Maid whom God had called to that task. Moreover, the people of France who knew her as Jehanne the Maid would feel that she had betrayed the faith they had given her. No one would ever give honor to a craven Jehanne du Lys, hiding safely at court.

She found herself in a real entanglement. Knowing that she would never ask for anything for herself, Charles had given her something that he truly thought would please her. Because he had given it, she had to accept it. But she would never surrender her God-given name. If He were willing, she would be Jehanne the Maid always, to the grave.

*   *   *

Much of France was swallowed in a violent blizzard by Christmas morning. The storm persisted throughout the day, and was still roaring by the time Jehanne attended Mass in the late afternoon. A wistful sadness took her to thoughts of her parents. She had never missed a Christmas with them in all her life, and she ached with the recollection of how impatient she had been to leave them a year ago. Soon after the Nativity she had indeed gone away to change her life and theirs forever. Now they would have to celebrate the birth of the Lord without three of their children.

The King's chapel at Bourges was hung with bright red and green ribbons. From the alpine regions of the German Empire boughs of fir, entwined into cheerful wreaths with red-berried holly and crimson satin, decorated the rafters and walls. Candles shimmered between the adornments framing the windows, throwing flickering reflections upon glass faintly brightened from outside by muted winter daylight. Before the statue of Our Lady, Baby Jhesus slept in His crèche under the adoring gaze of shepherds and His earthly parents. The chapel smelled of incense and mountain pine.

Jehanne was dressed in a new suit that Charles had given her. The shirt beneath her bright red tunic was a thick wool embroidered in gold. Over that she wore a deep royal blue surcoat lined with ermine, covered by a short scarlet mantle which fastened at the throat by a gold clasp. The King had also made her a gift of soft calfskin boots that ended three inches short of her knees. On this freezing day she was thankful for them and for the heavy woolen hose that warmed her legs to the waist. A soft hat reinforced with fox fur and embellished by a long pheasant feather sat at a cocky angle upon her hair.

Most precious to her was the ring on the third finger of her right hand, a present not from Charles but from Jehan. Her brother was strangely bashful when he gave it to her, for it was not very expensive or of high quality, but a simple band of base metal plated with gold. His new pedigree notwithstanding, he had no more money than he had when he was Jehan Darc, and what he did possess came from money the King gave to Jehanne. That did not matter to her. He could not have guessed when he purchased it in the town how pleased she would be by his thoughtfulness.

Both of her brothers were draped in new clothing, also gifts from the King, and Jehanne thought she would burst from pride in their handsome appearances. In the months since they had joined her at Tours they had ceased being boys and had become stalwart young men whose dignity disclaimed their humble origins. They looked grand in their new suits. Jehan was quite the dandy in vivid green velvet, with the sword Jehanne had given him swinging gloriously from his silver belt. Pierre, not to be outdone by his elder brother, had selected for himself a brilliant orange brocade from the King's tailor that made him glow like the sun.

The siblings walked side by side behind the royal couple into the chapel, where the other members of Charles' court were already assembled. Organ music announced their arrival in a stately hymn composed long ago to honor the birth of Lord Jhesus. There was a rustle of damasks and velvets as those awaiting them bowed low to the King and Queen. Jehanne and her brothers followed Charles to within an armlength of the altar, and knelt upon the cold stone floor. Then archbishop de Chartres began the solemn High Mass.

"*In nomine Patris, et Filii, et Spìritus Sancti. Amen.*"

The congregation obediently made the Sign of the Cross. Jehanne raised her face to the golden crucifix above the altar. On this, the holiest day of the year, she felt the promise of peace that Christe's coming had foretold so long ago. The new year would perhaps give evidence of that pledge if God willed it.

Please, Lord Jhesus, give me another chance to save the kingdom. I have not accomplished what God commanded of me in my allotted year. I know that I have not much time left now. Please touch the King's heart that he might release me to do Your will.

And then They were with her, singing Christmas praises through the swirling, soaring music the court musician launched toward Heaven from the chapel organ. She could sense Them as surely as she felt her brothers, kneeling next to her.

DO NOT BE SAD, JEHANNE. THERE IS A TIME FOR EVERYTHING, AND THIS IS THE MOMENT FOR REST AND CELEBRATION. GOD HAS NOT FORGOTTEN YOU.

Without words Catherine showed her what the next few months could portend if men of power chose to make it so. Jehanne's eyes widened in disbelief at the vision of clashing weapons and banners lost in clouds of dust. Her Guides did not need to explain what it meant.

Like dream images when wakefulness has returned, they began to dissolve, slowly, until her Counsel were gone, leaving her with a pang of bereavement. The old haunting desire to go with Them had never departed altogether, not since she first heard Michel's voice commanding her to obey her parents and to keep faith with God. She could almost hear him now, saying as in an afterthought, *It is not yet time.*

She returned fully to her surroundings and stood with the congregation, who began making their way to the altar to receive Holy Communion.

When Mass ended, Charles took the Queen's arm and led the gathering through the lashing snowstorm to the Royal Hall. The lords and ladies bustled inside and made straight for the fireplace where immense logs were stacked in a burning tripod. As in the chapel, seasonal greenery hung from the walls in wreaths festooned with bright ribbons, their fresh, tangy smell mingling with the odors of woodsmoke and a hundred different dishes. Seven barrels, three of beer and four filled with wine, stood invitingly against a wall, and right away their spigots opened to the thirsty. The usual benches had been taken away from the long, piled table in order to allow the celebrants an easy path to the food.

Venison marinated in wine and spices, then grilled slowly over a spit; roast pork coated in a sugary glaze; cheeses of every size, color, and odor; breads both light and dark; capons by the dozens, crisply brown and heaped upon silver platters; roast lamb served in a cameline sauce; pink, headless salmon in a steaming mixture of leeks and almonds; greens braised with bacon; chilled chicken livers prepared in wine, cinnamon, and ginger; beans fried in garlic; peapods swimming in butter; thick rabbit and fish stews; meat porridge; spinach pancakes; oysters stewed in ale; beef ribs braised in cinnamon, saffron, and wine; deep-dish chicken pasties; apple fritters fried golden brown; custard tarts and elderflower cheese pie;

puddings made from sweet cream, cakes of every imaginable size and taste. The fare seemed to have no end but went on and on in a startling array of inventive cuisine.

At this time of the year, when the usual formalities were set aside for feasting and caroling, the castle's household were as welcome to partake of food and drink as were Charles' retainers. Stewards and stablemen, valets and cooks, mixed freely with noblemen and ladies-in-waiting in a topsy-turvy annual fellowship that would be set aside after the Epiphany. All wore splendid new clothing, gifts from their liege lord and King.

Jehanne wondered how much all of this had cost. Certainly more than Charles' treasury would allow. She pushed away the temptation she felt to resentment. If the King wished to be generous with Trémoïlle's money in celebration of Our Lord's birthday, she should be happy rather than bitter that he had not used it to equip the army. The joyful faces around her were a rebuke, and she let ill will pass as she searched for the King among the other faces.

She moved a few paces to her right and saw him standing across the room beneath a tapestry embroidered in an outdoor spectacle prominently featuring his late father. Charles was as usual in the center of an admiring circle, among whom were old Robert LeMaçon, the seigneur de Trèves; Madame de Gaucourt; and Jehanne's brother Pierre. She could not hear what the King was saying at this distance, but from the amused expressions on the faces of the listeners, she surmised that he must be relating a joke. That meant that he was in a good mood, which would make her task easier.

Jehanne elbowed her way slowly through the chattering, eating throng, past the table to the other side. As she drew up to the rollicking group, Pierre put a casual arm around her shoulder and gave her an affectionate, one-armed hug.

"Here is our beloved Jehanne!" the King exclaimed, lifting a jeweled winecup so that a little of the contents sloshed upon his hand. His eyes were slightly glazed from drink but he was not drunk, at least not yet. "Are you having a good time?" he asked her. "Have you had something to eat? Our cooks have prepared a most excellent feast. Or so we are told." He raised his goblet and everyone but Jehanne laughed. They were all feeling the wine a bit.

"Yes, Sire, thank you. I'm not very hungry just now." She smiled.

"Then have some wine," Charles suggested. "We cannot vouchsafe for the food, but we can tell you firsthand that the drink is excellent." The group chortled again.

"Later, Sire," Jehanne replied, feeling her patience attempting to run away. "I'm sorry, my lord, but I must speak to you in private."

"Oh, must you?" He groaned like a peevish child. "Come now, Jehanne, this is a party. Let us leave off serious things today."

"It's important, Sire." She frowned. "Please."

He hesitated. "Oh, very well. Come with me."

The courtiers bowed to him as he moved away. Pierre grabbed her arm and whispered, "Don't make him angry, Jehanne, he's in a good mood."

"Mind your own business, Pierre," she snapped. She wrenched her arm from his grasp and went after the King.

He took her to the far end of the hall and opened a door to a much smaller room where she had never been before. She could tell from the laden bookcases that this was a library. A large desk sat next to the thickly frosted window, through which she could nonetheless see that the snowstorm had not subsided even a little. The library was cozy, thanks to the neatly arranged, kindled fireplace.

Charles did not sit, nor did he invite Jehanne to a stool. He placed his cup on the edge of the desk and warmed his slender hands before the fire. "Now what is so important that it could not wait?" From the tone in his voice, she could tell that he was not angry, just impatient to return to his festivities.

"Sire, when we were in Mass, my Counsel came to me." She paused. "They told me that you are in great danger."

"Danger?" Fear widened his eyes and he became pale. "What kind of danger?"

"My lord, you must not sign any more truces with the seigneur de Bourgogne," Jehanne warned him urgently. "He plans to betray you by building up his forces for a spring offensive against Orléans. If you agree to his request to stop fighting until winter ends, he will only use that against you."

"How did you know about that?" Charles looked at her as though she had sprouted a tail and hooves.

"As I said, Sire, my Counsel told me, just a little while ago, in Mass." She took a couple of steps toward him, extending her hands in a pleading gesture. "Please, I beg you, do not sign any more treaties or you will certainly lose Orléans again. Think what that would mean, Sire! With the English and the Burgundians holding Paris, you would be back where you started and all the fighting, all the dying, would have been for nothing! Even now the English plan to bring their boy-king to Paris to be crowned. If that happens, the Loire towns and those in Champagne that have swung to your side may change their fealty back to your enemies."

The latter point was not, strictly speaking, something her Guides had told her, not in words anyway, but it was certainly something They had made known to her. She knew that young Henry was coming, she felt him as surely as she felt the apprehension in the young man standing before her.

Charles turned his gaze to the fire, alarmed at what he had heard. If she knew about his secret treaty to extend the truce, did she also know that he had lent Compiègne to Philippe?

He looked at her, smitten by a pinprick of conscience. She trusted him, believed in him; that was plain by the look on her young face. Her forthrightness was a censure to his double dealing, and for the first time since he had known her he saw that he had played her falsely every step of the way. God had sent her to him, and in rejecting her he rejected the King of Heaven.

He thrust the thought aside. What did she know of diplomacy or the heaviness of the crown that she had forced upon him? He was the one who had to carry the weight of monarchy, and he would make the policies that governed the kingdom, not Jehanne du Lys.

His face softened a little. "Jehanne, I have no intention of allowing enemies of France to overrun the kingdom. But I need to buy time with this treaty in order to build up the treasury again to pay for an army. We have no money for war! By springtime, I hope to be able to borrow enough to resupply my soldiers."

It was on the edge of her tongue to say, You have no money for an army yet you give new clothes to your court and hold this wasteful party.

She bit down on the words as they leaped to her mouth, and instead replied, "The soldiers would come without being paid. They would come for love of you and of France. You have only to ask them, Sire. And your good Loire towns are loyal to you; they shall not betray you unless . . ."

He raised an eyebrow. "Unless?"

"Unless you abandon them, Sire," she said softly.

"You sound very sure of that, Jehanne."

"I would wager my life on it."

You may very well be sure, he thought. But you certainly do not know that my councillors goad me daily to have done with you now that I am King. They tell me that you have served your purpose, and I am inclined to believe them. What a tiresome nuisance you have become since the coronation! Yet I cannot let you go to your fate, for I do love you, Jehanne the Maid, in my fashion, and I am grateful for all that you have done and tried to do. That is why I ennobled you.

Aloud he said, "Let us wait until spring. An army would be at a disadvantage in this weather anyway. I give you my word as King that in the spring I shall once again give you the forces for which you have asked. Is that fair?" He smiled.

"Yes, Sire," she answered, relieved. He had heard her after all. She only hoped that the fruits of his promise would not come too late. Still, this concession from him was better than nothing, preferable to what she had had half an hour earlier.

"Good. Now let us return to the festivities. After all, it is Christmas, and we have much to celebrate."

The carnival atmosphere hung on at court for another week, into the new year. On January 1, the Feast of Fools, Charles surrendered his throne to a stableboy for the day. Archbishop de Chartres and the King's confessor wore masks during the Mass, and instead of hymns they sang licentious songs and ate sausages before the altar, evoking sacrilegious laughter from everybody present but one.

Jehanne was shocked to the soul by this blasphemy. It was not that she was embarrassed for Charles, pretending with a wink that he was a servant. Everyone knew he was still the King, that was part of the game. In Domrémy it was carried out in a much smaller way. The mayor changed places with old Sagot, a near-penniless wretch whose wife and children were dead and who lived on the charity of his neighbors. But the disgraceful antics of the clerics were another matter. Back home the pious common sense of the villagers forbade the curé from be-having shamelessly, so he did not profane God. He was one of them in any case and would not have even considered doing so.

But this! Yuletide excesses among the wanton rich had been the subject of village gossip for years, so it did not altogether surprise her. Nevertheless, her stomach turned to see the archbishop and the King's personal confessor cavorting like heathens before the altar of the Lord. She was so nauseated by it that she quietly stole away from the chapel, taking Pasquerel with her. They went to her room, where her confessor said a proper Mass and she took Holy Communion. With the sacred Host melting into her tongue, she prayed that God would have mercy on poor suffering France and that the Year of Our Lord 1430 would bring peace to them all as the last had not.

The riotous merrymaking continued until the Epiphany, when the castle's servants returned to their duties and everything settled back to normal. Although Jehanne became eighteen years old on that day, she did not remember to mark the occasion. She was too busy fretting over her enforced inaction, and so overcome with worry that Charles would again withdraw from his promise to provide her with an army when spring returned, that she could think of nothing else. By now she had come to expect the worst from her King, who had kept so few of his pledges to her.

So she paced apprehensively back and forth across the floor of her room. When she could no longer bear it, she went to the chapel and prayed for a long time. Her Counsel comforted her with reassurances that all would be well, that God was with her, that she must abide everything with patience. She felt better then and returned to the warmth of her small chamber. She had not been there long at all when a hundred worries again swooped upon her like ravens. She walked the floor for another hour before she went once more to the chapel.

This pattern continued for nearly two weeks. During that time she thought she would lose her mind with frustration. She ate little and slept even less. Her household felt the sharp side of her tongue more and more often, and one afternoon Minguet burst into tears under the brunt of her sarcasm. Weighed down with remorse yet too proud to admit her wrong, she suffered through her sin in silence until chided by Catherine.

THEY WHO LOVE YOU DO NOT DESERVE THE CONSEQUENCES OF YOUR ABSENCE OF FAITH. IN YOUR DISTRUST OF GOD YOU HAVE INFLICTED NEEDLESS PAIN UPON THOSE WHO ARE INNOCENT OF ANY MALICE TOWARD YOU AND WHO HAVE SERVED YOU WELL. YOU MUST MAKE AMENDS.

How?

DISMISS YOUR PRIDE. LET A PROPER BEARING RETURN WITH HUMILITY. APOLOGIZE SINCERELY. AND YOU SHALL HEAL THEM AND YOURSELF.

She did as Catherine commanded. Summoning them to her room took more courage than it had required for her to assault the walls of Paris. When they were all together, she quietly surveyed their sullen faces.

Pierre and Minguet, the youngest of her troop, had gotten the worst from her. Her brother's resentment smoldered like a black fire in his eyes. She remembered what a pest he was as a child and all those times when he had teased her back in Domrémy. But then that memory was replaced by another, and she saw him protecting her from the Burgundians at St.-Pierre-le-Moustier. He was no paid servant to suffer her verbal attacks in silence; he was her brother. So was Minguet, adopted in Tours when he had no other to call family. Now he was sitting on the floor with downcast eyes as he scratched an absent pattern on his boot with a thumbnail.

Jehan and d'Aulon merely looked at her, their faces cool, unapproachable. She knew what they were thinking. To them, the woman they loved and admired had become an intolerable tyrant, no better than Bedford or Philippe de Bourgogne. Only Brother Pasquerel, who understood the turmoil in her soul, fixed a small smile on her. She had a feeling that he knew how difficult the waiting was and what fortitude it required for her to have called them together. It could not be avoided. Neither she nor they could suffer any longer. She cleared her throat and swallowed.

"Thank you for coming here," she began. "I suppose you've noticed how out of sorts I've been lately." A log crackled in the fireplace, shifting a little as the flames bit into it. She took another breath. God, this was hard to do.

"I have felt useless in this place since we've been separated from the army. God has told me that we shall get another opportunity to fight our King's enemies, yet I worry that we shall not." Pasquerel's ascetic features ached with sympathy for her, and encouraged, she continued. "I have sinned greatly by doubting God, and in my weakness I have thrust my failures on all of you."

She swallowed again so that she might finish this. "I had no right to do that. My faithlessness is not your doing; it is mine. I know that I have hurt you, and I—I apologize. I only hope that you can forgive me."

And then they were all on their feet, loving her, embracing her in their charmed circle. All of them had tears in their eyes; even her confessor's blue eyes were misty. They held her very close to them, their arms around each other as well. She kissed each cheek in acceptance of his pardon. In that moment she felt turmoil leave her. Its dense shadow slunk away toward the abyss from whence it had come. She vowed before God that she would not take them for granted any more.

It was as though the curse she had been under was magically dispelled. During the next few days she felt so uplifted that when she prayed, she knew she was heard and that God would deliver her from the deadlock of Charles' court. It was up to her to be patient and to have faith that all would be according to God's design. In return He would protect her and fulfill her destiny.

Then came an invitation from the burgesses of Orléans. It had been many months since they last saw the Maid who had rescued their city from the threat of annihilation. They wished to give her an overdue feast to express their gratitude. Would she consider returning to Orléans if she had no pressing interests at court?

She was so overjoyed when Pasquerel finished reading the letter that she forgot that he was a monk and kissed him soundly on the cheek. Beaming, he did not seem to mind the transgression.

She flew to Charles, at that moment in council with Trémoïlle, de Gaucourt, de Chartres, and LeMaçon. The King easily granted her request, saying that he thought the journey would do her good. He had no objections, he said, if she wanted to bring her household with her. Without her asking, he gave her one hundred and fifty gold crowns. He wished her Godspeed and said that he would see her soon.

Orléans was not as she remembered it. When she last saw the city, it still bore the scars of siege. The English *bastilles* had stood like wasp nests under a warm spring sky, desecrating the churches that formed their foundation. The Tourelles for which she had fought so hard lay in a burned-out ruin. Food, brought in by the relieving army, was scarce and had to be rationed. Last May, the burden of seven months of siege was reflected in the faces of the people.

Everything was different now. The Orléanais had dismantled the hated fortresses raised by the *goddons*, leaving no trace of them except for new-bricked churches which proudly defied the vanquished enemy. The shattered earthworks that had once barricaded the Tourelles were gone, and the hole in the bridge repaired so that traffic crossed the Loire without hindrance. Smoke still stained the Tourelles themselves in a reminder of what had occurred. But a stranger from another kingdom might not notice the soot as he passed beneath the towers into the city. He would not know from the tranquil, healthy friendliness all around him what had transpired during that harried and historical week.

As they had in the past, Jehanne and her comrades entered the city in the company of the Bastard, and all of Orléans turned out to greet her. God had granted a reprieve to France for its excesses by stopping the Christmas blizzard shortly after the new year. Snow was still piled high outside the city walls in soggy drifts, yet within Orléans itself the streets were for the most part passable. Citizens crowded the thoroughfares in spite of the nip in the air, cheering loudly for the Maid. She waved gaily to them from her horse, touched by their ardent affection and glad of the fur hat that covered her ears.

When they reached the city hall, she dismounted and climbed the steps. Then she turned and addressed the multitude.

"It's good to be back in Orléans!" she shouted, her breath creating little clouds in the frigid air. The wind picked up, carrying her words away. She pulled her cloak a bit closer around her shoulders.

A roar of approval nearly knocked her over, and she reeled from the impact of their love.

"There is no place on earth where I feel as welcomed as I do here."

The applause went on for a full minute. Jehanne was enfolded in a fervor that swept the crowd, binding her to them. This was as close to home as she had felt in months! Grinning broadly, she waved a gloved hand. The acclamation gradually quieted and the throng waited for her next words.

"I hope to be here for a little while. In fact, I plan to buy a house here. Would you like that?"

Another yell broke through the winter sunlight, this one so prolonged that she thought it would never stop. The old chant began, "Jehanne the Maid! Jehanne the Maid! Jehanne the Maid!"

The gooseflesh that prickled under her warm clothes was not from the cold. She held up her hands and the refrain finally stopped.

"Since I plan to be here for some time, I hope to get to know you, and I want you to know me, too. But I cannot do that unless you allow me to move freely about your fair city. I do not ask for riches from you, nor any special privileges. You have already given me more than I could ever have asked for, with your kind receptions and your generosity in providing the army I have led with what we needed to go into battle. All I want now is to be your friend and neighbor. I just want to be one of you. If you love me—"

"We do, Jehanne!"

There was another burst of raucous assent. She raised her hands in a plea for quiet that she might go on. "If you love me, then treat me as you would one of yourselves. For in truth, I am no different from you—"

She was interrupted by affectionate, disbelieving laughter.

"That is true!" she yelled above the noise. "I am just a girl from a village in Lorraine, and if you praise me too much, I might forget that what I have done, I have done at God's command. It is *He* who deserves your honor, not me. If you love me, help me to keep from sin by giving your praise to God, Who is the King of us all!"

She paused for breath, trying to read the mood behind the wall of attentive, bundled faces. "Thank you all again. May God bless you."

She waved to them once more in hopes that they had gotten the point. That was something she could not tell, for their spirited accolades followed her into the town hall.

The Bastard and his burgesses feasted her with a display that included capons, rabbits, partridges, and wine. Pierre and Jehan received new doublets, tailored by the Bastard's own man. The city's Canons of the Chapter gave Jehanne a lease on a house of her choice at a very modest price.

After the honors were presented, the dinner began. Jehanne had practically no appetite owing to her excitement at being back where she was treasured, so she ate sparingly, just a portion of pheasant and some bread. But she enjoyed the entertainments and laughed lightheartedly at the acrobatic clowns. She did not want to think of serious things, not tonight. God was with her and she was home.

Jehanne found her house the next day. It was a two-story structure in the rue des Petits Souliers, a mere stone's throw from an inn that had been damaged by a cannonball during the siege. The city had inherited the residence some two years earlier when its owner died without heirs. One or another bureaucrat lived in it during that time but it had been empty for eight months. When they learned that Jehanne intended to bring her parents to Orléans, the councilmen sent servants to clean away the signs of neglect. If it pleased her, it would be hers.

January daylight shone cleanly through the house's many windows, and as she passed from room to room, Jehanne's elation mounted. She pictured where Maman could put her wheel, next to the fireplace in the second-floor parlor. The downstairs room on the corner would be a perfect place for Papa to receive visitors. Across the hall the family would take their meals in the large space next to the kitchen.

She wanted to live here, to bring Jacques and Isabelle here *now*! It was all she could do to keep herself from sending Pierre to fetch them. Because she knew she could not, not yet. Catherine's warning of enemy plans to contend against Orléans after winter ended made it too dangerous. Her parents would be better off where they were, out of harm's way in Lorraine. If war chanced upon Domrémy, that would be the will of God and nothing could prevent it, but common sense dictated that she not bring them into a likely battlefield.

Yes, it would be safer for them to remain in the village for the time being. Besides, they would only worry about her more urgently if she were forced to take up arms to defend her new home. Papa might even try to stop her this time, and she might not be able to resist Isabelle's distress. When spring passed and Orléans was safe again, then she would send for them.

In the meantime she stayed with her old friends, the Bouchers. Once again she shared young Charlotte's room. The girl had grown an inch since Jehanne last saw her. Nevertheless, she was still a child in awe of her heroine, and Jehanne knew that Charlotte was thrilled during that first night and did not easily fall asleep beside her honored guest.

Madame Boucher escorted Jehanne to church and showed her the city. It was much changed. There, next to the wall at the Porte de Bourgogne, was where the market would be when the crops came in. Jehanne remembered the way it had looked last summer, with townsfolk scattering frantically in the opposite direction as she tore toward the battle at St.-Loup with her household on her heels. Now it was only an empty space where there was no commerce. The actual business district where craftsmen worked at their shoes and pastries and candlesticks was west of the marketplace. Beyond that, near the center of the city, the town hall where Jehanne had addressed the people sat like a hub squarely in the middle of the banking houses. The streets which converged there moved all the way to the surrounding walls, with those structures closest to the center housing the wealthiest of the Orléanais. The poorer people lived farther away.

Jehanne stayed in Orléans for a little over four weeks. She was delighted to find that the Orléanais had understood her and were willing to leave her alone. They waved to her and shouted in greeting when she was out with Madame Boucher or the Bastard, but did not mob her. She got to know some of them by name: Jacquot the cobbler, a former soldier missing an eye from a minor battle in 1416 against the *goddons*; Madame le Noir, the baker's wife, who never let Jehanne pay for bread; and Gustave the oilseller. Dignitaries sought her company in the evenings, and it was not uncommon for her to have to turn away invitations to dinner. She was often in the company of the Bastard.

One evening when they were alone, she told him about her fears that the English would try to retake Orléans. She did not say that the information came from her Guides. He listened quietly, his face sober but not surprised. While she spoke he nodded in anticipation of her words, and she had a feeling that he already knew what she did. She did not imagine that he knew more.

"That is Charles' way, to seek for negotiations and settlements," he said. "There's a very real chance that he won't—or can't—give us money to defend ourselves."

"Yes, and that's why we must keep the *goddons* north of the Loire," Jehanne insisted. "The King has promised that he'll send me back against them in the spring, but I am afraid that he'll change his mind again. At least we know that the loyal towns will send supplies to help us."

The Bastard gave her a long look, as though he were trying to decide something. Finally, he stood up from his desk and went to the door. He opened it. There was no one in the hall to overhear, so he closed it and returned to his seat.

"You have been quite isolated at court, haven't you?" he asked.

She nodded, wondering what bad tidings he had for her. "Yes. The King rarely speaks to me, and never about the war."

"Jehanne, there is something you must know." He rubbed his hands together slowly as he collected his thoughts. "Back in August, just a week or so before we tried for Paris, Charles signed yet another treaty with Bourgogne, one which for the life of me I cannot understand because it makes no sense."

"Why? What did it say?"

He made a sour face. "Charles agreed to 'lend' Compiègne to Philippe while we besieged Paris so that Philippe might have a supply base for his men holding the capital." The Bastard smiled grimly at Jehanne's aghast expression. "That's right, he gave Philippe permission to take a town loyal to him, vanquish it, and then turn around and use it against his own army!"

"That's the most senseless thing I've ever heard!" she exclaimed. "Why would he do such a thing? Do you think he's becoming mad like his father?"

He shook his head. "Charles may be a fool at times, but he's not mad. I think that Trémoïlle is somehow responsible. He must have talked Charles into it, although I can't imagine what logic he used to convince the King to do it."

She turned unseeing eyes to the fireplace, for once speechless at the extent of Trémoïlle's treachery.

"The point is that back in October, when the people of Compiègne were told that they were being 'given' to Bourgogne, they rebelled and rioted in the streets, even resisting the advice of their own garrison commander to obey the King and surrender the town. They said that they were loyal subjects of His Majesty and would never yield to Philippe."

"Good for them!"

"Well . . ." The Bastard made another face that said, There's more, and it gets better. "The people wrote to Charles, pledging their loyalty and asking for military assistance. Instead of granting their request, he sent archbishop de Chartres to dissuade them from breaking the King's treaty with Bourgogne. The Compiègnese—God bless them!—refused, and that angered the archbishop so much that he wrote to Philippe, telling him that if they wanted to take Compiègne, they would find no one there to stop them."

"What!" Jehanne shook her head in slack-jawed amazement.

The Bastard nodded, raising his eyebrows. "That's right. Incredible as it sounds, Charles has managed to betray himself, and with him, those who have pledged their loyalty to him."

"So has Bourgogne taken Compiègne?"

"No. At least, not yet. But the town is under siege, as it has been these past months."

Her eyes wrinkled at the corners. "How do you know this?"

He rubbed his thumb and forefinger together. "You would be surprised what a little well-placed silver can buy, Jehanne. You might consider garnering sources of your own, particularly since you are so sequestered at court."

"I have my Counsel." She frowned.

"They do not tell you everything, though, do they?"

She shook her head. "But They tell me what is necessary."

"You might consider my advice." His voice was not reproachful, simply matter-of-fact.

"But how? Where can I find these people?"

He smiled, looking again like the genial man she knew. "I shall provide you with the means to contact those who have served me well, and still do. You'll find them most valuable."

"Who are they?"

His smile became ironic. "There are some things it's better not to know. I don't know their true identities, only their *noms de guerre*. They come and go in the dead of night, in shadows where I cannot fully see their faces. But I do know this: Their news is without exception correct. They have told me something else which you may not have heard. Things are very bad in Paris. Ever since we tried to take the city, Armagnac bands have been harrying the area around it. Near Christmas a dozen of them were captured and executed."

"Oh, my God." She shivered.

"Do you see now why it might not be possible to reinforce the Loire towns, even Orléans? The army—or what is left of it—has its hands full against Charles' enemies everywhere. Unfortunately, they cannot contend against those at court," he added with an uncommon bitterness. "The towns that have come over to him since the coronation, though willing, are unprotected. They may have to fight for their own lives if the English move on Orléans."

She let his declaration penetrate her brain. "Then I guess we'll just have to take what we can get."

"That may not be enough. You cannot hope to win without proper arms and men. And if there is no money to pay them—"

"They will come for me." Jehanne set her jaw stubbornly.

"Excuse me, but they did not come for you at La Charité, did they?" The Bastard's smile was not unkind.

She looked at the floor and did not answer.

"Be very careful that you do not attempt to assault a larger force than you have yourself," he cautioned. "I know that God is on your side"—he cut her off when she started to speak—"but you are not invincible, no matter what you think. I tell you this for your own good, Jehanne. Be careful. At court and in the field."

She put the advice into a mental chamber, where it rested alongside the Bastard's incredible news. She had known for some time now, since at least before the coronation, that Charles was weak and uncertain, but she had never dreamed how gullible he was, to the point where he could be persuaded to injure his own kingdom! She had to get back to court, she had to demand an army from him. But she also realized that he would wonder how she had discovered all that had come about, when she was not supposed to know about his secret agreements. She could not betray the Bastard and his confidence in her. She would therefore have to think of a plan for dealing with the King upon her return to court.

Meanwhile, she had to remain in Orléans until he sent for her. She found, on the heels of her immediate shock, that that was not so hard to do. The greater part of her needed a rest from politics and the sorrows of war. And in a secret place in her mind, she hoped that it would be a while before Charles interrupted the good time she was having.

From the Orléanais came nothing but praise and devotion. No one ever mentioned the defeats she had sustained at Paris and at La Charité. Little gangs of children followed her when she was out, shyly in the beginning. But their tongues loosened after she asked them about their families, and soon she knew their names, their ages, and where they lived. She gave generously to the poor, which made her feel wonderful inside, better even than when she tried on new clothes for the first time. All the struggle and pain had been worth it to have these rewards for her efforts.

And then, during the second week in February, just when she was most at ease and comfortable in her adopted city, Charles unexpectedly summoned her to rejoin him at Jargeau.

"Come!"

A servant opened the tall oaken door to admit Stafford into the duke's parlor. His master was sitting across the room next to the fireplace, the only source of light in the high-ceilinged chamber, and when he came in Bedford shifted the unmistakable profile, hawk-nosed and chinless, toward him. Stafford could see by the way the shadows fell across his face that he was smiling.

He stood up, still holding a large piece of parchment which he had been examining when his subordinate knocked on the door. "Welcome to Paris, Stafford." The deep voice was confident and warm. "I did not think I would be seeing you so soon, what with this weather."

Stafford glanced at the window and the screaming blizzard that had pounded February into deepest winter. "Thank you, sir, it's good to be here at last."

"Come over here, closer to the fire."

The soldier did not have to be coaxed. His boots echoed across the floor through the half-darkness, bringing him past the table and Bedford's halted chess game to the enlivening comfort of the burning wood. He spread out his hands, loving the near-painful tingle that warmed his blood again and made his hair virtually crackle. Almost immediately, his woolen clothes became so hot that they seemed ready to ignite.

"Better, eh?" Bedford grinned.

"Aye. It was snowing some when I left Dijon, but not like this. I didn't run into this bloody storm until I reached Reims." He turned his backside to the fireplace and rubbed the cheeks, which were still numb thanks to the saddle as well as the cold. "I encountered some rather deep drifts after that, and for a while I didn't think my horse would be able to make it. It's God's mercy that I'm here."

The duke smiled again. Robert, the earl of Stafford, was a brave man, and one whom he was certain had performed his duties well in Dijon. Those cold blue eyes no doubt had been fixed upon Burgundy throughout their talk, emphasizing Bedford's own uncompromising stance.

"Well, here then, have some hot wine." Bedford leaned over into the fireplace and picked up the copper kettle resting on the stone bed near a mound of ruby coals. He stood up and grabbed a ceramic-handled tankard from the mantel, then gave it to Stafford. The soldier could smell the tantalizing odor of cinammon ascending from the steam filling his cup.

"Thank you, sir." Slurping hesitantly, he decided that it was still too hot to drink. It did, however, give comfort to his chilled hand.

Smiling again, Bedford gestured to the second stool before the fire. Stafford sat down with a fatigued grunt and flung back his cloak. The duke poured more wine for himself, then also sat.

"I suppose you would like your report now, sir," Stafford said. He sipped noisily from the tangy cup.

Bedford laughed. "Only if it's good news." He could afford to be jovial about this, because every instinct told him that Philippe would be accommodating. Instinct and his experience with Burgundy's famous greed.

"It's good. The duke was most grateful for your offer, you were right about that." He inhaled a little wine between his teeth, appreciating the way the spices warmed his throat and made his nose run slightly. "I must say, giving him Compiègne and telling him that he may have the whole of Champagne if he can take it from the Armagnacs was an inspiration on your part, sir. He even agreed to your proposal to have Henry crowned in Reims after the city falls to him."

"Excellent!" Bedford clapped his hands and rubbed them together. "When the king is finally crowned King of France as well as of England and comes into his inheritance, Charles' illegal coronation will be wiped away in the minds of those miserable wretches who have rallied to him. Then we can regain the cities near here."

He shivered at the gust of wind which blew in from the bolted window. God's balls, how he hated this miserable palace! "I do not like having Charles' forces so close to the capital."

"What about the traitors here in the city? Have you caught any more of them since I went to Dijon?"

"A few. We tortured them, of course, but were unable to learn who their leaders are." The duke's mouth turned downward into a frown, leveling his insignificant chin. "We hanged them out there in the courtyard, as we did with the others, and left their bodies out for a few days so the people might see what we do to rebels. I've put it about that we'll pay handsomely for the chance to bring the rest to justice."

Stafford wiped his mouth with the back of his hand, then the sweat from his forehead. Sitting this close to the fireplace, his face was flushed and even more florid than usual. The carrot-colored hair seemed made of flames in the dancing light.

"We'll catch them, sir, you can wager that," he said. "What about Orléans, are we still going to move against it when the weather clears?"

Bedford shrugged. "That depends on Philippe and how successful his campaign against Champagne is. We cannot very well go against the Loire if Champagne is still hostile at our rear. But if Burgundy does manage to take Reims and Soissons, we can attack Orléans and Troyes at the same time. That will force Charles to divide his army, which naturally is not large enough to fight in two places at once."

"And the king? When will you bring him across the Channel?"

His lord glanced at the glistening, pockmarked face. "No later than April, I hope. I've given Warwick instructions to make ready His Majesty's apartment in Rouen Castle. I want you there as well, Stafford."

"Me, sir?" The earl's hard blue eyes, clouded a little by the wine but still as emotionless as ice, were staring at him as though he had not heard correctly.

"That's right. I'll want you to help Warwick command the garrison."

"But why? Won't you need me in the field?"

Bedford smiled, recalling Warwick's own astonishment and similar response when ordered to Rouen. "If Philippe keeps to his end of the bargain this time, we can let the Burgundians have the field around Paris and in the Loire while we protect the king. These days, the Armagnacs are so unpredictable that we cannot tell where they will strike next. We cannot chance that they'll decide to move on Rouen, especially if they should learn that Henry is there."

He leaned forward slightly in his chair, frowning. "Arthur of Richmond is back in the field these days with those wild Bretons of his, and I'm certain that he would give half his black soul to get his hands on the king. That must not happen, Stafford."

The earl's forehead creased thoughtfully. "Aye, sir. You are right, of course." It was clear that he had not considered the possibility of Armagnac activity in Normandy.

"When we bring the king from England, I shall have him accompanied by an additional thousand men. They shall be under your command, and it will be your task to see that they serve as guards to the king in the event that the worst happens. Warwick shall continue to command the garrison already there."

The younger man nodded. "I shall do my duty to serve the king, as always."

"Good man." Bedford smiled.

"There's one other thing, sir." Stafford's square jaw hardened and his eyes became slits of hatred. "You mentioned Richmond. Everyone knows that he was responsible for the massacre at Patay, and that he would not have been there at all if that damnable Armagnac whore had not interceded with Charles on his behalf. We can handle Richmond, but what are we going to do about the sorceress? If she is working her black magic in the field again, we may not have the means to contend against the Armagnacs. Will the king be safe, even in Rouen?"

The duke put his cup down on the floor and held his hands out to the fire. He rubbed them vigorously, detesting the question he had asked himself a hundred times.

"My spies tell me that Charles is displeased with her since her witchery failed to take Paris for him," he answered. "He has kept her on a leash, ever at his side as he's moved from one château to another." He gave the earl a wry smile. "It seems that our little king of Bourges does not quite know what to do with her now that she's an embarrassment to his 'royal' pride. And contrary to what we believed at the time, he was not at all eager to accept Richmond's feeble display of loyalty, even when advanced by the girl.

"That was her first mistake, Stafford. Not even Charles is stupid enough to really trust our demonic earl, and no one—not Charles, nor Burgundy, and certainly not I—wants him on his side. My faithful servants of England inform me that her sponsorship of Richmond was the beginning of her downfall in Charles' eyes. Why, he was so dismayed at Richmond's avowed support that he forbade him from taking part in his so-called coronation! And now, with the witch's losses at Paris and at La Charité, the Armagnacs are generally disillusioned with their most popular whore.

"But just in case she does manage to bewitch Charles into giving her another army, I have taken measures of my own to ensure that her military adventures are cut short."

Stafford wrinkled his eyebrows in bemusement.

Bedford held up the page in his hand. "There is a reward on her head now, my dear earl. Twenty thousand pounds."

The soldier's cut-glass eyes opened wider and he whistled softly. "That's a great deal of money, my lord."

"Indeed." Bedford chuckled. "I am most confident that sooner or later, someone will betray her. Sooner or later, some impoverished man-at-arms, or knight, or duke, will decide that it's a great deal more than he can afford to resist. And on that day, the halls of Heaven will thunder with joy at her destruction and our victory."

A blast of wind sent a fierce assault against the north side of the palace and whistled through the cracks around the window. It would snow all night, no doubt, and probably through the next day.

Bedford reached for his goblet, then drank from it. He was not worried, not really. In another two months spring would arrive, and with it they would take back what Charles had stolen from the king: 1430 would be a glorious year for England.

He suddenly thought of something that had earlier bedeviled and gotten the better of him. Without bothering to put his cup down again, he stood up and walked over to the table where his chess game sat undisturbed. He smiled at the few pieces remaining on the checkered board, seeing it all with fresh eyes.

He picked up the white knight and leaped it over his own white bishop standing in his way. It was a move that was so obvious that he had completely overlooked it before now. He set the piece down behind the black castle within easy reach of the black king.

"Check," he whispered.

Jehanne lowered her head and pushed against the freezing gale, glad that the drifts were not deep enough to breach her knee-high boots. The wind whipped against her face in stinging pellets and tried to fling back the hood that clung to her hair. Gritting her teeth, she grabbed the end of it and pulled it back in place, restoring her anonymity. Not that it really mattered. On this punishingly cold early March day, hardly anyone was about in the streets of Jargeau. Of those few who were, no one would have expected to see Jehanne the Maid out in the middle of a snowstorm in the first place, much less in such a disreputable section of town.

She had returned to Jargeau three days ago, after pleading with Charles to grant her a respite from the monotony of court life. She brought none of her companions with her, nor did she reveal the purpose behind her reappearance in Jargeau. Pasquerel, bound by his confessor's vow to secrecy, was the exception. He had read the communication to her, which she consigned to the fireplace after committing its contents to memory. The Bastard had kept his word and provided Jehanne with a most valuable contact, whom today she would meet for the first time.

Twenty minutes earlier she had left behind the solid, bourgeois district where she was again lodged with the burgher de Barneville and his wife. It was all right, Jehanne told Paulette de Barneville, for Madame not to accompany her to church in this storm. Jehanne had an urgent need to communicate with God, and the blizzard would guarantee that she was unrecognized and able to pray in peace. There was a time when telling a lie like that would have burdened her conscience, but it did not trouble her today. It was necessary that she go out, but equally vital that her destination be kept secret.

The commercial area where the tradesmen made stained glass, shoes, and silver candlesticks faded behind her, replaced by the hovels bordering the riverbank. In this section, unfamiliar and somewhat sinister in a rather exciting way, the gray shanties were like sores upon the rest of the city, old and crumbling into disrepair, windowless, lacking doors, the apertures covered by soiled pieces of burlap nailed to ill-fitting sills in an impotent endeavor to keep in some heat. Outside one of them a rheumy-eyed beggar, shivering pathetically under a thin blanket and holding a large, mangy dog close to him for warmth, huddled against a wooden wall cracked and split by many seasons' exposure to the elements.

Jehanne made herself take little notice of him. She staggered onward, and turned into an alley where the sun never shone. Someone opened a window above her head and tossed something out of it which splattered right in front of her. The nauseating stink of human waste steamed from the desecrated snowbank, mingling with the woodsmoke drifting from dilapidated roofs and the odor of cooking cabbage, perhaps the only food that the family boiling it would eat this week. In two different dwellings, pauper children were crying loudly, wailing for the meals, or heat, they did not have and would not obtain. There was a slithering shuffle ahead in the shadows as the rats who had been feasting upon the frozen carcass of a cat scattered at Jehanne's approach. Above it all floated that rancid river smell, created by rotting mud reeds and runoff from the city's sewers.

She shut out all of it, for these lives had nothing to do with her. She wrapped an alert, gloved hand around the hilt of her sword, knowing that even in these somewhat threadbare clothes—the same suit she had worn to Chinon a year ago—she looked wealthy in comparison to those who lived here, a temptation to those possible robbers who eyed her suspiciously from darkened doorways.

At the end of the alley she turned left, onto the street which ran alongside the Loire. It was snowing so hard that the river was hidden behind that blinding curtain of punishing icelets, but even so Jehanne knew that there were no barges sailing upon it, not today. Ahead of her, a sign painted with the weather-worn image of a rooster swung crazily on its hinges, and already she could hear drunken laughter and song issuing from behind the inn's closed door.

She quickened her step and walked past it, taking care not to slow down lest she be noticed. On the corner opposite the inn was the colorless, ordinary building with the faded red door where the Bastard had told her she would find her informant. She stopped in front of it and, hugging her cloak tighter about her shoulders, knocked as she had been instructed. Two raps, a pause, three more, then one.

No response.

Jehanne glanced anxiously down the street on either side of her. She was alone except for the wind and the powdery drifts. For the first time since she had ventured out today, her teeth began to chatter, and she pulled the cloak closer. A fresh gust of wind blew the scent of death to her nostrils. She looked down to see a dead rat, squirming with maggots, lying against the wall with its curled paws grasping the frozen air.

She did not know what to do next. Surely the Bastard had not gotten his information wrong. She was just raising her fist to knock again when the door opened a crack.

The face looking back at her was a woman's, smeared with the grime of ten years and surrounded by a mass of tangled, unwashed hair. "What do you want?" the voice snarled.

"The Loire is red and green at Orléans," Jehanne answered, reciting the code she had been given.

The door slammed shut.

Jehanne stared perplexed at the mottled, blood red wood. Could this really be the wrong place? If it were, she would be better off away from here. She was getting ready to leave when it opened again, wider this time.

"Don't just stand there, come in," the woman ordered. She had very few teeth, and those few were rotting stumps.

Jehanne scooted inside and the woman closed and bolted the door behind her.

The room was very dark, lit only by the fire in the hearth. Something disgusting was cooking in an iron pot which hung from a hook over the burning logs, and its contents bubbled beneath the lid and hissed into the coals. To her right, a rickety table held the skinned, headless remains of what could have been a rabbit, or worse. Aside from the short bench behind it, there was no other furniture. The dead air reeked with the musk emanating from the woman's long-unbathed body and that of the dog which lay panting before the fire.

"Back there." The woman pointed to the rear of the room and the tattered linen hanging over a doorway. Candlelight shone through holes in the cloth.

Jehanne looked at it apprehensively and wrapped an unwitting hand around the hilt of her sword. She did not move.

"Go on," the woman urged, giving her a toothless grimace intended as a smile. She waved Jehanne on with a motion of her skeletal claw.

Jehanne walked gingerly to the door, almost stepping on a rat which skittered out of her way. She wrinkled her nose and lifted the flap.

The candle she had seen burning through the curtain dripped streams of wax upon an old crate in the middle of the tiny chamber. Against the wall was a sagging, filthy bed, and a hooded man sat on its edge.

"Come in, but stay near the door." His voice was little more than a whisper, uttered in an accent as familiar and as teasing as a half-remembered song. He did not remove the hood, nor did he look directly at her. In the tenuous light, she could see only that he was wearing a plain tunic, thick pants, and boots. She remembered what the Bastard had said, that his messengers never showed their faces.

"Do you know who I am?" she asked.

"Of course. And I know why you are here. Do you have my money?"

"Yes." She reached into her doublet and fumbled for the leather sack she had crammed between her shirt and the band of her hose. Withdrawing it, she started toward him.

"Stay there. Throw it to me."

It clinked as he caught it. He untied the string around its mouth and opened it. Satisfied that he had not been cheated, the man closed the bag, tied it again, and stuffed it into his shirt.

"The Armagnacs have been busy in Paris," he said in that unsettling whisper. "Not only are the remains of Charles' armies daily harrying the outlying areas and the Anglo-Burgundian forces massed there, but there is also a plot within the city itself to topple Philippe and Bedford's combined power. The conspirators meet at a place called the Bear Inn, and its owner is one of their leaders."

"Who are they? The others, I mean."

His shrug was barely perceptible. "Lawyers, merchants, men of the Church. It does not matter. Brother Pierre d'Allée, the abbé of the Carmelite monastery at Melun, is their courier to Armagnac forces outside the city, and he also takes messages between Paris and Melun. They are trying to rouse the other Parisians to revolt. They hope that once the people rebel from within, Charles' army can attack the capital at the same time.

"But the English are on to them. They still do not know who all of the leaders are, but the inn is being watched by those loyal to Philippe, and house-to-house searches for hidden weapons are becoming commonplace. The fools underestimate the English. They will not yield Paris without a fight, nor France for that matter. They are convinced that the kingdom rightfully belongs to them, and no other race in the world can match their single-mindedness. There is nothing they will not do to hold on to what they consider theirs."

"They're wrong! God has told me that it belongs to Charles and to no other." Jehanne scratched her shoulder idly, so engrossed in the conversation that she was only half-aware of the fleas nibbling through her woolen clothes.

The man shrugged again. "Tell that to the English. As I've said, they are determined to hold Paris."

"What about Compiègne? Is the city still under siege?"

"It is. The latest word is that Melun is also making ready to attempt to throw off the English yoke they've been under for ten years now. Bedford has given it to his brother-in-law, Philippe de Bourgogne, but the people there have had enough of their foreign masters. Do not be surprised when in a short time you hear that there are riots in Melun."

She let the information soak into her mind. If all of this was true, she would somehow have to convince Charles to let her lead an army to Melun. And to Compiègne.

"Is there anything else?"

He paused. "Yes. The English are offering twenty thousand pounds for your capture, dead or alive. Preferably alive, because they want the pleasure of burning you at the stake for a witch."

She gasped. The taunts from the Tourelles and Talbot's threats flew at her like bats, sucking the saliva from her mouth. She remembered Guyenne and the fate that would have befallen him had Orléans not been taken by God's army.

She stared at the man, suddenly gripped by a fear greater than any she had ever known. How carefully he had counted the money in the sack she tossed to him . . . She took a step backward, and was on the brink of running from the room when he spoke.

"Don't worry. If I had it in mind to betray you, you would have been dead the minute you walked in here. But I am not interested in English gold, regardless of how much they offer for you."

The corners of her eyes wrinkled suspiciously. "Why not?" She barely breathed in anticipation of his reply.

"As you said yourself, this kingdom belongs to Charles. And I am no holder of English interests in France. That is all you need to know."

She considered his reply. His reasons were actually unimportant. The only thing that mattered was that he sounded convincing, and his thinking was sound. He indeed could have overpowered her and slit her throat, or impaled her with an arrow, when she first arrived. But even now he simply sat there, unmoving.

She eased a little. "What else?"

"There is nothing more. For now. Should you need to reach me again, contact the Bastard of Orléans as you did this time."

She nodded. "Thank you, sir." She turned to leave.

"Jehanne."

She looked at him over her shoulder. He had not moved. "Watch your back. Trust no one. Twenty thousand pounds, remember that."

She practically ran out of there, past the sleeping dog and the woman who did not look up from the vile-smelling contents of the pot she was stirring.

In the middle of the night Jehanne awoke beside the softly snoring form of Paulette de Barneville and sat up with the realization that had come to her in a dream. The mystery in the man's voice had plagued her for the rest of the day like an aching tooth, and no matter how diligently she had sought its source, it persisted in teasing her. But now, at four o'clock in the morning, she knew the elusive accent.

Her messenger had been an Englishman.

"Our mind is made up, seigneur chancellor. We are following sieur de Gaucourt's advice, and shall send the Maid to Melun."

"But Your Majesty, you must consider—"

"That is enough, Your Excellency." Charles turned a frown to the archbishop, daring him to disagree again. Clasping his hands behind his back, he walked the three steps' distance to the open diamond-paned window and looked out at the brownish-green expanse that was Trémoïlle's lawn. A pair of peacocks were waddling across the spring grass with their tails folded. One of them screamed at the other.

Charles smiled at the scene, loving the beautiful trees lining the riverbank that curved toward the castle from the other side of the lawn. It was difficult to imagine that there was a war at all in this peaceful château of Sully-sur-Loire. Perhaps one day he would be able to induce Trémoïlle to cede the estate to the crown. It would be another fine jewel in the strand of royal châteaux draped along the Loire if he could wrest it from the fat man's grasp. At any rate, it was a lovely dream.

The minister spoke now, interrupting the King's reverie. "Sire, as I have long pointed out, you must honor the terms of the treaties you sign with Philippe, or he will not take your attempts at reconciliation seriously." Trémoïlle's plump forefinger stroked the gold medallion engraved with the figure of an eagle that hung about his neck and rested against the massive, velvet-covered chest.

Charles had to restrain himself to keep from slapping the smug simper from the chancellor's mouth. He glowered at the man instead. "Are we not to take him seriously?" he sneered. "For months now, we have been most accommodating to him, even going so far as to lend him the use of Compiègne while we attacked Paris. But it appears now that our dear cousin Bourgogne will not return it and in any event is not content to have that town alone, he wants the whole of Champagne!"

The King fixed a determined look upon his three ministers, of whom only de Gaucourt nodded in silent agreement. "We shall not tolerate it! Philippe is playing a game of some sort with Bedford to publicly humiliate us—as well as steal our kingdom—and we need to teach him that he cannot get away with that. We are sending Jehanne back into the field."

"I have heard it said that she no longer has the same hold over the army as she once did," mused de Chartres, pulling his rubbery lower lip. "Perhaps her losses at Paris and La Charité are an indication that God has withdrawn his support from her. She said herself that He had given her only a year to accomplish His will, and it has been more than that now." He pretended to count on his fingers. "That is right," he nodded, "she first came to you in February of last year, and it is now the end of March." His smile was a triumphant flourish.

Charles shot a disgusted look at him, then lifted his arched eyebrows in a question directed to de Gaucourt.

"The men will still follow her, Sire," said the old soldier with a grim look at the other two. "They know that she did not lose Paris through any fault of hers, but because the army was undermanned and undersupplied." De Gaucourt pierced his old enemy Trémoïlle with a glare that communicated his disgust. "And because Your Majesty was persuaded to break off the attack too soon."

"Can she take Melun?" Charles wondered, almost to himself.

"I think so, my lord. She must. In the last week alone there have been three separate attempts on the part of the townspeople to expel the Burgundians holding the town, and many of them have been hanged, a few beheaded and their heads stuck on pikes. Our scouts report a large Burgundian buildup bound for that town and for Compiègne as well. If the rebellions are squelched in those places, the others towns of Champagne—including Reims and Soissons—will probably decide that it's too much trouble and too dangerous for them to resist." De Gaucourt's eyes enfolded Charles in a level urgency. "Particularly if Your Majesty makes no move at all to save them. In that event, they will no doubt feel that you have abandoned them, and before God, Sire, you may never get them back again."

Charles allowed the apocalyptic statement to sink into the others' heads. It was something he had already considered, a prospect which had, in fact, kept him awake at night for a while now. Coming from a professional soldier, and one with more field experience than the chancellor, the news stood a better chance of convincing these obstinate fools than his word alone.

"Sire, if you move on Compiègne, Bourgogne will certainly accuse you of reneging on your agreement to give it to him—"

"I did not *give* it to him, Chancellor, certainly not permanently." His eyes narrowed into an acid smile. "And now I want it back." The King shifted an icy expression, dignified in its authority, to de Gaucourt. "Is the Maid still waiting outside?"

The man nodded. "She was, my lord, when I got here."

"Fetch her then. We have that assignment that she has been begging for since before Christmas."

De Gaucourt inclined his head and went to his task. There was nothing more for the councillors to say, and they knew it. More important, Charles knew it, and he reveled in the power he felt at having successfully resisted them. He turned back toward the idyllic tableau down there beneath the window. What a lovely, clear day it was, surely like a day in Heaven must be.

He had to admit that Jehanne had served him well. Her losses were just strokes of temporary bad luck, he was sure of that. He would give her another chance. Both she and the army had had an opportunity to rest through the winter and would be fresh for their rejoined assaults against his enemies. This time there would be no reversals, or so he prayed. Yes, he owed it to her. One more chance to redeem herself.

From her vantage point upon the battlement Jehanne could see the light of late afternoon moving in shadows across the small gray hills around the town, and flickering like fireflies on the River Yonne. The countryside lay undisturbed all the way to the horizon, giving no sign of the retreating Burgundian troops she had not been able to engage. Within Melun's walls, slate-tiled roofs made an uneven, jagged floor which fell beneath the rampart in some places and rose to eye level in others. The usual day-to-day sounds of city life were absent, absorbed in loud music and the drunken songs of a thousand celebrants.

Jehanne had not been this close to the capital since the lost attempt on it. She had taken her household and two companies, but they did not have the chance to see any action. Informed that the Maid was en route to help them, the people had made a final life-or-death effort and risen of their own accord against the self-satisfied, unprepared Burgundian garrison who thought them cowed by their brutal restraint, expelling them from the town. By the time Jehanne got there, the townsfolk were already celebrating in the streets. She met briefly with city officials, then climbed the wall surrounding the town that she might view the retreating enemy. But they were long gone.

God bless these good people! Jehanne thought. Like brave Compiègne, Melun had stood up to the enemies of France, and won. She was pleased that her coming had inspired them to take matters into their own hands. Now she could turn her attention to rescuing Compiègne as she had saved Orléans. Surely when word spread throughout the kingdom that she was again in the field, soldiers from all over France would rush to help her to lift the siege. She would stay in this congenial, loyal town while she raised a larger force, taking them even closer to Paris, to Lagny-sur-Marne, only six leagues from the very heart of the city. There she planned to connect with a greater company under the command of the mercenary Italian, Bartolommeo Barretta.

The most recent news from Paris, which she had heard from soldiers who had actually been there, was grim though not hopeless. A week ago a detachment of Armagnac irregulars had made a foray against the outworks. The Burgundian garrison and a mob of Parisians rode out to engage them, but Charles' men beat them back and took some prisoners. The tools of England were now being held for whatever ransoms their captors deemed them worth. As Jehanne's mysterious informant had predicted, two days after the Armagnac success the English had ruthlessly put down the budding rebellion within the city. Brother Pierre d'Allée was captured, and under torture accused the other conspirators, among them the proprietor of the Bear Inn. They were arresting anyone even suspected of being an Armagnac sympathizer. The fall of Paris was again delayed.

An abrupt gust of cold spring air swept across Jehanne, and she shivered. Something was not right. A feeling that only a moment ago had not existed started humming in her ears and with it came a deadly weightiness. Out of the realm of nightmare, a bird of prey the color of midnight suddenly came at her with its talons poised for attack. Her mouth went dry at this unforeseen confrontation with a thing both appalling and inevitable.

What is it? she asked, paralyzed into a state of knee-shaking terror.

WE HAVE COME TO TELL YOU THAT IN A SHORT TIME, BEFORE ST.-JEHAN'S DAY, YOU SHALL FALL INTO THE GRASP OF THOSE WHO CALL YOU ENEMY.

Oh my God, oh no, no!

She felt the blood drain from her face, and she plummeted toward swooning. She looked around helplessly, panic compressing her lungs into short breaths. She wanted to run, to get away, but there was no place to go.

Oh, please, you cannot mean it, God cannot allow that to happen to me!

IT MUST BE, JEHANNE. IT IS GOD'S WILL AND NOTHING CAN PREVENT IT. DO NOT BE DOWNCAST BUT HOLD ON TO YOUR FAITH AND TAKE EVERYTHING IN STRIDE, KNOWING THAT HE WILL HELP YOU.

Then please, let me die right away when they take me! I could not bear imprisonment, especially a long one. I would rather die a quick death than linger in a dark cell. Oh please, say that it isn't so!

YOU MUST BE RESIGNED TO WHATEVER HAPPENS; IT IS YOUR DESTINY, THE COMPLETION OF ALL YOUR EFFORTS. WE CAN TELL YOU NO MORE AT THIS TIME. JUST REMEMBER THAT YOU SHALL NOT ENDURE IT ALONE.

The wind changed direction, taking Them with it across the battlements.

Jehanne stood for a long time looking out over the plain, not seeing the way the sun lengthened the shadows across the fields of March gold. She heard none of the songs, none of the laughter rollicking through Melun's narrow streets. The whole world had become dark and silent within the space of a few minutes, and hopelessness yawned beneath her feet like the maw of her nightmare's wolf. Her allotted year had slipped through God's hourglass, and with its end would come hers.

She had never considered before now what that portended. Captivity was the one fantasy with which she had not played. Life at Orléans in her new house, in the loving enclosure of her family, shattered before this explosion with reality. St.-Jehan's Day was only seven weeks into the future! She shuddered again, filled with an unwilling knowledge that in less time than that she would be a prisoner. Catherine had hinted that there would be no reprieve, no matter how many prayers she said that it might be otherwise. And the saint had never lied to her.

She pulled her cloak tighter about her shoulders. It would be a clear night. Already stars were blinking through the purple sky. Jehanne walked to the ladder and slowly climbed down to the street now shrouded in twilight.

Her life became a walking dream, her movements driven almost without thought. She tried to focus on her duty. Sometimes she was successful.

When she reached Lagny two weeks later, she was reunited with Ambroise de Loré, now in joint command of the two-hundred-man force along with Barretta and a Scotsman named Hugh Kennedy. In a rushed conference they explained to her that a band of Burgundians under one Franquet d'Arras was lately rampaging through the neighborhood. He was a particularly vicious cutthroat who gave no orders against his men raping farmers' wives and daughters while comrades disemboweled their children and burned their houses around them. D'Arras' name was uttered in terrified whispers in the town, for it was feared that he would attempt an assault on Lagny. The mad dog had to be stopped while he was still snarling about the countryside in the open.

Satisfied that she understood the situation, Jehanne insisted that they begin at once. The battalion left the city two hours after her arrival.

They had only gone a few leagues when scouts returned to the column with news that the Burgundians were just beyond the trees ahead of them. They were moving at a languid pace and would soon be surrounded on three sides by a thick forest. If the army charged them now, they could entrap the enemy with no route available for an escape.

The plan worked very well. When they realized that they were caught, the Burgundians dismounted and planted their already prepared stakes toward the

412

King's men in the English fashion. Desperation turned them into howling, mad-eyed demons, and they repulsed two waves of Armagnac attackers, killing thirty with their deadly, well-aimed arrows. Jehanne was starting to fidget in frustration when reinforcements arrived from Lagny and neighboring towns, bringing culverins and crossbows, townsfolk and garrisons. The battle resumed at a higher pitch, and within three hours was all over.

So hated had the enemy been that the victors put most of the survivors to the sword. City dwellers and men-at-arms alike ignored the pleas for mercy and hacked the prisoners to pieces, continuing long after some of them were dead. Even the women who had come with them took part, pummeling the objects of their hatred with hoes and pikes until their heads split open. They spat upon the corpses and cursed them to eternal damnation in a raging Hell. Normally civilized people who had families and performed their civic duties, the people of Lagny had become hideous agents of the Devil's vengeance.

Appalled by the spectacle, Jehanne ran about the battlefield calling for an end to the massacre. She was not heard. They did not listen when she said that God would turn against them for their hatred and would surely punish their sins. At last, overwhelmed by helplessness, she gave up and mounted her horse. She took her household with her, away from the horrors.

That evening the captains brought Franquet d'Arras to her lodgings in Lagny. Jehanne's prisoner radiated evil. He was muscular and rather short, and had ink black hair with bushy eyebrows that overhung a pointed, remorseless nose. Jehanne could see the slimy stumps of his teeth between thin, wide lips that sneered at her in hate-filled defiance. A long scar that began at his right ear came to an end at the corner of his mouth, and with his long, sparsely bearded snout he resembled a gutter rat.

De Loré pushed him to his knees before Jehanne. A chill shook her as the man grinned up at her in a sickening leer. He was not a man at all; he was Satan's own son.

"We should kill him, Jehanne," said Barretta. No angel himself, the captain was a mercenary who only fought for Charles as long as Charles could pay. D'Arras was a longstanding rival.

"I agree," affirmed de Loré with a firm nod of his shaggy head. "This scum doesn't deserve to live."

Jehanne stared at the man, trying to wear him down under the onslaught of her Power. But his blackness of soul was so potent that soon she could no longer look at him.

"We shall not kill him. There is a man in Paris whom my sources say is a good Armagnac as well as a good man. He is the owner of the Bear Inn, and was captured in the rebellion." She lifted her gaze from the floor to the captains. They were frowning at her through a veil of rising resistance. "I want to keep this prisoner to exchange for my man in Paris."

The three commanders argued with her as she knew they would. D'Arras was a rabid beast who had murdered hundreds of innocent people for his master's gold and for the sheer pleasure of killing. He deserved to die. If they ransomed him, he would again be free to return to his evil occupation.

413

Jehanne could not deny the truth in what they said. At the same time, she did not know if God wanted d'Arras' death. She would leave it up to Him.

"I won't change my mind," she maintained. "Send word to Paris that they may have this one if they release the Armagnac to me. I have commended the matter to God."

They took the prisoner away. Now that she had made her decision, Jehanne had to remain in Lagny until the courier returned from Paris. Then it would be on to Senlis, where she hoped to overtake the enemy. She had heard shortly after the battle that an Anglo-Burgundian division under the personal command of the duc de Bourgogne was marching north from Paris toward Compiègne. Once she had her answer from the enemy within Paris, Jehanne intended to meet Philippe in the field.

By late morning the following day she still had heard nothing. So she rode to the church down the street from her inn to pray for guidance. She had only just finished the *Pater* and was starting into an *Ave* when a group of women came rushing to her.

A young mother among them held in her arms a three-day-old infant. Still wrapped in its swaddling, the tiny bundle's face was blue and lifeless. The distressed woman fell to her knees before Jehanne and begged for her prayers.

"I cannot give life, Madame," she cried, aghast at the suggestion. "Only God can do that."

"Then pray with me, please!" implored the woman, "I know He will hear you."

Jehanne knelt with the other women and crossed herself. They bowed their heads. For several moments nothing happened. The women prayed in silence, their lips moving fervently. Then without warning the baby stirred a little and gave a feeble yawn.

His mother broke into a keening wail as one of the women raced to the holy water fount. She returned, and making a quick baptismal Sign of the Cross, splashed the infant's fuzzy head. The tiny creature gasped, then died.

The women heralded the event as a miracle. God had listened to His *L'Angélique* and resurrected the infant long enough for its small soul to be baptized, and now it would be escorted by the blessed angels into the Kingdom of Heaven! They clung to Jehanne's cloak and tried to kiss her boots.

Shaken, she pushed them away from her as politely as she could and left the church. If experience meant anything, she knew that the tale would soon be all over town, probably exaggerated so that it bore little resemblance to fact. They would forget that it was God Who had restored the baby to its brief moment of life. The glory that should go to Him would fall like a burden upon her.

She returned to the inn to find de Loré and Kennedy waiting for her at a table in the busy tavern. The messenger had returned from Paris, bringing bad tidings. The Armagnac Jehanne had wished released was dead, executed the day she sent her request. The bailiff of Senlis wanted to know, What did she want to do with d'Arras now?

Jehanne was tired of the matter. It was plain that by allowing the Armagnac to die, God had judged d'Arras a murderer and a thief, and commended him to man's law. She wanted no more of this. She had her own problems to deal with, and needed to be alone to ponder this strange day.

"He is your prisoner. Since the man I asked for is dead, do with him what justice requires," she replied impatiently.

She got up from the table where the men were still sitting and went upstairs to her room, closing the door against the lively atmosphere of the inn. She flung her cloak upon the bed, then sat down beside it. For a long time she stared out the window at the gray city sky.

She could not get the awestruck faces of the women out of her mind. L'Angélique, they had called her, just like all the others, praising her name to new, undeserved heights. She pictured what would surely happen next. Her horse would be mobbed again by wild adoration when she tried to leave town. Once more, she would have to wave at the people while struggling to resist the temptation to steal glory from God. But this time the conflict would have a bitter ally to torment her further.

Within a few hours of learning her future, it had seemed to Jehanne that she could not possibly have heard Catherine correctly. Her looming captivity was unlikely. God had promised that Charles would expel the English and win the war. Who would continue the fight if not her? There was no one else to inspire the army. The King needed her to give the soldiers heart.

And yet . . . she could not lie to herself. In a short while she was to become a prisoner. During those intervals of quiet resignation she told herself that she must accept God's will. He had created the world wherein all had meaning and He had created her to enact His will. She was obliged to obey with courage. God would help her; she had His promise.

But why would He will that His servant be captured? Perhaps it was only what Pasquerel would call "a test." Perhaps it was not true at all.

The argument within her was so noisy and violent that she had not slept last night. Today, she tried to wish it away, but it had surfaced in recurring irritability directed first toward the ecstatic women who had proclaimed the infant's brief return to life a miracle, then at the captains and d'Arras.

Is it true? Must it be?

YES.

But why?

All she heard was silence. Then at least tell me when I'll be taken, what day. No use. Catherine was gone.

When Jehanne reached Senlis, she met with discouraging news on two fronts. First she learned that the King had appointed archbishop de Chartres to command the army. Charles had done that to keep an eye on her; she knew it. But battlefield tactics required a decisive, steady head, and the old man was a ditherer who in his laughable negotiations with Philippe de Bourgogne could be counted on to yield too much and thereby lose everything. With him leading the King's men, they were sure to fail unless Jehanne executed a greater hold over them than she had recently.

Ever since Paris, she had sensed her inspiration slipping in their minds, although none of them said anything outwardly disrespectful or disloyal, and yet there were little things. The coarseness in their language had returned, now seldom shushed altogether in her presence. The bolder among them and those who had not served with her in previous campaigns gambled openly in the camp. Jehanne had seen suspicious women hanging around the camp who always disappeared whenever she tried to approach them. There were no encounters with anyone, which rendered fighting discontent and tarnished faith akin to struggling against a smoky phantom.

Remembering that they were here to fight, Jehanne made the best of things. She resolved to outflank old Regnault somehow if his ideas became perilous to the campaign. The prospect of having to deal with him was a major nuisance, but the second bit of information was downright alarming.

Philippe was personally in the field and already within sight of Compiègne with a massed army twice the size of the Armagnacs. They were presently besieging Choisy-au-Bac, where the Oise and Aisne rivers connected. It was vital that the army of Charles beat the Burgundians off at Choisy, otherwise they would have to fight them at Compiègne. That might prolong the siege until reinforcements could be gathered together from the scattered garrisons of France, and that could take weeks, perhaps months.

Both pieces of bad tidings collided when the archbishop decided that the army would have to use its heavy artillery in the battle for Choisy.

"We can't do that!" Jehanne cried, appalled at the old man's lack of battle sense. "The rivers at Choisy are shallow enough for light cavalry and men-at-arms to cross, but they're too deep for us to ford the cannon. We would lose them to the rivers!"

His disdain for her opinion came as she had feared. "I do not intend to cross at Choisy, but at Soissons. The Aisne is shallow enough there."

They were in a temporary council of war room on the second floor of an inn in Senlis. Barretta, Poton de Xaintrailles, de Loré, and Kennedy were crowded around the improvised map table which the landlord had ordered moved to this chamber. Normally serving as the master's writing desk, it sat delicately out of place, overladen with folded and refolded parchments, dead center in the circle of armor-burdened veterans.

The men said nothing in response to the archbishop's retort. They shifted their feet and avoided looking at Jehanne.

"Soissons is farther from where we are than Compiègne is!" Jehanne shouted. "It's three days' march or more, and by the time we get there, Compiègne could fall! Don't you see that?" She looked around to the others for support.

None of the captains acknowledged her plea.

"We must pray that we will be on time." De Chartres' chin whiskers moved like a billy goat's. He raised his feathered brows dramatically. "Surely you have not lost faith in God, Jehanne?"

Enraged at the sting, she flung back, "God gave us common sense and He expects us to use it! We can't just sit back and let God do all the work, we have to take the opportunities He sends us. If we dilly-dally and take the long way around to Soissons, we'll be wasting the chance for a quick attack that will take them by surprise and drive them away from Choisy! That is what God wants us to do."

"You are presumptuous to think you know the mind of God," the archbishop said, filled with stern indignation, "and in you is the sin of pride. You must be careful, Jehanne, for the sake of your soul, or God will tumble you down as He raised you up!" Spittle flicked at the corners of those purple lips. His yellow old eyes crackled.

"I know what God expects of me because my Counsel tell me, and They urge me onward by giving the army chance after chance to win victory. It is not the sin of pride; it is right here in front of us—the prospect of winning! Anyone with half a brain could see that!" The same voice that had urged men to take the Tourelles climbed in volume until she was bellowing.

"I will forget you said that, Jehanne." De Chartres delivered his attempt at a parry with lofty assurance. "I shall pray that you may see the arrogance that prompted it."

"You fool!" she yelled, not caring about his office. "If we go all the way around to Soissons, we'll waste three days there at least, and another three coming back to Choisy! With Choisy gone, we'll have to fight the Burgundians at Compiègne, and they have more men than we do. And since our objective is to raise the siege at Compiègne, we need to hold Choisy." Her voice sounded as though she were speaking to a simple-minded child pretending to be wise.

She could hear the traffic outside the window, and the inn's denizens downstairs in a steady hum of conversation occasionally punctured by laughter. A ragseller in the street was calling out prices for his wares. Xaintrailles shuffled his feet and folded his arms across his chest. All of them were staring at her, the captains with her but neither willing nor able to speak up.

The archbishop gave her a tiny, poisonous smile. "You have overstepped yourself this time, young woman. You forget to whom you are speaking."

"I know full well who you are, Your Excellency," Jehanne responded, her voice crisp with meaning. "I also know that you will cause us to lose Choisy."

She was right, although in a way she did not foresee. When after three tortuously slow days they reached Soissons, they found the gates closed and entrance to the bridge across the Aisne denied them. The captain of the town, a Picard named Guiscard Bournel, accused them of not wanting a way to the other side of the river at all, but of being hungry for Soissons' hospitality. He had the civilians so provoked over the prospect of having to billet three thousand men that they would not listen to Jehanne and de Loré's argument that this was not so, they desperately needed to relieve Choisy. Soissons refused to relent.

It was then that de Chartres decided to return the army to Senlis, citing God's will to explain his retreat. Jehanne refused to accompany him anywhere else. He was too stupid to have been given command in the first place, and she would have nothing further to do with him. She went instead to Compiègne in the company of Barretta and two hundred others, while the archbishop took the main army back to Senlis.

Her brother Jehan did not accompany her. When he made ready to mount his horse, she stopped him. Handing him her standard, she told him that she wanted him to ride to Ste.-Cathérine-de-Fierbois. He was to give the symbol of her victories to the monks there for safekeeping. That was where God had hidden the sword for her to use, and it was in that place that her standard was to remain.

Jehan refused at first. Why did she want to do that when she was still in the field?

She could not tell him the truth. If she did, he would again become the protective older brother and attempt to block God's will, thereby harming his soul. So she replied casually that since they would soon see action in another siege, she did not wish to risk losing the emblem that she so valued.

Jehan was doubtful, but eventually agreed. He hugged her and kissed her cheek in farewell, then climbed onto his horse.

She ordered herself not to cry until her brother had ridden out of sight. As he disappeared over a hill she whispered his name, knowing she would never see him again.

The diminished battalion rode all evening and through the night. They darted over the moon-forsaken landscape, dodging trees and fallen logs, their horses pounding across fields planted with new seeds. The sky was starting to pinken with dawn light when they dashed through the gate at Compiègne. The city welcomed them as saviours and gave them lodgings in inns and private homes. Jehanne stayed with the magistrate and his wife. Completely worn out from foreboding and the long ride, she slept dreamlessly through the morning and into afternoon. Her hosts were careful not to disturb her.

When she awoke, Jehanne sought out the town's military commander, Guillaume de Flavy, who showed her a map of the area. They were here at Compiègne, he said, pointing to the yellowed parchment, on the south bank of the River Oise. The city's rear was protected by the thickly treed Compiègne Forest, so they did not have to worry about an attack from that quarter. But directly across the bridge the village of Margny lay a little under half a league northwest of the city, and it was swarming with Anglo-Burgundians under the command of Baudot de Noyelles. Upriver, Clairoix sat at the junction between the Oise and the Aisne. Flavy's spies had reported only this morning that a division of men loyal to Jehan de Luxembourg, comte de Ligny and a steadfast partisan of Bourgogne, controlled that village. Three and a half leagues to the southwest was another hamlet called Venette, also in enemy hands, in this case English.

But these smaller battalions were nothing compared to the main force led by Philippe de Bourgogne himself, due north of Clairoix. Altogether Philippe had under his authority more than five thousand men.

Jehanne studied the map very carefully. The enemy strongholds, though close to the city, were some distance apart and could not offer rapid assistance to one another in the event that the King's army attacked one of them. Bourgogne was farther away still, and it would take some time for him to muster his lumbering forces against Jehanne's light cavalry. By that time, she could take one of the villages and be safely across the bridge, back within the walls of Compiègne. It was a tactic that had worked splendidly at Orléans, when the army had taken out the *bastilles* one by one. No matter that numbers favored the enemy, God was with her. This would be easy.

She rested comfortably that night and the next morning, May 23, sallied forth from Compiègne wearing a fine cloth of gold over her armor, intent upon assaulting Margny. Archers and culverins at the Compiègne gate shielded her rear, supported by crossbowmen bobbing in small boats upon the Oise.

The plan went at first as Jehanne had foreseen. Her band of two hundred were not noticed as they streaked toward the village. A short distance south of Margny, they fell upon the unprepared garrison like the wrath of God, killing a number of them before they could scramble for their weapons. This time Jehanne was armed with a Burgundian sword, booty taken in the conflict at St.-Pierre-le-Moustier. She swung it over her head, daring anyone to engage her, and managed to beat back several retreating adversaries. The remaining Anglo-Burgundians, panicked by the unexpected invasion, began to struggle toward Margny proper.

"After them, men!" Jehanne shouted. "We have them on the run now!" Her battalion gave a great yell and tore after the limping garrison.

Suddenly, eight or ten armored gentlemen in colorful *huques* descended from the northeastern bluff, intent upon giving aid to the Burgundians. The Armagnacs crashed into them with ferocious zeal, hacking and jabbing with their great broadswords, and screams of surprise and agony filled the warm, dusty air. The enemy knights, outnumbered and faltering, were gradually pushed back toward Margny.

Caught up as she was in the thick of battle, Jehanne did not immediately see the several hundred knights and men-at-arms rushing toward them from the direction of Clairoix. By the time she heard their warcry, they were close enough for her to see the patterns upon their flags. Their faces were twisted in rage and they waved weapons above their heads as they came at her.

"Jehanne," Barretta called out, "we must retreat back into the city! They will outnumber us here!"

Her troop had by now seen the advancing division, and the line was starting to break as the soldiers realized the sudden peril of their position. Without waiting for orders, most of them wheeled about their horses and started back for the bridgehead.

"Stand firm!" shouted Jehanne at her dwindling company. "Their defeat depends on you!"

She was now practically alone except for her household and twenty or so others, with the enemy bearing closer and closer. She had no choice but to withdraw.

"Let's go!" she yelled, jerking her horse around.

The men followed her. They raced toward the Aisne, closely pursued by four hundred screaming Burgundians. A quarter of a league ahead, most of the King's detachment were hurrying through the iron-toothed portcullis into the city.

Jehanne glanced over her shoulder. Her spirit took a dive into a black place as she comprehended the gravity of her situation. *They were right behind her, less than two hundred yards!*

The gate yawned before her, drawing nearer and nearer.

She gouged her horse's flanks with her spurs, drawing blood in a desperate effort to urge him onward, and sensing her terror, the animal surged ahead. Safety lay just ahead now, easily reachable.

But her pursuers were gaining on her, undaunted by the storm of arrows from the boats that hurled some of them into the dirt.

Understanding blasted into her brain with the force of a thunderbolt. If she led her men into the city, there would not be enough time to lower the gate before the Burgundians also entered, and then the struggle for the city would begin within Compiègne itself, endangering civilians as well as the thinned ranks of Armagnacs garrisoned there.

Without thinking, she raised her hand in a signal to halt and pulled on the reins, then whirled her horse about, within only a few feet of the gate. Jehanne's remaining men turned to protect her.

They were hit almost immediately by the enemy. They kept coming, on and on, increasing the pressure against the badly outnumbered guard until each of Jehanne's comrades was fighting five or six enemy knights. The reduced band hacked fruitlessly at the swelling numbers arrayed against them.

An ominous sound suddenly penetrated Jehanne's mind: the familiar creak of a portcullis chain as the wheel moved it. Flavy's men were lowering the gate.

"No!" she shouted. "Don't do that!"

She was ignored. Relentlessly, the door lowered until it pierced the ground. There was no chance now that they could find refuge in Compiègne.

"This way!" Jehanne called to her handful of men.

She prodded her horse into a short leap to the riverbank below, then hastened alongside the city wall, toward the northeast, her household hard upon her. She had no idea where she was going, she simply had to get away. Somewhere out there was safety.

They were dashing up the hill at the end of the wall when they saw a swarm of enemy horsemen heading toward them at full gallop. Jehanne looked to their rear. The Burgundians pursuing them had also left the bridge and were bearing down upon the tiny group.

They were surrounded on all sides. The river, to their right, was too deep to ford. They would have to fight if they wanted to survive. Lightheaded from the unreality of the situation, Jehanne shouted to her family, "Stand your ground! We shall fight them off!"

All of them, even Pasquerel, readied their weapons. The enemy divisions had slowed their pace and were tightening the trap. Jehanne licked her lips with a dry tongue, watching in disbelief as the circle became smaller. Her heartbeat thundered in her ears.

This is not happening, she told herself.

The Anglo-Burgundians cantered to within a few yards of Jehanne's household, swords bristling. "Surrender, in the name of Philippe, duc de Bourgogne!" someone commanded.

"Never!" Jehanne called back. "You surrender in the name of Charles, King of France!"

There was a howl of laughter. They kept coming. The circle became steadily

420

smaller. Jehanne held her sword ready in a sweaty hand, determined to fight them off.

The chant started, "Yield! Yield!"

"I will not!"

The words had barely left her mouth when she was pulled backward with a sudden jerk. Earth tumbled over sky and she hit her nose against the dusty ground.

She lifted her head, scarcely able to see through the gritty cloud invading her nostrils and her mouth. She was still spitting out dirt when rough hands grabbed her arms and pulled her to her feet.

She was squarely in the middle of them. Someone forced her hands behind her back, and she felt a rope looped over her arms.

"Look at the cloak on this one!" a man-at-arms declared. "He'll make a fine ransom, I'll warrant."

His comrades laughed. A youngish archer said to her, "Yield to me. I am Guillaume, in the service of the Bastard of Wendonne, and I demand your sword."

"I shall not yield to any man, only to the King of Heaven," Jehanne retorted.

The archer's eyes widened with understanding and he broke into a smile. "See here, boys, we've captured Jehanne the Maid!" A whoop of exultation clamored about her.

She suddenly remembered her household and craned her neck to look around for them. All had been overrun and forced from their horses. She caught sight of Pierre, on his knees in the dirt, already bound into a cocoon of heavy rope. A knight had a sword to his neck.

"Don't hurt my brother!" she yelled, contending against frightened tears.

Pierre heard her and raised his head. "Jehanne!"

Tied tightly, she was whirled around. Hostile hands forced her upon a horse. From this height she could see that her entire band was lashed as she was and, one by one, was being set upon a mount.

"Pierre!" she cried as he was yanked to his feet. "Tell Maman and Papa I love them!"

He did not have a chance to acknowledge that he had caught her words. In the next moment they lifted him onto a horse. She tried to turn to look at him but saw instead the stern-faced men riding around her.

Oh, God, help me! she begged. She had not wanted to believe it, but it was true; it had really happened. She was a prisoner.

CHAPTER FOURTEEN

Leap of Faith

May 23–December 16, 1430

A short way past the bridgehead south of Margny, English and Burgundian soldiers were lining the corpses of their slain comrades into a dripping, limbless row. Before the sun went down, the dead would be buried in the mass grave gradually taking shape just behind them. When they saw Jehanne coming toward Margny under the escort of forty guardsmen, they stopped collecting the casualties. Forming a gauntlet, they spat at her and shook their fists, hurling curses with the fury of culverin blasts.

"Slut!"

"Armagnac whore! Witch!"

"Let's burn her, lads!" cried an Englishman in badly accented French. They reached out to grab her, intending to pull her from the horse.

Her captors aimed their weapons at their comrades and pushed them back. An Englishman in a hatlike helmet threw a rotting head of cabbage at her, and it smacked wetly against her cheek, then plopped into the dust. With her arms bound, she could not wipe away the mess, which would later dry into a greenish-brown crust that cracked when she spoke.

The townsfolk watched her pass from their doorways and from the steps of the church in disbelieving silence. Jehanne rode impassively with her eyes straight ahead and her head held high, to all appearances indifferent to both the hateful catcalls and the kneeling women who crossed themselves as she was led past them to an unknown fate.

Inside, she felt nothing at all. None of this was real; it shimmered like a dream. In fact, it reminded her of a specific dream, but in her dazed condition she could not remember which. She only knew that she seemed to be watching what was happening from outside herself in a manner disconnected from any emotion.

She saw herself paraded through the small town's main artery to the north. At the end of the street, the retinue broke into a trot, then a canter, toward the high tower on the other side of a distant stand of trees. Jehanne had never ridden like this, bound, handless, at a full run across an uneven field. She gritted her teeth and clasped her knees tightly against the horse's sides. The warm wind whipped her face with bits of grass and earth flung from pounding hooves ahead of her. She closed her eyes into narrow slits, praying all the while that she would not fall off and be trampled.

A château appeared beyond the trees. With her eyes half-shut Jehanne could not see it very well, but it appeared fairly small and ringed by a low, crumbling enclosure. A window in the very top of its turret, the one visible from the town, was darkened. But there was a light burning on the ground floor, and silhouettes moving across it like black ghosts. As they came closer, the column began to slow. Their horses' hooves rumbled across a wooden drawbridge spanning a narrow moat and into a courtyard.

The party drew rein. The men dismounted around Jehanne and two of them dragged her from the horse. Her leg muscles throbbed from the effort she had made to remain horsed, and she crumpled to her knees. The two captors yanked her roughly to her feet. They shoved her through a door, into a deserted main hall. Forming ranks around her, they took her to a staircase against the hall's left side. The tramp of their boots clapped against stone steps, which spiraled upward in a staggering circle. Down below, the wind blew a scattering of leaves through the door and across the flagstones of the dark and empty room.

In a short while they came to a door, then proceeded unflaggingly up again, to what Jehanne supposed was the tower. Another door, this one opening to daylight. Three steps up and a turn to the right put them on a parapet extending a short way to the *donjon*'s coned peak. Margny sprawled across the field below, and in the late afternoon light Jehanne could see the tiny soldiers burying their dead. Across the small, shimmering river, Compiègne and the safety that she had not reached seemed a thousand leagues distant.

One of the guards took a key from his belt and unlocked the door. It creaked noisily on its hinges, and when it was wide enough, rough hands propelled Jehanne through it. She tried to brace herself for the fall, but landed on her knees anyway. The door slammed shut behind her.

Struggling to her feet, she considered her surroundings. The sole windows were arrow slits perhaps four inches wide, enough to allow meager light into the circular room. The chamber itself, about nine feet across, was empty but for the straw scattered across the planked floor and tiny pellets of rodent droppings. The air was stifling, musty, as though it had not been used for some time.

Jehanne paced anxiously, confusion hammering in her ears. What next? Would they kill her? God knows, they had threatened to do just that ever since she took up arms against them. With a shudder, she remembered her messenger's words and the price on her head.

She went to a window and looked out. Compiègne was not visible from this side of the tower. All she could see through the narrow space was a slice of dark forest and a field, lit by a now-setting sun whose gold burned out of sight behind her. A flock of birds winged overhead, southward bound, and she craned her neck to see them better.

When they disappeared out of view, she started pacing again. Her body and mind were charged with anticipatory dread, and every sense hummed with a heightened alertness. She was so filled with energy that she could have walked to Paris quite easily. Around the room and then across, her thoughts as disjointed and overlapping as her steps.

Will they kill me tonight or wait until tomorrow? What has become of Pierre? He had seemed in danger of execution when she last saw him. And the others? Have they already been done to death? How long will it be before the King is able to ransom me? Will the *goddons* allow him to do so? Or will they kill me before he even knows I've been taken?

She knelt, and commanded her heartbeat to slow down and her breathing to stop its open-mouthed panic. Speak to me, she implored, I need you now.

They were only faintly present in the coming darkness, as though They lacked the will to materialize fully. Catherine whispered through her like an illusion: BEAR EVERYTHING WITH COURAGE. GOD IS WITH YOU; and then was gone.

Jehanne stood up and walked to a window. The air was cooler now, and crickets had begun their night song. She eased herself into a sitting position beneath the slit and leaned against the thick wall. For the first time, she noticed how tight her bonds were. The fetters wound over the breastplate held her hands firmly behind her back, gouging her upper arms painfully. When she tried to shift them, metal jabbed into her muscles and she gave a sharp cry. She found herself also unable to move her wrists. The ropes binding them made her sweating hands buzz with numbness. There was no denying it; she was trussed up like a goose ready for roasting. There was nothing to do but sit and wait.

She could not tell how much time had passed when they came for her, an hour, two at most judging by the declining light. First she heard the stamp of boots on the stairs, and then the rattle of a key in the lock.

The torchlight made her blink as they poured through the door, eight or ten of them. One came toward her and said, "Don't you give us any trouble, or I swear we'll kill you."

He pulled her to a standing position. A second held his sword to her throat while the man who had spoken unfastened the thick coil binding her arms. Someone else behind her loosened the fetters around her wrists.

Jehanne thought she would collapse from relief. They would not be releasing her if they intended to kill her. But in the next moment she knew that they had no plan to leave her unbound. The man who had removed the larger rope now pulled her arms toward him and wound a cord around her wrists. He grinned at her and gave a savage tug to the knot he had tied, making her wince.

"That'll hold you, I guess," he said. Then he looked down at her hands and the rings glinting in the firelight. "What's this?" the man asked, grabbing her hands.

Jehanne tried to pull away, but he said, "Hold her, boys," and then she was struggling against the strength of three of them.

"No, that's mine, my father gave me that!" she shouted angrily.

The man pulled off her rings with such force that one of them cut her knuckle. He bit into the band from Jehan. "Not worth much," he shrugged, "but a good souvenir, eh, men?"

"Give that back to me! It's mine, not yours!"

" 'It's mine,' " he mimicked. His comrades laughed. "Come on, you," he said, wrapping a powerful hand around her arm. A sword prodded her toward the door, and she knew that she had no choice but to let them take her.

They went back down the way they had come, winding down narrow stone steps so dizzily that Jehanne tasted nausea at the back of her throat. Her stomach tried to heave. I won't be sick, she chanted. Her legs clattered down the stairs as though belonging to a toy with no will of its own.

At the bottom floor they turned sharply to the left and headed down a corridor. The guard halted at the end before an open door. They pushed Jehanne through it roughly. The captain and two of his men followed.

"Here she is, my lord," said the man who had stolen her rings, drawing a sword up in front of her face.

Jehanne scarcely heard the gloating comment. She was gazing in wonder about the candlelit apartment, richly decorated with the finest wall tapestries she had ever seen anywhere and illuminated by four large torches, one at each corner. In the glow of their dancing flames the room emitted well-appointed comfort and confidence. Two darkwood stools on either side of a solid desk were occupied by stylishly dressed gentlemen, one of whom wore a black eyepatch. It was all so mysterious, this beautifully appointed room and the elegant men amidst this ruin of a castle.

A third man was sitting behind the desk, and when he saw Jehanne, he stood with a smile and came around it toward her. "And here is Jehanne," he beamed, as though greeting an old friend. "Welcome! I am so delighted that at last we have the chance to meet."

She thought he must surely be a prince. He was magnificently attired in a surcoat of gold thread that glimmered in the firelight, and around his neck hung a sparkling medallion set with a circle of diamonds around a large emerald. His dark brown hair, freshly barbered, carpeted a long skull out of which shone close-set gray eyes that on the surface gamboled like the torches. Deep lines furrowed his cheeks all the way to the chin, above which pursed a small, red-lipped mouth. He drew closer, and Jehanne caught a whiff of his perfume, as light as that of a lady-in-waiting. His mouth smiled at her again, though the eyes did not.

"I think we can remove those fetters, Captain," the man said affably.

"You better watch this one, my lord," the soldier cautioned, bringing the sword closer to her nose. "She'll surely bewitch you."

"Nonsense. You can put down the sword now, fellow," said the man, still pleasantly. The guard hesitated. "Come on," the gentleman ordered in a clipped rhythm, "do as I say, cut her bonds."

With his free hand the man-at-arms reached for his belt and, withdrawing a dagger, cut the cord around Jehanne's wrists. They had not broken skin but the welts hurt anyway. She rubbed them and flexed her stiffened hands.

"I also think that she will not need her armor any longer." The lord snapped his fingers loudly.

Two men came forward and began to disarm Jehanne, removing first the belt, then the torn cloth of gold, which they lifted over her head. "That is better, don't you think?" the man asked as the plates came away from her to reveal the simple tunic and hose beneath.

"Leave us now," the man said when they were finished.

The guards did as they were told without further protest. The man who had stolen her rings grinned at her as he went.

"Who are you?" she demanded, vexed by the lord's pretended kindliness. "Where are my men?"

"Oh, please pardon my manners," he replied, as though genuinely dismayed at having offended her. "I am Philippe, duc de Bourgogne." He gave her a small nod. "And this is Jehan de Luxembourg, the comte de Ligny"—he gestured to the one-eyed man—"and my secretary, Enguerrand de Monstrelet."

The gentlemen had risen from their seats while Jehanne was being disarmed, and now they stood on either side of the duc. The three of them were beautifully dressed, shaved, manicured—and dangerous. Jehanne sensed that Monstrelet was more than a secretary; he was the duc's adviser and chronicler, the official voice of the House of Bourgogne. As for Jehan de Luxembourg, he would sell his own mother if the price satisfied his ongoing quest for wealth. He looked particularly menacing, with that disturbing eyepatch and the hideous scar running across the bridge of his nose.

Jehanne summoned the Power and gave Philippe a solid stare. "One of your men took my rings. He is a thief, and should be punished for his sin."

"Oh, my goodness, how sorry I am!" His eyebrows wrinkled with concern. "I must of course get them back for you."

"Where are my household?"

"They are quite safe, have no fear." The duc smiled. "I give you my word that both your men and your property shall be returned to you undamaged."

"Like you have given your word to the King? When was the last pledge to him that you kept?"

An eyebrow shot up. He studied her for several moments, and she could tell by his dark smile that his mind was working busily.

Finally, he said, very quietly, "Charles is not a true king despite his coronation, and I shall tell you why." He took a step toward her. "Charles is a fool, the most recent rotten limb of the Valois dynasty. His father before him was a madman who gave his kingdom away to the English by legal treaty. He is not fit to rule France, all he is equipped to do is lose himself in his books and his pretty playmates.

"But a king must be strong! He must take what is rightfully his by every means possible, and then he must hold on to his crown with his dying breath. A true king has a sacred duty to protect his people and bring order to his realm. He cannot trot languidly behind the monarchy, hoping to catch up to it!"

The other men laughed.

"Charles *is* the true King of France!" Jehanne glowered, outraged by this insult to her liege. "He was anointed in Reims Cathedral with the holy oil of St.-Clovis—"

"Oh, yes, I remember. By the way, thank you for your gracious invitation that

I attend the ceremony. You understand of course why I could not." The dissembling smile crept in a shiver up her backbone.

"As for Charles' sham of a coronation, it was you who brought him to it, or dragged him if what I've heard is correct." Philippe looked at her searchingly without getting a response. "Do you honestly suppose that he would have taken himself there had it not been for you? He would have continued to dance in the moonlight at Chinon while the English overran his kingdom. Now I ask you, what kind of king is that?" He put a confidential arm around her shoulder and she stiffened at his touch.

"Jehanne, Jehanne, don't you see? You have put your faith in the wrong party," he whispered loudly. "The Armagnacs can never win against my armies and those of the English, surely you know that? You want the war to end, I want the war to end, the English want the war to end. Only Charles stands in the way of peace! And since you and I want the same thing, don't you think that it is time that we worked together instead of against one another? You want your freedom and to lead an army? I can give you both."

She pulled away from him, seething. "It is not my King who is unfit to rule, it is you, you and your little English master! You spoke of order? Hah! Together you and the English have made a wasteland of France, have brought it nothing but death and misery, and for what?" She sneered. "That you who do not have God's support could rule."

She was unable to stop now. "Neither you nor the *goddons* care about the people whose lives you have ruined and the suffering kingdom, you only want the spoils. You may be rich, but you are still a vassal of the King and you have betrayed him, and for your sins, God has condemned you! Charles is the true King appointed by God, and while he may not be clever in the ways that you count important, he has a good heart and for that God made him King. God, seigneur Bourgogne, not me!"

She stopped to breathe. "I will never serve you," she panted. "I serve God and my King."

His eyes had stopped dancing and were deadly cold, like the man behind the mask. "Perhaps I should tell you the reality of your situation. I am glad that we have captured you at last, not because I bear you any personal ill will but because you have been the most powerful weapon Charles could throw against us, although in keeping with his nature, he does not realize it. I know that because I know Charles very, very well. And I also know that a weapon that can be used for one can be used for another.

"But, you see, the English, they cannot be altogether dismissed. Simply put, they want you dead, and they will pay any price, make any concession—within reason, of course—to bring about your death. Yet, you are not in English hands, you are the prisoner of the comte de Ligny." Philippe inclined his head slightly to Luxembourg. "The comte is in turn my vassal. If I order him to release you, he must."

The duc stared intently into her obstinate face. Lowering his voice, he continued, "But if I tell him that he may do with you as he wishes, then he is free to ransom you to Charles, or to keep you in a *donjon* until you rot, or"—he smiled again—"to sell you to the English. So which shall it be, Jehanne? Are you to be a living standard for the House of Bourgogne, or a traveler to an uncertain fate?"

Jehanne's mind seemed to whirl in a hundred different directions all at once, and she forced it to the heart of the matter. Of course she could not betray the King, that was out of the question. But was Bourgogne telling the truth? Would he keep his word not to interfere if she remained in Luxembourg's custody? The disfigured man would surely ransom her. Though a Burgundian, he was French; maybe she could remind him of that and persuade him to contact the King instead of the English. Charles had borrowed ridiculous sums just to give *soirées*; surely he would willingly go into debt again to save her.

She looked hard at Bourgogne, trying to read his intentions behind the perfumed, shaven mask. Could she trust him in this one instance? It made no difference. However slim it might be, it was her only chance. Perhaps she would get an opportunity to escape.

She turned the Power fully upon him. "You are not my lord, and I will never serve you."

"Very well." Philippe sighed. "You give me no choice. Guard!"

The door opened and the men entered with weapons unsheathed. "Take her back to the *donjon*." Bourgogne looked at her indifferently. "Good-bye, Jehanne."

They returned her to the tower, but did not bind her again. She sat in the dark for a long time. There was no moon, only a sprinkling of stars sometimes stroked by long, ghostly clouds. When she grew tired of standing at the slit in the thick stone wall, she sat down once more. She folded her arms across her knees and lowered her head. She dozed.

A noise wrenched her awake, the unmistakable crunch of masculine boots upon the parapet. The key turned in the lock and then she was momentarily blinded by torchlight. She blinked, and her vision cleared well enough for her to see her fellow prisoners pushed into the room. Their faces glowed for only a moment before the lights went.

"Jehanne!"

"Minguet! Brother Pasquerel, is that you?" She grabbed a hand in the dark.

"No, it's d'Aulon! Jehanne, are you all right?"

"Yes. How are all of you?" They murmured that they were well. "Where is Pierre?"

"We don't know," said d'Aulon. "Last I saw, he was slung across a horse, same as we all were. I don't know where they took him. He wasn't with us."

"What have you heard?"

They hesitated.

"What?" she demanded.

"About Pierre, nothing," said Pasquerel. "But do not worry, Jehanne. He is ennobled now, and ransomable. They will not harm him."

"You said that you've heard nothing about Pierre, but what *have* you heard?" She hated it when they tried to keep things from her.

"Just rumors, nothing more," the monk replied. His sigh came out in a wheeze.

"Some say that you are to be brought to Paris and made to stand at the altar when the English king is crowned there."

Jehanne snorted contemptuously. "What else?"

"They say that we—that you—are the prisoner of Jehan de Luxembourg," Minguet answered.

"Yes, I know that. I met him, and Philippe de Bourgogne."

"What?"

"Really, Jehanne?"

She told them about the interview, and although she could not see her family in the dark, she felt them grow quieter as she told about Philippe's offer and her refusal. They did not say a word for an uncomfortable length of time once she was finished.

Finally, d'Aulon cleared his throat and said, "Jehanne, I think you have to take his threat seriously. He'll order Luxembourg to exchange you for English gold."

"That's a chance I'll have to take. In God's name, do you expect me to throw in my lot with Bourgogne? Shame on you, d'Aulon."

"I'm not saying that you should join Philippe, but Jehanne, you must control your temper and not blurt out everything that's on your mind! They're more likely to treat you well and even ransom you to Charles if you don't try to battle against them. You don't have any arms now, and they have the upper hand. You are defenseless."

"I have God. I don't need anything else."

They talked to her urgently for a long while, and she could feel the fearful love behind their voices. She listened without interrupting and ended by promising what they requested. Then she lay down on a meager patch of straw and went to sleep.

The bell in the tower had just begun summoning students to their classes, and they scattered quickly across the atrium with their black gowns billowing behind them. From his window overlooking the courtyard, the bishop watched them as he absently tapped a piece of paper against his fingernails. He often stood here when he wanted to think. He filled his lungs with a deep, appreciative breath as he took in the fine summer afternoon, the gray-bottomed clouds floating like ships high above Paris, drifting very slowly toward the east. The prelate smiled. God had been good to him this day.

The letter he had just read brought the news for which he had so long prayed. His friend and brother of the late King Henry had sent an astonishing report from Rouen that the infamous heretic who had caused so much trouble for the crown was at last in the hands of the duc de Bourgogne, having been dragged from a horse when she failed to take Compiègne. Bedford was so delighted that his triumph almost leaped from the page. Now that they had her, they wanted her brought to trial on charges of sorcery, sedition against the king, and heresy. Most of all, they wanted her burned. Her condemnation, which would also un-mask the pretender Charles before the French people and the whole of Europe, would rid them of two enemies. No genuine monarch, consecrated by God, allowed himself to be used by an agent of the Devil, as this one surely was. The woman claimed to be from God, a lie which should be easy to disprove, given that she was an unlettered peasant, a cowmaid, and no match for the learned doctors of the University of Paris.

Would that august institution consent to overseeing the trial? Bedford wondered. The Holy Office of the Inquisition would naturally be consulted about sending a representative if the bishop concurred. As for the man who successfully prosecuted this case, King Henry had a very special reward in mind. The archbishopric of Rouen was currently vacant.

There remained one obstacle: Bourgogne. He would not ransom the woman to the throne cheaply. He had, in fact, asked for a fortune, the full twenty thousand pounds Bedford had pledged to whomever brought her down. Bedford was attempting negotiations to lower the price, but the king's slippery ally persisted in delaying with empty excuses. Of course, Bedford had the authority, as the young king's Regent, to order Bourgogne to release the woman to the English. But Philippe was not entirely trustworthy and might switch sides if subjected to pressure. Bedford wondered if perhaps Philippe were already communicating with Charles, intent upon selling the witch to the highest bidder. He could not allow that to happen. If Philippe demanded twenty *million* pounds, it must be collected. In the meantime, Bedford asked the bishop to pray that an ample ransom be raised quickly so that God's nemesis and theirs could be brought to justice.

The churchman smiled and, folding the page, put it into his sleeve. The small object that had been enclosed with the letter glinted evilly in his hand, and he closed his palm around it.

He would of course be happy to grant the duke's requests. For almost a year, since the Armagnacs invaded Beauvais and drove him from his diocese, the bishop had dreamed of vengeance against this demon in the form of a woman. Soon it seemed he would have his chance. God had been good to him today, as He had been throughout the bishop's life.

At sixty, Pierre Cauchon was within sight of reaching another goal in his illustrious career, begun when as the cleverest student in his class, he had enjoyed renown for his single-minded, ruthless intellect. Upon receiving a master's degree in theology from the University of Paris, followed by a doctorate in ecclesiastical law, Cauchon had commenced to Rome, where industry and ambition brought him office after office and the favor of Pope Martin V. Returning to Paris, he was appointed first a lecturer at the University, and by the age of thirty was its rector. His uncompromising zeal won the attention of the English, and when it came time for him to choose sides politically, he had accepted their advances.

He admired everything about them: their language, their culture, their pragmatic notions of chivalry, and their dedication to ridding the earth of heretics. Even as they wooed him with promises of higher offices, he had made himself available to their service, and was the primary negotiator in the Treaty of Troyes which confirmed King Henry V as the legal heir to the French throne. For his good work, the young English monarch had made him bishop of Beauvais and a wealthy man, which satisfied his yearning for power and gold.

Cauchon wanted even more. Bedford's hint regarding the archbishopric of Rouen made his heart leap, for he saw it as a preliminary to his becoming cardinal. From there it would be just a step up, into the seat of St.-Pierre. It was his destiny to rule Christendom with the same skill that had governed the University and his diocese of Beauvais, and until last summer it had seemed that his ambition was easily within grasp.

Then, without warning, *she* had come to turn the people of Beauvais against him and to make him a refugee, fleeing first to Paris, then to Rouen, and now back to the capital.

Cauchon's ice blue eyes narrowed at the thought of her and his lips fixed into a grim line. How he hated this woman he had never seen! Manifesting from the very bowels of Hell, she had first bewitched that imbecile Valois, then the Armagnac traitors at Poitiers, once his esteemed colleagues at the University. Entranced, they had voted to give her an army—Satan's own—and she immediately set about bringing the God-cursed Armagnac soldiers under her vile power. Not content with that, she next cast a spell upon the English at Orléans, rooting them where they stood while her diabolic legions slew them by the hundreds, indifferent to their cries for mercy. It was a pattern she repeated throughout the summer as her minions took Patay, Jargeau, and eventually, Beauvais.

Surely the most heinous blasphemy ever uttered by a living soul was her claim to be the mouthpiece of God. The Heavenly Father saw no difference between English and French; both were His own Christian children. Had He been so inclined, the English claim to the throne of France was honorable and legally binding, made in solemn vows to Heaven. Thus consecrated, Henry's young son and heir had God's support in this just war.

That this impudent cow-wench, this profane sorceress, had the temerity to claim Heaven's mandate made Cauchon's blood rage. Not even he, with his academic degrees and position in the Church, had ever heard God's voice, in spite of long years of theological training and steadfast devotion to duty. Why then should God bestow the greatest gift possible upon an illiterate farmgirl—particularly one of low morals—rather than giving it to an ordained prince of Holy Mother Church?

Now proof of Divine favor had broken through the darkness like sunshine after a summer shower. The so-called Maid—and was that not another profanity, when everyone knew that she had committed the sin of fornication with the entire Armagnac army!—had exhausted her Hell-sent power and been delivered by God into the hands of Bourgogne. What had seemed lost to him during his flight from Beauvais had been restored, through God's grace. Jehanne the Maid was known throughout Europe, and her trial and resulting execution would bring immeasurable prestige to the man who brought her to judgment. Cauchon's fate, ordained by God, would be realized after all. One day Pierre Cauchon would be the Holy Father of the One, True, Holy and Apostolic Church.

He did not worry, as Bedford did, that Bourgogne would not release her to him. Philippe, greedy though he was, was no fool and knew where his best advantage lay. He was simply endeavoring to extort as much gold from the English as possible before they ordered him to give up the girl. No doubt Bourgogne would eventually be paid a handsome sum once the English duke's political posturing satisfied Philippe's vanity and guaranteed his equality within the alliance.

And then Cauchon would have her.

He opened his hand and looked at the ring that Bedford had sent him. A square bezel dominated the nasty thing, impiously engraved along one side with the letters MAR and on the other, JHS. The letter M was scratched into the left shoulder, and on the other a cross. The imp had used God's own name against Him.

Oh, what a beautiful trial it would be, and what garlands he would gather in Heaven and on earth! He was destined to be remembered for a thousand years to come.

From a distance Château Loches in the moonlight looked like a giant, multi-tiered cake. Its turrets and spires, ivory against the night sky, seemed nothing more than cleverly spun sugar crowned by a layer of frosting made to resemble a tiled roof. The high encircling wall which had long been its first line of defense embraced the castle's creamy shine. Commanding a hill, the citadel overlooked the little town clinging to its walls, its crest rising from the dark countryside in an indolent yet splendid way that made the land seem created for the castle, rather than the other way around.

Or so it was to the man who had stopped to rest his horse. From beneath the largest oak in a long line of trees hugging the dirt road, he beheld the château now as though seeing it for the first time instead of the thousandth. He always felt as awed as a child whenever he came here—indeed, as awed as he had felt when he actually *was* a child.

He cupped his hands around his eyes in order to see its finer details. Most of the hundreds of windows were dark, yet he knew that Charles was in house tonight, undoubtedly in the royal residence hidden behind the wall. True to form, the King was not easy to keep pace with these days, but at the moment he was spending time in this, his most beautiful château. Word was that he would winter at Loches this year. Unless, of course, he changed his mind.

The man nudged his horse forward, using his spurs. He had ridden through the whole of last night and most of today to get here. If what he had heard was true, it was critical that he speak to the King even if he had to drag Charles from his bed. But it was still early evening, and that possibility was unlikely.

The sense of urgency he felt goaded him to slap his horse with the reins. The animal shot forward, its sturdy haunches grinding hungrily over the narrow road, bringing the man closer to his destination. Glimpsed through the tunnel of trees, the castle loomed ever larger and grander upon the hill. He did not slow the horse when he reached the town, but pressed him onward with his spurs more viciously than before, until they were at the spot where the road began to climb toward the arched gateway and the raised portcullis.

The watch upon the wall had seen him coming and shouted an alert to the gate sentinels. Two of them, Scotsmen from Charles' elite bodyguard, stood blocking the route into the courtyard with their *guisarmes* held blades outward, pointed in the rider's direction. He halted in front of them and pushed back the hood of his cloak.

"Identify yourself and state your purpose," one said.

"I'm the duc d'Alençon, and I have urgent news for the King."

The soldiers stepped aside, allowing him to pass through the gate. Slapping the lathered horse with his reins, he again put the spurs to it, somewhat more gently this time, and they cantered up the slope to the graveled courtyard. He stopped the animal at the marble steps leading into the royal hall, then dismounted stiffly and tossed the reins to a page who came running to him.

"Take him to the gate," d'Alençon ordered. "I'll let you know if I intend to stay."

Without wasting any more time, he bounded up the steps and into the golden-candled anteroom. He passed through it quickly, into the feasting hall. Charles must have hosted a later supper than usual tonight. Servants of both sexes were packing up the remains of the meal to return to the kitchen, and to judge by the number of platters yet upon the lengthy table, their work had just started. D'Alençon's stomach rumbled noisily, and he remembered that he had eaten nothing since last night. The table's leavings called to him, setting his mouth to watering. But he could not sate his hunger yet.

He returned his mind to more important things. He could see and hear laughing, chatting courtiers through the doorway at the hall's rear, which opened onto a parlor. The sound of a lute commenced, stopping conversation and turning heads toward an unseen singer at the end of the room. D'Alençon groaned aloud. He hoped to God that Charles was not among those being entertained. He would never be able to drag him away from the kind of mindless amusement the King loved.

He went to a serving girl who was putting stray fruit back into its basket and grabbed her arm. "Where's the King?" he demanded in a gruffer tone than he had intended to use.

The girl curtsied. "Last I saw, sir, he was in the company of His Excellency the archbishop and the seigneur de la Trémoïlle. They went up there"—she pointed toward the second floor where the King slept.

D'Alençon released her arm, knowing exactly where they had gone. From this floor the only passages upstairs were through the parlor where the musicale was starting. The last thing he wanted was to make his presence known to the entire court. It would be necessary to use the outside stairs instead. He turned and strode past the table, then back down the steps to the courtyard.

The guards cast curious glances at him, but did not speak to this gentleman who was now trotting around the corner to the building's left. Ahead of him was the west terrace. Gravel crunched beneath his boots as he made his way to where the tower shot up through the night sky. As he had expected, a light was burning in the apartment next to it. He quickly darted into the door at the bottom of the spiral stairway and began to climb.

The duc was perspiring heavily by the time he reached the second floor. At the first landing he bolted through the door. He turned sharply to the left, his bootheels smacking the flagstones emphatically, bringing him closer to the open door straight ahead of him and the chamber whose every detail he knew by heart. There were no guards in attendance at the portal tonight. A light burning in the room and the moving shadows it cast, larger than the figures they represented, stirred across the fireplace projecting from the eastern wall. He pressed on, determined to accomplish what he had set out to do.

Charles was hunched over a small table with his ministers on either side of him, the three of them examining a sheet of parchment whose curl hung over the edge of the delicate rosewood furniture. Straining to adjust his failing eyes to the page, old de Chartres leaned very close to the paper. Trémoïlle, toadlike as ever, stood back from the table a little to allow room for his massive stomach.

What a picture they make, thought d'Alençon.

Charles looked up at him, startled. "Jehan!" The King's wan complexion changed to a smile. "What are you doing here, of all places? I thought you were with your wife at Beaumont!"

"I need to speak to you. Alone." He did not bow nor acknowledge the other two men. His feet were planted slightly apart, fists clenched at his side. His face was as grim and pale as a death mask.

"Now, see here, young man, you cannot just burst in upon His Majesty when he is in conference, even if you are his kinsman!" Indignation flooded Trémoïlle's bloated countenance, shaking the flab in his jowls.

The duc fastened him with a cold, quiet stare. "Get out."

Trémoïlle lifted his head. "I shall not unless the King commands me."

D'Alençon's sword hissed from its scabbard. Pointing it at the minister, he took a step forward. His eyes bulged within the beautiful skull.

The archbishop gave a little squeal and clasped his hands together. Trémoïlle instinctively reached for his own weapon. Finding none in its customary place at his side, he rasped at Charles, "Are you going to allow him to threaten us?"

The King did not appear frightened. He looked at d'Alençon with an intent calm in tandem with something the young duc could not identify. A knowing pity. Contrition. Sadness. None of them fit. Still, there was something.

"Go now," Charles said, addressing his councillors. "We would speak to our cousin alone as he requests." They looked at one another uncertainly. "Go. We shall summon you again later."

The older men bowed to him and brushed past d'Alençon, whose unyielding stare remained fixed on the King even as he let his sword slide back into a state of rest. When their footsteps had receded and he knew they were truly gone, the duc turned and closed the door after them.

Charles sat down in a chair behind the table where his paper was spread. He smiled and moved his hands apart in the air. "We are alone now, Cousin. What is this terrible urgency of yours?"

D'Alençon folded his arms. "Is what I've heard true? Was Jehanne captured by the Burgundians at Compiègne about a month ago?"

The seated man let his eyes slip to the page in front of him. "Yes, Jehan, it is true."

"Well, what are you going to do about it? Is that"—he nodded at the page—"an offer to pay her ransom?"

"This is our plan for a feast we hope to give the Castilian ambassador in another month. He is coming to Tours with a design for a fine new sword—"

"And what about Jehanne?" the duc cut in, astounded by the King's casual tone. "What measures are you taking to arrange her release?"

Charles lifted a stolid gaze to him. "None."

"What?" D'Alençon's eyes narrowed. "You are going to abandon her? Don't you know what will happen to her when Philippe sells her to the English, as he most certainly will?"

"She's in God's hands now."

"God's hands?" cried the duc. "You are the King of France! You have enough money in your coffers to feast foreign dignitaries, yet you will not spend anything at all to save her? Where is your gratitude, Charles?"

His royal kinsman continued to stare wordlessly at him.

"She took two wounds for you at Orléans and delivered the city from bondage as she had promised! She was wounded again trying to take Paris. If it weren't for her, you would not be King at all!"

Charles bolted from his chair and crashed his fist down upon the table so hard that the inkwell on it jumped. "*God* made me King, Jehan, not Jehanne the Maid! He made me King when He drove my poor father mad and when He took my brother Louis, who would have worn the crown before me! If Jehanne had not forgotten that and lapsed into arrogance, God would not have caused her to be taken in the first place!"

"That is the archbishop speaking."

"It is the truth!"

"Oh, yes, I've heard how he wrote 'the truth' to your loyal city of Reims!" D'Alençon scoffed. "That vile old man said that she deserved what happened to her because she was puffed up with pride and chose to follow her own will instead of God's, although, typically, he didn't even have the courage to express such calumnies as his own, but attributed them to some young shepherd he has acquired who professes to manifest the Stigmata! That doddering moron wouldn't know a true sign from God if it were borne to earth by angels right before his eyes!"

"I have seen the shepherd's stigmata for myself," Charles answered calmly. "Bleeding wounds from his hands and feet—"

"Please, Charles," the duc begged, forcing his own voice to descend to a semblance of composure. "For the love of God, offer a ransom for her."

The King once more gave him that silent look.

"Philippe will release her to you, I know it. He has nothing to gain politically by selling her to Bedford, he cares for nothing except money, and you can match an English offer. If you wait until the English get their hands on her, getting her back will be almost impossible."

"Philippe has asked thirty thousand pounds for her."

D'Alençon's jaw dropped. He felt the blood melt into his head. A ringing buzz deafened his left ear. "So he has been in contact with you!"

"That is correct." Charles nodded. "But I do not have thirty thousand pounds to ransom her. As you have observed, I am King, and my overwhelming duty is to the kingdom. I must conserve what remains in the royal treasury for conducting the war, and I cannot allow sentiment to override my judgments in order to save one person."

"We are not talking about 'one person'! We are talking about Jehanne the Maid, who in partnership with God has given your kingdom hope!"

Charles frowned at him.

"Since Bourgogne's price is prohibitive, perhaps when Bedford comes into possession of her he will accept less than that amount. Write to him instead. If you throw in seigneur Talbot, whom you are still holding captive, along with other English prisoners they consider dear, and some silver, then Bedford will at least have the choice of letting her go. If he refuses, the sin will be on his head, not yours."

D'Alençon paused for a response he did not get. His eyes swept the room with an almost mad sense of desperation. Finding what he sought, he said, "At least give me an army to rescue her! I have it on good authority that she is being held at Jehan de Luxembourg's château at Beaurevoir. It is lightly defended, and I know that if I summon them, forces loyal to you and to her will waste no time gathering there."

"I cannot afford to pay them for that. All of my money is tied up in equipping the armies in the Ile-de-France and Champagne. If they fall—especially Champagne—our enemies may move on Orléans again, endangering the Loire."

"They will come whether or not they are paid."

Charles permitted himself a small smile. "That is Jehanne talking."

"And she is right," the duc shot back. His eyes filled with tears. "She has always been right."

"Come, Jehan, you are a military man, you know very well how much it takes to equip and feed an army, even without their wages."

"Are you doing this because she sponsored Arthur de Richemont?" D'Alençon demanded abruptly. "I know how much you hate him, but—"

"This has nothing to do with Richemont." The King raised his arched brows. "Actually, he has—at least, so far—turned out to be quite loyal, and his Bretons are wreaking a terrible destruction among the enemy ranks, especially among the English, whom he hates far more than I could ever hate him. For that, I am quite gratified, although to be sure I still do not trust him and would not want to be in the same room with him. His manners are appalling." Charles shook his head. "Richemont is quite beside the point when it comes to the Maid."

"What is it, then?" d'Alençon prodded. "Why are you really so determined to let her go to her fate?"

Charles half-closed his eyes and lowered them toward his pale hands. "She began as our servant, but since that time has become a power unto herself. I tried to explain to her, time and again, how important it is for us to woo Philippe de Bourgogne from his confederacy with the English. But Jehanne has insisted on actions that would damage our advances to Philippe and undermine his faith in the integrity of our word." He fastened his narrow brown eyes onto d'Alençon. "A kingdom can have only one ruler, Jehan. And I am he."

D'Alençon returned his stare, having for the moment no response. Then he sighed despairingly. "So you will do nothing?"

"I give you permission to equip your rescue party yourself," Charles replied softly.

The duc reeled under the force of this verbal slap. Despite his title, he was destitute, left without even his ancestral lands, which were still in the hands of the English. Every *sou* he had ever possessed had gone to pay his own ransom two years past.

"By all the saints, I shall never forgive you, Charles," he murmured. "God might, but I shall not, and I'll have the satisfaction of knowing that when He calls you to your Judgment, you will go full aware that you murdered one of His servants as surely as though you had struck the blow yourself!"

He did not wait for any further discussion, but spun around and stalked to the door. When he slammed it behind him, it sounded like a cannon blast.

He fled down the stairs with his knees shaking. He made straight for the door by which he had entered nearly an hour earlier, and when he stepped outside breathed deeply of the night air. His skin felt as though it were on fire, his blood surging through his body at an alarming rate. He wiped the dripping sweat from his forehead. Something prompted him to look up at the château.

The figure in silhouette at the window was turned toward him, the golden candlelight behind his head a mocking halo. D'Alençon sensed the eyes burning into him. He could not remember having ever hated anyone as much in his life.

From this moment, Charles, we are enemies, you and I. It may take months, or even years, but by the Holy Virgin I swear that I will take my revenge upon you. I pledge that before I leave this life I shall see you suffer the loss of that which you hold most dear.

He wiped his eyes, and began to run as fast as he could across the courtyard. When he got to the gatehouse, he found the page still there, holding his horse's reins. D'Alençon snatched them from him and swung up into the saddle, then jabbed the horse viciously with his spurs. The beast cried out in surprise and pain, and reared its front legs. It bolted through the gate, barely missing the Scots guardsmen.

He fled Château Loches pursued by memories, good and bad, that he felt powerless to suffer. He would not stop until he was far away. He would stay the night out there somewhere in some fleabitten country inn, rise before dawn, and then make his way home. But first, he would get very, very drunk.

"You spin very well, my dear," the old woman said with a brittle, searching smile. "Did your mother teach you?"

"Yes, Madame, when I was very young." Jehanne let the thread slip smoothly through her fingers, giving it enough lead slack to make its way around and around the spindle. "But it has been a little while since I did it." Indeed, she thought, the last time was in Moulins when she was the guest of the goldsmith, Cordier, and his wife.

She rejected the memory before it could fully form. It was important for her not to look back. Her survival perhaps depended on it, for she would certainly go mad if she thought about it too much. She had to live in the present regardless of what happened.

She was still a prisoner, no matter how gracious these kind ladies were. It was true that she had a room with a real bed instead of a cell, and was not ill-treated. But although the comte de Ligny referred to her as his "guest," allowing her to wander about unrestrained, that did not change the fact that she was watched day and night by either armed guards or the comte's female relatives, in whose comfortable presence she now performed labors they deemed suitable to women. She knew that things could have been much worse for her. Nevertheless, a pleasant cage was still a cage, and she prayed daily that she might regain her freedom.

Three months had passed since she was captured. Those first two days at Margny were the hardest, when neither she nor her companions knew if they would be allowed to live. At dawn on the third day the Burgundians took away Minguet and Pasquerel. Jehanne could still hear her confessor pleading that they spare the boy, but take him alone if they wanted to execute someone. She managed to embrace them both before they were seized, whispering to Minguet that she loved him and was proud of his courage, as she knew his parents would have been. The monk blessed her quickly before they snatched him away. Then Jehanne was left alone with d'Aulon.

An hour later the guards returned. They herded the two prisoners down the stairs and from the château. Once outside, they were bound again and set upon horses. A number of armed men surrounded them, and over the next three hours they were taken seven leagues north, to the duc's castle at Beaulieu. Jehanne was permitted to keep d'Aulon with her in the tiny cell. They were well fed twice a day and suffered nothing but loss of freedom and anxiety for their futures. Whenever the guards were out of sight, they whispered together and at last came up with an escape plan.

For almost two weeks they pretended to accept their situation, thereby lulling the guards into inattention. When they judged the time to be right, they pried apart the floorboards of the cell in the small hours of the morning, and d'Aulon helped Jehanne to squeeze through, lowering her to the first floor. She was in the process of turning the key to lock the guards in the tower when she was spotted by the porter. He gave a frightened yell that echoed through the cold stone darkness. Her mind thundering in panic, Jehanne ran only a short distance before she was caught. The squad of soldiers who brought her down tossed her into another cell, separate from d'Aulon. She did not know what became of her squire after that.

The next morning they moved her again, even farther north, to Beaurevoir. She did not know precisely where it was, only that it was far from Paris and even further from freedom. She had been here ever since, a prisoner not a guest of the comte de Ligny. This castle was his own home and comfortable in a crude way, for as his wife Jehanne de Béthune explained, the comte was not a wealthy man like his overlord, but the younger son of a younger son. What prosperity he did have came from his benefactor and liege.

Luxembourg's aunt, whom everyone called Tante Jehanne, was the primary force behind Jehanne's good treatment in this place. The old woman had taken an immediate liking to her, recognizing in the Maid a bluntly outspoken kindred soul fearful of no man. At the very outset she forbade her nephew to toss his prisoner into a long-unused storage chamber, but insisted that she be given a proper room and opportunities to hear Mass with the family. Tante Jehanne agreed to the presence of armed guards everywhere, on condition that Jehanne not suffer the indignity of being bound.

The comte consented, though with no small degree of reluctance. Since that time, Jehanne had been somewhat free to go where she liked, and because she preferred the company of the ladies to solitude and its sinister phantoms, she often sat with them like this, spinning or sewing in the comtesse's bedroom.

"Jehanne?"

"Hmm?"

"Did you not hear what Tante Jehanne said?" The comtesse's painted brows arched in concern. "She wanted to know if you would like the cloth you are making for a dress."

They had been after her since she came here to abandon her hose and tunic for women's clothing. She politely declined every time they asked, explaining that God had not given permission for her to change her mode of dress. The clothes she had on were what she preferred. They pretended to accept her reason, but every so often brought up the subject again.

She wished she could have a bath. They offered, of course, but aware of their disapproval of her clothing, she was afraid that if she removed her garments at all, they would take them away from her and give her only a woman's gown to wear. She could not loosen her vigilance; it would be a mistake for her to remove even so much as her boots when she slept. Catherine had spoken to her after Mass last night, and afterward Jehanne knew that her male clothing might be her sole protection in times to come.

"No, thank you," Jehanne mumbled.

"Perhaps Jehanne has other things on her mind, dear," Luxembourg's aunt remarked. "Come now, out with it, child. There's no use hiding that something is troubling you. I am an old woman and have seen many things, and I always know when someone is downcast. So come on, tell us." The wrinkled eyelids blinked twice, very rapidly, making her look like an ancient owl.

"I heard the guards talking. They said that Compiègne is about to fall, and that everyone within its walls is to be put to the sword, even the children." Jehanne gulped, trying not to cry. She had not wept since she was captured. Every emotion she might have felt was buried in a deep vault, far beneath a knowledge that she had to live day by day now that she was in enemy hands. When she was free again she would allow herself to feel, and to weep. But today was not that time.

"I know that you are not of my party," she continued, "but I ask that you pray with me for the innocent people of Compiègne. I have seen for myself, many times, that it is always the people who suffer the most in war."

"Of course we shall pray with you," the comtesse consoled, forming her tiny mouth into a smile. Her eyes were too close-set in a rather long face for her to be considered attractive, but her nature was generous and modest. She was thirty-six, married for a second time and the mother of a thirteen-year-old daughter, sired by her late husband, the younger son of the late duc de Bar, René d'Anjou's father.

The child, Jhanette, was also present, and now she volunteered, "I shall say a special prayer to St.-Jude for them, Jehanne."

"Thank you." She could feel Tante Jehanne's intrepid eyes boring into her, and she looked down at the thread that continued to race through her fingers.

"What else?" came the inevitable query. "Compiègne is only part of what is ailing you." The aged noblewoman could be imperious as well as kind, and now she was in no mood for evasions.

The wheel stopped whirring. Jehanne swallowed the lump of fear, but it came back up again and lodged in her throat. She looked at the ladies. Jhanette was curious; the comtesse full of apprehensive affection. Behind the brusque facade Jehanne saw something almost fearful in the wrinkled face that barked, "Well?"

"I have heard that I am to be sold to the English."

A quick glance darted between the comtesse and her daughter. "Nonsense!" Tante Jehanne scoffed. "The guard who told you that, what is his name? I shall have my nephew punish him for frightening you like that. The very idea is preposterous!"

"Excuse me, Madame, but it was not a guard," Jehanne replied, her face burdened with misery.

"Who then? One of the servants?"

"No, Madame." She looked into the indignant, frightened old eyes. "God."

The rapid tramp of masculine feet in the hall prevented Tante Jehanne's response. Luxembourg entered the room as he always did, unannounced and overbearing.

"Good afternoon, all," he said, stooping to kiss the top of his wife's head. "You should see the rabbits old Robert and I caught during the hunt. We'll feast well tonight if the cook doesn't burn the meat like she did the last time we had fresh game. You really should replace her, you know," he said to the comtesse, "or at least have her punished."

"Is it true, Jehan?" his wife begged, looking up at his scarred, one-eyed face.

He raised an eyebrow. "Is what true?"

"That you intend to sell this child to the English as though she were a horse," Tante Jehanne answered for her niece. The birdlike scowl dared him to confirm the rumor.

Luxembourg tried to laugh. "Now wherever did you hear that?"

"Is it true?"

He looked away, out the window, down at the floor.

"If you sell the girl, you will blacken your name and bring shame and dishonor upon this House!" his aunt admonished in a voice creaking with stern authority. "You know what the English will do to her as well as I do, and believe me, young man, her death will be on your soul."

"I have no choice, Tante Jehanne," the comte complained. "Philippe de Bourgogne has ordered me to turn her over to him, and my duty is to obey him."

"Your duty is to do what is right! God stands above Philippe de Bourgogne and above all the kings of the earth, and your first obligation is to Him. 'Thou shalt not kill,' Jehan. In battle it is different, because you must defend yourself. But to release an unarmed person to certain execution is a sin, as damnable as though you had performed the deed yourself! And who shall pay for your sin? Will Philippe burn in Hell in your place?"

"It is already done!" he shouted back. His one eye shot quickly to Jehanne. The blood drained from her face. "The English are raising the ransom. It is too late to withdraw from the agreement."

"You have sold your soul to the Devil!" Tante Jehanne's withered face was crimson. "I am disgusted with you, I am ashamed that you are of my blood!"

"We are poor! Doesn't this run-down barn remind you daily that we live worse than peasants? If I don't take their gold, someone will, and that someone will be Philippe, who has all the money he could ever possibly need! Why should I not partake of the spoils, when it was my vassal's man who brought her down?" He glared at Jehanne. She imagined the missing eye glowing behind the black shield.

His aunt grasped the arm of her chair and hoisted herself slowly to her feet. She walked to the comte and said, "You want to end this contest, Jehan? Is it your wish that I go down on my knees to you? Very well." She lowered her arthritic body to the floor and grasped his legs. "I beg you, do not sell the Maid to the English. Do not bring dishonor to the name your father left you, and do not endanger your immortal soul! I shall die soon. If you spare this girl, all I have shall become yours. Please, Jehan, there is still time."

Greed flashed through his remaining eye. He hesitated. "I'll do what I can." Then, unable to face his aunt any longer, he disengaged her hands and walked out the door.

Jehanne was not comforted by his promise, for she knew it to be false. He would wait until Tante Jehanne went to Heaven and then he would sell her, pocketing both his inheritance and the English blood money.

It is already done.

Luxembourg's words chanted in Jehanne's brain over and over again throughout the night and into the next day. They stayed with her, hovering ominously overhead, growing louder as the weeks passed and nothing unusual occurred. But it was done; it was a matter of time before they came for her.

Summer ended suddenly in a cool blast from the north, and still there was no movement. Jehanne found no peace in the tranquillity of her now familiar daily life, seemingly as placid as the browning hills beneath the tower. Something terrible was coming, something so repugnant that she could not stand to look at it. She tried to pray it back into its lair but it was stronger than her pleas to Heaven.

She often daydreamed about rescue. Although the King had not ransomed her, soon he would send a mighty army to take this place; it was nearly undefended and would be easy to conquer. Perhaps d'Alençon himself would ride at the head of her deliverers, d'Alençon and La Hire and the Bastard, just as in the old days. Once she was safely reunited with her comrades, she would order the soldiers to spare everyone, and grateful for her charity, the comte would change sides and ally himself with Charles. It was a beautiful dream.

But here on the rampart, at the top of the castle where she frequently took fresh air, her Counsel said otherwise. Where formerly They had brought her nothing but the greatest joy, now she dreaded Their coming and the constant instructions to bear all things faithfully. She had been faithful to God her entire life, and had willingly put herself under Their tutelage. She did not understand why God had brought her to this place. She could not stay in it, waiting for greater enemies than these mild folk to swoop down and carry her off. She would have to escape.

She took a quick look around. The guards were some distance from her, chatting together. Jehanne could not hear what the man was saying, but when he finished, his companions laughed. As she hoped, they were paying no attention to her. This kind of outing was routine, and she had never given them any trouble.

Very gradually, she inched toward the edge of the parapet. It was a long way down to the grassy bank that merged into softly rolling countryside. Compiègne lay over there, beyond that stand of trees, three days away by horse, five or six on foot. If she jumped to the ground, she could make it to the woods before they noticed she was gone. Bearing south would eventually bring her to a friendly farmhouse and a horse, and she could then sneak into Compiègne as she had before, under the cover of darkness.

Still, it was a great distance to the ground from here. What if she broke her neck?

She shook her head. That would not happen; God would not let it happen when she had tried her best to be His faithful servant. But—Lord be merciful!— if it were His will, so much the better. Death in this hospitable place was preferable to life in an English stinkhole.

Do not do it. It is God's wish that you stay where you are.

But Compiègne is in danger! I have heard that everyone above the age of seven is to be killed. I must get to them, I must save them!

The city is under God's protection and shall not be destroyed. Do not be troubled by these imaginings any longer.

Then what of me? You told me yourself that I shall be sold to the English, and the comte has confirmed that. I cannot bear this waiting any longer, I have to get away!

You do not know everything, only a part. Bear with the destiny you can no longer change, knowing that you are loved by God. You shall not be Delivered from your ordeal until you have seen the King of England.

I do not want to see him, I don't care if I never do. I must escape!

She looked down at the liberation calling to her, whispering her name more compellingly than Catherine's instructions. She closed her eyes. She made the Sign of the Cross.

Lord Jhesus, please bear me up and bring me safely to the earth. But if it is Your wish that I not survive, then I beg You, let me into Your Kingdom.

Jehanne took a step into empty space. The air rushed past her and she was flying toward the setting sun. She smiled. Freedom was on the other side of the trees.

The weight of a cool, damp cloth on her forehead brought her back. She tried to see who had put it there, but could not focus her vision, for the light was too intense and its onslaught like a stab into her brain. Somewhere a drum was beating an agonizing rhythm, and it forced her eyes shut again. Her head, swollen to grotesque proportions, threatened to pull her eyeballs into its whirling black waters.

A gentle hand removed the cloth and touched her brow for a moment. Jehanne heard the swish of the cloth in water and the dripping stream that came when it was wrung dry. It returned to a place above the bridge of her nose, temporarily calming the disturbance in her head. Whoever was with her caressed her hair.

"Maman?" she whispered.

"No, Jehanne, it is the comtesse de Ligny," the soft voice apologized.

Jehanne made another attempt to see. The room careened woozily through what she now realized was daylight, summoning salty bile to her mouth. When she closed her eyes again the swaying stopped, the nausea ebbed.

"Where am I?" she asked, dreading the answer.

"You are here, at Beaurevoir," came the expected response.

"I wanted to escape. I was afraid of what would happen to me if I stayed," she recited without emotion.

"Shh, shh, I know." The comtesse placed her hand over the cool, wet fabric. "But you could have been killed. When the guards found you, they thought at first that you were dead. It is a miracle that you survived such a long fall, and an even greater one that nothing was broken."

"My head is broken," Jehanne murmured, "I can feel it. I can't see you, even though I try. Something in my head is broken."

"It's all right, dear," the comtesse soothed. "The doctor says you will recover after a few days' rest. Are you hungry?"

Jehanne shook her head, feeling queasy at the thought of food. "How long have I been here like this?"

"Let me see . . . two days."

Two days. If she had been successful, she would be more than halfway to Compiègne by now. But she had failed, and stupidly injured herself in the bargain.

"Are you sure you want nothing to eat? You must, if you are to get well."

"No, thank you. I think I'll sleep again."

She let go of the room and was instantly swept into a place of revolving shadows, deep within a hole in the earth. A long way overhead a tiny light flickered like a star, calling to her that she should leave this murky, damp place, but she was trapped here in the darkness, alone. Yet not alone after all; squinting, she could just see indistinct shapes moving all about her. When the growls began, gurgling upward from the bottom of their throats, she felt the hairs on the back of her neck prickle. She froze.

The apparitions, now changed into English soldiers, suddenly rushed at her in a snarling pack, causing her to grapple desperately toward the light far above. They seized her legs and began to pull, trying to drag her back down to them. Something whispered that if she paid no mind to them, she could pass through their grasp without hindrance.

She stopped struggling and bolted toward the light.

Catherine and Marguerite were waiting for her. She knew who They were even though They lacked any defined shape, for Their essences pulsed with familiarity. The brightest of Them all, a great, burnished oval, hovered in the background, distant yet glowing with a love as constant as the heart of God. Their sublime authority and wisdom brought her back to what was Real in an implicit admonishment of her small unworthiness. She knelt before Them and put her arms over her head.

Please forgive my disobedience, she pleaded. I am not worthy to be God's servant, for deep down I do not believe that He will save me.

DEEP DOWN, YOU KNOW THAT HE WILL. IT IS FEAR, CLOSER TO THE SURFACE WHERE THINGS OF THE WORLD APPEAR IMPORTANT, WHICH INTERFERES WITH YOUR CLARITY OF VISION. THOSE THINGS ARE PHANTOMS, NOTHING MORE. CAST ASIDE DREAD, AND YOU SHALL SEE THAT IT IS A MEASURE OF GOD'S LOVE THAT HE BELIEVES IN JEHANNE, AND WILL GIVE HER A PLACE OF HONOR IN HEAVEN.

Compiègne—

RELEASE YOUR WORRIES; THE CITY SHALL BE RELIEVED BEFORE MARTINMAS BY FORCES LOYAL TO YOUR KING.

And me? Is my captivity a punishment for my sins?

IT HAS MANY DIMENSIONS OF SIGNIFICANCE WHICH YOU WILL NOT UNDERSTAND RIGHT AWAY. BUT IN GOD'S TIME, EVERYTHING WILL BE CLEAR AND YOU WILL KNOW THAT IT HAD TO BE.

Dear Jehanne, the God that is Love does not punish. It is important that you remember that through the times to come, and equally important that you do not hate those who persecute you. Your fellow beings are not demons; they are strangers upon the earth, as you are, and merit your compassion. Hold to that with all your strength when temptation tells you otherwise.

Their thoughts came over her in a mighty wave of light, pulsating all around and through her, filling her with a resurrection of her lost trust and conviction. Their purity bore her up, and she floated cloudlike into genuine unconsciousness.

She was able to take nourishment the next day. By week's end she was back on her feet as though nothing had happened. Everyone from servants to family remarked upon her extraordinary recovery, and although she replied that God had helped her, she knew by the looks they gave her that they suspected that she might be a witch after all. Luxembourg was all for throwing her into that dank hole that had been his first choice for her lodgings, but once more the old comtesse forbade it. He grumbled a bit, and that was that. Jehanne resumed her life at Beaurevoir much as she had before her attempted escape. The only difference was that now the guards never let her out of their sight.

By this time word had reached the outside world that Jehanne was being held at Beaurevoir. Over the next two weeks, the gloating comte brought men to see his prize, most of them boyhood friends and old comrades-in-arms. They mainly gawked at her worn and dirty clothing without saying anything. They came and went, oftentimes nameless, and soon all looked the same to her. But two stood out from the others, rendered unforgettable for different reasons.

One was young Haimond de Macy, a knight from an ancient family and Luxembourg's lieutenant. At his request, Jehanne received him alone in her room while the ever-present guards stood duty just outside the door. At first she found herself liking him for his well-bred manners and friendly air. They spoke of many unimportant things, of horses and fashion and pastimes pursued at the very different courts they had frequented.

Just as she was starting to ease into a comfortable reminder of d'Alençon, he suddenly grabbed her by the shoulders and pulling her to him, fumbled clumsily for her breast. He pressed his mouth to hers, hard, and she was repulsed by the tongue he tried to force between her clenched teeth. She rallied in half a heartbeat and fought him like a wild creature, shouting her resistance, pummeling and scratching his face with all her might.

With an abrupt motion he released her and staggered backward, holding a hand to the long red welt bleeding from his cheek.

She was breathing rapidly, blood pounding in her ears, as she raised her fists and bent her knees into a defensive stance. The glare she unsheathed dared him to take a step toward her.

The guards, having heard the commotion, flew through the door expecting to have to apprehend her. De Macy glanced at them, then grinned at Jehanne. "My God, it's true, isn't it?" He laughed. "You really are a virgin."

"Get out of this room," she commanded, her voice trembling with outrage. "You heard me, go!"

By now the guards knew what had transpired, and their chuckles made her flush with embarrassed indignation. Unabashed, de Macy swept the hat from his head and, still grinning, gave her a mocking bow. They left her without pressing the advantage their numbers would have given them.

When she was alone, her legs gave out and she sank onto a stool, dazed and trembling. She was angry at herself for having forgotten that she was in enemy territory where none could be trusted. From that moment forth she would only have to think of him when she met anyone for the first time, and caution would return to be her armor.

It was a lesson she held to when she met the second memorable personage. He was one about whom Charles and d'Alençon had spoken on that night months ago in Troyes, before the coronation. At the time, she had laughed at his name, never expecting to meet him.

But now he stood next to Luxembourg in the room where Jehanne slept with young Jhanette, a real man in the burnt rose gown of a bishop, his gray hair visible beneath the cap denoting his office. An ice blue intelligence measured Jehanne across the bridge of his strong nose, drinking in her shabbiness with a contemptuous lift of his brows.

She imagined that she was wearing the suit from the duc d'Orléans and corrected her posture. With a proud lift of her chin, she wordlessly proclaimed herself Jehanne the Maid.

The bishop's thin lips curved into the semblance of a smile. He held out his hand for her to kiss. Without hesitation she went down on one knee and put her lips to the ring. His spotted hand was as cold as a corpse's. "Your Excellency," she murmured, rising.

He might have been handsome as a boy, before bitter ruthlessness took hold of his soul and hardened there, settling grimly into the corners of his mouth. Jehanne saw no piety in the supremely confident man who regarded her with such outright disdain, and she knew that she would get no mercy from him. The words he spoke in a sweeping baritone confirmed her intuition.

"I have heard that you tried to kill yourself. Do you not know that suicide is a sin, damnable in the sight of God?"

"It was not that, Your Excellency," she answered calmly, set upon not allowing herself to be bullied by those impassive, satisfied eyes. "I am a prisoner in this place. I sought only escape and a return to my own people."

His lips twisted into a malicious grimace. "You will find, young woman, that you cannot escape God's justice."

"I have no fear of God's justice. He knows me better than anyone else, for it was He Who sent me to serve the King."

"In serving the pretender Charles, you have seriously erred, and your error has been compounded by your having listened to the voice of the Devil."

Jehanne's gaze did not waver. "My instructions come from God, not the Evil One. It is you who serve the Devil, Your Excellency, and his name is Henry of England."

For a few moments Cauchon regarded her silently. Then, finally, he said, "Very soon all of Christendom shall know which of us is from God and who is the agent of the Enemy." He reached into his pocket and withdrew a shining band. With a tormenting smile, he held it up for her to see. "You have already condemned yourself with enchantments such as this."

"My father gave me that!" She reached for it, but he snatched it away and returned it to his pocket. "That belongs to me, Your Excellency!"

"No longer." As though suddenly abhorred by her presence, he brushed past Luxembourg without uttering another word and rushed from the room. The comte's solitary eye scowled at her momentarily before he hurried after his guest.

Oh, Papa! Her eyes filled with tears and a sob leaped to her throat. It was as though her parents were now also in enemy possession. All of Domrémy and everything she loved was captive. But something much worse started to clamor in her mind. Jehanne's Counsel did not have to tell her that this brief meeting was in reality an inspection of bought goods. It was done; her fate was carved in stone, and nothing could undo it. An odd sense of relief came over her. November had brought its icy north wind and with it the waiting game had ended.

Never in her life had Jehanne been near the sea. Travelers who chanced upon Domrémy when she was a child had tried their best to describe its turbulent grandeur, yet in that long-ago time, as she listened to their stories with her serious little face rapt in the firelight, she had sensed that the tales were pitifully wanting. Someday, the girl told herself, she would see the great ocean firsthand. Someday when she was all grown up.

Shortly after Cauchon's departure, Luxembourg personally took her to Arras in the company of Anglo-Burgundian soldiers. It was there, while confined in a residence belonging to Philippe de Bourgogne, that she was shown a fanciful picture of herself painted by a Scot. The scene depicted her in full armor, kneeling before Charles, whose outstretched hand was prepared to receive a letter she offered him. The event had never actually occurred, but the painting was wrenching and filled her with regret for her lost glory.

Where was the King now? Surely by this time he knew that she had fallen into captivity. She ignored the taunting smiles of her enemies and maintained a fixed expression, all the while praying desperately that Charles would send his detachments to rescue her.

But he did not come for her at Arras, nor at the neighboring castle of Drugy, where she was attended upon by the monks from nearby St.-Riquier. Many visitors came to see her while she was there, mostly people from the town. She spoke to them of her confidence in God's esteem and mercy, of His love for the bleeding kingdom, and of her family, whom she missed more than words could tell.

While she heard herself talking, she wondered, Where is Jehan? Had her brother reached Fierbois safely? And the others, were they being held for ransom? She knew now that Pierre was alive. Recently she had begun to feel that he was still in the world, something Catherine confirmed. He would live to see his children grown, of that she was certain.

From Arras she was taken to Le Crotoy, a castle on the northeastern shore of Picardy, built a hundred years earlier by the English pretender who had started this ghastly war, Edward III. Constructed to protect the mouth of the River Somme, it jutted on a finger of land toward the Narrow Sea and was encircled by water on three sides.

Her first sight of the tossing gray expanse that the *goddons* called their "Channel" made her gasp in awe. There could not be so much water in the world! It stretched on to forever, covering the whole earth in rollicking whitecaps. Nearing land, they swelled to a high, foamy crest, then flung themselves forward in a rolling wave which crashed against the long strand of pale yellow beach. It lapped the rocky sand only to be sucked back from whence it had come, in waves endlessly returning, its power as alluring as the currents of a dream. For a moment Jehanne smiled and inhaled cold air misted with the odor of wet salt and marshweeds.

Way out there, a tiny boat bobbed up and down, its sail like an angel's wing pointed up to the cloudy sky. White seabirds circled against the clouds in graceful abandon, yelling their dominion over this place that had belonged to them long before humans had claimed it. When their webbed feet touched upon the sand, they lost their dignity and waddled across the damp brown glass, leaving tiny footprints imprinted there until the next wave washed them away. In that brief instant, as her senses filled with God's great gift to man, Jehanne felt a happiness she had not known for many months.

Her joy was short-lived. A detachment of English soldiers rode out to meet Luxembourg, and after a few minutes' exchange in the coarse-sounding language which Jehanne did not understand, she was handed over to the castle's garrison. They rushed her to the highest tower and confined her in a room facing the landward side of the castle. All that remained of the ocean for her were the tangy air and the faintly swooshing roar the waves made when they embraced the unseen beach.

Jehanne remembered that d'Alençon had been a prisoner here for three years, perhaps kept in this same crudely furnished room, with only a small cot for rest and a slit for a window. She wondered if confinement had been as boring for him as it was for her, with nothing to do but sit on the bed and yearn for home while day turned to night and then dawned again to the same monotony. How tedious it must have been for him while he waited for his family to raise the ransom the *goddons* were wresting from his dwindling estate. His wife had told Jehanne that they had taken it all, bit by bit, until he had nothing left. In this desolate place, he must have pined for her embraces, knowing that it would be a long time before he was with her again. Had there been no fire to warm him in the winter months as there was none for her?

She had been captured wearing this light summer tunic underneath her armor, and because the Burgundians were outraged by her men's clothing, they refused to give her warmer, or cleaner, ones. In her reeking state, she thought wistfully of the bathhouses in Orléans and Jargeau, and of something fresh to wear. By now her hair had grown nearly to her shoulders and fell into her eyes. She had no hope for small personal comforts, so when they came it was as though she had received a temporary reprieve.

The ladies of Abbeville brought them with their visit. Four women from the town came to see her, borne by boat down the wide mouth of the river. Less partisan than their menfolk, they carried in their baskets welcomed respites from the thin gruel that had become her diet: fresh bread, cheese, a small capon, and dried fruit. Jehanne was wolfing down these delicacies when the ladies took out their sewing. At the sight of the scissors, she begged them to cut her hair. At first they objected, but her tears moved them so that in the end they did as she asked.

They spent four hours with her. What was the news from Compiègne? she wondered. Her English jailers would tell her nothing.

The women replied that the siege had been lifted shortly before Martinmas by troops loyal to Charles.

Had the people suffered much, was there a great loss of life?

The ladies did not know, for warfare was not in their province. But they agreed to pray with her for any who had died, and when they were finished, the women asked Jehanne if there was anything she needed.

Yes, she responded, warmer clothing than she had.

They answered that they could not help her with that, not because they did not want to see her more comfortable, but would it not be better if she had a woman's dress?

God had not given her permission, she said.

Before they left her, full of tears and promises that they would pray for her safety, one of them took pity on her and gave Jehanne her cloak, a fine woolen robe lined with rabbit fur. She kissed them good-bye and told them that they would be in her prayers, also. And then they floated away, down the river toward the city where they lived.

It was during her time by the sea that she had the good fortune to meet Père Nicolas de Queuville. A kind man and a steadfast Armagnac, he had been the chancellor of the cathedral at Amiens when he was thrown into irons for refusing to disavow the true King. The guards allowed Jehanne to make her confession to him, and afterward he said Mass for her every day until the morning when another squadron of English soldiers came to take her away.

They shackled her at the wrists and tethered her by a short chain to one of the horses, forcing her to walk while they rode, all the way across the bridge spanning the broad Somme to St.-Valéry. Wrapped in the cloak the lady from Abbeville had given her, she was at least somewhat protected from the blowing north wind. They gave her no water. By the time they reached St.-Valéry, she was exhausted, her throat dry, and she greedily gulped the water they finally allowed her to have before they confined her in the tower until morning. From there they followed the ocean along its rocky beaches to Eu, where they spent the night in the castle. The following day the party traveled to Dieppe at the mouth of the Seine, stopping again to rest before resuming the final leg of the journey.

A little over a week before Christmas they put her on a barge and sailed her upriver to their final destination, the English capital in France: Rouen.

BOOK FOUR

Resolution

And when they bring you before the . . . magistrates and the authorities, do not be anxious how or wherewith you shall defend yourselves, or what you shall say, for the Holy Spirit will teach you in that very hour what you ought to say.

LUKE 12:11–12

CHAPTER FIFTEEN

Prisoner of the King

February 20–March 24, 1431

𝔐 y lord bishop, as I told you yesterday, I regret that I am unable to comply with your request," said the slender man with a proud lift of his chin. "I have not yet been appointed by my superior to represent the Holy Office on his behalf."

He searched the sober faces of his fellow clerics, apparently hoping for some glimmer of support from any one of them. But they stared at him mutely, none willing to offend the robust man at the head of the table.

Cauchon gave him an enigmatic smile. He picked up the page lying before him and waved it in front of the monk's nose. "Is it not true that with this document Master Graverent delegated to you responsibility for all activities pursued by the Holy Office in Rouen as long ago as 1424? I have not seen any further instructions from him rescinding that appointment."

"It is true that the Grand Inquisitor appointed me Vicar-General in his stead. However—"

"Then why do you object to performing your duty now?" asked Master Beaupère, his thick lower lip turned downward in a pout. He smirked at Jehan Le Maistre in an unwitting imitation of the bishop's dangerous smile.

"I do not object to obeying Master Graverent's instructions," the Inquisitor responded testily. "As I was trying to say, Your Excellency"—he shot a brief glare at the man who had interrupted his explanation—"my appointment extends only to the diocese of Rouen. Since this woman was captured in your diocese of Beauvais and not in Rouen, I have no jurisdiction over this case."

"I suppose that you also suggest that His Excellency has no authority here either, given that he is bishop of Beauvais and not of Rouen," remarked the thin-faced, swarthy man whom Le Maistre recognized as Nicolas Midi.

"I have no quarrel with Bishop Cauchon's role as judge," was the confident answer, "for I know that he has received permission from the University to sit in judgment of the case. I speak for myself, not for him or anyone else. Yet, it does seem to me that this is a matter for the University alone to prosecute."

"Oh, come now, Le Maistre," whined another monk, "you know very well that for any trial seeking to expose heretics, it is necessary to have a representative of the Holy Office present; otherwise, the proceedings have no legality."

"Nevertheless, it is the University which has brought charges against this woman," the Inquisitor stated firmly. "The Holy Office has found no legal grounds on which to try her. *Ergo*, the University must prosecute the case, not the Inquisition."

The group was assembled in the bishop's home on this snowy evening. After a comfortable meal, during which the churchmen made light conversation, Cauchon had brought the discussion around to the matter at hand. Not present was Jehan d'Estivet, the promoter whom Cauchon had selected to prosecute the sorceress once the preliminary interrogations were finished and the indictment formulated. His role lay properly in the future. Otherwise, Cauchon was surrounded this evening by those he deemed most trustworthy.

For months now he had traveled tirelessly from Rouen to Paris and back again, gathering together the finest ecclesiastical scholars to serve as assessors in the trial, men who would advise the court in matters of canon law. Among those seated at his table were University masters of the Augustinian and Dominican orders, and cathedral canons of Rouen. Handpicked for their legalistic talent and loyalty to the King, they would serve the bishop well. The only member whose intentions were questionable was the one whose role was most important. This meeting was designed to sway him to the side of justice.

Cauchon had anticipated Le Maistre's public refusal after their private meeting yesterday afternoon. At that time the little weasel had tried to squirm out of his obligation by using the same threadbare excuse to which was he was now resorting, namely, that he had not been given the authority to perform his duty. But the truth was that the Vicar-General of the Holy Office of the Inquisition into Heretical Error was a bureaucrat, a mere clerk with no stomach for prosecuting matters of such grave import as this trial. It was not a matter of political loyalties; Le Maistre had none but to his superior, Master Graverent. Yet, that devotion was the solution to the bishop's present dilemma. Unknown to Le Maistre, a letter from Cauchon to the Grand Inquisitor was at this moment en route to him, urging Master Graverent to order the junior official to represent the Holy Office at the trial. Unfortunate that he was unable to be here himself. It was a matter of bad timing that Master Graverent was presently overseeing a case in St.-Lô.

Cauchon eyed Le Maistre carefully. The younger man, to all appearances the essence of legal scholarship in his white Dominican's robe, was self-possessed and obviously trying his best to appear calm. Nevertheless, he would relent in the end; his feeble power was no match for the bishop's.

He let the page slip from his fingers onto Le Maistre's hand. "Read this again, very carefully"—the bishop smiled, sending an icy shiver up the monk's spine—"and I think that you will see that you do indeed have the right to appear at the trial as my fellow judge. In this document, Master Graverent says, and I quote,

'We make, create and constitute you our vicar in the town and diocese of Rouen, giving you entire authority against all heretics and those suspected of heresy.' This harlot who calls herself Jehanne the Maid has been thoroughly investigated, and the University has decreed that there are indeed sound legal grounds to suspect her of the gravest possible heresies.

"*Ergo*"—he mimicked Le Maistre in a voice no less menacing for its softness— "you have *de facto* authority already granted to you by Master Graverent."

Le Maistre pushed the page away. "What grounds do you mean? And what investigation? I know of no such undertaking."

"May I reply, my lord bishop?" asked Pierre Maurice, doctor of theology.

Cauchon nodded amiably, enjoying the eager support of his underlings. "Of course, Brother. I think it is time we made our findings known to our esteemed delegate from the Holy Office." His words dripped with venom.

"His Excellency has been most diligent in his endeavors to gather evidence against the woman," said Maurice with a condescending sneer. "He has summoned witnesses against her from all stages of her life, and they have given exhaustive depositions attesting to her scandalous conduct, evidence that we shall use with great zeal during her trial."

"Such as?" queried Le Maistre, peeved at the scholar's tone.

"The list is unfortunately long, and I say 'unfortunately' for her sake, poor misguided child," answered Thomas de Courcelles. At thirty, he was already bound for a great career within the Church. Gifted with a shining brilliance and an ostentatious humility, he was a favorite of Cauchon. "Her sins are as numerous as the stars, a pity for one so young."

"That does not answer my question, Brother. What evidence do you have?"

"To begin with, she claims that she was sent by God to have Charles de Valois crowned King of the French, a sacrilege that no man can deny," replied Midi, his dark eyes flashing with malice. "And it is well known that she used ritualistic magic to defeat the King's forces at Orléans. In addition, she was a follower of the apostate Brother Richard, who as we all know was driven from Paris for spreading blasphemy among the common people. One of his female consorts, a certain La Pierrone, was burned six months ago for claiming to have had audiences with the Almighty. This girl who calls herself the Maid has made similar claims."

The other monks muttered their shocked disapproval.

"Furthermore," Midi continued, "we have sworn testimony that she also employed the tools of Satan to find lost objects, such as the sword of Fierbois which, by the way, was rumored to have been profanely inscribed with five crosses. So potent was her compact with the Evil One that she seduced her Armagnac minions into capturing butterflies for use in her dark arts. There is more, a long list, as our dear brother Thomas has said."

"Then there is also the matter of her dress," added Beaupère with a prim smirk. "Even in her prison cell, she stubbornly refuses to put on a woman's gown, but insists on wearing the same tunic and hose she was captured in, a most outrageous indecency. Who but a sorceress would flaunt such immodest attire?"

"For a woman to wear man's dress is not *ipso facto* the mark of a witch, Master Beaupère." Le Maistre smiled. "During times of war, other women have assumed masculine attire to defend their castles and homes while their men were away."

"Those were excusable matters of necessity," Maurice retorted, "which in any case were abandoned when the men returned. This girl is different, I tell you. She has taken on the aspect of a man and refuses to relinquish it even away from the battlefield."

Le Maistre grimaced and waved his hand. "That is a very minor point, Brother. Have you nothing else?"

"In accordance with customary procedures set forth by the Holy Office," said Nicolas Loiseleur, "three days ago I introduced myself into her cell, disguised as a peasant from Lorraine. I told her that I was a fellow prisoner, a loyal Armagnac, if you can believe that." Maurice and Midi glanced at one another and chuckled. "At any rate, she took the bait and told me some very interesting things."

The Inquisitor frowned. He had not met this man until tonight, although he knew him well by the name he had made for himself as a diplomatic courier to Rome on behalf of the English. Loiseleur's pockmarked countenance mirrored the glee he felt in the performance of his assignment as false confessor, and Le Maistre found himself hating him for it. Although truly a ploy routinely used by the Inquisition to gather information from suspected heretics, Le Maistre found it distasteful, for he preferred the more direct method of questioning the accused in the open.

"Well, what did she tell you?" the Dominican asked.

"At first she asked only of news from the province," admitted Loiseleur, "so I contrived some for her. But then, with that out of the way, I urged her to speak of any concerns that she had regarding the trial. The little whore had the temerity to say that this sacred body has no right to judge her since God is her only Judge, and that, furthermore, she is being brought to trial for her actions in the field against the English rather than for her own misdeeds."

"Blasphemy!" breathed Midi, a black scowl creasing his forehead.

Le Maistre looked at the suspicious faces staring at him. So far he had not heard anything actually damning about the prisoner. Indeed, her anxiety was understandable considering her predicament. He let his eyes wander to the page granting his commission.

"Whatever your reservations, I can assure you, Brother, that we have conducted a most thorough inquiry into the woman's conduct," the bishop said. He was tired of Le Maistre's stubbornness, yet knew he must be careful. He did not want his fellow judge to be outwardly compliant while remaining unconvinced of the justness of their cause. That would create possible dissension within the tribunal and might even jeopardize the trial.

"We sent to Domrémy where she was born, and found that from her earliest days, she was schooled in the black arts by those closest to her. Her so-called miracles could have been accomplished only with the aid of the Enemy. She has employed magical rings and mandrakes in her mischiefmaking, and has caused otherwise innocent people to worship her as though she were a living saint. She has—"

"Excuse me, my lord bishop, but I was informed only yesterday by a very reliable source that she was recently examined to determine her virginity by no less prominent a lady than the duchess of Bedford herself." Le Maistre looked at Cauchon's glowering face without flinching. "If that is true, then all these purported evidences must be false. How can she possibly be in league with the Devil, since as we all know, the Evil One cannot have had commerce with one who is pure?"

The clerics shifted uncomfortably in their seats. Cauchon's nostrils flared angrily, but when he spoke his voice was composed. "The Devil has many means available to him to work his evil through the human race, lord Inquisitor. He may, for example, promise great riches or power in exchange for seeing his will accomplished. This girl has the necessary *diffamatio*, the bad reputation, on which a case of heresy and witchcraft may be based. If you are unconvinced of that, I can assure you that your superior will not be when I present the evidence to him. You shall preside at her trial, make no mistake about it."

He stood up abruptly, scraping his chair against the floor with a screech.

"I bid you a good evening, Brothers. The trial begins tomorrow morning at eight o'clock in the King's chapel." He glared at Le Maistre. "I suggest that you be present, Brother. Otherwise, Master Graverent will undoubtedly be most displeased to find that you have committed the sin of disobedience."

The bishop turned on his heel and left the room. The theologians looked at one another, then one by one rose to leave. They bundled into their cloaks and braced themselves for the late winter storm. Martin Ladvenu, of the same Order as Le Maistre but not connected to the Inquisition, gave the Vice-Inquisitor a haggard smile.

"May I walk with you, Brother?" he asked.

Le Maistre nodded. "Of course." He was more shaken than he had dared reveal. Cauchon would compel him to participate in this trial, and his heart and mind were not in it. There was something about the whole thing that made him extremely uneasy.

Outside, Ladvenu hung back several paces from the black habits who scuttled to their lodgings, resembling a flock of ravens in their haste to get in from the harsh cold. When they were out of earshot, he murmured to his colleague, "You must be careful, Brother. Our lord bishop is not to be trifled with. He could make things most unpleasant for you."

"I do not like this," Le Maistre whispered, his words barely audible in the howling wind. It was snowing as hard as it had been when they arrived at Cauchon's house, and deep drifts piled in the deserted, narrow street. The tower where the girl was being held loomed above the rooftops one block away. Le Maistre wondered idly how she was faring.

Ladvenu said, "You have every cause to feel ill at ease. There are many irregularities about this trial which I confess make me uncomfortable as well."

"Yes? Go on."

He stopped walking and turned his thin, ascetic face to his taller colleague. "For one thing, the girl should not be where she is, chained and guarded by English soldiers picked from the lowest ranks of the army. Have you met her yet, in her cell?"

"No." Le Maistre shivered and drew his cloak more tightly about him. The black cowl hung over his face, shielding it from the cold, and his breath blew in little clouds from the darkness within the hood.

"Well, I have, and I can tell you firsthand that she's at the mercy of five of the most despicable vermin in the King's army, three of whom are with her all the time." Ladvenu lowered his voice again. "I heard it from my brother Isambard de la Pierre that early on they tried to violate her, and it was only through Warwick's intercession that she was spared that ordeal. I saw her when they first brought her here, and again tonight. My heart quite went out to her. She has lost weight, not that she was very big to begin with, and there are circles of fatigue under her eyes. It's obvious that she's not getting much sleep, and who can blame her if she has to be constantly vigilant with those ruffians! If this is an ecclesiastical matter, she should be in a church prison, watched by nuns."

Le Maistre frowned from the shadows of his cloak. "That does indeed sound like a serious transgression of Inquisitorial policy. The secular arm of the law cannot have custody of any but a condemned heretic, and then, of course, it must mete out justice. But this trial has not yet begun; she has not been condemned as a lost soul."

Ladvenu crossed his arms, hugging the warmth of his body to his shivering frame. "That is because this is actually a political trial, everyone from the meanest beggar in the street to the duke of Bedford knows that. The English want her dead, and the only way they can have their wish fulfilled is if she is found guilty of heresy, since they do not have the prerogative to execute a prisoner of war, as her treatment would indicate that she is.

"And by the way, you were correct in insinuating that the bishop of Beauvais has no right to try a case in Rouen because it is not in his jurisdiction. Nicolas de Houppeville—do you know him?"

"Indeed I know of him, though I've never actually met him," the Inquisitor replied. "He has a fine reputation as one of the best masters at the University."

"Well, he had the nerve to tell Cauchon to his face that he has no authority in Rouen. He also pointed out that the girl was already examined by an ecclesiastical commission at Poitiers before the Dauphin gave her arms, and they discovered no culpability in her. Cauchon became incensed and ordered de Houppeville thrown into prison. He is there even now."

"What about what Cauchon said, about her training in sorcery? And the information that she used magic to perform so-called miracles? If true, they certainly constitute grounds for heresy and witchcraft."

Ladvenu looked over his shoulder. When he was certain that he would not be heard, he said, "It is true that a commission was sent to Lorraine to investigate her background, but they established nothing damnable concerning her. In point of fact, one of the team reported to Cauchon that he had discovered nothing in her which he would not wish to find in his own sister, and he said as much in the presence of witnesses, one of whom told me this himself. Cauchon flew into a fit of rage and called the unfortunate man a traitor, then refused to pay him for his work. The other two investigators came to the same conclusion, and the bishop reviled them as Armagnacs in disguise.

458

"But I know them, Brother, and they are not traitors. If they say that what they found in her was good, then it is so. As for the rest"—he shrugged—"I am not convinced that the testimonies were freely given, or accurately reported. It is important to remember that this is first and last a *political* case. I have no use for the Armagnacs or their false king, but I do value justice, and I am afraid that we shall not see it done in Cauchon's court. That, Brother, shall weigh upon all our souls."

"Oh, my God," Le Maistre moaned, putting a hand to his forehead. "What are we going to do?"

"I have no choice but to participate, because I have been so ordered." Ladvenu frowned. "You will be too, I'm afraid. Cauchon will convince Master Graverent to compel your presence in the courtroom. But you have more power in this than I do. I am only an assessor, compelled to advise the court, while you will be a judge."

"That does not make me feel any better, Brother Martin." Le Maistre smiled weakly. "How can I defy Cauchon? And how dare I defy the King's will?"

"Yes, that is the gist, is it not?" Ladvenu looked toward the tower. "What the girl told Loiseleur is true. She is being brought to trial for having defeated the English in the field, regardless of what the charges against her say. I shall do what I can for her."

"What can you do? As you said yourself, you are only an assessor."

Ladvenu shook his head. "I do not know. I pray that God will show me the way. May He help us both."

"May He indeed, Brother Martin." Le Maistre nodded toward the *donjon*. "And if she is truly innocent, may He help that poor child."

The usher, Massieu, came for her as he had said he would and brought her down the steps to the courtyard. Grey, Billy, and Barrow, and a fourth sentinel who stood outside her cell, followed them, *guisarmes* in hand. Jehanne folded her arms across her flimsy, ripped tunic, shrinking from the wind which cut through the fragile winter sunlight, stirring the clouds overhead toward the south. The heavy chains around her ankles clanked noisily in the snow and pulled at her feet, and she stepped very carefully so as not to lose her balance on the slippery, ice-covered stones. She appreciated that Massieu slowed his steps to match hers, as though he were in no hurry. He said nothing, just gave her a reassuring smile.

When they reached the chapel on the other side of the square, he opened the door for her and she entered before him and the three guards.

Cauchon, overbearing in his dark rose robe, sat in a high-backed chair in front of the altar, facing the door. On either side of him clergymen, most in black habits, filled the choirstalls; sprinkled among them like the seabirds at Crotoy were the Dominicans in their distinctive white robes. Ladvenu and Isambard, the monks who had summoned her last night, sat together in the front row nearest the bishop. Behind the stalls, helmeted English soldiers were standing with their lances pointed upward. The notaries who would record the testimony and inter-rogations manned two long tables, positioned before each double row of assessors.

Conspicuous among the monks were the masters of this place, the English lords whom Jehanne recognized from their visits to her cell. Warwick was there, dressed all in black and sitting with folded arms next to a hard-faced man whose short hair was the color and consistency of thatch. Directly in front of him was a cardinal of the Church clad head to foot in brilliant scarlet. Jehanne remembered that he had also been to her cell. He was Henry Cardinal Beaufort, whom the English called the cardinal of Winchester. He was related somehow to the little English king, that she knew. An old man like Cauchon, his demeanor was pleasant and jovial, and his cheeks perpetually flushed, the color of near-ripe apples.

I will fear no evil, her mind sang, Lord Jhesus is my strength.

A low, three-legged stool waited in the center where all could see it. Her stomach twitched but she kept her face calm. The chains rattled in the uneasy stillness as she lurched across the floor and took her seat. She looked around at the serious men staring at her, and when she came to one of them, she gasped.

The last time she saw him in her cell, he was dressed in the plain clothes of a peasant. Now he wore a black monk's habit, and the satisfied smile he gave her made her dizzy with a sudden sense of betrayal.

The guards had tossed him in with her a few weeks after the English brought her to Rouen. He was a prisoner, too, he said, a loyal Armagnac from her own native Lorraine, Loiseleur by name. Remembering the priest at Le Crotoy, she had warmed to him instantly. The guards had removed him the following morning—to another cell, she assumed at the time.

Her mind scampered about like a wild rabbit ensnared far from its warren. What had she told him? She could not remember now. Only that she hoped to be rescued, she thought, certainly nothing else. Definitely nothing about her Counsel, probably not a word regarding the King. She wished she could recall—

"Jehanne, you who call yourself 'the Maid,' you were apprehended at Compiègne in our diocese of Beauvais." Cauchon's deep voice echoed through the hollow hall, its tonelessness startling her from the struggle to remember her words to Loiseleur.

"Many of your actions, not only in our diocese but also throughout the kingdom of France and through all of Christendom, have brought harm to the orthodox Faith. Our most serene and Christian Prince, the Lord our King, has delivered you to us to be tried in matters of faith, according to law and reason.

"Therefore," the bishop continued, "considering the public rumor and common report as well as certain information already mentioned, after mature consideration with men learned in canon and civil law, we decreed that you should be summoned and cited by letter to answer truthfully the interrogations in matters of faith that shall be put to you."

A shrewd smile creased his mouth. "As it is our office to keep and exalt the Catholic faith, we charitably admonish and require you that, so as to more quickly unburden your sinful conscience and end this trial, you shall answer in full honesty the questions put to you upon these matters of faith, eschewing subterfuge which hinders truthful confession."

She did not understand half of what he had said, but grasped the gist of it well enough to know that she must be careful. Be with me now, please, I need you.

460

SPEAK BOLDLY, LITTLE ONE, DO NOT BE AFRAID.

A black-clad monk approached her carrying a fat book, and when he held it out to her, Cauchon said, "Put your hands upon the Holy Scripture and swear before God that you shall speak the truth in answer to such questions as we shall put to you."

"I do not know what you will ask me. Perhaps you might ask things I cannot answer."

A verbal drone rumbled through the chapel, and robes rustled as the assembly shifted in their seats. Deep lines appeared at the corners of Cauchon's mouth. "Will you swear to speak the truth about what you are asked concerning the Faith and everything else you know?"

"Your Excellency, I will gladly swear to tell the truth about my parents and about everything I've done since I left home, but I have never told anyone about my revelations from God except the King." Her heart pummeled in her chest, but she met him stare for stare. "I shall not reveal them even if you cut off my head, for I have promised Heaven that I shall not. Give me a week, and I will ask my Counsel if They will give me permission to speak of them."

The disturbed whispers resumed. Cauchon's face reddened, and he again demanded that she swear to tell the whole truth. Once more she refused, the Power filling her with steadfastness. Finally, she agreed to take a limited oath that she would speak about what she knew on condition that the vow not include her revelations. She knelt before the Bible and placed both hands upon it. Then she took the oath.

A stocky, thick-lipped man, whom she would later learn was Master Beaupère, stood up. Where his right hand should have been was a stump covered with a black cloth. "What is your name?" he asked.

"At home I was Jhanette, but since coming into France I am called Jehanne."

"And your surname?"

"My what?"

Beaupère made an exasperated face. "Your other name. Your last name."

"I have no other name. My father is Jacques Darc, and my mother is called Isabelle Romée."

"So your name is Jehanne Darc."

She shook her head. "I have never been called that. In Lorraine, it is customary for a girl to take her mother's name, so sometimes I was called Jhanette Romée in my village."

"Very well." The interrogator waved a weary hand. "What is your age?"

Her age. She could not remember. When she left Domrémy, she was seventeen, but that was so long ago, so much had happened since then. How many Twelfth Days had passed in the meantime? Two? There was Christmas with Charles at Bourges, then this last which they had not allowed her to mark.

"Your age?" Beaupère prompted impatiently.

"I'm nineteen, I think."

Cauchon asked where she was baptized, and who her godparents were. She replied to the first, Domrémy, then named her godparents. She provided the name of the village curé. The bishop asked if she knew the *Pater*, the *Ave Maria*, and the *Credo*. She answered in the affirmative.

"Will you say the *Pater* for us now?"

"Yes, Your Excellency, if you will hear my confession, I will gladly say it."

The bishop sent a scowl to Beaupère, who shrugged and shook his head. "There is no need for that. If you know the *Pater*, we require that you recite it. You may say the prayer to one or two notable French-speaking men if you prefer."

"Not unless you or one of them hears my confession."

It was all she had. She would not speak the sacred words in order to pass his test of her faith; the prayer meant too much to her to be used in such a manner, and surely Lord Jhesus had never intended that His words be uttered for that purpose. They were trying to keep Him from her by denying her the sacraments. Well, she would not dance to their tune.

The court erupted into disorder as six of them spoke at once. "Why do you refuse to utter the holy words?" Cauchon thundered.

"Who taught you the black arts as a child?"

"Was your mother in a witch's coven? Did she teach you to worship Satan?"

"What is the significance of the Fairy Tree?"

"What magic did you use at Orléans to defeat the King's army?"

"Do you have plans to escape?"

"Please, good sirs, one at a time!" she cried, dismayed at the hostility bombarding her from all sides.

The bishop raised his hands in a command for order, and the tumult gradually died down. His eyebrows creased the otherwise smooth forehead and his eyes burned at Jehanne. "We have heard enough for today. You shall now be returned to your cell. Upon pain of conviction for the crime of heresy, I forbid you to attempt to leave the prison. Do you understand?"

"Yes, I understand," she replied with a calmness she did not feel. "But I have never given my oath that I shall not escape, and if I do, then no one can accuse me of having gone back on my word."

There was another rumble from the benches.

"I am sorely mistreated in prison," Jehanne complained. "I am held by men who have threatened me physically and who torment me in other ways as well. You know that, Bishop, because seigneur Warwick saved me from being violated by the guards. Day and night, I am kept in chains, fettered to a large block of wood."

"That is because you have tried more than once to escape. You are kept in chains that you may not make another attempt." Cauchon beckoned to the guards who had hung back near the chapel door. They approached Jehanne's stool, and the bishop intoned, "You men who oversee this prisoner, I charge you to guard her well and faithfully, and to allow no one to speak to her without our express permission. Do you swear this before God?"

"We do, Your Excellency." Grey nodded solemnly.

"Then place your hands upon the Holy Scripture and take the oath." The men did as they were instructed, then Cauchon stood up. "We adjourn this court until eight o'clock tomorrow morning, when we shall resume the interrogation in the King's Robing Room."

The first day had ended. Massieu and the guards returned Jehanne to her captivity. The *goddon* soldiers kept her awake almost all night with their singing.

"Please, Brother Jehan, may I stop here a little?" Jehanne asked. "It has been so long since I was able to pray in a real chapel, and I need the comforts of Lord Jhesus' presence."

The two of them were alone in front of the chapel door, since this morning the guards were too drunk to accompany them to the second session.

Massieu took a quick look around at the empty courtyard. He shook his head. "The court is waiting for you, Jehanne."

"Please," she implored him. "I will not be long, I promise. You may fetch me when you choose."

The monk hesitated. Jehanne's hollow, dark-rimmed eyes tugged at his compassion, pulling him away from the resolve he had sworn not to abandon. "Very well," he said at last, moved by her earnest entreaty. "But hurry."

She pulled open the door and walked as quickly as the fetters would allow to a place near the altar, where she knelt and crossed herself. Looking up at the golden crucifix, she said the prayer she had refused to utter for the court. Then she whispered in her mind, Oh, God, give me courage!

That you have in abundance; it is a deep well from which you can always draw. God shall not abandon you. Speak the truth, and you serve Him, Your Creator.

They are so powerful and learned. Oh, why did I not learn to read at Jargeau when Brother Pasquerel offered to teach me!

You have a greater wisdom than can be found in their books. These men of the Church are not men of God or they would not be persecuting you. If they truly could hear God's voice, they would know that their efforts will bring them only loss, for they have no right to judge you. They do not know that they serve the powers of Darkness, and that before seven years have passed, the anointed King shall see the greatest victory he has yet had in this Kingdom of France.

"Jehanne!" Massieu was at the door, his homely face wan with fright. "Come quickly, you must hurry!"

She stood up and struggled for the door, but before she could reach it, a black shadow fell across the threshold.

The man was tall and gangly, and his dark face seethed with indignation. Jehanne had seen him before, in her cell, when he tried to pass himself off—as Loiseleur had done—as a fellow prisoner, but Catherine had whispered caution, so Jehanne held her tongue. She wished ruefully that Catherine had been as forthcoming about Loiseleur. This man was Jehan d'Estivet, promoter of the bishop's case against her.

"What is the meaning of this?" he demanded. Turning to Massieu, he shouted, "Traitor! Who gave you leave to allow this excommunicated whore into the

King's chapel? If you do so again, I will have you tossed into a *donjon* where you will see neither sun nor moon for a month!"

Massieu flinched and licked his lips but did not answer the prosecutor. "Come, Jehanne," he said quietly as she reached them, "the court is waiting."

Those in the Robing Room hardly noticed her entrance. Their attention was given over to a slender Dominican who was speaking to Cauchon. Jehanne came in just in time to hear him say, "My lord, so that this trial shall not be null and void because the Holy Office's representative is not present, I will take part. I wish you to note, however, that I do so with reservations."

Cauchon alone saw Jehanne come in, and now his gaze fixed upon the scruffy figure in the doorway. Following his hostile stare, the others turned toward her in silence as the Dominican who had spoken sank into his seat next to the bishop. Jehanne, her head held in proud defiance, walked to the empty stool and sat down.

Cauchon once again pestered her to take an oath that she would speak the truth about everything she was asked.

"I took it yesterday. That should be enough."

"Young woman," he growled, "you seem to be unaware that not even a prince can refuse to take an oath when required in matters of faith!"

"I swore yesterday. You may well ask me some things that I can tell you and others than I cannot." She shook her head wearily. "You are putting a great burden upon me."

"Burden or not, you are required to tell the truth in matters of faith!" he shouted.

"You are asking that I betray my oath to God. If you were really well informed about me, you would wish that I were out of your hands. The truth, Your Excellency, is that I have done nothing except by revelation."

The assessors stirred in their benches, filling the small room with whispers.

"We demand that you tell the truth, woman," said the robust monk in black who had questioned her the previous day, rising to his feet. "We do not have time to waste with this frivolous haggling."

"Very well," she said, wiping her sweating palms on her hose. "I promise before God to answer you truthfully in those matters that concern this trial. That is all that you will get from me."

The monk turned to Cauchon and held up his hands, then let them fall in a dramatic gesture of exasperation. "Continue, Master Beaupère," the bishop instructed, still glaring at Jehanne.

The man asked how old she was when she left home, and if she had learned any skills during her childhood. She responded that she was seventeen, and that yes, her mother had taught her to spin, adding that she did not fear any woman in Rouen when it came to spinning and sewing and other household crafts. Upon his questioning, she told them about her family's flight to Neufchâteau to avoid the skinners, and how they had stayed at an inn there owned by a woman named La Rousse whose dead husband had been a friend of her father. Yes, she replied, she confessed her sins at Eastertime as required by the Catholic faith.

464

"These supposed revelations of yours," Beaupère sneered, "how old were you when they first began?"

"I was thirteen."

"What were the circumstances? How did you react?"

"A voice came to me near noon on a summer's day, in my father's garden, from the direction of the church. I heard it on my right hand, and it came in a great light. At first, I was very afraid."

"What did this voice tell you? Did it call you by name?"

"He told me to be good and obey my parents, and that I should go to church often. He called me 'Daughter of God.' "

"Anything else? Did this voice identify itself?"

She took a deep breath and sighed. Now it was here, the real reason she was in this dreadful place. "He told me he was St.-Michel, sent by God to summon me to go to the Dauphin, who would give me an army to raise the siege at Orléans, and that afterward I should accompany the Dauphin to Reims for his coronation."

"And you believed him, this supposed St.-Michel?"

"Yes."

The courtroom began to buzz, and she raised her words above the tumult. "He had the voice of an angel, my lords, and I knew that he was truly sent by God. He has always given me good counsel. He told me that I should go to sieur Robert de Baudricourt in Vaucouleurs and he would give me an escort to Chinon. I told him that I was only a poor girl who knew nothing of warfare, and he said that God would protect me, for I had been born to see the Dauphin become King. And everything happened as St.-Michel said it would."

She told the court how Baudricourt had refused her at first but relented in the end. Upon further questioning, she recounted her summons to the old duc de Lorraine and of his concern for his health, which she could not cure. The assessors and judges heard the details of her journey to Chinon in the company of Metz and Poulengy, and of her first meeting with Charles. Jehanne talked so long that her throat became dry, and she wished they would simply leave her alone.

"When you saw the Dauphin, did your voice tell you it was he?"

"Yes."

"Was there a light around him then?"

She waved a tired hand. "Pass on to the next question."

"Did you not see an angel above the Dauphin?"

"Spare me that. Continue."

"Why did Charles de Valois believe you?"

"God gave me beautiful revelations that I shared with him."

"What kind of revelations?"

"I will not tell you. Send for the King and let him tell you himself. I made a vow to Heaven that I would not reveal them."

Cauchon crossed his arms, his malignant glare unrelenting. "Why do you wear men's clothes?" Beaupère fired. "Who told you to do that? Your voice?"

"No one did. I took them of my own free will."

"Did anyone else at court except the Dauphin hear your voice?"

"Everyone present did. That is why they believed me."

"Do you still hear it?"

"Every day."

"What rewards have you asked of it?"

"Nothing, except the salvation of my soul."

"Were you aware that when you attacked Paris, it was a feast day of the Church?"

"Yes."

"Do you think it was a good thing to make war on a feast day?"

Beaupère was leading her onto shaky ground. "Pass," she responded softly.

The monk asked her to relate the details of her attempt to take Paris, and she told him how she was wounded and refused to leave the field, but that her companions had constrained her to do so. Yes, St.-Michel did tell her to stay, she lied. In truth, Michel had not spoken to her at all since before Paris, though she could feel his muted presence even now.

Cauchon adjourned the court until the following day, when once more it assembled in the Robing Room. In this place, amidst the clerical vestments that the English king's chaplain regularly donned before Mass, they questioned her every day for a week.

After the second session, Jehanne noticed that the reluctant Dominican, whom she learned was Le Maistre, Vice-Inquisitor for Rouen, was absent. But even with him gone she knew that this, too, was a war, every bit as serious as the battles for Orléans and the Loire towns, except that now her only weapon was the truth, to be uttered or withheld.

Every campaign began with an assault from Cauchon in which he tried to force her to take the oath. She steadfastly deflected the blow, contending that she had made a vow to a Higher Power than they possessed.

"I say to you that you should beware of saying that you are my judge, for you are taking upon yourself a great responsibility, and you burden me too much."

"If you refuse to tell the truth," the bishop snarled, "you render yourself suspect, and this court will have no choice but to assume you guilty of heresy."

She parried the attack by taking a limited oath as she had before. And then Beaupère rose to take his part in the fray.

Did she still hear the voice? Yes, she did, every time the bells rang and sometimes when they did not. What was she doing when she last heard it? She was asleep. Did it waken her by touching her? No. Was it in the room? She did not know, but it was in the castle. Did she thank the voice and kneel? She thanked it from her place on the floor and asked it for help and advice. What did it answer? That she must answer boldly, and God would help her.

These tiresome questions made her want to scream. For weeks now, she had been locked up in a small, dark cell with guards whose life purpose seemed to lie in making her miserable beyond endurance. Catherine had counseled patience and faith, while Marguerite's soothing words bespoke charity, and Jehanne had borne it all as she was instructed. But now she had had enough, and her frayed temper snapped. The chains around her wrists jangled as her hand shot out and she pointed a grubby finger at Cauchon.

"You say that you are my judge, and perhaps you are, as the world values justice. But you should beware of what you do, for the truth is that I *have* been sent by God, and you are placing your soul in great danger!"

An appalled hum echoed through the room, steadily increasing until it became a roar. Several assessors crossed themselves. Cauchon's mouth worked into a wrathful grimace, hostility crackled around him, but he did not speak. Beaupère raised his black-sleeved arms and extended his hands, palms out. Once more, a hush fell upon the chamber.

"Does the voice ever change its advice?" he continued, unperturbed by her outburst.

"I have never heard two contrary words from Them in all the time They have been speaking to me," she swore.

"Has it told you not to answer this court?"

"I will not tell you about that. Give me some time to seek counsel, and then I will answer you."

"This voice, is it an angel from God, or a saint?"

"It comes from God. I will not tell you everything I know, for I will not displease my Voices."

"How can you displease them if you tell the truth?"

"There are some things that I know about the King that I may not tell you, for they are private as they relate to him."

Beaupère asked if she could make her Counsel send a message to Charles. Perhaps, she replied, it if was the will of God. Without God's grace, she could do nothing. When she heard the voice, did light still accompany it? The light comes before the Voice. Did she see anything else? She would not answer, for she did not have permission. All she would say is that the Voice was good and worthy. Could the voice see, did it have eyes?

"There is a children's saying that sometimes men can be hanged for telling the truth."

"Jehanne, are you currently in the state of grace?"

One of the assessors, Jehan LeFèvre, the bishop of Demetriades and a master of theology, sprang to his feet, indignation blazing from his eyes. "My lord bishop, I must protest that question! Not one of us could answer without endangering his soul."

Cauchon smiled slightly, his cold blue eyes chastising the man. "You forget that you are not the accused's advocate, Bishop LeFèvre. The prisoner will respond as required."

A pall of silence dropped upon the room.

Jehanne searched the chamber. Cauchon's right eyebrow was raised in a flag of victory, while those whom she now knew as Midi and Loiseleur smiled, their hope that she would stumble as evident as though they had proclaimed it. Ladvenu bit his lower lip. His friend Isambard touched an instinctive hand to his sleeve. The notaries had stopped their scribbling; Guillaume Manchon, youngest of the bishop's three scribes, was so intent upon Jehanne's response that he did not notice that a drop of ink had splashed from the pen he held poised above the parchment, obscuring part of a word he had previously written.

Jehanne lifted her chin. "If I am not, may God put me there. If I am, may He so keep me. I would be the saddest person in the world if I knew that I was not in God's grace."

A stupefied, common gasp exploded into the air, then for a heartbeat there was silence.

All at once the court broke into a jumble of awed discussion. Ladvenu glowed with relief, and Jehanne saw in Isambard's open-mouthed nod a new respect. For the first time many of the assessors smiled at her as they bent to their debates, the sound of which grew louder. Cauchon's brilliant blue eyes hardened with hatred.

Jehanne flushed, triumphant, aware that she had somehow outwitted Beaupère but uncertain as to the reason.

The turbulence persisted until Cauchon called for order, and when it had diminished, Beaupère cleared his throat and continued. "When you were a child, did the voice tell you to hate the Burgundians?"

"After I saw that They were for the King, I did not like the Burgundians."

"Did your voices tell you that the English would come into France?"

Jehanne gaped at him as though he were stupid. "Sir, the English first came into France long before I was born."

Some of the assessors hid smiles behind their hands, Ladvenu among them. Coming on the heels of her last, stunning answer, her humor was a lure that she could feel, pulling them to her side.

Beaupère blushed, humiliated by the retort and by his colleagues' manifest amusement, but he continued undaunted. "As a child, did you have a great desire to defeat the Burgundians?"

"My only 'great desire' was that the King should have his kingdom."

"In your village there is a tree called the Ladies' Tree, is there not?"

"Yes."

"Is it not true that people believe it to be a meeting place of fairies? And is it not also true that you danced and sang at that tree, and it is there where you first heard your voice?"

Jehanne shrugged. "*Some* people believe there are fairies at the Tree, but I have not since I could think for myself, for I have never seen them and do not believe they exist. When I was a child, the village children often sang and danced there, because it was a place where we met to spend time with one another. But after the Voices first spoke to me, I no longer went there. My brother told me that people have said that They spoke to me at the Tree, but that is not true."

"Is there not also a forest nearby called the Bois Chenu that is surrounded by a legend regarding a virgin deliverer? Do you believe that fairies meet at that place?"

"There is a wood called the Bois Chenu about half a league from my father's house, but as I have already told you, I do not know anything about fairies. When I first came to France, people said that there is an old prophecy that a virgin would come from the forest to redeem the kingdom. That is something I paid no attention to, for my calling comes from God, not from legends."

468

"Are you willing to forsake the men's clothing you are wearing and to put on a woman's gown?"

"Give me one to wear if you are ready to release me. Otherwise, I will continue with what I have on, since it pleases God that I wear it."

"These voices of yours, who are they?"

May I tell them?

YES, CHILD OF GOD.

"They are St.-Michel, Ste.-Catherine, and Ste.-Marguerite."

"What do they look like?"

"They are very beautiful. Their heads are covered with beautiful crowns, very rich and jeweled. If you doubt me, then send to Poitiers where I was examined before the King granted permission for me to relieve Orléans, and those men of the Church will tell you what I said."

"How do you know that your voices are who they claim to be?"

"They told me and I believe Them."

"How are they dressed? What age are they? Which of them appeared to you first?"

"I will tell you nothing about that. But I can say that it was St.-Michel who first came to me, and he was in the company of all the angels of Heaven. I saw Them with my physical eyes, as clearly as I see you before me, and when They departed, I wept and wished that They would take me with Them."

"What did St.-Michel look like? What did he tell you?"

"I will not answer the first question. As to the second, I have already told you that, and will not answer it again."

"Was it your voices who told you to dress as a man?"

Jehanne made an impatient face and waved her hand. "My clothing is a small thing. Everything that I have done has been at God's command, and if He ordered me to do otherwise, I would."

Beaupère returned to Jehanne's arrival at Chinon. How did she distinguish the Dauphin from all the others? Her Counsel told her it was he. What was the truth about Ste.-Catherine-de-Fierbois' sword? Jehanne related how it had been found after Ste.-Catherine told her it was there. Did she leave it at the abbey at St.-Denis with the rest of her armor? No, she no longer had it at that time. What happened to it? She could not remember. Why did she leave her arms at that place? Did she want people to worship it? No, she replied. It was customary among soldiers to leave their armor there when they had been wounded in battle, as an offering to God and thanks to Him for having spared their lives.

The interrogator asked her to describe her standard, which she did. Why did she insist upon having the inscription "Jhesus-Maria" put upon it? She had done so at God's command. Where was it now? She did not know what became of it.

(It is in a place where you will never find it, you men of the Church. You may have me; you may have stolen my rings; through God's grace, the standard is safe.)

Which did she prefer, her sword or her standard? She loved her sword because it was found at the shrine of her beloved Ste.-Catherine, but she much preferred her standard. She carried it herself in battle in order to avoid killing anyone. And no, she had never killed any man.

Beaupère then produced the letter she had sent the English at Orléans, and read it to the court. Was that the letter from her? he asked. Yes, except that instead of saying "surrender to the Maid," she had written, "surrender to the King." Why did she refuse to conclude a peace treaty with the English garrison? The English would not accept her terms for their surrender.

"Have you ever been in a place where the noble sons of England were being killed?"

"In God's name, yes," she said, her temper returning. "How gently you speak of them, and with what concern! Why don't they leave France and return to their own country?"

"Truly, this is a good and brave woman!" remarked an English lord to his neighbor, loudly enough to be heard by everyone. "Pity she isn't English, eh?"

A titter scampered through the courtroom, squelched in the next moment by Cauchon's threatening glower. "Do you hate the English, Jehanne?" he asked.

"I love what God loves, and hate what He hates."

"Do you think that God hates them?"

"I know nothing about what God loves or hates, but I can tell you one thing: Before seven years have passed, they will suffer a defeat worse than at Orléans, and at that time they will lose everything they have gained in France." The Power swept through her, and she met their incredulous stares unflinchingly. "I do not know the exact date, but you shall see this happen within seven years, and all of you shall remember this moment when I predicted it, and then you will no longer doubt that I was truly from God."

The assessors shuddered, some of them visibly, and a few made the Sign of the Cross. Warwick glowered at her through narrowed eyes and the muscles in his jaw twitched.

"How do you know this?"

"My Counsel have told me."

"Are you saying that all the English now here shall leave France?"

Jehanne nodded. "Except for those who die here."

"When St.-Michel appeared to you, how was he dressed? Was he naked?"

She snorted in contempt. "Don't you think that God has the means to clothe him?"

"Does he have long hair?"

"Why should it be cut short?" she retorted.

"Do your saints have mouths or any members?"

"I don't know."

"Well, come now"—Beaupère smiled condescendingly—"if they don't have mouths, how can they speak?"

"I leave that to God. All I know is that Their Voices are sweet and beautiful."

"Does Ste.-Marguerite speak to you in English or in French?"

"Since I do not understand English, she certainly speaks to me in French," Jehanne answered, her temper turning into sarcasm. "And anyway, why should she speak English when she is not on the English side?"

"When you were captured, you were wearing two rings," Cauchon intruded. "One of them is inscribed 'Jhesus-Maria.' Where did you get them? Did you use them in witchcraft?"

"That one you mentioned was a gift from my father, and you have stolen it from me," she countered. "The other one was given me by my brother. I will give that one to the Church, but I want the ring from my father, for it means much to me." She swallowed the heavy plug of sadness and loss sticking in her throat.

Cauchon ignored the request. Instead, he asked, "I put it to you again: Did you use the rings for magical purposes to heal?"

"No." Jehanne dug her fingers into the skirt of her tunic. "I have never cured anyone with my rings."

"What promises have 'Ste.-Catherine' and 'Ste.-Marguerite' made to you?"

"That has nothing to do with your trial," she replied, meaning the unforgettable visions They had sent her over the years. "The only thing I can tell you is that They said the King shall regain his Kingdom whether his enemies wish it or not."

"Anything else?"

"Yes, but nothing that concerns your trial. Within three months, I may tell you."

"Did your saints tell you that you shall be freed in three months' time?"

There was something that would occur three months hence, Catherine had whispered, but the feeling that evoked in Jehanne was one of undefined dread. She did not want to think about it. "That has nothing to do with your trial. I shall be free one day, but I do not know when."

"Did your voices prohibit your telling the truth about the one you call King?"

"I may not tell you anything about my King. There are many things that have nothing to do with this trial. The King shall have his kingdom; that is all I can say."

"What else do your voices tell you?"

"They give me great comfort every day. Without Them, I would die," she said simply.

"Did an emissary from comte Jehan d'Armagnac come to you, requesting your opinion regarding the Great Schism and asking which of the three contending popes is the true Holy Father?"

Jehanne gasped, amazed that they knew about an incident she had nearly forgotten. She nodded. "Yes, I was on my way to Paris and—"

"How did you answer him?" Beaupère mused, glancing at the bishop.

"I told him that I couldn't speak to him then, but that I would think about it and send the comte his answer after I reached Paris."

There was a general murmur in the courtroom. Jehanne knew immediately that she had answered wrongly, but she did not understand the reason.

"I was in a hurry at that time," she maintained. "My comrades were waiting for me, and I did not have time to speak to the man. So I sent him on his way."

"What did you do with your mandrake?" Cauchon asked. His tone was low and poisonous, and it was obvious that he had intended to catch her offguard.

"I do not have one and never have," she frowned, taken aback by his absurd question. "In fact, I have never even seen one. Someone once told me that there was one near my village, but I never saw it."

"Do you know what they are used for?" the bishop queried.

Jehanne shrugged. "I know that they are evil and dangerous to keep, but I don't know what they're for. My Counsel have never told me anything about them."

"When was the last time you saw 'St.-Michel'?"

"Not since I left Le Crotoy," she lied.

"Did he have his scales with which he weighs the souls of the dead before they enter Paradise?"

"I do not know."

"What did you feel when you saw him?"

She smiled. "I felt the greatest possible joy, and my soul was so clear I knew that I was not in a state of mortal sin."

"Have you ever confessed to 'Ste.-Marguerite' and 'Ste.-Catherine'?"

"Yes."

"Did you feel that you were in a state of mortal sin when you confessed to them?"

"I don't know. I only pray to God that I never was and that I shall never burden my soul like that."

Beaupère returned to the signs Jehanne had given the Dauphin. She repeated for the fiftieth time that the question had no place in the trial. Was anyone else present when she showed it to him? Yes, many others of Charles' court. Did she see a crown from Heaven above the Dauphin's head? She would not answer; she would not violate her oath to God.

"Does St.-Michel have wings? What do your other saints look like?"

"I have told you all I know," she replied, blinking away tears of frustration. These men, these learned, stupid men of the Church, were asking her to describe the unworldly, Beings existing beyond time and space in Eternity and therefore beyond description or explanation. Catherine had been correct when she said that, without any knowledge of God but what they read in books, the clergymen possessed no wisdom at all.

"Did you see their forms? Does 'St.-Michel' have a natural head?" Beaupère persisted.

"I saw Them as clearly as I see you right now, and I believe it was They as firmly as I believe in the existence of God."

"Do you believe that God made them in the shape in which you saw them?"

"Yes."

"Did God create them that way from the beginning?"

"You will have nothing else from me; I have already answered."

"What did your voices tell you about your escape from prison?"

"That does not touch on your trial. Do you expect me to endanger myself? They have told me that I should bear it all with faith and God will help me."

"What did you take that to mean?"

"That God will help me. In what way, I do not know."

"Did the commission at Poitiers ask whether you assumed male dress at the command of your voices?"

"I do not remember. Send for the Book of Poitiers and you can read my answer for yourselves."

"Did the Dauphine ask you to put on a woman's dress?"

Indeed, she had at first before Orléans, and again last winter at Mehun-sur-Yèvre. "That does not relate to your trial," Jehanne maintained.

"Did the comtesse de Ligny request it at Beaurevoir?"

"She did. I told her that I did not have God's permission. If I had had it, I would have done so for her as I would for no other lady in France except the Queen."

Beaupère paused to scratch his long nose. "Did you order your men-at-arms to have standards made for themselves like yours?"

"Some of my companions did in order to identify themselves as belonging to my command, but I did not order it."

"Did you sprinkle them with holy water, or so cause them to be sprinkled?"

"I know nothing about that. If it was done, it was without my authorization."

"Did you see it done?"

"That is not in your trial."

The monk asked her how she met Brother Richard, and she told the court about his coming to her in a delegation from Troyes. No, she was not one of his followers. He attached himself to the army at Troyes, and did not leave it until after the coronation when it was disbanded. Did she know that Armagnacs had had Masses said for her? She did not know, but if they did, it was not at her urging. Even if they did pray for her, she said, what was wrong with that? Did the people of her party believe her to be sent by God?

"I do not know what they believe; ask them, not me! But no matter if they don't believe it, I *am* sent by God."

"What do you suppose people were thinking when they kissed your hands and feet?"

"Again, I do not know their thoughts. I tried as hard as I could to prevent them from worshipping me, but I could not distance myself altogether from the poor because they came to me for help. I gave them what money I had."

"Did women touch your rings with their own?"

"Many people touched my hands. I do not know their intentions."

"Did people of your party catch butterflies in your standard at Château-Thierry?"

It had been said by simple folk that a swarm of white butterflies was sighted fluttering around her standard, but it was only a tale. "That is a story created by my enemies," Jehanne swore.

"Did you find lost gloves for a knight at Reims?"

"No. I heard that someone lost his gloves, but I was never asked, and never promised, to find them."

"Have you ever received the sacraments while you were dressed as a man?"

"Yes."

"Have you received them wearing armor?"

"I don't remember. I don't think so."

"Why did you steal the bishop of Senlis' horse?"

Jehanne made a wry face at the witless question and sighed heavily. "I did not *steal* it. When I arrived at Senlis, the bishop fled to Paris, and he left his carriage horse behind. A soldier gave the horse to me, but I found that it was too delicate to carry both my armor and its own. So I gave two hundred gold *saluts* to the seigneur de la Trémoïlle to send to the bishop as payment. At that time, I wrote to the bishop saying that he could have the horse back again if he wanted it."

She was asked about the dead infant at Lagny. Did it come back to life after she prayed over it? Yes, for a short time, until it could be baptized, but she was only one of a group of women who prayed for its soul. Did the women say that it was her prayers that restored the baby? Jehanne did not know; she had not inquired.

"Are you acquainted with one Madame Catherine de la Rochelle?"

"I met her twice: once at Jargeau, then again at Montfauçon-en-Berry."

"What were the circumstances?"

Jehanne plunged into a labored account of Madame Catherine's visit to her wherein she told of the White Lady. She went on at length about the test she gave the woman and how no vision appeared, just as Ste.-Catherine had foretold. Jehanne related the advice she gave Madame Catherine that she return home to her family. "And that is all I know of her."

"If your voices are from God as you say they are, why did you fail to take La Charité?"

"Who says They commanded me to take La Charité? My real intention was to return to the Ile-de-France, but it was men of my party who wanted me to attack La Charité."

"Which men?"

I will not speak against the King. "I do not remember."

"Do you remember why you jumped from Beaurevoir Tower? Were you trying to kill yourself?"

"No, I was not. I had heard that Compiègne was to be put to the sword, and I wanted to get away to help them. I had also been told that I was going to be sold to the English"—she glanced sullenly at the clump of great *goddon* lords, two of whom were taking notes—"and I wanted to escape."

"After you were found, did you become angry and blaspheme God?"

She shook her head vigorously. "I have never done that, not ever, and when I was found I was knocked senseless. I could not eat or drink for three days, so I certainly was in no shape to say much of anything, much less to blaspheme God."

"Did you cry out against God when you heard that Guiscard Bournel returned the town of Soissons to the allegiance of my lord duc de Bourgogne?"

"No. Anyone who says differently is mistaken."

Cauchon creaked to a standing position. "Brothers, gentlemen"—he bowed with grave solemnity to the English noblemen—"it is growing late. This court is adjourned for the present." With a snap of his cloak he turned abruptly and stalked from the room.

The assessors stood, beginning the inevitable discussion among themselves in a storm of overlapping words and accents. Two guards bearing *guisarmes* grabbed

Jehanne by her arms, squeezing so tightly that she winced, and hoisted her roughly to her feet. She had trouble standing; her behind was numb from the hard stool, her legs as fluid as pudding.

In the next moment Massieu was beside her. "You do not need to hold her," he told the men. "Come, Jehanne, here is my arm." He escorted her back to prison.

"Welcome, dear Brother!" Cauchon rose from his desk and with a hearty smile opened his arms to his visitor. The black-clad monk embraced him indifferently.

Jehan Lohier was taller than Cauchon but about the same age. A respected Norman canon lawyer, his was one of the most brilliant intellects in France, and he enjoyed a farflung reputation for his scholarship and equitable evaluation of judicial evidence. Confident and handsome, with a strong jaw and a pleasant demeanor, Lohier was also well liked by all who knew him. He had arrived in Rouen only yesterday after the court adjourned, and had spent the evening poring over the minutes of the trial. Called to the bishop's house after breakfast, he now held in his hand a thick sheaf of papers.

"Have you had an opportunity to read the trial records?" Cauchon asked amiably. With Lohier's support, another cachet of respectability would be attached to his beautiful trial, and those faltering assessors, won over by the Maid's impudence and the work of Satan, would quickly fall into line.

Lohier tossed the pages onto the bishop's desk and turned his steady gray eyes to the shorter cleric. "Yes, I have, Your Excellency, and I must declare these proceedings invalid."

"What?" Cauchon's face drained of color, and he gaped at the composed man in black. "On what grounds?"

"To start, it does not follow the procedure rendered by the Church for prosecuting heretics." He touched his left forefinger with his right. "Item: The trial is being conducted most often *in camera* with only one judge—you, Your Excellency—and an as yet uncommitted representative of the Holy Office. Furthermore, the assessors are not free to object to questions put to the girl, nor to express their views when they run counter to your own, and they do not have the privilege of reading the trial minutes."

Lohier ticked off another finger. "Item: Questions touching upon the honor of the French King have been introduced into the record, yet he has not been requested to attend this trial nor invited to send a representative in his stead.

"Item: Neither the charges nor the articles which the court are deriving from them have been made public. In addition, the accused has not been provided with counsel, and since she is only a simple girl from Lorraine, of all places, she cannot possibly defend herself adequately. She has been left alone to respond to masters and doctors of the Church upon matters of the gravest import, particularly as concern her revelations.

"Item: Not one shred of evidence has been produced that the prisoner is guilty of the crimes of which she is accused, namely, sorcery and heresy. I know very well that she was examined and found *puella intacta*, and since it is a fact that the Devil can have had no influence over a virgin, she cannot possibly be a witch. As for heretical leanings, she has consistently spoken of her devotion to God and denied any thoughts or actions contrary to the orthodox Catholic faith.

"Item: She is being detained in a military prison rather than in an ecclesiastical setting, as required by accepted judicial procedure. If a matter of canon law, she belongs somewhere other than where she is. If this is a military trial, then the girl was more correct than she perhaps knew when she said that you have no right to judge her under *canon* law."

The monk, still vital at fifty-eight, loomed above Cauchon, unafraid of the fuming, wide-eyed bishop. "This so-called trial of yours is biased in the extreme and motivated by political considerations; it is a travesty. The only really impressive thing about it is the accused herself, who has answered the questions put to her with an astounding sagacity. Truly, she must be inspired to handle herself so well." He shook his head, gravely serene. "I will not endanger my own soul by participating in this farce you call a trial."

Cauchon's mouth contorted with rage, spittle flecking the corners, and he exploded: "*I am in charge of this trial and I order you to attend and to give it your support!*"

Alarmed at the extent of the bishop's fury, Lohier involuntarily stepped back a pace as Cauchon pressed on, his blue eyes afire.

"I have been given the authority of the University of Paris and King Henry to prosecute this case, and you, with your scholarly pretensions and pride, *dare* to criticize the way I am fulfilling my obligation! I will not allow you to ruin all we have worked for!" Cauchon, older in body than Lohier, was breathing rapidly. "You are a traitor to the King, and like any traitor you merit a *donjon* and a trial yourself, followed by a hanging! You shall take part in this trial!" he yelled, louder than before.

Lohier stared implacably at the ranting man whose veins stood out in purple ridges at his temples, realizing for the first time that there was more to Cauchon's interest in his "beautiful trial" than a desire to rid Christendom of another heretic. This was personal. What demonic secret lay snuggled in the bishop's bosom like an adder waiting to sink its fangs into its chosen victim? the monk wondered. What could be that powerful, that deadly, and that frightening?

"Your Excellency," Lohier said in a quiet voice, "I shall return to Amiens tomorrow morning after Mass. I will not be a party to your hatred, I will not give my support to your sin." He tilted his head into a bow designed to convey a minimum of respect. "Good-bye, Your Excellency." He did not wait for Cauchon's response, but turned and left the bishop's house.

Cauchon brought his fists down upon his desk with a violent blow that shook the candle in its holder. He pounded it again and again, muttering his wrath and frustration.

That girl, that damnable whore, she was the cause of all this! She mocked his authority and now had jeopardized his hold upon the courtroom with her impudence and glib answers that these fools mistook for piety. Not even the deprivation of food and sleep that he had sanctioned was sufficient to wear down her vitality to the point where she was malleable. How he detested her, that blasphemous, lying, shameless little slut who derided all womanly decency by having the affrontery to appear dressed as a handsome boy! Her cropped hair, her confident virility, her maddeningly defiant composure, like that of a young captain of war, sent his mind into a whirligig of despairing passion, and there were times when he was certain that he could reach across the tribunal, seize her, then strangle the life out of her with his bare hands.

And Lohier! He was as bad as the Armagnac-in-disguise, Houppeville, and the idiots Cauchon had sent to Lorraine, worse than they because his reputation evidently hid a black, treacherous soul which would burn in Hell for all Eternity. The bishop's teeth itched at the fresh memory of the humiliation he had experienced from the monk's verbal flailing. No one could speak to the bishop of Beauvais in such a vile and condescending manner and get away with it! He would have the man punished for his disobedience to an ecclesiastical superior.

Still violently angry, Cauchon sent messengers to his staunchest supporters, commanding their presence at his house that same morning, and as he waited for them he paced the floor, planning his next strategy. When they arrived in a fluster because of the urgent summons, his outrage had not abated.

They had barely been seated when Cauchon poured forth an impassioned account of his conversation with Lohier. He had built a model trial, painstakingly put together for the past eight months, with the full authorization of the University and after considerable labor.

"And now, here's Lohier, who wants to ruin our trial by giving his interlocutory judgments!" the bishop railed. "He condemns the whole thing and says it's worth nothing. If you are to believe him, we should start all over again, and everything we've done will have been to no end!" Cauchon's eyes narrowed and an ugly satisfaction chattered upon his shoulder. "It's easy to see which side he's on. He would have us return the heretic to her Devil-inspired King! Well, by St.-Jehan, we'll do nothing of the sort; we'll go on with our trial as we have begun."

Beaupère lifted his bulky frame to a standing position and scanned the faces of his colleagues. "My lord bishop, I think I can speak for all of us when I say that you have, and shall continue to have, our full support." Midi and Loiseleur nodded in agreement. "Pay no mind to Lohier's opinions, Your Excellency, they count for nothing here."

"The first order of business should involve Le Maistre." Midi uttered the man's name with a contemptuous sneer. "He must be compelled to attend *all* the interrogations, regardless of his spineless excuses that he has not been assigned to the case. Have you had further word from the Grand Inquisitor?"

A frown darkened the bishop's brow. "Master Graverent has written to us that Le Maistre is his chosen representative from the Holy Office and must participate in the trial as required by law. Yet the little toad is full of excuses, as you have said, Brother Nicolas. But never fear, I shall deal with him in my own way."

There was a moment's silence as the implications of his statement settled upon each of them. None doubted that henceforth the Inquisition would be legally represented.

"What is also needed is a change in strategy," Courcelles said in a characteristic soft tone, his lowered eyes marking the humility he hoped to project. "I fear that unless we remove the sorceress from view, she may gather to her side those whose resistance to Satan is weak. That is the greatest danger to our successfully prosecuting this case."

Cauchon nodded, pleased at the young theologian's suggestion. "Well put, Brother Thomas. I have the same thing in mind."

"Might I suggest, Your Excellency, that she be examined in her prison cell?" Loiseleur smiled. "It is a most unwholesome environment, and it may weaken her resolve further if she is not free to move about, even if only to and from the Robing Room. Her spirit may not remain as defiant as it has been if she is questioned still chained to a wall."

The bishop bobbed his gray head affirmatively as his mind churned. Then he said, "Very well. I shall so order it. But before we resume the interrogations, we must adjourn for a few days. That will give us the opportunity to examine the trial minutes in a detailed manner and to formulate further questioning." He surveyed the men carefully. "Have you any proposals for who should participate in subsequent sittings?"

"My lord, so as to avoid contaminating the assessors any further with the woman's sorcery, I think it would be wise to consistently retain two or three men whose virtue and constancy are above reproach." Beaupère smiled at his master. "As to the other members of the tribunal, they should vary from one sitting to the next. I nominate Brother Nicolas"—he bowed slightly to Midi, who returned his vote with a smiling nod—"and also Brother Jehan de la Fontaine and as notary, Nicolas de Hubent."

Cauchon's delight spread across his face. Surely Master Beaupère was inspired! The latter two were ciphers, cringing nobodies who would do as they were told. "That is an excellent idea, Brother Jehan. Does Brother Nicolas accept the assignment?"

"I do, Your Excellency, with pleasure."

"What about the others?" Courcelles wondered.

"We shall summon them as they are needed," the bishop assured him.

"There is another thing, my lord," said Beaupère. "I am afraid that you must include another Dominican."

Cauchon made a face. "Le Maistre will be there, and Fontaine. Aren't they enough?"

"No, Your Excellency," answered Beaupère. "If the Dominicans feel that they are not being properly represented, they may make trouble for us. Already they have been heard muttering about the so-called irregularities in the proceedings, and their suspicions may be further aroused if you exclude them."

"Which of them is safe?"

"The only one among them who is not a sentimental idiot is Isambard de la Pierre," offered Midi. "The man is most prudent in his deliberations."

"Very well." Cauchon sighed. "Are there any other matters of business to be discussed?"

The monks looked at one another. Midi shrugged.

"Then let us start the examination of the minutes," Cauchon went on efficiently, having dismissed but not forgotten his earlier consternation. "We must prepare our next lines of questioning."

The cathedral was already filled with clerics, soldiers, and townsfolk when Lohier made his way to a quiet corner near a column and knelt within its protective shadows. Turning his cowled head to the crucifix, he removed the beads from his belt and made the Sign of the Cross. The Mass had not started yet, and he would have time to say at least a good portion of the rosary.

He had finished the *Credo* and was on the third *Ave* when he sensed someone near him. The theologian swung his limited view to his right and saw a young monk standing a few paces behind him.

Manchon smiled when he saw that Lohier's concentration was broken. He went down on his knees beside the older man and crossed himself. "I am sorry to disturb you, Brother," he whispered. "You are Master Jehan Lohier, are you not?"

"You have the advantage," the cleric mumbled back. "Who, may I ask, are you?"

"Guillaume Manchon, sir. I am one of the notaries in the Maid's trial."

Lohier gave him a sharp look. "What do you want?"

"Excuse me, Brother, but I must ask—" He paused to make certain they were not being overheard. "Have you read the trial minutes?"

"Why do you want to know?" He was in jeopardy enough already without giving his opinion to another possible adversary, for he did not take Cauchon's threat lightly. If this man were a spy, the bishop could accuse Lohier of openly trying to obstruct the trial, further endangering his life.

He took the young man's measure. Upon closer scrutiny he noticed that there were circles of sleeplessness under the earnest brown eyes seeking his answer. Lohier withheld his response, waiting for a reply.

Manchon licked cracked lips and lowered his voice. "Because I think it's possible we may have both come to the same conclusion."

"And that is?" Lohier asked, still wary.

"I do not like the way this is proceeding, Brother," the notary replied in the same low whisper. A crease of anxious remorse dented his forehead. "His Excellency has ordered me to alter some of the testimony to reflect badly upon the Maid, and when I refused he threatened me with the *donjon*. And I am not the only one. Master Houppeville was actually imprisoned for a few days and upon his release departed Rouen in haste. Others have gone, too, Bishop LeFèvre among them, and still others are considering leaving. I must confess, Brother, that I am in a great turmoil of conscience."

Lohier smiled at him for the first time. "You must stay, young man, and I shall tell you why you must. When this tragedy has run its inevitable course and Cauchon has condemned that unfortunate creature and caused her to be executed, there must remain an *accurate* record of what happened here. Tell me, how did you feel when he said that he would toss you into a *donjon*?"

"Terrified."

"Then take the weight of his threat and measure it next to what *she* faces, and then tell me that you are terrified. Think of spending Eternity in an everlasting lake of fire if you betray the truth, and then come to me with tales of how frightened you are." Lohier scowled more at the specter of Cauchon than at the notary.

Noticing Manchon's crestfallen face, visible even in the shadows of the cathedral and his hood, Lohier's features softened. "You have done well to defy the bishop," he said. "You have taken a stand for Christe's mercy and compassion, and even should Cauchon make good on his threat, you shall certainly earn a place in Paradise *if* and only if you continue to do your duty to God. As for me"—he shrugged—"I am returning to Amiens this very day."

"So you have read the records!"

"Shh! Not so loud. Do you want everyone to hear you?" Lohier cast a furtive glance over his shoulder. No one was paying any attention to them at this distance. "Yes, I have read the minutes, and that is why I am leaving."

"Did you tell the bishop what you think?"

"Indeed," he answered grimly. Lohier then disclosed to Manchon the grounds on which he objected to the legality of the trial and everything that had passed between him and Cauchon.

"You can see how they'll proceed," he murmured. "They will catch her if they can by her own words—that is, when she says, 'I know for certain,' touching her apparitions, she is lost. But if she says, 'it seems to me,' instead of, 'I know for certain,' then no man can condemn her." He shook his head. "I think they are going forward with this more from hatred than anything else, and therefore I will not stay here any longer, for I want nothing further to do with it." Lohier turned again to the notary. "Do you understand now why you must remain at your post? You cannot save her life, but you may make her rehabilitation possible after she is dead."

"Rehabilitation?" Manchon asked, stunned.

"Dear Brother Guillaume, do not underestimate God. His ways are oftentimes inscrutable, and the future is His greatest enigma for us mortals, however much we might give ourselves airs and assure ourselves that we know everything about Him."

"You don't believe that she is a heretic, do you?" the younger monk asked softly.

Lohier hesitated. "Based on what I have read, I think she has told the truth for the most part. And where she has lied, the questions were trivial anyway."

"Then if she has told the truth"—perplexed lines crisscrossed the notary's forehead just above his nose—"then that means that she must be a . . ." He could not bring himself to say the word.

"Precisely." Lohier's tone was wry, and he smiled again. "It means that she is exactly what she claims to be, and may God have mercy on Cauchon when he takes his last breath." He took another look at the dumbfounded younger man. "May God forgive anyone who persecutes His servants. Stay here in Rouen, Brother Guillaume. Do your duty."

A tiny bell tinkled from the altar, and the congregation rose for the start of Mass. Manchon dedicated it to the prisoner and asked God for strength, for himself and for her.

An early spring storm was brewing in the ironclad clouds above Rouen when Cauchon and his subordinates entered the courtyard from the King's chapel. The bishop led the way across the square, taking rapid strides that dared the other clerics to keep pace with him. After three days' deliberation, his closest cohorts had reached agreement regarding the more salient points derived from the heretic's testimony, and the bishop was eager to begin again. It was his sacred duty to rid Christendom of this contaminant who had so divided and threatened to infect the community of God.

Behind him, Isambard de la Pierre and Jehan de la Fontaine walked with anxious gaits, their sandals *clip-clipping* against the bricked pavement. Neither was particularly pleased to be part of the bishop's team, especially Fontaine, to whom had fallen the office of interrogator. Not an aggressive man by nature, he looked forward with distaste to harrying the prisoner. He had no firm conviction that she was heretical, and clandestine conversations with some of his brothers had corroborated that he was not the only one upon whom this trial had cast a pall of unease. He would, of course, perform his duty as ordered by the bishop. What else could he do?

Like Fontaine, Isambard was a morass of reservations. His friend and brother, Ladvenu, had been most insistent that the trial was illegal from the beginning, and after prayers for guidance, Isambard diffidently agreed. He had shared his thoughts with no one at all, not even Ladvenu, because although he trusted his brother, the walls had suddenly grown ears within the past few weeks and English spies were everywhere. The whole of Rouen hummed with disaffection and divided loyalties.

Isambard swallowed the metallic taste in his mouth and drew his cloak closer about his rounded shoulders, disliking the purple-robed autocrat who hurried before him to the far side of the square.

When they reached a door, Cauchon opened it and the monks followed him through the half-darkness up the eight steps to Jehanne's cell. The ever-present English guards stood up and one of them unlocked the door, a solid wooden portal whose barred window offered a glimpse of the dancing torchlight within. The guard swung the door open with a rusty creak, and the prelates entered the chamber.

Isambard took in the depressing scene with a sour, all-encompassing glance. The three English soldiers were lounging half-drunk on their stools near the door, and at the sight of Cauchon's bitter visage, they stumbled to their feet. A disgusting scent of urine wafted from the bucket where the guards relieved themselves, and flies buzzed above it. Partially obscuring the odor was another, created by stale air, a musty smell like that of death. Dirty straw lay here and there in small heaps, interspersed with the bony, ant-covered carcasses of capons and portions of lamb. Disturbed by the new arrivals, a rat scurried across the floor near the far wall, away from the menacing humans.

Jehanne was sitting on the floor beneath the slit of a window, knees drawn up to her chest. She raised her head and looked at the churchmen.

Isambard had not seen her for several days, and his heart cringed at her appearance. She had lost more weight, and the page's costume she was wearing hung loosely upon her small body, made all the more poignant by the chains around her wrists and ankles. The circles of fatigue outlining her eyes had deepened, yet within the eyes themselves was a defiant spark. With a slow, painful movement, she climbed to a standing position, swaying a little as she stood.

"Out!" Cauchon barked at the guards, who wasted no time absenting themselves. He turned toward Jehanne. "Are you ready to begin again?" A smile curled a corner of his mouth but the eyes remained hard.

"Does it matter?" Her posture, though slack, radiated antagonism.

Cauchon ignored the question and seated himself upon John Grey's stool. Hubent the notary took the other, and spread a clean parchment upon the guards' rough table, next to which he placed the inkwell. Fontaine took the third stool, leaving Midi and two assessors chosen for their docility to fend for themselves. Isambard sat down next to Jehanne on the long block to which her feet were still chained, and Massieu positioned himself to the Dominican's right.

Fontaine began as Beaupère had, by asking her to take the oath. As before, she refused. Cauchon lost his temper and yelled at her, but she was unmoved by his wrath. After several quarrelsome minutes she once more took a limited vow to tell the truth as it pertained to the trial.

The assessor asked for details surrounding her capture at Compiègne. Had her voices instructed her to go there? No, They had told her that she would be captured before St.-Jehan's Day but did not say exactly when, and if she had known that she would be taken at Compiègne, she would not have gone there. When pressed for further information, she told them that she had begged her Counsel that she not be taken, but They advised that it must be and that she should take it all with a good heart, and God would help her. She recounted her sortie against the Anglo-Burgundian garrison at Compiègne and the manner in which she was captured.

Fontaine asked if she had been given heraldic arms, and she replied that the King had given them to her brothers, not to her. She described the shield: a blue field on which were two fleurs-de-lys with a sword between them, supporting a crown. Did she have a horse when taken? Yes. How many horses did she own? Five chargers, gifts from the King, and more than seven hacks.

"Did you ask for any other gifts from the one you call King?"

"I never asked for *any* gifts. All I requested was enough money to pay and equip the army."

"So you have no treasure of your own?"

"The King gave me ten or twelve thousand *livres* Tournois, and almost all of that went to wage war. My brothers have the rest." Actually, Pierre had had it when they were captured.

"What sign did you give the Dauphin when you met him at Chinon?"

She sighed, tired of the same old question, yet determined not to reveal what had passed between Charles and herself. Michel had told her Charles' secret prayer, and for her to speak of it to anyone else would mean the breaking of a sacred vow.

"It is fair and honorable and most believable," she answered, "the richest in the world. But I shall not tell you what it was."

"You asked Catherine de la Rochelle for a sign, did you not? Then why won't you do the same for us, that we might see and believe?"

Jehanne frowned. These men of the Church wanted a tale? Very well, she would give them one. She had not sworn to tell the whole truth.

"I would not have asked for a sign from Madame Catherine if hers had been as well known and been seen by as many people as the one I gave the King. Besides," she shrugged, "Ste.-Catherine told me that there was nothing to Madame Catherine's story."

"Which people?"

"The comte de Clermont, the seigneur de la Trémoïlle, the duc d'Alençon, and many other knights all saw and heard it as clearly as I see and hear you now."

"Does this sign still exist?"

"Yes, and it will for a thousand years to come."

"Where is it?"

"With the King's treasure."

"Is it made of gold or silver or any precious stones?"

"I won't tell you, except to say that it is rich beyond description. The sign you really need is for God to deliver me out of your hands, the most certain sign that He could show you."

Fontaine was not satisfied. He insisted that she tell them more about the sign, so she made up an elaborate fable about how the angel gave her the sign to give to the King, and when he received it he said it pleased him well. Everyone present, more than three hundred strong, had witnessed the sign, and afterward she repaired to the chapel where she thanked God for it. It was then that the churchmen of Poitiers bestowed their benediction upon her.

Did the angel who brought the sign say anything to the Dauphin? Yes, that he should send Jehanne to raise the siege at Orléans. Was this angel the same who had appeared to her in Domrémy? Yes, it was always the same one. Did not the angel fail her when she was captured?

"It was God's will that I be taken."

"Has not this angel failed you as to your spiritual well-being?"

"How could he, when he comforts me every day?"

"Does he come himself, or does he send others like him?"

"He sends Ste.-Catherine and Ste.-Marguerite."

"Do they come uninvited, or do you have to call for them?"

"They come when I need Them, and sometimes after I ask God to send Them to me."

"Do you ever need them and they do not come?"

"No."

"When you pledged your virginity to God, did you speak to Him directly?"

"It is enough that I made that promise to those He sent, to Ste.-Catherine and Ste.-Marguerite."

"Why did you cite a certain man from Toul for breach of promise?"

She blinked at the question. How on earth had they managed to dig up *that*? "I did not cite him; he cited me, and I swore to tell the truth before the judge, which I did."

"Did you not break your pledge of betrothal to him?"

"I did not," she insisted. "I have never pledged myself to any man, for I promised God when I was thirteen that I would remain pure as long as it pleases Him, and I have kept that vow to this day."

Cauchon exchanged a meaningful look with Midi, whose dark smile struck Jehanne like a knife. Something was very wrong, but she did not have time to place it.

"Did you ever speak to your parish priest or any other clergyman regarding your voices?"

"No, only to the King."

"Jehanne, do you think you did well by leaving your parents without saying good-bye?"

The old pang of remorse tried to well in her eyes. "I always obeyed them in everything except that. Later, my father told me that they forgave me, although they almost lost their minds at first when I left home."

"Wasn't leaving them that way a sin?"

"It was at God's command that I went into France, and if I had had a hundred fathers and mothers and been a king's daughter, I still would have had to obey God." She was breathing indignantly, stung by his questions. She would not tell them how difficult leaving her village had been for her.

"Have you ever received a letter from St.-Michel or your other voices?"

Jehanne smiled in spite of herself. Two days ago the guards had brought her a letter which they claimed was from her Counsel. When she asked Catherine about it, she was told that it was a clumsy trap, devised because her captors underestimated her and thought her stupid.

She gave Cauchon an even stare, still smiling. "No, They do not communicate to me in that fashion."

"Have your voices ever called you 'Daughter of God,' or 'Daughter of the Church,' or 'Great-Hearted Maid'?"

"They call me 'Jehanne the Maid, Daughter of God.' "

"Why have you been unwilling to say the *Pater* if they address you as 'Daughter of God'?"

"I am not unwilling to say it if I am allowed to be confessed and receive Holy Communion."

Fontaine returned to the subject of her parents. Somehow the churchmen had unearthed the story of her father's dream that she was riding in the company of armed men, and she now wearily confirmed it. Did Robert de Baudricourt suggest that she put on men's clothing? No, she had done it of her own accord. Did her voices command it? Everything that she had done that was good was at Their command. Didn't she believe that for her to wear men's dress was wrong? No, and if she were now among her own people, she would still wear it, because it would be for the greater good of France for her to do as she had before she was captured.

How would she have liberated the duc d'Orléans from England? She would have taken enough English prisoners to ransom him, and failing that, she would have crossed the Narrow Sea to fetch him home. Did her voices tell her that she would do so within three years? Yes, she lied, and if she had remained free for three years she would have been successful.

At this point in the interrogation, Le Maistre joined them, having been so ordered by the Grand Inquisitor. He said nothing as he took a seat on the floor. A significant look, so small that Jehanne was not sure if she really saw it, darted between him and Isambard.

Questioning resumed on the subject of the King's sign. Jehanne was sick to death of the topic. Why wouldn't they just let it go?

But Fontaine again pressed to create what they wanted to hear, so Jehanne further ornamented her story with intricate details of the angel accompanying Jehanne from the chapel, then bowing to the King and presenting him with his crown. All the angels of Heaven were with them, she said.

"Did God send the angel on account of your merits?" Midi asked sarcastically, his mouth twisted into a sneer.

"God sent him on account of the King's merits, and because He had pity for the suffering people of France."

"Why were you chosen instead of someone else?"

"For His own reasons, it pleased God to use a simple girl to drive out the King's enemies."

"Did your voices tell you to assault Paris?"

Another raw wound. "No. It was at the request of knights and men-at-arms in the King's army."

"Was it a good thing to attack Paris on the Feast of the Nativity of Our Lady?"

She shifted in her seat. "It is always good to keep the festivals of the Church."

"Did you order those inside the walls to surrender in the name of Lord Jhesus?"

"What I said was, 'Surrender in the name of the King.' "

"Why did you jump from the tower at Beaurevoir?"

"I have already answered that," she groaned, exhaustion taking hold of her, body and spirit. "Why do you keep asking me the same questions when I have already told you?"

"Tell us again," Cauchon insisted.

She spoke at length of her attempted escape from Beaurevoir, going on so long that her throat ached and became hoarse. Was she trying to kill herself? No. Had her voices consented to the leap? No, They told her she must put her trust in God. But she jumped anyway; was that not a sin? Her saints told her later that God had forgiven her, and she understood that the injury she suffered was a penance for her disobedience.

Did her voices ask for a delay before they answered her? Sometimes They answered immediately, but sometimes Jehanne had a hard time hearing them for the interruptions by visitors to her cell and by the guards. Did the voices respond on their own, or did they refer to God? When she asked Them something, They in turn relayed the question to Our Lord for her and then responded at His instruction. Did a light always accompany them? Yes. They came to her every day and there was always a light that preceded Them. What did she request of them? She asked Them for three things: that they should deliver her from prison; that God should help France and guard the towns in the King's possession; and for the salvation of her soul.

"Why did you tell my lord bishop that he was putting himself in danger by judging you?"

She frowned at Cauchon. "I told him that so that if God punishes him I would have done my duty by warning him."

"And what is the danger in which he finds himself?"

"Ste.-Catherine has told me that I shall have help, but I don't know whether it will free me from prison, or if while I am being tried there will be a disturbance that delivers me. I think it will be one or the other."

"What else have the voices told you?"

"They say that I shall be delivered through a great victory. They say, 'Take everything in good spirits; do not despair in your martyrdom, for you will finally come into the Kingdom of Heaven.'"

Midi gave a sharp look to Cauchon, whose frown deepened. Isambard's plain face paled and he appeared to have been struck. The reluctant Inquisitor looked as though he would cry.

"Martyrdom?" Fontaine asked with a start. "What did you take that to mean? Are you certain that you understood them correctly?"

"Yes, They spoke to me simply and in a firm voice, and that is the word They used. I believe that They meant the suffering I have to bear here"—her eyes swept the miserable cell—"but I do not know if I shall have to endure a greater one. I put myself in God's care."

Fontaine's voice shook as he asked, "After that revelation, do you believe that you cannot commit a mortal sin?"

"I know nothing, but rely entirely on God."

"That is a weighty answer, Jehanne," Isambard said softly.

"I hold it as a great treasure," she whispered, fighting back tears.

"If your voices have assured you of salvation, why do you have such an urgent wish for confession?" This from Midi, whose dark eyes narrowed.

"If I were in mortal sin, I think that Ste.-Catherine and Ste.-Marguerite would abandon me. As for confession, one cannot purge one's conscience too much," which was something she had always told Pasquerel.

"Have you ever cursed God while you have been imprisoned?"

"No! Sometimes I have said, 'in God's name,' or, 'God or Our Lady willing,' but I have *never* cursed God. Those who said I have certainly . . . misunderstood."

"Do you remember a soldier of my lord duc de Bourgogne by the name of Franquet d'Arras?" Cauchon queried with a malicious smirk.

"Yes, I remember him."

"Was it not a sin to take a man for ransom and then have him executed?"

"I did not do that. When the man in Paris for whom I wished to exchange him died, I gave d'Arras into the custody of the bailiff of Senlis and the burghers of Lagny for trial. And he was not a soldier; he was a skinner who had murdered innocent people."

"Is it not true that you rewarded the man who captured him with payment?"

"I am not a master of the mint or the treasurer of France to give people money!" she snapped.

Midi stood up and read to her a list of five charges: She had attacked Paris on a feast day; she had stolen the bishop of Senlis' horse; she willfully jumped from the tower at Beaurevoir; she wore male clothing, a heinous indecency condemned by Divine Scripture; and she had consented to the death of Franquet d'Arras. Considering these charges, did she still maintain that she was not in a state of mortal sin?

Jehanne gritted her teeth and replied that, as to the first, she did not believe that she was in mortal sin, but if she were, it was for God to know it and the priest who heard her confession. She had paid for the bishop's horse and tried to return it. The jump from Beaurevoir tower was an escape attempt, not an endeavor to commit suicide. Afterward, she had confessed to disobeying her Counsel, and Ste.-Catherine told her she was forgiven. And when it came to her dress, she did it at God's command and in His service, and she did not believe it to be wrong.

"When it pleases God to command otherwise, I shall put it aside at once."

"Will you submit to the judgment of the Church?" Midi wondered.

"My testimony should be given over to clerics to examine, and if I have said anything contrary to the Catholic Faith, I will consult my Counsel. If there is anything wrong or against the Faith ordained by God, I would not want to uphold it but would be willing to change to a contrary opinion."

Cauchon made a great show of hiding a smile behind his hand, and Midi chuckled at her simplicity. "Perhaps we should explain something to you, Jehanne," the bishop said. He nodded at Midi.

The monk told her in a tone one usually reserves for dimwitted children that there were actually two branches of the Church. "The first," he said, "is called the Church Militant, and is the Church on earth: the Pope, cardinals, archbishops, bishops, the clergy, and all devout Christians who uphold God's will on earth. The second is the Church Triumphant, that is, God the Father, Lord Jhesus, and the Holy Spirit, as well as Our Lady, the saints, and the souls of all who have attained Paradise. Do you understand?"

"Yes."

"Then you must also see that you must submit all that you have said to the judgment of the Church's earthly representatives, the Church Militant."

Jehanne glared at him. "I will not give you any other answer for the present."

"Have your voices given you permission to escape from prison?" asked Fontaine.

"I have asked for it many times, but so far I've not had it."

"Would you escape if the opportunity presented itself?"

"If I found an open door, I would take that as God's permission and escape, yes. Help yourself, and God helps you."

"You have requested more than once to hear Mass. Don't you think it would be more appropriate for you to hear it wearing a woman's dress?" The question was Cauchon's, and as he expelled it he toyed idly with the cross around his neck.

"Promise me that you will let me hear Mass and I will answer you."

"All right, I promise that you may hear Mass, but you must wear a woman's dress."

"And what would you say if I told you that I promised the King that I would not change these clothes? All the same, make me a dress, long to the ground and without a train, and let me go to Mass, and when I return I will put back on what I'm wearing now."

"You must renounce those scandalous clothes and put on acceptable clothing, simply and absolutely!" the bishop shouted.

Jehanne scowled at his baleful countenance, the two of them locking eyes. "I will not," she replied firmly.

"Are you or are you not willing to submit to the judgment of the Church?"

"All my deeds and words are in God's hands, and I submit to Him. I do not wish to say or do anything contrary to the Christian Faith."

"How do you know that your voices are good spirits?" Fontaine asked, leaving Cauchon to fume in silence.

"St.-Michel assured me of it before the others came to me."

"How do you know that he was really St.-Michel?"

"Because he spoke to me in the language of angels."

"How do you know that it was the language of angels and not the voice of the Devil?"

"I had the will to believe it."

"If the Enemy appeared in the form of an angel, how would you know the difference?"

"I could tell very easily by what he said and tried to teach me."

"What doctrine did St.-Michel teach you?"

"That I should be a good child and God would help me. He told me of the great misery that is in the kingdom of France, and that I should bring God's help to the King."

"What form did St.-Michel take?"

She sighed, so fatigued that she could hardly hold up her head. "I have already told you that."

"Tell us again."

"He was in the form of a very true and upright man. He was in the company of a great host of angels, which I saw clearly with my own eyes, and I believe that it was he as firmly as I believe that Lord Jhesus died for our sins. I believe in him because of the good counsel and comfort he has sent to me."

"Will you submit all your deeds and words, both good and evil, to the judgment of Holy Mother Church?" Midi hammered.

"I love the Church and support it with all my power, and I should not be prevented from going to Mass. Any evil in me is for God to forgive. As for the good I have done, I commend myself to the King of Heaven."

"Will you submit to the Church?" the monk insisted, determined that she answer his question directly.

"I refer to Our Lord, who sent me, and to Our Lady and all the blessed saints in Heaven."

Again Midi explained the difference between the Church Militant and the Church Triumphant. It was necessary for her, as a good Catholic, to acquiesce to the Church Militant, represented by the court.

"It is at God's command that I was sent to aid the King, and it is to Him I yield all my good deeds and everything I have said and done."

"I ask you again: Will you put on a woman's dress?"

"Not unless I am found guilty. Then I want a long dress and a hood."

"Why, if you wear man's apparel at God's command, do you want a woman's dress at your death?"

"It is enough for me if it be long," she mumbled, half to herself. They would do it; they would surely kill her. Oh, God, please do not abandon me, I beg You!

"Do you think it pleases God for you to say that you will dress as a woman if we release you?"

If we release you. Was that still possible?

"If you release me in a woman's dress, I will put on a man's dress again and do as God commanded me, and I will not take any kind of oath promising that I will not arm myself and continue my part in the war, as is God's will."

"Did you put your armor on the altar in the cathedral at St.-Denis so that people would worship it?"

"No."

"Why did the sword found at Ste.-Cathérine-de-Fierbois have five crosses on the blade?"

"I don't know," she groaned.

"Who suggested the design for your standard, with angels having limbs and wearing clothing?"

"I have already answered that."

"Were they painted as they appear to you?"

"They were painted as they appear in churches."

"Did you carry it in battle because you thought it would bring you good luck?"

"I carried it at my Counsel's instructions. They told me to bear it bravely, and God would help me."

"Did you help the standard most, or did it help you?"

"Whether the victory was mine or the standard's, it was all through the grace of God."

"Have your voices told you that they would no longer come to you if you lost your virginity?"

Cauchon leaned forward slightly.

"That has not been revealed to me," she answered, though not as confidently as before.

"If you were married, would they no longer come to you?"

"I do not know. I give that up to God."

"Did he whom you call King do well by killing or causing to be killed my lord duc Jehan-sans-Peur de Bourgogne?"

"I do not believe he did that," she replied, shaking her head. "It was a great tragedy for France. But regardless of who killed him, God sent me to help King Charles."

"Although you have told my lord bishop that you would answer this tribunal as you would the Pope himself," Midi said in a snide tone, "there are a number of questions you have refused to answer. Are you not bound to tell the truth to the Pope, God's vicar on earth, regarding the Faith and your conscience?" He accented the final word.

"Take me to him and I will answer him."

"Why did you gaze at the ring marked 'Jhesus-Maria' before you went into battle?"

"For the love of my father and mother, who gave it to me. Please," her voice shook, "give it back to me. It can be of no use to you."

"Was your standard ever flown at your king's side?" Midi asked as though he had not heard her.

"I do not remember." She sighed. She was so tired that she felt she could fall over any second, and so worn down from the battery of words assaulting her that it was almost as though she bore physical wounds. Oh, dear God, please make them leave me alone.

"Why was it brought to stand beside your king during his coronation, rather than that of someone else, say, one of the Peers?"

She gave Midi a mordant smile. "It had borne the burden; it was only right that it should have the honor."

The men of the Church ceased their interrogation. Jehanne did not yet know it, but the preliminary trial was concluded. All that remained was the indictment. Her Counsel spared her the knowledge that the worst was yet to come.

CHAPTER SIXTEEN

In the Devil's Name

March 25–May 8, 1431

On Palm Sunday, Cauchon came to her again with his henchmen: Beaupère, the one-handed interrogator; Courcelles, whose soft-spoken humility masked a cold, sharp opportunism; the swarthy, pockmarked Midi, ruthless and terrible in his hatred; Loiseleur, the spy; and Pierre Maurice, a bucktoothed man who consistently spoke to her as though he were a sage and she simply an ignorant child. She glared at them as they entered the cell and walked with confident dignity to where she lay propped against the ever-present block of wood.

"Have you come to question me again?" she asked, moving her mouth with difficulty. Yesterday, while she was trying to look out the slit of window at the emerging spring sky, the guard called Billy had taken hold of the chain linking her foot to its shackle, and with a quick jerk brought her to the floor. Her face struck the block, splitting open her upper lip, and now it was swollen and scabbed. The guards, outraged by her resistance, were becoming bolder.

"We are here because yesterday as we were leaving, you asked to be allowed to hear Mass on this holy day," the bishop announced with an officious frown, drawing himself up to his full height.

A tiny hope brightened Jehanne's emaciated features.

"We have come to give you that opportunity if you are prepared to put aside that scandalous costume and assume attire suitable to a woman."

She sighed, and her eyes filled with tears. It was the same old contest. Nothing had changed.

It had been ten months since she was captured, and her release seemed more and more distant. In this terrible place, bereft of the solaces of companionship and the sacraments, there were times when she feared that she was losing her soul to despair, and it was in those dark hours that she knew for certain that everyone she had ever loved had forgotten her and would not save her.

As much as she tried not to think of the past, the relentless questions of her persecutors brought the faces vividly to life. Who were her parents and what was their character? Why had she gone there, and done that, and said this, and written those damnable words? They were experts at taking the truth and twisting it around to suit their own purposes. They kept her alive in this unspeakable existence, this Hell, and would not release her until they judged it time to kill her. And no one had come to rescue her.

Her parents, her companions-in-arms, her King, all of them were no doubt going about their own concerns, ignorant of the sufferings, large and small, that she had to endure. When it was at its most powerful, the black animal whispered that she was doomed, that even God had turned His face from her. She was a fool, it hissed, not to renounce Him as He had her, and to surrender to the demands of those who kept her imprisoned.

It was the Counsel who always pulled her free of the beast. Early on she had learned to take little catnaps to ward off the fatigue brought on by sleeplessness, and now she never slept long or deeply enough to see Them in dreams. Yet she felt Them very near her in the damp, stench-filled dimness. Catherine had promised that God would send a great triumph to deliver her, and it was to that that she clung as her last hope on earth. They had never lied to her. If They said that she would gain her freedom, she would. She reminded herself of that when things seemed at their most hopeless, and then the darkness would lift. They were with her now as she answered the bishop.

"Please, Your Excellency, I want very much to hear Mass and to take Holy Communion today and on Easter Sunday."

"Answer my lord bishop's question, Jehanne," Midi ordered sternly. "Will you renounce that outrageous suit and accept a woman's dress to hear Mass?"

"I have not yet received permission from my Counsel to do that."

"If your voices gave their permission, would you do it then?" wondered Beaupère.

"I want to hear Mass more than anything," she said. "But I dare not change what I am wearing." She sneaked a quick look at the guards who stood across the room snickering at her.

"Dare not?" Cauchon asked with a lift of his brows.

"I am not safe here," she whispered. "I am afraid of what would happen to me if I had to stay here dressed as a woman. You do not know what it is like for me to have to guard myself night and day. Please, Your Excellency, it is in your power to be merciful. Let me hear Mass as I am."

"Jehanne, the sacred Scripture forbids women from taking on the appearance of men," Courcelles admonished in his gentle, singsong way. "If you would hear Mass, you must be appropriately attired so as not to offend God."

"Would not God also be offended if I were violated?" she countered, anger springing to her defense like a sword. "I made a vow to Him that I would remain pure, and how can I continue to promise that if I put myself in danger by surrendering my only protection?" She looked Cauchon full in the eye. "I love God with my whole heart and soul, and I want to receive His sacraments at Easter as all good Catholics must."

Loiseleur rolled his eyes in disbelief. A nasty smile appeared at the corners of

Midi's mouth, and he shot a glance at Cauchon. The bishop's face was an unreadable mask.

"Dear child," Maurice condescended, literally spitting his words from his protruding teeth, "if you truly love God as you claim, then you must obey His injunctions."

"And he expressly forbids women to receive the sacraments dressed like that." Loiseleur gestured with distaste at her worn and dirty suit.

"I cannot," she mumbled, shaking her head.

"Perhaps if you asked your voices, they would give you permission to wear a woman's dress," offered Courcelles. "If they are from God, as you maintain, surely they want you to hear Mass and to take Holy Communion?"

Jehanne looked at the stalwart enemies who had come to tempt her. They were as determined as she not to yield. "My clothing does not burden my conscience, and I do not believe that God would wish me to break the vow I made to Him."

"Is that your final answer?" Cauchon growled.

She nodded. A sad, mute helplessness enveloped her. How she wished that Pasquerel were here to defend her. He could have spoken to these churchmen in the only language they understood.

"Then you give us no choice but to deny your request," the bishop pronounced. He looked at the clerics. "Come, Brothers, we are wasting our time arguing with this heretic."

He wheeled away from her and made for the cell door with the others close behind him. Jehanne watched them go, torn in mind and soul. She had to restrain herself from calling them back, from telling them that she would do whatever they asked if only they would allow her to receive the sacraments.

The door slammed shut after them. She sat down again and put her face in her hands. Oh, merciful Lord, please accept my confession and give me Your absolution. I am a miserable creature, unworthy of Your love, and I have sinned by doubting You. Give me courage and the strength to know that You will deliver me as You have promised.

"You're going to burn in Hell for all eternity, witch," rasped one of the guards, Julian Floquet, from the other side of the chamber. He scratched his fleabitten chest and grinned at her, relishing the anguished countenance that begged him to leave her alone.

"But first, we'll burn your body," Grey swore. He spat upon the filthy floor. "What a lovely flame you'll make when we lash you to the stake! There won't be enough left of you to bury in consecrated ground, even if the bishop allows that. We'll toss your ashes into the Seine and let the river take you to the sea." His toothless gums spread into an aspect of evil humor. "To our *English* Channel."

His comrades laughed and Billy slapped his shoulder. They looked like drunken village boys who had died in sin and gone to the Devil.

Jehanne turned her head from them and again buried her face in her hands.

Dear God, she prayed, send Your victory to me soon! I don't know how long I can endure any more of this.

* * *

"I, Jehan d'Estivet, do swear before God that I hereby assume the office of Promoter on behalf of Holy Mother Church without fear nor desire for favor, but through Christe's love and a zeal for the Faith. Given this Wednesday, the twenty-eighth of March, in the Year of Our Lord, 1431, at the castle of Rouen."

The prosecutor removed his hands from the Bible and kissed it. Giving Jehanne a haughty stare, he said, "Since the prisoner is not learned in letters or theology, she may now choose from our distinguished body here assembled an advocate to answer the articles which the court has formulated."

Jehanne considered first him, then the forty or so assessors. This morning they had returned her to the Robing Room where the first few sessions were held, and now she sat on a bench at a small table before the rows filled with theologians. The table directly across from her was reserved for the notaries, who waited for her response with their quills poised above parchment. Manchon gave her a slight, private smile. Her eyes swept past him, taking in the smug coterie of English lords, and settled upon Cauchon, seated in a great, high-backed chair at the room's end.

She shook her head. "Thank you for the offer, but I must refuse. I have no intention of separating myself from the Counsel of God."

"As you wish," the promoter said, a disdainful indifference to her choice evident in the lightness of his tone. "Before we begin, it is my duty to explain the procedures we shall follow, that there be no doubt in your mind as to what is transpiring. I shall read each article to you—"

He was interrupted by a sudden bustle at the door. Isambard and his brother Dominican, Guillaume Duval, hurried into the room. Both were out of breath and flushed.

"I ask your pardon, Your Excellency," Isambard panted, "but we were detained elsewhere and could not get here on time." He threw a swift look to Ladvenu, and in it Jehanne felt the glimmer of a conspiracy.

Cauchon did not see it. "Assume your seat, Brother Isambard, and do not allow it to happen again," he ordered with a reproving scowl.

"Yes, Your Excellency."

The Dominicans looked around them in apparent bemusement. Every seat was taken except for those on Jehanne's bench. Isambard scrambled to a place next to her, while Duval situated himself to the older monk's right. A titter of amusement floated among the assessors, then vanished.

"The promoter was explaining this court's protocol to the prisoner," Cauchon reminded them. He glanced at d'Estivet. "Continue, Brother."

"Thank you, Your Excellency." D'Estivet gave Cauchon a slight bow. "As I was saying, I shall read each article to the prisoner, one at a time, after which she will be given an opportunity to respond. Is that clear to you?"

"Yes." Jehanne nodded.

She was astonished to feel Isambard's elbow prodding her arm as though in a signal. But when she turned her head toward him, he was looking at d'Estivet with a bland innocence.

The promoter shifted her attention from Isambard by launching into a long-winded summary of their case against her. He began by restating Cauchon's right to judge her due to her having been captured in his diocese of Beauvais. D'Estivet followed that up with a pointed reference to the legal role of the Inquisition, allowing Le Maistre's absence to underscore that institution's importance.

Then he moved to the matter at hand, his denunciation of Jehanne.

All honest and sober people had vehemently suspected, defamed, and rejected her, he said, and as such the judges should declare her a witch, a false prophet, an invoker of evil spirits, superstitious, opposed to the Catholic Faith, schismatic, sacrilegious, idolatrous, blasphemous toward God and His saints. She was scandalous and seditious, an obstructor of the peace, an inciter to war, bloodthirsty, encouraging others to violence. At the command of the Devil she had shamelessly abandoned the modesty befitting her sex and dressed as a man-at-arms; she was an abomination to God and man, having rejected the natural order; she had misled princes and the common people; she allowed herself to be adored and venerated, giving her hands to be kissed.

According to the divine and canonical sanctions, she should be punished and corrected canonically and lawfully, as befitted these and all other proper ends. He, Jehan d'Estivet, canon of the cathedrals of Bayeux and Beauvais, appointed by the bishop of Beauvais, intended to prove and duly inform the minds of those present of the charges against Jehanne. The promoter expressed that it was not his intention to prove what was superfluous, but only what conformed to law and reason.

"As to the articles: First, do you oppose the role of the Church in rooting out heretical doctrines that threaten to infect, contaminate, and destroy the unity of Holy Mother Church?"

Isambard touched his foot to Jehanne's. She ignored the prompting and replied, "I believe that the Pope and the bishops should protect the Christian Faith, and I support their right to punish those who fall from it." She licked her cracked lips. "But I submit myself to God and Our Lady and the saints. I do not believe that I have failed in the Faith."

Cauchon's eyes narrowed and a baleful smile played about his mouth.

"Second: The accused was born of a union between Jacques Darc and Isabelle Romée, his wife, in the village of Domrémy on the Meuse in the duchy of Lorraine, in the diocese of Toul. From earliest childhood she was not, as she has stated, instructed in the principles of the Christian Faith, but instead schooled in the black arts and taught to worship fairies and evil spirits." D'Estivet regarded her with a neutral expression. "How do you answer?"

"The first part is true, about my parents and where I was born," she said, frowning angrily. "But the second part is a lie. I was raised to be a good Catholic and to attend the sacraments faithfully and to love God! If you read what is in your book, you will see that I've already told you that I know nothing about fairies, and I certainly know nothing about witchcraft, which is a great evil. You have twisted my words around to use against me."

Isambard prodded her leg with his knee in warning, but again she disregarded him.

"The notaries will strike that response from the record," Cauchon ordered. "Young woman," he glowered at her, "you will control your outbursts and answer the questions. Do you understand?"

She frowned back at him and did not answer.

D'Estivet raised his eyebrows and continued reading. "The prisoner has been guilty of a great number of sacrilegious acts, to whit: She has invoked, consulted, and frequented demons, has entered into pacts with them, maintaining that these demons are from God and her actions praiseworthy. In addition, she gave herself over to the common people to be adored and worshipped, as properly befits Our Lord and His blessed saints."

"None of that is true," she said. "My Voices *are* from God, whether or not any of you believe it. And I did not encourage anyone to worship me. Read what I said when you questioned me before and you will see what I actually said about that."

As though she had not spoken at all, the promoter read in the same mild tone, "The accused, from childhood until she was about seventeen, danced and chanted spells about a certain evil tree known as the Ladies' Tree. She kept a mandrake in her bosom, hoping by it to have prosperity in wealth and temporal things. How do you answer?"

"They are lies."

"At approximately the age of sixteen, the accused departed her village without the consent of her parents and went to Neufchâteau, where she took up residence at the home of a certain woman known locally as La Rousse. This establishment was in fact a house of prostitution, and the accused consorted with all manner of men in the sin of fornication, and when her betrothed learned of her scandalous behavior, he refused to marry her, as a good Christian should."

"That is a lie!" Jehanne shouted, shaking with rage. "I went to Neufchâteau with my family to escape the skinners, and we stayed at a respectable inn. I never promised to marry anyone. As for the rest, you all know that the duchess of Bedford examined me and proved that I am a virgin. For you to say otherwise is evil!"

Her eyes swept the room, daring anyone to contradict her. Several assessors looked away in shame. "Let the record state only that the accused denied the charges," the bishop directed.

"The prisoner, of her own free will or at the command of evil spirits, gave up and rejected female dress, had her hair cut short, and put on clothing appropriate to a soldier, and with these she went into battle, claiming that she was sent by God through revelations made to her on behalf of God. This is in violation of canon law, abominable to God and man, and prohibited by the sanctions of the Church under penalty of anathema.

"Moreover, she did not confine herself to the simple attire of a man-at-arms, but adopted sumptuous and ostentatious clothes of expensive material, of cloth-of-gold and fur, and it is well known that when she was captured, she was wearing a cloth-of-gold *huque*, open on both sides. To attribute the wearing of such clothes to God, His angels, and His saints is blasphemy."

"I have not blasphemed God or His saints, but only did what He commanded."

496

"The accused has repeatedly refused to change her dress for a woman's gown, and to perform other labors suitable for women."

"God has not given me permission to change what I'm wearing. As for womanly duties"—she shrugged—"there are plenty of other women to do them. Only I can do the Work I was charged to do by the King of Heaven."

"The prisoner took herself to the Dauphin Charles, to whom she made promises of glory, and then used occult, magical means to fulfill them."

"That is not true! I went to the Dauphin, all right, but at the command of God. What I told him was that I was God's messenger, and that if he would put me to work, I would raise the siege at Orléans, and have him crowned King at Reims, and through God's grace we would drive his enemies from the kingdom, *all* the kingdom, and if the seigneur de Bourgogne did not return his obedience to the *true* King of France"—she hurled a defiant glare at the English lords—"then the King would drive them out by force!"

She paused to take a breath. "That is what *really* happened, and I swear it before God."

A murmur escaped from the assessors like a great sigh, then dissipated into the stuffy chamber. Again Cauchon intervened. "Let the minutes record simply that the accused denied the charge."

The pages rustled in d'Estivet's hands as he exchanged the finished sheet for a new one. "The accused dissuaded the one she calls king from negotiations and incited her party to murder and the effusion of human blood, saying that peace could be obtained only at the point of a lance."

Jehanne shook her head once more. "That is not true. On more than one occasion, I wrote to the seigneur de Bourgogne asking that he make peace with the King. I even invited him to the King's coronation! It was he who insisted on war, not me."

The promoter dismissed her statement and continued reading. "The accused found the hidden sword at Ste.-Cathérine-de-Fierbois by divination, or fraudulently caused it to be found by the priests of that monastery. She put spells on her rings and her standards that they might bring her victory in battle. She blasphemously put the names of Our Lord and Our Lady and the Holy Cross on the presumptuous letters she sent to my lord the duke of Bedford and his most serene majesty, Henry VI"—a mutter rose from the English lords—"letters written at the dictation of evil spirits."

"They are all lies," Jehanne maintained through clenched teeth, barely able to hold back her wrath. "I refer you to my previous answers."

"The prisoner presumptuously took it upon herself to respond to the comte Jehan d'Armagnac's request for her opinion regarding the true Pope, when that matter has been settled in favor of Martin V for some time now. In so doing, she proved herself to be rash and erring in the Faith, as well as arrogant in her presumption that she, an unlettered peasant, had the right to answer a question more appropriately put to a master or doctor of the Church."

Jehanne had no reply except, "I refer you to my previous answer."

At this point Cauchon got stiffly to his feet and adjourned the court for the remainder of the day. As the assessors began to file out of the room, whispering among themselves, Massieu came forward to help Jehanne to her feet. She avoided meeting Isambard's eyes.

The Dominican frowned reflectively, watching her stumble slowly into the sunlight, supported by the usher and followed by armed English guards.

He went to her that afternoon in the company of his fellow Dominicans, Guillaume Duval and the man who had questioned her at Cauchon's command, Jehan de la Fontaine. After ordering the guards to vacate the cell so that the churchmen might question the prisoner in private, he quickly crossed the filthy floor and sat down beside her on the block.

"Jehanne," he whispered with some urgency, "Bishop Cauchon has sent us here to ask you again to submit to the Church, but we have come with purposes of our own." He placed a gentle hand on her arm.

"What purposes?" The corners of her sunken eyes creased in suspicion, and she was tempted to cast off his hand.

With a swift look, the monks renewed the promise of support they had made to one another in secret. Fontaine nodded to Isambard, an encouragement for him to continue.

"Brother Guillaume and I deliberately arrived late at today's session," Isambard said, softly enough that the guards would not hear him. "I wanted to sit next to you so that I might give you counsel, unobserved by the court. Why didn't you pay attention to my signals?"

She stared at his pleading countenance without answering, uncertain as to his sincerity.

"I know what you are thinking," he said with a small smile, "but you are wrong. My brothers and I are not your enemies. In fact"—he paused to look up at Fontaine, who stood with his hands in the sleeves of his white habit—"we think that you are being prosecuted for reasons that have nothing at all to do with matters of the Faith. You may not know it, but there are others, probably half of the assessors involved, who are convinced that the bishop has no legal right to act as judge in your case, as Rouen is out of his jurisdiction."

"The English want me dead."

Struck by her plaintive tone, Fontaine hunkered down in front of her, his expression softening. "We know that, Jehanne. We are also aware that that is the main reason you are here. But we can help you."

"How?" She recoiled from him, recalling his former role as interrogator.

"To begin with," he said, "when Brother Isambard gives you a sign that you should answer, or not answer, in a certain way, you need to do as his actions suggest. He is putting himself in great danger by attempting to advise you. Our Brother, Jehan Le Maistre, the Vice-Inquisitor himself, is serving the court under duress and against his will. You may have observed that he makes it his habit to be absent from the sessions."

He waited for a reaction from Jehanne which she did not give.

"At any rate, others have expressed opinions favorable to you, and Cauchon threatened them with severe punishments. A few have departed Rouen in haste, fearful for their lives. So you can see how serious this is, and what risks Brother Isambard is taking on your behalf."

"Not only I," Isambard added. "Another of our brothers, Martin Ladvenu, whom you probably remember from the night when we summoned you to the first session . . . ?"

She shrugged, then nodded.

"Brother Martin has been warned to keep his mouth shut, and is being watched by the English. That is why he is not with us tonight. He told us to tell you that he is praying for you."

"You must control your responses, Jehanne," advised Duval, kneeling next to Fontaine. He was very young, not much older than Jehanne. A square, earnest face mirrored his good faith, despite the angry pimple that seemed to the point of bursting from the end of his nose. "When you call the court liars, that angers Cauchon and his friends all the more, hardening their resolve to ruin you."

"And it also sways toward the bishop those who might otherwise be inclined in your favor," Fontaine asserted.

"But they *are* lying!" she protested. "They claim things that I never said or did."

"We believe you." Isambard kept his voice to a patient whisper. "And you can continue to maintain your innocence, but you must do so in a way that does not offend the court."

"What of their offenses against me?" she asked angrily. "And what of the offense to God and His saints whom He sent to me? They are not evil spirits, and to call Them that is certainly an affront to God!"

The monks exchanged an uneasy look. "Jehanne, I will be blunt with you," Isambard responded. "You must set aside your pride and any offense you feel. Every time you answer in anger, every time you toss out pert, clever comments, you take a step closer to your death. You are not in a position of power here; you have no right to challenge the court by direct means. If you intend to survive, it is necessary that you show humility and respect when you are questioned."

"You have some legal rights that you probably have not been informed of," Duval said. "For example, any prisoner accused of heresy has the right to make an appeal to the Pope. Did you know that?"

She shook her head.

"It is true," Fontaine assured. "And you also have the right, as one who is being tried by an ecclesiastical body, to be housed in a Church prison where nuns could look after you. Cauchon has no legal prerogative to keep you in this place." His thin upper lip curled in abhorrence as he quickly glanced about the dank, reeking cell.

"If you request these things in open court, they shall be entered into the trial record, and not even Cauchon could refuse to grant them," Isambard promised.

Confusion roared in her head, making her temples throb. She had been deceived so often—by the guards, by false prisoners, by other men of the Church. The concerned countenances of the monks implored her assent. She did not know what to say.

"There is something else," ventured Isambard in a way that told her that she would not like to hear it. "You must agree to submit to the Church Militant as regards your dress and your voices."

Jehanne sprang to her feet, wrath shaking her emaciated frame. "So that's why you've really come here, to get me to betray God and myself! I should have known from the first that none of you honestly meant to help me." She brushed away a tormented tear. "Return to your master and tell him that I said what I have told him before, that I submit only to God!"

"Be quiet, you little fool!" whispered Isambard with a frightened glance toward the door. "The guards will certainly hear you."

"Please, Jehanne, sit down, calm yourself," Duval urged. "I promise by Our Lady that we have come to you with the most honorable intentions. Brother Isambard was telling the truth when he said that we are not your enemies. Please," he added, patting the space where she had been sitting.

She gave them a rebellious glower, then reluctantly did as he asked.

"We know that the commission at Poitiers declared that there is nothing blameworthy in your manner of dress," the youngest monk assured her gently, "and we also know that you continue to wear men's clothes because you fear for your virtue in this place. Frankly, I cannot say as I fault you for that, for I know what animals your guards are. That is all the more reason why you should insist upon being moved to a Church prison."

"If you agree to submit to the Church," Fontaine explained, "Cauchon will have no choice but to declare you repentant, and then he will be forced to move you to a better place. But if you continue to defy him, not only will he leave you here, he will condemn you as a heretic and will give you to the English to be burned."

"But I cannot speak against my Counsel!" Jehanne wailed. "I cannot say that They are demons when They are not."

A glance leaped between Isambard and Fontaine. "Jehanne, how can you know for certain that your voices are from God?" Isambard asked.

"Because They are!" Her mind groped in frustration for the words she could not catch. "I cannot explain Them to you, for I do not know how, I do not have the words! But They have shown me some wondrous things and have never lied to me. They have never spoken to me of evil, only of God's love. Would demons do that?"

Fontaine released his breath in a weighty sigh. "Perhaps they would, if their intention was to prod you into committing evil acts."

"I have not done evil. All that I have done has been at God's command." She wiped away the tear that slid down her thin cheek.

Fontaine stood up and looked down at her with a smile. "Think about all that we have said to you, and ask God's guidance. You have our pledge that my brothers and I will continue to pray for you, that you might understand how you can save yourself, body and soul."

Isambard gave her hand an affectionate squeeze, then got to his feet. The youngest monk also stood. Isambard made the Sign of the Cross over Jehanne, and she crossed herself and folded her hands. The four of them bowed their heads as the Dominican murmured the *Pater*. When he was finished, he whispered, "God bless you, Jehanne."

The monks glided to the door. Fontaine called in a loud, authoritative tone for the guards to open it.

Isambard's last sight of Jehanne tore at his heart. An air of abandonment loomed over her like the Angel of Death, and she seemed small and helpless, her ravaged face the picture of blank despair. In that instant, the monk knew that she would not survive. And he also divined in a prophetic flash that the world would come to judge the court for her death and declare all of them guilty.

He did not have time to give the insight any further consideration. Waiting for them at the bottom of the steps was the earl of Warwick.

The Englishman stood with muscled arms folded, blocking the doorway that opened to the courtyard. He was dressed in a black leather tunic and leggings, and a menacing sword hung from his belt. A dreadful anger crackled around him. Seizing Isambard with fierce gray eyes, he came straight to the point.

"I saw what you did during the session today, friar. Why did you help that God-cursed bitch, giving her signs and nudges? By the Black Death, if I catch you trying to warn her again, I will waste no time in throwing you into the Seine!"

The blood drained from Fontaine's face, and he crossed himself. Duval's lower lip trembled with fear. The two of them bolted past Warwick, out into the spring sunlight.

Isambard stood his ground and glared at the nobleman with a courage he had not known he possessed. He said nothing.

Warwick turned from him abruptly, bound for the King's apartment.

With peril gone, Isambard's knees buckled and for a moment he thought he would fall. Instead, he forced himself to inhale a couple of deep breaths. When his heartbeat resumed its normal pace, he walked into the square, then made for the chapel. He felt a sudden, urgent need to speak to God.

The court reconvened in the Robing Room the following morning. True to his word, Brother Isambard took his place at the table next to Jehanne, and to her surprise, so did Brother Martin. She vowed that she would pay heed to their signals only if they did not disturb her conscience.

D'Estivet stood up and began reading from the indictment. "The accused has boasted of supposed revelations that she claims to have been sent to her from God, yet will not state their precise nature, which gives suspicion that they are, in fact, apparitions sent by the Devil. She maintains, presumptuously and rashly, that she can foretell the future, thereby accrediting to herself an aspect of the Divine. How do you answer?"

"My revelations come from Ste.-Catherine and Ste.-Marguerite. It is They who tell me what is to come, for without Them I know nothing. I shall stand by that until my death."

The assessors muttered. Cauchon seemed pleased with the response and eager for the charges to continue.

"The prisoner Jehanne, a simple and unlettered country girl, ignorant of theology, claims that God has sent His messengers to her rather than to one better versed in affairs of the Church and therefore more worthy of Our Lord's trust."

The muscles in her jaw flexed at the insult. "It is in God's power to send His messengers to whomever He chooses, and if He chose me, it is for reasons known to Him."

There were approving nods among the assessors. "That is a good answer, Jehanne," whispered Isambard, confident of support from the benches.

"Silence!" ordered Cauchon. "Continue, Promoter."

"The accused boasts that she is able to distinguish whom God loves and whom He hates."

"That is not what I said. If you read what I said before, you will know that that is not true."

"When the accused jumped from the tower at Beaurevoir, she did so either because she had no revelations, thereby perpetuating a sacrilegious sham, or because she went against them, which was an act of the greatest impiety."

Isambard touched his knee to hers.

"I refer to what I have already said. I do not know if I sinned, but in case I did, I asked God's forgiveness, and I know that He heard me because I asked Him in all sincerity and humility and repentance."

D'Estivet smiled, thinking to trap her with the next article. "Although even the most just man sins, the accused has stated that she has never committed a mortal sin, and is in the state of grace."

It was Jehanne's turn to smile. "That is not what I said at all. Everyone here knows that because they heard me. Read your book to see what I said."

"The accused has stated that she would rather kill herself than fall into the hands of the English."

"I said that I would rather *die*, and that is very different. I have no intention of killing myself."

"The prisoner says that her voices come from God, although she is unwilling to give even a single sign to prove it. Furthermore, she sought no spiritual advice from a worthy clergyman, but wanted to hide her apparitions from the Church, preferring instead to reveal them to simple and ignorant lay people."

"It is not my fault if those who demand signs from God are unworthy for Him to send them," she retorted, ignoring the pinch Isambard gave her and his soft moan of dismay. "I have often prayed that God would reveal them to people of my own party, if it were His will. I believe as firmly as I believe that Lord Jhesus died for our sins that my Voices come from God."

Again, the assessors murmured, this time giving her looks of reproach. The bishop beamed with pleasure.

"The accused has worshipped evil spirits, kneeling to them; embracing them; thanking them with clasped hands; invoking them daily."

"I refer to what I said before. I will call Them to give me aid and comfort as long as I live."

"How do you call them?" Cauchon interrupted. "What words do you use?"

"I say, 'Most sweet God, in honor of Your holy Passion, I beg You if You love me, then please tell me how I should answer these men of the Church. I well know that You commanded that I wear men's dress, but I do not know if I should forsake it. Therefore, please inform me if it pleases You that I continue wearing it.' "

Cauchon smirked at d'Estivet, who raised his eyebrows, then shook his head in dismissal of her answer.

"The accused has said that she was promised to enter the Kingdom of Heaven by her apparitions, provided that she kept her virginity, which is the sin of pride."

"I refer to my previous answer. I promised God to keep pure until my Work is finished."

"Although the judgments of God are impenetrable, the accused states that she is able to recognize God and the saints."

Isambard bit his lip, furious at the statement. The Church's greatest mystics, from St.-Paul to St.-Augustine, had received visitations from Lord Jhesus, and many more had seen His Blessed Mother. The promoter's charge insinuated that no one could know God through His saints. Yet Isambard was helpless to respond on Jehanne's behalf. Others among the assessors undoubtedly felt the same, for they stirred restlessly in their seats.

"I refer to what I've already said," Jehanne answered. "Their words are good and true and are the voices of angels."

"In an attempt to mislead, misinform, and make mockery of this court, the accused fabricated a tale regarding the sign she gave to the Dauphin at Chinon, which was not only an outrageous lie, but an affront to the dignity of the court and to all who seek for truth and justice." D'Estivet's voice slid into derision. "She claimed that an angel walked with her and held her hand, and that together they approached the Dauphin, to whom the angel bowed and presented a crown. To speak thus of angels is the most heinous of lies, for nowhere in the Holy Scriptures do we read of angels making obeisance to mortal beings, not even to the Blessed Virgin, the Mother of God!" D'Estivet glared at her, his chest heaving in anger.

Jehanne flushed and licked her lips. "Nevertheless, it is true," was all she could bring herself to say.

"The accused disregarded what the Church and all decent men deem proper and went to war dressed as a man."

"Read what I said before. I went at God's command."

"Reveling in the sins of pride and vanity, the accused dressed herself in sumptuous garments above her appointed station."

"I never asked for anything, but accepted what I was given as gifts from God."

"In a desire to be worshipped, the accused placed her armor before the statue of Our Lady in the cathedral at St.-Denis."

"I refer to what I said about that."

"When questioned by masters from the University of Paris, a certain Catherine de la Rochelle swore on oath that the accused told her that she consorted with apparitions whom she called her 'counselors of the spring.' Madame de la Rochelle was of the opinion that the accused should be carefully watched, lest she escape prison with the aid of the Devil."

"*What?*" Jehanne's breath escaped in a burst of astonishment, and her eyes widened.

"Does the prisoner wish for the article to be read again?" Cauchon smiled.

Jehanne shook her head. "No, I heard it." The blood drained from her face as she reeled under the impact of this unexpected falsehood. "I just can't believe that she would. . . ." Mustering her composure, Jehanne eyed d'Estivet firmly. "I do not know what she meant by 'counselors of the spring,' because I never said anything like that. And if the Devil showed me an open door, I would prefer to remain in prison even if it meant my death."

There was another stir from the assessors. D'Estivet switched to another page. "The prisoner has consistently refused to answer questions put to her regarding the one she calls king and concerning any signs she may have given him."

Jehanne did not hear the statement. She was still in shock from Catherine de la Rochelle's betrayal. With a pang of dismay, she remembered her Counsel's instruction to treat the woman and her pretensions with gentleness. At the time, she never thought that it would come to this.

Oh, Catherine, may God forgive you!

"Jehanne," Isambard whispered, nudging her with his elbow, "you must answer."

"What?" She raised her head and saw that they were all staring at her. The chamber was as quiet as a tomb.

"Does the accused wish the charge read again?" Cauchon was smiling broadly. She nodded.

D'Estivet repeated the article.

Jehanne frowned, once more in the thick of battle. "I made a vow to God that I would not reveal anything about King Charles, as what God told me about him was private to the King. Do you want me to break my oath to God?"

"It is for us to ask the questions, woman, not you!" Cauchon growled. He nodded to the promoter.

D'Estivet cleared his throat and continued. "Warned that she must submit to the Church Militant, after having been charitably admonished and following an explanation of the relationship between the Church Militant and the Church Triumphant, the accused stated that she would submit only to the Church Triumphant, referring her deeds to God and the saints and not to the earthly authority of the Church, as granted by God. She has made no attempt to mend her ways despite the patient admonition of this court. How do you respond?"

"I have not done any of the things you've said I've done," she answered, knowing that she was on slippery ground. A mantle of confusion wrapped itself around her. "Give me until Saturday, after dinner, and I will give you my response."

Cauchon rose to his feet, and as he did the cross hanging from his neck caught the light from the window. It glinted briefly at Jehanne, making her blink.

"Brothers, gentlemen of England"—the bishop bowed cordially to the lords—"this court is recessed until further notice."

Massieu rushed to Jehanne's side and took her left elbow, giving her a kind smile. With Isambard supporting her other arm, they helped her from her seat. Just as she was turning toward the door, her eye happened to catch the group of English lords.

Among them was a boy, splendidly dressed in a red velvet tunic, who could not have been any older than seven or eight. His dark brown hair was cut very short, above his ears, and partially covered by a soft cap adorned with a small ostrich feather. He was staring at her with a serious curiosity, his little face like that of a small, red-lipped cherub. Next to him, a tall man in black whom Jehanne knew to be the earl of Warwick noticed the child looking at Jehanne. He bent to the boy and whispered something to him. The boy nodded somberly and gave the man his answer.

Jehanne gazed at him over her shoulder until she was brought outside, into the courtyard. Her legs were as unsteady as tubes of water, and she nearly collapsed. A great bell tolled in her heart as she remembered Catherine's prediction, made upon the battlements at Beaurevoir.

The time had come. She had seen the king of England.

Cauchon was too busy to notice Jehanne's escort from the courtroom. With the session adjourned, he was immediately surrounded by his admiring subordinates. But scarcely had Beaupère launched into a flowery plaudit when Warwick jostled him aside.

"I must speak to you, Bishop," he confided in an imperative whisper. Over his shoulder, he ordered one of his men-at-arms, "Escort His Majesty to the royal apartment, Robert." Remembering the boy, he smiled at the serious, pinched little face. "Go along with Robert, Sire. I shall join you soon."

Henry responded with a nod of resigned submission. Warwick watched the little king go with his bodyguard, marveling that a child could be so unlike his father. Where Henry V was vigorous and charismatic, a natural leader even had he not been born to rule, his son showed a listless aversion to the art of weaponry, preferring the company of books and monks instead.

What would become of such a king? Warwick mused, hopeful that he would be dead by the time Henry VI reached full manhood. But at present there were other matters to consider.

He turned his attention to Cauchon, who waited with practiced forbearance for what the bishop surely knew was coming. The assessors and soldiers were still filing out of the hall. Midi glanced anxiously at Cauchon, then whispered something to Beaupère, who shrugged. The two of them followed the others into the April sunlight.

When Warwick and the bishop were alone, the earl gave him an even look. "Why are you prolonging this? It has dragged on since February; surely you have enough to convict the witch?"

Cauchon nodded, knitting his brows. "We have taken our time with this particular case because we want to be certain that the prosecution is thorough."

"Thorough?" Warwick said, on the verge of temper. "You have it from her own mouth that she will not yield to your authority. Convict her and be done with it!"

A subtle sneer lifted the bishop's lip. "My dear earl, you evidently do not understand legal protocol. We cannot simply condemn the accused before we exhaust all possible means of saving her wretched soul from perdition. We—"

"I don't give a damn about her soul!" Warwick seethed through clenched teeth.

"What I want is to burn her. Thanks to her, we're in danger of losing our grip on this blasted country. Charles' army is razing everything in Champagne and the Loire region in an attempt to limit our forage, and between you and me, Bishop, supplies from England are a mere trickle. Parliament is loath to tax the people any further, for there have been grumbles among the populace, and they do not want to bring on another peasants' revolt. It looks as though my Lord Bedford may be forced to levy another tax on Normandy in a year or so, and if Charles is still as popular then as he is now, there will be Hell to pay!"

He paused to catch his breath. Cauchon saw a glimmer of desperation in the soldier's passionate gray eyes. "It is the king's will that the witch must die. With her gone, the miserable rabble will know that they cannot prevail against the power of England and will yield their fealty to Henry, especially when they realize that Charles was the dupe of a Devil-sent sorceress. And make no mistake, we shall make certain that they do realize it."

Cauchon smiled. "Please be reassured, my lord, that your aims and ours are in perfect accord. The heretic will be condemned. But we must see to it that the sentence of excommunication is pronounced only after we have made every effort to restore her to the Church. Otherwise—"

"And what if she yields?" Warwick shouted, his eyes flashing. "Then there will be no condemnation and we shall not be able to execute her."

"Otherwise," the bishop went on as though he had not been interrupted, "some may have doubts regarding her guilt, which will in future—shall we say, cloud?— our findings. Unless her guilt is unequivocal and final, you will not succeed in convincing everyone that her king was a tool of the Devil, and your problem of allegiance to the crown will still exist. We must follow canon and civil law to the letter."

"You have not answered my question, Your Excellency," the earl said with haughty defiance. "What happens if your plans go awry and the girl submits to the Church? You will not be able to excommunicate her in that event, and we will not be able to carry out the sentence of death."

Cauchon gave him a satisfied smile. "If she submits, she will soon recant, of that you may be assured."

"Oh?" The Englishman crossed his arms and looked at Cauchon full of skeptical sarcasm. "And how can you guarantee her relapse into evil?"

"Ahh." The bishop's smile broadened. "That is where you come in, my lord. I have a plan."

He began to speak, and as the inner workings of Cauchon's mind emerged, Warwick was struck by the sweeping ruthlessness that moved the bishop. Reassured by Cauchon's gleeful expression of hatred for the girl and by the undeniable power of his scheme, Warwick smiled for the first time.

"Yes." He nodded. "I see the logic in that. Very well, Your Excellency, proceed as you have. But do not allow it to continue much longer. My lord Bedford has communicated that our time is running out, and we must be done with this as soon as is humanly possible."

"It will be done." Cauchon assured. "But you must be patient. In God's time it will be finished."

"On Thursday morning, in the presence of the assembled court, you swore that on Saturday, after dinner, you would give us your answer regarding your submission to the Church Militant," Midi reminded Jehanne. "Today is Saturday, and seeing as how we have all dined"—the men with him chuckled—"we have come for your response."

She groaned aloud. Here they were in her cell, Cauchon and his small group of devoted followers, returned to pester her once more. She let her eyes take in the stony, merciless expressions, and when she could divine no compassion in any of them, bowed her head in silence.

"Well?" Cauchon insisted. "Are you willing to submit to the judgment of the Church Militant concerning everything you have said and done, good and evil, as relates to your trial?"

She lifted her gaze to his hate-filled countenance. "Yes," she whispered, "except to those things that ask the impossible of me."

" 'The impossible'?" he snarled. "Explain what you mean by that term."

Jehanne sighed. "It is impossible for me to revoke the things I've said and done at God's command, and since it was He who sent Ste.-Catherine and Ste.-Marguerite to me, I cannot deny Them, either. I will not do that for any man alive."

Midi smiled darkly at her, then tossed a significant look to Beaupère. The latter asked, "Would you submit to the Church Militant if it told you that your revelations were illusions or diabolical superstitions, sent to you by the Enemy?"

Had she possessed the vitality, she would have reacted angrily, but she could not reply; she was utterly worn down.

Please, dear God, she implored, make them stop. Give me the strength to resist their evil. "I would pray to God for an answer," Jehanne whispered, "and would do whatever He commanded me to do."

"Dear child," Courcelles sang in his hallmark cloying style, "don't you believe that you are subject to the Church of God on earth, *id est*, our Holy Father, the cardinals, archbishops, bishops, and other devout prelates of the Church?"

Jehanne nodded. "But above them all stands God, and I must serve Him first."

"Have your apparitions ordered you not to submit to the Church?" asked Midi.

"I don't just say whatever comes into my head," she replied, a spark of her old temper reappearing. "I speak at the command of my Counsel and through Them, God, and although They have not told me to disobey the Church, I know very well that my Lord, the King of Heaven, must be honored above all else."

Jehanne lowered her head again. Leave me alone, you men of the Church, she enjoined them, I am so weary of you. I can no longer hear you, you who have never heard me.

To her amazement, they did just that, without putting to her any further challenges.

She had no doubt it was only a temporary reprieve. They would be back when the time suited them, same as always. But they were done with her today. She sighed with relief and murmured a heartfelt thanks to God.

She did not know that Cauchon was beside himself with joy. His mood was almost boyish as he adjourned with his confederates to the comfortable house given him by Bedford. The group seated themselves around the grand desk where he had worked so passionately on the case. When he had poured wine for all of them, he lifted his cup and, eyes shining with elation, said, "Brothers, to justice and the stake!"

"Aye!"

"To justice!"

The clergymen imbibed the excellent wine, each imagining the advancement of his respective career.

Cauchon broke the stillness by saying, "I have been giving much thought as to how we should proceed next. Now that the charges have been filed, the assessors must give their opinions on the case. Before that can occur, the articles must be reduced from seventy to the twelve most crucial points. Brother Nicolas"—he smiled at Midi—"I entrust you and Brother Loiseleur with the completion of that task."

"My pleasure, Your Excellency," responded Midi with a tight-lipped simper.

"Yes, Your Excellency." Loiseleur inclined his head to Cauchon.

"Be very careful when you are evaluating the documents," the bishop instructed, suddenly sober. "It is important to eliminate entirely any of the questions put to the heretic, as well as her impudent answers. What we want is simply a compact list of charges, couched in terminology that is as abstract as possible so as to avoid any sympathy for that creature on the part of our more soft-hearted brothers."

"Or the more soft-headed," drawled Beaupère.

Cauchon chuckled, delighted with his apprentice.

"How many copies should we order the scribes to make?" Loiseleur wondered.

"Enough for every doctor and master in a position to give an opinion. Issue with each copy a statement directing that the assessor give a written pronouncement upon the document in matters of the Faith. When we have collected the responses, we shall send them with the twelve articles to the University for its ruling, the conclusion of which is foregone." He took another swallow from his cup.

"That may not be entirely true, Your Excellency," Midi remarked idly.

Cauchon's wrinkled visage darkened. "What do you mean?"

"Merely that you cannot count on concurrence among the assessors. We should consider the Dominicans."

There was a collective mutter at the mention of the men in white. "Yes, of course," Cauchon said, "those miserable cowards! Despite my injunctions, Le Maistre has attended only two of the sittings, and I fear that he has been spreading his calumny among the others. What do you propose, Brother Nicolas?"

"Rather than send the assessors' responses *and* the articles to Paris, it would ensure a successful conclusion if we send only the articles themselves. Thus, the University shall not be unduly influenced by any contaminating sentiments."

"I agree with Brother Nicolas," affirmed Courcelles, "and in addition, I propose that he, together with Brother Beaupère, should accompany the document to

Paris. Their presence will give added weight to the significance of the court's findings."

"What about you?"

"If it please Your Excellency"—the young man lowered his gaze to his lap—"I humbly submit myself for any services you may wish me to perform here."

Cauchon beamed warmly at Courcelles, gratified by his loyalty. "That does indeed please me, Brother Thomas. It is an admirable offer, one most suited to a loyal son of the Church." He looked at the others. "Do you accept the assignment that Brother Thomas has suggested?"

"Yes, Your Excellency."

"I do, my lord bishop." Beaupère nodded in concurrence.

Cauchon pushed back his chair and stood. "Then, Brothers, I recommend that you begin your work now, tonight. There is still much to be done before we can fully celebrate."

"There is one other matter I would like to broach, Your Excellency, before we begin our work."

"Yes, Brother Nicolas?" The prelate smiled, his right eyebrow cocked in surprise.

"It seems to me," Midi observed, "that the sorceress has become quite thin since she has been imprisoned, and her health appears to be deteriorating. That may be one reason—aside from the deceit of the Dominicans—why certain of the assessors have expressed sympathy toward her."

Beaupère snorted in derision. "Well, what of it? As her constitution declines, so perhaps will her resolution to resist the Church's authority."

"We cannot condemn a corpse, Brother," retorted Midi. "Our English friends would be most distressed if the witch who defeated them by such atrocious means were to escape secular justice. And what I said about the assessors' sympathy toward her is sound advice."

"What do you have in mind?" Cauchon frowned.

"Merely that she be given nourishment to restore her to a reasonable measure of good health. Not a feast, certainly, but something more substantial than she has obviously had until now. I suspect that those ruffians who guard her have been eating what was intended to be shared equally among them, including the woman."

For a moment Cauchon considered Midi's counsel without responding. Then he nodded slowly and said, "It would be an act of charity and mercy to provide the prisoner with something. I shall consider what you have said, Brother Nicolas. Meanwhile, do your duty, all of you, to God and to the Church."

The monks rose and bowing to him, departed.

Cauchon turned toward the window and looked out at the purple dusk hanging over the rooftops of Rouen. He did not see the wineseller who plodded down the deep-rutted street at the reins of his wagon, bound for who knew what inn, nor the little group of drunken English soldiers staggering noisily toward their barracks. The bishop was lost in thought and oblivious to everything his eyes beheld.

He had been brimming with confidence until Midi's wise caution about the damnable Dominicans. That little toad Le Maistre continued to plague him with an outward compliance that hid his obstinate refusal to cooperate by participating in the trial. Well, Master Graverent would certainly hear of his subordinate's iniquities. Cauchon would advise the Grand Inquisitor to reprimand Le Maistre in the strongest possible terms. He wished he could be there when the full weight of the Holy Office chastised the miserable traitor for not performing his duty as ordered. He would not be so defiant then.

Worse than Le Maistre's open rebellion was the more subtle insubordination of the monk's brothers. Although he had no tangible proof, at least not yet, Cauchon suspected that they were giving private counsel to the heretic. How could she have eluded so many of their traps unless she had somehow garnered information from those in a position to know in advance what she would be asked? His hands itched at the prospect of catching them in the act, for when he did he would make good his threat and have them executed as the woman's fellow apostates. Warwick had told him that Brother Isambard attempted to aid her in the courtroom, but the table had been placed at such an angle, and Cauchon's attention had focused so entirely on the witch, that he had not observed anything suspicious.

He could not believe that Isambard, that level-headed and scrupulous man, would resort to such a trick. He would watch him carefully from now on, just in case the Englishman was correct and not merely overreacting in his customary fashion. If Warwick was right, he would order the Dominican's hanging without hesitation, whether or not it was legally endorsed. His execution would give Cauchon tremendous satisfaction.

But not as much as that vile strumpet's. His heart raged every time he thought of her, and he knew that he hated her now more than ever.

He had underestimated her wickedness and her deluded stubbornness. "Daughter of God," indeed! Spawn of Satan was more like it. Her refusal to abandon her outrageous, Devil-inspired clothing galled him almost as much as her persistent clinging to the demons who had led her from the path of decency and meek obedience to the Church. Every time he saw her, clad in that heinous costume, looking so eerily like an attractive—albeit somewhat scrawny—boy, he could rip the clothes from her ragged body and fling both them and her into the Seine. He could barely wait until the court found her guilty and he had the opportunity to watch her burn.

And watch he would, until she was reduced to ashes. Then, and only then, would she no longer haunt his dreams and shake him to the sultry wakefulness that so shamed and reduced him to begging for God's clemency. With her dead, he would no longer be under her immoral, profane spell.

But first, he would force her to recant, to kneel before him as her ecclesiastical father. As a penitent, she would have her head shaved and be dressed in a long linen gown. She would be sentenced to life imprisonment, leaving people to acclaim Cauchon's skill as a jurist and his triumph over heresy.

The archbishopric was in sight. He would soon become the most famous man in Europe. The College of Cardinals rose like the Celestial City over his horizon. He did not worry that recantation would save her from the fire, for as he had confided to Warwick, he had a plan to bring that about after she abjured her demons and yielded to the Church. The law was a useful tool for those who knew how to manipulate it. The bishop would attain both of his goals.

Nighttime had fully come, and now Cauchon was able to see the stars scattered across the heavens like diamonds on a blanket of black velvet. He breathed deeply of the evening air. Midi had a point. The girl was thinner than she once was. Tomorrow he would send her something to restore her health. The English would be most displeased with him if she were to die a natural death.

Jehanne was asleep, curled up on her side, when the rumble in her stomach gushed upward in a flood of bile and pain. She instinctively sprang to her hands and knees. Opening her mouth, she splattered the floor with a thick torrent that splashed all over her tunic. She gave a violent shudder, then opened her mouth to vomit again.

John Grey awoke from his place on a stool and snapped his head away from the wall where he had been leaning. "What's this?" he shouted.

Leaping from his seat, he loped to where the trembling prisoner knelt on the hard floor. He reached her just as another river of green slime soaked the filthy straw, covering it with a nauseating stench.

"Whew! She really stinks!" said Billy, drawing up beside the captain, his face contorted in disgust.

Jehanne's mouth opened again, this time offering a puddle of bloody, yellowish malignancy to the wooden planks. Teary-eyed, she turned a waxen face to her jailers. "The bishop—the fish he sent me"—she croaked—"I think it was poisoned."

The soldiers, now joined by the fat Floquet, exchanged an anxious look. "What should we do?" Billy asked.

"We have to call the guard," said Grey, "otherwise, if she dies, it'll be on our heads. *Guard!*" he yelled without warning, taking the younger Englishman so by surprise that he jumped.

Jehanne was still hunched over the steaming mess her stomach had rejected. Another wave of nausea grabbed her midsection, but when she gaped to release it, nothing came up.

Her memory darted briefly to the alleyway in Orléans, but that had been much different. Overindulgence in wine had not left her as she was now, with every pore aching in flaming ice and her starved body shivering beyond her control. She tried to vomit again yet could not. A thin strand of spittle hung from her mouth, then plopped into the puddle. She crawled weakly to a place near the wall, where she collapsed onto her side, drawing her knees up to her chest. The pain in her stomach was more intense than any she had ever known, as though a strong hand were squeezing and twisting it, and she knew all at once that she was going to die.

"A priest," she mumbled. "I must make my confession."

Through a fog of agony and exhaustion, she was aware that the cell door had opened and there were new presences in the room. Far and away, she heard the rough voices discussing her.

"What did she say?" asked a guard whom she took to be John Barrow, one of the group stationed outside the cell.

"Something about a priest," said Floquet.

"You'd better fetch the earl," Grey commanded. "Tell him that the witch looks to be dying. And tell him to bring a doctor," he shouted as Barrow hurried to the door.

The first deluge of nausea was passing. Jehanne's burning cheek lay almost comfortably against the wooden floor. She opened an eye. A few inches away, a large rat hugged the wall, its pointed nose twitching anxiously. Beady little eyes regarded the helpless creature, too spent to move, whose flesh offered such a tempting meal.

It took a step toward her.

Before coming to this place, Jehanne had always taken vermin for granted as an unpleasant feature of daily life, for they were everywhere, in gutters, in the grandest castles, in the marketplace where they skittered over vegetables and ran from irritated humans. But since she had been here, chained to the wall and the block with her feet restricted, she had come to loathe and fear them. They scampered across her lashed body at night while she tried to sleep, and more than once she had been wakened by sharp little teeth sinking into her legs and hands. The guards were free to swat at them with half-awake curses. Jehanne could only wriggle in her cocoon of chains while panic clattered through her chest.

This one inched closer, taking two steps, then two more. Jehanne watched in dazed horror, too weak to frighten it from her.

A heavy boot suddenly stamped the floor in front of the rodent, making it scamper away from Jehanne toward the other end of the cell.

Had she possessed the strength, she would have thanked whoever had come to her rescue. But although her tongue labored to form the words, no sound came out, and her eyes closed again as she drifted into the merciful half-shadows of consciousness.

She was moving dizzily through a black tunnel, out of control, at such a speed that she thought she would vomit again. On and on she went, slowing at long last, little by little, until finally the darkness lifted, changing into a cloudy, silent light.

Indistinct figures floated within the vapor, and Jehanne was aware of thousands of heartbeats pulsing all around her, just beyond her vision. The light strengthened, bringing with it a low, buzzing hum that broke into many parts and became voices. Now Jehanne was able to see that she was in a large courtroom, not in it exactly, but hovering somewhere above it.

An empty chair which she knew to be the seat of Judgment rested beneath a large stained-glass window depicting Christe with His hands open in benediction. There was no crucifix, no altar beneath the circle of colored glass, so Jehanne knew right away that this was not a church. The benches were filled with an astonishing array of hundreds of people. Men and women, young and old, some with skin as dark as midnight, yet others with slanted eyes and golden complexions, all packed together in a jumble of strange and unusual garments. Charles was among them, sitting not in the exalted position of Kingship, but in a place designating him as simply one of the spectators. Next to him was a beautiful young woman with golden hair whose heart-shaped face was turned toward him, her eyes glowing with love. The King kissed her lightly, then looked straight ahead, wearing the saddest expression Jehanne had ever known to burden him.

She moved away from Charles' sorrow. Others she knew were there. Her parents sat between her brothers, and over them flew a pennon bearing a sword between two fleurs-de-lys on a blue field. The Bastard was present in that strange setting, with d'Alençon, and Minguet and Pasquerel, and all those others whom she loved. In that place her childhood friend Hauviette sat with those who had come to watch and to pray.

There were many others, some of them very eccentric, who took up the assessors' seats. On the front row, a man was writing on a thick sheaf of paper. He was dressed all in white, in a rumpled coat that buttoned down the front, its wide, bizarre flaps resting upon his chest, a stringlike tie around his neck. His hair, as snowy as his clothes, was wild and unruly, and beneath the large nose a bushy white mustache hid his mouth. A righteous yet humorous light burned like a hearth beneath his considerable eyebrows. Next to him sat a small-breasted, aristocratic-looking woman with short dark hair and large brown eyes, dressed like a man in boots which extended to her knees, trousers flaring at the thighs, and she, too, held a pen and paper in her lap. Clustered around them, others of both sexes in similarly astounding apparel appeared to be taking notes. A sense of expectation pervaded the great hall as though the multitude were waiting for some momentous occurrence. Jehanne marveled at the scene, feeling honored to be here, in this company.

A sunbeam suddenly filtered through the window and shone upon the Judge's chair, and the light gradually took on the shape of a Being whose features were so bright that they were an indistinguishable gold; even so, Jehanne could still see the smooth, ageless face, as calm as glass and wiser than time.

"Let the accused approach the court." The Being's voice rang, masterful and lovely, like a great cathedral bell.

Two spirits of lesser brilliance appeared in the center of the courtroom, escorting a man in the ragged, dirty purple robes of a bishop. He was heavily chained at the ankles and the wrists, his gray head bowed in disgrace. The crowd booed him soundly, and some of them threw scraps of paper and stones at him. He knelt before the Judge and put his hands over his head.

"Who will defend this man?" asked the Judge.

From a distance Jehanne saw herself. The armor she had sacrificed at St.-Denis looked as it had when it was new, and around her pulsed a soft illumination. She bore her unscathed standard with graceful stateliness down the center aisle, stopping at the man's side.

"I will, my Lord."

A respectful "ahhh" wafted from the assembled throng.

"What is his defense?" the Judge inquired in the voice of a dove.

"There are no evil men," the dream-Jehanne replied, "only men who perform evil deeds. In life this man was so frightened by the force of his own darkness that in his fear he rejected the Truth and embraced the Lie, thinking that it would save him. In the name of God, I call upon Your mercy and compassion, for that is the Truth which will reclaim him."

The bishop burst into piteous sobs and clasped her feet. Those in the benches bowed before her.

"All praise and Eternal glory to Jehanne the Maid, Child of Paradise, whom the Divine Fire has purified and exalted!" cried the Judge. "In her the curse of the past is lifted and abolished; in her the dawn of Spring has come to brighten the earth and to give glory to her Father, the King of Heaven."

"Jehanne the Maid! Jehanne the Maid!" the people sang, filling the chamber with the musical sound of her name.

The dreaming Jehanne overflowed with tears. In prison she had thought that she was absolutely alone. With nothing of God but snatches of intuition and occasional whisperings from her Counsel, her reality had sunk into the darkness of the cell and the interrogations and the overhanging intimation of death. An insight exploded within her head and she realized that every day, while verbally upholding God, she had actually despaired of Him. But He had not forgotten her.

The tableau vanished in a blast of lightning, replaced by the soft, glowing features of a man from Eternity. The energy sparkling about him was light and airy.

Who are you? Jehanne asked.

I am Gabriel, born from the burst of a Star, and I have come to join with the others who guide and teach you. I shall be with you until your earthly days are finished, just as those who have been with you are with you always.

What does all this mean? she wondered, transfixed by his luminescent beauty.

It prophesies your reward for having kept your faith with God and His devoted servants.

Catherine?

YES, LITTLE ONE.

What will become of me? Will the English kill me as they have sworn to do?

LIFE AND DEATH ARE BUT TWO SIDES OF THE SAME ILLUSION. IN TRUTH, THERE IS ONLY LIFE, AND YOU SHALL NEVER DIE. HOLD TO YOUR FAITH IN GOD, AND HE WILL GIVE YOU EVERYTHING YOU NEED.

What of the Church? The bishop demands that I yield to his Church Militant.

THERE IS NO CHURCH MILITANT; THAT IS A FANTASY CREATED BY MAN. GOD IS THE ONLY REALITY THAT ENDURES THROUGH ETERNITY.

I understand. Please, help me to keep to these things you have shown me.

It is not appropriate that you retain a memory in your mind, yet it shall linger in your soul long after you think you have forgotten it, until it is time for you to see it again. A thousand blessings upon you, Child of Light.

Don't go! Jehanne pleaded, please don't leave me yet.

WE ARE NEVER FAR FROM YOU.

Someone lifted the back of her head and put a foul-smelling cup to her mouth.

"No." She turned her head away, but it followed her, insistent that she drink.

With great difficulty she lifted her eyelids. Everything swung wildly in a circle. A man in a dark robe and cap was probing her face, and under his thoughtful hazel eyes he held the draught he wanted her to drink.

"Come," he said with unexpected courtesy, "this will make you feel better."

"I can't," she murmured.

"Come." He coaxed the mixture to her lips and she took a sip.

It was bitter and burned all the way down. She coughed. The second taste was not as bad, but after that she could not drink any more. She shook her head and whispered, "That's enough, please."

The man took the cup away and gave it to someone else. Jehanne's eyes closed and she laid her head back, and it was then that she realized that, though still in her cell, she was lying on a bed.

Not really a bed, a low cot. She could not see her feet. When she moved them the chains jangled, so she knew she was still chained. But her hands were free. The man took her arm and gently held her wrist. He placed his fingers to it and concentrated intently, as though he were listening for something. Another man, also in black, knelt on her other side and put a cool hand to her forehead. Then stretching forth large hands, he pushed on her stomach.

She yowled as a quick pain stabbed her.

"Will she live?" asked a voice in accented French.

Now she saw him, the earl of Warwick. He was standing behind the physicians, glowering apprehensively at her. The torchlight next to the cell door brightened half the patrician face; the rest was like the dark side of the moon. Both eyes were narrow gray slits.

"Probably," replied the first man. "We shall have to bleed her."

"Out of the question," came the clipped statement.

"Do you want her to live or not?"

"Oh, I want her to live, you can be sure of that." The cultured utterance was deadly quiet.

"Then you must let us bleed her," snapped the second man. "The duchess' physician knows what he is doing, my lord."

Warwick was still. The eyes did not leave her. "Very well. Just watch her carefully; she's quite cunning and might manage to kill herself."

The doctors looked across Jehanne at each other. "Look at her, she's half-dead," the first man muttered, annoyed by the absurdity of the warning. "She's hardly in a position to kill herself."

"Well, mend her then," the Englishman said crossly. "My lord Bedford paid dearly for her and does not want her to escape justice."

The man who had felt her midsection picked up a bowl from the floor. In it was a long piece of cord and a sharp knife. The other doctor pushed the sleeve of Jehanne's tunic up past her elbow, then reached for the bowl that his associate passed to him. He placed it on her stomach and withdrew the cord, which he then tied very tightly across her upper arm. He took the knife while the assistant held the bowl next to her arm.

"Stretch out your arm a little and make a fist," he ordered her.

She did as she was told, feeling a sharp coldness as he sliced a vein in the crook. A small red fountain squirted into the bowl, then stopped. The man made another cut, a little larger this time, and the blood came in a steady geyser.

Jehanne closed her eyes. Nausea tossed through her stomach and her head grew lighter. Just before she fainted away altogether she heard Warwick chide the guards, "You men watch her but leave her alone. It is the King's wish that she recover. And clean up this bloody mess! It stinks to high heaven in here."

Jehanne slept through the night and into the morning for the first time in months.

The physicians brought her a bowl of vegetable soup swimming with a few bits of meat. It was from the king's own table and would give her strength, said the man who had bled her. She was still too frail to sit up, so he removed his cloak and placed its folded bulk behind her head. He fed her as he would an infant, lifting the spoon from the bowl with a nurturing patience. She chewed slowly, every time she swallowed opening her mouth for more like a baby bird. The first two bites seemed strange, for it had been a long time since she tasted cabbage and onions. The soup warmed her shrunken stomach, and when she had finished the bowl, she lay back, sated, and fell asleep again.

She woke at sunset to find that the doctors had returned. This time they brought slices of dried apple, a small cheese, bread that was recently baked, and a bowl of roast venison marinated in wine and spices. The cup they offered Jehanne contained clean water. She ate with greater vigor than she had displayed in the morning, although her stomach filled quickly, allowing only a few bites from each dish.

The doctor's name was Jehan Tiphaine, he replied when she remembered to ask, and he was the duchess' personal physician as well as one of the court's assessors. His assistant was another churchman, Guillaume de Chambre. Jehanne thanked them for nursing her and went back to sleep.

The monks were there when she woke again the following morning. So was d'Estivet the promoter.

He stood at the foot of her cot, glaring at her. "Why are you putting it about that you are ill?" he demanded. "Are you trying to prolong your trial?"

"I *am* ill," she whispered. "The bishop sent me a carp, and it made me sick."

"Liar!" the promoter shouted. "You wanton whore, you told the guards that Bishop Cauchon tried to poison you! The truth is that you have eaten shad and other rich food that did not agree with you."

Jehanne laughed feebly in spite of herself. "Now where would I have gotten any of that, seeing as how the guards eat everything that comes here? It was the fish Bishop Cauchon sent."

D'Estivet's smile was full of venom. "If the bishop's gracious gift made you sick, it was because you tried to cram the whole fish down your throat all at once instead of dining upon it as a civilized person would. I heard what a pig you made of yourself, tearing into the carp with both hands and stuffing your mouth. You gluttonous slut!"

"Civilized?" she asked incredulously. "Is it civilized for the English to keep me here like this, in the company of men who are themselves little more than ani-

516

mals? You try going without food for days at a time, grateful for any pitiful scrap that these *goddons* leave behind, and we'll see how delicately you eat when you have the chance!"

"You are trying to disrupt the trial," he accused her. "You think that you can escape justice by feigning illness, but it will not work on us. We know that you are guilty of heresy and witchcraft, and when we so rule we shall give you over to England to be burned!"

"You have no right to judge me!" Jehanne shouted back. "Your precious trial has nothing to do with me or what I've said and done. You're trying to discredit the true King of France through me, by saying that my help to him came from the Devil and not from God. Nevertheless, I *did* come from God, and it is *you* who are of the Evil One!"

"That is a lie, like everything else that issues from your fiendish mouth! You have rejected the Church, revealing what you truly are, and the Church shall declare you apostate and schismatic, and when you are dead your excommunicated corpse will be thrown into a common sewer to be devoured by vermin!"

"Your fate, Promoter, not mine! Look to your own black soul, for God shall judge you a thousand times more guilty than you judge me!" Jehanne's chest was heaving with rage, and she could feel the fever rise again in her face.

During this exchange, Tiphaine had been about his duty, feeling for Jehanne's pulse. By now passionate hostility between the girl and d'Estivet was racing through her blood. The royal physician looked at the beaded, colorless face with some alarm, aware that a decline could bring her back to the point of death.

He pushed himself from the floor where he had been kneeling next to Jehanne's cot and touched the promoter's arm. "Master d'Estivet, this woman could die if her fever returns, and now it appears that it may. You are not making my task to heal her any easier. Please save these matters for the courtroom."

Tiphaine spoke with an even-tempered dignity. He did not want to offend the promoter, yet was reasonably confident that his position within the royal House endowed him with a measure of authority.

D'Estivet looked from the doctor to Jehanne. "I shall tell the court what you have said," he promised her, "and when they hear of it, your death will be assured." He spun around and abruptly left the cell.

Jehanne fell back into the hard cot, spent from the emotional assault. The invisible hand around her stomach suddenly twisted her midsection into a knot, and she burst into a puddle of clammy sweat. She was getting colder and colder with the pain, as though her blood were a river of ice. She erupted into uncontrollable, shivering convulsions. The promoter's attack had thrown her into the front lines of battle before she was ready. She was not yet well enough to wage war against the Church.

Tiphaine and de Chambre knew it, too; she could see that on their worried faces. Tiphaine felt her forehead, then removed his cloak and covered her with it.

Jehanne's teeth chattered from the cold. She looked at the doctors with eyes that begged them for relief. But the fever only got worse, and before long she was carried away by its heat into the nighttime of awareness.

They bled her again.

Cauchon brought his associates to the cell shortly after sunset. D'Estivet was not with them, but Le Maistre was. The Inquisitor's nose wrinkled distastefully as he followed the bishop to the dark corner where Jehanne lay. She could feel his pity for her and his wish to be anywhere but in this depressing hole. Jehanne saw civil war, birthed from doubt and confusion, in his eyes.

There was no such conflict within the others. They were all there, the same men with whom the bishop plotted for her death. She had groaned when the door opened to admit them, and now she lay on the hard bed dreading their mission.

"In the name of Our Lord Jhesus, we have come to again put to you our charitable admonition that you unburden your conscience and submit to the authority of the Church Militant." Cauchon sounded as though he had rehearsed the statement, and Jehanne knew that its official language was for Le Maistre's benefit.

She did not reply.

"Since you are an illiterate woman, ignorant of the Scriptures," Loiseleur spoke up, "we again invite you to choose a counsel from among us to represent your interests. If you refuse, you are placing yourself in the gravest peril."

"It seems to me," Jehanne breathed, "considering the illness I am suffering, that I am already in great danger of death. If that is God's will for me, I beg you to hear my confession and give me my Saviour in Holy Communion, and then let me be buried in consecrated ground."

"If you wish to have the rights and sacraments of the Church, you must behave like a good Catholic and submit to the Holy Church," growled Cauchon.

Jehanne's eyelids fluttered, then dropped. "I have nothing more to say to you right now." She did not have the strength to fight him, and even this brief confrontation was sapping her fragile vitality.

"The more you fear death from your illness, the more you must amend your life," Maurice said, hoping to wear her into submission. "You cannot have the solace of the Church unless you yield to its authority."

"If my body dies in prison," she mumbled, "I trust that you will bury it in consecrated ground. If you do not, then I put my trust in my Lord."

Courcelles and Loiseleur shifted their feet. The Inquisitor's compassion took a blow from Jehanne's dismissal of the offer. Cauchon had told him that her obstinacy testified to her guilt, and the temptation to believe that loomed before Le Maistre in her willingness to die rather than capitulate. He decided to try another angle of questioning.

"Jehanne, during your trial you said that if you had done anything against the Christian faith, you would not want to uphold it. That very faith rests upon the structure of the Church, an authority that Lord Jhesus Himself gave to St.-Pierre and to all his successors and bishops from that time to this. Every good Christian must accept that."

"I refer to the answer I have already given, and to Our Lord." Jehanne's temples were throbbing, nausea sat like metal in her mouth.

Le Maistre gave Cauchon a concerned glance which the bishop did not see.

His cold, scholastic eyes were fastened upon the sallow-faced girl whose labored breathing wheezed with every rise of her chest.

"You claim to have had many revelations from God, from St.-Michel, Ste.-Marguerite, and Ste.-Catherine," the bishop pressed. "Could any good creature come to you saying that he had revelations from God regarding you, and you would believe him?"

Jehanne moved her weak head in denial. "No Christian in the world could come to me without my knowing whether or not what he said was true, for my Counsel would tell me."

"Could you not imagine that God could reveal something to a good man without your knowledge of it?"

"Of course He could." Her tongue licked cracked lips. "But I would not believe that person unless I had some sign that he was telling the truth, either from him or from my Counsel."

"Do you believe that the Holy Scriptures were revealed to man by God?"

"Yes. We both know that is true."

"Then if the Scriptures say that God wishes man to place himself under the authority of the Church, you also accept that."

"Whatever happens to me," Jehanne murmured, "I can't do or say anything other than I have already said in the trial."

"The Scriptures clearly say, in Matthew 18: 15–17, 'Moreover if thy brother shall trespass against thee, go and tell him his fault between thee and him alone; if he shall hear thee, thou hast gained thy brother. But if he will not hear thee, then take with thee one or two more, that in the mouth of two or three witnesses every word may be established. And if he shall neglect to hear them, tell it unto the Church; but if he neglect to hear the Church, let him be unto thee as heathen and a publican.' Unless you obey the Church," Maurice warned, "the Church will have no choice but to abandon you as a heathen and a Saracen."

"I am a good Christian," she insisted, irked by his gibberish. "I was baptized in the Church, and I will die a good Christian."

"You claim to wish to receive Holy Communion," observed Cauchon. "If you are allowed it, will you submit to the Church?"

"I cannot answer contrary to what I've already said." Jehanne's sunken eyes pleaded with him to stop. "I love God, Your Excellency. I am His devoted servant. And I support the Church with all my power."

"Come, Jehanne," he said with a ghastly attempt at a smile, "would you not like a beautiful and worthy procession to receive your Lord and put you in a state of grace, if you are not already there?"

"All I want is that the Church and all good Catholics should pray for me," she whispered, slipping into the familiar waters of insensibility.

Cauchon smiled triumphantly at Le Maistre, who was by now frowning at the unconscious creature who looked so much like a wasting child.

"Have you heard enough, Inquisitor?" the bishop inquired.

Le Maistre did not respond. He turned away and went to the door. The guards opened it, and the other assessors took that as an indication that the session was over and they also departed.

Cauchon stood over Jehanne for several moments, his mouth curved into a satisfied bow. She was as good as dead.

He waited until an hour after matins tolled at midnight, then slipped out the monastery's kitchen door. Concealed within the darkness, the man in the black robes crept toward the street with his heart galloping in his ears. He clung to the hidden security of the shadowed walls, darting in and out of the moonlight, until he came to the cathedral. With a look back over his shoulder to make sure that he had not been followed, he dashed up the steps on the cathedral's north side and pushed his way through the heavy oaken door. He closed it behind him, careful not to make a sound.

He was at the transept closest to the chapel of Ste.-Anne. Votive candles flickered in colored glass lamps before the statues and shrines nestled in recessed nooks between the vast columns. The high altar to his left burned with a dancing light from two tall tapers. Except for the candles, the cathedral was clothed in an eerie darkness.

Getting his bearings, he shunned the nave and turned to the right, walking very quietly and slowly along the side aisle toward the main entrance at the western end of the building. He passed the chapel of St.-Nicolas, then the sacristy and St.-Eloi. Beyond them, at the feet of St.-Julien, his brothers were waiting for him. Like him, they had cast aside their customary white habits and were covered in cowled black robes. They huddled together in a little clump, and when they saw him they turned expectantly.

"Were you followed, Brother?" asked Ladvenu.

"No," whispered Le Maistre, "at least, I don't think so. I didn't see anyone. God willing, even the spies are in bed." He looked over his shoulder without realizing it.

"How's the girl? Did she recant?" Fontaine queried, hope making him impatient.

"She thinks she's dying, and from what I could tell she's probably right," the Inquisitor murmured. "Cauchon offered her Communion if she would submit to the Church, but she maintained that she will yield only to God." He shook his head, feeling very close to awed. "Even at the brink of death, with salvation or Hell before her, she still resists. I have never seen anything like it. She does not seem to understand the implications behind her refusal. That, or she actually is possessed."

His brows wrinkled in thought within the cowl. "But I do not think that is the case; she does not resemble anyone in the grip of Satan whom I've ever seen. She does not curse God or anyone else. It is most extraordinary, this constancy of hers."

"What was Cauchon's response?" asked Isambard.

"He took it as proof that he was right and I wrong." Le Maistre smiled wryly. "That gave him great satisfaction, I am sure." The humor left him. "I am also certain that he will press me even more vehemently to join him now."

"All of us are approaching a time of choice," warned Ladvenu. "By placing a few innocuous-seeming questions abroad, I've learned that the bishop is most displeased with the rulings that are coming to him from the assessors. Or rather, I should say, that are not coming in. Just under half have not given him anything."

"Good to know we're not the only ones," Isambard remarked. "Tell our brother Le Maistre what Cauchon *is* getting."

"Many insist that they lack proper documentation," continued Ladvenu, "because they were given only the articles on which to make a ruling and none of the actual minutes, and after the first few sessions most of them were not present to hear the questions or the girl's responses. I agree with them, for I was not present either."

"If you had been, you would know as I do that she consistently denied any devotion to the Devil and maintained an implacable love for God," muttered Fontaine, recalling the interrogation in her cell. "There is a foundation for serious doubt in all this."

"There's more," Isambard told Le Maistre. "When our brother Guillaume Adelie asked Cauchon how the accused responded to these twelve new articles, the bishop did not answer him. Adelie later found out quite by accident that they have not been read to her and thus she has not been given an opportunity to respond."

"I've learned that three assessors have written that if Jehanne's revelations come from evil spirits, then many of her statements are suspect," murmured Fontaine. "But they also went on to say that if her voices come from God, what she has said should not be interpreted as evil."

"Everywhere there is unease," Ladvenu whispered. "Everyone feels intimidated, not just us, and there are few who are wholeheartedly convinced of her guilt."

"And there are those who are muttering what three months ago was unthinkable."

"What is that, Brother?" asked Le Maistre.

"That the girl is what she says she is," Isambard said with a tired smile, "that she actually was sent by God."

A somber silence fell over the men. Until this moment something had lurked within each of them, unbidden and unrecognized, but now that Isambard had summoned it into the open, none could force it back into its lair. It sat there, staring at them triumphantly.

"Still, she does refuse to submit to the Church," Le Maistre pointed out, desperate for a shred of uncertainty.

"I inquired from the bishop of Avranches what he thought, and do you know what he said?" asked Isambard with a rhetorical lift of his brow. "He said, 'Young man, what did St.-Thomas Aquinas say about submission to the Church?'

" 'That in cases of doubt such as this touching the Faith,' I said, 'one must have recourse to the Holy Father or to the General Council if it is in session.' The old man smiled then, and shook an approving finger at me. And that, Brothers, is the answer to all this. Cauchon does not have the legal right to try this girl, and he is behaving at variance to canon law. Her case should be brought before the Council at Basle."

"And who among us will bring that to the bishop's attention?" the Inquisitor countered. "You, Brother?"

"No." Isambard smiled. "The girl herself."

"I thought you said that you and Brother Jehan"—he nodded at Fontaine—"advised her to do so in her cell. She has made no mention of it to the bishop, or to anyone else that I know."

"I do not think she really heard us. This trial has sapped her health, and I do not think that she understood what we were saying." And she does not trust us, poor creature, he thought; that really is why she does not hear. Isambard cleared the rasp in his throat. "Furthermore, I do not think that she understands that when she is asked to submit to the Church, it does not mean only to Cauchon and the court but to the Church as a whole. She needs to be told that those attending the Council comprise churchmen from other kingdoms and those of her own king's party. She must be given to understand that if she is willing to yield to their judgment, then no one can legally condemn her."

"Are you offering to be the one who enlightens her?" Le Maistre wondered.

Isambard looked around at his brothers. "Yes."

"Cauchon will be very angry if his prey escapes condemnation," the Inquisitor cautioned. "And that's not considering what you'll have to deal with if the English discover that you've helped her."

"I know," Isambard replied, his eyes grim at the memory of his verbal assault by Warwick. "But my conscience insists upon it. I cannot rest knowing that there is a chance that she can be saved, particularly in view of all this mystery and these pernicious half-truths and outright lies. This is no ordinary heretic. Had the Dauphin never given her an army, no one would be bothering to prosecute her, least of all the English."

"And if she were just another soldier who had never mentioned God in connection with her supposed mission, she would be held for ransom, nothing more," Ladvenu pointed out.

Le Maistre looked down at the sandaled feet, guilt gnawing at his fears.

"You represent the Holy Office, without which no trial for heresy can be taken seriously because that is the Inquisition's sole, duly appointed function. You are in a position to use the power that comes from it. We need your support," Ladvenu urged him. "We need to know that if Cauchon discovers that we have spoken to her, you will not allow him to harm us."

"What we need most," said Isambard, looking the slender monk in the eye, "is that you are as disturbed and revolted by these proceedings as we are, and are as sworn to see justice done. The accused deserves to know that other choices exist by which she can prove her love for both God and the Church."

The Inquisitor turned to Fontaine. "Are you part of this too?"

Fontaine licked his lips and nodded. "I am frightened," he admitted, "but I want to act with compassion as Our Lord commanded. I could not bear it if an innocent person were condemned when I could have prevented it."

Le Maistre's gaze passed from one to the other and rested on Isambard. "After you have informed the accused, what if she will not agree to send an appeal to the Council? What if she still refuses the Church?"

Ladvenu bit his upper lip thoughtfully. Shuffling his feet, Fontaine avoided the Inquisitor's question.

Isambard bowed to his superior's unrelenting stare and said, "Then we shall have no choice but to condemn her. But there remains the possibility that that will not happen, and because of that possibility we must make an attempt."

The Inquisitor sighed, then nodded, their resolve having empowered him into a decision. "Very well. Do your duty. I pledge before St.-Dominique that I will serve as your faithful advocate should it become necessary."

"Thank you, Brother." Isambard embraced Le Maistre and kissed his cheeks. The other monks followed his example. Then they said a quick *Pater* and sneaked, one by one, out of the cathedral and back to the monastery at the half-finished church of St.-Ouen.

By the beginning of May, Jehanne was well enough to be brought back to the Robing Room to face her accusers. While the guards unlocked the chain linking her waist to the wall of her cell, Massieu the usher explained that she was being taken to a public admonition, where the court would give her one more opportunity to confess and repent her errors. She recalled that two days ago the Dominicans had come to her and explained what would happen in this next session. They also told her something very important which she could not remember now. It had gotten lost somehow.

There was no world away from this, no other actuality but the long hours she spent chained to the cot by her feet in the cell's darkest corner, at a safe distance from the drunken, quarreling guards. Her illness had left her unable to think clearly and drained of any physical stamina she still possessed after weeks of little food and haphazard rest. Life in the bleak hole had taken on a shimmering, unreal quality that flitted across the menacing torchlit faces of the soldiers and obscured the merciless linguistic distinctions the interrogators put to her almost daily. She could still recall events that had happened long ago, but could not distinguish one question from another; they all sounded the same, gobbledygook in some strange language, though she knew it was French. In defense against the battering questions, Jehanne retreated into herself, no longer hearing anything that was said to her. Her mind had traveled past weariness into a void where there existed an inability to string two thoughts together and no feeling at all, a place of transcendent pain.

Like a refrain from a recurring nightmare, she was overtaken by a single thought: She was going to die in Rouen very soon. If disease did not kill her, the men of the Church and the English would. The prospect seized and bound her in a panic that shortened her breath and made her want to leap from her body. They would cut off her head and toss the corpse into an unconsecrated ditch without giving her the Last Rites to escort her soul to God. She would be damned forever and barred from Heaven.

As terrible as that possibility was, there was a worse one bearing the same spiritual results: the stake. Ever since she burned her hand on her mother's stove at the age of two, Jehanne had had a wary respect for fire and handled it when she must with great care. She could not contemplate what it would be like to be burned to death. When the horrific imagining elbowed aside death by decapitation and leered at her, its tongue lolling insanely, she ran, shrieking, into the arms of her Counsel.

She rarely heard Them any more. They had been with her when she was ill, yet she could remember none of it, only that St.-Gabriel had come, bringing comfort to her. But although They did not speak, They were still with her, in movements Jehanne saw from the corner of her eye, in the resignation that settled over her despairing spirit and signaled her return to faith when the river of terror had run its course. They whispered that she would not die, and she clung to Their assurances like a drowning person to a boat. She could not renounce Them, no matter what her enemies, and God's, threatened her with. God would release her through a magnificent victory; she had Their pledge. It was the only thing that kept her alive and willing to continue the fight.

As she sat down on the stool in the middle of those learned men, she knew that she was as ready as she would be. Isambard was not allowed near her. He was on a bench next to Ladvenu under the hawk-eyed gaze of the bishop. Something important was to happen today, a thing which Jehanne did not fully comprehend. More questions, to be sure, but something else.

Isambard looked at the chains around the frail wrists with a grim smile. He knew all too well how she felt. As agreed, he and his brothers had gone to her the morning after their surreptitious meeting with Le Maistre, and they patiently explained that she could save herself, body and soul, if she requested in open session to be taken to the Council of Basle. She did not answer; indeed, she seemed not to have heard them. Ladvenu repeated the proposition, very slowly and deliberately, hoping in vain to make her understand. A numbed, uncomprehending gaze from those enormous sunken eyes was their only response. With a sudden start Isambard realized that to her, the Dominicans were no different from Cauchon and his men. At that point he broke off the attempt and, his heart weighted by failure, returned to the abbey with his brothers.

Within a few hours the bishop had demanded the trio's presence in the refectory. Isambard, Ladvenu, and Fontaine had been betrayed by Jehanne's English guards. Cauchon was awesome in his fury, and after a long harangue during which he called into question both their manhood and their piety, he promised to have them hanged. Not one of them doubted he would do it. Pale and shaken, they were dismissed. Fontaine went directly to his horse and galloped out of Rouen as though all the demons in Hell were after him.

Ladvenu and Isambard wasted no time going to Le Maistre, who renewed his promise to protect them. They were still with him when Cauchon arrived in person to condemn their treachery. In the confrontation that followed, the Inquisitor told him that if the bishop harmed his brothers, he would permanently absent himself from the trial, thereby depriving it of the Holy Office and rendering it invalid. Checked for the time being, Cauchon stormed from the abbey, leaving them free to worry about Jehanne now that death no longer hung over their own heads.

Cauchon stood up, wrenching Isambard's thoughts to the present.

"Brothers in Christe, my lords," he bowed to the English. "After she had been thoroughly interrogated, this woman replied to the articles judicially prepared against her by the Promoter, and we sent the digest of her confessions, drawn up and summarized in the form of twelve articles, to doctors and other persons educated in canon, and civil law, for the purpose of obtaining their advice."

There was an uncomfortable rustle among the assessors. In one way or another, most were caught in the storm of intrigues and counterplots swirling about the city, and they all knew of the desertions and threats. Now many suspected that the accused had not confessed to anything.

Unperturbed, the bishop continued his speech and said that although firmly convinced of Jehanne's guilt, he nevertheless had not yet ruled in the case. In private interrogations, the Devil had prevented her from renouncing her evil spirits. Many honest, conscientious, and learned men had therefore advised that the court had a duty to exhort and reprimand the prisoner in a public session of admonishment, and to that end they were assembled that day. He introduced Jehan de Châtillon, archdeacon of Evreux, "an old and learned master of theology, one particularly understanding in these matters," who would charitably admonish the accused, uttering many things profitable for the salvation of her body and soul.

Did Jehanne understand what he had said?

Yes, she replied.

A venerable cleric with wisps of white hair sticking out beneath his cap creaked to his feet. His face was kind and gullible. The archdeacon explained to Jehanne that all faithful Christians were compelled and obliged to believe and hold firmly to the Faith and its articles. She must, he said, correct and reform herself, her words and her deeds, in accordance with the advice of the distinguished doctors and masters who were trained in the interpretation of divine, canon, and civil law.

"Read your book," Jehanne said, nodding at the collection of papers he held, "and then I will answer. I am in the hands of God, my Creator, whom I love with all my heart."

"What reply do you have to the general admonition?" Châtillon asked, peering at her near-sightedly.

"I await the words of my Judge, the King of Heaven and earth." Jehanne's response was a colorless recitation. She felt empty inside and completely alone.

The old man then read a condensation of the twelve articles. Jehanne was proud and arrogant; she believed that she understood more about matters of faith than educated and lettered men; she refused to submit her words and deeds to the Church Militant; she persisted in wearing that abominable clothing; her apparitions were lies and vanities; and in the darkness of her soul, she insisted that she had not sinned. Châtillon repeated the meaning of the Church Militant, forcing Jehanne to listen to it for the hundredth time.

"I believe in the Church on earth," she sighed, worn down by the repetition, "but as I've said before, I refer my words and deeds to God. I believe that the Church Militant cannot err or falter, but I refer myself to God, Who commanded me to do and say all I have."

"Do you not recognize the authority of any earthly judge?" the archdeacon asked. "Do you not recognize the authority of the Holy Father, the Pope?"

Ladvenu and Isambard leaned forward in their seats.

"I will say nothing more about this," Jehanne answered with a fatigued shake of her head. "I have a good Master, God, Whom I trust in everything."

"Woman, if you do not acquiesce to the power of Holy Mother Church"—Châtillon frowned, raising his voice—"you will be excommunicated as a heretic and be sentenced by other judges to be burned."

"I can say nothing more," she mumbled. "If I saw the fire, I would continue to say what I already have and nothing else."

"Would you submit to the judgment of the Pope?" he insisted, his wrinkled visage reddening in frustration.

Something tried to whisper in her ear, but she did not grasp it. "Take me to him, and I will answer him."

"My lords." Isambard got up from his seat. "The accused has requested to be taken before the Holy Father. I respectfully advise that she be given that right as an avowed Christian."

The assessors murmured, some venturing to nod in agreement. Low growls hummed among the English.

Cauchon jerked his head around at the young man. "The Holy Father is in Rome, at a great distance from Rouen," he snarled. "If the woman does not submit to his representatives in the form of this court, it is the same as her not submitting to the Pope."

"The central question in this case is this," Isambard said, refusing to be cowed. "Are the prisoner's apparitions from God or from Satan? It is a matter so vital to the well-being of both the accused and the Church that it should be left to the highest authority to decide." The monk continued speaking even as he saw Cauchon's anger mount to the point of breaking. "Let the case be brought to the Council at Basle, where many of our brothers from the accused's own party have assembled, along with doctors and masters from the whole of Christendom."

Jehanne's ears perked up at Isambard's last words, and she finally realized what the Dominicans had said to her while she slept through their visits to her cell. The fog surrounding her lifted. She suddenly saw everything with an animated clarity.

"Oh, yes!" she cried, hopeful for a way out of this nightmare. "If there are gathered together churchmen of my party, I will gladly submit to their judgment!"

"Your Excellency," an alert Isambard interceded, "I submit to the court that the defendant is willing to yield to the supremacy of the Council."

"*In the Devil's name, be silent, both of you!*"

An eerie hush hit the courtroom like a slap.

Everyone—the defendant, assessors, even the English—stared at the glowering, wild-eyed bishop, dumbfounded by what he had said. For the first time Ladvenu saw the extent of Cauchon's madness, and a premonition of dread began to form in his soul. Isambard sat down slowly, his face wan and still. No one else moved.

Many moments passed.

It was Manchon the notary who finally disturbed the quiet. "Your Excellency," he ventured in a timid voice, "do you wish that I record the prisoner's response?"

"That is not necessary." Cauchon shot a heavy load of malice at Isambard; the monk felt it between his eyes like the impact of a lance.

"Oh, yes, of course!" Jehanne shouted, very close to tears. "You write down what is against me and nothing that is for me!"

A spontaneous roar erupted among the assessors, then swept into a windstorm, liberating weeks of constraint and doubt. Disordered, they congregated in little cliques, no longer bothering to whisper their skepticism but openly communicating their disapproval of the trial's now flagrant irregularities. Isambard looked over the heads of the theologians and saw Cauchon standing in front of his chair, rigid, red-faced, inarticulate with rage. The decrepit archdeacon was looking about helplessly.

Jehanne watched it all in a daze. She did not understand precisely what was going on, but she was struck with the realization that not everyone here was against her. It was apparent from the half-hidden black glances being thrown at Cauchon that many of these men would set her free if given the chance. The Dominicans had told her that there was discord within the court, but she had not believed them. Since coming to Rouen, she had come to consider all churchmen as adversaries. Ladvenu caught her eye and in his smile she saw him at last.

The heavy boom of a book impacting upon a table, the sound overlaid with a basso cry of "Order! Order!" sounded through the chaotic babble.

When no one responded, Cauchon again crashed the tome onto Manchon's table and shouted further commands for quiet, this time louder than before. Many years of training came to the fore and the monastic tongues stopped in mid-sentence, one or two in the middle of a word.

Cauchon was standing at the table with the battered book in his left hand. His hair stuck out from his cap like wings on a bird of prey, and his wrinkled countenance sagged in a furious mask. He let the book fall again. It sounded like a door slamming shut.

In ones and twos, the masters and doctors began to retake their seats. The more rebellious lingered for a few moments before they, too, sat down.

"I would like to remind our young colleague," the bishop said in a voice charged with malevolence, "that the accused was twice offered to choose a counsel from the membership of this court, and twice she refused, claiming that all the counsel she needed could be found in her demonic apparitions. She has repudiated her right to be advised, and has not been granted you to fill that role. And the Church does not sanction it."

Cauchon bore into the young monk with all his strength, twisting his arm behind him. "The Church admonishes you to remember your vow of obedience, to your Order and to your ecclesiastical superiors. You have strayed very close to the violation of that vow today, Brother Isambard. You will not do so again."

Isambard blinked and looked down at his hands. His face burned with a mixture of personal humiliation and outrage at the bishop's blatant disregard for justice. Dozens of eyes avoided the burning gaze with which Cauchon swept the room.

He sat down with a calculated dignity. "Master Châtillon, resume the admonition."

The archdeacon stood and squinted at Jehanne. He cleared his throat importantly. "Abandoning all womanly modesty and decency, you have insisted, and continue to insist, that you will not forsake that disgraceful costume, as ordered by the Church."

"I will put on a woman's dress to go to Mass and receive Holy Communion," Jehanne replied, firm in her wide-awake resolve, "but when I return, I must put on what I'm wearing now."

"But, dear child," the old man crooned, "you have no need of man's clothing now that you are not leading an army and are in prison."

"I have every need of it, for my guards have tried to violate me, and it is my only protection."

A stunned murmur raced through the room. The English lords whispered furiously among themselves.

"Don't write that down, you fool!" Cauchon shouted at Manchon, frightening the young man so that he knocked over his inkwell. He quickly righted it, but not before spilling a thin trail of ink across his table.

Soon, Cauchon told himself, his brothers would return from Paris with the University's ruling, without doubt an unqualified judgment of excommunication and abandonment to secular justice. That task would be carried out by the other party in this venture. The bishop nearly smiled. Behind him, like an elder brother, loomed the full power and might that was England.

"Master Châtillon?" He gestured for the old interrogator to begin again.

"The Church demands that you put on a woman's gown, permanently and absolutely."

"When I have done what God sent me to do, I will wear a woman's dress."

"It is blasphemous to say that God and His saints have commanded you to dress like that," the archdeacon fumed, "and when you declare otherwise you stumble into error and evil."

"I do not blaspheme God or the saints."

"The voices that told you to dress as a man are evil! For you to give them your faith is a corresponding evil."

"They are from God." These men did not know anything, for all their books and their schooling. They had not been with her when she spoke with her Counsel; they had not seen the soul-whistling, transformative visions. If they could, they would know that her Teachers were what she knew them to be.

"Concerning your sign to the one you call king," Châtillon muttered, turning to another page, "would you be willing to refer to the archbishop of Reims and the others, knights and squires, who you claim were present when this event occurred?"

"Bring them here and I will answer," Jehanne stated. "Otherwise, I will not submit to you about that."

"Are you willing to submit to the cathedral at Poitiers where you were examined?"

Jehanne threw back her head and looked at the ceiling. She started laughing, painfully, making no sound. It was funny, these toys they kept dangling in front of her. Today, in Cauchon's refusal to allow her to take her case to Basle, she had seen his holy pretensions stripped away like a peeled onion, rotten within, revealing the scorn for real justice and the magnitude of the hatred in his decaying center. He had invoked the name of the Evil One. There was no way out for Jehanne, and this present offer was another trap.

She looked past the fragile graybeard at Cauchon. "Do you think that you can catch me this way and draw me to you?"

"Under pain of excommunication and abandonment by the loving protection of the Church," shouted Châtillon, "the court demands that you submit to the Church Militant!"

Jehanne said nothing.

"If the Church abandons you, you will be in great danger; your soul in peril of Eternal fire, and your body ravaged by temporal fire."

She shook her head in slow denial. "You will not act against me as you say without your suffering evil in body and soul."

There was a collective gasp. The monks crossed themselves in a commotion of fluttering sleeves. Two Englishmen made signs against the evil eye.

"You are required to give one good reason why you will not submit to the Church."

Jehanne held him in her wavering sights. She wanted to cry out, Because you are all fools who know nothing of God! But they would only pick that up and fashion it into a weapon with which to bludgeon her.

She did not answer.

Battered down, defeated by her obstinacy, the old man shook his head. "I have no more arguments, Your Excellency."

Cauchon invited the court to admonish her at will. Maurice railed at her; Courcelles the same. They went back over identical territory and received similar answers until even the assessors were tired of it and wanted nothing better than to adjourn. Cauchon was pleased that this assembled body, comprised of many rebellious and tempted men, could now put their minds and consciences to rest, having seen the heretic's recalcitrance for themselves. When the third assessor who had made the attempt seemed ready to explode with frustration, Cauchon raised his hands. The weary monk sat down.

The bishop gave Jehanne a twisted smile. "You must give serious consideration to the admonishments you have heard today, and you must declare your answer."

"How long do I have to think about it?"

"You must respond here, now."

She looked down at the tips of her boots. When it was clear that she would say nothing more, Cauchon adjourned the court and Jehanne was removed to her cell.

CHAPTER SEVENTEEN

The Great Victory

May 9–30, 1431

hen they came for her that morning, Jehanne found the climb to the *donjon* of Rouen Castle much more arduous than she had expected it to be. A year ago she could have taken these steps at a brisk trot, but now it was all she could do to lift one foot to the next step above it. Her legs were weak and ached from disuse as though stabbed with fiery knives. A reeling dizziness throbbed in her head and she nearly swooned.

Once she did stumble when she foolishly looked down and was assailed by a sudden lightheaded spasm. The English jailers behind her seized her arms, then roughly forced her to her feet. Ahead of them Massieu stopped and looked down at her, his plain face recoiling in pity and a flickering shame. When he saw that she could continue, the usher resumed his climb. Their steps clapped against the stones in a weighty, portentous chorus, taking them to a destination known to all but Jehanne.

The top of the staircase opened into the circular keep. Cauchon was waiting there, and the white-robed Inquisitor, looking very ill at ease. Present also were Loiseleur, Courcelles, and six other assessors whom Jehanne knew by sight. Two laymen were with them, not soldiers from the looks of them but townsfolk of the lower class. One was beefy and barrel-chested, with a matted beard covering his round, florid face. The second man was smaller, thinner, though not one who could be considered a weakling. Both were wearing leather jerkins and pants stained with spots from past meals and what appeared to be dark splotches of blood. Their dull faces took in the fabled Witch of Orléans with a twinge of disappointment. Jehanne knew what they were thinking, that she was just ordinary after all.

"Do you know why you were brought here?" Cauchon asked.

Jehanne looked at the tips of his shiny red boots and shook her head.

"Take a look around you," he ordered with a tiny smile.

She raised her head. The room was crowded with instruments the likes of which

Jehanne had heard about in hushed whispers but never actually seen. There was an iron cage hanging behind the bishop's head from a thick chain, bolted into a crossbeam running the length of the ceiling. Anyone locked into it would be fastened into place by shackles, unable to stand or to sit; left there indefinitely, a prisoner could die of hunger or thirst. Below it and off to the side, a long trestle of rough-hewn wood, its planks blackened with bloodstains, jutted out from the wall. At either end of it strong leather straps attached to pulleys, and the pulleys to a wheel from which extended handgrips. Next to that a low table held a viselike apparatus with a screw that could be turned to crush fingers; like the rack, it was caked in old blood. A hollow, hinged boot prickling with long spikes waited on the floor. Implements of various sinister configurations—some bladed, others bearing hooks and saws—hung from pegs protruding from the wall. Embedded next to them were shackles for hands and feet, and nearby an iron rod was being prepared in the glowing coals of a brazier. In case the poker did not prove persuasive, rusted knives of many different contours and sizes sat on a table within easy reach of the brazier.

Jehanne's face drained of color and her knees buckled under a torrent of horror that nearly swept her to the floor. Deliver me from evil, she chanted, deliver me from evil, God give me strength!

"Now," Cauchon said, taking a step toward her, "do you know why you are here?"

"You are going to torture me." She knew now who those two men were and why they were present.

"Perhaps," the bishop replied with a lift of his eyebrows, "perhaps not, if you submit to the Church."

"What is the truth about the sign you gave your king?" demanded Loiseleur, beginning the attack.

"I have already told you," Jehanne muttered, swaying a little, "and I stand by what I said."

"Will you submit to the Church and confess that your voices are minions of the Devil?"

"I recognize that the Church cannot err, but I submit to God Who made me and to Him above all others." The answer was rote, having been given a hundred times already. She could not keep her eyes from darting to the knives and the boot.

They cannot torture me! Oh God, my God, give me courage!

"Will you submit to the Church Militant as regards your dress?" asked Courcelles.

She bowed her head and after a moment, sighed. No matter what they did to her, she could not let them have her soul. It was the only thing they had not taken from her. She shook her head. "I must continue as I am."

Loiseleur glanced with helpless frustration at the bishop.

"Jehanne, the Church has available to her many means of bringing her stray lambs back to the fold. Do you want to be put to the torture?" Cauchon asked sternly.

She gave the rack and the cage an involuntary glance.

All at once, she knew that they would not do it. Her Guides had never hinted that she would be tortured. It was another trick. She raised a defiant stare to Cauchon's impassivity.

"If you pull me limb from limb and drive my soul from my body, I will still say what I have. And if you do torture me, I shall say afterward that whatever I confessed was forced out of me and did not reflect my true thoughts."

She saw a glimmer of uncertainty flash through the bishop's eyes, and under her breath prayed that it meant that she had outmaneuvered him.

Before he could respond, Le Maistre pushed himself forward. "Jehanne, for the love of Heaven, submit to the Church!" the Dominican urged, his slender body shaking with fear for her. "Do you want to die?"

Her face softened at his genuine anguish. "On Holy Cross Day, St.-Gabriel came to me and gave me great comfort. I asked whether I should submit to the Church since that is what all of you want from me, and he told me that if I want God to help me, I must trust Him for all my deeds."

She took her time to look at each of the men. They were moving at the same angle as the floor, in and out of focus. She had to catch them one at a time. "I have always known that God is my only Master," she told the man in the violet mantle, "and that the Evil One has no power over me."

"How do you know that this new spirit is St.-Gabriel?" inquired Loiseleur.

"Because he told me so, and my Counsel told me so." Her reply came out in a moan. The weight of his stupid question was like a stone added to a growing mound that threatened to bury her. Loiseleur had not been there, he had not seen, none of them had. And she did not have the words to tell him what he wanted to know.

"How can you be certain that he was not lying, that he was not in fact another demon?"

"Because of the great comfort he gave me," she answered without hesitation.

"What else did he tell you?" A barely hidden wonder colored Le Maistre's question.

"I asked Them if I am to be burned, and They said what They always say, that I must trust God and He will help me."

Le Maistre wiped his mouth with a shaking hand. Three of the assessors exchanged wordless communications, comprehensible only to themselves. Loiseleur shook his head, resembling a man trying to shake water from his ears. When he looked at Jehanne again, she saw sudden disquiet sprint across his face, settling into creases at the corners of his eyes. He asked her silently, Who are you? What are you?

The bishop simply held her in his unrelenting sights. "About the sign of the crown that you showed the archbishop of Reims," he finally said. "Would you be willing for us to consult him?"

"Bring him here and then I will answer you," she said, feeling a small stirring of the old Power. "He would not dare contradict what I have told you."

Cauchon's eyes narrowed. Something was eating at him; something had made him uneasy. He turned to the two laymen and said, "You may go for now, but be available in case we need you."

"But Your Excellency," protested Courcelles, "she must be put to the torture, for the sake of her errant soul!"

"We need to deliberate further before we take such a drastic step, Brother," the bishop replied. He nodded at Massieu. "Take her back to her cell."

"But Your Excellency—"

"I said that is all, Brother," Cauchon lifted his voice to Courcelles like an angry hand. "We shall convene at my house in two days' time to discuss this further." He waved his arm at Massieu and the guards. "Take her away."

The soldiers grabbed Jehanne's arms and dragged her from the torture chamber. Lightheaded with relief, she almost collapsed as they made their way slowly down the twisting steps to the courtyard.

Thank you, Lord, she sang, thank you for my life. She had won a reprieve, for now.

Jehanne lay on the cot they had not taken away from the time she fell ill. Her feet were chained to it instead of to the large wooden block, which remained where it had been for five months. Hands folded behind her head, she looked sightlessly at the ceiling, indifferent to the dice-tossing guards on the other side of the cell. Her heart was racing because of what had just occurred.

A short while ago, when she lay much as she did now, she suddenly heard laughter and the sound of jubilant, masculine voices coming toward the cell. They were not churchmen, for the theologians always came so quietly that she did not know that they were there until the key rattled in the door. She could hear this high-spirited crowd a long way off, out in the courtyard and in through the door at the bottom of the steps, drunk and singing. When they were just outside the cell door, she caught the cadences of English accents among the French. There was a brief commotion and the door swung open.

The guards immediately bolted to their feet as Warwick, his aide the earl of Stafford, and three other gentlemen entered. All were elegantly dressed as though they had come from a party. It was the first time Jehanne had seen the military lords in anything but leather and chainmail. The golden threads in their wide-shouldered tunics shimmered in the torchlight at odd variance with the dismal prison, and the perfume wafting from their fresh shaves overpowered her own longstanding putrescence.

With a start, Jehanne recognized among them Jehan de Luxembourg and young Haimond de Macy, the same Burgundian who had tried to take liberties with her at Beaurevoir. She did not know the last man, dressed in bishop's robes, but reasoned from his resemblance to Luxembourg that he must be a close relative, a brother perhaps.

She sat up slowly as they approached her.

"Well, Jehanne," said Luxembourg, staring with his good eye, "your fortunes have much declined since I saw you last." His words were slurred, and it was obvious that he was drunk.

Go away, she thought, I do not want you here.

"But cheer up, I have come to ransom you." His teeth spread so that he looked like a grinning, one-eyed cat.

The other men chuckled. Macy nudged Luxembourg's brother with a confidential elbow. Warwick pursed his lips and impaled Jehanne with hate-filled gray eyes. He was most definitely sober, unlike his Burgundian cohorts. So was Stafford. His wide, pockmarked face was deadly quiet.

"No, you haven't." She sighed.

"Indeed," the nobleman insisted. He lightly fingered the end of his mustache. "I have come to ransom you, on condition, of course, that you vow never to take up arms against us again."

There was another mirthful exchange among his companions. Even the Englishmen smiled.

"In God's name, you are making fun of me." Jehanne scowled. "I know that you have neither the wish nor the power to set me free."

"It is true!" The picture of wounded truth, he spread his hands apart mockingly. "I have given my lord Warwick here"—he smiled at the Englishman—"a great deal of money to ensure your liberty."

"I do not believe you." She put her hand to the dull pain hammering between her eyes. Leave me alone!

"Oh, you do not believe me," he crooned with exaggerated offense. "The Maid does not believe me, gentlemen, when my intentions are most honorable and generous, considering that I am a poor man." Macy chuckled at the joke, enjoying the torment to the girl who had so fiercely spurned him.

Jehanne snorted ironically and rolled her eyes. Then she secured Luxembourg with the fragile strands of her Power. "You are lying. I well know that these English will kill me, thinking that after I'm dead they will overrun France."

She moved her sights to Warwick. He smiled, very slowly, telling her with his eyes: That's right, we will; and I shall light the fire. His arrogance, his supreme confidence and determination, the ruthlessness behind his smile, all combined to resurrect the anger which she thought had died to sadness.

"But what they do not know is that killing me won't help them because they do not have Heaven's support, and even if there were a hundred thousand more *goddons* in France than there are now, they still would not gain the kingdom!"

She saw the knife flash in Stafford's hand almost before she had finished speaking. Firelight from the torch Macy was holding caught a glint of steel as the weapon began its descent.

Jehanne instinctively raised her hand to deflect the blow that never came.

"No!" Warwick caught his assistant's arm just inches from its target. Leaning very close to the soldier's ear, he whispered loudly, "We have something much better than this waiting for her."

Stafford made no move but maintained his grip on the dagger. Jehanne could see the desire to slit her throat in his fierce features, and strangely, a part of herself wished that he would. His narrow eyes impaled her as though he would disobey Warwick's order regardless of the cost.

Then, suddenly, he loosened his stance and frowned at his superior.

"You'll have your revenge," said Warwick, taking the knife. "Come, let us leave this place."

Jehanne's enemies did not linger after that. They departed as quickly as they had come, except that when they left they were no longer laughing.

She willed her face into an expressionless mask, and ignoring the black scowls of her jailers lay down again on her back. Grey and his men muttered against her, using the same obscenities to which they customarily resorted, but made no move to bother her. Soon they were once again slurping their ale and tossing dice for pennies, having forgotten all about her.

We have something much better than this waiting for her.

The headsman's ax? The stake? They had threatened often enough to burn her; was that what he meant?

No, it wasn't just that. There was something else which Stafford would do, hinted Warwick; and she had seen that other thing in the earl's eyes and in the way Stafford looked at her when he relinquished the knife. It slithered across an unprotected place at the bottom of her spirit, leaving a cold, slimy trail with its passage.

She was not able to calm her sprinting heart. Something was coming. For the past week she had begun to feel the relentless rise of events toward some calamitous end, growing steadily nearer with every passing day. As much as she tried to obey the instruction of her Counsel to remain firm, there were moments such as this when the gnawing fears rushed to overtake her, and then as now her soul cried with all its power for release from these terrible circumstances.

Her Counsel had vowed liberation through a magnificent victory, and They had never, ever lied to her. But where was that liberation, she wondered, why was it taking so long? The English would never hold her for ransom no matter how much the King offered to pay, so that path to freedom was blocked. Was Charles having difficulty raising the money to pay for the mercenaries necessary to descend in vast numbers upon Rouen, was that it? Failing a military operation, would God send a mighty storm of vengeance to level the castle in rain and wind, a mark of His omnipotent hand that even the English would not be able to withstand or disregard?

Whatever it was, she pleaded silently that He would dispatch it soon, for she knew that she could not live much longer in prison. It was apparent from the looseness of her rank clothing that she had lost a great deal of weight, and the frailty of her body told her that starvation lay in her immediate future unless God intervened.

She sought solace in the past. Her thoughts drifted back to Domrémy, to the days of her childhood before the advent of the visions which had set her upon her path. How simple life was then. She had had nothing to worry about but marauding skinners. Her more immediate concerns had revolved around the day-to-day habits of village life, dictated by the seasons.

She remembered how, when she was very small, she used to lay her head in Maman's lap and Isabelle would brush her long, thick hair, crooning a folk song that Jehanne loved about a little bird who flew to Heaven and returned with a sunbeam to build his nest. If she closed her eyes and kept very still, she could see her mother's round, apple-cheeked face and feel the gentle hand stroking her hair.

Oh, Maman! she wanted to sob, I didn't even get a chance to kiss you good-bye!

Stop this, Jehanne! If you think about the past you will start bawling like a child, and then at the least these English will think you weak and laugh at you, or worse than that, you will indeed finally tumble into a raving madness. There is no past for you until you can have a future again.

She made herself think of something else.

What was happening with the war? She had not thought about that since the trial began. It would be useless to ask anyone here for news. Even if they deigned to answer, they would probably lie. Charles must still be King, for if he were not, his enemies would certainly be gloating over the fact. Likewise, Paris presumably remained in enemy hands; the *goddon* soldiers would have raged had it fallen to the Armagnacs.

But what of d'Alençon? Was he still alive, or had he been slain in an attempt to regain his ancestral estates? She knew from her Counsel that Pierre was not dead, but They would not tell her more about his fate. Was he in a cell like this one; would he be ransomed as Pasquerel had predicted? And the others? Had any of them passed through death to God?

Questions without answers; her head ached from the speculation. The only thing she knew for certain was that she was not to be tortured. Something had changed the bishop's mind about that; she had seen it in the sagging frown, in his wavering eyes. Perhaps even he was open to some spark of God's love within him, however feeble.

Dear God, please help me, please do not abandon me. I am so afraid of this thing that I feel approaching me.

She waited for a response from her Counsel, and when none was forthcoming, she drifted off into a battle-ready sleep.

"We have decreed that you shall once more be urged to return to the way of Truth for the salvation of your soul and your body," Cauchon intoned, leveling a majestic look at his exhausted prisoner.

"In accordance with the solemnity of these proceedings, we have sent to our mother, the University of Paris, for her ruling in your case. Our messengers have returned with the verdict given by the Faculties of Theology and Decrees, and our brother Pierre Maurice will now read them to you." He sat down in the grand, carved chair that Warwick had provided for him.

The room directly beneath Jehanne's cell had a window, and she marveled at the foreign sunshine which cast a square, quartered frame upon the floor. Present to hear this latest remonstrance were the Dominicans, Le Maistre, and Isambard, together with Jehanne's particular antagonists, the promoter d'Estivet, Midi, and Beaupère. Bishop Louis de Luxembourg, whom Jehanne now definitely knew to be comte Jehan's brother, was there, among the half-dozen other assessors. They sat on benches with their backs to the warm sunlight and their hostile faces turned toward Jehanne. Two *guisarme*-wielding English guards stood at the door.

Maurice rose from his seat and cleared his throat, then began to read from papers bearing a green ribbon. "Firstly, Jehanne, you have said that from the age of thirteen you have had revelations and apparitions of angels, of Ste.-Catherine and Ste.-Marguerite, whom you have frequently seen with your bodily eyes; and that they have often spoken with you and told you many things set forth at length in your trial.

"The clerks of the University of Paris have considered the manner and end of these revelations, the matter of the things revealed, and the quality of your person; and having considered everything relevant, they declare that it is all false, seductive, pernicious, that such revelations and apparitions are superstitions and proceed from evil and diabolical spirits."

Of course. Jehanne lowered her eyes to her folded hands, giving them an ironic smile. It makes no difference what you think, she thought, only half-listening to him. Soon God will send His victory to take me away from this place.

One after another, the monk read the verdicts of damnation. Her story of the sign she gave her king was presumptuous, a misleading lie, an undertaking contrary and derogatory to the dignity of angels. She had declared that she knew her visions to issue from angels because the spirits told her that they were so, and in believing them Jehanne displayed an eager credulity, deviating from the Faith. In admitting that she knew future events she gave evidence of her being superstitious, vain, presumptuous (again), and guilty of the sin of divination.

She blasphemed God by wearing masculine clothing and charging that she did so at the command of the Almighty; she was full of vain boasting and was given to idolatry and self-worship. By taking up arms against the English and the Burgundians, she committed herself to treachery, cruelty, sedition, and bloodthirstiness.

When she left home without her parents' permission, she broke the commandment to honor her father and mother, causing them great distress; unrepentant, she claimed that she did so at God's command, which was blasphemous and an error of faith. Her leap from Beaurevoir tower was an attempt at suicide, brought on by the sin of despair and compounded by a greater sin of presuming God's forgiveness for her action.

She had said that her spirits promised to lead her to Paradise if she pledged her virginity, and in this she was rash and erred in the Faith. Jehanne asserted that God loves some people and hates others, and that moreover, she had learned from her voices that He did not love the English. In this, also, she was blasphemous and a transgressor of the commandment to love one's neighbor.

She knelt before her spirits and kissed them; she believed they issued from God and she could tell that they were angels, not demons; and in doing so she revealed herself to be an idolatress, an invoker of demons, an apostate from the Faith, a maker of false statements, and a swearer of an unlawful oath.

Finally, she refused to submit to the wisdom of Holy Mother Church as related to all the above matters, stubbornly declaring that she would submit only to God. For that, the University masters and doctors found her to be schismatic, an unbeliever in the unity and authority of the Church, apostate, and obstinately erring in the Faith.

Maurice lowered the pages and gave her a look of tender regard overflowing with transparent hypocrisy. "Jehanne, dearest friend, it is now time, near the end of your trial, to think well over all that has been said. Although you have been admonished four times by our lord bishop of Beauvais and by the lord vicar of the Inquisition, and by other doctors appointed by them, for the good of your soul and the ease of their consciences, you have not wished to listen."

She stared at him from her stool. You are all fools, she thought, and God will deliver me as He has promised. I am not your "dearest friend" nor are you mine. I have no friend here but God.

The monk went on to exhort her to return to the true Faith for which Lord Jhesus had died to save her from sin. She had believed lightly in her apparitions, he said, without consulting prelates or learned ecclesiastics who could enlighten her, as she should have done considering her ignorance in such matters.

"Take an example," he said. "Suppose your king had appointed you to defend a fortress, forbidding you to let anyone enter. Would you not refuse to admit whoever claimed to come in his name but brought no letters or authentic sign?"

Jehanne gave no indication that she had heard him. Her sunken-eyed glare unnerved Maurice a little, but he forged on.

"Likewise Our Lord Jhesus Christe, when He ascended into Heaven, committed the government of His Church to St.-Pierre and his successors, forbidding them to receive those who claimed to come in His name but who brought no token but their own words. So you should not have put faith in those which you say came to you, nor ought we to believe in you, since God commands the contrary."

You do not know what you are saying, she told him silently. You have never seen God; you have only your old books.

"Jehanne, consider this: If a soldier or other person born in your king's realm said, 'I will not obey the king or submit to his officers,' would you not say this man should be condemned? What then should you say of yourself, a baptized daughter of the Church, if you do not obey Christe's officers, the prelates of the Church? What judgment shall you bring upon yourself?

"I beg and exhort you, cease from uttering these things if you love your Creator; obey the Church and submit to its judgments. Know that if you do not, if you persevere in your error, your soul will be condemned to eternal punishment and perpetual torture, and your body will perish. Do not allow pride and empty shame to hold you back because you fear the loss of the great honors which have come to you from the world. The honor of God and the salvation of your soul must come first.

"Therefore, on behalf of your judges, I beg, admonish, and exhort you to correct and amend your errors, return to the way of truth by submission to the Church. By so doing you shall redeem your soul and save your body from death. If you do not, know that your soul will be lost and your body destroyed. From these ills may Our Lord preserve you!"

The chamber went silent. His duty done, the monk sat down next to Beaupère.

Isambard was watching her carefully, probably praying that she would yield. The Inquisitor looked sadly at the cross the windowpanes made on the sunny floor in front of him. The others waited. Cauchon's face was remorseless.

It does not matter what any of you think. Very soon God will deliver me from your evil. "As for my words and deeds, which I declared in the trial," she answered in a cracking voice, "I refer to them and will maintain them."

The assessors released their dismay in a communal sigh. The bishop sent a conspiratorial glance to d'Estivet.

"Do you not think that you are bound to submit yourself to the Church Militant or to anyone other than God?" asked Beaupère.

"I submit to what I have always said during this trial."

Midi looked at Beaupère and shrugged.

"If I were condemned," Jehanne ventured, "and if I saw the fire and the executioner ready to kindle the faggots, and if I were in the middle of it, I would say nothing different from what I've already said, and would maintain it until my death."

The assessors murmured at her fearlessness. Isambard could no longer look at her, and she knew that he considered her lost. Cauchon stood up slowly. "Do you, Promoter, or you, Jehanne, have anything further to add?"

"No, Your Excellency," d'Estivet replied.

Jehanne shook her head.

"We, competent judges in this trial, according to your refusal to answer further, declare this trial ended," the bishop stated. "With this conclusion pronounced, we assign tomorrow as the day on which you shall hear us give justice and pronounce sentence, which shall afterward be carried out and proceeded with according to law and reason." He beckoned to the guards. "Return the prisoner to her cell."

Jehanne went with them, dragging the chains between her ankles.

Please, dear Lord, now is the time. I beg You, send me the liberating victory You promised me!

She stayed awake through the night, alert for the sound of cannon on the horizon. Toward dawn she realized that she had been in captivity for exactly one year.

Beaupère came to her cell with Massieu not long after sunup that Thursday. The assessor explained that she was to be taken to a scaffold especially erected in the cemetery adjoining the abbey of St.-Ouen, where she would hear a sermon and be sentenced. She listened through a haze of fatigue, barely comprehending what he had said.

"Do you understand?" He frowned.

Jehanne looked at him with sunken, red-rimmed eyes. She nodded.

As in a dream, she saw the guard unlock the chains binding her feet to the cot. Massieu took her arm very gently and helped her to stand. The room spun around and for a moment she felt that she would faint. She put her hands on either side of her head to steady it. The sensation ebbed slowly, and she waited, wobbling a little, while the soldiers reattached the shackles to her ankles. Then, with the monks in attendance and followed by the guards, she walked shakily down the familiar eight steps to the courtyard.

Jehanne blinked at the sharp light and put up a hand to shield her eyes. It was a bright, fair day, and across the mild sky razor-sharp clouds that looked as though they had been flattened by a giant hand were scudding toward the east. The small procession—Beaupère leading the way, followed by Jehanne and Massieu, then the soldiers—crossed the square and passed through the south gate where a horse-drawn cart was waiting.

Jehanne and the monks got in. The soldiers positioned themselves on either side of the transport. With a click of his tongue, the driver flicked the reins, and the vehicle wended its way down a narrow, twisting street past a church, and onto another lane as far as the corner where the street made a sharp left turn.

There were suddenly scores of people lining the streets, and Jehanne gasped at the sheer weight of their numbers and the emotions assailing her. It had been so long since she had seen people—ordinary, normal people—that they seemed alien to her, part of a world to which she no longer belonged and could never return. As the cart took her past them, townsfolk gaped in silence at the infamous, emaciated prisoner whom they had been told they should hate for her wickedness. Many women and some of the men crossed themselves at the sight of her. Jehanne could not remember the last time she had seen a woman, much less a child, and now as they clattered slowly down the street there were many of all ages, little ones brought to witness her passing. On the whole everyone was very quiet, a few women wept, and Jehanne recalled that this was actually a French town in spite of the longtime English presence. The people did not want her death.

A rush of Power bolted through her, making her at once attentive as she had not been in quite a while. Today was the day that God would set her free; it would occur once she reached the destination the Church had appointed for her. She needed to keep her wits sharpened.

An even larger crowd was gathered at the wall separating the abbey's garden from the cemetery. Within the grounds, surrounded by headstones marking those who had gone to God, the foundations of the incomplete church's annex covered the ground in gleaming stones. Civilians stood shoulder to shoulder between the graves and upon the spring grass.

Two wooden scaffolds had been hastily constructed against the wall, and above both flew the banner of Henry's England: golden lions upon a crimson field, quartered with the purloined lilies of France. Upon one of the platforms Cauchon, Warwick, and other dignitaries were awaiting the cart and its unwilling burden. Jehanne recognized the cardinal of Winchester among them by his scarlet robes and wide, flat-brimmed hat. Fifty or so English soldiers in shiny hatlike helmets held the crowds back as the wagon made its way to the rear of the empty platform. Strangely, considering the size of the crowd, there was an unnatural stillness in the air, prophesying the violent encounter all could feel coming.

The driver pulled on the reins and the cart came to a stop. Massieu jumped to the ground with an agility that surprised Jehanne, and he reached up to help her down. From out of nowhere, it seemed to her, Loiseleur emerged around the front of the cart and took her arm.

"Jehanne, listen to me!" he said in an ardent whisper. "If you mean to live, accept the woman's dress they offer you and do everything you're told, or you are in imminent danger of death." His face was drawn as though he, too, had not had much sleep. She plumbed his eyes, trying to discover his motives, and saw to her amazement only a desperate sincerity.

"If you do as I say, not only will your soul be saved but your body as well, and you'll be turned over to the Church for safekeeping. Do you understand me?"

Mute with lingering surprise, she nodded.

"Good girl," Loiseleur whispered. "Now go; they're waiting for you. Do not forget what I've said."

He released his hold on her and Massieu took her other arm. The usher brought her around to the steps and together they climbed to the floor of the scaffold. Ladvenu and Isambard elbowed their way to the front of the crowd and stood beside the steps. Both were haggard and drawn. A forest of English *guisarmes* bristled around them and all through the multitude.

Guillaume Erart, one of the assessors and a fervent supporter of the bishop, mounted the steps and joined Jehanne and Massieu. He took a book from the small table at the front of the platform. Erart looked at Cauchon for a signal to begin. The bishop nodded.

"Our text is from the gospel of St.-Jehan, the beloved apostle of Our Lord Jhesus," the theologian said, loudly enough for all to hear, " 'As the branch cannot bear fruit of itself,' " he read from the book, " 'except it abide in the vine; no more can ye, except ye abide in me.' "

The crowd waited eagerly for his next words, many straining to see the small figure in a filthy linen tunic who listened with her head bowed and her eyes fastened upon a dark knot in the wooden planking.

"All those baptized in the Catholic Faith remain in the true vine of Holy Mother Church. Yet this woman"—he pointed at Jehanne—"has separated herself from the unity of the Church by her manifold errors and grave crimes, and has scandalized Christian people in many ways. Through the authority granted to me by the University of Paris, which proceeds from the Pope himself, I admonish and charge her to relinquish her false presumptions and return to the way of faith."

Erart spread his arms in a gesture of drama. "Ah, noble House of France, always the protector of the Faith, and you, Charles, who call yourself king and governor, have you been thus deluded, to attach yourself to a heretic and schismatic, to the words and deeds of a wicked woman, ill-famed and dishonored? And not only you, but the entire clergy and nobility of your party, by whom she was examined and approved, as she has said?"

At the mention of Charles' name, Jehanne ripped her eyes from the scaffold floor to the assessor. This departure was for the benefit of the English. Her nostrils flared angrily at this insult to the King.

Erart's arm shot up and he pointed a long finger. "I am speaking to you, Jehanne, and I tell you that your king is heretical and schismatic!"

"That is not true!" she shouted, no longer able to contain her indignation. "I tell you with all respect, on pain of my life, King Charles *is* the Most Christian King!" She was thinking about the honorific which had earlier been bestowed upon all French monarchs by a grateful Pope. "No one loves the Church more than he, and he is not at all what you say."

"Make her shut up!" Cauchon shouted to Massieu.

"Shh, Jehanne! Do you want to make matters worse?" the usher murmured in a low voice quivering with fear. His eyes were wide, and there were beads of sweat like a mustache on his upper lip. "Don't underestimate the English!" he hissed.

"Here are the lord judges," Erart went on, "who have many times summoned and required you to submit all your words and deeds to Holy Mother Church, warning you that in those words and deeds were many things which, the clerics decree, are not good to say or maintain."

Jehanne lifted her chin, flexing the muscles in her jaw. "Regarding submission to the Church, I have said that all the works which I have said and done should be submitted to Rome to our lord the Pope, to whom, after God, I submit myself."

Voices among the crowd rumbled, many nodding their agreement.

"As for my words and deeds, I did them on behalf of God Who sent me."

Ladvenu crossed himself quickly and folded his hands. Isambard grimaced. Warwick's hand instinctively flew to his sword. Next to him, the cardinal of Winchester whispered something to Cauchon, whose grim countenance grew even more grave. The soldiers stirred restlessly at the foot of the platform, grumbling like dogs.

"The responsibility for all my actions is mine alone," Jehanne shouted, "and not any other person's, neither the King's nor anyone else's, and if there was fault in them, it was mine only."

"Will you abjure and submit to the Holy Church?" Erart raised his voice.

"I refer myself to God and to the Pope in Rome."

"The Holy Father is too far away from here," he said, shaking his head, "and the bishops here present, as well as the lord cardinal of Winchester, are judges in their own dioceses, duly appointed by the Holy Father to administer matters of faith in his name. You must accede to what the princes of the Church and learned clerics have said and determined."

Ladvenu and Isambard, on tiptoe at the bottom of the steps, were waving frantically. Isambard silently formed the word "Submit," his eyes pleading with her. She smiled at them. It was not their fault that the plan to appeal to the Pope had failed. But it was all right. Any minute now God would send the rescue He had promised her.

Clenching her fists, she looked at Erart defiantly. "Then if I cannot see the Pope, I refer myself to God."

The Dominicans groaned. Ladvenu put his face in his hands.

"I ask you again," Erart bellowed, "will you yield to the authority of the Church and abjure your evil ways?"

"My ways are not evil, for they were commanded by God!" she yelled. Her pulse hammered in her ears, and for the first time in months she felt truly alive.

"I order you, in the name of Jhesus Christe, to submit to the Church Militant!"

"I yield only to God!" she hurled back at him.

By this time the crowd had grown restless, and what had begun as a grumble whipped into a uproar. "Get done with it and burn the witch!" cried an English soldier.

An angry mutter of support rose from the ranks of his comrades, and with faces crimson with outrage, they began to shout in a chorus for the Church to burn her. Their hatred came at her in a series of blows, and she reeled backward a

542

pace. Everyone else in the crowd, it seemed, was shouting at her to save herself, body and soul.

"Please, Jehanne, do as they say!" called out Isambard.

"Jehanne, for the love of God, abjure!" echoed his friend Ladvenu.

She shook her head. "I cannot." Her words were scarcely audible above the din. Subjects and soldiers were yelling at one another, each faction trying to beat its opponent in insult and volume. Housewives squared off against burly soldiers in helmets and chainmail. Alarmed by the violent atmosphere, toddlers wailed in fear. Cauchon stepped forward and held up his hands in a command for silence. Few noticed him. The French were imploring Jehanne to recant; the English were shouting at Warwick to execute her. Midi walked to the edge of the stage and shouted twice for order. It took several minutes before his patience was rewarded and a semblance of peace restored.

With a final barren glance at Jehanne, Cauchon took a page from the table before him and began to read in a solemn tone. " 'In the name of the Lord. Amen. As often as the poisonous virus of heresy obstinately attaches itself to a member of the Church and transforms him into a limb of Satan, most diligent care must be taken to prevent the foul contagion of this pernicious leprosy from spreading to other parts of the mystical body of Christe . . .' "

Massieu seized Jehanne by the shoulders and stared deeply into her dark-circled eyes. "Jehanne, he is reading the sentence of condemnation! You probably don't know this, but already the English have built a stake in the marketplace, and when the bishop finishes reading, they will take you there."

"No, that cannot be," she denied with a determined shake of her head. "My Counsel promised that God will deliver me."

"It is true!" he swore. Massieu forced her to look at him, and lowering his tone, said, "Your voices have lied to you. There will be no great victory to set you free. The English will burn you today, now, unless you abjure! The only thing that awaits you is death by fire!"

"No, that can't be true, They have never lied to me." Her head felt ready to explode from the confusion raging within it. She licked her lips and pleaded without words for him to admit his mistake. "They cannot burn me; my Counsel promised that it would not happen!"

Loiseleur had climbed the scafford while Jehanne's attention was on Massieu. Now he thrust his face very close to hers and said, "Your apparitions are not from God, Jehanne, or they would not have led you to this fate. Brother Massieu is telling the truth! There is indeed a stake piled high with wood waiting for you just a short ride from here. Do you want to die?"

She looked from one desolate face to another. Massieu was without a doubt sincere in his terror, and not even Loiseleur was so good a liar as to feign the dread and remorse written across those unshaven, pale features.

Jehanne shook her head in disbelief. It could not be true; Michel and Catherine and Marguerite, her only anchors to God and to all that was good in her life, would not lie to her, They never had!

But reality was colliding all around her in extreme opposition to the mystic memories that she struggled to summon. A wave of giddiness like the sudden break in a turbulent ocean covered her, and she rose to the top, trying to grip onto some tattered flotsam of hope.

Oh God, my God, help me as You have promised!

She was immediately covered in a drenching despair. This was really happening. The monks were telling the truth this time; it was no tortuous jest of their devising. No trumpet sounded from the gates of Rouen, no one was calling in alarm at the sight of Charles' galloping hordes; there was only the sound of the throng, exhorting her to abjure and yield. The fact of her impending death screamed from the anguished eyes of the French townspeople and gloated within English grins.

Her Counsel receded into misty dreamland and blinked out of existence. The reality was that she was here, on this platform, and in the marketplace a short distance away the English had constructed the instrument of her death. They would take her there.

Today. Now. When Cauchon finished reading.

Jehanne fell into the Void, where she found herself small and solitary and in imminent danger of death by fire.

"What must I do?" she whimpered, now genuinely frightened as she had never been during the trial.

"Yield to the Church," Loiseleur instructed, his face lightening now that he saw that she realized at last the direness of her situation. "Abjure as they ask."

"Abjure?" she repeated, like a child hearing a word for the first time. "What does it mean, 'abjure'?"

"It means to take back everything you've said in the trial," Massieu replied, sighing with relief.

"How do I do that?" Jehanne looked around uncertainly.

A jumble of confusion had broken out among the multitude, and now everyone was calling out conflicting admonitions in a tumult that promised to become even more violent than the earlier one.

Cauchon stopped reading and looked at her, his brow wrinkled in a question. An English cleric, secretary to the cardinal of Winchester, grabbed the bishop's arm and said something sharp to him. Cauchon retorted angrily, but Jehanne could not hear the words.

She could not hear anything in spite of the noise. Abjure! her inner voice screamed, abjure, or be damned!

Jehanne sank to her knees and clasped her hands. "St.-Michel," she pleaded aloud, tears streaming down her thin cheeks, "tell me what to do!"

An English priest ran up the scafford steps with a piece of paper in his hand. Thrusting it at Massieu, he ordered, "Have her sign this."

Massieu and Loiseleur pulled her, still praying, to her feet. "Jehanne, you must sign this," Massieu said.

"I cannot read," she answered simply, "what does it say?"

"It says, 'I, Jehanne, known as the Maid, hereby abjure the false statements I have made during the course of my trial, and return with a faithful heart to the bosom of the Church, which is my rightful Christian home. I swear before God that I will put aside my mannish garb in exchange for a penitent's gown, never

544

to wear them again, and I promise before God that I will not take up arms against His Royal Majesty, Henry VI, King of England and France. I swear further that I will abide by the terms of penance imposed upon me by Holy Mother Church, so help me God.' "

Jehanne stared at the few lines squiggled in black upon the page trembling in Massieu's hand.

"Come," he said, taking her arm. He pulled her toward the table and the inkwell. Then he dipped the quill and gave it to her. She looked at it as though she had never seen a writing instrument in her life.

"Sign now," Loiseleur hissed, "or end your life in the fire!"

Jehanne put the pen to paper. But it had been so long since she wrote her name, and even in the old days when she did it frequently, Pasquerel had always been there to watch for any mistakes she made. Her memory was as blank as the space beneath the writing. She drew a small circle.

"Sign your name," the Englishman ordered brusquely.

She made a cross with the pen. Massieu covered her hand with his own and together they traced the outline of her name.

The English cleric snatched the page and waved it triumphantly.

A howl of protest sounded from the soldiers and they began shouting that they had been betrayed by the bloody Church.

"Traitor!" Warwick shouted at Cauchon. "You have been too lenient with her, and now she has escaped us!"

"You are lying!" the bishop yelled at him. "My profession compels me to seek the health of this miserable sinner's soul and body!"

All at once there was not a single person who was not yelling at someone else. Townsfolk and soldiers shouted at one another across a barrier of *guisarmes*. A fistfight broke out between a blacksmith and a soldier, and alarmed witnesses hurried to break it up. A soldier on the ground below pushed Ladvenu, who stumbled backward but did not fall. Several small stones pelted Cauchon, and he held up his arm to ward them off.

The long months of hunger and fatigue and strain collapsed upon Jehanne. She began to laugh insensibly at the scene. Soon she was unable to stop the mad, despondent cackle that had welled up from some dark cavern to seize her in a fit of numbed abandon. The laughter hurt so much that tears of pain distorted her face, giving her the appearance of a silent, open-mouthed gargoyle. Her entire body shook and her heart flip-flopped within her breast. The force of her release stabbed deep into her side.

"Abjure," she repeated the ridiculous word, "abjure."

"*Silence!*" roared a thunderous voice. Henry Beaufort, cardinal of Winchester, raised his scarlet arms and again commanded quiet from the warring rabble. At first no one paid him any mind. He had to exhort them for five full minutes. Gradually, order was restored and an expectant hush replaced the chaos.

The only sound was Jehanne's sobbing laughter. She knew she sounded like a choking dog, but she could not stop herself. Her mind was blank. Massieu must have known that she had crossed over the edge. He put an arm around her quaking shoulder and tried to shush her.

Cauchon picked up the book and turned to another page. " 'Inasmuch as you have openly renounced your errors and have with your own lips publicly abjured all your heresies, according to the form appointed by ecclesiastical sanctions, we unbind you from the bonds of excommunication which chained you, on condition that you return to the Church with a true heart and sincere faith.' "

He glared darkly at Jehanne, by now exhausted into docility. " 'But inasmuch as you have rashly sinned against God and the Holy Church, we condemn you for salutary penance to perpetual imprisonment, to eat the bread of sorrow and drink the water of affliction, that you may weep for your faults and never henceforth commit anything contary to what you have sworn.' "

"Perpetual imprisonment?" she whispered to Massieu. "Am I to be kept chained?"

"No," he replied, "now you are in the custody of the Church."

A vision of gentle surroundings with nuns for company swam briefly before her. She would at last be given enough to eat—even if only bread—and would not have to fear for her virtue and her life.

Oh, thank You, Lord God!

"That is good." She smiled, wiping her face with the back of her hands. She raised ghostlike eyes to Cauchon. "Take me to your Church prison, that I may be out of the hands of the English."

The bishop gave her an unreadable smile in return. "Take her back where she came from," he ordered the guards.

"No!" Jehanne shouted, panic and anger at his treachery filling her eyes. "You promised that I would be guarded by the Church!"

Two English guards dashed up the steps and grabbed her roughly by the arms. They began dragging the feebly protesting prisoner down the steps.

"You promised!" she wailed.

Isambard shouldered aside the soldiers in his way and moved rapidly to the edge of the platform where Cauchon was standing. "Your Excellency, I must protest! The prisoner has abjured, and as a penitent she belongs in a prison attached to the cathedral. For the love of Heaven, I urge you to act according to canon law!"

"You overstep your authority, Brother Isambard," the bishop rebuked him. "The prisoner is tricky and might well recant unless she is diligently guarded. Take her away!" he commanded the guard.

Jehanne tried to struggle against the soldiers, but their hands were painfully squeezing her upper arms. They hauled her to the cart and slung her into it like a sack of oats. Massieu jumped in beside her.

As the cart began to move away from the scaffold, he said to the tearful, trembling girl, "It's all right, Jehanne. They will send you where the law demands that you be kept. Do not worry."

"But I can't go back there!" she wept, despair written in her frightened eyes. "Those soldiers will certainly kill me now, I know it!"

Ladvenu and Isambard leaped into the moving cart, disregarding the English soldiers who spat at the occupants and hurled verbal garbage. "You lying slut! You God-cursed witch!"

546

"We'll burn you yet, witch, just you wait, and may Hell swallow all you filthy priests!"

Isambard ducked as a stone made straight for his head. The driver, his face pale with fright, slapped the reins against the back of the wide-eyed horse, and the carriage lurched out of the cemetery and sped down the street.

All the way back to Rouen Castle, the monks tried their best to comfort Jehanne. All would be well, they promised her. Once she put on the penitent's gown, she would be moved to a Church prison. Now that she had submitted to its authority, Holy Mother Church would protect her.

She was manacled again to the block of wood and to the wall. The guards did not immediately close the door of the cell but gathered at the threshold, muttering together in their rough native language, as they always did when plotting mischief. Jehanne knew they were discussing her from the hateful sneers they flung toward the dark corner where she sat upon the bed. At one point, one of them said something that made the others laugh. Billy leered at her with a nasty grin.

Take your last look at me, she thought, for I shall soon be gone.

By the time the cart returned to the castle, she had been persuaded by the monks that she would be moved from this place, very soon. She must be patient while arrangements were being made, Ladvenu had said.

But the churchmen were not allowed to escort her to her English prison. The guards stopped the monks at the foot of the stairs, and after hurling profane curses at them, seized Jehanne and yanked her ruthlessly to the cell. Then they returned her to the irons she thought she would never wear again.

That was hours ago. Since that time, the soldiers had left her in peace while they planned God knew what.

Jehanne tried to pray, but there was a blockage in her heart and the words did not come. One thought kept bouncing around in her mind: Her Guides had failed her. They had pretended to be from God and for all these years had been lying to her. Fool that she was, she had believed Them, trusted Them, permitted Them to order her all over France while like an unsuspecting child she had followed Them, declaring to the King and to everyone else that she had Heaven's support.

Who were They? Demons as the churchmen contended? Jehanne could not believe that either. After all, They had shown her some wondrous things. But the Devil would do that in order to have her soul. She shuddered. How close she had come to losing both her life and that eternal core that belonged only to God! And for what? That Charles should be King?

Yet, Charles *was* the true King of France; she could not doubt that. She would know it in her heart even without Them to tell her that it was so. Why then would the Evil One want him on the throne? It was a fact that France had had bad Kings—and unfit ones, too—in the past, despite their having been duly anointed at Reims as Charles had been. Still, Charles was not evil, nor could Jehanne believe that he was unfit, although he did waver annoyingly.

And anyway, bad or not, unfit or not, there was a sacred bond between the King and God. So why would the Devil have sent demons to tempt Jehanne in a manner that touched upon that bond? It made no sense for Them to be agents of the Devil. Neither did it make sense that the King of Hell would have wanted Orléans to be delivered from enemy hands, particularly if Charles was God's own King. God loved His people and did not want them to suffer needlessly. Perhaps their sins had brought them to a state of siege, and perhaps God truly had abandoned them until Jehanne the Maid rode out of the east and persuaded His noble Dauphin to allow her to rescue the city.

But it still made no sense. The English did not belong in France. That was a fact. God had made people to live in their own countries and speak their own languages. It was evil for them to do otherwise, to attempt to overrun someone else's country, torching the homes of peasants and stealing their food and murdering them while they slept. And if the English performed evil acts, was it not clear that the Devil had supported them in their rampage across the kingdom? So why would he have sent demons to tempt her into making Charles King and saving Orléans, that France should at last be free of foreign dominion? She was not so arrogant as to think that it had been simply for the sake of damning her soul, not when so many other lives had been affected in the bargain. It made no sense at all. Unless—

A sinking feeling began to creep slowly up her spine, and when it reached her brain it burst into the unthinkable.

Unless she had been right all along and They truly *were* from God.

She tried to push it away but could not. It returned with a vengeance and forced her to look at it in spite of her wish to do otherwise. What if They had not betrayed her? it taunted. What if she was the traitor, to Them and to God?

Close to panic, her eyes swept, unseeing, past the conspiring guards. What had she really done when she renounced her faithfulness and signed her name to that paper, when she "abjured"? She put a hand to her forehead and rubbed the space over her eyes. Think, Jehanne.

She had been very close to death when she accepted that there would be no victory, no freedom. But They had promised that she would be free, and liberation had not come. Was that not a lie on Their part?

Then something else occurred to her. Was it possible that she had misunderstood Them?

No, that could not be. Catherine had told her very directly, in plain French, that God would send a great victory to set her free. That could only mean exactly what it sounded like. Or could it?

Not caring if the guards saw her, Jehanne clasped her hands very tightly and bowed her head.

Oh, dear God, give me some sign that will let me know, in a way I cannot doubt, whether I did the right thing by saving my life, and if I have sinned, I humbly submit myself to Your Judgment. I will accept any penance You impose upon me. Oh God, please have mercy on me, I do not want to lose my soul!

There was the sound of footsteps coming up the stairs, and even from her corner Jehanne could see the guards stiffening. "Halt!" cried a soldier who was out of view. "What are you mangy priests doing here?"

"We have come at the behest of Bishop Cauchon and of my lord earl of War-wick," someone answered.

"Go on, get out of here," said another soldier, Floquet, Jehanne thought. "We don't want you traitor priests here!"

"If you do not allow us to pass," rejoined Isambard's calm voice, "you will have to answer to the earl, and I do not think that you really want that, now do you?"

The guards hesitated. After a moment, one of them grumbled, "Very well. But be quick about it, and don't try anything tricky, or I swear by the bowels of Christ, we'll lop off your bloody heads!"

Isambard was the first into the cell, and across his arm was folded a neat bundle. He was followed by Courcelles, Midi, Le Maistre, and finally, Loiseleur. All of them were smiling.

"Dear Jehanne," said Isambard, his haggard face gently alight, "we have come to tell you how much we rejoice in the great mercy that God has shown to you this day."

"God has indeed forgiven you, Jehanne, and restored you to His grace," Cour-celles confirmed with a pious nod.

"When will I be able to leave this place and go to a Church prison?" Jehanne asked, glancing with some uneasiness at the guards. They were listening to the exchange from their place at the front of the cell, grinning in an ominous, un-settling way.

Le Maistre averted his eyes from her imploring stare and bit his lip. Courcelles peeked at Loiseleur, who fixed his gaze upon the narrow window chink. Uncertainty flashed across Isambard's gaunt countenance.

"All in good time," Midi said smoothly. "There are many arrangements still to be made. Before you can be moved, you must obey the wishes of the Church and show your good faith by putting aside those clothes"—he gestured at her garb with his head—"and putting on the gown of a penitent."

Isambard took a step toward her and held out the homespun folded across his arm. Jehanne looked at it, then at the monks. They begged her obedience without saying a word. She reached for the grayish-white dress, which was scratchy but clean.

Floquet whispered something to Billy, and the younger Englishman giggled. Frowning, Isambard turned toward the guards. "You there," he said to Grey, "unchain the prisoner, and you other men get away from that door," he ordered. "Jehanne requires privacy that she might change her clothes."

Grey spat on the floor, then grinned. "We're under orders to watch her at all times." There was a titter from his comrades.

"For the love of God, man," Le Maistre rebuked him testily, "have you no decency at all? Go on now," he waved to the other soldiers, "leave this cell, and shut the door behind you."

The captain of the guard shrugged. "Come on, you lot, do what he says. There's nothing for you to do yet."

The men grumbled but obeyed. Grey ambled to Jehanne, groping at his belt for the key. He unfastened the heavy band around her waist chaining her to the wall, then he tossed the iron with a loud clang onto the floor. Next came the fetters around her wrists, followed by those at her ankles. For the first time in months Jehanne felt so free it seemed that she could fly if she wanted.

When Grey was out of the room, the monks turned their backs to her. She put the gown upon the bed and sat down next to it. The foul odor steaming from the boots she had not removed since she was hauled from her horse at Compiègne made her gasp in disgust. When she pulled them off, they took a layer of damp, wrinkled skin, leaving pink patches on the bottoms of her feet. With shaking fingers, she untied the lace at her throat and slipped the tunic over her head. The strings holding up her hose took a little longer, for the strong knots were bound very securely. Finally, they were loose enough, and she peeled off the lower garment that had become like a second skin. Deep red creases crisscrossed her hips where the laces had been almost embedded. She unfolded the penitent's gown and slipped it over her head.

"I'm ready now," she said in a voice not unlike a child's.

The churchmen had of course known that she was female, but the full impact of that knowledge did not hit them until they turned to look at her, clad now in the simple dress that ended just below her knees. Surprise registered in their faces.

"When may I go to the Church prison?" she asked again.

"There is one thing more to be done," replied Midi. Reaching into the sleeve of his habit, he withdrew a pair of large scissors. "We must remove that masculine haircut, in order to prepare you for a new growth more suitable for a woman."

Jehanne nodded, her eyes upon the shears. With a resigned sigh, she walked to the block and sat down. Courcelles moved to where her old clothes lay discarded upon the cot and picked them up. He stuffed them into a sack, then tossed it indifferently into a corner.

Midi glided to her and took a shock of the hair that had grown to her shoulders and fell into her eyes. The scissors snipped finality, and she felt a slight tug.

The last time anyone had cut her hair was at Le Crotoy, when the ladies of Abbeville reluctantly granted her wish because they felt sorry for her. How different that had been from the first haircut she had ever had, long ago in Vaucouleurs. Metz had been so careful with her, and Madame le Royer so scandalized. What was it he had said as he cut? Oh, yes, something about how certain the citizens of that town thought her to be a witch, while others were of the opinion that she was a saint. She recalled her answer, that she was neither.

How right she had been. She was only Jehanne the Maid from a tiny hamlet in Lorraine called Domrémy, a country girl who had dared think that she was worthy to hear voices sent by God. But that seemed the folly of another life. Now she was simply a humble penitent in the custody of the Church. She wiped away the tears trickling toward her chin.

Midi finished cutting. He stooped to the floor and gathered together the fallen hair. Jehanne hesitated, then put a hand to her denuded scalp. It was gone, all of it. Nothing but stubble remained.

The monks were already leaving the cell. Isambard was the last to go. He looked back at her, consolation brightening his gaunt face, and he seemed to be silently apologizing for all she had been through. "Bless you, child. Don't worry, the bishop will keep his promise to you." Then he, too, left her alone, still sitting upon the block.

Their footfalls had scarcely receded down the steps when the guards filed back into the cell, even the ones who usually kept watch outside. The one Jehanne knew as Barrow, with the strange, wandering eye that always seemed to be looking at a space above his head, held a footlong stick which he was clapping rhythmically against his palm. All five wore malignant smiles as they began to form a loose circle around her.

Every instinct she had hollered in alarm, and Jehanne knew that she was in terrible danger. Her mouth was suddenly as dry as dust.

"So it's a girl after all," said Floquet with a grin that chilled her blood.

"Do you think so?" Billy asked in mock bewilderment. "Looks like a slimy French pig of a witch to me."

"A lying French pig of a witch." His captain snarled a correction.

The circle grew tighter. A bitter hostility replaced their grins. Jehanne looked desperately over her shoulder for a way out. There was only the dim corner behind her.

"I've heard tell that if a witch bleeds, she loses her power," remarked Floquet.

"There's a way to tell if that's true," growled Barrow through gritted teeth.

His stick flashed in the torchlight like lightning. Jehanne's head exploded into pain.

She fell to the floor. A trickle of blood seeped into her eye, temporarily blinding the numbed left side of her face.

"That was for your lies," rasped the man with the stick.

"And this is for Orléans." Grey's boot connected viciously with the small of her back.

She screamed.

They were all around her now. The force of another foot cracked one of her ribs. Before she could get up, Barrow's club came down hard across her shoulders, knocking her flat on her face.

I've got to get away!

She tried to crawl toward the corner, but someone said, "No, you don't, witch," and two of them seized her shoulders with violent hands and hoisted her to unsupporting feet. Grey's arm swung back and he hit her with all his strength.

Blood gushed from her fractured nose and she saw vivid pricks of light as she collapsed against the wall. Pulling her up by the arm, Floquet twisted it behind her back, and she howled at the sudden, sharp wrench that felt as though he were trying to rip it from its socket. Billy punched her violently in the stomach with his fist.

Air shot out of her lungs. She sank to her knees, panicked by a wheezing, passionate effort to inhale. She could not catch her breath, could not breathe, could not—

A kick in the jaw flung her onto her back, splitting her upper lip all the way to the root of her nose. Her front tooth cracked in half, and she almost swallowed it.

Her left eye was swollen shut, but with the other she saw the stick descending to her head and without thinking, rolled away just in time to avoid the blow. The pole cracked loudly upon the floor.

Grey laughed and pulled her to what would have been a standing position had her legs upheld her. He clenched what remained of his teeth and pulled her close to his reeking, sweaty face. "And this is for Patay," he spat.

His hand struck first one side of her puffed, bleeding face, then the other. He tossed her to Floquet, who brought a two-fisted grip down between her shoulder blades.

They're going to kill me, she thought, hitting the ground. They're going to beat me to death. Oh, merciful God, help me!

A hail of buffets from the stick rained down on her back; their boots kicked her, hard. Jehanne sensed her lifeforce draining from the gash above her closed eye, from the shattered bridge of her nose.

Dear Lord, accept my soul into Your Kingdom!

"Stop this!"

When another whack of the stick crashed onto her shoulder she hardly felt it.

"I said, Stop it!"

The beating miraculously ceased. Breathing heavily from their efforts, the men swung toward the door. With a weakened lift of her head Jehanne squinted through her good eye, just able to make out the earl of Stafford at the entrance to the cell. The nobleman stood with hands on his hips, glaring at the men under his command. Exasperation flashed in the wide-set blue eyes. He was so angry that he forgot to speak French: the terse orders he barked at the soldiers were delivered in a gibberish of incomprehensible English.

Jehanne's battered face sank against the floor. Thank You, Lord Jhesus, she thought as her consciousness dimmed. She was aware of footsteps moving away from her and of the sound of the cell door closing.

She was not alone. The unmistakable clack of boots sauntered slowly to where she lay.

"Jehanne the Maid." Stafford uttered her name in a colorless, understandable whisper as though it were a curse.

She attempted to look at him but failed. She could not move.

"You said recently that we would never have this kingdom regardless of our numbers. Perhaps now you begin to appreciate the power that is England. Perhaps you see at last why we shall indeed have this realm for our own." The words were all the more deadly for their quiet. "Get up," he snapped.

Jehanne put her palms flat on the floor beside her fallen head. Her side felt as though impaled with a broadsword. Lacking the strength to push herself up, she collapsed.

"I said, Get up." Stafford seized her and lifted her aloft like a broken doll. Her wounds shrieked in outraged agony, and she screamed along with them.

He lugged her to the cot and flung her onto her back. "We are great, Jehanne, greater than France," he said in the same dangerously calm tone. His hands were moving at his waist. "Because unlike the French, we have the courage and the means to take what we want."

He finished unfastening the laces and pushed his hose down over his hips.

"No!"

She tried to roll off the bed, but his full weight was suddenly on top of her. Horrified panic gave her strength, and unmindful of her injuries, she struggled against him with the strength and resolution of a wild animal, scratching and slapping helplessly at his round, thatched head.

Furious, he struck her hard across the face. The blow opened another bloody gash over her eye.

Her head was still reeling when he pushed her dress to her waist. She clenched her legs together, infuriating him, and he slapped her again, and again. Burning her face with hot, panting breaths, he forced her arms behind her back into an unmovable grip. Another smack from the callused hand smashed against her unfeeling head.

A sudden sharp pain invaded the space between her legs as he jabbed his evil into her.

"No!" she sobbed. "Oh, merciful Jhesus, *help me!*"

The face of the Devil above her was beaded in a sweaty, clenched grimace. He delivered the thrusts with teeth-gritting hatred, and it seemed that he would split her in two. Her protesting flesh stiffened in revulsion, her mind unaccepting of what he was doing to her.

Oh, God, make him stop!

It seemed to go on forever.

Eventually, he shuddered in a great spasm of released venom, then crumpled heavily upon her. He gave her another, needless slap. Then he got up and looked down at her as he pulled the hose over his blood-smeared manhood. Coughing up a wad, he spat in her face.

He strode quickly to the door.

She could hear bawdy laughter coming from outside the cell. Shame and outrage seized her in great wracking sobs, and she hastily pulled the skirt down to cover her violated body.

The door opened and the laughing soldiers reentered. "Well, lads, I believe what we have here is Jehanne-What-Once-Was-a-Maid," Grey cackled. "And now that the earl has had his fill, it's our turn."

Jehanne tried to get up. She had to get away, to go anywhere, far from this nightmare that was not really happening.

The captain was on her before she had a chance to stir. His gamy odor attacked her, made more disgusting by his fumbling hands. A new pain shot into her pelvis like the penetration of a lance, and she screamed through her terrorized sobs.

Dear God, forgive me my sins. I am so sorry for having offended You! Her consciousness started to slip from her grasp. It would not stop, no matter how hard she prayed.

He finished with a sound like a rutting pig. Billy was waiting.

Jehanne fainted, mercifully unaware of what happened next.

When she awoke, she was unable to open her left eye, which was sealed shut by congealed blood and mucus. Her face burned as though cut with hot knives, just as the stick had broken her head and covered her in throbbing bruises. The nightmare the Devil's whim had called to life stung her loins, and she felt an urgent need to urinate, to purge herself of memory.

When she tried to move, she found that she was lashed tightly to the cot by a long chain. It cut across her cracked ribs, jabbing her with each labored breath. Dark brown blood covered the front of her shift.

It was daylight. Mid-morning light lay in a slit across the filthy floor. The devils in human form were gambling again, tossing their dice against the wall next to the door.

"Let me up," she mumbled. Like a lazy hand, her tongue grazed the sharp end of her broken tooth. Her lips were swollen and numb, her words barely understandable.

They looked at her. "What did it say?" Barrow asked. His google-eyed stare loomed over a bearded smile.

"Let me up," she croaked louder. "I need the latrine."

The men laughed.

"Ret ne op," aped Billy, imitating her fractured speech. They laughed again.

"Please." Her whisper shook with humiliated tears.

Grey stood up and went to the bed. He hung over her like a threat of death, and she prayed that he would not strike her again. He took the keychain from his belt and stooping, unfastened the lock. Not at all gently, he pulled the tethers from her, and she cried out as the chain raked across her bruised and broken ribcage.

She counted to three. With a shuddering, resolved effort, she managed to sit up and place her hands on the cot. But before she could stand, Grey grabbed the end of the gown and pulled it over her head.

Jehanne instantly hunched over to hide her nakedness, shame surmounting the affliction that stabbed her side.

Lewd laughter spouted from the soldiers, and Floquet whistled in derision. Grey beckoned toward them. Billy grabbed a sack from the table and walked to his commander, who reached inside and took out her old clothes.

"Put that on," he ordered, flinging them at her.

She clutched them to her. "I cannot wear this," she said. "I promised I wouldn't."

"It's that or nothing, slut." Grey's toothless grin hovered above her.

"Please."

"Prease," Billy mocked. He had moved into position behind her. She recoiled from the breaths raising the short hairs on her neck.

"I cannot wear these clothes," she protested. Her bad eye stung from the salty tears dropping like acid into the open cuts on her face. "I gave my word."

Grey spat on the floor. "Since when is the word of a French whore worth anything?"

Jehanne winced.

She felt a sword tracing the outline of her spine, and whirled around. From the look on his face, the reeking young man behind her was enjoying his role as torturer. He pursed his lips in an imitation kiss.

"Please, sir, for the love of God! I swore on oath." A great sob leaped from her chest. Her insides were near to bursting, and she urgently craved the latrine. Her one horror at that moment was that she would disgrace herself if they did not let her up.

"Witches have no need of God," the captain replied, shaking his stringy hair.

"I'm not a witch," she whispered, blinded now by a sorrow sharper than all of her combined injuries.

"Well, the Church says that you are," he insisted. "And we know you are, don't we, men?"

"Aye!" they chorused.

So this was how it would end. Nothing would move these evil men. Jehanne accepted that she had no choice.

She bent over double to conceal her breasts and her privates. With tortuous difficulty, she pulled the tunic over her head and down to her waist. Still sitting, she slipped her feet through the hose and pulled them up. Just tying the laces required most of her strength. "You know that this is forbidden me," she said in a dull rhythm.

"Accept it," Grey stated. "This is the way things are. You cannot hope to win against us."

True enough. She was beyond all redemption now. A cell door slammed shut in her mind, and she knew that, one way or another, she was doomed.

Somehow she managed to get to her feet. Somehow she was able to limp painfully down the steps, into the courtyard briefly, and then to the latrine, with Grey and Floquet behind her every step of the way.

As she relieved herself of the bloody, stinging urine, she wept from the depths of her desecrated soul. She was alone upon the earth and in perpetual imprisonment. Jehanne the Maid was dead.

After she put on the forbidden clothes, the men of England did not mistreat her further. Grey returned her to the old chains, and he and his guards resumed their drunken dicing as though nothing had happened. For the most part, they ignored her altogether. Every now and then they tossed a hard hunk of bread to her, which she could not eat because of her aching, purpled face and loosened teeth. She did not want it anyway. She lay on the cot, shivering with a fever that she hoped and at the same time feared would carry her off. She no longer had the will to live.

The men of the Church did not remove her to the gentle prison they had promised her, not that morning. Jehanne drifted in and out of fevered consciousness, half-expecting that upon waking again she would find Isambard or Midi or Loiseleur standing over her, ready to take her away. But daylight turned to darkness, and there was no sign of them.

They did not come for her the next day, nor the day after that. The long hours dragged by as though time itself had died, and in the aftermath of Hell made manifest, Jehanne tumbled into the anguish of a far greater and more searing Abyss.

The Church had broken its word. Bishop Cauchon intended that she stay with these *goddon* animals until she died. Understanding flashed into her head and she knew that that had been his plan all along; that or the stake. Mercy had never had a place in his grand design. He hated her that much. All of them did. Anger and degradation raged through her, contributing to her sickness in spirit and body, but as much as she tried to blame the clergymen, she knew that she was equally at fault.

She should have let them burn her. Had she done so she would have gone to the stake as Jehanne the Maid, with her body and her soul intact. During all these months her Counsel had cautioned her to stand fast and God would help her, but the threat of a fiery death had forced her to betray that in a foolish attempt to save herself. On the platform before all those people, she had proclaimed that They had never been real. Somewhere was a paper with her signature on it attesting to the great lie. When it was already too late she had prayed that God would send a sign that she had sinned, and He had done so. As she had cast Him and His saints from her, so God and her Counsel had withdrawn Their protection and support.

Now she was defiled and damned to Eternal fire and the deprivation of Heaven. The most loathsome rat had more value. She was nothing. She was not worthy to live, for she had squandered faith.

It had always been so, from the beginning. How often she had importuned Them, begging like a stupid child for some bauble to hold up her fragile loyalty, and time after time, again and again, everything They had ever told her had come true, even as she secretly believed it would not. Their love, always constant, forever patient, had dragged her along, unworthy as she was. She had lost Paris because she went without Their blessing. She had rebelled when They told her that she would be captured. Even though They forbade her to attempt to escape from Beaurevoir, she had done as she pleased. And all along God, through Them, had been testing her faith to see whether she was deserving of Heaven.

She felt tiny, insignificant. Her failures had been her fault.

They had never lied to her. The victory They had promised would have come had she kept to her faith in Them and in God. A great thunderclap could have ignited the skies, awing everyone present with God's blessing on her. But now she was beyond rescue, and would never know what Ste.-Catherine's prophecy had meant.

She was to die in prison. The guards were only resting for a bit. Soon they would have another go at her, and when they did, they would kill her anyway. Execution in the flames would have been quicker and ultimately more charitable than this slow, shameful demise. But one way or another, God willed that she die for her sins. For rejecting Him and Those He sent to guide her, she did not deserve life.

Jehanne turned away from the soldiers raucously flinging coins against the wall. Unmindful of the damage to her side—even welcoming it as a small penance—she drew her legs up to her waist and bent her head toward a clenched fist, which she bit hard until her teeth broke skin. Her shoulders shook in stifled sobs. Despair wrapped its black shroud around her, and she was lowered into a tomb where nothing worse could happen, for there was nothing worse than the prospect of a terrified and short life in prison and the loss of her soul.

She scolded herself for having been stupid enough to believe the men of the Church. She knew that they wanted her death, yet hoped that somewhere within them there was a kernel of God's love. Truth was, she thought that they could be trusted because she *wanted* to believe it. Everything that they had done in the trial, everything they had said proved that they were determined to ruin her. Nevertheless, she had feared the fire so much that when the final moment came for her to choose, she forgot their evil and turned to them instead of to God, Who had never betrayed her faith. Had she accepted His will and let them burn her, she would be safe in the arms of her Lord. In choosing physical life, she had rejected the Life that never ends.

Her Counsel were gone from her. No trace of Them remained. They did not come to comfort her as They had when she was ill from the bishop's fish. She had never known such aloneness as this. She folded her hands and closed her good eye.

Oh God, Whose face I was never worthy to see, I am the vilest of sinners. I do not deserve Your mercy, but please accept my death as penance for having betrayed You. It is all I have left to give You.

Exhausted, she slipped into a shadowy doze.

A noise brought her back to wakefulness. Jehanne opened her eye in time to see the cell door swing open. The guards stopped their gambling as Cauchon entered, followed by Le Maistre, Courcelles, an English monk and another Jehanne did not know, and Isambard.

Jehanne forced herself to sit up on the bed. Her vision spun around violently, and she had to put hands to her head to keep from falling onto the floor. When she could focus, she saw that the Inquisitor had gone pale at the sight of her. He held a shaking hand to his throat.

Isambard murmured, "Oh, my God," then swung a shocked, accusing look at Cauchon.

"Behold, Brothers, an obstinate and relapsed heretic!" The surprise that should have accompanied the bishop's words was absent.

All of her pent-up resentment and anguish sprang to Jehanne's throat. "If you had kept your promise and sent me to your Church prison where I could have been watched by women, none of this would have happened!" Tears filled her uninjured eye and poured down a ravaged cheek, dampening her tunic.

She turned a pleading look to Isambard. "I want to go to Mass and receive my Saviour in Holy Communion, and I want to be put in a decent prison where I don't have to be chained any more. If you take me there, I promise to be good and do as the Church commands."

"But, dear child," said Courcelles, "you have put on the scandalous clothing that you abjured. You have recanted, as Bishop Cauchon observed."

"Look at me!" she shouted, sobbing in disbelief that he could be so dense. "Do you think I did this to myself?" She turned on Cauchon, thrusting her disfigured face and bruise-covered arm at him. "I had every intention of keeping my vow to the Church. I warned all of you that this would happen if you left me alone with these English! You do not know what violence they have done to me since the Church forced me to dress as a woman!"

The Dominicans were seething by now. Cauchon's arrogance had made him careless, and now his intentions were out in the open for all to see. Isambard in particular looked as though he wanted to strangle his superior. Le Maistre's face was blank, as one who has just been drenched in cold water.

"Since last Thursday, have you heard your voices?" asked Cauchon hurriedly in a plain attempt to turn away the antagonism coming from Le Maistre and Isambard.

Lightning flashed through Jehanne's mind, and in the silence that followed she heard the voice of redemption.

It was all so clear. She knew what Cauchon wanted; she knew what God willed. He had accepted her penance, and was giving her a second chance. Lies had stolen her soul away. It was a lie that would reclaim it.

Thank You, Lord God! Thank You for returning my soul to me!

"Yes," she whispered.

"What did they say to you?" Cauchon asked, eagerness etched across his cold features.

"They said, 'God sends word to you of the great pain He has felt in the treason to which you consented when you denied Him and us, His servants. You did that in order to save your life, but in saving your life you damned your soul.' "

"Do you still maintain that they were Ste.-Catherine and Ste.-Marguerite?" interrupted Courcelles.

"Yes." She nodded. "And They truly are from God."

"Did they say anything else?" The bishop toyed idly with the cross hanging from his neck.

"Before Thursday, They told me that I should stand firm and God would help me. They told me even as I stood on the platform that I should answer the preacher boldly, that he was a false preacher, because he said many things that I had not done. Everything I swore to when I signed that paper was a lie. The truth is that I really *was* sent by God to send the English from France, and I really *did* hear St.-Michel and Ste.-Catherine and Ste.-Marguerite! I denied Them that day only because I feared the fire."

An ugly smile spread across Cauchon's face. He had won. At last.

But Jehanne was not finished; she was filled with the Power again, as vibrant as though it had never left her. "I was wrong to . . . abjure without God's permission. I was confused and didn't understand what was in that paper I signed. If you want, I'll return to female dress *after* you take me to the Church prison. But in everything else, I refer myself to God."

She took a breath and plunged into God's will. "I would rather do the ultimate Penance than stay one day longer in this awful place."

Cauchon nodded slightly. Jehanne could hear the thought he did not utter aloud.

His violet robe whirled around, and he left the cell, with his partisans at his heels.

Wordlessly, Isambard blessed her and Le Maistre whispered the *Pater*. Jehanne bowed her head, ignoring the sacrilegious buffoonery of the guards. When the prayer ended, she looked up to see that both monks were weeping. Her pummeled face and the hopelessness of her plight were more than they could stand, and they left her without saying anything else.

Jehanne eased herself back onto the cot. The guards went to their dice.

She had no doubt what this meant. Now the Church would turn her over to the English for execution. She felt calm, almost joyful. She would certainly die, but damnation was no longer assured.

Thank You, God, for this second chance. I was not worthy of Your absolution.

She lay on her side facing the wall whose every notch was more familiar now than her mother's face. Released from the horror of Heaven's loss, Jehanne went to sleep.

Michel came to her during the night to tell her that God had never actually abandoned her. That was just the shadow her fears made, he said, fears springing from the guilt she felt. But God understood and felt pity for her. She was His dearest touchstone.

The Archangel reminded her that life does not end. All of Them would be with her, he promised, to escort her Home in glory.

Massieu was the first to arrive. He came very early, bringing with him Pierre Maurice. Allowed entrance by Grey, the monks ignored the snoring Billy and Floquet, and crossed the cell to where Jehanne lay chained by her feet to the cot. Massieu knelt next to her and took her hand.

"Jehanne, the council met last night to deliberate your fate." He paused, and when he spoke again his voice was shaking. "They have declared you a relapsed heretic. You are excommunicated."

She pushed herself to a sitting position. "Will I be given Last Rites?"

"Yes," he said. "Brothers Isambard and Martin insisted upon it, and Inquisitor Le Maistre backed them up."

So it was truly to be death for her. She thought she had accepted it, but now that the moment was here, terror swooped upon her like a flock of hungry ravens. She would die today, never to know night and the dreamtime again. Jehanne's breathing began to come in shallow, rapid pulses, and her eyes widened as though she were possessed.

"Oh, Brother Massieu," she cried, reminding the usher of a terrified child, "where will I be tonight?"

"Have you no faith in God, Jehanne?" Maurice answered for Massieu.

She gulped, then nodded. "Yes, and by God's grace I shall be in Paradise." She could not allow herself to doubt that, not now, after having accepted repentance. She would have to step out into empty space with only her faith to hold her up.

I'm only nineteen, she thought bleakly. I shall never see twenty.

"If I may ask, Jehanne, why did you resume male garb?"

She stared at Massieu as though he had lost his mind.

Reading hers, he said, "Yes, I know *why* you did. But what was it that really made you do it? Where did those clothes come from?"

She was too ashamed to tell him the whole truth, and besides, Maurice was no friend of hers. So she told them only about how the guards took the dress away from her and would not allow her to leave the cell to relieve herself until she had put on the tunic and hose. Even that memory throbbed like a bleeding wound, and as she recounted it her tears spilled onto Massieu's hand.

Jehanne dragged her sleeve across her wet, tender face. When she could see again, Ladvenu and his young acolyte Jehan Toutmouillé were coming through the door. The other guards had awakened, and Billy was rubbing the crusts of sleep from his eyes with a filthy hand. He frowned at the presence of the detested monks.

"Jehanne, I am come to hear your confession," Ladvenu said. "Afterward you may take Holy Communion."

She tried to smile but was not entirely successful; fright and her beaten features allowed only a half-curve to her swollen lips. She knew by the numbness that she must have looked like a strange creature, part human, part demon.

The churchmen exchanged a silent communication, and Massieu and Maurice rose to leave. "I shall see you in a little while, Jehanne," promised the usher. They left her alone with Ladvenu and his young assistant.

"How am I to die, Brother Martin?" Jehanne asked, already knowing the answer. "The ax?"

He shook his head. A sigh escaped through his mouth. "The stake."

"Oh, God!" she sobbed. "I would rather they took my head!"

Ladvenu put a comforting arm around her shoulder as she wept into her hands. He jerked his head at his acolyte. Toutmouillé moved to a discreet distance while Ladvenu shushed Jehanne, and began waving the half-awake guards from the cell. Ladvenu pressed his lips to the cut over Jehanne's eye. When she was able, she made her confession to the gentle Dominican.

She told him everything. At first, she spoke haltingly of how frightened she had been upon the scaffold, and of the lie she had spoken to save herself. For a little while afterward, she admitted, she had doubted her Counsel and God Who had sent them to her. She told Ladvenu of her prayer that God would send her a sign to let her know if she had done right or wrong. The monk's eyes widened in revulsion and horror as she relived the beating that followed her assuming the new dress, and when she got to the part concerning Stafford, she broke down altogether and could say no more.

Ladvenu put his arms around her and she cried desolately into his rough linen habit. Overcome with shame, she confessed in a torrent of babbling outrage the defilement the Englishman had thrust upon her.

Ladvenu's whitened features contorted into a grieving pity. "Oh, my poor child," he murmured, "I had no idea it would come to that. Please forgive me, Jehanne. I told you that you would be sent to a Church prison, but I did not know—" He broke off, unable to speak further. He wiped his eyes on the sleeves of his habit.

"It's all right," she said, "I think it had to be this way. I sinned by denying God, and that was my penance."

He sniffed loudly. "Then I can give you no other." He recited the Latin words of absolution, then, "Come, let us say the *Pater* and the *Ave Maria. Pater Noster.* . . ."

"*Pater Noster* . . ." Jehanne could not remember the rest of it. Her mind grappled in desperation for some memory of it, but it eluded her. She could not believe this. The prayer she had said thousands of times throughout her life from the time she could speak at all was utterly forgotten.

"*qui es in Coelis . . .*," Ladvenu prompted with a patient frown.

"*qui es in Coelis . . . sanctificétur nomen tuum . . .*"

She managed to finish it with him without further prodding. The *Ave* came a little easier, although she lost her way in the middle of that, too.

When they had completed the prayers, Ladvenu turned to Toutmouillé. "Go, and see why it is taking so long for the Host to arrive."

The young monk jumped to his feet and made for the door, almost bumping into Cauchon.

"Ah, Bishop!" Jehanne cried. "It is through you that I go to my death."

"It is through yourself only." He frowned. "You die because you did not keep your promise but returned to your evil ways."

She would not release him. "If you had put me in a Church prison and in the hands of nuns as *you* promised, this would not have happened. That is why you shall one day have to answer to God's Judgment, for He knows you, Bishop, and He knows what you have done!" She hesitated, then gave him an even look. "And for what reasons."

Cauchon reeled back a pace, flinching as though she had struck him with a sword. He looked from Jehanne to Ladvenu. The monk no longer feared his ecclesiastical superior, but unabashedly glared at Cauchon, the dignified lift of his chin proclaiming the full extent of his disgust. The bishop of Beauvais, aware that he had no defense, melted under the double assault and fled.

Toutmouillé returned in a few moments carrying only a paten on which the sacred Host lay exposed and unprotected.

"What's this?" demanded Ladvenu. Jehanne had never imagined the normally quiet but sympathetic young man angry, as he was now. His face was crimson, and fire raced through his eyes. "Where's the rest of it, the chalice and the cloth to cover the Host? Where are the monks who should accompany it, and the candles? And where the Devil is my stole?"

The youth looked at Ladvenu and Jehanne in consternation. "I had them with me, honestly! The guards stopped us at the bottom of the steps, and this is all they would let me bring."

"Go back down there," Ladvenu ordered in a firm tone, breathing between his teeth, "and tell them that I demand that they release the others and allow them to bring me what I need to give Jehanne Communion! Tell them that if they don't, I shall personally go to the cardinal and they may explain to him why they took it upon themselves to interfere with a holy ritual! Go!" he shouted at the babbling monk.

More afraid of Ladvenu than of the English, Toutmouillé dashed from the cell. Ladvenu took Jehanne's hands. He raised his sad, temperate eyes to hers, peering into their depths, searching, as it seemed, for her soul. "Jehanne, I must know the truth before I give you Holy Communion: Are your voices truly from God?"

Their presence ran up her backbone, tickling her with Their energy. "Oh, yes!" she whispered. "They are most truly from God."

"And the angel? The one who gave the king his crown?" the monk continued, probing her.

She smiled as the tears trickled to the edge of her mouth. "It was not a lie. *I* was the angel sent to the Dauphin, and I really *was* sent by God."

Ladvenu blinked. His look changed to complete, unashamed awe, and she knew that he finally believed her.

Toutmouillé came back, this time accompanied by two solemn, cowled Dominicans bearing lighted candles and a veiled chalice. Ladvenu picked up the narrow purple stole, kissed it, then put it around his neck. While Ladvenu chanted the rite of death and his brothers made the required responses, Jehanne prayed for her soul's salvation and for the courage to face her death. At the right moment, she raised her chin and opened her mouth. Ladvenu placed the Host on her tongue, and as it dissolved she felt renewal merge into her spirit. Now she could go to God with no blemish on her soul.

"You there!" Ladvenu shouted to Grey. "Unfasten these chains."

The captain of the guard swaggered to them. He unfettered Jehanne without comment, then returned to his comrades, who also had sneaked back into the cell. The three of them whispered together, laughing.

"Get out of here!" the monk said sharply. "Your duty is done. Jehanne is in the hands of the Church now."

"Not for long, friar," Grey rejoined with a rancorous growl. But he did not defy Ladvenu's authority. The soldiers went, banging the door behind them.

Massieu came back as he had pledged. Isambard was with him, and he carried the gown she was required to wear. It was smeared with a foul-smelling yellowish powder. "What is this powder?" Jehanne asked, accepting it.

The monks looked at one another, then at the floor. "Sulfur," Isambard mumbled.

She stared at it. When the fire reached her, she would go up like a torch. Her face twisted into a lament, and she was rent by a fresh wail.

"Come, Jehanne, put it on. God loves you, dear child," said Isambard. "He will not let you suffer too long."

Michel had said something very like that last night. Remembering that gave her strength, and she thrust panic away from her.

The monks turned to give her the privacy she needed. Jehanne took off the tunic and hose for the last time, then pulled the gown painfully over her bruised torso. It came to just above her ankles. "Ready," she whispered.

Ladvenu draped a long bonnet over her head. The flaps were like blinders on either side of her face, and the top hung over so far that the most she could see was her bare, dirty feet. She had heard that it was customary for a condemned person to wear something like this, lest a witch give the evil eye to innocent people.

They brought her down the steps and across the courtyard. With her injured eye and her vision further limited by the bonnet, she could see only the stones covering the square. She knew the guards were right there, on either side of Ladvenu and Isambard. She could hear the sharp tapping their boots made against the bricks.

562

Jehanne was put into a cart, and for a moment she felt a sense of recall. This ride would be different, though, from the one she had taken last week. There would be no return to prison today. The conveyance moved slowly through the streets. At first, there were not many people, but the closer the cart drew to the marketplace, the denser the crowd became, and Jehanne could feel them all around her, could hear their weeping despite her inability to see them.

Suddenly, an energy detached itself from the crowd and rushed at her. "Jehanne, forgive me! I am guilty of a great sin!"

She moved her head to look at him. Loiseleur was running alongside the cart behind the wall of English guards assigned to keep the crowds back. He was white with fear and there were tears streaming onto his black habit. He looked like one who had seen the Devil beckoning to him with a satisfied grin. He tried to reach the cart, but was pushed back by the angry guards.

"Get back, priest!" one of them rasped, raising a threatening hand.

"Please, Jehanne!" the assessor begged, undaunted. His pace kept up with the cart although he did not try to break through the line.

"Yes," she shouted as best she could. "I forgive you."

Loiseleur dissolved into the throng, which now had grown larger. Many were moaning and crying aloud for God to be merciful, to her and to them. The vehicle entered the city square, and Jehanne gasped at the presence of what she sensed were hundreds of people. If she raised her head, she was able to see some of them. They hung from windows and packed the marketplace so densely that they could not move. A great many soldiers held them back, away from the platforms that the English had constructed at the southernmost end of the triangular space, alongside the church of St.-Sauveur.

There were three such scaffolds close together, two hung with brightly colored banners of the English monarchy. Cauchon, Le Maistre, Midi, and the cardinal of England stood upon one, while a second held Warwick, Stafford, and their officers. Jehanne did not see the boy-king. A third was empty, and it was at the base of that one that the cart halted.

Isambard, Massieu, and Ladvenu quickly disembarked and reached up to help Jehanne down. She had to move with care for her injuries, and when Isambard put his hands into her armpits, she howled at the sudden jab to her battered side. The monk muttered an apology as he gently put her down. Massieu climbed the steps to the empty platform ahead of her, while the other monks followed. She moved carefully, trying not to stumble. She felt nothing inside.

When she reached the top, she was able to see everything clearly enough if she turned her head to take in a little at a time. As far as she could see, there was only that stirring mass of humanity. Every window of every building ringing the marketplace held several people craning their heads for a glimpse of her. People sat on rooftops; children in the crowd perched upon their fathers' shoulders; women clasped their hands, weeping and praying. Between them and the scaffolds, a long line of helmeted soldiers stood as sentinels, clutching their dangerous, bladed pikes.

Then Jehanne saw it.

At the western end of the square, only fifty or so yards away, was a gleaming plaster stand, built very high and large enough to hold only one person. The base was heaped with resinous dark wood that shone in the sunlight. The bonelike stake rose toward Heaven, and near the top the executioner had nailed a sign inscribed with many lines of heavy black writing.

Jehanne could not look at it any more. It was too real. She forced herself to see only the expectant multitude. "Rouen, Rouen," she murmured, surveying the spectacle as best she could through her undamaged eye, "am I really meant to end my days here? How I fear that you will someday suffer greatly for my death."

Upon the clerical rostrum, Midi stepped forward with an open black book in his hands. " 'And whether one member suffer, all the members suffer with it,' " he read in a loud voice. "Such are the words of blessed St.-Paul, who set forth this warning that none might, through the crime of heresy, infect Holy Mother Church and her children, severing them from God's love."

Jehanne lost his words not long after he had begun. Her fear was starting to build again. Sweat sprang to her palms, and her heart beat faster. Ladvenu slipped a secretive hand into hers and squeezed it in encouragement, although he continued to look at Midi as though intent upon the sermon. Midi went on and on and on. He spoke for almost an hour. The soldiers shifted their feet restlessly, and even at this distance Jehanne could hear them growling with impatience.

"Jehanne, go in peace," the theologian said in conclusion. "The Church can no longer protect you, but hands you over to the secular arm." He stepped back a few paces.

Cauchon came forward, a powerful figure in violet. " 'You have returned to the errors which you had abjured as a dog returns to its vomit,' " he read from the paper in his hands. " 'That is why, as one self-willed and obstinately adhering to the aforesaid offenses, excesses, and errors, we pronounce you in the name of the law to be excommunicated and a heretic. It is our resolve that you, a rotten member whom we would not have infect other members with your rottenness, shall be separated from the body of the Church and given over to the secular arm. We cast you forth and abandon you, praying that this same secular arm may moderate its sentence so that it fall short of death and mutilation. May God have mercy on your miserable soul!' "

The latter was just a formality, not meant to be acted upon. Everyone present knew it, including Jehanne. She fell to her knees and clasped her hands tightly. An engulfing terror burst from her heart and tears poured from her chin onto the frock, creating damp, yellowish cakes in the sulfur. She turned her battered face up to the crystalline blue sky.

"Oh, Father God Who are in Heaven, I beg You, accept Your child into Your Kingdom!" she called out feverishly. "You alone know the extent of my sins and how unworthy I am of Heaven! You have seen that there were times when I pushed ahead against the advice of the loving Counsel You sent me, out of impatience and a belief in my own will instead of faith in Yours. You know the anger that has so often come over me, and the pain that it must have caused those who were in my path. Of these great sins, I most humbly repent and implore Your forgiveness!

"Dear Ste.-Marie, Mother of Lord Jhesus, I pray that you will guide me through the darkness that I might see your Divine Son. Catherine! Marguerite! Michel! Be with me now at the moment of my death as you have been with me since you first came to me in that long-ago time! Do not abandon me now, when I have such great need of you! Please know that in my heart I never lost faith in you, even when my mind faltered and I fell into fear."

Jehanne lowered her gaze to the multitude. Most of the English soldiers were laughing and pointing at her. But others watched solemnly, and she saw in their faces that they were moved by her words. Women and men throughout the marketplace were weeping, flooding the square with the awful sound of their remorse and fear of God's retribution. Jehanne saw the cardinal of Winchester's secretary wipe his damp face with a quivering hand, and when she turned toward the ecclesiastical podium, she beheld through her tears the anguished, sobbing countenance of the Inquisitor.

From the foot of the bishop's podium, the young notary, Manchon, stared at her with a rapt, tear-stained face. His fingers were moving through a rosary, his lips fluttering in silent, helpless pleas for God's mercy. There was not a dry eye among the assessors. As the import of what they were doing fell over them, almost all turned and fled, overwhelmed by remorse and unable to listen to more.

But Cauchon stood looking at her with an implacable hatred, his hands clenched at his sides. Warwick's aristocratic lip turned his mustache upward into a smile.

She could not let them win. The last word would be hers. There was nothing more that they could do to her. She took the bishop's dare.

"All you people of France, know that your King, Charles VII, is blameless in everything concerning me," Jehanne shouted. "Everything that I have done and said is my responsibility alone, and no fault of his! If I have done the kingdom any injury, I ask the King's forgiveness and yours, and I ask also that you pray for me. You men of the Church," she cried above the rising murmur, "those of my party and those who give their loyalty to England, I ask your prayers for my soul, and if you can be moved to charity, then please say a Mass for me."

She looked in Cauchon's direction. "And all you judges, I ask your pardon, and in turn I grant forgiveness for the great wrong that you have done me. I cannot claim to be perfect as Lord Jhesus commanded us to be, but I am not as bad as you have come to believe." Jehanne hesitated. She picked up the strongest weapon she had always possessed and flung it at the bishop. "If I have been guilty of anything, it was in my imperfect faith that God was always with me, even in those dark times when I foolishly thought that He had turned His face from me."

She paused, breathing in great gulps. The communal lament had reached the point of a monumental wail, joining nearly everyone in grief and wonder at the inevitability of the moment. Stunned, the soldiers were looking apprehensively about them at the rising mood of the crowd.

"I beg you, do not forget me," she whispered.

A monk dressed in black came up the steps, bearing a rounded paper cap. Wider at the top than at the bottom, it resembled a judge's hat, except that three hideous demons were painted on it in black ink. The cleric removed Jehanne's bonnet and crowned her with the headgear of a condemned sorceress. A gasp ascended from the multitude at the sight of the purple, beaten face, replaced a heartbeat later by even sharper clamors of bereavement. The magistrate, who should have pronounced the sentence, was too overcome to speak. He looked helplessly at the ground, his shoulders shaking with sorrow.

A grumble stirred in the English ranks. Someone shouted, "Be done with it and burn the bloody witch!" His exhortation caught on with his comrades and soon many were shouting noisily for her death.

Cauchon signaled Isambard and Ladvenu to remove Jehanne from the scaffold. "Come," Ladvenu whispered to her. The monks took her arms and helped her to stand. With her knees trembling so that she could barely walk, she descended the steps leaning against Ladvenu's shoulder.

Jehanne suddenly thought of something. "Brother Isambard! May I be allowed to have a cross?"

He nodded, then said to Ladvenu, "I'll be right back. Take care of her; make them wait until I return." Without a backward look, he elbowed his way rapidly through the crowd, bound for the church behind the officials' platforms.

An older soldier standing at the bottom of the steps had heard Jehanne's request. His eyes searched the ground until he spied a crooked stick, which he picked up, then broke in two. The man ripped a strip of cloth from his own tunic and tied the sticks together into the form of a crude cross. He offered it to Jehanne, and when she looked at his face she saw a tear trickling into his gray-flecked stubble.

"Thank you, sir," she whispered, accepting it. She kissed it and thrust it into the dress between her breasts.

Massieu and Ladvenu were waiting for the magistrate to pronounce the sentence. They looked at him expectantly. Still too overwhelmed by emotion to speak, he lifted his arm feebly and waved his hand in a resigned signal. A victorious cheer from the English blasted into the sunshine.

The monks took Jehanne's arms, and the three of them began walking toward the stake. Wobbling slightly, she grabbed onto Ladvenu as tightly as her fragile strength would allow. The crowd parted to let Jehanne and the monks make their way through. The homely faces grieved for her and jeered at her, all the while stepping aside that she might die.

The moment froze. She could not take her eyes off the stake. The top bore the written condemnation on a fluttering white page, and from there it descended to its wood-heaped base. A man stood upon the pile, clad head to foot in black, the mask on his face terrible to see. In his hands he held a long chain.

Jehanne's heart thundered furiously, growing louder and stronger as she steadily approached her death. Her chest tightened with fear. And yet she could not look away from it. She wiped the perspiration dripping from her palms against the shift. This was no nightmare; this was real. She was going to die. By fire. She could see the brazier burning in front of the pitch-smeared beams and the torches protruding from it. The scaffold was several feet from the ground, higher than a man's head, and between the wood and its very edge was a low plaster barrier.

Oh, Michel, keep your promise to me! she prayed, do not allow me to suffer long!

Just as they reached the scaffold, Isambard came running up to them, out of breath and bearing a long pole crowned by a silver crucifix. Jehanne seized the cross in an embrace and bowed her head over it. She would call Lord Jhesus' name every time the fire hurt her, to remind herself that it was through the flames that she would find her way to Him.

"Hold it up high so that I can see it," she told Isambard. "I want to know that it's there."

"Of course, Jehanne," he mumbled back.

"Come on, you miserable priests!" a soldier shouted. "Get on with it! Do you want to make us take our dinners here?" His angry words were met with loud consensus from his comrades.

Jehanne kissed the crucifix, then released it as Ladvenu pulled her to her feet. She looked at his grief-stricken face and nodded. Half afraid that she would fall, she mounted the ladder propped against the platform where the retaining wall was lowest. Massieu held it in place for her. She pulled herself up with difficulty, stabbed by the pain in her side at every step. Still holding the cross, Isambard climbed the ladder behind her. When she reached the top, the executioner grabbed her arms and helped her to step over the low wall. His black clothes were rank with sweat.

She was standing a little behind the center of a very large pile of wood smeared with glistening tar. At the very edge of the wood was the stake. She would have to stand on the pyre in order to be tied in place.

The executioner knelt before her. Dressed as he was, covered head to foot in black, his face masked by a dark hood, he looked like a repentant demon begging entrance into Heaven. "Do you forgive me for what I must do?"

"Yes," she whispered, looking in horror at the wood.

He stood up again and held out the thick chain. Jehanne stepped upon the sticky heap and positioned herself against the stake. She reached for the crucifix Ladvenu held out to her from the ladder, and took it in her embrace one last time. The executioner fastened the chain at her feet and wound it around her legs and up her torso. Jehanne released the cross, and he bound her arms to her side. Then he vaulted to the ground and accepted the lighted torch his assistant held out to him.

"Brother Isambard," Jehanne cried, "get down from here! Do you want to burn too?"

The monk gave her a look filled with pity and contrition. Worn down by Cauchon's command, he had voted with the majority for her death. In the wordless exchange, Isambard asked her forgiveness and she gave it. He jumped from the ladder and took his place beside Ladvenu and Massieu. Jehanne could scarcely see the tops of their heads.

She heard the executioner signal his men to light the fire. Torches sailed over the enclosure and fell onto the resinous wood. Less than two feet in front of her, flames shot like lightning through the pile, crackling and snapping as they embarked upon their rampage.

"Hold the cross up where I can see it!" Jehanne shouted through the solid curtain of black, suffocating smoke. It invaded her lungs and she coughed.

The flames crept toward her. A breeze brushed against her face, parting the smoke so that she could see the crucifix through the shimmering waves of heat. Every time it hurt, she would call on her Lord for comfort and redemption. Her heartbeat was like thunder.

Snapping and biting, the wall of fire surrounded her on all sides and moved with mindless certainty toward her. She could feel its burning breath grow hotter and hotter, determined to eat her alive. She fixed upon the cross with all her might.

The wolf sank its sharp, crackling teeth into her feet. "Jhesus!"

Whimpering with terror, she tried frantically to stamp it out, to kick it from her, but she was tied too tightly to move. She did not dare to look down, to see her skin sizzling, her flesh being burned bloody and raw. It sank its jaws into her again and began to chew.

"Jhesus!"

Jehanne could smell the sickly-sweet odor of her own flesh burning, like the smell of pigs in a burned-out barn. Her toes disappeared into the blazing maw. There was a deadly hiss as blood from her feet sizzled into the flames. The gown caught fire, flaying the skin from her legs all the way up to her clenched hands.

"Jhesus!" she screamed, her eyes still fixed on the cross.

Oh dear God take me!

No longer able to stand, she slumped a little toward the mouth of the beast. It chomped hungrily upon her hands and moved up her arms. It had devoured her legs and was creeping through her pelvis, feasting on her backside in thorough, remorseless bites. The heat was high enough now for the paper cap to ignite and be blown away.

She wanted very badly to vomit. "Jhesus!" she whimpered.

Nausea punched her in the stomach. She could no longer see the cross; she was encircled by the orange-red, chortling figure of the wolf. The little cross between her breasts ignited and the brute nibbled toward her heart.

"Jhesus! Jhesus!"

Oh God, this is more than I can bear! Michel, if you love me take me! Take me now!

"*Jhesus!!!*" she shrieked.

A great invisible hand seized her by the scruff of the neck and yanked her from the flames. She shot up into the sky with a tremendous *Whoosshhh!*

An English soldier standing behind Ladvenu had been laughing, but now he followed her with dumbfounded eyes, his mouth ajar in dazed astonishment. He sank to his knees, babbling incoherently, his finger pointing straight at her.

He could actually see her!

She rose higher and higher. The poor man lost sight of her and collapsed into the arms of a comrade, still mumbling something about the dove he saw fly out of the flames. Jehanne continued to move upward, and when she was able to see the whole marketplace, she stopped. She was in no pain, nor was she saddened. She was amazed.

The scene beneath her was very clear. The tiled rooftops of the buildings were like tiny gray mirrors under the spring sun, and in the middle of them the anonymous masses, packed shoulder to shoulder, were lamenting the day. Although driven back a short way by its heat, Ladvenu and Massieu were weeping before the raging pyre. Dazed, Isambard still held the cross toward the flames, all the while expelling his grief in slack-jawed sobs. Many churchmen were praying. Those assessors who had not already deserted the site wrung their hands and crossed themselves, moaning with fright and contrition. A resonant howl bellowed through the packed square, and people were crying inconsolably into one another's arms. Contrary to instinct, the human wall tried to move toward the fire, but the determined soldiers held them back, hurling threats at the populace, many of whom were now openly muttering against Warwick.

"My God, we are all damned!" cried a voice in English from the royal platform. "We have burned a saint!" Tressart, the cardinal's secretary, was wringing his hands and weeping.

Jehanne tried to call to them, It's all right, I'm here, I'm alive. But they did not hear her.

She felt no pain, no suffering at all, just a sense of release. Joy hummed around her in a bright light, and she knew that she had not failed God or her Counsel. She had not failed in anything. In some mysterious way, she had done everything God had meant for her to do. She knew that as certainly as she knew her name. She was surrounded by a curtain of pastel light. And she was free.

In that timeless moment she understood.

They had told her the truth; there was no liberation that could possibly surmount this. She would not know pain again, or confusion, or frustration, or sorrow. Never again would she feel the sting of betrayal. No one would exhort her and force her to endure the agony of loss. She was free and in a place where none could do her any harm; in a perplexing way which she could feel, yet not entirely comprehend, she had been triumphant after all. Her spirit overflowed with elation.

She tried to look down at the marketplace, but it was far away and very small. There was only the inferno and the thing roasting within it.

Come away now, Jehanne. There is nothing left for you here.

She lifted her sight to a place just above her head. Sloping down toward her was a swirling tunnel of misty gray light that ended in a much greater Illumination some distance away. Tiny twinkling particles like dancing sunbeams began to dart around her playfully, back and forth in front of her face, and up and down her arms and legs, until she felt coated in the sheen they made. She laughed in delight and let them coax her onward, into the formless, glowing tunnel whose heart emitted all knowledge and munificence and tranquillity. Jehanne moved, unafraid, toward the authoritative Figure glowing in its center.

From a distance he looked like a throbbing ball of bright light, but as she drew closer she found that if she looked carefully, she could see the aspect of a golden Man in magnificent, sun-polished armor. He was even more beautiful than he had ever appeared in her dreams. His features, wispy and delicately etched, were smiling at her, and in his eyes, older than time, she saw humor and an acknowledgment of everything she had ever done, everything she was, unquestioned by a pure and constant love. Slightly behind him floated two softly glowing Beings who held Their arms outstretched in her direction. Like the heavenly Knight, They had faces. Lovely, perfect faces.

Jehanne willed herself to run to Their arms, toward the Light shining at the end of the tunnel like the promise of Salvation.

Ashes

Upon orders from Henry Beaufort, cardinal of Winchester, the executioner gathered what remained of Jehanne's body into a blanket, then unceremoniously tossed the grisly bundle into the Seine. He would later claim that he had been unable to reduce her heart to ashes no matter how much fuel he had put to the task. At roughly the same time La Hire, Poton de Xaintrailles, and Gilles de Rais, on campaign in Normandy, were beaten back before they could reach Rouen. Whether their raid was an attempt to rescue Jehanne, or simply a continuation of their King's strategy to reconquer that duchy, is a subject of scholarly debate to this day.

When the news reached Domrémy, Jacques du Lys (né Darc) withdrew into his grief and two months later was dead. His widow remained in Lorraine until 1435, when she moved to Orléans accompanied by her recently ransomed son Pierre, himself soon to become the owner of the Ile-aux-Boeufs in the Loire River. Isabelle Romée lived there at the city's expense until her own death some thirty years later. Jehan du Lys returned to Lorraine and eventually inherited Robert de Baudricourt's old job of military governor at Vaucouleurs. The family's last descendants—from Pierre's line—would die out in the seventeenth century.

In the years following Jehanne's execution, the young men who had shared the greatest adventure of their lives in her company also rose above their stations. Ennobled by Charles VII in 1444, Jehan de Metz continued to live in Vaucouleurs, and while his fate is unknown, it is certain that he lived well into his sixties. Bertrand de Poulengy was appointed an equerry of the King and likewise enjoyed a long life. Minguet (Louis de Coutes) became first a squire, then the lord of Novyon and of Reugles. In later life, Jehan d'Aulon, Jehanne's competent, no-nonsense squire, earned the rank of seneschal of Beaucaire.

Following the debacle at Paris, Georges de la Trémoïlle's power and influence became eclipsed by the battlefield heroics of his longtime foe, Constable Richemont, against whom he continued to intrigue. In a violent encounter between the two at Chinon in 1433, the earl attacked Trémoïlle with a dagger; his life was spared, however, because of his corpulence. Fully recovered but having learned nothing from this vivid consequence of his machinations, he later took part in the adolescent Dauphin Louis' revolt against the King, an act which finished him at court. He died at his castle of Sully-sur-Loire in 1446, expiring— against all expectations—of natural causes.

Regnault de Chartres, archbishop of Reims, lived until 1445. He also died peacefully in his bed and went to his grave laden with honors.

La Hire (Etienne de Vignolles) continued to fight tirelessly for his King. He was instrumental in keeping the English from regaining Lagny in 1432; taken prisoner at Beauvais in 1437, he was free by the following year, when in the service of René d'Anjou he engaged in guerrilla warfare in Lorraine. He died in battle at Montauban on January 12, 1443.

Gilles de Rais left the army not long after Jehanne's death and retired to his estates in Brittany, where he proceeded to become involved in alchemy and ritualistic Satanism. In 1440 he was tried, convicted, and executed as a sorcerer and mass murderer of children, most of them boys. For generations, his name was invoked by French parents as a warning to their disobedient children. He became the inspiration for the seventeenth-century French novel, *Bluebeard.*

Pierre Cauchon failed to realize his ambitions when the duke of Bedford re-neged on his promise to appoint Jehanne's judge to the archbishopric of Rouen. As a consolation prize, he was given the episcopal seat at Lisieux in 1432, and ten years later died a wealthy man after suffering a heart attack while he was being shaved. A fine procession with full episcopal honors accompanied his body to its tomb in the cathedral at Lisieux. But when the findings of the Trial of Rehabilitation were made public (see "Author's Note"), an outraged mob stormed into the cathedral and disinterred the corpse, which they then threw into a common sewer to be kicked, spat and urinated upon by passers-by. Their verdict has endured for centuries, with a supremely ironic—and poignant—twist given to the tale in modern times: While alive, Pierre Cauchon lusted for fame and believed he would earn it as a result of his condemnation of Jehanne, yet his role as a judge in her trial has made him one of the most universally detested figures in history. Even so, few people outside of France—apart from medievalists—even know him by name.

Nicolas Midi, one of Cauchon's favored associates, died of leprosy sometime after 1438; that same year, Jehan d'Estivet, the promoter who had so ruthlessly prosecuted Jehanne, was found beaten to death in a sewer. By that time the Inquisitor, Jehan Le Maistre, had mysteriously disappeared; whether he was still alive is unknown.

In 1437 Jehan, the Bastard of Orléans, honored by Charles VII in recognition of his military exploits and his loyalty to the king, received the title comte d'Aulnoy (or Dunois), thereby finally earning a legitimate name to pass on to his heirs. He remains one of history's "good guys," a rare embodiment of the medieval chivalric ideal: conscientious, brave, honest, constant.

It is unfortunate, given his potential, that the Bastard's cousin, the duc d'Alençon, did not fare as well. In 1432, barely a year after Jehanne went to the stake, the young man suffered the shattering death of his wife; although arranged, the marriage appears to have been a genuine love match. Apparently grief-stricken past his capacity for endurance, he took to drink and acquired several mistresses, one of whom introduced him to magic.

In 1440 he suddenly changed his allegiance to the King and participated in the revolt staged by the sixteen-year-old Dauphin Louis against his father. To Charles' credit, after putting down the rebellion the King treated his cousin with leniency, only stripping him of his office as lieutenant-general. But instead of reconciling with Charles, the duke complained openly and bitterly that his liege had treated him unfairly by refusing to restore his ancestral Norman lands. Shortly thereafter, d'Alençon entered into conviviality with the English. He was arrested for treason in 1456 on the eve of giving his testimony in Jehanne's Trial of Rehabilitation, and condemned to death by his peers in 1458. Once more Charles pardoned him, but it was not until the accession of Louis XI that he was released. In 1474, he was again tried, convicted, sentenced to death—and pardoned. It must have seemed to Jehanne's "beautiful duke" that he could not extinguish whatever demons haunted him by dying, but finally he did die—poor, embittered, and alone—in 1476.

D'Alençon's father-in-law, Charles, duc d'Orléans, returned home from English captivity in 1439, ransomed in large part by—of all people—Philippe of Burgundy, the only man in France wealthy enough to meet the enormous price. The poetry Charles d'Orléans wrote while imprisoned in England is now included in university curricula throughout Europe and North America.

Philippe of Burgundy was never brought completely under control by King Charles and died, wealthy and powerful, at Dijon in 1467. It would remain for Charles' heir, Louis XI ("the Spider King"), to break the power of the disobedient House of Burgundy.

By 1435 the deathbed promises he had made to Henry V—to hold on to Normandy regardless of the cost, to press his heir's claims to the French throne—had completely exhausted John of Lancaster, duke of Bedford, and he died in Rouen on September 14. His role as manager of English military affairs in France passed to Richard Beauchamp, earl of Warwick, an office Jehanne's warden held until his own death in 1439. But by then Fortune's wheel had turned against England: Bereft of Bedford's conscientious and unselfish leadership, the English monarchy lost its fragile grip on France and the kingdom tumbled into the disastrous civil conflicts known as the Wars of the Roses.

At the outbreak of those wars Henry VI found himself the pawn in a political tug-of-war between the houses of Lancaster and York. In 1460 the latter's partisans captured and imprisoned this frail heir to the Valois madness, later deposing him in favor of York's son, Edward IV. Upon his release, Henry wandered listlessly in an uncertain exile while his wife, Marguerite d'Anjou, plotted to place their son on the throne. He was eventually captured by the Scots and turned over to King Edward, who ordered his murder in the Tower of London in May 1471.

As for the war in France, eleven days after Bedford's death, Burgundy refuted his part in the Treaty of Troyes and entered into a solemn alliance with Charles VII, whereupon Philippe wasted no time sending his own forces against his former allies. In February 1436, Arthur de Richemont, by that time fully reconciled with

Charles and Constable of France, besieged the capital assisted by the Burgundians and by its citizens. Following a month-long battle, Paris fell to them, and with great pomp the royal army entered the city on April 13, almost five years to the day after Jehanne predicted in open court that "within seven years time, the English will suffer the greatest defeat they have yet had in France, greater than at Orléans."

But it was not yet over. Another seventeen years would pass before the last battle of the Hundred Years War was fought at Castillon on July 17, 1453, during which Jehanne's old nemesis at Patay, John, Lord Talbot, was slain. Finally, with all of France otherwise returned to the King's control, Charles allowed the English to retain Calais out of deference to his ally Burgundy, who needed the port in order to conduct his Flemish wool trade with England.

Charles VII became known to his subjects by the well-deserved sobriquet "the Victorious." In addition to winning the longest war in European history, he centralized the bureaucracy serving the monarchy, established the first standing national army on the Continent, and brought about the period of peace and prosperity that would set his kingdom on the road to the Renaissance. He died in 1463, after thirty-four years upon the throne of France.

Author's Note

People sometimes ask me if I found it difficult to write this book. I usually respond that I felt challenged by it, excited, occasionally frustrated; it involved an extended period of considerable research and labor over a word processor. But these are superficial answers that do not genuinely explain how I put together the pieces of this historical novel.

I was fortunate to have been drawn to a subject whose story is so well recorded that it presented only occasional research problems, for few historical figures—and none in medieval European history—have led lives more thoroughly documented than that of Jehanne the Maid (Joan of Arc). This is due both to the efforts of contemporary chroniclers and to the extraordinary fact that her life was examined at not one but two trials: the first, and more widely known, which condemned her; and the second—the result of her family's wrongful death lawsuit against the dioceses of Rouen and Beauvais—which exonerated her twenty-five years after her execution.

The minutes from the first trial were written in both Latin and French, while those of the Trial of Rehabilitation were taken down exclusively in Latin. During the nineteenth century the eminent French historian Jules Quicherat undertook the exhaustive labor of translating the Latin records from both trials into French. In 1932, W. P. Barrett translated the French minutes from the Trial of Condemnation into English and these, together with other commentaries, were published under the title *The Trial of Jeanne D'Arc*. Subsequent historians have used these collections as primary sources and have based their biographies upon them.

While the proceedings from the first trial contain Jehanne's own account of her life, there are obvious gaps in the testimony, due no doubt to the court's political agenda. The minutes from the Trial of Rehabilitation—in which more than a hundred witnesses were called to testify, people who had known her during every stage of her life: childhood friends, comrades-in-arms, people with whom she lodged—fill in the blank spaces, offering to posterity her story's richest and most thorough details. Thanks to these individuals, we have an impression of what she looked like; we know where she went, what she wore, what she said and did, even what she ate. The testimonies of the monks who witnessed her imprisonment and trial of condemnation were invaluable in painting a portrait of how she conducted herself during her final ordeal.

With all of this in mind, writing this novel was "easy" in the sense that I had at my disposal day-to-day accounts of Jehanne's life from the time she first heard her Voices until the moment of her death. For additional insight, I read biographies of those individuals whose own lives figured prominently in hers, as well as books concerning life in medieval France. I was even fortunate enough to stumble across facsimiles of a few letters she dictated and signed; it is her actual signature at the end of her famous—and quite real—letter to Bedford that appears in Chapter Five. My objective was to tell the story as authentically as possible, the story not of a perfect, plaster saint but of the complex, flesh-and-blood human being who peeks at us from behind the stone wall of unsubstantiated legend and cold fact alike. I also felt challenged to write it primarily from Jehanne's point of view, and thus to give the reader an opportunity to imagine what it might have felt like to *be* Jehanne the Maid.

To this end, I included in the narrative events that would reveal Jehanne's character and the complexities of the Hundred Years War, while leaving out others that, although interesting, seemed less important to advance the action or deepen character development. Virtually every event in the novel, and much of the dialogue, is based on historical fact; this is particularly—although not exclusively—the case in the chapters involving the trial, where the dialogue is taken directly from court records. Even scenes that may appear to be contrived are actually documented: One such instance occurs during the final battle for Orléans when Jehanne pulls the arrow from her own shoulder; this scene, which might seem the melodramatic product of a novelist's imagination, arose from the testimony of Jehanne's confessor, Jehan Pasquerel, who was present when she was wounded. Another example involves the sudden change in the wind's direction at Orléans, which was witnessed and later described by a small crowd.

Nonetheless, as rich as the source materials are, I did run into obstacles from time to time. Some of these obstacles were due to the medieval propensity for ignoring the inner life while stressing outer deeds, itself a reflection of the scant importance people of that age attached to individuality. In other words, while accounts of Jehanne's actions are plentiful and detailed, they do not always include character motivation. We know, for instance, that she wept over the bodies of dead English soldiers, but we have no account of how she reconciled the bellicose requirements of her mission with a mystic's sensitivity.

This question came into particular focus when it came time for me to depict Jehanne's first encounter with actual warfare at Orléans. As a novelist, I drew upon what I knew of her character to put forth what seemed the most reasonable representation of the inner conflict she may actually have felt yet never publicly revealed. It made sense to me that someone who was capable of keeping her mission secret for three years before she first announced it in Vaucouleurs would have remained adept at hiding her emotions after she had gained a measure of fame. The emotional suffering I described in the aftermath of Orléans' liberation—Jehanne's internal monologue in her bedroom, and the subsequent party at which she becomes sick on wine—are the results of my own attempts to depict the inner contest between saint and soldier for domination of her personality.

The issue of character development surfaced again when it came to getting a grasp on Jehanne's parents, brothers, squires, pages, and friends from Vaucouleurs. These were actual people, yet the bare facts presented by medieval accounts fail to bring them to life. Thus, I was free to let my imagination roam when fleshing out these characters, an advantage I did not have in describing the members of the upper classes. The personalities of Charles VII, the duke of Bedford, the Bastard of Orléans, the duke of Alençon, and others of noble rank are so well known that I was constrained to describe them as they appear in the history books. (Indeed, La Hire's personality is so vibrant that it shines through the darkened window of the chroniclers' rather pedestrian narratives; his prayer— "Lord, I pray that today You will do for La Hire what La Hire would do for You, if You were a man-at-arms and La Hire, God"—is all his own.)

Occasionally, I was confronted with tantalizing gaps in the story. For example, after her failure to take Paris, how did Jehanne find out about the Armagnac plots in the city and the danger to Compiègne, when she was closely seques- tered—even imprisoned, one might say—at Charles' court? The answer is un- known, but this information not only came to her notice but launched her upon her last, fateful military adventure. To account for this revelation as the narrative demanded, I decided to invent the mysterious messenger whom she met in Jargeau and, for an added touch of irony, made him an Englishman.

In a similar vein, while there is no first-hand account of the physical abuse Jehanne suffered at the hands of her jailers between her abjurement at St. Ouen and the monks' return to her cell three days later, important circumstantial evi- dence suggests that such mistreatment did occur. Isambard de la Pierre testified during the Trial of Rehabilitation that when he and the other churchmen entered her cell and found that Jehanne had returned to men's clothing, her face was "disfigured, and wet with tears"; moreover, that she cried out that the priests "did not know what violence the English had done to her since the Church forced her to dress as a woman." Jehan Massieu, the usher (bailiff) who had conducted her to and from the interrogations, described for the Rehabilitation court how Jehanne's guards took away her dress and would not allow her to put it on again, forcing her to resume male garb, a story he claimed Jehanne herself told him. And Martin Ladvenu, who had heard her last confession, also testified that Jehanne informed him that during that three-day gap "a great English lord" had "tried" to rape her but that she had repulsed him.

I found it difficult to believe that such an attempt, if it occurred, would have been thwarted, given her documented physical weakness at that time. It seemed to me either that, while Jehanne told the truth insofar as her mind allowed her to recognize it, she was in a state of shock and denial, or that Ladvenu lied under oath to avoid besmirching the name of "Jehanne the Maid," already revered in France by the time he gave his testimony. Initially, the first solution appealed to me until I realized that a person in the grip of denial would most likely block the trauma entirely, never mentioning it at all. So if Jehanne did not reveal the incident, how could Ladvenu have known that there had been an attempt in the first place? Unable to answer this question with any other explanation, I wrote both the rape scene and Jehanne's confession to Ladvenu as I think they probably happened.

I also called upon my imagination to depict Jehanne's meeting with Colette de Corbie. It is known that both women were in Moulins at the same time, and since Jehanne frequently went to Colette's convent chapel to pray—and since both were famous mystics of their day who shared common political sympathies—it seemed possible that they may have had occasion to meet. The content of their conversation is of course pure invention on my part.

My greatest challenge certainly lay in how I chose to depict Jehanne's "Voices," something I could not avoid if I were going to write the novel predominantly from her viewpoint. In the end I opted to present them simply as characters.

One final note: The reader will find that the name I use for her is Jehanne the Maid (in French, Jehanne la Pucelle). This was the name by which she was actually known to her contemporaries. During her trial, she testified that she was never called Jehanne d'Arc in her village, but was known as Jehanne (or Jhanette) Romée, a surname belonging to her mother, as was customary in that time and place. Contemporary documents refer to her father variously as Jacques Darc, Tarc, Day, d'Ay, or Dart, suggesting that it was not assumed at the time that his name meant "of Arc." The name "Jeanne d'Arc" is an invention, dating from the sixteenth century. I interpret this discrepancy symbolically: "Jeanne d'Arc" (Joan of Arc) is the name of the legend, perfect and unapproachable, while Jehanne the Maid is the name of the actual person. It is the latter whose story I have tried to tell.